"A meticulously researched alternate history, a tantalizing glimpse of the free America we have lost, and a thrilling story of warfare in the Napoleonic era."
—GENE WOLFE, author of *The Wizard Knight*

"A thought-provoking and gloriously action-packed saga . . . Flint charges into [the story] like a saber-swinging general on a white horse, delivering battle scenes of cinematic grandeur while warmly rendering all of his characters as relatably human . . . This is simply fine, action-packed entertainment."
—SFReviews

"Flint did an excellent job of seamlessly blending fact and fiction, and his deft characterizations make the story memorable."
—Blogcritics.org

"His characters, historical and invented, are plausible for the time and place, and he makes neither an icon nor a demon of anyone."
—*Booklist*

"Essential for fans of alternate history."
—*Library Journal*

D0017604

1812

THE RIVERS OF WAR

ERIC FLINT

BALLANTINE BOOKS • NEW YORK

2006 Del Rey Mass Market Edition

Copyright © 2005 by Eric Flint
Excerpt from *1824: The Arkansas War* copyright © 2006 by Eric Flint

Published in the United States by Del Rey, an imprint of The Random House Publishing Group, a division of Random House, Inc., New York.

DEL REY is a registered trademark and the Del Rey colophon is a trademark of Random House, Inc.

Originally published in hardcover as *The Rivers of War* in the United States by Del Rey Books, an imprint of The Random House Publishing Group, a division of Random House, Inc., in 2005.

ISBN 978-0-345-46568-9

Printed in the United States of America

Map illustrations © Jeffrey L. Ward

www.delreybooks.com

OPM   9   8   7   6   5   4   3

"To Quatie, who gave her blanket"

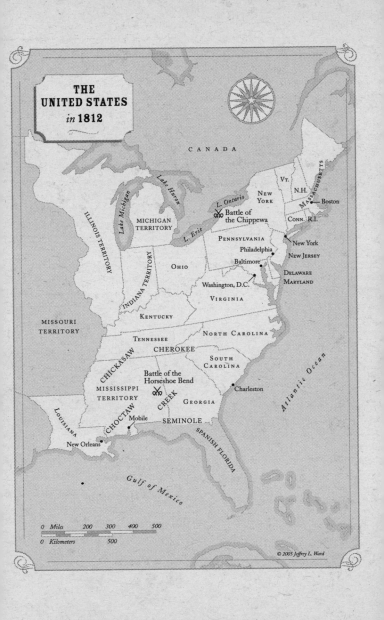

THE
UNITED STATES
in 1812

CANADA

ILLINOIS TERRITORY

Lake Michigan

Lake Huron

L. Ontario

MICHIGAN TERRITORY

L. Erie

Battle of the Chippewa

NEW YORK

VT.

N.H.

MASSACHUSETTS

Boston

CONN. R.I.

New York

INDIANA TERRITORY

OHIO

PENNSYLVANIA

Philadelphia

NEW JERSEY

Baltimore

DELAWARE

MARYLAND

Washington, D.C.

MISSOURI TERRITORY

KENTUCKY

VIRGINIA

NORTH CAROLINA

TENNESSEE

CHEROKEE

CHICKASAW

SOUTH CAROLINA

Battle of the Horseshoe Bend

Charleston

MISSISSIPPI TERRITORY

CREEK

GEORGIA

CHOCTAW

Mobile

SEMINOLE

LOUISIANA

New Orleans

SPANISH FLORIDA

Atlantic Ocean

Gulf of Mexico

0 Miles 200 300 400 500

0 Kilometers 500

© 2005 Jeffrey L. Ward

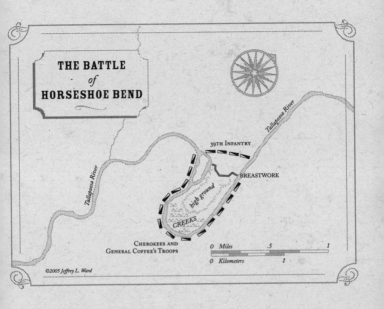

THE BATTLE
of
HORSESHOE BEND

Tallapoosa River

Tallapoosa River

39TH INFANTRY

BREASTWORK

high ground

CREEKS

CHEROKEES AND
GENERAL COFFEE'S TROOPS

| 0 | Miles | .5 | 1 |
| 0 | Kilometers | | 1 |

©2005 Jeffrey L. Ward

DRAMATIS PERSONAE

American Characters

JOHN QUINCY ADAMS: U.S. negotiator at the peace talks with the British being held in the Belgian city of Ghent; son of John Adams, the second president of the United States.

JOHN ARMSTRONG: U.S. secretary of war.

CHARLES BALL: Freedman; U.S. Navy gunner.

JOSHUA BARNEY: Commodore, U.S. Navy.

JACOB BROWN: U.S. general in command of the Army of the Niagara.

JOHN COFFEE: A close friend and associate of Andrew Jackson, as well as his top subordinate officer.

HENRY CROWELL: Freedman; teamster, owning his own wagon.

PATRICK DRISCOL: Sergeant, U.S. Army.

SAM HOUSTON: Ensign in the Thirty-ninth U.S. Infantry; adopted son of the Cherokee chief John Jolly; his Cherokee name was Colonneh, which means "The Raven."

ANDREW JACKSON: Commanding general of the Tennessee militia; later, major general in the regular U.S. Army, in command of U.S. forces in the southern theater in the War of 1812.

FRANCIS SCOTT KEY: Lawyer and poet.

MARIE LAVEAU: New Orleans voudou queen.

JAMES MADISON: President of the United States.

ANTHONY MCPARLAND: Private, U.S. Army.

JAMES MONROE: U.S. secretary of state.

LEMUEL MONTGOMERY: Major in the Thirty-ninth U.S. infantry; personal friend of Andrew Jackson.

DAVID MORGAN: Brigadier general; commander of U.S. forces

on the west bank of the Mississippi River in the New Orleans campaign.

DANIEL PATTERSON: Commodore, U.S. Navy; in command of American naval forces during the New Orleans campaign.

JOHN PENDLETON: Corporal in the Baltimore United Volunteers, a militia dragoon unit.

JOHN REID: Andrew Jackson's aide.

WINFIELD SCOTT: Brigadier general, U.S. Army; Brown's top subordinate officer.

WILLIAMS SIMMONS: Accountant, formerly employed in the War Department.

WILLIAM WINDER: Brigadier general, U.S. Army, in command of the defense of Washington, D.C.

Indian Characters

THE RIDGE: A major Cherokee chief; took the name Major Ridge after the battle of the Horseshoe Bend.

JAMES AND JOHN ROGERS: Tiana Ross's half brothers, nephews of chief John Jolly.

CAPTAIN JOHN ROGERS: Father of Tiana, James, and John; although a Scots-American, he was an informal member of the Cherokee tribe and adviser to John Jolly; his nickname was "Hell-Fire Jack."

TIANA ROGERS: Niece of Cherokee chief John Jolly.

JOHN ROSS: Young Cherokee leader; very influential in the tribe, although not a chief.

SEQUOYAH: Cherokee warrior; developer of the Cherokee written language.

NANCY WARD: Leader of the Cherokee women's council, holding the title of *Ghighua,* "War Woman" or "Beloved Woman."

WILLIAM WEATHERFORD: Principal war leader of the Red Stick faction of the Creeks during the Creek War; also known as Chief Red Eagle.

British Characters

SIR ALEXANDER COCHRANE: Vice admiral, in top command of Britain's operations against the U.S. south of Canada.

GEORGE COCKBURN: Rear admiral, British navy.

SAMUEL GIBBS: Major general; Pakenham's top subordinate.

JAMES MONEY: Captain, Royal Marines.

THOMAS MULLINS: Lieutenant colonel; commander of the Forty-fourth Foot Regiment.

SIR EDWARD PAKENHAM: Major general; replaces Robert Ross as commander of British land forces in the New Orleans campaign.

ROBERT RENNIE: Colonel; commander of the Forty-third Light Infantry.

PHINEAS RIALL: Major general, commander of British forces on the Niagara front.

ROBERT ROSS: Major general, commander of British army forces in the Chesapeake Bay campaign.

WILLIAM THORNTON: Colonel, in command of the Eighty-fifth Foot Regiment.

PROLOGUE

MAY 30, 1806
Harrison's Mill
Logan County, Kentucky

The duel was to be held just across the state line in Kentucky. The government of Tennessee would enjoy the luxury of looking the other way. Although the illegal affair involved some of its more prominent citizens, their activities would be taking place outside its legal jurisdiction.

Kentucky would do the same, of course, simply because the perpetrators would be out of the state as soon as it was over. And they were all a bunch of cussed Tennesseans, anyway.

The first group was in high spirits as they made their way to the agreed-upon dueling ground.

"Twenty-four feet, you say?" asked Charles Dickinson, who was to be one of the principals in the duel. He said it with a smile on his face; as well he might, since it was a pointless question. He'd already asked it a dozen times that morning, and received the same answer every time.

Dickinson had finished reloading his pistol. He waved it toward a nearby tree. "That tree looks to be standing about eight paces away. Pick a leaf, gentlemen, if you would."

His companions—half a dozen of the "gay blades of Nashville," as the newspapers liked to call them—were feeling just as festive as Dickinson. After a short and energetic wrangle, they settled upon a particular and distinctive leaf.

No sooner had they done so than the pistol in Dickinson's hand came up, quickly and smoothly. The gun fired, and the leaf fluttered to the ground. Dickinson's shot had severed the stem.

*   *   *

By contrast, the mood of the other party was grim.

"You don't stand a chance against him," stated the principal's second, General Thomas Overton. "Dickinson's probably the best shot in the whole of Tennessee."

His companion, a fellow general of the Tennessee militia, nodded silently. The nod was somewhat on the jerky side, though the man showed no sign of nervousness. His bony head was perched atop a narrow neck, which connected it to a slender body that looked to be all bone and gristle.

"I'll have to take the first shot," he declared. "No point trying to beat Dickinson there."

Overton winced. "You may very well not *survive* that first shot," he observed bleakly.

The principal shrugged. "Oh, I think I'll be all right. Long enough, anyway. And I don't see where I've got any choice, anyhow. I said I'd kill the bastard, and I intend to be true to my word. Whatever it takes."

The surgeon who accompanied the two generals said nothing. He didn't even wince, although he'd be the one who'd have to keep the general alive afterward, if that was possible.

There was no point in wincing. A man might as well wince at the movement of the tides.

Once both parties had arrived at the dueling ground, the lots were drawn. Dickinson's second, Dr. Hanson Catlett, won the choice of position. Overton would have the count.

There was no point in delaying the affair. As soon as the principals had taken their positions, at the twenty-four-foot distance they'd agreed upon, Overton's voice rang out.

"Are you ready?"

"I am ready," Dickinson replied cheerfully.

"I am ready," came the stolid voice of his opponent.

"Fere!" cried Overton, pronouncing the word in his old-country accent.

Dickinson's pistol came up like a streaking lizard. The gun fired the instant it bore on the target.

The Tennessee general hadn't even lifted his firearm yet. A puff of dust rose from the breast of his coat. He staggered back a couple of paces, clenching his teeth. Slowly, he raised his left hand and pressed it to his chest.

But he never lost his grip on the pistol in his right hand.

Dickinson gaped, drawing back a step. "Great God!" he cried out. "Did I miss him?"

"Back to the mark, sir!" roared Overton. He raised his own pistol and aimed it at Dickinson. "Back to the mark, I say!"

Dickinson's face went blank. He stepped forward and resumed his position at the mark, his pistol now lowered to his side. He'd had his shot, and by custom, he had to wait his opponent's return.

All eyes moved to the opponent. The situation was clear. Honor had been satisfied, beyond any shadow of a doubt. A magnanimous man would respond by refusing the shot, or simply firing into the air.

This particular Tennessee general was already famous for any number of things. Magnanimity was not one of them. Slowly and deliberately, he raised his pistol and took aim. He squeezed the trigger.

Nothing, beyond the slight click as the hammer stopped at half cock.

Everyone held their breath. What would the general do now?

His companions, who knew him very well, didn't hold their breath for more than a second.

The general drew back the hammer and fired again.

Dickinson reeled, struck below the ribs.

His friends leaped to his side, catching him even before he fell. They lowered him to the ground and began stripping off his coat. Blood was spilling everywhere.

"Passed right through him!" one of them called out. "He's bleeding buckets!"

Overton strode over to the wounded man, but the surgeon didn't bother to follow. From his experience, he knew Dickinson would die from such a wound, no matter what anyone did. And he had his own principal to attend to.

"Let me see your wound, General," he said quietly. "You *were* hit, I believe?"

The general took his eyes off the sight of his opponent, lying there on the ground. As always, the surgeon was struck by the color of those eyes. A sort of bright blue that wasn't particularly pale, but still always reminded him of ice.

The blue eyes were startled now. "I believe he did pink me a little. Forgot all about it."

He opened the coat. After some probing, the surgeon determined that Dickinson's bullet had broken two ribs and was buried somewhere in the general's chest.

He shook his head. "I don't think I'll be able to remove it. It'll be too close to your heart."

The general shrugged, without even wincing at the pain that movement must have caused him. "I'll just have to live with it, then."

Overton left the group of men clustered around the fallen Dickinson and walked back. "He won't want anything more of you, General. He'll be dead by tomorrow."

He then took the general by the arm and began leading him away. As he did so, two of Dickinson's companions rose from the shattered body and came charging toward them. Overton half raised his pistol by way of warning.

But the two men, though furious, were not armed. Or, at least, they didn't have any pistols in their hands.

"That was ungallant, sir!" one of them cried. "*Ungallant,* I say!"

The general glared at him. Before he could speak, though, the other man joined in.

"And you may be sure that we will publish a report on this affair! There will be a scandal! Be sure of it, sir! Charles Dickinson is a popular man in Nashville!"

"Publish what you will," snarled the general, "but I caution you not to publish anything like Dickinson did, or I'll challenge you, too."

Then the pain from his wound caused his teeth to clench, for a moment. The general's long and gaunt jaws lent themselves well to teeth clenching.

"He insulted my wife, once," he continued. "I let that pass after he apologized, since he'd spoken the words while drunk in a tavern. But then he called me a coward, and a blackguard, and a worthless scoundrel, and did so in print. Be careful, sirs, I urge you."

The general turned away, then, finally allowing Overton to guide him off the killing field.

One of Dickinson's companions looked to the surgeon. "It was *ungallant,* sir. I say it again."

The surgeon spread his hands. The gesture wasn't a pacific one, just a recognition of reality.

"He said he'd kill Dickinson, and he did. Even—deliberately, mind you—took the first shot in order to do it. What did you expect from him, sir? He is Andrew Jackson. Such is the nature of the man."

Part I

⁓

THE TALLAPOOSA

CHAPTER 1

The first time Sam Houston set eyes on Andrew Jackson, the general's left arm was in a sling, and he was losing his temper.

"Do I make myself clear, sir?"

Jackson's eyes were like small blue volcanoes erupting under bushy blond eyebrows and an even bushier head of sandy-gray hair. The scar on his forehead actually seemed to be throbbing.

Sam had heard tales about that scar. Supposedly, it had been put there decades ago, during the Revolution, by a British officer. After seizing the home occupied by Jackson and his family in the Carolinas, the Redcoat had ordered a thirteen-year-old Jackson to shine his boots. Jackson had flat refused, and hadn't changed his mind even after the officer slashed him with a saber.

When he'd first heard the story, Sam had been skeptical. Now, watching Jackson with his own two eyes, he didn't doubt it any longer. The general's jaws were clenched, his bony fists were clenched, his whipcord body was clenched. He seemed ready to jump right out of his uniform and start pummeling the officer who was facing him.

"Answer me, blast you!" Jackson bellowed. Shrieked, rather, since he had a high-pitched voice. The general thrust his head forward so aggressively, his chin leading the way like the ram on an ancient war galley, that his fancy hat fell right off his head. The two-cornered general's hat landed on its side, like a shipwreck on a reef. Jackson paid no attention to the mishap.

The officer who was facing him—somebody in the Tennessee militia, judging from the uniform—was doing his level best not to wilt under Jackson's fury. But his level best . . .

Wasn't good enough. Not even close.

The man sidled backward a step, his eyes avoiding Jackson's accusing gaze. "Tarnation, General," he muttered, "you can't just—"

"*Yes, sir, I can! And, yes, sir—I most certainly* will! *I've done it before, and I'll do it again!*"

For the first time, Jackson seemed to catch sight of the two officers who had entered his command tent. He glared at General John Coffee first. But the glare was fleeting, nothing more than a split second's reflex.

"Coffee," he stated tersely. The greeting had an approving air to it, from what Sam could tell.

But then the glare turned on Sam himself, so he didn't have any time to ponder the matter.

It was quite a glare, too. Easily worthy of one of the heroes in Sam's treasured *Iliad*. Maybe not quite up to the standards of Achilles, but certainly the equal of anything Agamemnon or Menelaus could have managed.

"And *you,* sir!" the general barked. "You're wearing the uniform of a regular soldier in the army of the United States of America. Can I assume that *you* will follow orders?"

The general's eyes flicked to the militia officer. Jackson said nothing, but the glance alone was enough to make clear what he thought of the fellow.

Sam might have been amused, except he was starting to become angry himself. He didn't like bullies, never had, and the general looked to be about as bad a bully as he'd ever encountered.

"Yes, sir," he said stiffly, straightening up to his full height of six feet two inches. "I took the oath and I'll obey orders. Presuming the orders are lawful, that is."

With that, he fell silent. For a moment, it looked to Sam as if the general would literally explode. His pale face seemed so suffused with blood and fury that his temples threatened to burst. Both of them were throbbing now.

Then, to Sam's surprise, the general grunted a little laugh. "Ha! Got some backbone, do you? Good."

Jackson pointed a stiff finger at the target of his rage. "The issue in question here, young ensign, is whether or not these miserable militiamen will be allowed to desert their country in its time of need. I have informed this—this—this—*individual* that I will have shot any militiaman who attempts to desert."

The fact that the general's left arm was in a sling only added emphasis to the rigid, accusing finger of the other hand. For two reasons. First, because Jackson seemed to have an uncanny knack for striking dramatic poses. *The lion, wounded, yet still able to challenge the hyena.* Second, because the militia officer knew—so did everyone, including Sam himself—that the wound in question was the result of a recent shootout at a hotel in Nashville between Jackson and his friend Coffee and the Benton brothers. The pose might be histrionic, but Jackson's capacity for violence was by now a legend on the frontier.

Again, that jaw thrusting forth. "*Damn me* if I won't, sir!" he roared. "I'll shoot them myself, if I have to!"

The jaw receded, leaving the man a sinking wreck. Jackson's eyes turned back to Sam. "I will trust you to carry out the order, young ensign. If you've got spine enough to stand up to me, you ought to have spine enough to shoot a worthless deserter."

The officer, though sinking, hadn't quite dropped out of sight yet.

"General," he pleaded, "the terms under which the men enlisted—"

"Blast your terms, sir! *Blast them,* I say!"

This time, Jackson's finger pointed out of the tent. "Do the Red Sticks care about your 'terms'? I'll crush those savages, so help me I will—and you'll be there to help me do it. You will, sir! Don't doubt it! Or I'll crush you first!

"Now get out of my sight. Your protest has been heard, adjudged wanting in all right or reason, and summarily dismissed."

With that, the general took a half step back himself, as if he'd encountered a bad smell. The officer took advantage of the momentary space and scuttled out of the tent.

After he was gone, Jackson shook his head. "God save us from militiamen," he growled. "Lawyers, every one of them. And shysters at that."

His eyes came back to Sam, ranging, for a moment, up and down the uniform that identified him as a regular in the Thirty-ninth Infantry, U.S. Army. While European armies had adopted close-bodied coats or jackets in the course of the Napoleonic wars, American uniforms remained the traditional cutaway style, with elaborate lapels, facings, and turnbacks. Coats were still closed with hooks and eyes rather than buttons.

Sam's uniform was typical. The coat was blue and long-skirted, with scarlet cuffs and a standing collar. The woolen trousers were white, plain, and tucked into his boots. He had his tall leather infantry cap—often called a "tombstone shako"—tucked neatly into the crook of his arm.

After an inspection that lasted for several seconds, Jackson seemed satisfied. "Fortunately," he continued, "I now have *real* soldiers on the spot. What's your name, Ensign? And how long have you been serving the colors?"

"Sam Houston, sir. I enlisted in March of last year."

Jackson's eyebrows lowered slightly. "Houston. I believe I've heard about you. Aren't you the one who was adopted by the Cherokee?"

The sentence seemed almost like an accusation, but . . . not exactly. Sam couldn't really tell what lay beneath it.

"Yes, sir," he replied. "When I was sixteen, after I ran away from home. I lived for three years with John Jolly and his people. He's the one adopted me, and gave me my Cherokee name."

"And that is?"

"*Colonneh,* sir. It means 'The Raven.' "

Jackson sniffed. "Nasty birds, ravens. On the other hand, they're also tough, and smart. Let's hope they picked the right name. Do you speak the language?"

"Yes, sir."

"Fluently?"

"Yes, sir."

"Do you get along with the savages?"

"Very well, sir." Sam's big shoulders shifted. "And I don't take kindly to people insulting my family."

Jackson surprised him again. The general grinned—rather cheerfully, it seemed. "It's against the law to challenge a superior officer, youngster, so you'd best leave the rest of that thought unspoken. I'd have to shoot you dead, and I'd prefer not to do that. Still and all, I'll refrain from using the term. In your presence, at least." There was a hint of sarcasm in his voice.

The general rubbed his long chin. "I can use you for liaison then, if Coffee needs it. We've got five hundred Cherokees al-

lied with us in this campaign, and about a hundred friendly
Creeks. Do you speak their language, too?"

Sam hesitated. That was a hard question to answer. The Creek
Confederacy was an amalgam of a number of tribes of different
origins, further divided between the so-called Upper and Lower
Towns. The term "Creek" itself was a white man's word.
Creeks were more likely to think of themselves as Coweta or
Alabama or Tuskegee.

"Well . . ." he began.

But apparently Jackson understood the reality of the situation. "Any of the dialects?"

"I can get along, sir, with some of them. I speak a little
Choctaw, also."

"No Choctaws with us on this campaign, so that doesn't matter. It might later, though. Once we're done with the Red Sticks,
we'll be facing the British, you can be sure of it. Maybe the
Spanish, as well. John? Do you want him? If you do, I'll have
Colonel Williams detach him from duty with his regiment."

The officer who had accompanied Houston shrugged his
shoulders. "I could certainly use Ensign Houston, General, but I
don't really need him. At least a third of the Cherokees speak
English. The Ridge doesn't, true enough, but he's got that
young John Ross fellow to translate for him." Major Coffee
chuckled. "Of course, I don't think Ross really speaks Cherokee all that well. But we'll get along, true enough."

Jackson nodded. "All right, then. To tell you the truth, John,
it'd probably be better to keep the ensign with his unit. I'll be
counting on the Thirty-ninth to keep the ragtag-and-bobtail in
line." He glanced at the flap of the tent through which the militia officer had beat a hasty retreat. "I think I did a pretty good job
of bullying the little piglet. But you know as well as I do that
they need bullying on a regular basis. How *was* my tantrum, by
the way?"

Coffee smiled. "Pretty good. Not your very best, though."
The major looked down at Jackson's hat, which was still lying
on the floor. "For a really top performance, you should have
stomped on the hat."

The general stared down at the object in question. "Tarnation.
I didn't think of that." He seemed genuinely aggrieved.

Jackson stooped over and picked up the hat, brushed it off,

then jammed it back onto his head. By the time he was finished, Sam was thoroughly amazed at the transformation in the man. The general who now stood before him, smiling and relaxed, seemed like a completely different person.

Jackson gave him a cool, thin smile. "A lesson here, Ensign Houston, which will stand you in good stead. A reputation, once developed, is as valuable as a fine sword."

Then the smile became very thin. "But don't forget that it has to be a valid reputation. Or the sword's got no edge. I *will* shoot the bastards, if I have to."

There didn't seem to be much to say to that, so Sam kept his mouth shut. After a moment, the general turned away and motioned for them to follow him to a table that stood in the corner of the tent. "And now, John, let's discuss the campaign."

There was a large map spread across the table. "The Georgians are worthless, as usual," Jackson growled. "There's nobody quicker to steal land from Indians, but whenever it comes to having to actually *fight* the savages—"

He broke off, tossing Sam a sly glance. "Excuse me, Ensign. I should have said 'the gentlemen of the red-skinned race.' But whatever you call them, the Georgians run for cover every blasted time they appear. I just got word that General Floyd has retreated—again—and relinquished command to Colonel Milton at Fort Hull. Who'll probably be just as useless as every Georgian seems to be. So it'll be up to us Tennesseans to put an end to the Red Sticks."

Coffee studied the map intently, as did Sam. It was hand-drawn, and showed the terrain of the Territory of Mississippi, where the Red Sticks were concentrated. The Red Stick faction of the Creeks, the southern allies of Tecumseh, came mainly from the Confederacy's Upper Towns. By and large, the Lower Town Creeks had either remained neutral or were allied with the United States.

American newspapers tended to portray the Red Stick war as an attack on white settlers. It was that, certainly, but it was more in the way of a civil war among the Creeks themselves. The people massacred at Fort Mims by the Red Sticks a few months earlier, on August 30, had mainly been Creeks, not whites. Mixed-bloods, true, most of them—but the same could be said of the Red Sticks, especially their leaders. Tecumseh and his brother The Prophet had sought to unite all Indians against the whites. But, like most Indians, they viewed the distinction between "red men" and "white men" more along cultural lines than strictly racial ones. Many of Tecumseh's followers, especially the Creek warriors of the Red Stick faction, had some white ancestors themselves.

Tecumseh himself was dead now, killed in Canada in October, when U.S. forces under the command of General William Henry Harrison had defeated the British and their Indian allies at the battle of the Thames. It was reported that Colonel Richard Johnson, who'd led the final cavalry charge and had been badly wounded in the affray, had shot Tecumseh personally. But the fires Tecumseh and his brother The Prophet had lit among the many Indian tribes were still burning in the southern territories of the United States.

Coffee rubbed his chin. "Are you sure you don't want to wait for the Georgians to regroup, General?" His finger traced the lines of the Coosa and Tallapoosa rivers. "We're not going to move easily through this terrain. It's pretty much pure wilderness, by all accounts I've received."

Jackson shook his head impatiently. "We haven't time for a slow campaign, John. The real enemy is the British, don't ever forget it. We've got to crush this uprising as soon as possible or we'll still be tied up when the British arrive."

"You may be jumping to conclusions, General. Napoleon might beat them, you know, even after his defeat at Leipzig. If he does, the British won't be in any position to send more troops all the way across the Atlantic."

Sam was a little surprised that Coffee didn't hesitate to argue the matter. After witnessing the Homeric temper tantrum Jackson had just thrown, Sam himself would have been a little hesitant to disagree with him under any circumstances.

But the general didn't seem to mind. "All my hopes are with Napoleon, to be sure. But . . ." He sighed. "The bastards are already into France itself. Marching on Paris, according to the latest news. I just can't assume that he'll win. And if he loses, which at this point I'd have to say he probably will, then the British Empire is going to bring all its power down on us. With the Spanish holding their coats. Before that happens, we've *got* to have the savages under control."

Again, he gave Sam that sidelong glance. "Begging your pardon, Ensign."

Sam suppressed a sigh of his own. He had a sneaking suspicion the general was going to needle him on the subject for . . . quite some time.

Jackson turned back to the map, his own finger tracing a route along the Coosa. "I intend to start our march as soon as possible. We'll follow the Coosa down to here, at which point we'll move eastward toward Emuckfaw. From there, we'll just be a short distance upriver from the horseshoe bend on the Tallapoosa, where Chief Menawa and Weatherford and about a thousand Red Stick warriors have forted up.

"John, I'll want you and your cavalry—you'll be working with the Cherokees, too—"

CHAPTER 2

When The Ridge and his companion saw the militia officer come scuttling out of General Jackson's tent, they said nothing, but they did exchange a little smile. Some of the Creeks had already started calling the American general "Sharp Knife," and The Ridge was pretty sure it wouldn't be long before the Cherokees who were Jackson's allies would be doing the same.

The smile faded soon enough, however. When it came to the Americans, there wasn't much for Cherokees to smile about.

Many Creeks, and a fair number of Cherokees and Choctaws, would explain it on the simple grounds that the Americans were white people, and, as such, a fickle and treacherous race. But The Ridge didn't think even the Red Sticks really believed that. Maybe in the North they did, where Tecumseh himself had come from. The Ridge didn't really know that much about those tribes, even though the stories claimed the Cherokee themselves had come from the North, long ago. Those stories were probably true, he mused, since the Cherokees spoke a language that was similar to the Iroquois.

But racial explanations didn't make much sense to The Ridge, and never had. He was himself mostly a full-blood, yet all he had to do was look around him to see the extent to which "the Cherokees" had long ago begun to change, on that level which the whites called "race." Even the name "Cherokee" was of white origin. The term the Cherokee themselves used was *"Ani-Yunwiya,"* which meant the "Real People" or the "Principal People."

All he had to do was look at the man squatting next to him, in fact. Young John Ross.

To all outward appearances, John Ross was a white man himself. His skin was as pale as any white man's; his hair was red; his eyes were blue. Nor was that a freak of nature. Measured by blood, John Ross *was* a white man. The Ridge didn't know him well yet, since he'd only just met him on this campaign, but he knew some of the man's ancestry. Seven of his eight immediate progenitors were white people, mostly of Scot extraction. Only one of them, his great-grandmother Ghigooie of the Bird Clan, had been a Cherokee.

But the way the Cherokee measured such things, that made John Ross a member of the clan. The fact that he looked like a Scotsman simply didn't matter, as far as they were concerned. The *Ani-Yunwiya* traced lineage through the mother's line, not the father's. The white man's concept of "race" was an alien one. The people whom the Americans called "Indians" actually belonged to a wide variety of peoples, who spoke different languages and had different customs.

No, The Ridge wasn't really an Indian, except insofar as the white people placed him in that category. But because they did, he had to deal with it, because he had to deal with them.

From his own viewpoint, though, he was *Ani-Yunwiya,* because he belonged to one of the seven Cherokee clans. The Deer Clan. Beyond that, he recognized kinship with many other tribes, since Cherokees often married outside the seven clans.

John Ross probably had a better understanding of the white way of thinking, even if he didn't agree with it. Despite his youthful age, Ross had already acquired a reputation among his people, and he was emerging as a Cherokee leader. Certainly no one doubted his loyalties to the Bird Clan.

Things were no different with their Red Stick enemies. Somewhere in the distance to the south, the Red Stick faction of the

Creeks had forted up on a bend of the Tallapoosa River in an attempt to withstand Jackson's coming assault. Their loyalties to their own leaders were fierce, but had little to do with race. Their central war chief was a man who, like most Indians of the time, had two names. Red Eagle, and . . . William Weatherford.

Like Ross, Weatherford had more white than Indian ancestors. That hadn't stopped him from leading the successful attack on Fort Mims, although rumor had it that Weatherford had tried to prevent the massacre of the fort's population. But The Ridge was quite sure that race had nothing to do with the massacre, either. Most of the people massacred at Fort Mims had been Creek half-bloods, just like Weatherford himself and many of his Red Stick followers. The different ways in which white people and red people measured difference to begin with was just one of the many problems they had faced, separately and together, for over two centuries now.

The Ridge had seen the sea, several times since his youth, and had never forgotten the inexorable power of the tides. They couldn't be stopped, certainly. But perhaps they could be channeled.

Perhaps.

John Ross was somewhat in awe of The Ridge, and so he took his cue from his older companion's unreadable countenance, and his still manner of watching things.

"Stoic." That's what white Americans would have labeled The Ridge. The word wouldn't have meant anything to the man himself, since he spoke no English and was basically illiterate. But John himself was fluent in English—more so than he was in Cherokee, in fact—and he was a voracious reader.

Still, John was a Cherokee, and he thought like one. So he knew that "stoic" was a misnomer. The Ridge's manner did not derive from the ancient philosophies of the Romans, whom most Americans saw as their political forefathers. John Ross had read some of those Roman texts in school, as did most educated children, but he was sure The Ridge had never even heard of them.

No, The Ridge's manner came from the traditions of his own people. The stillness of hunters waiting for prey; the patience of the river bottoms where a people grew its beans, squash, and corn.

The Ridge was in his early forties. He was well known among the Cherokee as an advocate of finding workable compromises with the whites, and even adopting many of their practices, when it made sense. But, in other ways, he was something of a throwback. One of the great ancient ones, John Ross liked to imagine, come back to life in the Cherokee time of need. The Ridge wasn't entirely a pureblood, since his mother's father had been a Scot frontiersman. But there was no trace of that ancestry in his form and figure. The Ridge was as dark-skinned as any Cherokee, with the dramatic nose and cheeks to go with his powerful build. He'd been named for his hunting prowess. "The Ridge" was an English translation of the Cherokee *Kahnungdatlageh,* which meant "the man who walks on the mountaintop."

He had been a blooded warrior at the age of seventeen, killing one of the white Tennesseans who had been allied with the Unakas. By the time he was thirty, he was one of the Cherokees' most influential chiefs. He was often referred to as *asgá siti.* The term was usually translated into English as "dreadful," although for Cherokees themselves the connotations were more that of "terrifying" or "formidable."

Still, The Ridge had for at least a decade been the principal voice among the Cherokee, advocating an end to the ancient Blood Law that kept the Cherokees—like most Indian nations—continually embroiled in clan feuds.

John's own musings were interrupted by new movement at the entrance to the general's tent. Two more American officers were emerging.

The Ridge was already studying them. One of them, rather.

The man on the left, John Coffee, wasn't the object of his scrutiny—he was already well known to the Cherokee. It was the young officer who accompanied Coffee whom The Ridge found interesting.

Physically, at least, he was certainly impressive. Very tall, broad-shouldered, and with a muscular physique. But The Ridge could outwrestle almost any man he'd ever met, so that was of no interest to him. Instead, he focused on the young officer's face.

That face had possibilities, he decided. The blue eyes looked to be intelligent, and the mouth seemed to be one that smiled easily. Better still, one that could tell jokes.

"Is that the one?"

John Ross nodded.

So.

The adopted son of Oolooteka, "he who puts the drum away"—or John Jolly, as he was often called. John Jolly was a fairly minor chief among the Cherokee, but his older brother Tahlonteskee wielded great influence. Mostly a bad influence, The Ridge thought, since Tahlonteskee was the most prominent advocate of moving the tribe to the West. Indeed, Tahlonteskee had already done so, leading a thousand people in his own clan across the great river into the region the Americans called Arkansas.

At best, The Ridge thought the decision had been premature. But Tahlonteskee wasn't the only one who was advocating that course of action. His younger brother John Jolly did so as well, although he hadn't yet made the move himself. Their position was especially influential among the purebloods.

So.

"I think we will talk to him," The Ridge announced.

John Ross started to rise. The Ridge placed a hand on his forearm and drew him gently back down. "Not now. After the battle."

Ross shot him a questioning glance. The Ridge allowed himself another little smile. "Whatever else is different about Americans, one thing is not. They prize courage as much as we do. So. After the battle. He will be a great deal older then than he is now, once that day is over, and everyone will know a great deal more about him."

Finally, Sam couldn't keep the question from bursting out.

"He was *faking* it?"

As they walked away from Jackson's tent, General Coffee cast the young ensign a sidelong stare.

"I have known Andy Jackson for ten years, both as a friend and a business partner. I married his wife's niece, and I fought a duel with Dickinson's friend McNairy two months before Andy killed Dickinson. I know him as well as anyone does. Andy Jackson doesn't *fake* anything.

"It's just . . ." Coffee looked away, as if gathering his thoughts. "It's a little hard to explain. Let's just say that the general is a lot smarter than most people think he is."

Something in Sam's face must have made it clear that he wasn't satisfied with the explanation. Coffee issued a little chuckle.

"All right, then let me put it this way. With Andy Jackson, you just never know. He does, in fact, have a temper that can shake buildings. And he can be as cold-blooded and ruthless as anyone you'll ever meet. You heard about the time a company of militiamen tried to march back to Tennessee—it happened last November—because their term of enlistment was up? Andy rode out on his horse, planted himself square in front of them, and leveled his rifle at them. Said he'd shoot the first man who took another step."

Sam nodded. By now, the story was famous—notorious, more like—all over the frontier. He'd even heard that it was stirring up a ruckus in Washington, D.C.

"And there's the time Hall told Jackson his brigade was planning to desert—this happened at Fort Deposit, a month later. The story goes that Jackson had two cannons trained on them. Then mounted his horse and swore that he'd have them fired on, despite the fact that he and his horse were right there in the line of fire. You heard that one, too, I'd wager."

Sam nodded.

"Well, both stories are absolutely true. In every detail. I was an eyewitness to the first one myself. And I can tell you there wasn't a single one of those militiamen who doubted for a minute that Andy would pull the trigger. They don't call him 'Old Hickory' for nothing."

The two men walked on in silence for a moment, negotiating their way around a group of soldiers who were squatting at a campfire. After they were past, they found themselves picking their way a little more slowly, now that the sun had set. Coffee spoke again.

"You just never know, that's the point. And that's the way Andy likes it. Did they tell you when you were a kid that bullies are always cowards?"

Sam laughed softly. "Yeah, but I didn't believe it, even then."

"Smart lad. It's pure horseshit—and Andy Jackson is the living proof of it. He's a ferocious bully, and he's a sneaky, conniving bastard who won't hesitate for a second to trade on that reputation. But he doesn't have a cowardly bone in his body. Even his fingernails have guts."

Coffee stopped then and turned to face Sam straight on. The general was as big as Houston, so their eyes were on a level. There was still enough light shed by the sundown to enable Sam to make out his features. Coffee's round face was surmounted by a mass of black hair and centered on a prominent nose. He had very dark eyes. Despite the natural solemnity of the face, Sam thought he detected a trace of a smile playing across the general's lips.

"And I'll tell you what else is true, young man. The British probably *will* beat Napoleon. And if they do, they'll send their crack units here—Wellington's veterans—to crush the only republic left on the face of the earth."

Sam thought that was a bit of an exaggeration. The Swiss were a republic, and they were likely to survive the fall of Napoleon. However . . .

He wasn't inclined to argue the point, since he understood what Coffee was saying. The Swiss had been around for centuries, and they weren't any sort of threat to the aristocracies that ruled Europe. The United States, on the other hand, really stuck in their craw.

"If they can get away with it," Coffee continued, "don't think for a moment that the British wouldn't love to throw our little revolution here into the waste heap. If they can land and seize control of the gulf, along with the mouth of the Mississippi, they'll have us by the throat."

He stopped talking for a moment, and cocked his head questioningly.

Sam nodded in agreement, and firmly. He'd already come to the same conclusions.

"Okay, then." Coffee turned and resumed walking. "So here's what else is true. Just be damn glad that conniving, way-smarter-than-he-looks, bullying son-of-a-bitch Andy Jackson is in command. We'll need him, before this is over."

CHAPTER 3

MARCH 27, 1814
The Battle of the Horseshoe Bend

The next time Sam Houston encountered Andrew Jackson, the general was hollering again, but this time Sam couldn't make out the words.

First, because Jackson wasn't the only one hollering. So were a thousand Red Stick warriors hemmed in behind their barricade on a horseshoe bend in the Tallapoosa, with about two and a half thousand white soldiers and militiamen facing them.

Secondly, because the hostile Creeks trapped behind their own fortifications were beating war drums. *Lots* of war drums, from the sound they were making.

And, thirdly, because up close, even two cannons make an incredible racket.

It was late morning when Sam and his superior officer, Major Lemuel Montgomery, came up the rise where the general had set up his field headquarters. Topping the rise, Sam saw the two cannons Jackson had hauled with him across the wilderness positioned atop a small hill overlooking the fortifications the Red Sticks had erected. Sam had been in the army long enough now to recognize the cannons as a six-pounder and a three-pounder.

Field guns. No more, and the three-pounder was something of a lightweight, at that. Nevertheless, Sam had been hearing the racket they made ever since the Thirty-ninth Infantry had arrived at the battlefield and had taken up their position. The Thirty-ninth was at one end of a field that sloped down toward the other end, which was closed off by the Creek fortifications. Now that he was close enough, he could see that the guns hadn't done any damage worth talking about to the enemy's fieldworks.

He wasn't really surprised, though, getting his first good look at those fortifications. The Red Sticks had had months to prepare for this attack, and obviously they hadn't wasted the time. The barricade they'd put up across the neck of the peninsula was impressive. Very, very impressive.

Moments later Montgomery and Houston were just a few feet away from Jackson. Seeing them, the general waved his hand in the direction of the fortifications. The nearest part of the wall stood less than a hundred yards from the position Jackson had taken on the hill. The farthest part of it, Sam estimated, was another three hundred yards distant.

"Have you ever seen anything like it, Lemuel?" Jackson demanded. His tone was half angry; the other half contained grudging respect. "Tarnation, who would have thought those savages would come up with something this well made?"

Jackson's blue eyes flitted to Sam, and a sarcastic little smile came to his lips. "Begging the ensign's pardon."

Sam decided to ignore the remark. Truth be told, he wasn't any too fond of the Red Sticks himself. He didn't consider them savages, as such, the way most white people did. But they'd certainly behaved savagely since they'd organized themselves in response to the religious preaching of Tecumseh's brother, the prophet Tenskwatawa. That had been true even before the massacre at Fort Mims.

Sam frowned as he studied the fortifications. The breastwork that the Red Sticks had erected across the neck of the peninsula consisted of heavy timber—solid logs, most of it—laid in a wall ranging anywhere from five to eight feet tall. The solidity of the structure made it effectively impervious to the small cannons Jackson had with him. The double row of firing ports and the zigzag design of it gave the defenders the ability to bring enfilade fire on anyone advancing across the open field that stretched in front.

True, as was almost invariably the case in Indian wars, the Creek warriors were poorly supplied with guns. They were probably just as poorly supplied with ammunition. But, with those fortifications, even the bows with which most of the Red Sticks would be armed could be devastating.

Houston could see Major Montgomery's face tightening, the way a man's will when he's arriving at a very unpleasant conclusion.

"We'll have to try a frontal assault, then, General."

Jackson nodded. "I'm afraid so. I'd hoped the cannons . . ." He waved that thought away impatiently. "I'll need to rely on you and your regulars, Lemuel. Pass the word to Colonel Williams to get ready."

"Yes, sir." Montgomery winced slightly, as the six-pounder went off again, just a few feet away. "How soon?"

"I'm not sure, yet." Jackson took off his hat and ran long, bony fingers through his hair. Because his left arm was still in a sling, he had to use the same right hand that was holding the hat. The result was to dishevel his stiff, sandy-gray hair all the more.

Then he gestured with the hat toward the Tallapoosa. The river wasn't far off, but it couldn't be seen through the heavily forested area. This late in March, this far south, most of the trees already had foliage on them.

"I sent Coffee and his cavalry and all of the Cherokees to ford the Tallapoosa two miles away, then circle around to the other side of the river. Mainly, I just wanted to make sure the Red Sticks were trapped. I intend to crush them here, once and for all, and I don't want any of them escaping. But . . ."

He clamped the hat back on his head. "John's an energetic officer. He may be able to distract their attention with a diversion of some kind. So let's wait another hour and a half. In the meantime, I'll keep peppering them with cannon fire. Even if it doesn't look to be doing any good, that should keep their attention fixed on us, instead of the riverbank."

Montgomery pulled out a watch. "That'd be half-past noon, General. I'll tell the colonel."

Jackson nodded. Montgomery squared his shoulders. "I'll lead the assault myself."

The general nodded again. Then, abruptly, he stuck out his hand. "Take care, Lemuel." There was quite a bit of warmth in his tone. Houston had heard that Jackson and the major had been personal friends since before the war started.

To his surprise, after Jackson finished shaking hands with Montgomery, the general thrust his hand at Sam. "And you, as well, Ensign Houston. I will rely upon you to carry forward if . . . anything untoward happens to Major Montgomery."

Jackson's grip was firm. Sam hoped the same was true of his own. "I will, sir. You can count on it."

He even managed not to wince when another cannon went off. Fortunately, it was only the three-pounder.

Slowly, The Ridge moved a branch, just enough to afford him a good view of the opposite bank of the Tallapoosa. Behind him and spread out on both sides, hidden in the forest, hundreds of Cherokee warriors crouched. General Coffee and his cavalry were somewhere farther back, having agreed to follow The Ridge's advice and stay well out of sight of whatever Red Sticks might be watching the river.

In theory, Jackson's Cherokee allies were led by their chief, Gideon Morgan, to whom the Americans had given the rank of colonel. But that was mainly due to Morgan's fluency with the English language. In practice, as the campaign against the Red Sticks had unfolded, it was The Ridge who'd come to be the central war leader, and the one whom General Coffee relied upon. The Ridge had started the campaign with the lowly American rank of lieutenant, but now he was a major.

Observing nothing on the other side except a line of beached Creek canoes, The Ridge examined the river itself for a moment. The muddy waters of the Tallapoosa were moving fairly quickly, but he didn't think it would be impossible to swim across. Not even difficult, really, since the distance wasn't that great.

He went back to studying the opposite bank, with the patience of a hunter.

Nothing. There might well be some warriors in the vicinity, but it was becoming obvious the Red Sticks hadn't thought to place a guard on the river.

He wasn't surprised. He could hear the sounds of fighting off in the distance, and had been hearing them for quite some time. By now, the Red Stick warriors would be concentrated at or near the fortifications that stretched across the neck of the peninsula, hundreds of yards away from the river's curve. The terrain directly opposite The Ridge's location was flat, once the riverbank itself was surmounted, and it wasn't as heavily forested as most of the region.

Somewhere in the distance he thought he could see the high ground that was reported to form the center of the peninsula, and he was pretty sure the Creek village itself would be located at the foot of it. That area would be guarded, but the river itself wasn't being watched. Not closely, at least.

Moving slowly again, The Ridge let the branch slide back into position, no more abruptly than if it had been moved by the wind. Then, he turned his head and considered the Cherokees who were clustered nearby.

He dismissed John Ross without even a thought. The youngster seemed stalwart enough, but had no real experience in this sort of fighting. The Americans had made him an adjutant, and had given him the rank of a second lieutenant. But, again, that had been mostly due to his familiarity with English. For something like this, The Ridge wanted a more experienced man. Besides, it would take a good swimmer, and The Ridge had no idea how well Ross could handle himself in the water.

His eyes fell on The Whale. The man's name wasn't simply due to his size. The Ridge made a subtle summoning gesture with his head, and The Whale eased his way forward.

"Right across the river," The Ridge murmured. He slid aside a little so The Whale could take his own peek.

After carefully parting the branches and examining the canoes on the other side, The Whale grunted softly. "I'll take two men with me. Won't take long, so have everyone ready."

He turned away and softly called out two names. As the men rose from their crouch, The Whale led them a short distance upstream. They'd start their crossing far enough above the beached canoes that the current wouldn't sweep them right on past.

Then The Ridge glanced at John Ross again. If the youngster harbored any resentment because he hadn't been chosen for the task, there was no sign of it on his expression or in his posture. The Ridge was pleased, but not surprised. He'd already come to the conclusion that Ross was exceptionally levelheaded, and as such not subject to public bravado that infected most men his age.

There remained, of course, the question of Ross's courage. The American ensign wasn't the only young man in the group for whom this would be the first real test in battle. But there, too, The Ridge expected the young Cherokee to acquit himself well enough.

Well enough was all The Ridge asked for this day. The Cherokees already had enough warriors who had proven their fighting abilities. The Ridge himself was one of them. What they lacked were leaders who could negotiate their way through the tangled thicket of politics that confronted their nation in a world being swept over by a tide of white settlers.

He had high hopes for John Ross. Because of his background, Ross had a far greater familiarity with the subtleties of American customs than did most Cherokees. Certainly far more than The Ridge himself. The Ridge had never visited the home of the Ross family, near Lookout Mountain, but he had heard tales about it. The two-story log house was said to be full of books and maps and newspapers—even newspapers from England. John had been brought up in Cherokee country, in a Cherokee family, but as a boy he'd been tutored by a white man; and, as a youth, he had attended a white man's academy in Tennessee.

The value of such an education was unquestionable, in these difficult days. The proof of it was an even greater marvel than a two-story house full of books. John Ross had formed a business partnership with Timothy Meigs, the son of the well-known Indian agent Colonel Meigs. They had taken good advantage of the lucrative government contracts produced by the Americans' wars against the British and the Creeks. In the short few months before Ross had joined the Cherokee force that now fought alongside Jackson, he'd become a prosperous man, even as white men measured such things.

A Cherokee—not more than twenty-three years old—becoming wealthy from trading with white men! That was what the American missionaries called a "miracle."

As he ruminated, The Ridge listened for The Whale and his two companions. That was a waste of effort, really, since he knew full well that the men would perform their task soundlessly.

Sure enough, the first sign The Ridge got of their progress was the sight of the three warriors, coming down the river. The Whale and his companions, all of them expert swimmers, were crossing the stream without trying to fight the current, moving quickly, surely, and quietly.

"Get ready!" he hissed. The words were pitched in such a way that, while they wouldn't be heard by anyone across the river, they would alert all of the nearest Cherokee warriors. He could rely on them to pass the word along to the remaining hundreds crouched farther back in the forest.

That left only . . .

The Ridge hesitated. On the one hand, he wanted to observe the young man next to him under fire. On the other hand, it was also critical that the American cavalrymen didn't work at cross-purposes with what the Cherokee warriors were going to be doing. Once everyone started piling across the river, there was a serious risk that the allies would start killing one another in the midst of the chaos. White soldiers, even regulars, were notorious for not making fine distinctions between friendly and hostile Indians, especially once their blood was up.

Granted, most Indians didn't make fine distinctions between friendly and hostile whites, as well. But in situations like this one, the white soldiers had the advantage of wearing uniforms, which the Indians didn't.

For this campaign, it had been mutually agreed that all the Cherokees would wear two distinctive feathers and a deer tail in their headbands. The Ridge was hoping that would be enough to keep the American soldiers from firing on Cherokees by accident. Still, it would be smart to make sure that Coffee knew exactly what they were doing—and Ross was the obvious person to send as his liaison. The young Cherokee's English was fluent. More than fluent, really, since English was his native language.

So The Ridge arrived at his decision. "Find General Coffee and tell him we're crossing the river," he ordered Ross. "Do what you can to make sure the Americans don't start shooting at us, once they follow us across."

Ross's mouth quirked. "They're cavalrymen, don't forget. By the time they finally bring themselves to abandon their precious horses—since there's no way to get them across the river easily—it'll probably all be over, anyway."

The Ridge chuckled softly. There was quite a bit of truth to what Ross said, but . . .

"Do it anyway."

Ross hesitated. Just long enough, The Ridge understood, to make clear that he wasn't afraid to join the fight. It was very smoothly done, for such a young man. Then, moving not quite as quietly as an experienced warrior would have, Ross faded into the forest and was gone.

The Ridge turned his attention back across the river. The Whale and his companions had reached the canoes and were already sliding three of them into the water. They were big canoes, and they'd have only one man guiding each one. The current being what it was, they'd come across the river quite a ways farther down from his position. He did a quick estimate of where they'd land, rose from his crouch, and started heading that way.

His own movements, unlike those of Ross, were almost completely silent. That was simply long habit, so ingrained that The Ridge wasn't even conscious of it. The noise of the battle being waged somewhere on the other side of the small peninsula was such that even if he had set off an explosion on his side of the river, it probably wouldn't have been noticed.

Major Montgomery pulled out his watch.

"Fifteen minutes," he announced.

"We're ready, sir," stated Houston. The two officers were standing twenty yards in front of the arrayed lines of the Thirty-ninth Infantry, facing the enemy fortifications.

Montgomery took the time to move back and inspect the ranks himself. That wasn't because he doubted the ensign's assessment; it was simply because Montgomery had learned—largely from watching General Jackson—that soldiers were steadied by the immediate and visible presence of the officers who would lead them in an attack.

"God, I love regulars," the major murmured. Montgomery himself was only a "regular" in a purely formal sense. Still, even in his short military career, he'd come to share Jackson's distrust of militia volunteers.

Taken as individuals, militiamen were no different from regular soldiers. Better men, actually, in most ways. Certainly, as a rule, more successful men. The regular army was notorious for attracting vagabonds and drunkards to join its ranks, just for the sake of the steady pay and regular provisions; whereas militiamen were frequently respected members of their communities.

But even those members of the militias who weren't lawyers soon enough adopted a lawyerly view of their rights and obligations. That usually meant a keen sense of the right to leave the service the moment their short term of enlistment was up.

As he walked slowly down the well-formed ranks of the Thirty-ninth Infantry, here and there giving a soldier a careful inspection, Major Montgomery's lips twisted into a half-sarcastic little smile.

Regulars, God bless 'em.

Most of the men were armed with the older-style Model 1795 .69-caliber musket that Jackson had wanted for this campaign. The weapon wasn't as handy as the Model 1803 .54-caliber Harpers Ferry musket that was the standard issue for regulars, but it had the advantage of a fixed bayonet mount—and all the bayonets were fixed. Jackson believed in the value of cold steel.

They looked splendid, too, in their real uniforms with their high-collared blue coats and white trousers. Best of all, Jackson's quartermaster had somehow managed to finagle iron cap plates for the Thirty-ninth's tall headgear. The men would go into battle with their heads shining the regiment's name in the sunlight, instead of having to make do with painted imitations.

Vagabonds or not, when the time came these regular soldiers could be counted upon to do their duty, and do it well. Whatever coat of mail they might pass on to their offspring, assuming they knew who their bastards were in the first place, it might well include a half-empty bottle of whiskey as part of the insignia. Should, by all rights, for at least half of them. Still, there'd be no petticoats there. Not a one.

Montgomery came back forward to stand alongside Ensign Houston. He pulled out his watch again.

"Five minutes to go. And, yes, we're ready."

CHAPTER 4

There were some Creek warriors not far from the riverbank, as it turned out. Even if they hadn't been posted as guards, they were too alert not to notice when The Whale and his two companions started sliding canoes into the river.

With a great shout, several of them rushed down to the water's edge, waving the crimson-painted war clubs that had given the Red Sticks their name. Most of the clubs were the type known as *atassa,* which were very similar in shape and design to a sword, concentrating the force of the blow on a narrow wooden edge. Many, however, were ball-headed clubs, or tomahawks with flint or iron blades.

The Whale's two companions got their canoes into the river and started paddling them across. But The Whale himself had some trouble untying the tether on his chosen canoe. By the time he got the canoe freed, it was too late. The Red Sticks were right on him.

The Whale hadn't encumbered himself with weapons when he swam the river, so all he had for defense was the canoe's paddle. The Ridge saw him rise up and smash the first Red Stick in the ribs with the edge of it. The Creek warrior went down instantly. His rib cage must have been shattered, and he might even be dead. The Whale was very strong.

But there were four more Red Sticks surrounding the intruder. He was only able to block one club strike and break another warrior's arm before he was struck down himself, his head bleeding profusely. Half-dazed, The Whale dropped his paddle and scrambled into some brush by the riverbank.

No doubt the Creeks would have followed him and finished him off, but by then one of them had caught sight of the hundreds of Cherokees massed in the woods on the other side of the river. He gestured to his fellow warriors, and the expression on their faces almost caused The Ridge to laugh.

Meanwhile, the two canoes were already more than half the distance across, and it was obvious to the Creeks that they would soon be facing an invasion of their fortress on its unprotected river side.

So, they left The Whale unmolested and began running back to alert the rest of the Red Sticks. By the time they were all out of sight, the captured canoes had reached the southern bank. The Ridge was the first to pile in. The Whale and his companions had taken care, right off, to seize the paddles for all the canoes and stack them in the ones they'd seized. So all the Cherokees who crammed into the canoes could help drive them back across the river. As experienced as they were with such things, it took less than a minute before they were starting to clamber onto the opposite bank.

The Ridge didn't bother giving any orders, now. Cherokees

might not have the mindless discipline of white soldiers, but they didn't need to be told the obvious. Several Cherokee warriors, each holding a paddle, were already untying the rest of the canoes. They'd paddle them back across to load up more warriors. Within a few minutes, the vanguard that had crossed in the first two canoes would be reinforced by hundreds more.

"Can The Ridge handle it alone?" General Coffee asked, leaning forward in the saddle.

John Ross nodded firmly. "Yes, sir. And, ah . . ." His voice trailed off, as he searched for the right words.

Coffee frowned. "Yes, I think I know what you're getting at. He's more worried about being shot by my soldiers than he is about the Creeks, isn't he? Can't say I blame him."

Coffee pursed his lips and stared into the distance, examining what he could see of the river.

"All right, then. I'll keep my cavalry on this side for an hour. But I'll have them spread out all the way around the horseshoe, with orders to shoot any Indian who tries to swim across. The one thing General Jackson is determined about is that we're going to crush the Red Sticks, here and now. They'll either surrender or die. None of them are going to escape."

He looked down at Ross again, his expression bleak. "You understand? Make sure you tell The Ridge to keep his Cherokees on the other side, once they've crossed, no matter how desperate it gets. Those fancy feathers and a deer's tail won't look like anything once they're soaking wet and dragging behind heads of men swimming across the river. They'll just get shot in the heat of battle . . ."

He didn't finish the sentence, because he didn't need to. Ross understood the harsh realities as well as anyone. To most white men, one Indian looked just like the next. There were some who could tell the difference between the hair styles worn by the different Indian tribes, but not many. All the more so because of the habit men had in the southern tribes of wearing turbans as often as not.

John suppressed a sigh. This was no time to dwell on the unfairness of life. There was still a battle to be fought and won, this day.

"I'll tell him, sir," he said, then he raced off.

*   *   *

A horseman came charging up the field toward Montgomery and Houston, where they were standing in front of the Thirtyninth. Even at a distance, Sam was pretty sure it was the same militia officer he'd seen harangued by Jackson the day he arrived in Fort Strother. Houston had good eyesight.

Montgomery had been on the verge of ordering the attack. But, seeing the oncoming officer, he held off. "Better see what he has to say. Jackson must have sent him." The major snorted. "The blasted fool. On a field like this, he'll break that horse's leg if he isn't careful."

Even on an uphill slope, at the pace he was driving his mount, the militia officer would arrive within seconds. Sam was already certain he knew the message he was bringing. The officer had plucked off his hat and was waving it frantically toward the Creek fieldworks, using only one hand to guide the horse.

"Blasted fool," Montgomery repeated.

"Sir, I think General Coffee—or the Cherokees, more likely—just launched an attack on the enemy from across the river," Sam said.

Montgomery squinted at the log fortifications. The open field which led to that barricade sloped from a rise to the north of the peninsula. The Thirty-ninth was arrayed on that rise, ready to start its charge. Most of the charge would be on level ground, since the rise ended less than half the distance to the wall. But their current position did give them, at the moment, a decent view over the top of the enemy fieldworks.

"I think you're right. I can see Red Sticks—quite a few of them—scrambling away from the barricade."

Sam was pretty sure his eyes were better than the major's, and he'd already seen the same thing.

But there was no longer any need for them to guess. The militia officer finally came within shouting range.

"The general says to attack at once! Coffee has launched a diversion in the enemy's rear!"

"That's it, then," Montgomery said. He drew his sword, which, like Sam's, was scabbarded on a two-inch waist belt. Thereafter, the swords parted company. Officers were expected to purchase their own weapons, and Montgomery was a prosperous man. His weapon was a fine clipped-point saber, silvermounted with eagle pommel and an ivory grip. Sam's was a straight sword he'd purchased from a down-at-heels artillery officer who'd resigned from the service. The sword could best be described as utilitarian.

On the positive side, Sam had also bargained well enough to get the man's pistol in the deal. He didn't think much of the sword, but the sidearm was a dandy Model 1805 Harpers Ferry cavalryman's pistol. It was against regulations, true, but he'd stuffed it into his waistband that morning, and Montgomery hadn't done more than look at it cross-eyed for a few seconds.

Jackson hadn't looked at it at all.

Montgomery hawked up some phlegm and spit on the ground. Then, loudly, he said, "Ensign, give the signal!"

Trying not to smile, Sam waved his hand, and the drum began pounding the signal to advance.

Their one and only drum. When Jackson's army had marched out of Fort Strother on March 13, to begin what everyone hoped would be the final campaign against the Red Sticks, it had been discovered that there was only one drummer boy left in the little army. All the others, it seemed, had reached the end of their enlistment, and had gone home.

Another commander might have been nonplussed by the fact. But Old Hickory, after five minutes worth of yelling about worthless thirteen-year-old lawyers, had simply snarled that men could march as easily to a single drum as they could to a thousand. They'd just have to listen a little harder.

So as the drum began its own battle against the din, the men began to move.

They had several hundred yards to cover, and Montgomery paced the charge accordingly. At the beginning, it was more in the way of a fast march than a "charge," properly speaking. Sam was eager to close with the enemy—just to get rid of his nervous energy, really, not because he felt any bloodlust. Still, he appreciated the major's foresight.

Maybe Homer's ancient Achaean heroes could run hundreds of yards and fight a battle at the end—though Sam had his doubts—but their feebler modern descendants would be winded if they tried to do the same. The pace Major Montgomery established wouldn't tire out soldiers who were accustomed to frontier wilderness terrain. Sam guessed that the major would only order a real charge once they were within fifty yards or so of the breastworks.

True enough, that meant they'd be exposed to enemy fire that much longer, out in the open. Still, better that than to try to scale those fieldworks exhausted and out of breath.

It was hard, though, at least for Sam, to maintain that disciplined pace. Already, the Creeks were starting to fire arrows at the oncoming Thirty-ninth. They'd save their powder and bullets until the infantry regulars were within a hundred yards.

Sam's mother routinely accused him of being "high-strung." True, his mother was a harsh woman, given to exaggeration when she criticized someone—which she did frequently, especially her children. Still, he knew there was at least some truth to it.

So, he did his best to dampen the instincts that were shrieking to send him racing toward the enemy. He still didn't feel anything resembling the wrath of Achilles—which, in and of itself, suited him just fine. Sam had never much liked Achilles. He'd always found the Trojan Hector a far more appealing character.

No, it wasn't bloodlust or fury, he finally decided. He had no particular desire to pitch headlong into battle, no matter how much he wanted to make a name for himself. He was simply wound tight and ready to run, like a racehorse, now that the contest was under way.

That realization helped him to focus. Sam Houston had determined that he would pass through his life like a fine thoroughbred, not a plow horse. Better a short and glorious life than a long and dull one.

"Better yet," he murmured, "a *long* and glorious life."

"I'm sorry, Ensign, I didn't catch that," said Major Montgomery, marching along next to him.

Embarrassed, Sam cleared his throat and tightened his grip on the sword. "Nothing, sir. Just talking to myself."

Sam eyed an arrow that was speeding in his direction. More and more were falling now, though few were yet finding their targets. He didn't break stride, but he did edge slightly to his right, almost crowding Montgomery. The arrow passed safely three feet to his left.

"Don't," said the major. The word was spoken firmly, even sternly, but the tone wasn't accusatory. "In a fight, you can't see every danger. Just ignore it all, young man. That'll help steady the men—and it's in God's hand now anyway."

"Yes, sir."

And that, too, young Sam Houston filed away for later study.

He suspected the major was right—but he still thought it was a foolish way to fight a battle. Of course, that might just be his Cherokee upbringing at work. Cherokees, like all Indians Sam knew of, generally thought that the white man's headlong way of fighting was just plain stupid.

Perhaps it was. But it was also a fact that white men eventually won their wars with Indians, if not always all the battles. Maybe this was part of it.

He chewed on that concept, too, for a time. Indeed, he became so engrossed in thought that Montgomery's bellow caught him by surprise.

"Charge!"

Breaking into a run, the major led the way, waving his saber. The fieldworks weren't more than fifty yards distant now.

By the time John Ross got back to the river and crossed on the first available canoe, the battle on the other side—between The Ridge's Cherokees and the Red Sticks—was well under way.

It was a swirling, confused melee; hundreds of Indian warriors fighting singly or in small clusters, clubbing and stabbing one another among twice that many tall trees. John heard some shots ring out, as well. The Cherokees had been provided with guns by Jackson. Not enough to arm every warrior, to be sure; but they had gotten far more guns from the Americans than the Red Sticks had been able to obtain from the British and Spanish enclaves down on the coast.

But there weren't that many shots, for this size of a battle. Even someone as inexperienced in fighting as John Ross could tell as much. He wasn't surprised, though, now that he saw the terrain. The fight between Cherokees and Creeks on the southern end of the peninsula was simply too close up, too entangled in forest and brush. By the time a man could see his opponent, his gun usually wouldn't be any more use than a large and clumsy club. That being so, why not use a real war club from the outset?

John, on the other hand, was no more proficient with traditional Cherokee weapons than he was with the Cherokee language. His loyalties to his nation were clear, but the truth was that he was far more comfortable with the white man's ways of doing most things.

So, like any young white man would have done in his first battle, Lieutenant John Ross drew his pistol and charged forward. He would have preferred a rifle, but proper officers didn't carry such.

Less than fifteen seconds later, John was glad he'd been armed with only a pistol. A Red Stick came around a tree, screaming out a war cry, and tried to brain him with his war club. John barely had time to throw up his arm and block the blow. Fortunately, his forearm intercepted the club well down the shaft, or he would have had a broken arm instead of just a badly bruised one.

The Red Stick drew the club back for another blow. He was a terrifying sight, in that moment. His mouth was open in a rictus of fury, and his painted face made him look like a demon.

John never knew, then or later, whether he pulled the trigger of his pistol out of fear or rage, or just pure reflex. Probably all at the same time, he concluded.

He wasn't even aware that the gun had gone off—the sound of it was overwhelmed by the chorus of war cries and the confusion of the moment. Then he saw the Red Stick's left leg flung aside and a spray of blood erupt from his thigh. The warrior's strike missed him by a good foot, and the warrior himself staggered for two paces before collapsing.

But to John's dismay he rose again, almost instantly, screaming another war cry. The .62-caliber bullet would have shattered the bone, had it struck the leg squarely. But it had only inflicted a flesh wound. A bad one, to be sure—the man would eventually bleed to death if he didn't tie up his leg—but not bad enough to stop him.

John stepped back, wondering what to do. Even against a half-crippled opponent, his pistol with its twelve-inch barrel was a poor match against a real war club, especially when the club was being wielded by a religious fanatic. What was worse, he certainly didn't have time to reload.

The Red Stick lurched toward him, still screaming. The smartest thing for John to do was simply to run away, of course. Fanatic or not, the Creek would have no chance of catching him, not with that bad a leg wound. Or by the time he did, at any rate, John would have been able to reload.

But John couldn't stomach the thought of being seen as a coward. So, he braced himself, took a firm grip on the pistol butt, and decided he'd try to deflect the coming blow—

Then another Cherokee came around the same tree, as silent as a ghost, and shattered the Red Stick's skull with a single blow. From the amount of blood and hair and gore that was already covering his ball-headed war club, this wasn't the first brain he'd spilled that day. The warrior paused to stare at John.

"Stupid," the Cherokee growled in English. "Why didn't you just run away?"

The newcomer was no older than John himself. He glanced around quickly to make sure there were no other enemies in the immediate vicinity, and then grinned at him. "Stupid will make you dead," he continued, but he said it quite cheerfully now. "I'm James Rogers. You?"

"John Ross."

He'd never met Rogers, but he'd heard of him. He was one of the sons of Captain John Rogers, the Scottish sometime-adventurer and sometime-adviser for John Jolly's chiefdom. The sons were said to be close friends, in fact, of the American ensign Houston whom The Ridge had found so interesting.

Rogers grin widened still further. "You're John Ross?" He switched to Cherokee, in which he proved to be quite a bit more fluent than John himself. "From the way you look and the uniform you're wearing, I thought you were an American. *The* John Ross, from Ross Landing? The same one who made a fortune swapping stuff with the Americans down on the river by Chatanuga?"

In keeping with the language, Rogers used the Cherokee name for Lookout Mountain.

John nodded.

"In that case," Rogers jibed, switching back to English, "you've got *no* excuse. I'm only half Scot. You're supposed to be much smarter than me."

Ross grinned back. "That's only if you believe what the Scots say."

Rogers pointed at John's pistol with his gruesome club. "Better reload that thing now. This fight is turning into a mess."

Trying to keep his hands from shaking, John did as Rogers suggested. "I'm looking for The Ridge," he told Rogers. "I've got to warn him that Coffee has all his men lined up on the river, ready to shoot anyone who tries to cross back over. That means Creeks, not us, of course, but . . ."

Rogers barked a laugh. John grimaced.

"Exactly. So I need to find—"

"It doesn't matter. The Ridge has no intention of retreating, believe me. We'll stay here until it's done." Rogers waved his club in a little half circle. "As for where he is, who knows? Best advice I can give you is just to follow the screaming. Wherever it's loudest, you'll probably find The Ridge. He does love that sword the Americans gave him."

Rogers eyed the pistol. "You reload pretty well, I'll give you that. So if you don't mind, I think I'll stay with you. I'll handle any Red Sticks who make it past your deadly gunfire."

"That probably means most of them," John admitted.

"Probably," Rogers agreed amiably. "But 'most' is still better than 'all.'"

They encountered two more Red Sticks before they finally found The Ridge. Ross fired twice, missing both times. Rogers did all the killing, although Ross had one of the men grappled by the legs before James brained him.

"You'll make a good diplomat, people say," Rogers commented idly, as they moved through the trees.

John hoped he was right. He'd certainly never be famous as a warrior.

CHAPTER 5

Sam ran pretty well for a man of his size, but he couldn't match Montgomery.

The major was a big man himself, as tall as Sam if not as heavily built, but he just seemed to bound through the hail of arrows and bullets now being fired at the oncoming Thirty-ninth by the Red Sticks forted up behind their barricade.

Sam took his lead and example from Montgomery, not knowing what else to do. There was something bizarre about the whole experience. It just didn't seem reasonable for a man to race through deadly missiles with less thought and concern than he'd give so many raindrops in a shower.

It wasn't that Sam was scared, really, although by all rights he should have been frightened out of his wits. This was easily the most dangerous thing he'd ever done in his life, and he wasn't a cautious man.

He'd been even less cautious as a teenager. Plenty of his Tennessee townsmen in Maryville had thought the sixteen-year-old boy had been a lunatic to run away from home and travel through sixty miles of wilderness to live with savage Indians for three years. But it had seemed a reasonable proposition to Sam, at the time, compared to working on his mother's farm or as a clerk in his brother's general store. Still did, for that matter. Clerking wasn't what it was cracked up to be, and farming was worse yet.

So, he'd enlisted and given his oath, even pressed for a commission as an officer. The government having carried out its part of the bargain, Sam was now obliged to make good on his end of the deal. And if that involved charging a log wall armed with nothing more than a sword and a pistol, well, so be it. The Red Sticks pelting him with arrows and bullets were just . . .

Irrelevant, he decided. Sam, who'd memorized two-thirds of the poem, conjured up something from Alexander Pope's marvelous translation of the *Iliad* to steady himself.

> But know, whatever fate I am to try
> By no dishonest wound shall Hector die;
> I shall not fall a fugitive at least,
> My soul shall bravely issue from my breast.

When Montgomery reached the wall he was ten feet ahead of Sam. The major clambered up the log fortifications using only his left hand, still waving his saber in the right.

He shouted something. Sam thought it was *Follow me!* but he wasn't sure. Between the gunfire and the screams of the Red Sticks on the other side of the barricade, he couldn't hear himself think.

Not that there was any thinking to be done, really. It all

seemed very simple. Climb the wall, get on the other side, do your best to beat down your enemies before they did the same to you.

Montgomery reached the top of the wall and dropped into a crouch, ready to leap across.

Then he shouted again. It was a wordless cry, this time, nothing more than a dying reflex as lungs emptied for the last time. Sam was sure of that. He could see the blood and brains erupting from a bullet that passed right through Montgomery's head.

The major fell back to the ground, his body passing Sam as he clambered up the wall.

"Follow me!" Sam shouted. Pretty damn good and loud, too, he thought. But he didn't try to wave the sword he carried in his hand. He'd save that for when he reached the top.

Finally he was at the top of the wall. It had seemed to take forever. Since Montgomery's crouch hadn't done much good for him, Sam decided to emulate what he imagined an Achaean would have done. Achilles, anyway, if not Odysseus.

He started to rise. Started to raise his sword, ready to wave it about now and shout *Follow me!* again. The painted faces of the Red Stick warriors staring up at him from the ground below were just a colorful blur in his mind.

He never even saw the arrow coming.

Fortunately, his foot slipped just as he started to stand, and what would have been a heroic posture turned into an ungainly sprawl. *Fortunately,* because had he kept his footing, that arrow would have plunged deep into his groin. As it was, the missile simply sliced a gash along the outside of his thigh before caroming off to the side.

It didn't even hurt. Sam realized he'd been wounded only when he spotted the blood soaking his trouser leg.

But he just shrugged it off. He was a big man, there was a lot of meat and muscle there, and the wound wasn't spouting the way it would if an artery had been severed. It was, quite literally, nothing but a flesh wound.

Besides, Sam had far more pressing concerns. Sprawled across the wall the way he was, his head was now within reach of the enemy—and, sure enough, a Red Stick was trying to brain him with an *atassa*.

Frantically, Sam brought up the sword. By sheer good luck more than any conscious intent, the blade intercepted the haft of the club. There wasn't enough power in that awkward parry to do more than deflect the club, but deflected it was. Off balance, the Red Stick stumbled past.

Seeing nothing else to do, Sam threw himself off the wall and landed on his hands and knees on the enemy side of the barricade. Instantly, he came to his feet, feeling a rush of relief greater than anything he'd ever felt in his life. Whatever happened now, at least he'd be standing up to face it.

What *was* happening now was that the same Red Stick was trying to brain him again. For the first time since the battle began, Sam got angry.

That bastard was trying to kill him!

Stupid bastard, too. Most white men didn't really know how to handle an Indian war club up close. Guns and knives were a white man's weapons. But Sam had been trained in wrestling and hand-to-hand fighting by his Cherokee friends John and James Rogers. James, in particular, was a veritable wizard with a war club.

His reflexes took over. A sword wasn't quite as handy as a war club, but close enough. Sam parried the strike and returned the favor.

Then . . .

He discovered that a sword had both an advantage and a disadvantage over a war club.

The advantage was that it had a blade.

The disadvantage was that it had a blade.

Sam was strong, even for his size. He'd brained the Red Stick, sure enough. And now he had a sword stuck in the man's skull.

No time to work it loose, either. Two more Red Sticks were upon him, and still more were aiming their bows his way.

There was nothing he could do about the arrows that would be coming. He left the sword where it was, drew his pistol, and fired it at point-blank range into the chest of one of the two Red Sticks. Then, threw the pistol into the face of the other and grappled with him.

A good hip roll and the warrior was slammed into the ground with enough force to wind him and jar the war club out of his hand. Sam dove for it, eager to have a usable weapon. He didn't even notice that the headlong plunge took him out of the path of three arrows that sank into the wooden barricade behind.

He came up with the *atassa* just in time to see dozens of Thirty-ninth Infantry soldiers pouring over the wall. With their blue coats, they looked like a wave crashing over a too-flimsy dike.

The Red Sticks at the wall reeled back from the assault. Sam charged forward to place himself once again at the lead.

"Follow me!" he bellowed again, waving the war club.

Even at the time, he thought it was a silly war cry. He had no idea where he was leading them, after all. It just seemed like the right thing to do, under the circumstances.

When he was excited, Andrew Jackson's high-pitched voice was often unpleasant, even shrill. But it was a piercing voice on the battlefield, able to cut through almost any din of shouting and gunfire.

It was certainly doing so now. From his vantage point atop the hill, Jackson had acquired a perfect view of the storming of the barricade. There'd been a sharp pang of grief, of course, when he saw his good friend Lemuel Montgomery killed. But, as always with Jackson, grief would have to wait its turn when more pressing matters were at hand. Whatever else, the man was a fighter first and foremost. And, for him, the excitement of battle would always override anything else at the time.

He was excited now. Excited enough, even, to lapse into profanity.

"Goddamn me, but that's a *soldier*!" He snatched off his fancy hat and waved it like a sword. "Go for 'em, lad! Give the savage bastards Jesse!"

The men standing around him matched his grin. Most of them were artillerymen, and they were out of the battle now, so they had plenty to grin about anyway.

Jackson jammed the hat back on his head. Then, still grinning, he turned to one of his aides.

"Do remind me, however, not to call them savages in the presence of that fine young fellow. He might take umbrage, and I do believe he'd be dangerous in a duel."

The aide grunted. "Especially if he had the choice of weapons."

Jackson's grin became wider than ever. Wider, and more savage than any of the men killing each other on the field below, of whatever color.

Leading, Sam soon discovered, was pretty much indistinguishable from *chasing.* Once their fortifications were overrun, the

Creeks seemed to have no idea what to do. Not surprising, really. It was unusual enough for Indians to have built such an impressive line of defense. Sam would have been astonished to discover that they'd prepared lines of retreat, as well.

But they hadn't, as he expected. The Creeks reminded him of the Icelandic clansmen he'd read about in Sturluson's stories, based on ancient Icelandic sagas. Endless clan feuds which produced a race of hardy, resourceful, and ferocious warriors.

But not soldiers, really. Certainly not in the modern sense of the term. They just didn't have the ingrained customs and habits that produced ranks of disciplined men who formed what could properly be called an "army."

Sam knew that it would have taken all of Chief Menawa and William Weatherford's authority and political skills to have gotten the Red Sticks to build that breastwork at all. There was no chance they would have gotten them to build a secondary line of defense—or even, for that matter, have developed a battle plan that provided clear contingencies in the event that the fortifications were overrun.

So, now, everything was confusion and chaos. As individual warriors, the hundreds of Red Sticks still at large on the peninsula were as feisty as ever. More so, probably, since desperation had been added to fanaticism and the ever-present Indian courage, to keep them fighting. But they were fighting as individuals, now. Or, at most, in small clusters gathered around the figure of one of the chiefs or war leaders.

Following that initial heady charge after the retreating Creeks, therefore, Sam called a halt to the pursuit. He also was discovering that battles were incredibly exhausting, something Homer hadn't mentioned in his poems. Despite being in better physical condition than most of his men, Sam was just about winded.

Houston's voice had none of Jackson's piercing qualities, but it was still a big man's voice—and that of a man who'd never been in the least bit bashful. So when he called out the order, it brought the soldiers up short, quick enough. And, soon thereafter he had their lines reformed. He even took the time to make sure that every soldier had reloaded, and done it properly. In the heat of a battle, it was common for soldiers to forget to reload, or to double-load—and it was by no means unheard of for an excited man to fire a ramrod instead of a bullet. Which left him with neither a ramrod nor the means to reload his weapon.

That done, he ordered the soldiers forward in a steady march, ready to fire a volley as soon as any cluster of Red Sticks large enough to warrant a volley appeared. *They'll do so soon enough,* he thought. He could hear the sounds of fighting on the other side of the high ground, and he was sure that by now the Cherokees had crossed the river in large numbers.

Coffee's cavalrymen, too, perhaps, but Sam suspected it was mostly Cherokees who'd crossed the river. Coffee and his cavalry were probably still on the opposite bank, chewing on the matter.

John Ross and James Rogers found The Ridge, ironically enough, only by circling around in the chaos of the battle and coming back to the riverbank. Some of the Red Sticks were trying their best to escape across the Tallapoosa, and The Ridge was just as determined to see to it they didn't.

He was in the water himself, in fact, when they found him. Standing thigh deep in the muddy current and battling it out with a Creek warrior.

It was an arresting tableau, and for a moment John was transfixed by the sight. Somewhere along the line, The Ridge must have lost his sword—indeed, any weapon he might have been carrying. He was grappling the Red Stick, hand to hand. The Creek was the taller man, though he didn't have The Ridge's width of shoulder and muscular mass, so it was a fairly even match.

But he was much younger, too, and didn't have The Ridge's experience. In a wrestler's movement too quick for John to follow, The Ridge freed one of his hands, snatched a knife scabbarded at the Red Stick's waist, and stabbed him in the belly with it.

The Creek warrior screeched in pain and fury. He grappled The Ridge all the harder, ignoring the blood spilling out of his body. He got a better grip on his opponent, since that quick knife thrust had removed one of The Ridge's arms from the wrestling match.

Despite his terrible wound, John thought the Creek might still have a chance to win the fight. Hesitantly, he raised his pistol. He was afraid to fire, though. He just wasn't a good enough shot, even at this short range, to be sure he'd hit the right target.

James's hand on his arm brought the pistol down.

"Wait."

Rogers had seen what Ross hadn't—yet another Cherokee warrior ready to jump into the river from nearby brush.

The new arrival went into the water and with three powerful and steady strides came up next to the two combatants. He had a spear in his hand, and the thrust that followed had all the cold and terrible precision of a wasp sting. The blade of the spear sank deep into the lower back of the Creek, well away from any part of The Ridge.

The Cherokee withdrew the spear with an expert and vicious twist of his wrists. The Red Stick was paralyzed by pain and shock, his back arched like a bow. The Ridge pushed him away and stepped back, leaving a clear target.

The second spear thrust went right through the man. John, paralyzed himself by the spectacle, saw several inches of the blade protruding from the Creek's abdomen. Blood poured off the spear, adding its burden to water already stained bright red despite the muddy current.

James's hand went to John's shoulder, and gave it a little shake. "Come on," he murmured. "Let's give him the warning."

John shook his head to clear the moment's horror. "Yes," was all he could say.

As soon as he'd gotten out of the water, they told The Ridge of Coffee's plan. He gave the opposite bank of the river nothing more than a quick glance. By this stage in the battle, John realized, the warning was almost pointless. Coffee's cavalrymen were already visible all along the riverbank. They were dismounted, and had brought their rifles up, ready to shoot any Creek who tried to cross.

And anybody else, most likely.

But The Ridge seemed more interested in Ross himself. He looked the younger man up and down, slowly and carefully. John was suddenly glad for his scuffled appearance. Even more, for the bruise on his cheek that he'd picked up when James hadn't deflected a war club quite in time. Most of all, for the blood spattered all over his American-style uniform. True, none of it was his; and, true also, the enemy blood had been spattered onto him by the efforts of his companion. Still, it was living proof that he'd been in the thick of battle; and, whatever else, he hadn't flinched.

The Ridge grunted, and looked to James. "How is he doing?"

James smiled, in his easy manner. "Well enough. I think he'll make a better politician than a warrior, though."

Honesty compelled John to speak, then. "I can't do much worse."

The Ridge was back to studying him. Then, after a few seconds, he grunted again.

"You're here," he said softly. "Good politicians are harder to find than warriors anyway."

For the first time since John Ross had met The Ridge, the older man actually *smiled*. The expression looked almost weird, on that blocky and fearsome face.

But John thought it might be the best smile he'd ever seen. He'd never doubted his own loyalties—nor did anyone, he thought—but his upbringing had always left him feeling like something of an outsider in the Cherokee world. In much the same way, he suspected, that the American ensign who was about his own age must often feel among white people. How could an adopted Cherokee feel otherwise?

Yet, somehow, though none of the blood covering him was his own, nor had any of it been put there by his own deeds, he knew that he had just crossed a final line this day.

The Ridge had smiled upon him. Every Cherokee knew that The Ridge almost never smiled.

CHAPTER 6

Andrew Jackson found Sam Houston on the high ground, after it had been cleared of hostiles. The ensign was hobbling along in the company of two Cherokees, engaged in what appeared from a distance to be a cheerful and animated discussion. They might have been arguing about a horse race, for all the general could tell.

He didn't know either of the young Indians, but he knew they were Cherokees. They might have been Creeks, true, since there were about a hundred friendly Creeks participating in this battle on the American side, under the leadership of the headman of Coweta, William Mackintosh. But Jackson, unlike many white men, could see at a glance the subtle difference between Cherokees, Creeks, Choctaws, and Chickasaws. Sometimes even Seminoles, although it was always harder with them. The Seminoles were more in the way of a split off from the Creeks than a truly separate tribe.

There was no significant difference in the features between a member of one southern tribe and another. But they all had distinctive clothing, accoutrements, and ways of styling their hair.

White people coming from the long-settled East, when they first encountered southern Indians, were frequently taken aback by their appearance. The general had often been amused by the phenomenon. The southern Indians, except when they painted themselves up for war or ceremonies, or stripped down to loincloths to play the stickball game they were so fanatical about, just didn't *look* like "wild Injuns." They looked exotic, to be sure, but it was the exoticism of such long-civilized peoples as the Arabs or the Hindoos.

They wore European-style cloth shirts, often with wide and decorated collars, and leggings that were certainly not European in design but resembled Araby pantaloons more than they did an easterner's notion of "Indian leggings." And their headgear, if they wore any, would be a turban or an elaborate cloth cap. Not the feathered headband everyone seemed to expect.

In the last few decades, some of those distinctive features had begun to blur and fade—the elaborate facial tattoos of the previous century had almost vanished—as more and more of the southern tribesmen adopted the ways and customs of the white settlers. Many had become Christians, and the missionaries always encouraged the adoption of white habits and economic practices, as well as the religion itself. But even those who hadn't adopted the white man's religion had adopted much else.

The Ridge, for instance, still adhered to his tribe's traditional religious practices, but Jackson knew he'd been among the first of the Cherokees to erect his own separate log dwelling, in the American style, apart from the traditional Cherokee town. It was said that he had a chimney, in fact, and a well-built one at that.

He'd also abandoned hunting, despite his own fame as a hunter, in favor of tending orchards and raising livestock—much of the labor, as was true for prosperous whites in the South, being done by black slaves he'd purchased. From accounts Jackson had heard, The Ridge's plantation at Oothcaloga was the equal in size and prosperity to that of almost any white man's on the frontier.

The Ridge had even placed his oldest son, John, with some Moravian missionaries in a boardinghouse at Spring Place, at the age of seven, so that he might learn to read and write and speak English fluently. His daughter Nancy, too. And he'd convinced his brother Watie to do the same with his oldest son, Gallegina—or Buck Watie, as he was known in English.

The general had mixed feelings on the subject. On the one hand, he thought that the ideal solution to the Indian problem would be for the savages to adopt the white man's ways completely. He'd already decided that if they did so, he'd throw his considerable influence into granting them full rights of citizenship, and not just the limited rights possessed by freedmen.

For all that he clashed frequently with the missionaries and Indian agents like Colonel Meigs over what Jackson considered their coddling of the savages, he didn't fundamentally disagree with their assessment that Indians might be the equal of white men. As individuals, he'd always found many of the savages to be impressive people. He'd even taken into his household a little Creek boy named Lyncoya who had been orphaned in last year's battle at Tallushatchee, and intended to adopt him legally once the war was over.

But . . . that was the problem, when looked at from the other side. Impressive people were also stubborn, independent, and fractious people. Jackson didn't fault them for it—rather admired them, in fact, since he was stubborn, independent, and fractious himself. But what he could admire in an individual, he could *not* admire in nations that were opposed to his own. Certainly not when the British and Spanish empires he so utterly detested were always ready and eager to foment unrest among the savages, and use them as weapons against his beloved republic.

So, watching the young American ensign enjoying the comradeship of two young Cherokees, the general saw a very mixed blessing.

Something in his skeptical expression must have emboldened one of his aides to speak.

"And will you look at that! There's still a battle raging, and there they are, jabbering away like heathens."

The aide was a young officer, and new to Jackson's service. Knowing what was coming, the other officer who stood with them—Major John Reid, that was, who'd been Jackson's secretary for a year now—sidled back a step or two.

Fury was always close to the surface with Andrew Jackson, and it could erupt as instantly as a volcano.

The general spun around, his face red, and thrust his long jaw not six inches from the face of the aide.

"You, sir! When the day comes that I see *you* fearlessly charging the enemy, you may presume to criticize such a man. Until that day comes—and I am not holding my breath in anticipation—*you will keep your mouth shut*. Do I make myself clear?"

The young officer blanched, and his eyes went so wide Jackson could see the veins in the corners. Jackson's voice, filled with rage, cut like a knife. The aide was too shocked even to step back. He just gaped.

"Answer me, blast you!"

"Yes, sir," the man finally squeaked. *"Yes, sir!"*

The general continued to glare at him, for long and silent seconds. Finally, with a contemptuous gesture, Jackson waved him away.

"Get out of my sight," he growled. "Somewhere to the rear, where your talents might find some use. Count bullets or something, you miserable clerk. Better yet, count rations. You probably wouldn't recognize a bullet if you saw one."

His right hand went to the hilt of the sword scabbarded to his waist. There was no conscious intent to draw the weapon; it was just the instinctive reflex of a man for whom intimidation was second nature. The aide scurried off like a lizard on a hot rock.

As Jackson's temper settled, he saw that the altercation had drawn the attention of Houston and his Cherokee companions. The three of them were standing some forty feet away, staring at him.

Unwilling, for the moment, to take his right hand from the sword, Jackson summoned the ensign with a jerk of his head.

Houston came over, as quickly as he could given that he was limping. The two Cherokees followed at a slower pace. Something of a reluctant pace, it might be said.

When Houston drew near, Jackson nodded. "That was well

done, young man. Very well done, indeed. A most gallant charge. Please accept my admiration and respect, as well as the gratitude of your nation. I'll see to it that you get a promotion."

"Thank you, sir."

Jackson finally took his hand from the sword hilt and pointed at the bandage on Houston's leg. "Your wound?"

Houston stared down at the bandage, which had a few fresh red spots mixed in with the brown of old bloodstains. "Oh, it's not much, sir. It's still bleeding some, but I'll manage well enough till this is over. Certainly not as bad as it was for poor Major Montgomery."

A look of regret passed over the general's face. "Yes. Well, it's not over yet."

Houston smiled thinly. "Not hardly, sir." He turned and pointed toward the river. "Between us and the Cherokees, we've driven the Red Sticks off the high ground, but there are still plenty of them forted up here and there in the forest. This peninsula must comprise hundreds of acres, all told. As heavily wooded as it is . . ."

Jackson nodded, understanding full well the realities of warfare in the wilderness. The Indian warrior wasn't the match of the white man in a pitched battle on an open field, or in a siege. They lacked the organization and discipline for such. But in their own element they were unsurpassed; as dangerous as wild boars.

"Any chance they'll surrender?"

"I doubt it very much, sir. Not yet, anyway. There's still plenty of fight in 'em." The ensign gave the sky a glance, gauging the sun. "They'll for sure try to hold out until sunset, and then make their escape across the river."

Jackson glared again, although not with the sheer volcanic fury that he'd unleashed on the aide.

"Tarnation, I've given Coffee clear and firm instructions—"

The ensign was bold enough to interrupt. Jackson was rather impressed.

"And he's carried them out, sir." Houston gestured toward the two Indians, who were now standing only a few feet away. "This is my old friend James Rogers—he's the one on the left with the war club. And Lieutenant Ross. John Ross, that is. I just met him for the first time today, but I'd heard of him."

Jackson gave the two Cherokees a quick examination, most

of which was spent studying the war club Rogers held. Clearly enough, it had been put to good use.

He grunted his satisfaction, then cocked an eyebrow at the ensign. "And the point is? I'm assuming you didn't interrupt your commanding officer in the midst of a battle simply to introduce your friends."

Houston flushed. The ruddy complexion under his mass of chestnut hair turned pink. He looked like one of the brightly painted Christmas ornaments that German immigrants were starting to turn into a popular custom. It was all the general could do not to burst into laughter. Despite the severity of his rebuke, he approved of this young ensign. Approved of him mightily and heartily, in fact.

"Lieutenant Ross here serves as one of General Coffee's aides, sir," Houston explained. "He was the one Coffee sent to warn The Ridge not to cross the river again. Which he did—he and James spoke to The Ridge himself." Houston squared his shoulder and stood very straight. "That's because it was The Ridge and the Cherokees who grabbed some canoes and created the diversion that gave us our initial advantage."

The last statement was spoken in a slightly combative tone. Not belligerent, precisely. And not precisely aimed at Jackson. But Houston sounded like a man who felt he'd made his point, and had been proven right.

Yet again Jackson stifled a smile. For all that he routinely referred to Indians as savages, he understood them quite well. He wasn't all that different himself, in many ways. Like any Cherokee or Creek or Choctaw chief, he magnified his own influence by gathering young leaders around him and making them his protégés. Political authority, among white men on the frontier as much as the Indians, was mostly an informal matter.

But it wasn't enough for his protégés to be smart and capable. Not enough, even, to be physically courageous, as well. They also had to have the strength of character to stand up to Jackson himself, if need be. Without that, they were useless to him.

Andrew Jackson had been a bully as far back as he could remember. As a boy, he'd bullied other boys; as a man, other men. He'd bully anyone he could, and he'd do it in a heartbeat.

He was phenomenally good at it, too. That wasn't and never had been because he was an especially large man. Although, even there, Jackson's whipcord body was one that could do far better in a fight than many people would have suspected just looking at him.

Yes, Jackson was a bully, and he made no apologies for the fact. Indeed, he worked at it, the way a smart man works to improve his skills. It enabled him to get things accomplished he could not have accomplished otherwise.

But he also knew—he'd seen it all his life—that a stupid bully collected nothing around him but yes-men, fawners, toadies, and lickspittles. Who, as a rule, were good for absolutely nothing else. And what did that accomplish?

So. Ensign Houston was looking better all the time. Jackson was starting to develop great hopes for him.

But that was for later. Today, there was still a battle to be won.

He looked up at the sky. There were still several hours of daylight left, even this early in the year with the solstice just passed. Enough time, he thought, to drive the matter through before night fell.

Whatever else, Jackson wanted the Creeks defeated—no, more than that: broken and pulverized—before the sun set.

It wasn't so much that he feared fighting them in the dark, though that certainly wasn't something he looked forward to. But Jackson knew from long experience that the red men were in many ways a more practical breed than whites. They had their superstitions, to be sure, but they had their reason, as well. Indians preferred ambush and surprise attacks to open battle, and they simply weren't given to pointless last stands. Not, at least, if there was a viable alternative.

Which there would be, if hundreds of them were still at large come nightfall. There was no way in creation that John Coffee, even if he had thrice the force he had covering the riverbank, could prevent Creeks from escaping the trap under cover of darkness.

"All right," he said. "Is there any place in the peninsula where they seemed to be centered?"

Houston's eyes ranged the forested peninsula. "I don't think so, sir, but it's hard to tell. Everything's pretty confused right now, what with the Thirty-ninth and the militiamen milling around on this side of the peninsula and the Cherokees starting down by the river. We met them on the high ground—"

He grinned coldly for a moment. "I even managed to discourage the militiamen from shooting at The Ridge and his men, if you can believe such a wonder."

His hand slid to the butt of his pistol, which was stuck in his waistband. The ensign had apparently made a priority of recovering it, after that initial dramatic charge across the barricade.

Again, Jackson had to stifle a smile. He was pretty sure that Houston's "discouragement" had included threatening at least one militiaman with the nonregulation weapon. Possibly several of them. Under that genial, boyish exterior, Jackson suspected that Houston could throw an impressive temper tantrum himself.

"Indeed," the general said mildly, looking down at Houston's large hand covering the pistol butt. "I have found myself that militiamen generally need discouragement, from time to time. And even more in the way of encouragement. They're a flighty bunch."

Houston took the hand away from the pistol. The gesture was almost surreptitious. There'd be some complaints coming from the officers, Jackson knew, about the coarse young regular officer who'd had the unmitigated gall to bully—*outright bullying, sir!*—stalwart citizens of Tennessee who were temporarily serving under the colors.

Jackson wasn't concerned about it. He could bully militia officers in his sleep. With a handful of exceptions, he wouldn't trade the young ensign standing before him for all the militia officers in the United States. If they complained, he'd set them straight.

Hurrying past the awkwardness, Houston continued. "If I might make so bold, sir, I'd recommend that we take the time to reorganize, and then start driving the Creeks in that direction." He pointed toward a portion of the forest that seemed indistinguishable from any other. "I've been told there's a ravine down that way that'd wind up making the bottom of the trap."

Jackson ignored the presumptuousness of an ensign telling him that they had to "reorganize"—as if that wouldn't be blindingly obvious to the most incompetent general in history. The rest of the advice seemed sound enough.

"See to it then, Ensign. Pass the word to Colonel Williams yourself. I'll handle the militiamen."

CHAPTER 7

There were still skirmishes taking place here and there, but the immediate vicinity was relatively calm.

The Red Stick village had been all but destroyed. As he searched for Colonel Williams among the soldiers who were milling about, John Ross and James Rogers following close behind, Houston came upon a militiaman standing over an old Creek man. The Creek must have been addled as well as elderly, because—right there in the middle of a battle—he was squatting on the ground, pounding corn with a mortar.

The militiaman raised his musket and shot the old man in the head.

The bullet passed right through the skull, blowing blood and brains and pieces of bone all over the ground. Then, kneeling next to the corpse, the militiaman pulled out his knife and cut away the old man's breechclout. Following that, he started to make an incision in the corpse's leg, beginning just above the heel.

Houston froze. His companions also stopped, and stood silently.

The killing had been bad enough, since the old idiot was obviously no danger to anyone. Now—Sam had heard tales, but never really believed them—the militiaman was going to skin a long strap from the body, most likely to use it for a set of reins. Boasting rights, among his buddies when he got home.

The paralysis broke before the militiaman's cut got past the buttock. Houston limped over, feeling light-headed. Horror was replaced by fury.

"What in the blazes are you doing?"

The militiaman was so engrossed in his work that he apparently missed the meaning of Houston's tone.

"Finally killed me an injun," he said gleefully, not even looking up. "First chance I got today. Them cussed regulars—"

The rest was lost in a squawk of surprise when Houston grabbed him by the scruff of the neck and, in a single one-armed heave, hauled him to his feet. The man gaped up at him.

Sam batted the knife out of his hand, then backhanded him hard enough to split his lip.

The soldier shook his head, half dazed. That had been a powerful blow, even though it hadn't been delivered by a closed fist.

"Hey!" he squawked. His hand flew up to his bleeding mouth.

"Tell you what," Sam said thinly. "I just realized that while I've killed me some injuns today, I ain't killed me a single stinking militiaman."

He drew his pistol. The man stared at it, his face suddenly going pale.

"Hey!" he protested again, the word garbled by the hand that was still covering his mouth.

For a moment, Houston glared down at him. He was sorely tempted to drive the butt of the pistol right into the man's face. As strong as he was, and as angry as he was, he'd smash the man's hand, as well as his mouth. Probably break his jaw in the bargain, even with the hand absorbing the impact.

But . . .

No. He reined in his temper. Enough was enough. The old Creek was dead anyway, and he couldn't let the situation spin out of control.

He looked around. Three other militiamen stood nearby, staring at him. Two of them had brought their rifles halfway up.

He grinned humorlessly and cocked the pistol, though he didn't—quite—point it at them. "Go ahead," he said. "This worthless bastard's too mangy-looking to make me a good set of reins. But any one of you will do. Any one at all."

The three men all swallowed. Their eyes flitted back and forth between Houston and his two Cherokee companions.

John Ross didn't really know what to do. He looked to James to get some guidance, but realized immediately that would be no help. Like Houston, James was grinning now, too. He'd sidled over a few paces, clearly ready to hurl himself at the militiamen once Houston fired the pistol. They were close enough that he could probably get in among them with his war club before they could shoot him.

There'd be one less by then, anyway. John had no doubt at all that Houston was prepared to fire—and not much doubt that, at this range, he'd hit his target squarely. There was something almost frighteningly competent about the big young American.

Ross knew as well that, for James, the only issue involved here was what amounted to an incipient clan feud—and The Raven, white man or not, was part of his clan. That made it all very simple for him.

The murdered old man had been nothing to Rogers. Just an enemy—and killing noncombatants was as common among Indians as it was among whites. So was mutilating their corpses. In one of the atrocities committed by the followers of Tecumseh last year, which had triggered off the current war, they'd not only murdered seven white settlers on the Ohio but had disemboweled a pregnant woman and impaled her unborn baby on a stake.

Here and now, if Houston hadn't intervened, Rogers would have passed by without comment. He might have given the matter a second glance. Then, again, he might not have.

But Houston *had* intervened, and that made it a clan matter. So James was ready to kill as soon as the fight erupted.

For a moment, John wished that his own thoughts and sentiments were as clear and straightforward. But only for a moment. James Rogers's traditional way of thinking would lead the Cherokee to disaster, just as surely as Tecumseh's new way of thinking had led his followers to their doom. John could see that disaster coming, the way a man can see a thunderstorm developing in the distance.

He was pretty sure The Ridge could see it coming also.

He had no idea what to do about it, not yet. If there was anything that could be done at all. What he *did* know was that if there was any solution, it would come from people who could think a little crookedly. People like himself, who'd always felt somewhat twisted in the world.

And, maybe, people like this peculiar young ensign, who was prepared to start killing men of his own race over what amounted to a moral abstraction.

John decided that was good enough, for the moment. Who was to say how new clans emerged? It was all lost somewhere back in time, in a thousand different stories and legends. Maybe a new one was being born here. Or something similar enough.

He drew his own pistol and cocked it. Quite proud, for an in-

stant, that his hands weren't shaking at all. Granted, he'd probably miss his target. He'd missed just about everything else he'd
tried to shoot that day. But he'd give it his level best, for sure.

Hearing the sound of Ross's pistol being cocked, too, the militiamen suddenly broke. Houston could tell—knew it for a certainty—even though there was no visible sign beyond the fact
that one of them stepped a half pace back. It was just, somehow,
obvious.

Good enough.

The general wouldn't thank him any if Houston started a side
war between the Cherokees and regulars against the Tennessee
militia, who constituted not only the majority of Jackson's army
but, push come to shove, his political constituency as well. Certainly not over an issue like a murdered old Creek.

He uncocked his own pistol then, and shoved it back into his
waistband. "The general gave clear and direct orders," he announced loudly. "And you heard them. No killing of noncombatants."

He cleared his throat. "It's my responsibility to enforce discipline. Which—"

He glanced down at the militiaman he'd cuffed. Blood from
the split lip was seeping through his fingers. It was a cheery
sight.

"I have," he concluded. He waved his hand in a peremptory
gesture. "So go on about your business, men. That's an order.
I'm on an errand for the general."

With that, he turned away and began limping in the direction
he thought—for no good reason, really—he was most likely to
find Colonel Williams.

Ross hurried to follow. When James Rogers caught up to
them, he was still grinning.

"Too bad," he said. "It would have been a good fight. We'd
have won, too."

An hour later, Jackson was ready to start the final drive. By
then, hundreds of Red Sticks had already been slaughtered in
the fighting. As poorly equipped as they were with firearms,
they hadn't been able to fight very effectively once the Cherokees erupted into their rear and the Thirty-ninth breached the
barricade.

Jackson had indeed given orders before the battle started that the Creek noncombatants were to be spared. There weren't many on the peninsula, not more than a few hundred, since the Red Sticks had sent away most of their women and children and old folks before Jackson's army arrived. But any Red Stick warrior who didn't surrender was to be killed. And he knew perfectly well that his soldiers—especially the militiamen—hadn't bothered to ask.

Jackson didn't blame them. In this sort of chaotic brawl not even the regulars would follow the established laws of war, at least not very often, and the general wasn't about to ask any questions. It just didn't pay to do so.

Still, there'd been several incidents reported to him. In most cases, Jackson was inclined to accept the explanation that the killings had been accidental. They probably were, in truth, at least half the time. A woman running through the woods was just a blur of movement to a soldier whose nerves were at a fever pitch due to fear and battle fury. He'd shoot first and think later. So would Jackson himself, being honest.

However, there'd been one case involving a small boy that had angered Jackson as much as it had the officer who'd reported to him. Confused and frightened, the boy—he hadn't been more than five or six years old—had stumbled into a group of American soldiers. One of them had bashed his brains out with the butt of his musket.

Even then, for Jackson, the issue wasn't the killing as such. The officer reported that the culprit had justified his deed on the grounds that if the boy had lived he'd have grown into a warrior—so why not kill him now when it was still easy? It was a sentiment that Jackson didn't share—not quite—but he had no trouble at all understanding it.

Yet that was beside the point. The general had given his orders, clear and simple, and a soldier—a regular, too, to make it worse—had taken it upon himself to disobey them. If he could find out who the man was, he'd have him punished.

That wasn't likely, though. The officer who'd reported the outrage had been from a different unit, and didn't know the man's name. The odds were slim that the culprit's own superior officer would identify him—and the odds that his fellow soldiers would do so were exactly zero.

The general smiled thinly. Quite unlike—ha!—the instant

readiness of a militia officer to report to him half an hour before, hotly and angrily, that Ensign Houston had brutalized an honest citizen of Tennessee and threatened several others just because . . .

Well, you know how it is, General, the boys like to have their trophies . . .

Jackson had given him short shrift. But the incident was enough to crystallize his feeling that this battle had gotten a little out of control. He didn't object to killing Indians, not in the least. In fact, he'd planned the entire campaign in such a way as to trap the Red Sticks on this horseshoe bend of the Tallapoosa so he could kill as many of them as possible. Still, a civilized nation *did* have its established rules of war, and it had to follow them or it would become no better than the savages themselves.

"We'll give them a last chance to surrender," he announced.

The officers gathered around him exchanged looks. Finally, Major Reid was bold enough to speak.

"Uh, who, General? What I mean is, who's supposed to take them the offer?" Reid looked down at the ravine where most of the surviving Red Sticks were now forted up.

"Forted up" was the phrase, too. The Red Sticks hadn't had the time to build anything as solid and well designed as the barricade they'd placed across the neck of the peninsula. But the southern tribes were all woodsmen, and in the few hours they'd had, the warriors had been able to erect a rather substantial breastwork down there. Storming it would be a dangerous business.

Given the desperation and fanaticism of the Red Sticks, it would be equally dangerous taking them an offer to surrender.

Jackson's eyes moved past the little cluster of aides gathered immediately around him. He was looking for a particular officer, among the several hundred soldiers milling about in the immediate vicinity. He'd be there, for sure.

Sure enough, he found the young man quickly, even in that crowd. Partly because of his height, but partly because of the two Indians standing next to him. The three of them seemed to have become well-nigh inseparable in the course of the battle, and they stood out in a crowd.

Houston was perhaps thirty yards away, but his eyes met the general's immediately. Jackson suspected he'd been anticipating the summons. Indeed, the young ensign began walking toward him immediately, without even waiting for a command.

Limping toward him, rather—and the limp seemed to have gotten worse. Jackson wasn't surprised. A flesh wound is still a real wound, and even a man as big as Houston would be feeling the effects of it this many hours later.

Still and all, it was a very *firm* sort of limp. Whatever pain and weariness the ensign might be feeling, it was clear enough that his determination hadn't flagged.

When Houston drew near, he spoke without being asked to do so.

"I'll take them the offer, sir. But I can tell you right now it's a waste of time."

Houston jerked his head, indicating the ravine behind him. "Me and James and John snuck down there a little while back. I know the lingo well enough—James knows it even better—that we got the gist of it. They've got some shamans down there with them, and they've been busy firing them up for a last stand."

Jackson snorted. "Are they still claiming their magic will turn our bullets into water?"

"Yes, sir. They aren't calling out for all the cats to be killed, though. Of course, I doubt me there's a cat in the world dumb enough to be within a hundred miles of this place."

Jackson chuckled harshly. One of the Cherokee prophets following Tecumseh had been a half-blood by the name of Charley. His white ancestry notwithstanding, Charley had become famous for demanding that the Cherokees abandon all the cursed ways of the white man. *All* of them, not just the books and mills and orchards and clothes and featherbeds and tables. He'd been especially incensed by the new habit of keeping domestic cats. All cats were to be killed!

He might have even swayed the Cherokee, for he was eloquent enough, whatever you thought of his notions. But The Ridge had put a stop to it. He'd stood up at the council meeting after Charley had predicted the immediate demise of anyone who opposed him and challenged him to make good his claim. A small mob of Charley's followers had attacked The Ridge then, but he'd battled them off long enough for his friend Jesse Vann and other allies to rally to his aid.

The brawl that followed had been inconclusive, since one of the old influential chiefs had managed to stop the fray. But the fact remained that The Ridge had defied one of Tecumseh's prophets and lived. That had been enough to produce a rapid decline in the prestige of Tecumseh's adherents, at least among the Cherokee.

"But regardless of whether or not they've decided to spare the cats, sir, I can tell you that they aren't relenting about anything else." The ensign shrugged. "I'll take them the offer, if you want, sir. But I'd just as soon lead a charge on them right now and be done with it. I'd a lot rather get shot carrying a sword than a white flag. Stupid, that."

Then, more quietly: "They *aren't* going to surrender, General. There's not a chance in creation."

Jackson rubbed his jaw, pondering the matter. "You say you'll volunteer to lead the charge?"

"Yes, sir," replied Houston, calmly and firmly. "I will."

Jackson thought about it some more. His decision teetered on a sharp edge.

In the end, it was the ensign himself who decided the matter for him. The ensign . . . and his two Cherokee companions.

To blazes with the Red Sticks. Jackson didn't want to risk losing such a promising young man, certainly not in something as quixotic as a doomed parlay attempt. All the more so because this war with the Creeks was just the opening skirmish in the coming battle with the British. He wanted Houston around for that.

As for the charge . . .

Jackson's eyes moved to the two Cherokees who accompanied Houston, but had stayed back when he came up to speak to the general.

"Never mind. As you say, the offer's probably pointless. And now that I think about it, a straight-up charge is probably just as pointless.

"Can you find The Ridge?"

"Yes, sir." Houston jerked his head again. "He and his people are staying down by the river, to help General Coffee kill any Red Sticks who might still be trying to cross."

There was a slight twist in the set of the ensign's lips. A trace of bitter irony, Jackson thought. The general was pretty sure that the real reason The Ridge had taken his Cherokees away from the high ground was to avoid any clashes they might get into with the Tennessee militiamen.

So Jackson came to his decision. "Go find him, if you would.

Ask him to bring a number of his men with him. Provide them with an escort. Use your own platoon. Just bring them up here. They've got bows, yes?"

Houston nodded. "Quite a few, although most of them are armed with guns."

"Quite a few will be enough." Jackson pointed toward the ravine. "From every description I've gotten, those breastworks can be set aflame. Let's see if Cherokee fire arrows will do the trick."

They did. By nightfall, the ravine was a blazing inferno.

Every Red Stick who tried to escape was shot down.

The next morning, the killing continued, here and there, as occasional bands of Red Sticks were uncovered elsewhere on the peninsula. No quarter was offered; no quarter was asked for; no quarter was given.

Halfway through the morning, Jackson ordered a body count. To make sure that no dead hostile was counted twice, he ordered their noses cut off once the count was made. Scalping was pointless, since most of the dead Red Sticks had already been scalped the day before. Sometimes by white soldiers, sometimes by Cherokees—often enough, by other Creeks. The Red Sticks had waged a savage civil war against any Creeks who opposed them, and now the favor was being returned by their own tribesmen.

The nose count came to some five hundred fifty. When Coffee crossed the river and reported on the action that had taken place there, he told the general that he estimated he and his men had left another three hundred and fifty or so dead in the water. He didn't think more than a hundred, at most, had managed to escape.

Jackson thought that estimate was too optimistic. Creeks, like all the southern tribes, were as adept in the water as they were in the woods. He was pretty sure the number who had escaped across the river was higher.

Nonetheless, out of approximately one thousand Red Sticks who had forted up on the horseshoe bend of the Tallapoosa, at least eight hundred were dead. It was as complete and as bloody a victory as he could have hoped for.

*   *   *

There were only two dark spots on the victory for Andrew Jackson. The first was the death of his friend Lemuel Montgomery, who had died heroically leading the charge on the barricade.

The second was that both Chief Menawa and—even worse—William Weatherford had been among those Red Sticks who had escaped the trap.

Weatherford, as it turned out, had never been caught in the trap in the first place. Jackson discovered from interrogations of the surviving Creeks that Weatherford had left the horseshoe bend several days before the battle started, in an attempt to recruit more followers for his cause.

Weatherford had led the massacre at Fort Mims, the act that had triggered the Creek War. Jackson wanted him badly. But he'd catch him, sooner or later.

And then he'd hang him.

CHAPTER 8

APRIL 18, 1814
Fort Jackson, Mississippi Territory

As befitted the most junior officer in the gathering, newly promoted to the rank of second lieutenant, Sam Houston stood toward the back of the large tent in Fort Jackson. The canopy served as a field headquarters for the general whose name had been given to the newly constructed fort.

Houston was perfectly happy with the arrangement. Andrew Jackson was having another temper tantrum, and Sam didn't particularly want to have the general's attention drawn to him.

Not that there was much danger of that. Leaving aside the fact that Jackson had made his approval of Houston eminently clear since the Horseshoe Bend, there were other people in the tent to draw the general's ire.

Two colonels, to be precise.

Very shortly, it was reported, Major General Thomas Pinckney would be arriving at the fort. Once he did so, as the senior general, his authority would supersede Jackson's. But, in the meantime, Jackson was still in command—and the two colonels in question, having recently arrived at the fort with their units, had made it quite clear that they didn't consider him qualified for the position.

Homer Milton and Gilbert Russell were only colonels, but they were both commissioned officers in the regular army, whereas Jackson's majestic rank of major general was that of the Tennessee militia. Jackson might favor regular soldiers, but, technically speaking, he was nothing but a militiaman himself. Both colonels had stated outright that they considered Jackson's authority over them to be a simple formality.

To make things worse, while Russell had commanded his Mississippi troops fairly well—it had been his men who cleared most of the hostile Creeks from the lower Alabama River back in February—the same could not be said of Milton. He and the Georgia troops had been, in Sam's opinion, well-nigh useless all the way through the campaign.

"—good for nothing except plundering friendly Indians!" Jackson shrilled. "Couldn't be found, it goes without saying, anywhere near the hostiles!"

The general waved angrily toward the north. "I've already lost The Ridge and most of my Cherokees on account of you! When word came through that your stinking militia stole their livestock and ruined their fields and orchards while they were down here fighting the Red Sticks—"

Milton was no shrinking violet himself.

"General, you'd already discharged the Cherokees yourself before the word arrived. And since when have you cared what happened to any such savage?" he sneered.

Sam held his breath, and he could see General Coffee and Major Reid doing the same. Up until now, this had just been a run-of-the-mill Jackson tirade.

It was fascinating, really. Jackson was the only man Sam had ever seen who could somehow turn livid with fury and ashen with rage at the same time. "Bright pale," you might call the color of his face.

The general said nothing, as seconds dragged on. He just gave

Milton his patented double-barreled blue-eyed glare. And if the glare was as rigidly fixed as an iron bar, the rest of Jackson wasn't. His tall, whipcord body was almost vibrating like a harp string—or a bowstring being drawn.

Even the haughty colonel finally realized he'd gone too far. "Sir," he added lamely.

Jackson snatched off his hat and slammed it onto the table next to him, scattering papers in the process. There had been a big map which had covered it, and that spilled halfway onto the ground.

"I gave them my *word,* sir—and you made me into a liar! Savages be damned! My word is my word!"

For a moment, Sam thought the general might actually strike the colonel with his fist. It was clenched—so was his left one, even in the sling—and there was spittle coming from the corners of Jackson's mouth. If they hadn't both been in uniform, Sam was pretty sure he would have challenged Milton to a duel right there on the spot.

"*That's* the issue here, sir!" Jackson gritted. For an instant, his angry eyes flitted to the other colonel. "At least *he*"—a jerk of the head toward Russell—"had enough grace not to steal from his Choctaws and Chickasaws!"

It was all Sam could do not to grin. He'd gotten to know the general a lot better over the past few weeks, since the battle at the Horseshoe Bend, and one of the things he'd learned was that Coffee was right. Jackson's rages were genuine enough, to be sure—but that never stopped the general from using them with all the cold-blooded skill of a master swordsman in a fight. Milton's blundering arrogance had given Jackson the opportunity to peel Russell away from him, and the general hadn't missed the chance.

Russell, clearly enough, was by now just looking for a way out of the brawl. He wasn't any happier than Milton was at the situation, but he had enough sense to realize that Jackson's victory at the bend had made him the popular hero of the southwestern states and territories. That would draw plenty of favorable notice in Washington, D.C., as well.

A lot more favorable notice than it should have, he no doubt felt, but American victories on land in the war that had begun with Britain in 1812 had been few and far between.

Very few, and very far between. The American navy had acquitted itself well, even if many of its heroes, like Oliver Hazard Perry and Isaac Hull, were from the same New England that was largely opposed to the war with Britain. But the record of the American army had generally been poor, outside of Harrison's victory over Tecumseh at the Thames. And sometimes it had been downright dismal.

The very first major offensive launched by the United States, an attempt at conquering Canada led by the governor of Michigan, William Hull—he'd been made a brigadier general, for the purpose—had ended with Hull's ignominious surrender, along with the taking of the town of Detroit.

So Jackson's triumph at the Horseshoe Bend had given Americans a much-needed boost. Granted, Hull had faced British regulars, along with hostile Indians, while Jackson's victory had been over Indians fighting on their own. Still, a resounding victory was a resounding victory.

Now Colonel Russell edged back a pace. Colonel Milton, seeing him do so out of the corner of an eye, finally had enough sense to realize that he'd dug himself into a hole. So, he tried to climb out of it.

Unfortunately, he did so ass backward.

"I agree that it was most unfortunate, General, but—"

"It wasn't 'unfortunate,' Colonel—it was an outrage! And leaving aside the stain on my reputation, it presents me with a rather massive practical problem." Jackson snatched his hat back off the table and jabbed with it toward the tent's entrance. Once, twice, thrice.

"There are still, by all reports, at least a thousand Creek hostiles gathered around the Spanish forts at Pensacola and Apalachicola. And you can be sure the British agents there will be arming them—runaway Negro slaves, too—and keeping them in the fight while they bring their regulars to our shores. I was counting on having the Cherokees return to service with me in a few months. Now—thanks to you—!"

Jackson having given him the opening, Russell took it eagerly enough. Let his fellow colonel in the regulars sink on his own. "The Choctaws and Chickasaws are still with us, sir," he said righteously.

Jackson's glare never left Milton's face, even as he replied. "That's fine and dandy, Colonel Russell. The fact remains that I probably lost the Cherokees for the rest of the war, and I doubt very much if as many Choctaws will step forward to take their place. Much less Chickasaws. There aren't more than four thousand Chickasaws in the whole world to begin with." Jackson's glare intensified. "That's our situation, thanks to these Georgian thieves!"

Milton scowled, but looked away. "They're not *my* Georgians, sir," he grumbled. "Most of my troops are from South Carolina. The plundering was done without my knowledge by Georgia militiamen"—he tried one last sally—"and probably some Tennesseans with them."

If Milton thought Jackson would rise to that bait, he was mistaken. "Probably," Jackson grunted. "And so what? Since you seem so preoccupied with the formal matters of command, Colonel Milton, let me ask you a simple question. Which one of us was in charge of operations in the state of Georgia? Me, or you?"

There was no safe answer to that question, so Milton subsided into a mulish silence.

After a few seconds, apparently having decided he'd won his point, Jackson jammed the hat back on his head. That hat was something of a marvel. Somehow, despite all the abuse Jackson inflicted upon the innocent headgear—Sam had now seen him stomp on it twice—the thing still retained a visible resemblance to a general's official hat.

Of course, it might not be the same hat. Sam wouldn't have been surprised to discover that one of the chests in Jackson's baggage was chock full of the things. The general was perfectly capable of planning ahead of time to bring enough hats with him that he could stomp a dozen of them into oblivion and still appear the next day, as fancily dressed as ever.

While the officers continued their glaring match, Sam spent his time coming to a decision.

There were a lot of things about Andrew Jackson that he didn't like—some, he downright detested—but, overall, he had come to develop a profound respect for the man. Even admiration, for that matter.

Say whatever else you would about Jackson, Sam didn't think there was another man in the country who could have driven this campaign through so relentlessly and effectively, especially given the fact that the general's own health had been wrecked in the process. He'd probably never recover from the bullet wounds in his arm and shoulder that the Benton brothers had inflicted on him last September, in their brawl at the City Hotel in Nashville. He might have, if he'd followed medical advice. But Jackson had refused, as soon as word arrived of the massacre at Fort Mims, in order to assume command of the Tennessee militia. He'd started the campaign just a few weeks after the shootout, and had led the whole thing with his left arm wrapped in a sling.

Sam didn't share Jackson's intense hatred of the British, but he did agree with the general that the current war wasn't the meaningless joke that so many New Englanders thought it was. If the British got the chance, they'd crush the new American republic. Cripple it, for sure. And now that they looked to be on the verge of finally defeating Napoleon, they'd get their chance. They'd send Wellington's veterans across the Atlantic. Except for some of Napoleon's elite units, those were probably the best regular soldiers anywhere in the modern world.

The war was just heating up, in short—and Sam Houston couldn't think of a commanding officer he'd rather be serving than Andrew Jackson. Whatever his faults.

And being honest, there was the fact that Sam was ambitious. Like many young men who came from poor circumstances, Sam treasured the republic because it allowed for young men like himself to advance as far as they could, based on their own merits. Sam had every intention of taking advantage of that opportunity.

On the other hand, he wasn't naive, either. "Merits" were fine and dandy, but having a powerful patron would help an awful lot. The United States was a fine place for a young man to advance himself. Far better than any of the aristocrat-riddled countries of Europe, to be sure. But it was no paradise. Connections and influence mattered, plenty.

Jackson had already made clear that he was willing to make Sam one of his protégés. So far, though, Sam had held off from any definite commitment. Partly, because Jackson's harsh attitudes repelled him some; mostly, just because there had been no clear and specific way to do so.

There was now, however—and Sam wasn't surprised at all to see that, as soon as the two colonels finally left, Jackson turned to peer at the most junior officer in the tent. He could almost read the general's mind.

Sam cleared his throat. "I think I've got a way to bring the Cherokees back, sir, yes. But . . ."

The words trailed off. Sam wasn't a coward—he *certainly* wasn't bashful—but even he found that piercing, blue-eyed gaze a bit intimidating.

Jackson's smile was razor thin. "But there are some conditions. Yes, I thought there might be."

The general glanced at Coffee and Reid. "Gentleman, if I could have some privacy?"

Nodding, Coffee left.

Major Reid was already passing through the tent flap.

CHAPTER 9

When they were gone, Jackson took off his hat and gestured with it toward a chair on the other side of the table. "Have a seat, Sam."

It was the first time he'd ever used Houston's first name. After Sam took his seat, Jackson laid the hat on the table—gently, this time, taking care not to damage it even further—and pulled out a chair on his side. As soon as the general sat down, he spoke.

"I'm going to break them, Sam. All of them. The Cherokees and the Choctaws just as much as the Creeks. Don't have any doubt about it. Know that, right from the start."

Sam took a deep breath. Before he could say anything, Jackson waved his hand impatiently.

"Spare me your objections. Tarnation, I didn't say it was *fair*. What in the name of Jesse has 'fair' got to do with any of it? Is it fair that a Cherokee needs eight square miles of land to enjoy his customs and habits, but a crofter in Scotland or Ireland—or England, or Germany, for that matter—has to eke out a living on a tiny patch of poor dirt? Am I supposed to tell my kinsmen—

yours, too—who are pouring into America that they should go back and knuckle their foreheads to their noble betters in the old country?"

He laughed harshly. "Not a chance, Sam. I wouldn't do it even if I could. My loyalties are clear. They're to my own people, and be damned to anyone else. *That* I learned from my good old mother. And you're going to have to make the same decision, one way or the other."

Sam had been holding his breath all the way through, without realizing it. Now, he let it out.

"I don't have a problem with *that,* General. A man should have his loyalties, and live by them. But I do have a problem— might, anyway—with how it's done."

"I don't *care* how it's done," Jackson said firmly. He ran bony fingers through his hair. "If it can be done humanely, though, then that would be fine by me."

For a moment, his face came as close to softening as that intrinsically ferocious face ever could. "I know the Indians are calling me 'Sharp Knife,' and frankly I don't regret the fact. Not one bit. Rather like it, actually, since it makes things easier for me. But I don't cut people for the pleasure of it, either."

That was true enough. Andrew Jackson was probably the most belligerent man Sam had ever met, but he wasn't one of those people who took a sick enjoyment in inflicting pain. He could be utterly callous, yes, but you couldn't honestly call him cruel. By reputation, he even treated his slaves better than most plantation owners—although God help a slave who was insubordinate or tried to run away. Jackson would have them lashed, chained, and then sell them.

Sam thought about it. "It won't be easy," he said.

"To put it mildly! Say whatever else you want about the sava—ah, our noble red brethren—but nobody's ever accused them of being cowards. Sure, they'll resist. I'll still break them. If I have to, I'll crush them out of existence. Just like some of my none-too-noble ancestors crushed others out of existence. Where are the Ostrogoths and the Lombards now?" The general flicked fingers across his cheek. "Somewhere in here—and in your face, too—mixed in with everything else."

Sam wasn't surprised by the general's knowledge of history. Whether or not there were any extra hats in Jackson's chests, Sam knew there were books. And not just the Bible and *The Vicar of*

Wakefield that, by reputation, were said to be Jackson's only reading matter. The general's written English might be riddled with eccentric spelling and syntax, but Jackson was far better educated—self-educated, anyway—than most people realized.

"I don't care about that part of it either," Sam said bluntly. "The Indians aren't any different from our own barbarian ancestors. The Cherokees haven't been in their area for more than a few centuries, probably. They came from farther north, driven out by some other tribe—and I'm sure they didn't hesitate to drive someone else out to make room for themselves. The whole Creek Confederacy is a patchwork of conquered tribes, when you get right down to it.

"Still and all, they aren't Huns. Once the Creeks broke a tribe, they let them join. Are you prepared to do the same? Make them citizens?"

To Sam's surprise, Jackson nodded.

"*Real* citizens, I mean. Not that half-and-half business we do with the freedmen."

Freedmen weren't slaves, but they weren't really citizens, either. Not, at least, in any state Sam knew about it. They couldn't run for office—couldn't even vote, for that matter—and were restricted by law in any number of other ways. They couldn't marry whites, for instance.

Jackson shrugged. "I'm not the Almighty, Sam. I don't have a problem with letting the Indians become full citizens of the country—*if* they agree to give up their independence. But that's just my personal opinion. You know as well as I do that most states wouldn't agree to it. Not in full, anyway."

Sam was rather proud of the fact that his eyes—blue, like the general's, if a softer shade—never left Jackson's face.

After a moment, it was the general who looked away. "All right, tarnation. I'll promise to do what I can. Within reason."

Jackson usually couldn't stay seated for very long. He rose to his feet, and began pacing.

"But that's no real solution, and you know it as well as I do." Jackson jerked his head toward the entrance of the tent. "Is that John Ross fellow still here with you?"

Sam nodded. "Yes, he is. He and James Rogers decided to stay, when all the other Cherokees left. I'm pretty sure The Ridge—Major Ridge, he's calling himself now—told them to do so."

Jackson grinned. "*Major* Ridge, is it? He'll grab what he wants from us, in other words, and leave aside the rest. So, tell me, Sam: Is that young Ross, who looks like the spitting image of a Scotsman, any different from the rest? Is he more willing than any of them to give up his political independence?"

The worst thing to do when dealing with the general was to lie, or even to try fudging the truth. "No, sir. He's flexible, mind you. But he's just as determined as any of them to stay a Cherokee. There are some exceptions, but not many of them would want to become U.S. citizens, even if they had the chance."

"I didn't think so. And that leaves us with only two options. Let's face the truth squarely, Sam."

Again, the general jerked his head toward the tent flap. "The United States of America already has an estimated eight million citizens, with more coming across the Atlantic every week. There were eighty thousand Americans alone just in Tennessee when we got statehood twenty years ago—and the population's probably doubled since then. How many Cherokees are there, all told? For that matter, how many people in all the southern tribes put together?"

Sam spread his hands. "Who knows, really? At a guess—but it's probably a pretty fair one—I'd say there are about twenty thousand Cherokees. They're the biggest tribe, except for maybe the Creeks, so . . . All told? Maybe eighty thousand."

Jackson nodded. "And that's eighty thousand *people.* Not eighty thousand warriors. At best, I doubt all the tribes together could field fifteen thousand men in a war. Not all at once, anyway. And however fierce they can be in a battle, their tribes are fragile because of the way they live. I'll just burn them out, all of them, like I've been doing to the Creeks. They'll surrender soon enough."

The general's words were harsh, but Sam knew they weren't anything more than the simple truth. Jackson's soldiers had been systematically burning the towns and riverbank crops of the hostile Creeks as they marched. By now, the Upper Town Creeks were on the edge of starvation, and hundreds of them were coming in to surrender. Soon, it would be thousands.

The traditional way of war among the southern tribes was a thing of clan feuds and tribal clashes. Short battles and ambushes, usually, followed by a peace settlement. The kind of relentless total war Jackson was waging was simply not something they could deal with.

Jackson drove it home, as relentlessly as he'd driven the campaign. "They don't stand a chance, Sam, not in the long run. Leave me out of it. Leave the whole U.S. Army out of it. Then what? I'm not even their worst enemy. They can call me Sharp Knife, but what do they think those cussed Georgians are? Tens of thousands of rapacious little razors, that's what."

And that, too, was no more than the truth. Even by the standards of white settlers on the frontier, the Georgians were notorious for their land avarice. They were just about as notorious—among Tennesseans, anyway—for not being worth a damn in a straight-up war against the hostiles. But it didn't matter, not in the long run. Georgians might run for cover every time the Indians went on the warpath, but they were back again soon enough. Killing Indians whenever they had a chance, grabbing their land, burning everything they couldn't steal.

If they had the martial reputation of locusts, they had the voracity as well. And the numbers.

"You could . . ." But Sam didn't even have the chance to finish the sentence.

"Stop them? How?" Jackson's expression wasn't quite a sneer. Not quite. "How am I—how is the whole U.S. government, for that matter—supposed to stop hundreds of thousands of settlers from shoving in on Indian land? Stop playing the innocent, Sam. You know those people as well as I do, because they're our own. The 'people of the western waters,' some call them. They're Scots-Irish immigrants, the most of them. Being honest, not all that much different from the Indians. Just as feisty, for sure—and there are a sight more of them."

Sam couldn't help but smile. The truth was, the people who had produced both he and Jackson weren't very far removed from being barbarians themselves, even today. They were flooding into North America just like, in ancient days, the Gauls and Germans had flooded into Western Europe. Today's "people of the western waters" had been yesterday's border reivers, often enough.

"How is anyone supposed to stop them, Sam?" The general picked up his hat and, for a moment, looked like he might smash it back onto the table.

"What would it take?" he demanded. "I'll tell you what."

He *did* smash the hat back on the table. "We'd have to scrap our precious republic and replace it with something like the stinking tsars have set up in Russia, that's what. Turn everyone into serfs so we could establish a level of taxation necessary to keep a huge standing army in the field. That would keep the people in their place. Over my dead body!"

Sam studied the hat. He'd studied mathematics, too, when he'd been a schoolboy. And he could recognize an immovable equation when he saw one.

Jackson flicked the much-battered hat aside. "So that's one option," he stated flatly. "Give it twenty years—thirty, at the outside—and 'the Cherokees' will just be a name. Something schoolboys study in books."

Sam took another deep breath. He took off his own cap and ran fingers through his hair. "And the other?"

"You know it as well as I do. Relocation. Let the Cherokees— *all* of the southern tribes—move across the Mississippi. If they want to keep their independence, fine. Let 'em do it somewhere else."

Sam smiled crookedly. "You sound like my foster father—his older brother Tahlonteskee, even more. That's what they've been advocating for almost twenty years now."

Sam's hair was even bushier than the general's, so he could keep busy with it for a while. "Not with much luck, though, in terms of convincing most of the Cherokees. Their opponents keep asking difficult questions. Just for starters: What's to keep the same thing from happening down the road a spell? Give it another fifty years—a century, for sure—and there'll be more settlers wanting their new land."

The general started fiddling with his hat, trying awkwardly with one hand to press it back into shape. Sam's smile got more crooked still, and he reached across the table.

"Here, General, let me do that. Out of curiosity, by the way, do you have a bunch of these stashed away somewhere?"

Jackson handed over the hat, chuckling. "Of course." A long, bony finger indicated one of the chests in a corner of the tent. "I had Rachel send me half a dozen, after Coffee gave me the idea. I'd like to salvage this one, though, if we can. I've only got two left, and the things are blasted expensive."

As Sam did his best to knead the hat back into shape, Jackson went on.

"If that turns out to be the case, then to blazes with them. Am I supposed to be their nursemaid, too? Tarnation, Sam, if the Indians are given half a century to put together a real nation of their own out there—and they still can't manage the affair—then let them go the way of all broken nations. Let them join the Babylonians and the Trojans. That's just the way it is. Always has been, always will be—just like the British will break us if we let them."

That seemed fair enough, to Sam, at least in the broad strokes. The devil, of course, was in the details.

"I'll help you, sir, as best as I can," he said evenly. "I'll do my best to convince them. But you know as well as I do that there are a hundred different problems. The help that the U.S. government always promises the Indians somehow never materializes, or if it does so, it's always in dribs and drabs. Why? Well, let's start with the fact that most Indian agents are crooks and swindlers and thieves, and the ones who aren't—like Colonel Meigs or Benjamin Hawkins—are the ones you usually quarrel with the most."

Jackson glared at him. "Can't stand the bastards," he growled. "Nothing but blasted injun lovers, the both of 'em."

"So am I, General," Sam said mildly, "when you get right down to it. I grew up among them, and I've got as many Cherokee friends as I do white ones. If I'd stayed a few more years, I'd probably have wound up marrying a Cherokee girl. I can even tell you her name. Tiana Rogers, my foster father's niece." He handed the hat back to Jackson.

Jackson snatched the hat, still glaring. Sam sat up straight in his chair and returned the glare without flinching. "That's the way it is, sir. Take it or leave it."

After a moment, and not to Sam's surprise—no longer, now that he'd taken the general's measure—Jackson began to chuckle.

"My own injun lover, is it?" He placed the hat gently back on his head. "Well, why not? Maybe you can do with magic and your glib tongue what I'd have to do with a sword and a torch. Well, if you can, I won't object."

Sam took another deep breath. "That's not enough, General."

The glare flared up again. It was like staring into two blue furnaces.

"What?" he demanded. "You're adding *conditions,* too?"

Sam smiled easily, and spread his hands again. "I wouldn't call them 'conditions,' sir. Not exactly. Let's just say I want a promise from you that you'll back me up, when the time comes, as much as I'll back you up until then. I don't know when or where that'll be, I admit, or even if it'll ever be. But I still want your word on it."

At first Jackson didn't say a word, and, for a moment, Sam was sure that he was about to snap a flat and angry refusal.

But, whatever he would have done, he was interrupted before he could respond. A man stepped through the tent's entrance, pushing the flap aside, and came two steps into the tent. Then he stood still and very erect. He had a dark complexion, like a part-blood Indian, but he was wearing a white man's clothes.

Jackson's glare was transferred onto him. "Who in the blazes are you, sir? I don't recall inviting you to intrude upon my privacy!"

The man replied in perfectly fluent English. "Yes, you did. The word is in all the towns that you are looking for William Weatherford."

Jackson lunged to his feet, his anger instantly replaced by eagerness. "You know where the murdering bastard's to be found? Splendid! There'll be a reward for you, be sure of it."

The man's face showed no expression at all. Suddenly, Sam rose and reached for his sword.

But the man ignored him.

"I am not an informer. I *am* William Weatherford. Also known as Red Eagle. I led the attack on Fort Mims. They say you intend to hang me for it.

"Do it then, Sharp Knife."

CHAPTER 10

Jackson's eyes flicked to his own sword, still in its scabbard and leaning against a tent post. Then, seeing that Houston already had his pistol out, the general turned his attention to Weatherford.

"How did you get into the fort?" he demanded.

For the first time since he'd entered the tent, there was an expression on Weatherford's face. Not much of one, just a slight smile.

"You called upon all Creek chiefs to come in and surrender, didn't you? I was one of them. I came in and surrendered. The soldiers didn't seem to know what to do, so I just rode in past them."

"You were supposed to be brought here in manacles and chains!" Jackson snapped.

Weatherford's smile widened a bit. "And who was supposed to chain me?"

The smile went away. Weatherford spread his hands. "If you need the chains, Sharp Knife, send for them. I came unarmed. And I simply came to surrender."

It was the first time since Houston had met Jackson that the general seemed genuinely taken aback by anything. Confused, even, as if he didn't know what to do. It was an odd experience; unsettling, in its own way.

Jackson's angry eyes moved away from Weatherford and fell on Houston. Seeing the pistol in Sam's hand—half raised if not yet cocked—he made a sudden, abrupt, impatient gesture with his hand.

"Oh, put that away."

"Yes, sir." Houston slid the pistol back into his waistband—but only far enough to hold it there. He'd still be able to get it out quickly. "Do you want me to send for soldiers, sir? And manacles?"

Jackson glared at him. Sam just returned the glare with a mild gaze, saying nothing.

Jackson looked back at Weatherford; then, suddenly, slapped the table with his open hand. "*Tarnation,* sir! If you'd been brought to me as I commanded, I'd have known what to do."

"Why should your life be any simpler than mine?" Weatherford demanded. The Red Stick war leader shrugged. "I am in your power, Sharp Knife. Do with me as you please. I am a soldier. I have done your people all the harm that I could. I fought them, and I fought them bravely. If I still had an army to command, I would be fighting you still."

He seemed to shudder a little. "But I have none. My people are all gone. I can do nothing more than to weep over the misfortunes of my nation."

By the time he was done, the expression on Jackson's face had undergone a sea change. There was still anger there, yes, but . . .

Jackson rallied. "You massacred hundreds at Fort Mims! Women and children!"

"And you massacred women and children at Tallushatchee."

Even Jackson's innate self-righteousness couldn't prevent him from wincing. Sam hadn't been at that battle, since the Thirty-ninth Infantry hadn't yet joined up with Jackson's Tennessee militia. But he'd heard tales of it.

The Creeks at Tallushatchee, unlike those at the Horseshoe Bend, had been caught by surprise by Jackson's advance. Hundreds of women and children had been trapped in the village. Whether or not any of them had been deliberately massacred—and, given the temper of militiamen after Fort Mims, Sam was quite sure that some of them had—many had died as the village caught fire and burned. Sam had heard one Tennessee militiaman who'd been present describe to him, in a weird sort of half-horrified glee, how he'd watched a Creek child burn to death after crawling halfway out of a flaming cabin.

You could see the grease coming out of him, I swear!

Jackson's jaws were tight. "I gave no orders—"

"Neither did I," Weatherford said sharply. "I tried to stop the massacre. But my warriors were out of control by then—don't tell me you've never had that happen to you as well, General

Jackson." His face grew stony. "They even threatened to kill me, at one point, if I persisted in trying to stop them. Tempers were very high."

Jackson's hand came up, and he stroked his jaw, as if trying to knead out the tension. Then, he grunted.

The wordless sound was one of grudging recognition. The story that Weatherford had tried to stop the massacre was by now well known. Enough survivors had reported it that even many white settlers were inclined to accept the story. There was even a rumor that Weatherford had agreed to accept command over the Red Sticks only because the fanatics had taken his family hostage. Whether that was true or not, Sam had no idea.

And, clearly enough, Weatherford wasn't going to say anything more about it. This wasn't a man who was trying to beg for mercy, not even by pleading extenuating circumstances. Even his rejoinder concerning the massacre had been that of an accuser, not a criminal seeing leniency.

Jackson removed his hat and placed it on the table. The motion was precise, almost delicate, as if he were using the moment to marshal his thoughts.

"All right," he said quietly. "War's a nasty business at the best of times, as I well know. I won't hold the massacre at Fort Mims against you."

Sam could tell that the general was doing his best to appear solemn and grave. But he couldn't quite keep the admiration he so obviously felt for Weatherford's courage from showing, not so much in his face, but in his posture. More than anything else, Andy Jackson despised cowardice. And whatever else you might say about William Weatherford, he whom the Creeks called Chief Red Eagle, he was no coward.

"All right," Jackson repeated, uttering the words sharply this time. A command, now, not a judgment. "I'll give orders that you are not to be detained or molested in any way. But understand this, William Weatherford. The war is over, we won, and you have no choice but to surrender. If your surrender is an honest one, that'll be the end of it. But if—"

Weatherford made an abrupt gesture with his hand. "Please, General. We are both warriors. My nation is beaten, and I must now look to salvaging what I can. If I had a choice . . ."

He took a deep breath. "But I have no choice. Not any longer. Once I could lead my warriors into battle, but I have no warriors left. Their bones are at Talladega, Tallushatchee, Emuckfaw, and Tohopeka."

Tohopeka was the Creek name for their encampment at the horseshoe bend. Even though Weatherford hadn't been at that battle himself, he'd clearly heard the tales. He hadn't been able even to pronounce the name without hesitating a moment, in order to swallow.

The Creek war leader looked away, sighing for the first time since he'd entered Jackson's tent. "If I'd been left to fight only the Georgians, I'd still be fighting. I could have raised our corn on one side of the river and fought them on the other. But you came, and destroyed us. So it was. I will accept your terms, General Jackson, and urge others to do the same. I will fight you no longer. Such is my word."

Jackson nodded, and stepped to the tent entrance. Pulling aside the flap, he called for Major Reid.

The next few minutes were rather amusing, Sam thought, although he was careful not to let any of that humor show on his face. He wasn't sure which part of it he found the funniest—Reid's astonishment, Jackson's increasingly exasperated attempts not to explain himself, or Weatherford's none-too-successful struggle to hide his own amusement.

But, eventually, it was done. Reid escorted Weatherford out of the tent. He did so with an odd combination of diffidence, wariness, and uncertainty. Much the way an angel might have ushered a devil out of heaven, after God had pronounced him not really such a bad fellow, after all.

After they were gone, Jackson continued to stare at the now-closed flap of the tent. "They are a brave people," Sam heard him murmur, as if he were talking to himself. "That, whatever else."

Abruptly, he turned to Houston.

"All right, Sam. You have my word. If the time comes when you can work out a satisfactory solution, I'll back you. To the hilt."

The general grinned, and rather savagely. "Mind you, I may well be cursing you at the same time, and damning you for a fool. But I'll do it in private. Or perhaps to your face. I might prefer it that way."

Sam smiled. "Well, sure. I wouldn't expect anything else."

Jackson went back to the table and sat down. "Where do you plan to start?"

Seeing the look of confusion that appeared on Sam's face, Jackson barked a laugh. Cawed a laugh, rather.

"Thought so! Fine and sentimental speeches are easy, young man. The trick is in the *doing*."

Sam's mind was still a blank. The general pointed to the other chair. "Sit down. Let an old warhorse get you started."

After Sam took his seat, Jackson rearranged the large map so that it again covered most of the table. Then, he pointed to the junction of Tennessee, Georgia, and the Territory of Mississippi.

"Start there, Sam. The Ridge lives somewhere here in north Georgia, and most of the other major chiefs aren't far away. Take Lieutenant Ross with you. See if you can talk The Ridge—and any other chiefs, for that matter—into going to Washington. You'll serve as their guide and official liaison with the government."

That was the last thing Sam had expected to hear.

"Washington? You mean the *capital*?"

Jackson snorted.

"Where else? You want to guide an official Cherokee delegation to any other town named Washington?"

Sam's mind was still a blank. The general smiled smugly.

"Let them see Washington, Sam. Let them see for themselves that there's more to America—more strength, too—than the white settlers they usually encounter."

Sam winced. "I don't know if that'll do much good, General. The Ridge has already been to Washington."

Jackson frowned. "He has?"

"Several years ago. There was a dispute among the Cherokees—sharp one, too—when Tahlonteskee and Black Fox tried to get the tribe to agree to the first proposal for a big land swap. It was tied to relocation across the Mississippi. The Ridge was opposed to it, so the Cherokees elected him to be part of the delegation that went to Washington for further negotiations. I don't think he met with the president, but I know he met with Secretary of War Dearborn. John Jolly told me about it."

"Dearborn! That worthless old coot." Jackson scowled, looking at the map. "I didn't know that. Still . . . That was back when? 1808? Madison's administration is now in office, and Secretary of War Armstrong is a different creature altogether. He might actually *do* something."

Sam hesitated. True enough, John Armstrong was a very different man from the tired old general who had served Thomas Jefferson as secretary of war. But the country had been at peace in 1808, too, whereas today . . .

Doing something, whatever that might come to mean, would inevitably entail *spending money*—and plenty of it—or those were just two meaningless words. No Indian tribe was wealthy, at least not in terms of movable property. Asking them to relocate beyond the Mississippi without providing them with massive assistance before, during, and after the relocation was just a pipe dream. And given the demands of the current war with Britain, Sam doubted the government had much money to throw at anything else. Especially not the Department of War, which was legally charged with handling all Indian affairs.

Jackson seemed to read his thoughts easily enough.

"Patience, youngster," he said, still smiling. "You know as well as I do that no Indian tribe—certainly not those cantankerous Cherokees—will be making any big decision quickly. And they've got a few years, anyway, before the rope starts to tighten."

Sam looked at him skeptically. Jackson cawed another little laugh. "I said I'd break them if they tried to resist me for too long. I didn't say I was Attila the Hun. Besides—"

The general began tracing lines on the map. "The Cherokees—Choctaws and Chickasaws, too—are down the road. Quite a ways, unless I miss my guess. Our main enemies are the British and Spanish, don't ever forget that. So the first thing I intend to do, at the upcoming negotiations with the Creeks, is strip the Creeks of half their land. *This* half."

His finger quickly traced the area he proposed to seize from the Creeks. "That'll create a buffer zone between the Creeks and the Spanish territories. They won't be able to get war supplies from our enemies, any longer."

Sam grimaced. "General, most of that land belongs to *friendly* Creeks. The Lower Towns. The same ones who were allied with us in the recent battles."

Jackson glared at him. "Allies! That's just because the Red Sticks had them by the throat. They sent us a few hundred warriors, here and there, never more than that and never all at one time. And you know as well as I do that if the British had landed soon enough on the coast, and waved guns under his nose, that Big Warrior would have switched sides in a heartbeat."

That was true enough, so Sam couldn't argue the point. Despite occasional clashes—the last major one had been the battle at Etowah in 1793—the Cherokees had usually been allied with the United States since its creation, and before that with the colonists against the British. The same was true for the Choctaws.

The Creeks, on the other hand, had maintained close ties with the British and the Spanish for many decades.

Sam didn't trust Big Warrior's change of allegiance any more than Jackson did. Traditionally, the Lower Town Creeks and the Seminoles had been the southern Indian tribes most closely tied to the British and Spanish. The only reason the Lower Town Creeks had allied with the United States was because the civil war launched by the Red Sticks had been an immediate danger to them, and Britain and Spain had been too preoccupied with their war with Napoleon to provide much in the way of assistance.

"And it's all beside the point, anyway," Jackson continued. He jabbed his forefinger at a spot on the map, then at another. Both spots were on the coast. One was marked *Pensacola*; the other, *Apalachicola*. "Don't forget—ever—that the Indians are a sideshow. The real enemy is down here. Spanish Florida is a running wound in the side of our republic. As long as the Dons hold territory in North America, the British will use it as an invasion route whenever they can—and as a conduit to arm and stir up the Creeks and Seminoles against us year-round, year after year. As well as any other tribe they can reach and influence—and provide with arms."

As long as the British held Canada and the Spanish held Florida, Sam realized, the United States would be caught in a vise. Granted, the Spanish Empire was a shadow of its former self. But they'd let the British do the dirty work for them, and Britain looked to be emerging from the Napoleonic wars as the most powerful empire in the world. If the British could seize New Orleans and the mouth of the Mississippi, the two-sided vise would become a three-sided one.

So Sam could understand the cold-blooded logic of Jackson's

plans. By stripping away the southern half of Creek territory and opening it up to white settlers, the general would separate Spanish Florida from all the southern tribes except the Seminoles. Whatever clashes the Creeks—or the Cherokees, Choctaws, and Chickasaws, for that matter—had in the future with the United States, they'd have to fight them without access to guns and ammunition from the European powers. Which meant, in practice, that they couldn't really fight at all. The destruction of Tecumseh's forces had demonstrated graphically that poorly armed Indians couldn't hope to defeat the United States in an open battle.

That still left the Seminoles, of course. That breakaway portion of the Creek Confederacy was already entrenched in Florida.

Sam cocked his head, studying the general. "And that'll be stage two of your strategy, won't it? You'll go after the Seminoles."

"Blast the Seminoles, lad. I'll use the Seminoles as an excuse to go after the Dons." Then, scowling: "Not that I've got any problem at all with crushing the Seminoles. But if they were just down there in Florida on their own, they'd be a minor problem, at best."

Abruptly, he rose to his feet. "It's the Dons I'm after! I swear, I *will* have them out of North America entirely. I'd love to take Cuba from them, too—let the Negro rebels have Hispaniola, I don't care much about that—but I doubt I can. Still, I'll settle for driving the Dons off the continent entirely. Let them rot on their islands."

Sam couldn't help but laugh. It was like hearing a man complaining that he didn't think he'd be able to fly to the moon after he climbed the tallest mountain.

"Uh, General . . . you *do* know that official U.S. policy is to stay on good terms with the Spanish?"

Jackson snorted. "That'll change. If needs be, I'll *force* those fools in Washington to change it."

A light was beginning to dawn. "I see. My Cherokee delegation to Washington is just an excuse, really. What's more important is that I might have an opportunity to talk to someone while I'm there. Say, Secretary Monroe."

Jackson waggled the hand that was draped in the sling. "Well, not exactly. I actually do have hopes that something might come out of the Cherokees going back to Washington. It's not just a masquerade. But, yes. Monroe will be the next president, most likely. I don't have anything specific in mind, but from what I've seen of him he seems a substantial sort of man. Quite unlike—"

He broke off abruptly. Not even Andy Jackson was prepared to openly deride his own president. Not, at least, in front of a junior officer.

But he didn't need to say anything. The animosity between Andrew Jackson and James Madison was well known on the frontier. In Washington, too, for that matter, unless Sam missed his guess. It dated back to Thomas Jefferson's attempt to have Aaron Burr convicted of treason during the last year of his administration. The trial had become a national spectacle. Jackson had supported Burr. Madison, of course, being the secretary of state at the time and the man most people assumed would be the next president, had supported Jefferson.

Jackson, in his inimitable manner, had publicly pilloried Madison. He'd pilloried Jefferson, too, but that was nothing new. The animosity between Jackson and Jefferson dated back even further.

Once Madison became president, needless to say, he hadn't forgotten the episode. When the war with Britain erupted, he'd repaid Jackson by passing him over when he was selecting generals for the regular army.

Monroe, on the other hand . . .

Jackson continued. "I don't know Monroe well, you understand. But I was deeply impressed by his vigorous protest of Britain's policies when he was ambassador to the Court of St. James. He's likely to make a good chief executive, I think."

"I understand, sir," said Sam. "And if I get the chance to speak to him—"

"Oh, you will. Have no doubt about that." His tone was now harsh. "Whether those bast—ah, people in Washington like me or not, they have to live with me now. They're counting on me to keep the British at bay here in the South—and I daresay I'll have more success than *they've* had dealing with them in Canada."

He cleared his throat noisily, almost triumphantly. "I'll write several letters for you to take along, Sam. You'll get to see the secretary of state. Count on it."

Sam rose to his feet. "Best I be off, then. It'll take me several months to convince the Cherokees to send another delegation to Washington. If I can do it at all, which I rather doubt."

"Just do your best. If nothing else, just go yourself. See if young Ross will accompany you. He's said to be a rising man among the Cherokees. And he's too young, I assume, to have seen the capital?"

Sam shrugged. "So far as I know. I'll find out. But even if he agrees to come with me, he's not on the council. So he won't represent anyone but himself."

"Well, you never know how these things will work out, in the end. Ross might well grow into his new role. And, remember, you've still got a few years before . . ."

Jackson smiled grimly. "Before you call in your promise—or I drive over whatever promise you couldn't come up with."

Sam nodded. "And in the meantime?"

"I'll have Colonel Williams release you from the Thirty-ninth, for detached duty. But by the end of the year, I expect, I'll be facing the British. Either in New Orleans or Mobile. So come back from Washington as soon as possible. I could use an officer like you then, Sam. I'll find a suitable place for you, be sure of it."

"By the end of the year . . ." Sam mused. "That should be enough."

The general stuck out his hand, and Sam shook it. "In eight months then, Captain Houston. I'll expect you back no later than mid-December."

Sam raised an eyebrow. Jackson just grinned.

"One of those letters will include my strong recommendation that you be promoted to captain." He cleared his throat again, just as noisily and even more triumphantly. "And I daresay they'll listen to me this time. After the Horseshoe Bend, *I daresay they will.*"

Part II

~

THE NIAGARA

CHAPTER 11

Two soldiers manhandled each condemned man, forcing them to their knees just in front of the graves. The five condemned men were dressed in white robes, with hoods of the same color covering their faces. Their hands were tied behind their backs.

General Jacob Brown, commander of the small Army of the Niagara, had left the training of the regiments in the hands of his subordinate, Brigadier Winfield Scott. Scott was a stickler—many of his soldiers would have said a maniac—on the subject of camp sanitation, as well as discipline in general. "Efficiency," he liked to say, "is just one of many necessary soldierly qualities." The same bullets that slew the deserters would serve to transport them to their graves.

Four of the condemned men made no sound. The fifth, on the far right, was sobbing uncontrollably. The sound was quite audible, despite the hood that was covering his face.

And well he might sob, thought Sergeant Patrick Driscol harshly, as he made his final inspection. The condemned man's name was Anthony McParland, and he was a "man" in name only. McParland had tried to desert the army not two weeks after his seventeenth birthday. "Desperately homesick," the little puler had claimed at his court-martial.

Driscol wasn't moved by McParland's age, much less the puling. He might have been, except that the young soldier was another Ulsterman. Came from that stock, at least, even if he'd been born in America.

Like many of the United Irishmen who had taken refuge in

the United States after the British crushed the rebellion of 1798, Sergeant Driscol hated two things above all.

First, England.

Second, any man—or boy, and be damned—who capitulated to the Sassenach.

For Driscol—who'd spent several years in the French armies before emigrating to America—"capitulation" most certainly included desertion. And the penalty for desertion in time of war was death.

He came to the end of the line, and examined the trembling figure for a few seconds. Then, he straightened up and stalked off.

The five condemned men were well separated, to allow for the large firing squads. There were a dozen men in each squad—a preposterous waste of effort, to Driscol's mind, not to mention a waste of ammunition that could be better used against the enemy. But Brigadier Scott had been firm on the matter. He'd said he didn't want any one man knowing for sure that he'd been the agent of death.

There'd been a sixth man convicted of desertion also. But, in light of extenuating circumstances, the court-martial had not sentenced him to death as it had the other five. Instead, he'd had his ears cut off, the letter *D* branded into his cheek, and he had been dishonorably discharged from the service.

Once he was out of the line of fire, Driscol turned and squared his shoulders.

"Ready!" he called out. The sergeant had a loud voice, trained over the years to penetrate the cacophony of battlefields.

Sixty muskets were leveled, a dozen at each condemned man.

"Arm!"

Sixty hammers were cocked.

Driscol gave a last glance at the shrouded figure of young McParland. The front of his robe was stained wet.

Let the little bastard remember that, too. And if he forgets, I'll make sure to remind him.

He turned his head and looked at the general. Brigadier Scott was sitting on his horse, some forty yards away.

Scott looked every inch the officer, despite his youth. The sergeant had known plenty of peacock officers in his day. Scott might have the vanity of a peacock, but he had the soul of a fighter.

That was all Sergeant Patrick Liam Driscol cared about. He'd been born in County Antrim, in Ireland, of Scottish Presbyterian stock. His father and older brother had been members of the United Irishmen and had died in the rebellion of 1798. Patrick himself had participated in the final battle, near the town of Antrim, that had seen the rebels broken.

Patiently, he waited for the general to steel himself. Driscol knew the moment, when it came. The general had a little way of twitching his shoulders to steady himself. Another man might simply square them, but Scott was too energetic.

This past November, when he'd still been a colonel, Scott had ridden a horse through sleet and snow for thirty hours straight in order to join a battle. That alone, in an American army whose top officers were more prone to spending thirty hours straight in taverns or lying in bed complaining about their illnesses, had been enough to endear Brigadier Scott to the sergeant from County Antrim.

Scott gave him a little nod. Not bothering to turn his head—he had a very powerful voice—the sergeant called out the command.

"Fire!"

Sixty muskets roared. The sound of them—one-fifth, to be precise, an entire bloody squad—was off a bit.

He turned his head to see the results. Young McParland was lying curled up on the ground.

As if the pitiful wretch had actually been shot!

Worthless little shit. It was all Driscol could do not to heave a sigh. He had his orders, after all.

The sergeant's eyes quickly scanned the other four men. Three of them were no longer visible. The volleys had done their work, hurling them into the pits. To Driscol's disgust, however, one of the men was sprawled across the edge of his grave. His robe was soaked red, and the body under it would be a broken ruin. But the man seemed to be twitching a bit.

Driscol drew his pistol and stalked over, glaring at that particular squad along the way. He'd be having some words with those sluggards later that day, they could be sure of it. From the sickly look on their faces, they knew it themselves.

The sergeant reached the man lying at the edge of the grave. He cocked his pistol, took aim, and blew the deserter's brains out. Then, with a boot, rolled the corpse into the pit.

That done, he walked down the line, taking a moment at each grave to inspect the body lying in it. They were all dead.

That left McParland.

Driscol marched over to the white-shrouded figure, twitching and trembling on the far right. The sergeant still had his weapon in his hand, since the barrel was a bit hot yet. For a moment, he was tempted to pistol-whip the sobbing wretch.

Orders, orders.

Driscol was a squat, powerful man. He reached down with his left hand, seized McParland by the scruff of the neck, and jerked him to his feet.

"Get up, you sniveling bastard."

With the same hand, he snatched McParland's hood off. Under normal conditions, McParland's eyes were hazel, but the tears had left them looking more like slimy mud at the moment. The boy's legs were shaking, too.

"If you fall down," Driscol snarled, "I'll give you the boots. I swear I will. And my boots will make you think you're being trampled by cattle. I swear they will."

McParland stared at him. Then, slowly, he peered down at his own body.

"I'm still alive," he whispered.

"No thanks to me," Driscol growled. "You're a shame and a disgrace to Ulstermen. I'd have shot you dead and not thought twice about it. But the brigadier there"—the sergeant twitched his head toward Scott on his horse—"was of the opinion that a bawling babe might still be able to learn a lesson. Waste of time, in my opinion. But . . . he's the commander, and I'm the sergeant, and so you're still alive. The muskets of your firing squad were loaded with blanks."

McParland was still staring down at his unmarked body. Unmarked by blood and gore, at least. The urine stain was quite visible—as was the smell of feces. The boy had beshat himself as well.

"I can't believe it," McParland whispered.

"Neither can I," grumbled Driscol. "The brigadier also instructed me to pay special attention to your training from now on. God help me."

Driscol hefted the pistol, looking at McParland with a speculative eye. He smiled. It was a very, very, very thin smile.

"You'll be doing me the favor, I hope, of trying to desert again. Then we can just shoot you properly and be done with it."

McParland started shaking his head violently. "Never do it again!" he choked.

Driscol didn't try to suppress his sigh, this time. "I was afraid you might say that."

That evening, after Driscol had finished stripping the hides off the squad that had done such a slovenly job of executing their assigned deserter, the sergeant went to visit the brigadier. Scott had instructed him to make an appearance after the men were settled down.

Scott wasn't one of those officers who made a show of sleeping in a tent like his men, at least not when the army was camped at a proper base. There'd been a farmhouse on the grounds, vacated by its residents. Two years of fighting on the contested soil that lay between the United States and Canada had left half the towns on either side of the border nothing much more than burned shells. The house, however, remained intact, and the brigadier had cheerfully sequestered the building and turned it into his headquarters.

Most of the soldiers of the Army of the Niagara had ascribed that action to Scott's desire to sleep in a real bed, and eat his meals off a real table. There was some truth to that, of course, but Sergeant Driscol knew that Scott's principal motive had been more straightforward. The brigadier was bound and determined to make full and proper use of the months he'd had since General Brown had turned command over to him, while Brown himself returned to his headquarters at Sackets Harbor. Scott had used those months, that blessed lull in the fighting, to train an American army that, for the first time since the war began, had a real chance of matching British regulars in a battle on the open field.

Scott was a superb trainer of troops, as efficient with the business as he was energetic. Efficiency, however, meant that his headquarters was exactly that—a military headquarters, not a lounging area for officers looking to idle away the day in chitchat, and the evenings in drinking bouts.

So the brigadier had his feather bed, and ate on his table. But most of the farmhouse was devoted to keeping and maintaining the records of the army's training, supplies, and sanitation. And God help the subordinate officer whom Scott discovered using the headquarters for any purpose other than that.

The sentry ushered Driscol into the room that served Scott as a combination study and chamber he used for discussions he wanted to keep private. Then the man left to find the brigadier and tell him the sergeant had arrived.

While he waited, Driscol took the time to admire Scott's bookcase. That bookcase had become famous, in its own way—notorious to the soldiers who got the assignment of lugging it around. It was five feet tall, solidly built and heavy, and contained the brigadier's impressive military library. Scott took it everywhere he went—except directly into battle, of course.

As with so many things about Winfield Scott, the library was contradictory. On the one hand, the thing could be looked upon as an extravagant affectation. On the other hand . . .

Scott had *read* the books in that library. Done more than simply read them—he'd studied them thoroughly and systematically, with a mind that was acute and a memory that was well-nigh phenomenal. Each and every one of them: the writings of the great French military engineer Vauban, Frederick the Great's *Principes Généraux de la Guerre,* Guibert's *Essai Général de Tactique* along with several other French military manuals, Wolfe's *Instructions to Young Officers,* and dozens of other volumes relevant to the duties of an officer. Many of them were biographies of great military leaders of the past.

When Sergeant Driscol had first showed up in Scott's camp, he'd been astonished to discover that Scott was organizing and drilling his men using the same principles and methods that Driscol himself had learned in Napoleon's army. Granted, the brigadier's grasp of those methods was a bit on the academic side, but he'd been ready enough—even eager—to modify them in light of the practical suggestions made by Driscol and the handful of other men in the Army of the Niagara who had experience with European wars.

If Scott could be prickly in his dealings with other officers—and he could—he was never prickly dealing with competent sergeants. Driscol had also noted that Scott's abusiveness toward other officers was usually well deserved, and that the often-rude brigadier could get along quite well with officers who showed a fighting spirit.

General Wilkinson *had* been a sluggard, not to mention a thief, even if it had been most impolitic for Scott to say so publicly. And if Scott had initially been abrasive toward General Jacob Brown because he felt—correctly—that Brown was an amateur from the New York militia who'd been jumped over him due to political connections, he'd warmed to the man after Brown had demonstrated that he was willing to *fight* the British, instead of finding reasons to avoid them.

Since then, in fact, Scott and Brown had developed quite a friendly and productive relationship.

Driscol's musings were interrupted by the brigadier's voice, coming from the door.

"I've told you before, Sergeant, you're welcome to borrow any of those books should you choose to do so. Just make sure you bring them back in good condition."

Driscol turned and saluted. " 'Twould be a waste, sir. I know my letters, well enough, for practical matters. But those writings are a bit beyond me, much as I can admire them from a distance. I'm afraid my schooling was interrupted—permanently, as things turned out—by Lord Cornwallis. May he and all his ilk rot in hell."

Scott's eyes tightened slightly. The brigadier was six feet four inches tall, with a well-built frame and a head so handsome it would have suited an ancient statue. For a moment, as he peered down at the squat, broad-shouldered sergeant who was almost eight inches shorter than he was—and whose visage no classic sculptor would have even considered for a model—he resembled a refined aristocrat casting a cold eye upon a crude peasant.

It was all Driscol could do not to laugh. Despite the ease of his working relationship with Scott, the two men were very far apart in the way they looked upon matters other than military. Winfield Scott was as close as Americans ever got to having a nobility, born as he'd been into the Virginia gentry. And, leaving aside his birth, Scott's social and political attitudes were such that many people accused him of being a barely veiled Federalist in a poorly fitting Republican costume.

The sergeant, on the other hand, possessed—gloried in, rather—the kind of ferociously egalitarian ideology that made any proper Federalist splutter with indignation. Like all United Irishmen, Driscol had been weaned on the ideals of the French Revolution, and after his emigration to the United States, he'd promptly sided with the radical wing of Jeffersonian democracy. Insofar as he favored any American political figures, the most promising of the lot looked to be that notorious southerner Andrew Jackson. The man was said to be a maniac by the gentility, at least, which was always a promising sign.

And, needless to say, Driscol lifted his glass in salute once a year, on July 11. The anniversary of the day when Aaron Burr shot Alexander Hamilton dead in a duel, before the Federalist schemer could foist a new aristocracy on the great American republic.

The brigadier issued a little exasperated sigh. "Irishmen and their feuds," he muttered. Manfully, and as befitted a mere sergeant, Driscol refrained from pointing out that the record of personal feuds between officers in the U.S. Army made Irish history look like a chronicle of brotherly love. As frequently as the brigadier himself participated in those follies, he was by no means the worst offender, either.

Something of Driscol's sarcastic thoughts must have shown on his face, though, because Scott's glower was replaced by a wry smile. "Though I suppose the fault can be found elsewhere, as well." The brigadier clasped his hands behind his back and leaned forward.

"Patrick," he said, lapsing into rare informality, "I will repeat my offer. Just say the word, and I'll get you a commission."

Driscol gave his head a little shake. "No, sir. Thank you, but no. I'm a natural sergeant, and the rank suits me fine. Besides . . ."

He hesitated, gauging Scott's temper. Then, with a shrug so slight it was barely perceptible, plowed on. "If I were an officer, I'd be duty bound to treat British prisoners—especially officers—with respect and courtesy. That would be, ah . . . difficult."

Again, the brigadier issued an exasperated sigh. But he didn't press the matter. Scott was something of an Anglophile, as was commonly true for Americans of his class. But he had enough intelligence to understand that the world looked different to someone who'd seen his father tortured to death at the orders of British officers.

"So be it," he stated. "At least I'll still have the best sergeant in the army. So, have you spoken to the boy yet?"

"No, sir. I'll wait till later tonight. For the moment, the best thing for the little bastard's quaking soul is to wallow in the admiration of his mates."

Scott cocked his head quizzically. "Admiration? I'd have thought . . ."

Driscol smiled. "Oh, it'll be a very adulterated sort of admiration, sir. To the untrained ear, most of it will sound like ridicule and derision. But admiration it is, be sure of it—with more than a trace of envy."

The brigadier kept his head cocked, inviting Driscol to continue.

"It's like this, sir. Poor boys have little enough to brag about, and precious few accomplishments to their name—nor any great prospects of improving their lot. As it is, assuming he lives that long, young McParland will be able to brag to his grandchildren that he was once executed by a firing squad, and lived to tell the tale. Of course, by then the story will have changed a great deal. His offense will have become quite a bit more glamorous than desertion—something along the lines of heroic insubordination in the face of a tyrannical officer, I imagine—and there'll certainly be no mention of the sobbing and incontinence."

Scott chuckled. "I understand. Still, I'd think there'd be some of the soldiers who'll harass the boy."

Driscol's jaw tightened. "Never you mind about that, sir. Such matters are beneath notice for an officer of your rank. I'll deal with the matter, should it arise."

The brigadier studied him for a moment. Then, smiled thinly. "Yes. I imagine you will. Very well, Sergeant. It's a small thing, but I'd appreciate it if you'd check in on the boy tonight."

Then Scott unclasped his hand and pointed to a nearby table covered with papers. "Meanwhile, there is news. Some good, some bad. The bad news is that Napoleon has abdicated the throne. On April 6, according to the newspaper accounts I received from the capital. That means the British no longer have their hands tied. They'll be coming at us full force, now. Wellington's veterans, for sure; perhaps Wellington himself."

Driscol took a deep breath, absorbing the information. That part of it, concerning the future actions of the British, he gave but a moment's notice. The Sassenach were a given. Mostly, he pondered the fate of Napoleon, a man he'd once admired deeply, and had fought for until the emperor's overweening ambition had finally driven Driscol to leave his service and come to America.

"On a more cheery note," Scott continued, "I just received word from General Brown. He's on his way back to Buffalo and expects to arrive within the week. He proposes to advance on the enemy no later than the end of the month."

Driscol grunted his satisfaction. Say what you would about Jacob Brown, the man was a fighter. The New Yorker had no formal military training at all, and was hopelessly lost when it came to the fine points of tactics and maneuvers. But he was willing to leave such matters to Scott, and, best of all, he didn't get in Scott's way.

"You'll be commanding the First Brigade, sir?"

Scott nodded. "Yes. The Ninth, Eleventh, Twenty-second, and Twenty-fifth Regiments. Ripley will be in command of the Second Brigade." Scott's air of satisfaction faded a bit. "The ragtag-and-bobtail—the Pennsylvania and New York militia units; some Indians and Canadian volunteers, also—will be dignified with the title of 'Third Brigade.' Porter from New York will command them."

A politician. That figured. But Driscol didn't care about Porter and his puffed-up "Third Brigade" any more than Scott did. Whatever real fighting was done would be done by the regulars.

"I'll see to it the men are ready, sir."

"Thank you, Sergeant."

When Driscol entered the tent McParland shared with several other enlisted men, a quick and hard glance was all it took to send the rest scuttling hurriedly into the night beyond. McParland himself remained on his pallet, doing his best not to cower.

His best was . . . pitiful.

"Oh, be done with it," Driscol growled. "The monster from Antrim got his jollies today, well enough. I just came to see how you were doing."

The boy sniffed and wiped his nose with the back of his hand. "I'm all right, Sergeant." He was honest enough to add: "Once I got cleaned up, anyway."

Driscol studied him, for a moment. Then, pulled up the only stool in the tent and sat on it.

"I won't desert again, Sergeant. I promise."

"Promises are for officers and gentlemen, youngster. The likes of you and me have simpler ways. You tell me you won't do it again, and there's an end to the matter. If things turn out otherwise, I'll shoot you myself. Certainly won't bother wasting ammunition with another firing squad."

McParland wiped his nose again. "I wasn't scared, Sergeant. Of the Brits, I mean. I was just awful homesick. I miss my mother something terrible."

Driscol looked at him bleakly. "Homesick? Try watching your home burn to the ground, sometime, torched by British soldiers. Miss your mother? My mother passed when I was six, taken by disease like so many on the island. I have longer memories of my father. The most vivid of them was watching him die after being chained to a tripod in the center of our town and given five hundred lashes by a British soldier."

The sergeant's voice was low and level, but the cold rage that flowed underneath was enough to paralyze McParland's nose wiping.

"So fuck you and your homesickness, McParland," Driscol continued. "I don't want to hear about it. If the Sassenach win this war, you'll have plenty to be really sick about, believe you me. And in the meantime—"

He jabbed a stiff, stubby finger at the young soldier. "You enlisted in the United States Army and you will *damn* well do your duty. With no whining, no puling, no sobbing, and no pissing and shitting in your trousers. Is that clear?"

"Yes, sir. Uh, Sergeant."

Driscol nodded, rose from the stool, and left the tent. Once outside, his eyes ranged from one campfire to another, looking for his next target.

Corporal Hancock and Privates Lannigan and Wright were crouched around a campfire, exchanging sarcastic remarks about a certain incontinent teenager, when a figure stepped out of the shadows and cast a pall upon their comradely conversation.

Short and squat, he reminded Hancock of a troll, straight out of fairy tales. Without a word of greeting, the troll moved forward into the light and squatted by the fire. Then, drew forth his dirk and began heating the blade over the flames.

"There's always at least one nasty bully in every regiment," the troll commented. He rotated the blade, exposing both sides to the heat. "Pitiful, really, since they're always such wretched amateurs."

The troll said nothing, for a moment. Then: "Did you admire the way I cropped the sixth one's ears, lads? Efficient, I thought. The hot blade cauterized the wounds as soon as it made them. Saved the surgeon no end of work."

Hancock remembered flinching as the troll had done the manual labor involved in the punishment of the sixth deserter, who hadn't been executed. He'd severed the man's ears and branded his cheek—and his boot had been enough to send the man flying out of the camp.

Apparently satisfied with the temperature of the blade, the troll withdrew it from the flames. Then, slowly, he gazed from one soldier to the next. The troll had rather light-colored eyes, Hancock recalled, at least in the sunshine. An odd shade of blue-green that matched his pale complexion. At the moment, however, they were black pits. Above those sunken eyes, the low, broad brow seemed like a stone. The nose between them, a crag; the cheeks on either side, a pair of bony bastions. It was best not to think about the mouth and jaws at all.

"If there's any bullying of young McParland, I'll find out about it. Don't think I won't. If I question a soldier with my spirit in the work, his bowels will turn to water."

The hellhole eyes looked down on the blade, which was still shining slightly from the heat. "And when I do, the bullies will discover their true place in the world. Very quickly and, oh . . . so very thoroughly."

With that, the troll rose and left the campfire. You couldn't say he "walked," exactly. Human beings walk. It was more of a lurch, except that it was astonishingly quiet, and there was no air of unsteadiness about it at all. The three soldiers remained silent for long moments afterward.

"He wouldn't," Private Wright finally protested. "It's against the rules."

Corporal Hancock and Private Lannigan agreed with him immediately. But the conversation around the campfire failed to regain its former wit.

Before long, they went off to their separate tents.

CHAPTER 12

It had been quite a picture, although not one the brigadier would ever commission for a portrait.

As the American expeditionary force neared the Canadian shore of the Niagara, in the early hours of the morning, Winfield Scott demonstrated his leadership qualities by drawing his sword, waving it about in a splendidly martial fashion, and being the first man in his army to wade ashore, crying out *Follow me!*

A pity, though, that he hadn't waited until they'd actually reached the shore, or ascertained the depth of the water. The last sight Patrick Driscol had of the brigadier was the startled expression on his face. A moment later, all that could be seen was the sword, still above the surface. Not the hilt, though—that, and the hand holding it, had quite disappeared, although the blade itself was waving about energetically.

Of Scott himself, there was nothing to be seen.

There was always this to be said for Winfield Scott, though: he was never the man to let a minor mishap get between him and his conception of heroic destiny. Where another man might have dropped the sword and swum back to the surface, Scott plunged resolutely onward. Driscol and the rest of the soldiers tracked the brigadier's progress by following the sword blade as it cut its way toward the shore like the fin of a shark.

A very slow shark. And no shark's fin ever bobbed up and down and wobbled back and forth the way Scott's sword did. Driscol could just imagine the muddy and treacherous footing the brigadier was fighting his way through on the river bottom, while trying to hold his breath.

Still, he made it. Far enough, at least, that he was finally able to bring his head above the surface and cry out. And he still sounded like an officer barking out a command.

"Too deep!"

Not even Driscol could keep from laughing, at that point.

"Everyone's safely ashore, sir," Driscol reported to the brigadier a short time later. "There were some British pickets, but they ran off after firing just a few shots. Into the air, so far as I can tell. We suffered no casualties at all."

"Other than to my dignity," Scott chuckled, looking down at his still-sodden and somewhat bedraggled uniform. "I hate to think what it'll cost me to have the damage repaired."

On another occasion, the ruin visited upon his beloved uniform would have caused those words to be uttered in a snarl. But Winfield Scott was as pugnacious a commanding officer in the field as any Driscol had ever encountered, saving Napoleon himself. If he didn't love the carnage of war, he did love the excitement of the enterprise. The man was in his element, now, and his spirits couldn't be shaken by something as petty as a dunking.

Assuming the United States won this war, Driscol had already decided that he'd remain in the army. He was thirty-two years old, and after sixteen years of soldiering he figured he was too old to take up another occupation. However, he'd also decided that once peace had arrived, he'd find some quiet and discreet way to separate himself from Scott's entourage.

In a war—certainly in a battle—there wasn't another officer in the U.S. Army that Driscol would rather serve under. But in time of peace, he had no desire to be a master sergeant under Scott's command. For that, he wanted a different sort of officer. One who, at the very least, wouldn't be quarreling constantly with other officers and embroiling his subordinates in his personal feuds, just because he didn't have a real war to fight.

But that problem was for a later day—assuming Driscoll lived that long. He might very well not. The British forces charged with protecting the peninsula that jutted between Lake Erie and the Niagara were headquartered at Fort George, under the command of Major General Phineas Riall—who also had a reputation for being aggressive. There was sure to be a battle soon, and most likely a savage one. Riall wasn't the sort of officer who'd allow the American army to challenge British dominance on the open field, as General Brown and Brigadier Scott now proposed to do.

"Cousin Jonathan" was the derisive term British officers used to refer to the Americans. They were convinced that while Cousin Jonathan could manage well enough in a border fray, where half the combatants on both sides were savage Indians, the Americans had neither the skill nor the fortitude to match the British army on a battlefield.

And . . .

There was more than a little truth to the British sneers. The kind of battle that Sergeant Driscol had experienced in Napoleon's wars could only be fought effectively by a real army. Standing up to musket volleys at close range on an open plain was simply beyond the capacity of militias or poorly trained troops.

Indians wouldn't even try. As in almost every war that had taken place on American soil for the past two centuries, there were Indians fighting on both sides in this one. Scott had learned that Riall's army maintained several hundred Mohawks as allies. On the American side, Porter's Third Brigade had about as many Indians. From a different tribe, Driscol assumed, although he didn't know which one. The sergeant hadn't been in the United States long enough—and, then, not in the right part of the country—to learn the Indians' complex tribal and clan distinctions.

Nor did he care, in the end. Driscol didn't have anything against Indians in particular, but he considered them irrelevant to his business. Indians made fine scouts and skirmishers, from what little he had seen of them, and that was it. Such qualities didn't impress Driscol for the simple reason that the same could be said of his own Scots-Irish kinfolk back home in Ireland. And he'd seen with his own eyes how pitiful a reed that was when the iron rod of the British army came down.

Battles against the likes of Wellington's men wouldn't be won by scouts and skirmishers. They hadn't been in Ireland; they wouldn't be here in America.

Scott's voice broke into his musing. "And the supplies?"

"All ashore, sir. The quartermasters have the matter in hand. I checked."

"Splendid." The brigadier examined the sunrise for a few seconds. "We've got plenty of time to converge on Fort Erie by noon. Assuming Porter doesn't get lost, of course. But Ripley and his brigade are landing only a mile away upstream, so we should have established contact with them well before then. That's what matters."

When General Brown had divided the Army of the Niagara between his two brigadiers for this campaign, he'd given the bulk of them—four out of the six regiments—to Winfield Scott. Not because he thought badly of the other brigadier, Eleazar Ripley, but simply because he had *complete* confidence in Scott. Brown, a former county judge and state legislator, might not know the technical details of soldiering—Driscol suspected the major general couldn't even post camp guards properly—but he was an excellent judge of men.

There was a pitched battle coming, and General Brown wanted the bulk of his forces under the command of Winfield Scott. He was taking a risk in so doing, of course, because Scott was prone to rashness. But Brown was the sort of officer who'd always prefer to fail through acts of commission, rather than omission. The sergeant couldn't fault him for that. It was a refreshing change from the usual run of American generals, who could find endless reasons to avoid fighting British regulars.

Somewhat to Driscol's surprise, Porter and his Third Brigade didn't get lost. By midday, the three columns of the Army of the Niagara converged on Fort Erie, according to plan.

The siege that followed was a simple affair, even by the standards of warfare in North America. The British holding the fort numbered but one hundred and seventy men. They were facing a besieging force of almost four thousand soldiers, more than three thousand of whom were regulars.

"They'll hold out just long enough to satisfy honor," Driscol predicted, when Scott asked the sergeant's opinion. "You can expect them to surrender by sundown."

The brigadier scowled at the enemy fortress. "I hate to lose the rest of the day. I'm thinking perhaps we should just take it with a charge."

Driscol restrained a sigh. Scott's aggressiveness was an asset for the American army, but it did need to be checked from time to time.

"Sir, it'd take us till midafternoon anyway to organize and carry through a frontal assault," he pointed out mildly. "We'd gain but two or three hours, and at the cost of fairly heavy casualties, leaving the army exhausted. Storming a fortress is bloody and tiring work."

Scott was too good a general not to know that Driscol was right, but he kept scowling for hours. Driscol made it a point to remain by his side throughout the rest of the day. Just in case the brigadier needed to be gently restrained again.

Driscol's prediction proved accurate almost to the minute. At five o'clock in the afternoon, the British defenders surrendered Fort Erie.

As he watched his men escorting the captured British soldiers to the rear—a friendly enough affair, on both sides, since calm reason had prevailed over silly belligerence—Scott finally stopped scowling.

"Well, you were right, Sergeant," he commented gruffly to Driscol.

"You're quite welcome, sir," Driscol replied easily.

Moments later, though, Scott was starting to scowl again. Driscol decided it would be best to cheer him up with the prospect of looming difficulties and desperate circumstances.

"By now, of course, the main British army at Fort George will have learned that we've landed on their shores. The pickets would have brought Riall the news. He'll already have his troops marching south to meet us."

"Will he, then?" Scott clapped his hands together. "How soon, do you think?"

"Sometime on the morrow."

"That quickly? Fort George is well over twenty miles away."

Driscol gave him a level gaze. "That's a professional British army we're about to smash into, sir. Sometime on the morrow. Be sure of it."

General Brown didn't propose to wait for them, however. He arrived at Fort Erie soon after it was taken, and ordered Scott to move his First Brigade north the next morning.

"We should be able to seize the bridge over the Chippewa before the enemy arrives," said Brown.

Scott nodded. "We need that bridge, or we'll lose days. So far as I know, there aren't any fords across the Chippewa unless you go pretty far upstream, off to the west."

Driscol kept his mouth shut, as protocol demanded. In point of fact, he thought the American generals were indulging themselves in a fantasy. The Chippewa River was a bit closer to Fort Erie than it was to Fort George, true. But an officer like Riall would send out an advance force, to delay the American approach until Riall himself could arrive with the main body of his army. Driscol was fairly certain the British would get to the bridge first.

In this, as in so many ways, the level of professionalism of the British army was simply superior to that of the American one. Scott had done wonders with the Army of the Niagara in the months he'd had to train it. But months of training couldn't possibly match the decades of experience the British army had amassed in pitched battles and maneuvers on the European continent. Driscol thought that Scott had shaped the army well enough to match the British on the open field of battle, if not in the maneuvers that led up to it. And that was as much as the sergeant could ask for.

He'd have a chance, finally, to face the Sassenach on something close to even terms.

Somewhere on the plain south of the Chippewa, he thought to himself. *That's where it'll happen.*

It was as good a place as any for the man from County Antrim to get his revenge, or meet his death. Most likely both, he guessed.

JULY 4, 1814
Street's Creek

"God*damn* them!" Scott snarled, blatantly disregarding his firm and clear regulations prohibiting blasphemy.

Of course, other men took the Lord's name in vain when they did so. The brigadier didn't, since—surely—the Almighty was in agreement with his viewpoint.

Patrick Driscol wasn't going to argue the matter. First, because he was a sergeant. Secondly, because given his deist views, he didn't care much about blasphemy anyway. Finally, because he shared the brigadier's attitude toward the object of the curse—the Sassenach; who better deserved damnation? However, he didn't share the brigadier's surprise and disgruntlement.

Just as Driscol had foreseen the night before, within an hour after marching north that morning, Scott's brigade had begun encountering British detachments. The detachments hadn't sought any decisive engagement, where they would have been overwhelmed by Scott's numbers. They had simply been sent to delay the American advance long enough to enable Riall and his main force to seize the bridge over the Chippewa, and establish a firm foothold.

With the Chippewa bridge in their possession, the British would enjoy a very strong defensive position from which to resist any further American encroachment into Canada.

It was the best move for the British commander to have made. Brown's forces numbered almost four thousand men, of whom three-fourths were regulars. To oppose it, Riall had no more than two thousand men at his immediate disposal in Fort George, according to the intelligence Scott had collected. Granted, Riall probably didn't realize what a high percentage of Brown's army was made up of regular soldiers. Because of supply shortages, most of the American regulars were wearing undyed gray uniforms, barely distinguishable from the standard militia issue. Only a few actually had the regulation blue coats and white trousers.

Still, outnumbered two to one, Riall would probably wait behind his defensive lines until Lieutenant General Drummond could bring up reinforcements from other British units in Canada.

So, the entire day of July 4 was spent in a frustrating series of minor engagements with British skirmishers. Just to make things worse, the day had turned out hot and dry. For an army tramping up a road, that translated into "very dusty."

Again, Driscol was impressed with Scott's ability to keep driving the brigade forward. The sergeant hadn't expected to reach the Chippewa until sometime on the fifth, but Scott managed to get his brigade there by late afternoon of Independence Day. In the process, he left the rest of Brown's army lagging far behind.

Nevertheless, the brigadier's energy and determination turned out to be futile. By the time the First Brigade was in sight of the Chippewa, Riall and his army were thoroughly entrenched.

"*Damn* them!" Scott repeated. He sat back in his saddle and glared at the enemy force across the river. Then, sighing softly, he turned his head and scanned the terrain his brigade had just passed through.

Driscol waited patiently for the command, even though he knew perfectly well what it would be. Not even a commanding officer as impetuous as Winfield Scott would be rash enough to order a brigade of thirteen hundred men to attack a force of almost two thousand men who had a river to provide them with a defensive position.

A commander unsure of himself might have kept his brigade muddling around in the open field south of the Chippewa, but Scott was no indecisive muddler. Since he couldn't attack, the only intelligent thing to do was retreat half a mile and have his brigade take up defensive positions of their own.

"We'll move back across Street's Creek," Scott announced to his aides. "See to it, if you would."

The junior officers trotted off to attend to the matter. Driscol, as he usually did unless Scott gave him a specific order, remained behind.

Scott often asked his advice, though rarely when other officers were around to overhear. He was notorious for being self-confident to the point of rashness, but at least half of that was for public show. In private, Driscol had found that Scott was quite willing to solicit the opinion of his master sergeant. Whatever else, the brigadier was no fool.

"What do you think, Sergeant? Not much chance, I suppose, that we could get Riall to come at us directly."

From the vantage point of his own saddle, Driscol examined the terrain. Off to the right, the Niagara River formed the boundary to the east, and the Chippewa to the north. Without boats, there was no way to cross the Niagara at all, and no way to cross the Chippewa except at the bridge. To the south, where the American units were already starting to move back, lay Street's Creek, nestled a short distance back into the trees. The creek wasn't the barrier that the Chippewa was, but it would still provide the Americans with a reasonably strong defensive position of their own.

Between Street's Creek and the Chippewa lay an open plain one mile deep and about the same distance wide. There was a dense woodland to their left, on the western side of the plain, which completed the enclosure.

In short, it was a classic battlefield terrain. There was a clearly defined open area for the clash of arms, and no easy way for either side to maneuver around it. The trick, of course, would be to get the British to come out onto the field at all. Why should they? They were the defending force, and they were outnumbered to boot, with a very strong position from which to break any further American advance.

"Probably not, sir," the sergeant replied. "Although . . ."

A bit surprised, Scott lifted his eyebrow. "Although . . . *what?*"

Driscol paused for a few more seconds, studying the American troops moving to the rear.

"Well, it's the uniforms, sir. From a distance, they look just like militia uniforms." He turned his head and scanned the British forces across the Chippewa. "Riall's an aggressive sort of general, by all accounts. We're so far ahead of the rest of the army that he has *us* outnumbered, for the moment. And if he thinks we're just a militia force . . ."

"Interesting point," Scott murmured. "Yes, he does have us outnumbered at the moment. About seventeen hundred men, as best as I can determine, to face our thirteen hundred in the brigade."

Scott thought about it himself, and then shook his head regretfully. "It's still not likely he'll come out. Certainly not today, as late as it is in the afternoon. And by tomorrow, General Brown will have arrived with the rest of our army."

Driscol was amused. Most American officers would have been relieved to avoid an open battle with British regulars. Scott was disgruntled that the enemy wouldn't come out for it.

Driscol nodded. "You're most likely right, sir. Still, if he thinks we're militiamen, Riall might just think he could rout us easily."

"I fear it's not likely to happen, Sergeant. If I were in Riall's position, I certainly wouldn't take the chance."

With some difficulty, Driscol managed to keep a straight face.

He knew perfectly well that if the positions had been reversed, Scott would already have been marching his army onto the field.

But he kept all that to himself.

"I'll be seeing to the men's encampment then, sir. It's beginning to look like rain."

Scott nodded. "Thank you, sergeant. There's nothing else to do at the moment. *Damn* them."

CHAPTER 13

JULY 5, 1814
The Battle of Chippewa

Brown and the rest of the army began arriving just before midnight, in the middle of a downpour. Ripley's brigade made camp south of Scott's brigade, eager to get their tents up.

By the morning of the fifth, the rain had stopped, and the sun had returned. The heat soon dried up the traces, leaving the ground as dusty as ever. Scott's pickets started exchanging gunfire with British skirmishers who'd taken up positions in the woods to the west. The presence of the enemy there was a nuisance, but nothing worse than that. Still, after hours of it, Brown was annoyed enough to order Porter to take his Third Brigade of militiamen and their Indian allies, and clear the skirmishers out of the woods.

Porter and his men began moving into the woods late in the afternoon. While they did so, Scott decided that he would use the rest of day to march his brigade across Street's Creek and engage in a full drill in front of the main British forces. The brigadier was frustrated by inaction.

"If nothing else," he told Driscol, "we can thumb our noses at the enemy. Show them we're not intimidated. Besides, I don't want the men getting rusty."

Driscol thought it was a lot of foolishness, but he went about the brigadier's business, getting the men ready for the drill. As he did so, he noticed General Brown and several of his aides trotting toward the woods. Brown had apparently decided to see how Porter was getting along.

Not well, it seemed. There was a sudden burst of gunfire from the direction of the trees, which turned into what sounded like a small running battle. Driscol assumed the British had decided to reinforce their skirmishers in the woods.

But he didn't see anything further. Even if he hadn't been pre-occupied with his own affairs, the screen of trees and brush along the banks of the creek blocked his view of the plain to the north.

"We've got them pinned in the woods, sir," Riall's aide said to him, after he took the report from the courier.

Major General Riall nodded. Then, smiled rather ferociously. "Time to teach Cousin Jonathan what's what, then, wouldn't you say? Order the army across the bridge."

When General Brown saw the first of Porter's militiamen stumbling out of the woods, he scowled. His scowl deepened when he saw the cloud of dust starting to rise in the north.

He lifted himself up in the stirrups in order to get a better view. After a few seconds he started seeing British uniforms, flashing like gleams in the dust.

"Good God. They're coming across the bridge."

His eyes swept back and forth across the field. It was obvious that Riall had sent enough reinforcements into the woods to tie up Porter's brigade. If he moved his main army onto the plain quickly enough, he had a fair chance of capturing Porter and his men before they could disengage.

Instead of simply waiting behind defensive lines, Riall had decided to lay a little trap.

"Ha!" Brown's scowl changed into a grin. If Scott could get his brigade onto the plain quickly enough to forestall Riall's advance, that would allow them time enough for Brown himself to race back and bring up Ripley's brigade as a reinforcement . . .

He jabbed a finger in the direction of the woods. "Get in there—all of you—and stiffen up Porter. Tell him to hold."

Without another word, he turned his horse and began galloping back toward the bridge across Street's Creek.

*   *   *

Sergeant Driscol was in the leading ranks of the First Brigade as it began crossing over the Street's Creek bridge. He was on foot now, not on horseback, since in the coming drill he'd be assuming his normal position in the battle formation. General Scott and two of his officers were the only mounted men in the vicinity. They were ahead of him, and they weren't throwing up enough dust to obscure Driscol's vision.

As soon as the sergeant saw the cloud of dust to the north, he figured out what was happening. He began to alert the brigadier, but saw that it wasn't necessary. Scott was already perched high in his stirrups, staring at the sight.

Then, an oncoming horseman made the whole issue a moot one.

It was General Brown, galloping recklessly across the field, grinning like a lunatic.

He didn't even slow down. He thundered past Scott and Driscol, pointing behind him with a finger. "*You will have a battle!*" he shouted gaily, and then he was gone.

By now, Scott was grinning himself. He began bellowing orders. By the time those orders got to the master sergeant, Driscol had already taken care of what needed doing. Seeing that, Scott's grin widened even further.

"We shall whip them, Sergeant! Watch and see!"

Driscol shared the brigadier's hopes, but not his anticipation. Brown's entire army might outnumber Riall's, but Scott's First Brigade didn't. Driscol doubted if Brown could get the Second Brigade moved up before nightfall. In the battle that was about to take place, Scott would face something like seventeen hundred British regulars with only thirteen hundred men of his own.

No American army since the war began had beaten an equal-size British force on an open battlefield. Not regulars matched against regulars. Now, Scott proposed to do it while outnumbered four to three.

So be it. It seemed a nice countryside. Not Ireland, true, but still a pleasant enough place to die.

Half an hour later, the two armies were taking positions facing each other on the plain by the Niagara, and Private McParland was scared out of his wits. Drill was one thing. But finally seeing red-coated British troops maneuvering on a plain with all the precision of a machine—well, that was something else entirely. The enemy army reminded the teenage soldier of the brightly painted threshing machine he'd seen once at a county fair. With him and his mates as the grain about to be haplessly mangled.

Desperately, he tried to control his terror. And, like many of the men around him, he found his anchor in the sight of Sergeant Driscol.

He was there, of course. Where else would he? Stalking calmly back and forth in front of the troops, living up to the name his men had recently given him.

The troll.

Off in the distance, young McParland could see Brigadier Scott, shouting something to another group of soldiers. McParland couldn't make out the words, but he was quite sure that Scott was exhorting the troops. The brigadier was a fine speechifier, as he'd demonstrated in the past any number of times.

Sergeant Driscol's notion of "exhortation," on the other hand, was . . .

About what you'd expect from a troll.

You will not flinch. You will not quaver. Forget those wretched Sassenach, boys. If a man so much as twitches, I will cut him up for my soup. You will face lead with serenity. You will face bayonets with a laugh. Because if you don't, you will face my gaping gullet.

The beast went on in that vein for another minute or so. By the time he was done, McParland felt himself settling down. Not so much because he was scared of the troll's wrath any longer—the youngster would surely be dead soon, anyway, so what difference did it make?—but because he knew for sure and certain that the enemy was doomed. The British might have precision and training and experience and all the rest. But did they have their own troll?

Not a chance. McParland didn't think there were more than six trolls in the whole world. Eight, tops.

"We'll let them fire the first volley," Scott announced.

Driscol nodded and walked off. He wasn't entirely sure himself that was the right thing to do, but . . .

Maybe. That first hammering volley was a treasure for an army, to be sure. But if it was fired that little bit too soon, it wouldn't have any effect on well-trained troops except to prove to them that they could stand up to it. Thereafter, the force that had taken the first blow and rebounded had that little extra edge to their confidence.

And that was what it was all about, in the end. Confidence. For all the intricacy of the firing movements and the endless training it took to get men to do it properly in the midst of carnage, musket battles on an open field—where one line of men hammered at another at point-blank range—could only be described as sheer brutality. Driscol wasn't a learned man, but he knew something of the history of warfare. He didn't think there was really anything like it, unless you went back over two thousand years to the days of the Greek hoplites.

To win such battles, one thing was needed above all. The confidence—say better, arrogance—of Achilles and Ajax. Pain and suffering and wounds were irrelevant. All that mattered was that you did not break.

Ever.

You died, but you did not break.

Once he got back to his position, he decided to brighten up the spirits of the troops a bit more.

If you break, I will hound you to the gates of hell. If you waver, I will rend your flesh. If you hesitate—

"Oh, just shut *up,* will you?" McParland hissed under his breath. But he held his musket at precisely the right angle when he said it. The musket was properly loaded, and the ramrod back in its place.

By an odd quirk of the air, that little hiss made its way to the sergeant's ears. It was all Driscol could do not to laugh aloud. His exhortations had succeeded in their purpose. The spirits of the troops were as bright as the sunshine. In a manner of speaking.

The British fired the first volley. When the smoke cleared, Major General Riall watched the American forces maneuvering calmly to close the gaps left by the dead and wounded. Then he saw the first American volley coming like a thunderclap, with none of the raggedness he'd expected.

He rose up in his saddle.

"Those aren't militiamen. By God, *those are regulars*!"

One of his aides shook his head. "We still have them outnumbered, sir."

"So we do. Still and all, I wouldn't have thought Cousin Jonathan had it in him."

Some part of McParland's brain was astonished to discover that he was still alive. The man right next to him had been smashed flat.

The British had a small battery of nine guns with them. From the quantity of gore splattered all over McParland, the young soldier assumed his mate had been hit by a grapeshot and not a musket ball. There was something sticking to the seventeen-year-old's trouser leg that looked like a piece of intestine.

But he didn't have time to think about it. McParland brought his musket up on command. Noting, in some odd, new, confident part of his brain, that all of his mates had brought their muskets up at exactly the same time, and at exactly the same level. He could see them out of the corners of his eyes. Not as men, really, but simply as an endless gray line. Like a short cliff, standing on a plain.

He didn't aim the musket, of course. Just leveled it and pointed it in the general direction of the enemy. He pulled the trigger when he heard the troll's command.

Fire!

To Sergeant Driscoll, that first volley fired by his own men was like a taste of the finest whiskey. In times past, he'd always been able to tell the difference between an American and a British volley, just by the sound alone. British volleys were as they should be: crisp, like thunderbolts. American volleys were altogether different; haphazard gusts trying to match a hurricane.

Not here.

Not today.

On the field of open battle, the volley reigned supreme. That wasn't due to the tactics involved, but because a good volley reinforced what was essential in musket battles: *confidence*.

A good, proper volley stiffened the men. A ragged one tore at their certainty. It was as simple as that. Musket battles were won by morale, not bullets.

*   *   *

When the smoke cleared, McParland saw that the troll was still standing there, untouched by the carnage. He wasn't surprised. McParland thought the troll probably had a magical shield that deflected enemy musket balls and grapeshot. Or maybe it was simply that the lead bullets were terrified of him, too.

Reload!

McParland went through the motions, easily, quickly. He discovered that the concentration needed to reload a musket kept his mind off anything else.

Step forward! Ten paces!

Somewhere in the middle of those paces, another British volley ripped through the ranks. McParland saw a nearby soldier clutch his face with both hands, spilling his musket to the ground. An instant later, blood was gushing through the fingers and the man toppled next to his musket. There was no hole in the back of his head, but, from the completely limp and lifeless look of the body, McParland was pretty sure the big musket ball had jellied the man's brains.

But the teenager didn't really think about it. His mind was entirely focused on the need to close ranks to make good the gaps. Between them, over the months, Brigadier Scott and his troll of a master sergeant had trained McParland to do, and do, and do—and never to think. Not in a battle.

"I want that battery taken out, Captain! Do you hear me? Move your three guns forward. Charge them if you have to, but get close enough to take them out with canister!"

For all the fury of his words, Scott's tone was lively. Almost cheerful. Captain Nathan Towson was a good artillery officer, and Scott was confident that he'd get the job done.

He had other things on his mind, anyway. Porter's Third Brigade had been beaten, and they were in full flight out of the woods. Scott had to protect his now-exposed left flank.

"Major Jesup! Take your Twenty-fifth Regiment and swing them around to cover the left!"

Jesup was another good officer. Scott seemed to collect them like a magnet, in time of war.

It was going well. Driscol could tell, from long experience, despite not being able to see much due to the gun smoke that now obscured most of the field. The men had suffered casualties, but had kept moving forward despite them—and, now, with ever-growing confidence that they could do so.

So, another volley.

It was a given that men died in battles, winners and losers both. Victory was all that mattered.

Fire!

McParland wondered—not until he'd pulled the trigger, of course—how the troll managed to project his voice so well in the middle of a battle. The words were quite clear, even crisp—quite unlike the monster's normal rasp, which had always reminded McParland of a dull saw hitting a knot in a log.

That penetrating voice, in fact, was the only thing McParland had heard clearly since the battle began. Abstractly, he'd known that battles would be noisy affairs. But the reality made the word "noisy" seem meaningless. It was like being in the middle of a thunderstorm, except the clouds were light instead of dark. The volleys came like flashes of lightning. And with white gun smoke hanging everywhere, McParland couldn't usually see more than fifteen feet in any direction.

Reload!

Step forward! Ten paces!

"Good God."

Major General Phineas Riall stared at the battlefield. Four volleys had been exchanged, each at ever-closer range, and the American forces hadn't so much as wavered. If anything, their volleys were even surer than those of the British.

An aide next to him made a slight shake of the head. Riall had served in the British army for twenty years, and was as well trained as any British officer. But his service had been entirely in the West Indies.

The aide, he recalled, had fought Napoleon's army on the continent.

Towson's three guns along the Niagara were starting to silence the British battery. Scott peered at the other side of the field. Jesup and his Twenty-fifth had succeeded in anchoring the American left flank, but the movement had opened a gap in his lines. So Scott ordered McNair and his Ninth Regiment to move to the left. The fact remained that the British army was larger than his own, and there was no way Scott could match the lines without creating a gap somewhere. That was dangerous.

On the other hand, Riall's force had moved forward far enough that the British right was no longer anchored on the woods.

There was a maneuver . . .

Risky, of course, and not usually tried in a real battle. But if it was done well enough . . .

"Yes," Scott murmured. "In for a penny, in for a pound."

"Excuse me, sir?" asked one of his aides.

Scott grinned. "I was just remarking that the whole point of fighting a battle is to win the thing. Let us do so, Lieutenant.

"Take orders to Major McNair. Tell him I want the Ninth Regiment to keep moving left. When his forces meet up with Jesup's, I want them to wheel inward, facing northeast. Riall's right is hanging in the open, so McNair and Jesup should be able to bring enfilade fire on them, and roll up their flank. They'll break."

The lieutenant hesitated a moment, before racing off with the orders. Even he could see that Scott's maneuver was going to open a great, gaping hole in the center of the American force. If the British moved quickly enough, they'd smash through before the flanking attack could be brought to bear.

In effect, Scott was gambling that his American army could outmaneuver a British army in the middle of a battle, while standing its ground against superior forces in what was now practically a point-blank contest of musket volleys.

The lieutenant probably thought he was insane.

"He's *insane!*" snarled Riall. "What lunatic is in command over there?"

"I suspect that's Winfield Scott's brigade, sir," replied the aide. "He's said to be bold. Even, ah, rash."

"He's insane," Riall repeated. "Send forward the Royal Scots and the One Hundredth Foot. We'll smash this thing before it gets started."

One of the couriers raced off to give the command. The aide kept his own counsel. It was possible, of course, that Riall was right. But the aide couldn't help remembering that the word "insane" had been applied quite often to Napoleon, as well.

To be sure, in the end, they'd beaten Napoleon. But not before the madman had won a lot of battles.

* * *

For a moment, the clouds of gun smoke cleared enough for Driscol to see what Scott was doing with the other regiments. He understood the maneuver immediately—and it was all he could do not to whoop with glee.

Driscol's own Twenty-second Regiment had pinned the British, and now—finally, at last!—an American army had a general worthy of its soldiers. Scott would match their confidence with his own, using the kind of bold and daring stroke that Napoleon would have favored.

Suddenly, the sergeant was spun completely around. The blow didn't even register as such until he stumbled to one knee. Then, looking down at his left arm, he saw that a musket ball had struck it.

Destroyed it, rather. Driscol had seen more battle wounds than he could remember. If he survived the battle, he knew that he was looking at an amputation.

At the very least. The elbow was a shattered mass of flesh and blood. That meant an amputation somewhere in the upper arm, not the lower. Most men did not survive such, not in the conditions of a battlefield surgery. Not for long. If blood loss and shock didn't kill them, infection would.

So be it. It was a given that wounded men died after battles. Winners and losers alike. All that mattered was victory.

Then the pain arrived, in a searing wave that all but blinded him for a moment. He gritted his teeth, and pulled away from it by sheer force of will. Still on one knee, Driscol called out the commands.

Reload!
  Ten paces forward!
It seemed to McParland as if the troll's voice was a bit off. But he didn't give it much thought. Truth to tell, the young soldier was hardly thinking at all any longer. Reality had shrunk down to an endless cycle of repeated actions. There was nothing much beyond that, other than noticing—briefly, and without dwelling on the matter—the bodies of his mates as they were flung aside or crumpled to the ground, often showing hideous wounds.

So it came as a complete surprise when he stumbled across the troll's body as he stepped forward into the gun smoke.

Stumbled against it, rather. The troll was down on one knee, but he wasn't dead. His left arm looked to be a complete ruin from the elbow down, and he was awkwardly trying to bind it up with his one good hand. McParland realized that he had shouted the last orders even after he had been wounded.

Very badly wounded, from the look of it.

The troll glanced up at him. "Bind this for me, would you? Then help me up."

Confused, McParland looked down at his musket. How was he supposed to . . .

"Just put the bloody thing down!" the troll rasped. "Consider yourself on detached duty for the rest of the battle, young McParland. I promise I won't stand you before a firing squad."

McParland had been trained to dress wounds, so once his mind cleared, he set down the musket and went about the business, quickly and efficiently. That done, he helped the troll to get back on his feet.

"Where are the boys, lad? I'm feeling a bit light-headed."

McParland did a quick estimate, in the battle murk.

"They've made the paces, Sergeant."

The young private didn't think, with a wound like that, he'd have been able to do more than croak. Or scream. But the troll's bellowing, piercing voice had not a quaver in it this time.

"Fire!"

The volley hammered every other thought or sensation aside. It really was like standing right next to a lightning bolt. Or so McParland imagined. He'd never actually stood right next to a lightning bolt, since he wasn't insane.

Or hadn't been, at least, until some mad impulse he could no longer remember clearly had led him to volunteer for the army.

Amazingly, the troll was now grinning.

"It's going well, lad. I can tell. The volleys have that sure and certain victorious air about them."

McParland had no idea how the troll had come to that conclusion. As far as he could tell, the universe was a place of sheer confusion. The volleys weren't so much sounds as periodic, paralyzing bursts of chaos.

Still, the words cheered him up.

Why not? If anyone could make sense out of this madness, it would be a troll.

"Help me forward now, lad. I will not fall until I see the

Sassenach broken. In *front* of me, goddamn them. Lying at my feet, whipped like curs."

Again, that voice. Like a lightning bolt itself.

Reload!

Ten paces forward!

The aide saw the truth before Riall could bring himself to accept it.

"If we pull back now, sir, we can still salvage the army. Wait another few minutes, and . . ."

Riall glared at him. Then, went back to glaring at the battlefield.

The aide waited.

A minute went by. Then another.

The British army was caught in a vise from which they barely had time to extricate themselves. Scott's flanking attack, however reckless it might have been, had been carried out so well and so swiftly that Riall's forces hadn't been able to move quickly enough to counter it.

In truth, they hadn't moved at all. The American lines in front of them had never flinched. Indeed, had kept coming forward every time they fired.

"Never seen the like," Riall muttered. "What has Cousin Jonathan been eating lately?"

French food, the aide was tempted to reply. But, wisely, he refrained from uttering the quip. Riall didn't have a good sense of humor even on his best days.

Which this one most certainly was not.

"Order retreat. We'll fall back across the Chippewa, while we still hold the bridge."

The British soldiers didn't start breaking until the order came. Even then, stiffened by professional training and experience, they were never routed. But the last few minutes were ghastly. Captain Townsend brought his guns forward and added canister to the havoc being wreaked by the American musketeers, who were now firing from oblique angles into a mass of soldiers caught in the closing trap.

They got out, but not before they left more than five hundred men on the field, dead or wounded.

American casualties were only three hundred or so.

*　*　*

"I'm still alive," McParland said wonderingly. "Not a scratch on me."

The troll said nothing. Just watched, with a look of satisfaction on his face fiercer than anything McParland had ever seen, as the last British soldiers stumbled across the distant bridge. The ground that lay between them and that bridge looked like a red carpet, from the uniforms on the broken bodies covering it. And the blood, of course.

The most amazing thing happened then. McParland never told anyone, afterward, because he knew he'd be called a liar. But the troll's eyes filled with tears.

"Those bastards broke two of my nations," he heard him whisper. "They won't break this one."

After a few seconds, McParland cleared his throat. "Sergeant, we'd really better get you to the surgeon. That's a nasty wound. Really nasty."

The sergeant glanced down at his left arm.

"Oh, aye. I'll lose most of it. I doubt me if even a top surgeon in Philadelphia could fix this ruin—and there'll be no top surgeons in an army camp, you can be sure of that."

McParland turned him around and they began hobbling away.

"On the bright side," Driscol continued, "I'll just grow myself another arm."

By the time McParland got him to the surgeon's tent, he decided the sergeant was joking. He wasn't certain, though.

CHAPTER 14

For a wonder, the surgeon was sober.

Better still, from Driscol's viewpoint, he was a young man. The sergeant's experience had been that the practice of medicine affected men like alcohol affected those with the curse of drunkenness. The more they studied, the worse they got. Middle-aged doctors were as dangerous as vipers; elderly ones, deadly as the Grim Reaper himself.

"The arm'll have to come off, Sergeant," the young surgeon said firmly, leaning over Driscol where he lay on a pallet in the surgeon's tent. "You'll almost certainly get gangrene, with that bad a wound. Your elbow's pretty well gone, anyway. Even if we left your arm and you didn't get gangrene, you'd never be able to use it again."

He moved off, heading toward one of the tables onto which his assistants were hoisting a wounded soldier. After he was gone, Driscol rolled his head and gave young McParland a cheerful grin. He hoped it was cheerful, anyway.

"D'you ever hear such nonsense, lad? Even with a ruined elbow, I could still use my fingers to count money."

McParland even managed to return the grin with one of his own. Well, a sickly smile—but Driscol suspected his own grin was on the sickly side itself.

"What they pay us, Sergeant, I think you'll only need the fingers of one hand for that. And you're right-handed anyway."

Driscol pursed his lips, as if giving the matter careful consideration. "True enough. I'll take your advice, then." He raised his uninjured right arm, extending a warning finger. "Mind you, youngster, if we ever take Montreal and I don't get my fair share of the loot on account of my missing arm, I'm taking it out of your pickings."

McParland nodded nervously. The sergeant was sure the nervousness was due entirely to the horrid surroundings of the surgeon's tent, not his jocular threat. For all the boasts of American politicians and generals, the chances that the U.S. Army would ever take Montreal were about as good as Driscol's chances to survive gangrene if he tried to keep his arm.

Driscol didn't fault the youngster for being twitchy. Hardened veteran that he was, the sergeant found the surgeon's tent unsettling—and would have, even if he hadn't been one of the wounded men waiting his turn.

The sawdust in the boxes under the two cutting tables was soaked through with blood from the operations, and the blood was seeping onto the dirt floor. That was probably just as well, since it provided the flies swarming in the tent with a ready feasting ground, and distracted them from feeding directly off the wounds. Still, between the festering blood and the gore from intestinal injuries, the stench in the tent was incredible.

No such side benefit could be found from the noises that also saturated the tent, unfortunately. The screams and groans and moans and muffled prayers blended into each like a cacophony straight from hell. The surgeon almost had to shout, in order to be heard at all.

Driscol watched as the doctor and his assistants amputated a soldier's mangled foot on the table nearest him. For all the grisliness of the work, it was done swiftly and expertly. Two of the assistants kept the man's shoulders pinned and two others restrained the legs. Once the patient was securely immobilized and a tourniquet tightened around his leg, the surgeon cut the flesh all around the ankle, right down to the bone; then, peeled the flesh back so as to expose the bone farther up from the incision itself. He'd sever the bone as far up the leg as he could. That way, the resulting stump would have some padding over the bone's end, once it healed.

That was assuming, of course, that the patient didn't die before then, from one of several common diseases brought on by amputation. Which, he very well might. Almost a fourth of all men who had amputations done after a battle died later from infection.

No, Driscol reminded himself, never being one to shy away from the cold facts. That "one-fourth" applied to men who had their *lower* limbs amputated. The death rate was much higher for men who, like Driscol, had the cut made above the knee or elbow.

So be it. Driscol distracted himself, as best he could, by continuing to watch the surgeon at his work.

The blade the man used to slice flesh was no delicate instrument. It reminded Driscol, more than anything else, of a smaller version of the flensing blades used by whalers. It'd make a decent weapon in a tavern brawl, in fact, even if it wasn't quite long enough to be suitable on a battlefield.

Fortunately for everyone concerned, the soldier being operated on had fainted from the agony at that point. So he missed entirely the heart of the operation, which came when the surgeon took up a saw and hacked through the bone. Driscol was impressed by the surgeon's speed. No master carpenter could have done better, he thought.

The sergeant could only hope the man would cut off his arm as smoothly and efficiently.

That done, the severed foot was tossed onto a nearby pile of such horrid objects. The flies over there were a seething little mountain of insects. The surgeon sewed up the severed arteries; then, still working as quickly as ever, folded the flaps of flesh and skin over the end of the bone and sewed everything up.

A bandage was then placed on the bleeding stump, and it was done. The assistants heaved the unconscious soldier off the table and carried him out of the tent. He'd recuperate—and, hopefully, survive—in a different tent set aside for the purpose.

While the surgeon waited for his helpers to return, he washed his hands in a bowl of water. Then cleaned the blade and the saw using a sponge soaked in the same bowl.

Driscol couldn't really see the point of that. By now, the water in the bowl wasn't much thinner than blood itself, as often as it had been reused for the purpose.

The surgeon's eyes ranged around the tent, quickly examining the dozen or so wounded soldiers who lay in it. Experienced eyes, obviously, despite the surgeon's youth. Driscol could see him quickly dismissing about half the cases as either hopeless or so chancy that he wouldn't spend time on them while men who might survive were kept waiting.

That meant he dismissed almost any kind of major abdominal, chest, or head wound as beyond his treatment. About the only exception to that rule was that battlefield surgeons would usually attempt to extract a bullet that hadn't penetrated any deeper than a finger's length. If it had . . .

Well, they'd just leave it alone. If the man survived, the bullet would sometimes work its way closer to the surface, where they could eventually get to it. Driscol had known a soldier in the French army who'd survived such a bullet wound—and then, eight years later, finally had the thing extracted. By then, it lay just under the skin.

For all practical purposes, the job of an army surgeon was to cut off hands, feet, arms, and legs. Nothing else, really.

Fair enough, Driscol thought. Two-thirds to three-fourths of all battlefield wounds were suffered in the extremities, to begin with—and those same wounds accounted for almost all the survivors. Men shot or stabbed in the torso or the head almost invariably died, unless the wound was a superficial one.

The surgeon's gaze fell on Driscol. On his mangled arm, rather. The sergeant didn't think the surgeon had even looked at his face—and he was quite sure he wouldn't remember Driscol if they ever met again.

"You're next," he said.

Driscol saw the assistants coming back into the tent.

There was no point in dallying. "Do it, then."

"I've got some antifogmatic I can give you," said the surgeon. "Whiskey or rum?"

"Rum."

Driscol sneered. "And it'll be raw, too. Not that I'd touch any kind of rum. It'll be whiskey, or no drink at all."

"Sergeant, this is going to hurt. A lot."

Driscol's sneer remained firm and unwavering. "Is it, now? Sawing through my flesh and bone is going to hurt. I'm shocked to hear it."

Driscol decided he'd teased the surgeon long enough to maintain discipline among the troops, when word got back. "Never mind. I've got something better in my kit. Private, my tent's not far off. Rummage around in my pack and you'll find a bottle of laudanum. I keep it for just such a mishap. Bring it here, would you?"

McParland was gone in a flash.

Driscol closed his eyes. The pain had become constant and savage, but the sergeant was no stranger to suffering. The more so when he still had his duty to perform. Driscol had known for years that attention to duty was a better distraction from pain than anything else.

By the time McParland got back, the sergeant's reputation would have climbed still higher among the troops—or sunk lower, depending on how you looked at it. Word would spread like wildfire that the troll was delaying his amputation because he'd gotten into an argument with the surgeon over the respective merits of rum versus whiskey.

He grinned at the thought. Every corporal and private in the Twenty-second Regiment who heard the tale—which would be all of them, eventually—would see it as proof that the master sergeant was indeed an inhuman creature, and an insane one at that.

But Driscol was quite sure that, forever after, whiskey would be the spirit of choice of the regiment. Within a day, any new re-

cruit unfortunate enough to have smuggled in some rum would
be forced to get rid of it. The ridicule would be unbearable.

Henceforth, for the Twenty-second Regiment, rum would be
a drink for sissies.

Laudanum took a bit longer to take effect than raw spirits would
have. But it hardly mattered, since it wasn't as if the surgeon
had been kept waiting. Few lumberjacks in the world used a saw
more vigorously and more continuously than an army surgeon
after a major battle.

"And now we're back to you, Sergeant," the surgeon said finally. Through blurred vision, Driscol saw the young doctor
leaning over him again. The man's cheap frock coat was a
bloody mess.

Driscol was in a haze, now, but he had enough consciousness
left to peer up at McParland. The private's face was a blob, but
he could still recognize the anxiety, if not quite the features on
which that anxiety was displayed.

"Help the surgeon and his boys get me onto the table, McParland. And then help them hold the arm while he saws it off. I
may twitch just a bit."

The effort of moving to the table almost drained him of consciousness. He had just enough of his wits left to whisper one
last request.

"Do me the favor, youngster. If I scream anything untoward,
keep it to yourself, would you?"

Even with the laudanum, the brief time that followed was agonizing beyond belief.

But McParland assured the sergeant afterward that the only
thing he had screamed during the operation was *Fuck the Sassenach!*

"You hollered that mebbe a hunnerd times."

Driscol thought McParland might be fudging the truth. He'd
never know, since his own memory was thankfully nothing but
a blur. It didn't matter, really, so long as McParland passed the
same story along to the troops.

The surgeon, as usual, just tossed the severed arm onto the pile
of limbs, but McParland dug it back out. He was determined to
give the troll's limb a proper burial.

On the battlefield itself—with a squad to fire a proper salute. McParland would fire one of the muskets himself.

Winfield Scott came to visit Driscol the next day. The brigadier's first words were typical of the man—direct and to the point.

"Will you consider that commission *now*, Patrick? With only one arm, your days as an active-duty sergeant are over. The best you could hope for would be a position in the quartermaster corps. And you're not a good enough thief for that job. You'd wind up in the poorhouse."

Driscol squinted at him. "And is this your idea of cheering up the troops, sir? Offering them a choice between becoming a bloody officer, or a life of squalor?"

Scott looked surprised. "Well. Yes."

Driscol chuckled, though it came out rasping. "Napoleon would have handed me a miniature marshal's baton—just a promissory note, as it were, not the real thing—and given me a pension that'd vanish within eight months when he needed the money for another campaign. The assurances of the mighty. Water poured on sand."

Coming from someone else, those words might have angered Scott. As it was, the brigadier simply smiled.

"Well, to be honest, once the war is over a U.S. Army commission is likely to be about as valuable as one of Napoleon's little sticks. I'll try for captain, Patrick, but we'll probably have to settle for first lieutenant. Still, it'll be better than nothing."

Driscol had now been given several hours to ponder bleakly on his future, and had come to the same conclusion himself. "Aye, sir, I'll take it. And thank you."

"The thanks are entirely due the other way, Sergeant." The words were said forcefully, as well they might be. The brigadier's glorious victory at the Chippewa had ensured his career, and enriched his own future prospects—assuming he survived the war, of course. And while that victory was due in part to Scott's own skill and courage, a great deal of it was due to men like Patrick Driscol.

The brigadier cleared his throat.

"I must be off, I'm afraid. Riall's retreating to Fort George, and General Brown wants to press the campaign. Rightly so, of course. Now's not the time to give the enemy any breathing space."

He cleared his throat again. "Patrick, the worst place for you to stay is here in this tent."

Driscol's chuckle was even harsher, now. "Do tell. A man's got a better chance of surviving a battle in the first rank than he does surviving a stay in a camp surgery."

Scott nodded. "So I propose to transfer you to Washington. I'll send along orders to have you placed in military quarters there. And"—here the brigadier's face brightened—"I happen to know a splendid doctor there. A very fine gentleman by the name of Jeremy Boulder. He has real medical degrees and everything. Studied under Benjamin Rush himself! I'll also send a letter asking him to take you under his care."

That news did *not* cheer up Driscol. A real doctor, with real degrees—a fine gentleman, no less—who'd studied under the most famous medical practitioner in the United States . . .

He might as well just shoot himself in the head.

But he saw no point in arguing the matter with someone from Scott's class. There'd be time enough and opportunity to evade a "real doctor" once he got to Washington.

Assuming he got there in the first place. Driscol looked down at the stump that protruded below his left shoulder. It was all that remained of his arm. The bandages covering the stump were crusted with dried blood, and the thing ached constantly. It would do worse than ache, too, once the last of the laudanum was gone. There was no way that Driscol, even as tough as he was, could survive a journey to Washington unless he gave himself several weeks to heal first.

Alas, surviving several weeks in an army surgical camp was a chancy prospect.

From the look on his face, which was no longer cheery at all, it was obvious that Scott understood as much himself. The brigadier grimaced. "Very well. I'll leave instructions to have inquiries made with the local residents. There might be a farmer nearby who'd be willing to take you in."

Driscol barely managed to keep from laughing aloud. The chance was just about nil that any local resident, such as were left, would be willing to take in a wounded soldier. That was just as true of American citizens living across the river as Canadian ones on this side. The war had ravaged the area for two years—and, to make things worse, the American army had conspicuously failed to make good on its promises to carry the war past the border territories. For the citizens of upper New York, the slogan *On to Montreal!* garnered as much respect as continental money, bungtown coppers, and wildcat banknotes.

The assurances of the mighty.

Water poured on sand.

Driscol caught a sudden little motion out of the corner of his eye. McParland had more or less informally attached himself to the sergeant since the battle. As was usually the case, he was perched on a stool nearby in the tent.

He turned his head. "You wanted to say something, Private?"

McParland looked simultaneously eager and . . . worried. He cleared his throat. Cleared it again.

"Oh, just speak up, lad!" Driscol growled "I promise I won't have you shot. Neither will the brigadier."

"Well. It's just. Well . . . My family's not far away from here, Sergeant. We live on a farm just a few miles north of Dansville." The young soldier flushed a little. "That's why, uh, I tried to run away. My home being so close and all. It's less'n seventy-five miles away."

Eagerness pushed aside anxiety: "And my mother's a right slick healer." He gave Scott an apologetic glance. "Of course, she bean't a real doctor. Don't have any degrees or such."

Scott sniffed, as well he might. McParland's family was no doubt dirt poor. And while his mother might have some medical skills in the way of farmwives the world over, she'd be riddled with herbalist nonsense and have no proper sense at all of modern medical theories.

Driscol seized the offer like a drowning man seizes a lifeline.

"Done, then! I can survive seventy-five miles." He cocked an eye at the brigadier. "You'd need to place Private McParland on detached duty, sir, as my escort. I couldn't manage the trip on my own—and I'll need him for the introductions anyway."

To his credit, Scott didn't hesitate. Whatever his own opinion of a farmwife's medical care, he wasn't blind to the fact that anything was better than leaving Driscol to rot in an army camp.

"Very well. I'll write up orders sending both of you to the private's home. But I'll expect you"—here he shot McParland a stern look—"*both* of you, mind, to show up in Washington as soon as possible. Leaving aside the fact that you do need *proper* medical treatment as soon as possible, Sergeant Driscol, there's the little matter of your commission."

"Aye, sir. We'll be along to the capital as soon as I can manage the trip."

He meant it, too, although he had no intention of looking up Scott's precious *real doctor,* the fine gentleman Jeremy Boulder.

Driscol came from a poor family himself—albeit his father had been a village blacksmith rather than a farmer—and he had no illusions as to the joys of country living. A poor family like McParland's would be hard-pressed to provide for themselves, let alone another adult, especially one who was unable to work. To be sure, they'd eventually be recompensed by the government for the expense. They might even be lucky enough to get payment in some real currency, such as the Spanish reale, which was the most favored coinage in the United States. But they were just as likely to be paid in shaky state banknotes. And, no matter how they got paid, the money would take its sweet merry time getting to them.

Still, *anything* was better than an army surgery.

"It's settled then," Scott said firmly. "I'll look forward to seeing you again, the next time I'm in Washington. The Lord Almighty knows when that'll be, though."

Driscol spent most of the trip to Dansville in agony, and the exhaustion that came from it. Only long experience as a horseman and his own innate resilience kept him from falling off the saddle. By the time they arrived at McParland's home, the sergeant was hanging on to life by a thread.

It was as poor a farm as he'd expected, just a one-room log cabin with a puncheon floor. And his bed was nothing but a straw mattress and some cheap blankets, which he'd have to share with McParland and one of his brothers.

"So, Anthony," said Mr. McParland, after Driscol was tucked into his straw bed. The sergeant was still just conscious enough to hear the conversation across the cabin. "Is this sergeant a friend of yours?"

"Uh, he bean't exactly a friend, Pa. Uh." Smiling slightly, and with his eyes closed, Driscol waited to hear what lies the boy would tell. *They'd just be small ones yet,* he thought.

"That is, actually . . . Well, the sergeant was in charge of my firing squad."

"Your *what*?"

Driscol heard young McParland clear his throat. "My firing squad, Pa. I got charged with desertion. Which, uh, well, I did. Desert, I mean. Well, I tried, anyway. They caught me."

Another clearing of the throat. "Truth is, I didn't get five miles. Brigadier Scott's cavalry were a lot better than we thought they'd be."

Without opening his eyes—he didn't think he could have, anyway, the lids felt so heavy—Driscol managed a harsh little chuckle.

"Don't you be blaming the cavalry, youngster. We caught you because *I* was in charge. You think you lot were the first deserters I've ever been sent after? Ha. Sorry bastards tried to leave the emperor's service all the time. I know all the stupid little tricks."

There was silence in the cabin.

Then, Driscol heard the voice of one of the younger brothers. He wasn't sure which one, even though he'd been introduced to all of them when he arrived. *Thomas,* he thought, *who was about fourteen years old.*

"Well, if that don't beat all creation! What happened then? How come you're still alive?"

"The brigadier thought I was too young to get shot. So the muskets of my firing squad bean't loaded with real bullets. Just blanks."

Silence. Then, again, young Thomas: "Were you scared?"

Here comes the first lie, Driscol thought. But McParland surprised him.

"Scared as you can imagine. I pissed my pants. Even before the guns went off."

That was as far as honesty would take him, it seemed. But Driscol, even hovering on the edge of the grave, wasn't about to let him get away with it.

"And then you shat your trousers when the guns did go off. I could smell it five feet off."

Silence, for a few seconds.

"Well, yeah. I did."

Silence, again. Driscol was tempted to open his eyes to see if McParland's father was reaching for an ax, or if his mother was

busy rummaging in the bins to find something suitably poison-
ous. But it was too much effort, and he hurt too much really to
care anyway.

Besides, he'd grown up in a poor Scots-Irish family like this
one. He was pretty sure he was safe.

McParland, on the other hand, wasn't nearly as secure.

"Well!" exclaimed Mrs. McParland. "If that don't make me
crawl all over to think of it. But I'm glad somebody finally gave
you the whupping you deserve! You little wretch! Trying to
desert—when you'd given your *word*."

"And facing the Sassenach," growled the boy's father. "I
oughta shoot you for real myself."

Enough was enough. "Leave the boy be," Driscol rasped. "He
was just homesick, is all. 'Twas nae cowardice. He stood
against the bastards at the Chippewa, just the few days later. I
know, I was right by him. Never flinched the once, and fired
every shot on command."

By now, word of the great American victory had spread
throughout the area. Driscol knew it would be racing like wildfire across the entire nation.

Even with his eyes closed, he could sense the calm—no, satisfaction—easing into the silence of the cabin.

"Well," said Mrs. McParland. "That's true."

"Can't nobody dubiate that," agreed the father. "So I guess I
won't take down the musket after all. Not even the belt."

In the days that followed, young McParland's honesty slipped a
bit. Small crowds of people—young men and boys, especially—gathered about the farmhouse to hear Anthony's tales
of the glorious deed at the Chippewa. The story of his execution was a favorite bit—there was no way for him to avoid it, of
course—but there was never any further mention of his trousers
being soiled.

Nor was Driscol inclined to make good the lack. *Moderation
in all things,* he decided—*including honesty.* The boy had
learned his lesson, and even managed to be truthful enough with
his family. Anything more would be an exercise in cruel
ridicule.

If the sergeant from County Antrim was as harsh as Irish
poverty, he wasn't cruel. Cruelty was a vice of the wealthy, especially the Sassenach. Such, at least, was his firm conviction.

It hardly mattered, anyway. The glory of the Chippewa was enough to wash away all sins, and cover all blemishes. Within the week, young Anthony McParland—for the first time in his life—was a hero to his neighbors. And Driscol, a veritable legend.

Soon, Driscol was strong enough to move about and sit at the table for his meals. Thereafter, given his own iron constitution and the fare provided by Mrs. McParland, his recuperation sped up still further.

"It bean't much," she said apologetically, the first time Driscol sat down to dinner.

He examined the food. Looked at from one angle, "bean't much" was certainly accurate. Salt pork and potatoes sauced with hog's lard—the staple in the diet of poor Americans. There'd be pudding for dessert, maybe.

For breakfast, as he'd had every morning since he'd arrived, there'd been porridge. Porridge every day—and that would be true if he stayed here for ten years.

For lunch, nothing more than bread smeared with apple butter.

But . . .

There was plenty of it. And if the fare itself got tedious, Driscol could always cheer himself up with philosophical ruminations.

As, indeed, he proceeded to do right then and there. "It suits me just fine, Mrs. McParland. The Sassenach sneer at us, you know, for being a nation of drunkards, tobacco spitters, and fat eaters."

"Do they really?"

"Oh, yes. I've read some of the newspaper accounts." He ladled some salt pork and potatoes onto his plate. "But I recall that they used to sneer at us for exactly the same thing in Ireland—and added, to the bargain, the sneer that we were too poor to afford much in the way of whiskey or tobacco or fat."

He ladled more salt pork and potatoes onto the plate.

"Here in America, on the other hand, we can afford plenty of it. So . . ." He ladled still more onto his plate. "This suits me just fine."

Mr. McParland grunted his agreement. He grunted instead of speaking, because his mouth was full. After he finished swallowing that first great bite, he added his own philosophical observations.

"And we bean't forced to listen to Church of England sermons about our sinful ways, neither."

Young Thomas spoke up. "There's Church of England people here, too, Pa."

His father sneered. "So? They don't swagger about giving orders, do they?"

"And they've even got a sense of shame," Driscol pointed out. "At least here they label their cowardly Anglican superstitions by the name of 'Episcopalianism.' Might I have some more tea, Mrs. McParland?"

"Why, of course, Sergeant." She refilled his cup from a kettle she brought over from the stove.

It was a large kettle, full of the strong and bitter tea that was more or less the recognized national drink of Americans. When they weren't drinking whiskey, that is. Like most American farmwives, Mrs. McParland always had a kettle of it brewing.

"The Sassenach sneer at our tea, too," Driscol commented mildly.

"They're just jealous!" piped Thomas.

Driscol nodded. "Right you are, lad."

By the end of that evening, Mrs. McParland apparently decided that Sergeant Driscol was one of their own. Even if he had, in a manner of speaking, executed her oldest son.

So the next morning, Driscol got a treat for breakfast. Instead of the constant porridge, Mrs. McParland fished some eggs out of a barrel of limewater, where they were kept fresh. Then, she fried them up in the hearth, in one of the three-legged skillets that people called "spiders."

She tried to apologize again, but Driscol would have none of it.

"This will do me wonders, Mrs. McParland." He wasn't lying, either.

A few weeks later, word arrived. There'd been another great battle at Lundy's Lane toward the end of July, just a few miles north of the Chippewa. The British were claiming it as a victory, because they'd been in possession of the field when the day was done. But, after hearing the details, Driscol assured the anxious visitors to the farm that the battle had really been pretty much of a draw.

A draw, and a horrible carnage, from the sound of it. Each army had lost at least eight hundred men. Not to Driscol's surprise, an inordinate percentage of the American losses had come from Winfield Scott's First Brigade. The brigadier had been in the forefront of the fighting, leading his men with a white plume held over his head. He'd had two horses shot out from under him.

During the fighting, which continued into the night, Scott's shoulder had been smashed by a musket ball, and he'd been taken unconscious to the rear. General Jacob Brown had been badly wounded, also—and so had the Major Jesup who'd led the Twenty-fifth Regiment so ably at the Chippewa. Brown had been wounded twice, once by a musket ball in the thigh and then by a cannon ball that ricocheted into his rib cage. He'd had to relinquish command to General Ripley, who'd ordered the army to retire from the field.

The American army had retired in good order and there'd been no rout—no pursuit of any kind—so the British claims of a "victory" were more a formality than anything else. The British army had been so badly savaged itself at Lundy's Lane that it was in no position to do anything further.

Most important of all, Driscol knew, was that the U.S. Army had been able to withstand such a holocaust in the first place. Battlefield victories and defeats came and went. What mattered was the quality of the army that was shaped by them. Driscol doubted if the stalemate on the northern front would ever be broken. But more than ever, it seemed likely that the British would abandon their efforts to prosecute the war in that theater. The American forces that faced them there were simply too good, too well trained—and now, too well blooded in battlefield experience.

The loss of Brown and Scott would hurt, of course. From the news accounts, Scott would be out of the war for a number of months, recuperating from his wound. But Eleazar Ripley was quite competent, if not as aggressive a general as either Scott or Brown. He was certainly no poltroon or fumbler, like so many previous American commanders had been on the Canadian front.

So. The war would be moving elsewhere; to the eastern

eaboard, where coastal towns in Maryland and Delaware were
eing ravaged by Admiral Cockburn, and—above all—to the
;outh.

New Orleans was the prize the British would be eyeing now.
f they could seize the mouth of the Mississippi, they'd have
heir hands on the throat of America's commerce.

Driscol was becoming impatient, which meant that he was re-
:overing well. His arm still ached, and he was still much weaker
han normal, but it was time he got back to the fight. As much as
1e could manage with only one arm, at least.

"We'll leave tomorrow," he announced.

The family must have been expecting it, since there was no
;how of surprise.

McParland didn't try to talk him out of it. For a wonder, he
didn't even break into tears.

They were given a heroes' send-off. Mrs. McParland went so
far as to pack them a small cask full of her salt pork, which was
quite a sacrifice for such a poor family. The money from the
government, needless to say, hadn't arrived yet. But Driscol assured the good farmwife that once he arrived in Washington and
was able to snarl at a lazy War Department clerk, the money
would be sent off right slick.

By then, she wasn't inclined to doubt him.

Part III

THE TENNESSEE

CHAPTER 15

Tiana Rogers stared down at the arrow stuck into the side of the canoe, less than a hand's span from her hip. The tip of the blade had punched right through the thin wall of the craft and almost penetrated her skin. The shaft of the arrow was still thrumming.

For just an instant, she was paralyzed.

If I get killed on this trip, all because of Sam Houston, I'll kill him! I swear I will!

The circular absurdity of the thought caused her to burst into laughter. Her older brothers James and John were already rolling the canoe, and Tiana threw her weight into the motion also. So, to her regret a moment later, she fell into the river with an open mouth and came up under the shelter of the canoe shell coughing up water.

At least she'd had the satisfaction of knowing she'd die laughing. With the pride of a sixteen-year-old girl, that was not a small matter.

It was nearly dark under the canoe. The vessel's walls were thick enough to block out sunlight, so the only light in the small open-air space under the shell was coming up through the muddy water. Still, she had no trouble seeing the grin on the face of her brother James.

"What's so funny?" demanded John, always the more serious of the two.

James had an uncanny knack for reading her mind. "She's probably thinking how silly it'd be to get killed chasing after The Raven. Might as well chase a real bird."

Tiana saw no reason to dignify that with a response. Besides, John was still talking.

"Creeks, d'you think? We'd better start moving to the other shore. If they keep firing, they'll eventually rip it to pieces."

As if to illustrate his point, they heard two *thunk*ing noises in close succession. Somewhere toward the bow of the canoe. Tiana saw that more arrow blades had punched through.

Then came two muffled *booms*.

"That'll be John Ross and Sequoyah, shooting back from the other canoe," James stated. "John won't hit anything, but Sequoyah's a good shot. They might drive them off. Let me take a look."

James moved easily in the water, even though he was encumbered in travel clothing. He vanished from under the canoe shell.

He was back in less than half a minute.

"They drove them off, all right. For the time being, anyway. Let's roll the canoe. It'd still be a smart idea to push it to the other shore, using it for shelter—but it'll be a lot easier with the thing sitting right side up."

"Make sure all our gear is still tied in, first," John cautioned. "Washington is still a long ways off."

"What's the point?" James demanded. "If something came loose and went into the river, we'll never find it anyway."

But he was already moving under the shell, checking their goods, which were bound up in oilskins and lashed securely to the canoe frame. The American capital *was* a long ways off, and their journey had only just begun.

Some time later, on the southern shore of the river, they did their best to dry their clothes without taking them off. None of them thought the attack was over, and they didn't want to be caught naked. The first thing they'd done, of course, was patch the holes in the canoe.

"Wasn't Creeks," Sequoyah said in his usual terse manner. "I saw the war paint on one of them. Got a good look, before I shot him. Chickasaws."

John Ross frowned. It was an oddly mixed expression, Tiana thought, somehow managing to combine ruefulness and doubt at the same time.

"I missed my own shot. But why would the Chickasaws be attacking us? They're our allies in this war."

Seeing the annoyed look on Sequoyah's face, he hastened to add: "I'm not arguing about the paint. I didn't see it well enough myself to know. I just don't understand the reason for it."

James Rogers chuckled harshly. "You spend too much time reading American books and newspapers. What's the 'war' and 'allies' got to do with anything? This'll be a clan fight."

The last and oldest member of their six-person party spoke up. Nancy Ward, that was.

"I'm sure James is right. There was a killing nearly two months ago, farther down the river at a trading post below the Suck. One of James Vann's relatives—second cousin, I think—was said to have killed a Chickasaw."

James and John Rogers nodded, as if that explained the matter completely.

Ross, on the other hand, rolled his eyes, and Sequoyah shook his head. Like Tiana, both of them thought the situation was absurd.

She glanced at Nancy Ward, and saw that the old woman had a tight, disapproving look on her face. Clearly enough, Nancy was of the same mind.

It was odd, Tiana thought, how differently her brothers seemed to look at the world. James and John were just as mixed as she was—which meant, in terms of blood, that they were actually more white than Cherokee. But both of them held to a very traditional Cherokee viewpoint. One that she couldn't entirely embrace.

John Ross didn't think that way, either, which might be explained by the fact that seven of his eight great-grandparents were Scots.

But Nancy Ward was a full-blood, even if her second husband had been a white man. And her way of thinking was a lot closer to Ross and Sequoyah and Tiana herself than to her brothers.

"James Vann." Ross pronounced the words as if they left a bad taste in his mouth. Which, they probably did.

Vann had been a prominent Cherokee. He was dead now, murdered over five years ago by an unknown assailant. It could have been just about anyone, as many enemies as the man had made in his brutal life. No one, not even his own clan, had tried to find out who'd done it. But he'd left a legacy that continued to this day. Unfortunately, Vann had been a town chief, as well as a prosperous mixed-blood trader. He'd had more than one wife, a slew of offspring and relatives, and a small host of hangers-on. No doubt it was one of those who had killed the Chickasaw at the Trading Post.

The person who'd done it, like James Vann himself, wouldn't have given a moment's thought to the political repercussions of his violence. Neither, probably, had his victim. The Chickasaw was just as likely to be a mixed-blood as the Vann cousin, and just as loosely connected to his clan.

But that didn't matter. When a killing like that happened, the ancient customs came into play. The dead Chickasaw's clan would be out looking for revenge—and any Cherokee would do. The fact that there was a war going on, in which both the Chickasaws and the Cherokees were allied with the Americans, just didn't matter.

Angrily, Ross scuffed the soil of the riverbank with his boot. "It's no wonder the Americans always play us for fools! The British and the French and the Spanish, too. Half our people—every tribe's—are too busy with their idiotic feuds to even think about what's happening to us all."

James Rogers shrugged. "I'm not going to argue the point, since I probably agree with you. But so what? Before we start for Washington, we've got to get to Oothcaloga and meet up with The Raven. That's a fair distance itself—and those Chickasaws won't have given up. We probably just ran into a few of them, and now they'll gather their whole war party.

"This thing isn't over yet."

Oothcaloga
Cherokee Territory, in northern Georgia

"No, Colonneh. If I go, it will seem like an official delegation. And no such thing has been approved by the council."

Major Ridge smiled wryly. "You lived among us. You know how quick one chief is to suspect another of conniving with the Americans. If I go with you to Washington—and *especially* if I agree to anything while I'm there—I'll be accused of being bribed when I come back."

Sam tried to come up with some way to argue the point, and couldn't. It was true enough. On both counts, for that matter, since it wasn't simply a matter of suspicion. Bribing chiefs *was* a standard method by which the United States sowed division among the Indian tribes, and bent them to its will.

They were standing on the porch of Major Ridge's big house. Suppressing a sigh, Sam let his gaze wander for a moment across the landscape.

It was a prosperous-looking countryside, with its well-tended orchards and grazing cattle. Sam could see a few signs left of the depredations committed by the marauding Georgia militiamen, but not many. That wasn't surprising, given that Major Ridge had been home for weeks before Sam arrived, and had something like twenty slaves to do the work of repairing the damage.

Sam had wound up being delayed in Fort Jackson for some time before he set off on his expedition. In the meantime, James Rogers had returned to his uncle John Jolly's island on the Tennessee, with Sequoyah and John Ross in tow. James had wanted his brother John to join them on the expedition to Washington, and Ross wanted to visit his family in nearby Chatanuga before they left. Especially his wife, Quatie, whom he'd only married a few months ago.

They'd probably all be on their way back here, by now. They'd agreed to meet up at Major Ridge's plantation before starting off for the capital.

Alas, it looked as if the main reason Sam had set Oothcaloga as the meeting place had become a moot point. Major Ridge's refusal to accompany them had been stated in a friendly manner, but very firmly nonetheless.

Ridge was not considered *asgá siti* for nothing. If the man said "no," the word meant "no."

"However," Major Ridge continued, "if John Ross and Sequoyah go with you, as you say they plan to, I will promise to pay careful attention to what they tell me when they return."

He said nothing about James and John Rogers. That didn't surprise Sam. The two Rogers brothers were excellent warriors, but neither of them had a reputation for anything other than their fighting skills.

"John Ross and Sequoyah have earned enough respect for their words to carry weight, when they return," said Ridge. "But neither of them is a recognized chief, so we will avoid that problem. That will be better all the way around, Colonneh. We will get the advantage of a good discussion in the council, without the chiefly rivalries and suspicions. Trust my judgment, if you would."

Sam nodded. Started to, rather. The nod broke off into a frozen little gesture when he saw that the smile on Major Ridge's face had become *very* wry.

"However, there *is* a way you can keep me directly connected to the situation, without requiring my own participation."

Ridge turned and beckoned to someone who had been lurking inside the house, so silently that Sam hadn't known they were there. Two young boys stepped forward onto the porch, followed by a girl. The boys looked to Sam to be about twelve years old. The girl, perhaps two years older.

Ridge placed his hand on the shoulder of one of the boys. "This is my son, who is known as John Ridge, though his Cherokee name is Skahtlelohkee. And the girl is my daughter, whose American name is Nancy." His other hand came down upon the shoulder of the second boy. "And this is my nephew Gallegina—or Buck Watie, as he is often called. All three of them have been studying at Spring Place, at the school set up by the Gambolds."

Sam knew of the school at Spring Place, although he'd never visited it himself. The Reverend John Gambold and his wife were Moravian missionaries who'd emigrated to the United States from Germany. Since then, they'd devoted themselves to bringing learning and the Christian faith to Indians on the southwest frontier.

He had a bad feeling he knew what was coming.

Sure enough, Ridge continued:

"They came home just recently. The Gambolds are fine people, but I would like to place the children in a school which is more substantial, where they can continue their education in the American manner. Since you are going to Washington anyway, I wish you to do me the favor . . ."

So now I'm a nursemaid, Sam thought sourly.

He couldn't refuse, of course, given the nature of his mission. If he was to get any significant number of Cherokees to return to rejoin General Jackson's forces, Major Ridge would be the key to his success. Most of the other Cherokee chiefs were still too furious at the wreckage the Georgian militia had made of their homes and lands—while they'd been down in Alabama fighting as Jackson's allies, no less!—to even consider joining Sam's proposed expedition to Washington, much less volunteer to fight any further in the war.

Gloomily, he wondered what else could go wrong.

With the Rogers brothers involved . . .

A lot.

By sundown, Tiana and her companions had made it to a small island where they decided to rest for the night. The isolation gave them the advantage of enjoying a campfire. No revenge-seeking Chickasaws could attack them there without making some noise crossing the water—and Tiana's brothers had even better hearing than she did.

"Wait'll Colonneh sees you!" James laughed, as he fed fuel to the fire. He was grinning widely. "He thought you were joking when you told him, three years ago, that you'd have him for a husband."

"I *was* joking," Tiana said, with as much dignity as she could manage.

Was I? she wondered.

It was hard to remember. The difference between a sixteen-year-old and a thirteen-year-old girl was enormous. At the time, Sam Houston had seemed as glamorous and exciting a husband as any Tiana could imagine. Exotic, yet familiar enough with Cherokee life to make such a union seem possible. Not to mention witty, intelligent, good-natured. Even good-looking.

But she wasn't sure, anymore. She was a lot more practical-minded than she'd been at the age of thirteen. And Sam Houston had been gone from John Jolly's island for those three years, back to the American society he'd come from. So she'd had time to think about things without the distraction of his presence.

Marriage to a white American certainly wasn't out of the question. Her own mother had done it, after all. But whether it would be successful or not depended mostly on the man's ambitions.

The ambitions of Captain Jack Rogers had been those of an adventurer, who liked the frontier and intended to stay there. "Hell-Fire Jack," they called Tiana's father, and for good reason. He didn't care in the least about the good opinion of proper society, as Americans figured it. If they chose to call him a "squaw man," he'd return the sneer with plenty of his own. What did he care? It wasn't as if he was planning to run for office, or get appointed to some prestigious position.

Sam Houston, on the other hand, had different ambitions. Tiana was pretty sure of that. And whatever his other qualities, he was not a man to let sentiment get in the way of his goals. He wouldn't do anything immoral to advance himself, as he saw it—and Sam had a pretty good sense of morals. But he'd stay focused on his purpose, and not let himself get diverted by passion or desire.

Something of her skeptical thoughts must have shown in her face, even in the dim light of the campfire. Old Nancy Ward leaned over and asked her softly: "So why *did* you come, girl?"

Tiana shifted her shoulders. "I don't know. I guess I just needed to find out. Or I'd wonder about it for years."

"Good reason."

"You think so?" Tiana was genuinely interested in the old woman's opinion. Nancy Ward was a *Ghighua*. The Cherokee word had several translations into English. "War Woman" was one of them. But Tiana just thought of her as "wise."

The old woman smiled, wisely. "Oh, yes. Best reason there is to do anything, I sometimes think."

CHAPTER 16

JUNE 18, 1814

Tiana and her companions left the island before daybreak, hoping to elude the Chickasaws altogether. If they pushed hard, they'd be safe by midafternoon, and they could make it to Ross Landing by nightfall. The area around Chatanuga was not one any hostile Chickasaws would venture near.

Her brother James predicted that the maneuver wouldn't

work, and it didn't take long to find out that he was right. Just as the sun was coming up, they saw two canoes coming upriver toward them. Even at a distance, they could see that the canoes were packed with painted warriors.

"Chickasaws, sure enough," James said, reading the colors on the distant faces. That was enough, even if he couldn't see the specific patterns yet. He swiveled and studied the river behind them.

"Go back?" asked his brother. "Or go ashore?"

"Neither, I think. There's at least one canoe back there, although I can barely see it." His eyes quickly scanned both riverbanks. "And they've probably got warriors in the woods, too."

The canoe bearing John Ross, Sequoyah, and Nancy Ward drew alongside.

"What should we do?" asked Ross. The question was asked flatly and calmly. Technically, it could be argued that Ross was in charge of the expedition. But the young man was self-confident enough to know that James Rogers would have a better idea what to do than he would.

"Go at them directly. That'll keep the numbers closer to even. And they'll have the sun in their eyes, this time of day. If we can get past them, they'll never catch us."

His brother John winced. "True—*if* we get past them. They've got five men on each of those canoes, to match against our total of five."

Seeing that Nancy Ward was giving him a cold look, he hastily added: "Six, I mean."

Ward snorted, and drew a pistol from under her wrap. The Spanish-made weapon looked even older than she did. "I knew how to use this before your *grandfather* was born."

She wasn't bragging, either. Nancy Ward had earned the title of War Woman among the Cherokee following the battle of Taliwa, against the Creeks, sixty years ago. After her husband Kingfisher had been killed, Nancy had picked up his gun and led the final charge that drove the enemy off. She'd been eighteen years old, at the time.

"Does everyone have a gun?" asked Ross. The question was really aimed at Tiana. He already knew that the four men in the party did.

"No," she replied. "Just this." She unlaced a small parcel at her feet and drew out a knife.

James shook his head. "Actually, she does have a gun. Or will have"—he pointed into the other boat—"after you lend her your rifle."

Ross stared down at the weapon in question. It was a very expensive-looking rifled musket. The kind of hunting weapon that only a rich family like the Rosses could afford.

"Uh . . ."

"Don't be stupid," James said curtly. He bent down, lifted his own musket, and passed it forward to his brother John. "We've got three long guns. Sequoyah's got one of them, and he's a good shot. I'm giving mine to my brother, because John's a better shot than I am. And our sister is a better shot with a rifle or musket than either one of us. Probably with a pistol, too."

He flashed her a grin. "But I can still outwrestle her. So can John. Although neither one of us has tried in a while. Too risky, with her temper."

After a moment, Ross's face got that easy, relaxed smile Tiana had come to recognize in the days since she'd met him. He really was a very self-assured young man.

She decided that she liked him. It was too bad that he was already married, to a woman named Quatie. He'd probably make a better husband than Sam Houston, even if he wasn't as handsome.

Ross handed the rifle to her across the little distance separating the canoes. "I probably couldn't hit anything with it until we got close. And if I understand the plan right, we're going to keep as much distance as we can."

He cocked an eye at James. Tiana's brother smiled blandly.

"We'll go straight at the Chickasaw canoes until we get within musket range. Then we'll veer off and try to pass them on the southern side."

"Shooting all the way," his brother muttered. "As great war plans go, this one isn't going to be remembered."

"Best I could come up with." James hefted his paddle and began stroking again.

"We'll lead. You follow," he said to Ross and Sequoyah. Ross was in the rear of their canoe, Sequoyah in the bow. He'd stop paddling once they got near enough, then use his musket. In the middle, Nancy Ward had her pistol resting in her lap.

Tiana, also in the middle of her canoe, admired her newly acquired rifle. It was a beautiful-looking thing.

"I don't like Chickasaws," she pronounced.

"Who does?" said James, from behind her. "And when did you ever meet any Chickasaws?"

"This is the first time. I'm a good judge of character."

That was enough to make James laugh out loud. "Saying that! With you coming on this trip for no good reason than chasing after a bird!"

The plan went wrong right from the start. The first shot fired was by one of the oncoming Chickasaws. It was a stupid shot, made while they were still out of range.

Dumbfounded, Tiana saw her brother John twist suddenly. Then, clap one hand to his face.

She looked down and saw that his paddle had been shot right through, shattered by the lucky bullet just below John's grip, as he'd been raising it for another stroke. What was left of it, he tossed into the river while he pawed at his eyes.

"Splinters," he hissed. "Can't see a thing."

"It'll be up to you and Sequoyah, Tiana," James said grimly. "Don't miss."

He started picking up the stroke, to make good for their brother's incapacity. Tiana gauged the distance and shook her head.

"Stop paddling. The current's not bad, as long as you aren't rocking the canoe."

With a quick backstroke, James brought the canoe almost to a standstill. He was just as proficient with a paddle as he was with a war club. Next to him, moving more awkwardly, John Ross did the same.

"Have at it, girl," James said.

Tiana brought the fancy rifle up to her shoulder, sighting down the barrel. Ross's gun even had a rear sight, to match up against the front one. That'd be pointless with a smoothbore musket.

The range was long, well over a hundred yards, and probably closer to two. On dry land, braced properly, Tiana would have been confident enough in the shot, even with one of her father's muskets. Here, sitting in a canoe braced only with her own knees . . .

But the current was smooth, so the canoe was almost steady now that James had stopped paddling. And with the rising sun behind her, she had an excellent view of the target.

She'd trust John Ross, she decided. He might be a bad shot, but by all accounts the man was a shrewd trader. He'd have bought the best rifle available.

She aimed at the lead warrior in the canoe on the left. She'd try for a belly shot, as low as she could. If she missed, at least she might damage the canoe.

As always, when the gun went off, she was a little surprised. One of the reasons Tiana was such a good shot was that she knew how to squeeze a trigger instead of jerking it. She ascribed that to the superior virtues of women, trained in such practical and patient arts as sewing. Men, hunters, always tried to do things with a swagger.

"Hoo!" she heard James bellow. "Knocked him *flat*!"

She looked up and saw that he was right. Her shot must have caught the Chickasaw in the bow square on.

As good a rifle as Ross would have bought, her bullet might have passed right through the first man and hit the one behind him. The whole crew of that canoe collapsed into a confused pile, and the craft itself began yawing to the side.

She glanced at the canoe next to hers, and saw that Sequoyah had already assessed the new situation. He had his own musket up, aiming it at the other canoe.

Then, he shook his head and lowered the weapon. "Still too far, with my gun. If I miss the shot, I'll have to waste time reloading."

"Keep paddling ahead?" Ross asked.

"No," replied James. "Just keep the boats steady in the current, to give Sequoyah and Tiana as good a shot as possible. Let them come to us, while the sun's still half blinding them. The longer it takes, the better. Tiana will need a lot of time to reload that rifle."

He twisted in his seat, squinting back. "The canoe behind us is still a long way upriver. I'm sure they thought we'd go ashore. So they stayed back as far as possible. That way they wouldn't be swept past our landing spot by the current."

Tiana heard her brother John chuckle, even as he kept wiping his eyes. "Can you blame them? Who'd expect Cherokees to turn a simple river fight into a stupid formal duel? Good thing our father isn't here."

Tiana chuckled herself. Her father had fought a number of duels in his life, but not one of them had been what you could call "formal." Hell-Fire Jack's opinion of formality in a gun-fight ranked somewhere below his opinion of worms.

Best time to shoot a man is before he's even got a gun in his hand. Better yet, before he's even looking at you. Best *of all, when he's drunk or asleep, or both.*

"Stop pawing at your eyes!" Tiana snapped, trying to keep her mind focused. "Splash some water on your face." Unkindly, she added: "Even blind, you ought to be able to find some water. We're in the middle of a river."

John leaned over and stretched out his right hand. Then, started splashing water into his eyes.

"They say white men have tender and sensitive girls for sisters," he muttered. "Mothers, too."

"Not that I've seen," Tiana retorted. "Maybe in the East. The way Sam tells it, his mother—"

"Tiana!" James barked. "You'd better get started on your re-load. That's a rifle, not a smoothbore musket."

The reproof was unnecessary, since Tiana had already started. But, in the time that followed—it seemed like half a day—she realized why James had spoken so sharply.

Tiana had never fired a rifle before, and had been delighted by the result. Now, reloading one, she understood why warriors tended to curse the things—and why even American or European armies rarely used them.

A smoothbore musket could be reloaded in less than a minute. A rifle . . .

At one point, she almost despaired completely. Trying to force the bullet down that long and rifled barrel with a ramrod wasn't beyond her strength, as such. Tiana was a very big woman and had the muscles to match her size. If she'd been standing, she'd have done it readily enough. Not easily, no. But she'd have done it, since she could have leaned her weight into the task.

But sitting in a canoe! That required pure strength of arm and shoulder. Nor did she dare to use the measure of last resort, which would have been to slam the butt against the ground. As dangerous as that was on dry land—the gun could easily go off—it was impossible in a canoe. Any impact hard enough to force the bullet down past the rifling would punch right through the thin hull.

Somewhere in the middle of her labors, she heard Sequoyah's musket go off. Again, James gave out that exultant *"hoo!"*, but Tiana didn't look up.

"Just wounded him, I think," she heard Sequoyah say apologetically.

"Who cares?" came James's reply. "That other canoe just started moving again, and now this one will be slowed. We'll have time for at least one more shot for both of you. For that matter, we've got John's—"

Tiana shook her head. "No. I want to save John's musket until the end."

She glanced up quickly, then focused back on her task. "They're still more than a hundred yards off. I probably couldn't hit them with the musket anyway. I'm surprised Sequoyah did."

Eventually, it was done. Tiana had barely enough strength left to bring the rifle back to her shoulders, and she worried that she might be too weak to hold the gun steady.

It didn't matter. By now, the nearest Chickasaw canoe was within fifty yards. That was the one Sequoyah had targeted, not the one she'd shot at.

At that range, Tiana could hit practically anything, even with a smoothbore.

Two of the Chickasaws, she saw, had already fired their guns. One, a musket; the other—stupid fool!—a pistol. Vaguely, she could remember hearing the sounds of the gunshots.

That left one Chickasaw with a loaded gun, the man farthest to the rear. He was starting to bring his musket up.

Tiana blew him right out of the canoe. Ross's rifle was a heavy caliber, with a bore well over half an inch. The bullet must have struck the man in the middle of the chest. He almost did a full back somersault before his body hit the water.

Then Sequoyah's gun fired again. The Chickasaw with the pistol seemed to fold up and collapse into the canoe.

"Three down!" barked James. "Forget that one. We'll go around them, Ross. *Start paddling.*"

A moment later, both canoes were driving through the water again. Not a moment too soon, either. Out of the corner of her eye, Tiana saw something flashing toward them.

Turning her head, she saw an arrow plunge into the river, not more than five yards away. A second later, another one did the same, even closer.

Looking up, she could see several Chickasaw warriors on the north bank of the river. They were armed with bows. The traditional weapons were too awkward to use well in a canoe, so they must have given their few guns to the men who'd be carrying the attack onto the river.

They weren't awkward to use on land, though. And "traditional" didn't mean the same as "ineffective." They were within bow range, too, even if at the extreme edge of it.

Tiana had seen the results of wounds inflicted by arrows. Worse than gunshot wounds, usually, since it was impossible to draw out the barbed arrowheads. They either had to be cut out or pushed all the way through the flesh. Removing the hideous things often caused more damage than the initial wound itself. They *had* to be removed, too. Bullets, dull and blunt, normally did little further damage once they were lodged in a body. And they tended to work their own way out, over time.

Not arrowheads, with their sharp edges. They'd keep cutting up flesh every time a person moved—and the barbs would make them work their way still deeper.

James was obviously of the same mind. Instead of staying as far away from the enemy canoe as possible, he steered directly for it. The enemy warriors on the shore wouldn't dare fire at them, right next to one of their own canoes. Although they were still within bow range, they were far enough away that the Chickasaws on the shore couldn't aim very carefully.

"Get ready," he hissed. "There's still two of them left in that canoe."

Three, really, since the man Sequoyah had wounded wasn't completely out of the fight. In fact, he seemed to have the only remaining unfired gun. A pistol, which he could use even with one shoulder maimed. If he was tough enough.

He was. Tiana could see him raising the pistol, grimacing like a madman. At the point-blank range James was bringing them into, he couldn't possibly miss.

"Here!" she heard John cry out. Still blinded from the splinters, her brother had been coolheaded enough to follow the progress of the battle by hearing alone. He was holding up his musket, thrusting it in her direction, gripping it one-handed by the barrel.

Even if Tiana had had the time to reload Ross's rifle, she wouldn't have had the strength. But the musket was already loaded. All she had to do was shoot.

She brought it quickly to her shoulder. But then she realized that James had already brought their canoe almost even with the enemy's.

The Chickasaw canoe was on her right. Tiana was right-handed.

She didn't even think to shift the butt to her left shoulder. That would have made for an awkward shot, but still an easy one to make, at such close range.

Instead, from reflex and excitement, she twisted and rose to a crouch. Brought the musket up.

"Tiana!" James shouted.

She fired the gun. The Chickasaw with the pistol went over the side of his canoe, spraying blood everywhere. The bullet had struck him in the neck, just above the chestbone.

Tiana went right over the side of her own canoe, almost capsizing it. Her brother's musket had been as heavy a caliber as Ross's rifle. Half standing as she'd been, poorly balanced, the recoil had sent her sailing.

But she didn't let go of the musket. Tiana was almost as good a swimmer as her brothers, so she had her head back above the water within seconds. This time she'd remembered to close her mouth, too. She shook her head vigorously, to clear her eyes.

Unfortunately, that shook loose her turban, which must have starting coming undone somewhere in the course of the fight. Tiana's hair was long, and black—and she never tied it back when she was wearing a turban. So, at the same time that she shook water out of her eyes, she shook her hair into them.

By the time she clawed the hair aside, the two canoes were side by side. James was now standing, his legs spaced and maintaining his balance. He held his paddle as easily as a war club.

One of the two remaining Chickasaws swung his own paddle. James parried the blow easily and then batted the man off the canoe. It was almost a gentle swipe. James simply wanted to clear him aside so he could concentrate on the second warrior, and he didn't want to risk losing his own balance.

Fighting in a canoe was . . . tricky. As Tiana had just discovered.

The Chickasaw turned his plunge off the canoe into a fairly

graceful dive. He landed in the water not far from Tiana herself. But she paid him no attention, since her eyes were riveted on the battle between James and the last warrior in the canoe.

James would win it, she was sure of that. She'd been told by old warriors that James was as good with a war club as any they'd ever seen—and a paddle makes for a pretty fair improvisation.

But he never had to. Another gun went off, just as the Chickasaw was rearing up for a strike. A pistol, by the sound. That surprised Tiana, since—if she remembered everything clearly—by now Sequoyah would have had his musket reloaded.

She looked over at the other canoe and saw that the shot had been fired by Nancy Ward. There was something grim and merciless about the old woman's eyes as she watched the last Chickasaw topple overboard.

Nancy Ward was almost eighty years old. For a moment, Tiana was frozen by the sight. Half exultant—if she could be like that, at that age!—and half petrified. It was like watching some ancient, terrible creature, rising from its lair.

The voice of John Ross broke the trance.

"Tiana! Look out!"

Startled, Tiana tore her eyes away and saw that the Chickasaw whom James had sent into the river was now swimming toward *her*.

The half grin, half snarl on his painted face would have been enough to make clear his intentions. Even if he hadn't had his knife clenched between his teeth so that his hands would be free, allowing him to swim more quickly.

Tiana had been in a lot of fights, the way girls will. A couple of them had been ferocious, with Tiana leaving her opponent unconscious. In one case, the person had received a broken arm.

This had been her first real battle, however, fought with weapons and with deadly purpose. But of all the things that happened that day, this attack was the only one that made her truly furious.

Why is he doing this?

"You idiot!" she shrieked, as the man came up to her. His last breaststroke left his head completely exposed.

Tiana was six feet tall, strong for her size, and a very good swimmer. A powerful thrust of her legs sent her up. She raised the musket out of the water, holding it in one hand.

The Chickasaw's eyes widened. He hadn't spotted the musket.

"Idiot!" she shrieked again. Her grip on the musket butt felt like iron. So did the butt strike itself, when it came down on the warrior's head.

His eyes rolled up. Blood spurted from the corners of his mouth as his jaws clenched on the knife between his teeth.

Tiana brought the butt up for another strike, but by the time she could kick her legs again to get into position, the Chickasaw was gone. She thought she might have felt his fingers tugging on one of her leggings, for just a moment, as he sank beneath the surface.

But she wasn't sure. As hard as she'd hit him, he'd been too dazed to do anything that wasn't pure reflex. He'd probably drown, unless someone fished him out.

Which Tiana had no intention of doing. She started swimming back to the canoe. Moving more awkwardly than she normally would have. Whatever else, she wasn't going to let go of the musket. There were monsters in the river.

James hauled her aboard, none too gently. Just a powerful heave that sent her sprawling into the canoe, while he went back to paddling.

"Next time," he growled, "don't stand up to fight in a canoe. Unless you know what you're doing. Which you don't."

Tiana made no retort. She was too busy scrabbling to get her head above the side of the vessel, so she could see what was happening with the other enemy canoe.

Nothing.

It was now at least forty yards off. The three men left in it— she must have hit two of them, after all, with that first rifle shot—were just staring. Then, as if her gaze was the trigger, they suddenly started paddling away.

Sequoyah had never fired again, she realized. She looked over and saw that the lame warrior was just sitting in his canoe, calmly and confidently, his musket ready. He'd been waiting for the enemy to come closer so he could kill one of them.

But the Chickasaws had had enough.

Shakily, but proudly, Tiana realized that this fight on the river was going to become a small legend of its own. Six Cherokees—one of them an old woman—had faced almost twice that number of enemies. And they'd left seven of them dead or badly wounded, while not suffering a single casualty of their own.

She gloated too soon. The one and only casualty they suffered that day happened two seconds later. An arrow fired from the riverbank almost maimed her. Fortunately, the wicked arrowhead left only a gash on the back of her left hand, before slicing off into the water. If it had struck her wrist squarely, she'd have lost the hand.

"You're lucky," Nancy Ward said to her later, once they came ashore several miles farther down the river.

The old woman finished replacing Tiana's own quick dressing with an expert bandage. "It didn't cut any of the tendons. You'll have a scar there, for a while. But I think it'll eventually fade away."

Tiana hoped it wouldn't, although she didn't say it aloud. Nancy Ward had been her heroine since she'd been a little girl. And now, Tiana had the visible proof that she wasn't unfit to travel in her company.

"And don't get too swellheaded," Nancy murmured. "*That's* a much worse kind of wound. Most people never recover from it."

"I won't," Tiana promised.

Nancy patted her cheek. "Oh, yes, you will. Why shouldn't you? You were very brave, and very good—and you can take that from a woman who knows. Just don't let the swelling get too big, that's all."

Alas, James must have heard the softly spoken words. He had *very* good hearing.

"No chance of that," he chuckled. "The Raven'll shrink her head right down. Best-looking girl in John Jolly's band, and he won't pay any attention to her at all."

She scowled at him. That was probably true, but . . .

Her other brother was grinning at her, too! John had finally washed the splinters out of his eyes. Luckily, there didn't seem to be any permanent damage.

"What are you looking at?" she demanded. "Now that looking doesn't do anybody any good."

John's grin just widened. "Oh, how quick with a blade she is! What you'd expect, of course, from a great warrior woman. But you still shouldn't sneer at your brother, even if his own exploits didn't match yours."

Tiana glared at both of them. "The two of you are making fun of me."

"No, we're not," James said. To her surprise, his tone was firm and calm, not jocular. "We're just telling you the truth."

"You should find a different husband," John agreed. "Colonneh isn't right for you."

"Find me a better one, then!" Tiana snapped.

James and John looked at each other. Then smiled.

She'd been afraid they would.

"All right."

"We will."

CHAPTER 17

JUNE 28, 1814
Oothcaloga

"Of course we had to bring our sister with us," James Rogers said firmly. "She needs a better education than she can get with the Moravians."

He shot Sam a sly look. "She'd have been furious with us if we hadn't, seeing as how she insists that you're her future husband. But how can she manage that—you being a fancy officer now—if she doesn't get a proper American education?"

Sam rolled his eyes.

Tiana was the half sister of the Rogers brothers. He'd met her during the three years he'd lived with John Jolly and his people on their island in the Tennessee River. When he'd first arrived, Tiana had been ten years old and more or less oblivious to the sixteen-year-old white boy who'd dropped into their midst. By the time he'd left, however, she'd been thirteen and he'd been nineteen—and Cherokee girls married young. On the day he left, she'd publicly announced that she'd have him for a husband, when the time came.

Sam would have laughed it off, except . . . Tiana was ferociously strong-willed. John Rogers *had* laughed, at the time, and Tiana had promptly knocked him off his feet. Even at thirteen, she was a big girl.

In the weeks that had passed while Sam waited at Oothcaloga—even with such an informal party, the Cherokee notables insisted on lengthy discussions and extensive debates—James Rogers had made it back to John Jolly's island on the Tennessee. As planned, he'd picked up his brother John, who hadn't been at the Horseshoe because of a broken foot. Nothing spectacular, in the way of injuries—a horse had stepped on it.

What Sam *hadn't* expected was that he'd bring back his sister, too. But Tiana was here now, sure enough. Packed for travel, and grinning ear to ear.

Her father was off somewhere, on one of his mysterious—and probably illegal—expeditions. So he hadn't come. Neither had her uncle John Jolly. Sam's foster father usually didn't leave the island in the river where he'd created something of a refuge for his band of Cherokees. But it seemed that Jolly was in support of the notion also, even if—for the same reasons as Major Ridge—he didn't feel it would be wise for him to go to Washington himself. Jolly was a small chief, but he was still a chief.

And, besides, his ties to his brother Tahlonteskee were well known, and Tahlonteskee was a major chief—a status he had not lost simply because he'd led his thousand Cherokees to settle in the land across the Mississippi River. The "Western Cherokees," as they were coming to be known, were still considered by everyone—including themselves—to be part of the Cherokee Nation.

To Sam's absolute astonishment, however, Tiana had been accompanied by yet another woman. A woman who was so old that Sam was amazed she'd made the trip at all.

Nancy Ward. Or *Nan'yehi,* to use her Cherokee name. The last—and some said, the greatest—of the Cherokee *Ghighua.* The title was sometimes translated into English as "Beloved Woman," and sometimes as "War Woman." However it was translated, the *Ghighua* occupied an extremely prestigious place among the matrilineal Cherokee, perhaps none more so than Nancy Ward.

"Leave aside the girl's claims to be your future wife, Colon-neh," Nancy told him quietly in private, that evening. "That's as may be—and you could do worse anyway. She's even good-looking. What's important is that she's willing to do it."

"She has as much interest in further formal education as a she-bear," Sam complained. "John Jolly and Captain John practically had to hog-tie her to keep her in the Moravian school."

The old woman grinned. "Stop exaggerating. She's not as big as a bear. Not quite. I admit she has something of a she-bear's temperament. You should have seen her in the fight on the river! Even better than me in my first battle, and I was two years older.

"And so what? She'll be placed with Major Ridge's daughter Nancy, in whatever American school you find for them—and Nancy's just as strong-willed as Tiana, even if she's a lot quieter about it. She'll see to it that Tiana settles down, and even stud-ies."

The arguments of Nancy Ward—even the threats and en-treaties of Tiana Rogers herself—Sam might have resisted. In truth, the problem wasn't that he found the prospect of Tiana's company unpleasant. Rather the opposite, in fact. The girl *was* good-looking, now that she was sixteen years old—downright beautiful, in fact—and Sam had always appreciated her intelli-gence and good humor.

Yet . . .

That was the problem. If Sam had intended to make his life among the Cherokee, Tiana would make him a splendid wife. But, he didn't plan to settle with the tribe. Even before the Horseshoe Bend, Sam's ambitions had been turned elsewhere.

Now, with Andrew Jackson's friendship and patronage, he had the prospect of a career in the political arena, at the national level. Such a career, however, required a suitable wife—which no Cherokee girl, no matter how accomplished, would be con-sidered by proper American society.

Sam might regret that fact, but a fact it remained nonetheless. And he wasn't about to dishonor himself by playing with Tiana's emotions, as tempting as that might be. He'd never be able to look at himself in a mirror again.

"I don't know . . ." he muttered feebly.

"Do it," Nancy insisted.

Despite her age, Nancy Ward's voice was still firm—and her tone, unwavering. That wasn't surprising, really, given the way she'd first earned her position as *Ghighua* in the battle of Taliwa.

Since then, however, she had carved out a reputation as a shrewd diplomat and strategist for the entire Cherokee Nation. Ward was the leader of the women's council and she had a voice in the general council of the chiefs. For decades now, she'd advocated a policy of trying to find some sort of suitable accommodation with the American settlers, and had proven to be flexible in her methods. No Cherokee doubted her devotion to the nation, but she sometimes left them confused by her subtlety.

"Do it," she repeated. Then, giving Sam a considering look through very shrewd eyes, she added: "The girl's marital ambitions are irrelevant. So are yours, Colonneh. What matters here isn't Tiana anyway, but Major Ridge's children. It's Major Ridge who's the key. That's the reason I came down here at all. To talk to *him*."

Sam had wondered about that. The woman normally didn't leave her home at Chota any longer.

"You're not coming with us to Washington, then?" he asked cautiously, doing his best not to let his relief show. As hale and healthy as Nancy was, she was still close to eighty years old, and the trip to the capital would be a long and arduous one.

"At my age? Don't be silly." Nancy chuckled drily. "You're worrying too much, for a youngster. It'll work out, well enough. For one thing, I think Ridge's daughter Nancy is formidable in her own manner. She may even be able to keep Tiana from braining some stupid white girl."

The old woman shook her head. "Of which there are a multitude. How did those fools ever let their men shackle them so?"

Sam rubbed his jaw.

And that was *another* problem! White men and Cherokees had radically different notions of the proper place of women. One of the biggest complaints among the crusty and conservative Cherokee shamans, in fact, was that Cherokee women who married white men became unnaturally submissive.

There was some truth to the charge, too, although few if any

Cherokee women would ever be as submissive as most white women were. Sam knew of one Methodist preacher who regularly beat his wife with a horsewhip. The wife was white herself, of course. A wife among the Cherokee would never tolerate such treatment—and, even if she were inclined to, her brothers and uncles and cousins would soon wreak their vengeance on the husband.

Their actions would be supported by Cherokee law and custom, too. In white society, a woman became essentially her husband's chattel after marriage. If he divorced her, she would be left penniless and destitute. In Cherokee society, in the event of divorce, the wife kept all the property and the husband went on his way, taking only his personal belongings.

White Americans were often astonished to learn that a fair number of white women who'd been captured by Indians refused to return to white society after they were "rescued." But Sam wasn't, not with his knowledge of the frontier. To be sure, women of America's eastern gentility would be appalled at the living conditions of the Cherokee, much less the prospect of having a red-skinned husband. But most captured white women were frontier people themselves, and their conditions, living in primitive log cabins, were essentially no better than those of Cherokees.

The main difference was that while a Cherokee husband was just as likely to get drunk as a white one—probably even more likely, in truth—he wouldn't beat her.

Something of his gloomy thoughts must have been evident in his expression. Nancy Ward's old eyes seemed to get a little twinkle in them.

"Our people are not so different as all that, young Colonneh. Do not forget that I married a white man after Kingfisher died. Bryant Ward, from whom I took my new last name in the American way, and had children by him. It can be done. Even if—" She laughed. "That Scots-Irish man sometimes drove me crazy, the way they will."

Scots-Irish. Sam's own ancestry, as well as Jackson's and that of most white frontiersmen. A hard people, often a harsh one, shaped by centuries of conflict. As he'd said to the general, not very far removed from barbarism themselves.

But, like the Indians, always a brave folk. Perhaps, out of that mutual courage, something might be done. Granted, every *other* characteristic of the two nations worked against what he was trying to accomplish. Pigheadedness, first and foremost. The Scots-Irish even worse than the Cherokee.

"All right," he sighed. He didn't really have a choice, anyway. "I'll give it a try."

Part IV

THE POTOMAC

CHAPTER 18

Weeks later, they finally arrived at the outskirts of Washington. With no major problems or incidents along the way, to Sam's surprise. But just when he thought the worst was past, all hell seemed to be breaking loose.

Naturally, Tiana was grinning at him. Naturally, the girl was her usual disrespectful self.

"So much for impressing us with the famous American capital city!" she cackled. "We got here just in time to watch the British burn it down!"

"They haven't burned it *yet*," Sam growled. Honesty forced him to add: "Although I admit, from the rumors, they may be about to."

He started muttering under his breath.

John Ross, riding next to him, cast him a quizzical look. "What did you say?"

Houston sighed. "I was just quoting from Homer's *Iliad.*"

He watched gloomily as another carriage raced past them along the road. Sam and his small expedition had been on that road since daybreak, and the nation's capital was almost in sight.

The carriage, like all the others that had forced them to move aside that morning, was racing *away* from Washington.

Sam repeated the verses, this time loudly enough for John to understand them:

> *"In thronging crowds they issue to the plains,*
> *No man nor woman in the walls remains:*

In ev'ry face the self-same grief is shown,
And Troy sends forth one universal groan."

"You think it's true, then?" Ross asked.

Sam shrugged. "The danger must be exaggerated. I don't ac
tually think the British plan to gut and roast American babies fo
breakfast, after raping all their mothers. But, yes, the gist of i
seems to be true. The British have landed, and are advancing on
Washington. Worse, from what I can tell, nobody seems to think
the U.S. forces stationed there are going to stop them."

Another carriage appeared—no, two—coming around th
bend ahead, moving far too swiftly to be safe on such a poorly
maintained road. That would have been true even if both car
riages hadn't been overloaded with passengers and baggage.

Sam edged his horse still farther to the side.

The driver of the second carriage shouted at them as he raced
by. *"Flee for your lives! Cockburn is here!"*

Of all the British officers fighting against the United States in
the war, none had as unsavory a reputation as Rear Admira
George Cockburn. Cockburn was the top naval subordinate of
Alexander Cochrane, the vice admiral in overall command of
Britain's operations in North America, and he'd taken persona
charge of the British navy's campaign to destroy American
towns along the shores of Chesapeake Bay. Cockburn was so
feared and hated that one American had reportedly offered a re
ward of $1,000 for his head—and $500 for each of his ears.

Cockburn claimed publicly that his actions were justified
simply a retaliation for American outrages against the private
property of Canadian citizens. And . . .

Sam suspected there was plenty of truth to his claim. If there
was one subject on which Sam Houston had come to be in ful
agreement with Andrew Jackson—not to mention George
Washington, in times past—it was that militias were usually
more trouble than they were worth. Without a commander like
Andrew Jackson breathing fire on them, militias were prone to
run away in battles and spend more time pillaging and commit
ting outrages than anything else. Often enough, against com
pletely innocent parties.

Sam glanced back at the group he was escorting to Washing
ton. The smallness of that group was due, in fact, to the depre
dations of the Georgia militiamen. If it hadn't been for them

he'd probably have been able to convince half-a-dozen Chero-kee chiefs to come along.

Another carriage careened past them, even more heavily loaded. The driver gave no notice to the Indians who sat on horseback by the side of the road. He did, however, glare at Houston and John Ross.

That was probably due to the clothes they were wearing, and the fact that Ross looked like a white man. That morning, for the first time since they began their long journey from northern Georgia, Sam had put aside his traveling clothes and donned his army uniform. John Ross had done the same. Their new uni-forms, in fact, with the captain's epaulet on Houston's right shoulder, and the first lieutenant's epaulet on Ross's left. Jack-son's field promotions wouldn't be official until the War De-partment approved them, but the general had never been one to let clerks tell him what to do. If he said Sam Houston was a cap-tain in the U.S. Army, and John Ross was a first lieutenant, then so it was—and Jackson made sure they had the insignia to prove it before they left.

Sam cleared his throat, but before he could speak, Ross inter-cepted him.

"Yes, I know. We're officers in the U.S. Army, and we have a duty to help defend the capital." He grinned, broadly. "Even me, I suppose. Wonder of wonders."

Ross swiveled in his saddle and regarded the rest of the party. "I don't doubt that the Rogers brothers will accompany us, just for the sake of a good fight. But we'd be better off asking them to escort the children somewhere safe." He gave Sequoyah an apologetic glance. "And they'll need a wiser and more experi-enced head, of course, to keep them out of trouble."

That was diplomatically done, Sam mused, as he'd come to expect from Ross. Sequoyah's club foot left him somewhat touchy on the subject of his courage. No one doubted the bravery of the man, but the fact remained that he was lame and would hinder them if they found themselves forced to move quickly.

Which, alas, was very likely to happen.

Yet another carriage went careening by. From the look of the wheels, Sam suspected it would collapse into a heap of kindling within another five or six miles.

Before they could find out whether or not Sequoyah would object to Ross's suggestion, it all became a moot point.

"*I'm not a child!*" shrilled Tiana.

Almost immediately, the other children joined in. It quickly became obvious that unless Houston and Ross proposed to become a two-man firing squad, they had a full-fledged mutiny on their hands.

And the mutineers were winning.

"All right, then!" Sam finally shouted. "We'll stick together. But I'm *warning* you—I intend to fight the British, and it won't be my fault if you get yourselves shot!"

The Rogers brothers didn't say a thing. They just looked smug. The Ridge and Watie children responded with youthful bravado.

But it was Tiana's reply that worried Sam the most.

I love big fires . . .

Did not bode well. Either as a prediction of the future, or an indicator of the girl's temperament.

CHAPTER 19

Patrick Driscol gazed out of the upper-story window of his boardinghouse in Baltimore, at the crowd swarming in the streets below. The citizens of Baltimore, unlike those of the capital, had responded to the news of the British landing with determination, instead of panic. These crowds weren't loading carriages with their goods in order to flee the city before the enemy arrived. They were loading wagons with provisions and tools, in order to strengthen the fortifications that would keep the Sassenach from entering Baltimore in the first place.

"The difference is always in the quality of command," Driscol stated. "Remember that, lad."

He pointed a stubby finger toward Fort McHenry. "To be sure, having a real fortress helps. But those idiots in the War Department could have done as much for Washington—and still can, if they try. Well enough to hold off this sorry lot of invaders, who are gambling like madmen with this risky attack on Washington. But, sadly for us, and for reasons I cannot begin to imagine, Secretary Armstrong chose to place the capital's defenses under the command of"—he pronounced the name with clear disgust—"Brigadier General William Winder. Who is a complete and unmitigated incompetent ass."

"He was polite enough to you when you reported for duty," McParland pointed out. "Even if he did tell you there was no suitable military housing in Washington, and that you'd have to come up here to Baltimore."

"I didn't say he was an impolite bastard. I said he was an incompetent ass. The fact that a man may be a gentleman does not qualify him to be a commanding general.

"As a colonel, Winder undermined Smyth at Black Rock—no great accomplishment, though, seeing as Smyth was an incompetent ass himself. For that, the powers that be made Winder a brigadier. Then, he and Chandler botched the campaign at Stoney Creek. Even managed to get themselves captured while wandering around in the dark. Whereupon, after Winder was returned in a prisoner exchange, the War Department rewarded him *again,* placing the silly dolt in charge of the capital's defenses."

Driscol surveyed the mob milling below, noting the firm purpose in what easily could have degenerated into chaos.

"On the other hand, I've got to give credit here to the mayor of the town, who rallied its citizens. And to their own trust in Lieutenant Colonel Armistead and his regular troops and sailors manning Fort McHenry. Confidence, lad, that's the key. Even with militiamen and civilian volunteers, you can accomplish wonders so long as you are confident. Baltimore will stand, watch and see if I'm not right. Whereas Washington . . ."

He shook his head gloomily. "Winder is the sort of man who frets every morning over which boot to put on first. He'll dilly and dally and charge back and forth, issuing orders which contradict the orders he gave an hour before—and, all the while, preventing anyone more capable from taking charge."

McParland stared to the south, toward Washington. "Good thing we're here in Baltimore, then."

Driscol started to say something, but he was interrupted by a

knock on the door. He recognized the knock as that of their elderly landlady. Mrs. Young was a timid woman, and she never
presumed to enter the room without knocking at least three
times, each knock more hesitant than the last.

So it was a surprise to see that the door suddenly flew open
before either he or McParland had a chance to move toward it. A
beefy and imposing man came bursting through, almost pushing Mrs. Young aside.

"There you are!" the fellow boomed, half cheerfully and half
accusingly. He placed a large valise on the table by the door.
Judging from the clump it made coming down, the thing was
heavy. "The merry chase you've led me!"

Driscol didn't say anything, peering back and forth between
the man and his valise. That thing looked suspiciously familiar.

His worst fears were confirmed. The voice continued to boom.

"Winfield made me promise him I'd take you under my care!
I daren't do otherwise, you know, now that word's come down
that he'll survive his own wounds! So let's be at it!"

Driscol stared at him in horror. The lofty brow. The blue eyes,
gleaming with certainties. The firm mouth—no hesitations
there—and the chin, which was firmer still.

"Dr., ah, Boulder?" he croaked. "Jeremy Boulder?"

"The very same!" boomed the doctor. Then he saw the dismay so apparent on Driscol's face. "Oh, you needn't worry
about the expense, my good fellow! Winfield assured me that
he'd cover the bill, even if the War Department reneged."

Boulder opened the valise and began rummaging within.
"You're a very fortunate man, you know. I studied under Benjamin Rush himself."

Driscol, always calm in battle, felt light-headed and dizzy.
Benjamin Rush was the most famous doctor in the United
States, a towering figure in American medicine. It was also said
of him that he'd drained more blood than all the generals in
North America.

Sure enough . . .

"We'll start with the leeches, of course. Then put you on a
rigid regimen of daily puking and purging. Plenty of dosages of
calomel, it goes without saying. A wondrous drug! '*The Samp-
son of Materia Medica*,' Dr. Rush calls it."

Driscol didn't doubt it. Like Samson, calomel had slain its
thousands.

Benjamin Rush was nothing if not a theoretical man. One of his many theories, Driscol had been told, was that Negroes were caused by a peculiar form of leprosy. No telling what the great doctor might prescribe as the remedy for *that* condition. Skin the poor black bastards alive, probably, and smear calomel over the bodies. After bleeding them with leeches.

It was time for Driscol to demonstrate his own command qualities, now that he stared certain death in the face. He reached out his remaining hand, seized McParland's arm in a grip of iron, and propelled the youngster toward the door.

"I'm afraid that'll all have to wait, Doctor. Just got our orders. We're commanded—at once—to Washington, to join in the capital's defense. We'll face a firing squad if we dally."

He shouldered the doctor aside as he passed through the door. With his left shoulder, having no choice in the matter, which produced a spike of agony. The stump still hadn't completely healed.

But Driscol ignored the pain resolutely. Wounds, even great ones like the loss of an arm, could be dealt with. Death was absolute.

Boulder boomed protests behind them as Driscol hurried his young companion down the steep and rickety staircase. All water off Driscol's back. Far better to face the Sassenach in all their fury than a *proper doctor*.

At the foot of the stairs, he paused just long enough to retrieve their weapons from the closet where Mrs. Young had insisted they be kept. Then he located their landlady and paid her the rent due.

"Will you be back?" she asked in a quavering voice. She glanced nervously toward the stairs. The door at the top shut with a bang.

"May as well rent out the room to someone else," Driscoll gruffed. He could see the doctor's thick legs coming down the staircase. Each step, naturally, boomed. "Who knows when we'll be back, if at all?"

He hustled McParland through the front door before the doctor could make his way down. "The vagaries of a soldier's life, I'm afraid! S'been a pleasure staying in your house, Mrs. Young."

"You sure, Sergeant?" McParland asked, once they reached the safety of the street, and put some distance between themselves and the doctor. "Uh, Lieutenant, I mean. I guess."

Technically, the promotion still hadn't gone through. Neither had the pay increase. The wheels of the War Department turned very slowly.

"Am I sure?" Driscol snorted. "You must be joking. If I'm to be bled any further, thank you, I'll have it be done by bullets and bayonets. I'll have a much better chance of surviving."

Driscol continued to exercise his talent for decisive command by sequestering a wagon, three blocks away. This wagon, unlike most of the ones that were crowding the streets of Baltimore, wasn't heading toward the fortifications, laden with tools. Instead it was heading inward, toward the city center, loaded with foodstuffs.

Best of all, the driver was a black man. Driscol didn't have much experience with the Negroes of America, but he was reasonably certain that it would be easier to browbeat this fellow than it would a white man.

"And we'll need you to drive it, too," he finished. He lifted the stump of his arm. "Afraid my wagon-driving days are over, and . . ."

He left off the rest. There was no point in publicly humiliating McParland. His family was too poor to afford a wagon, so McParland had no experience driving one. The same had been true of Driscol's family, but he'd learned to drive a wagon as he had learned most everything except his personal beliefs and blacksmithing, during his years in Napoleon's service.

The lieutenant's tone addressing the Negro was firm but pleasant enough, as if he was unaware of the pistol and sword belted to his waist or the musket that McParland wasn't *quite* pointing up at the black man.

The wagon driver was relatively young, not more than thirty, and very powerfully built. At the moment, however, despite his Herculean physique, he bore a close resemblance to a rabbit paralyzed by the sight of a snake. The only thing that seemed firm about him was his grip on the reins.

"I'm a freedman, sir," he protested. "Was born free, too."

"All the better!" Driscol stated forcefully. "You won't need an explanation to keep your master from whipping you, after he finds out that you've gone."

Despite the assuredness of his words, however, Driscol was

taken aback. He *had* assumed that the man was a slave. His clothing was shabby, but the wagon he was guiding was well built, and obviously well maintained. From the look of the thing, Driscol had thought it belonged to a prosperous farmer. The sort of vehicle that could serve to haul produce on week-days, and the farmer and his family to church on Sunday.

The black man's dark eyes flicked back and forth from Driscol to the wagon. The *lovingly* maintained wagon, Driscol now realized.

The soldier from County Antrim felt a sinking feeling in the pit of his stomach. He was no stranger to poverty himself, and he knew how thin the shield could be that kept destitution at bay. He'd intended to write the mán a note, providing him with an official excuse to deflect the wrath of his master. Now that he understood the driver was a freedman . . .

He sighed and reached for his purse. With only one hand, the task was a bit awkward. But recent experience had taught him how to manage it, well enough.

"It's all I own, sir," pleaded the Negro. "Took me eight years working in the foundry to save up enough to buy it. Spend most every half cent I can raise to keep it up proper."

The purse now open, Driscol sighed again and dug deeply into it. That wasn't hard to do, alas.

At least the few coins he came up with were good Spanish currency. Unfortunately, most of those were rcales, what New Englanders called ninepence and Pennsylvanians called eleven-pence, but most Americans usually referred to simply as a "bit." A *reale* was worth approximately one-eighth of a dollar. "Two bits" was the standard slang for a quarter dollar, since, in normal exchange, Spanish coinage was a lot more common than Amer-ican.

Still, as modest as it was, a *reale* was real money, and nobody doubted it. So were the two American half-eagles nestled among them. Those were genuine gold, not paper issued from a state or wildcat bank somewhere.

The driver was still looking forlorn, although the sheer des-peration that had been on his face earlier was gone. Driscol ex-amined the wagon for a moment, estimating its worth, and then sighed again.

"Look, my man," he said, "the chances are that you'll earn

more money selling your produce in Washington than you will here—*and* you'll probably pick up a princely payment from people desperate to be taken out of the capital."

"And if I don't? What if the Sassenach burn my wagon, too?"

Driscol was startled, hearing that term issue so unexpectedly from the lips of a black man. He'd thought most Negroes in America were rather partial to the British, since one of the favored British tactics in the war was to free slaves and try to use them against their former masters. So, at least, claimed the shrill accounts in the newspapers.

The startled look he shot the Negro brought, for the first time, something other than fear and anxiety to the black man's face. Amusement, or something close.

"They're mostly Irishmen in Foxall's Foundry, sir," the driver said quietly. "I got along well with some of them."

The emphasis was on the word *some*. Driscol wasn't surprised. Plenty of his countrymen—even former United Irishmen—had begun acting like Sassenach themselves, once they arrived in America. They did so, not because they were any richer than they'd been in Ireland, but simply because they now had Negroes they could lord it over. It was a side of human nature that Driscol had seen many times. Give some men, be they never so wretched, a different breed of men they can sneer at and feel superior to, and they will often enough become the willing lickspittle of the rich and mighty.

The fact that Driscol understood the phenomenon did not make him despise it any the less. The Sassenach had left his father dying on an iron tripod, but that Scots-Irish blacksmith's ideals had not soaked into the ground along with his blood. Not so long as his son was still alive, anyway.

"Some colored folk can believe the promises of Englishmen," the driver continued, "but not me. I can read, sir. Not too well, but well enough to figure out that slaves 'freed' by Sassenach are just cannon fodder for 'em."

"And isn't that the truth?" Driscol growled. "Stupid bastards. Just as stupid as all the Irishmen and Scotsmen who choose to wear English colors."

For the first time, he studied the black driver as he might study any man. And found himself feeling slightly ashamed that it was the first time he'd done so, since he'd arrived in the New World.

"Not so 'new' after all, I guess," he chided himself under his breath. "Da would whup me good."

"I didn't catch that, sir."

"Never mind," Driscol muttered. He reached into the special pocket of the purse and drew out his prize. Four years, now, he'd hoarded the thing. A genuine Portuguese joe, a gold coin worth about eight dollars.

"Look here. You get us to Washington, and if anything happens to the wagon, I'll give you this. I know it won't replace the wagon, but it'll go a ways toward it. And . . . well, it's all I have.

"But one way or the other, I *am* going to Washington."

By the time they'd reached Baltimore's limits, the driver seemed to have relaxed. Enough to have exchanged names with Driscol—his own name was Henry Crowell—and even swap a jest.

"Never seen a man so eager to head toward trouble. You must be running away from a woman, Lieutenant."

"Worse!" barked Driscol. "I'm running away from a doctor. Did you know you have leprosy, by the way?"

Crowell's eyes widened. He glanced at Driscol, who was sitting right beside him on the driver's bench, and making no apparent effort to keep his distance. "If that's so, Lieutenant, you must be crazy."

"It's a special kind of leprosy," Driscol countered. "Only Negroes have it. That's why you're black. Not contagious to white people, not even Irishmen."

Crowell looked down at his dark hands, holding the reins in a sure and powerful grip. "Do tell. Where did you learn that, Lieutenant?"

"From the same doctor I'm running from."

"Oh." Crowell clucked and flipped the reins. The carriage sped up just that little bit.

The closer they got to the capital, the more they were slowed on their journey by refugee-laden carriages coming up the road. Fortunately, Crowell's wagon was a lot more substantial than most of the fancy carriages headed away from Washington, so the evacuees more often made way for him, rather than the other way around. As was generally the case, in Driscol's experience, only people of means could afford to flee a city that was coming under attack—and people like that typically owned carriages designed for elegance rather than endurance. Pound for pound and horse for horse, they were simply no match for Crowell's vehicle.

Had Crowell been alone, of course, he wouldn't have dared to bully his way through such a flood of gentility. But Driscol didn't hesitate to use his uniform to indicate his authority—or, for that matter, the threat of McParland's musket, on the one occasion when an offended party made a vehement protest.

Halfway to Washington, they even picked up an escort. Several dozen armed and mounted men were milling around outside a roadway tavern, appearing more confused than inebriated.

Driscol recognized the look of leaderless soldiers. Militiamen of some sort, going by the flamboyant nature of their uniforms. Cavalrymen, presumably, given that some of the men were on horseback, and most of the others had their horses by the reins.

"And who're you?" he barked, as soon as the wagon reached them. He stood up, giving them a full view of his uniform and sword, and the lieutenant's epaulet that sat on his shoulder. If the sight of his left sleeve, tied up just a few inches below the epaulet, detracted from the impression, he could see no sign of it.

"*Answer me,* blast you!" he bellowed.

One of the mounted men—they were all youngsters, most of them still teenagers—gave him a salute that was so awkwardly exaggerated that Driscol almost burst into laughter.

"I'm Corporal John Pendleton, sir. We're part of the United Volunteers. From Baltimore. Uh, we're supposed to be attached to General Tobias Stansbury's Fifth Regiment, but . . . uh, well."

Plaintively, another one of the would-be soldiers piped up: "Do you know where we might *find* the Fifth Regiment, sir? We haven't seen hide nor hair of General Stansbury."

Driscol snorted. "Threatening to level cannon fire against newspapermen, I should imagine."

He made no effort to disguise the contempt in his voice. General Stansbury's principal claim to fame in the war had been his refusal to protect the antiwar Baltimore newspaper, the *Federal Republican and Commercial Intelligencer,* when it came under attack at the outset of the conflict, from a prowar mob. When asked for his assistance by the sheriff, Stansbury had proclaimed that the newspaper deserved to be blown up, and that he was rather inclined to level it with his cannons than protect it.

The fact that, politically speaking, Driscol shared the general's attitude toward the Federalist newspaper in question was beside the point. He had no more liking for lynch mobs than he did for Sassenach.

"Ah, yes, Stansbury," Driscol sneered. "I can well imagine you're having difficulty finding the fine general, what with an actual armed enemy to face."

That bordered on gross insubordination, but he didn't really care. If there was any advantage to losing an arm, it was that it tended to put everything else into a certain perspective.

Still, there was no point in letting the youngsters stew on his words. Best to put them to good use.

"Since you're unattached, I'm assigning you to my unit. I'm on my way to special duty in Washington." That sounded better than *on medical leave, fleeing a doctor,* he thought. "As of this moment, you are attached to General Winfield Scott's First Brigade."

The eyes of all the young cavalrymen went wide. They were more like half-baked dragoons, really; at least two of them were having trouble with their horses. But it didn't matter. As Driscol had known it would, the name *General Winfield Scott* served as a talisman. Scott was a *genuine* war hero. Unlike such wretches as Stansbury, the brigadier had won a real battle against British regulars.

He pointed behind the wagon. "Most of you, take up positions in the rear. You, Pendleton, and you"—he pointed to the other youngster who had spoken up—"ride ahead of us."

From then on, they made excellent progress. Not even the most desperate or arrogant refugee would argue passage with a cavalry troop, small though it might be. Certainly not one that rode as confidently as one of *General Scott's* units, half-baked teenage dragoons or not.

They stopped only once, at Driscol's insistence. The young cavalrymen were all for pressing onward, but Driscol had too much experience to make that mistake.

"Never go into a battle on an empty stomach, lads. We can spare the few minutes for a late breakfast."

Fortunately, there were some smoked hams in the wagon.

Fortunately also, most of the youngsters came from well-to-do families living in Baltimore, and could afford to pay Crowell for them. For those few who couldn't, Driscol borrowed a pen and some notepaper from Pendleton—it seemed the boy was a budding Caesar, who had hopes of recording his exploits for posterity—and solemnly scribbled out "official War Department obligations." He gave them to Crowell to redeem . . .

Well, whenever and however. In truth, the notes were probably about as good as Driscol's well-nigh illegible handwriting.

"I'm sorry, Henry," he said softly, "but it's the best I can do. I just won't lead men, much less boys, into a fight when they're getting weak from hunger."

"Never you mind, Lieutenant," murmured Crowell, just as solemnly tucking the notes away in his waistband. "I'll make out fine. As much as you overcharged the rest of them."

Washington was a ghost town.

Almost all shops and offices were locked and shuttered by the time they arrived, in the sultry heat of midafternoon. The city's residents were either in flight or hiding in their homes. Before long, they found streets that were full enough, to be sure—but with soldiers, mostly militiamen, in full and furious retreat. Rout, it would be better to say.

By putting together accounts blurted out by fleeing soldiers, Driscol learned that a battle had already been fought. Just outside the capital, it seemed, at the town of Bladensburg.

General Winder had led the American forces, and it sounded as if it had been more farce than anything else. Commodore Barney's regular naval artillerymen and Captain Miller's marines had given a very good account of themselves, by the reports. But when the militiamen who were supposed to be guarding their flank ran away after firing not more than two ragged volleys, the artillerymen and marines had been overwhelmed.

For the rest, the less said the better. With uncertain and incompetent officers like Winder leading them, militia forces were about as reliable as rotten wood. At least Beale's men had put up a bit of a fight before deserting the artillery and marines. The Second and Thirty-sixth Regiments of militia hadn't even managed that much. The British had unleashed their newfangled and much-feared Congreve rockets, and as soon as they started hissing down like aerial serpents, those regiments had broken and run. Never fired a shot, apparently.

And General Stansbury? Oh, he'd made a splendid showing, in the beginning—riding up and down the lines loudly proclaiming that he'd have any man who ran away sabered by his officers. Fat lot of good that piece of loudmouthery had done him. When the Congreve rockets started flying, the officers had raced off the field just as fast as the men.

Driscol was tempted to rub salt in the wounds, but the abashed looks on the faces of his newly acquired dragoons were good enough. General Stansbury was a joke, and there was no pride to be found in being considered part of his regiment.

Leave it at that. By now it was obvious to Driscol's experienced eye that the young dragoons had shifted their tacit allegiance over to him. And why not? Their uniforms were too idiosyncratic to register any specific unit identity, and they were volunteers anyway. That being the case, far better to be associated with the name of the hero of Chippewa and his now-legendary First Brigade. Who was to say otherwise? No one, besides Driscol or McParland—and Driscol had no intention of doing so, and McParland would lead where he followed.

Leading them where, though?

Once they reached Pennsylvania Avenue, Driscol could no longer evade the question. Even if his little troop had been composed of grizzled veterans from the emperor's Imperial Guard, they'd be no match for an army of British regulars.

He didn't dare hesitate for long, either. Soldiers like the ones who followed him needed a confident commander even more than veteran regulars. Whether he made the right decision or not wasn't as important as that he made *some* decision.

In the end, he was the only one who appreciated the irony. He gave a firm order—

"To the president's house!"

—knowing full well he was just dodging the responsibility. Postponing it, at least. The brick building that housed the War Department stood right next to the president's mansion. Who was to say? Maybe Driscol would find someone in authority there, who would be able to take charge.

Besides, he told himself as his little troop began trotting

down Pennsylvania Avenue, if nothing else, the sight of the mansion would bolster his soldiers' morale. The official residence of the nation's chief executive was one of the very few things about Washington, D.C., that was genuinely impressive.

Even if, he'd been told, the roof still leaked.

CHAPTER 20

As Driscol and his party made their way up Pennsylvania Avenue, soldiers from various fragments of the army that had been routed at Bladensburg fell in alongside them. Judging from their loud complaints, it was obvious that all of them were disgruntled, and many were downright angry at the situation. These men hadn't been beaten, really. They'd been routed due to confusion and inexperience, or because they'd been given orders to retreat. Much against their will, in many cases.

"That blasted Winder's a traitor, I'm telling you!" shouted one young sailor. He and a dozen of his mates were from the artillery battery under the command of Commodore Barney. That was, by all accounts and not just their own, one of the few units which had fought well at Bladensburg. They hadn't retreated until the militiamen guarding their flank had broken, and Barney himself had been badly wounded.

"The only reason we're heading to Georgetown is because those are Winder's orders!" another sailor protested. "The hull army's supposed to gather and reorganize there. And don't that just cap the climax!"

Angrily, the naval artilleryman pointed down Pennsylvania Avenue. "Why in Sam Hill aren't we planning to defend the Capitol? A gang of Baltimore plug-uglies could hold the place!"

Looking back down the avenue in the direction the sailor was pointing, Driscol decided he was right. Pennsylvania Avenue was littered with soldiers and sailors plodding sullenly toward

Georgetown. There was a good-sized military force there, if it could be organized and given firm leadership.

The more so, because the nation's Capitol building could easily be transformed into something of a fortress. The twin buildings stood atop Jenkins Hill—what people were now starting to call Capitol Hill—so they occupied the high ground in the area. And the two wings were solidly built, with thick brick walls clad in sandstone, even if they were only linked by a covered wooden walkway. The central dome that was intended to connect the two houses of the nation's legislature hadn't yet been erected.

All the better, Driscol thought to himself. The British would be approaching from the east, and artillery could be emplaced between the two buildings. Riflemen firing from the windows could protect the artillerymen while they did the real slaughtering of the Sassenach as they were struggling their way up the hill.

He could see it all in his mind, quite vividly. The enemy could eventually seize the impromptu fortress, but that would take time and require heavy casualties, neither of which the British could afford. This raid of theirs, Driscol was well-nigh certain, was a risky gamble on their part. There was no possibility that the British forces could hope to hold the area for more than a few days. Washington was just too close to the centers of the U.S. population. Their real target was New Orleans and the mouth of the Mississippi. *That,* they could hold, if they took it.

This was simply a diversion, he thought, to keep Americans confused and befuddled while the enemy organized their main strike in the Gulf of Mexico. But, that being so, Admiral Cochrane couldn't afford to suffer many casualties here. He'd need those soldiers later. And if Cochrane allowed his little army to spend too much time in Washington, the risk would grow by the hour that they might be cut off and captured by American forces coming to the capital city from the surrounding area.

Driscol suspected that this entire operation was really Rear Admiral Cockburn's pet project, which he'd foisted on a somewhat reluctant Cochrane. Cockburn seemed to take a special glee in burning American property. He was said to be much offended by the way he'd been portayed in American newspapers, none more so than Washington's *National Intelligencer*.

Driscol looked down at the aggrieved sailor and his companions. They could be a start, coupled with his few dozen young dragoons . . .

Then, mentally, he shook his head. He was a practical and hardheaded man, and he knew full well that he was not the officer to rally broken and confused troops like these. His new rank notwithstanding, Driscol was a sergeant by training and by temperament. If someone else rallied some troops, then—oh, certainly—he would know what to do with them. He'd keep them firm, if nothing else. But the rallying itself had to be done by a different sort of officer.

It didn't even have to be a commander like Winfield Scott, for that matter. Military skill, knowledge, and experience wasn't really needed here. Someone like General Jacob Brown would do splendidly. Brown was almost as tall as Scott, possibly even more handsome and imposing looking, and every bit as decisive. And he could speechify well, too.

Decisiveness aside, Driscol was none of those things. He knew perfectly well how he appeared to the sailors who were staring up at him. Squat, troll ugly, weathered, and battered by life—and now missing an arm, to boot. A figure to bolster men, not to inspire them. The fact that he'd appeared before them on a wagon driven by a Negro instead of riding a horse didn't help any, of course.

Then again, maybe inspiration could be found up ahead. The president's mansion was only a short distance away.

"Fall in with us," Driscol commanded, pointing to the impressive-looking edifice. "Let's see if there's someone in command there who isn't a fool and a poltroon."

"He's a traitor, I tell you!" the sailor insisted. But he and his mates seemed to be relieved to find someone willing to take charge.

As the sailors started to take their positions, Driscol leaned over and bestowed a smile upon them.

"A lesson here, lads, which I've spent a lifetime learning. Never explain something on the grounds of wickedness, when simple stupidity will do the trick."

The sailors looked dubious. Driscol nodded his head firmly. "Oh, yes, it's quite true. Brigadier Scott even told me an ancient philosopher had proved it. Fellow by the name of Ockham."

He straightened up in the wagon seat. "The English, of course, being the exception that proves the rule."

"You know Brigadier Scott?" asked one of the sailors. For the first time, the expression on his face and that of his mates as they looked up at Driscol was not *and who is this ragamuffin?*

Before Driscol could answer, McParland piped up. The young private was sitting atop the foodstuffs stacked in the wagon bed.

"Sure does! He was the brigadier's master sergeant. Got a field promotion to lieutenant after he lost his arm at the Chippewa." Pride filled the youngster's voice. "He was in my regiment, the Twenty-second. I was right there when he got wounded. Sergeant Driscol never even flinched. Just had me bind up the wound while he kept shouting the firing orders."

Now they were genuinely impressed. That still wasn't the same thing as inspiration. But it was a start.

As his ragtag little army continued toward the president's house, Driscol turned his head, to give McParland a meaningful look. He'd learned by now that the seventeen-year-old boy was quick-witted, despite his rural ignorance. McParland took the hint, and slid off the wagon. He'd walk alongside the sailors the rest of the way, regaling them with tales of exploits.

Mostly his own, of course.

"Whatever you do . . ." McParland's voice drifted forward. The boy still hadn't learned that a "whisper" addressed to a dozen people carried almost as far as a shout. ". . . don't *ever* cross the sergeant. Uh, lieutenant, I mean." A few words faded off; then: ". . . not sure he's really human. A lot of the fellows thought he was one of those trolls you hear about in . . ."

It was all Driscol could do to maintain a solemn face.

". . . made the mistake of arguing with him over an order when I first showed up in the regiment. Next thing I knew he had me in front of a firing squad."

Driscol didn't need to turn around. He could practically see the wide eyes of the young sailors.

"—'strue! The muskets was loaded with blanks, o' course, or I wouldn't be here today to tell the tale. But I almost pissed my pants—and let me tell you, I never argued with the sergeant again.

"*Nobody* does, what knows him. He tells you to jump into a lake, all you ask is 'how far'."

A good start, indeed.

*   *   *

"I *will* have those twelve-pounders, sir!" Sam Houston insisted, rising in the saddle. "What's the gol-derned use of hauling the things all the way to Georgetown?"

After clambering aboard his own horse, William Simmons glared at him.

"None, Captain, for all I know! But General Winder has given explicit orders for all troops to abandon the capital and rally at Georgetown. Unless you intend to be insubordinate, you must follow his orders. And so must I—and I will *not* have these guns fall into the hands of the enemy!"

Sam studied the man for a moment. Simmons was an accountant for the War Department, for whom the entire day had been hours of sheer chaos. The intense heat of an August day in Washington didn't help matters. There were clouds gathering in the sky, but the humidity was as intense as ever. By now, in the middle of the afternoon, the man was a festering bundle of weariness, anger, uncertainty, and confusion.

Unfortunately, although he was a civilian, Simmons's position gave him something in the way of authority here, for the mob of militiamen who'd gathered around the president's house. The fact that Simmons had taken it upon himself to order the mansion's sole remaining servant to bring out the presidential brandy and serve it as refreshments for the soldiers had sealed the matter.

So.

There was no point in pulling out lofty citations from the *Iliad* in this situation. That left wheedling and conniving. Sam was good at both of those, too, if his mother's opinion was anything to go by.

Sam gave the accountant his most winning smile, then pointed to the carriage of the nearest twelve-pounder, perched beside the front gate of the president's house. "I ask you to consider something, sir. These are ornamental guns, you know. Look at the carriages. Purely decorative! Those wheels will break long before you could reach the heights of Georgetown."

Simmons stared at the two cannons. Sam's statements were . . .

Preposterous. The field guns were perfectly serviceable, and their carriages in splendid condition.

Before he could say anything, however, Sam hurried on, now

speaking quietly. "It's an explanation, after all, should General Winder ever inquire about the matter."

For a moment, Sam thought Simmons's angry expression was aimed at him.

"That's hardly likely!" the accountant snapped. Then, sourly: "I was dismissed from the War Department just last month, you know—after twenty years of service." His expression turned more sullen than ever. "'Twas due to a clash between myself and Secretary of War Armstrong, concerning proper accounting procedures. All the sense in the world is wasted on men like him and Winder."

For a moment, Sam considered using Simmons's newly admitted lack of authority against him. But that wouldn't do much good with the militiamen who surrounded them. In Sam's experience, men were prone to support any fine fellow who handed out free liquor.

Again, Odysseus was called for, not Achilles.

"It was certainly unfortunate that Secretary Armstrong chose to place General Winder in command of the city's defenses. What could he have been thinking?"

"What, indeed!" Simmons barked. He gazed for a moment longer on the twelve-pounders, before his eyes came back to Sam.

"And just what do *you* propose to do with them, my fine young captain? Two twelve-pounders will hardly hold off the enemy."

Truth to tell, Sam didn't really have a good answer to that question. All he knew was that the moment he caught sight of those two splendid guns, when he and his companions arrived at the president's house, he was bound and determined to do *something* with them.

But this was no time for public uncertainty. "General Jackson had but a six- and a three-pounder at the Horseshoe Bend, you know. I was there, and I can tell you they gave excellent service."

That was a black lie. The things had been completely useless, and Sam had the scar on his leg to prove it. Nevertheless, he pressed on with assurance and good cheer. "These will do well enough, Mr. Simmons."

"And how do you even propose to use them? You told me you

were an infantry officer, not an artilleryman. You're facing
British regulars here, Captain, not wild savages."

Mention of "wild savages" drew the accountant's skeptical
eyes to Sam's small group of companions.

Fortunately, Sequoyah and the Ridge children had donned
American clothing that morning. *Unfortunately,* the Rogers
brothers had done no such thing. James hadn't even bothered to
tuck away his beloved war club.

Tiana Rogers was a mixed blessing. On the one hand, she too
had outfitted herself in American apparel for the occasion. On
the other hand, the big girl was far too imposing and good-
looking, in her exotic way, not to draw attention to herself.

Skepticism was growing rapidly in the accountant's expression. Sam drew himself up haughtily.

"A delegation from the Cherokee Nation, sent here expressly
by General Jackson. Even includes two of their princesses."

Nancy Ridge looked suitably solemn and demure.

Tiana, alas, grinned like a hoyden.

Best to distract the accountant, Sam thought hurriedly. He
pointed a finger at John Ross, whose appearance and uniform
made him look like a white man. "Lieutenant Ross here is a wizard with artillery, sir. Very experienced with the big guns."

John's eyes widened. Sam ignored him and pressed forward.

"Oh, yes," he said, chuckling. "General Jackson gave him no
choice in the matter, seeing as how the lieutenant can't hit the
broad side of a barn with a pistol or a musket. But give him a
proper-size gun—!"

Wide as saucers.

Forward, ever forward.

"Indeed so. Ross is *murderous* with the big guns. He'll wreak
havoc upon the enemy, Mr. Simmons, be sure of it! Grapeshot
is his preferred ball, of course."

Then, Sam decided it was time to add a modicum of truth to
the matter. Just a pinch.

"Look, Mr. Simmons," he said softly, almost conspiratorially.
"I don't honestly know if the lieutenant can make good his
bloodthirsty boasts. Achilles himself would be daunted by the
task. But if nothing else, he and I are determined not to let the
British come into the city. Certainly not without at least firing
some shots. *We need those guns, sir.*"

By now, a large crowd of soldiers had gathered around the

two men on horseback. While they'd been arguing, a new batch of men had come up and pushed their way to the front of the mob. These looked to be under some sort of discipline, at least, even if the lieutenant in command had only one arm and was riding on a wagon instead of a horse.

On the positive side, the newly arrived officer was glaring at Simmons, not Sam. Quite a ferocious glare it was, too. The one-armed lieutenant's face looked as if it belonged to Grendel's brother, or one of the monsters in the Grimm brothers' fairy tales.

Simmons spotted the same ogre's glare. He threw up his hands.

"Oh, do as you will, then! The cannons are yours, Captain Houston, if you'd be such a fool."

And with that, he rode off.

Driscol arrived in time to hear most of the exchange. He didn't think he'd ever heard such a magnificent pile of lies, exaggerations, and pure hornswaggling in his entire life.

Whoever this big young captain was, he *had* to be a Scots-Irishman. Nobody else would be mad enough to entertain the idea of stopping the British with just two cannons and a small band of Indians.

He was a joy to behold.

The captain's blue eyes turned on him now, along with a grin as cheerful and confident as anything Driscol could have hoped for.

Oh, aye, he'll do splendidly. And who knows, he might even survive. Stranger things have happened.

Driscol returned the grin with a thin smile of his own.

"I dare say yon 'artilleryman' Lieutenant Ross wouldn't know one end of a cannon from the other. Judging from his expression. But as it happens, sir . . ."

Driscol swiveled in the seat. "Naval gunners, front and forward!" he barked.

The sailors trotted up as smartly as you please. The lieutenant turned back to the captain.

"Commodore Barney's men, these are, sir. They'll know how to handle the guns, once they're positioned at the Capitol."

There wasn't so much as a flicker in the young captain's expression, even though he had a subordinate officer tacitly telling him what to do. Then, just a second later, the grin grew wider still. The captain edged his horse alongside the wagon.

He leaned over, speaking quietly enough that only Driscol and Henry Crowell could hear him.

"I've got no idea what I'm doing, Lieutenant, save that I *will* fight the British bastards." The captain gave the black driver a cool, considering look, as if gauging his ability to keep from gossiping. "So I'll be delighted to hear any suggestions you might have."

The look impressed Driscol in a way that the ready grin, the handsome face, and the confident shoulders hadn't. The soldier from County Antrim had known plenty of young and self-assured officers, some of whom had made excellent leaders on a battlefield. Few of them, on the other hand, had been clear-eyed enough to understand that a menial was still a man, even a black one, and couldn't be dismissed with no more thought than you'd give the livestock.

Driscol, in turn, glanced at the captain's Indian companions. There was a tale there, too, he was certain.

He started to look away from the group, but a flash of teeth drew his eyes back.

Lord in Heaven.

Driscol hadn't paid any attention at the time to the big girl whom the captain had claimed to be an Indian princess of some sort. His focus had been entirely on the captain's argument with the officious clerk, and he'd dismissed the statement as just another of the captain's Niagara Falls of balderdash and bunkum. Now . . .

The "princess" was exchanging a jest with a young Indian warrior who looked to be some sort of relation. That big smile, on *that* face—perched as it was atop a supple body whose graceful form couldn't possibly be disguised, even in a modest settler's dress—

It took a real effort for Driscol to tear his eyes away. This was no time for such thoughts. It was hardly as if that smile had been aimed at him, in any event.

"I know what I'm doing, yes, sir," he growled, more gruffly than he'd really intended. "I served under Generals Brown and Scott in the Niagara campaign, and before that for some years with Napoleon. I was at Jena and Austerlitz both, and more other battles than I care to remember."

The captain's grin shallowed into a simple smile. "Oh, splendid. I'll give the speeches and wave my sword about, then, while you whisper sage advice into my ear."

"My thoughts exactly, sir. You lead the men, and I'll keep them steady."

The captain examined Driscol carefully. By the time he was done, there was but a trace of the smile left. "Steady. I imagine you're good at that."

"None better, sir. If I say so myself."

The captain nodded. "I'm Sam Houston, from Tennessee. You?"

"Patrick Driscol. From Country Antrim originally. That's in northern—"

Houston clucked. "Please, Patrick! Do I look like an Englishman? My own sainted forefather, the good gentleman John Houston, arrived in this country from Belfast almost a century ago. Hauling with him a keg full of sovereigns he claimed to have earned honestly, mind you. Though I have my doubts, just as I suspect my ancestors weren't really Scot baronets who served as archers for Jeanne d'Arc when she marched from Orleans to Reims. We Scots-Irish tell a lot of tall tales, you know?"

An impulse Driscol couldn't control took over his mouth. "Oh, aye. Tales of Indian princesses and such."

Houston glanced back at the girl in question. "That tale's taller than it should be, I suppose, but it's not invented from whole cloth. Tiana really does come from a chiefly family."

When his eyes came back, Driscol was surprised to see the shrewdness there. He hadn't suspected that, in such a man.

"I'll introduce you later," Houston said. "Mind you, I'd still like to get the children off to a place of safety, but . . . They're all from chiefly families, and headstrong as you could ask for. Tiana most of all. So I doubt me I'll be able to shake them loose."

Tiana.

Driscol shook his head, trying to concentrate on the task at hand.

For the first time, it dawned on him that he might have gotten more than he bargained for when he seized upon this brash young captain as his chosen champion. Champions always had a will of their own, of course. So much was a given. But could he possibly possess *subtlety* as well?

A little shudder twitched his shoulders. A big hand clapped down on the nearest, blithely ignoring the arm that was missing below. "And now, Lieutenant. The Capitol, you say?"

Houston looked at the president's mansion. "I'd thought to make a stand here, myself."

Driscol started to explain the superior merits of the Capitol as a make-do fortress, but Houston cut him off.

"I'll take your word for it. It doesn't really matter, now that I think about it. If I survive this mad adventure, I'll eventually have to report to General Jackson. And if I had to tell Old Hickory that I chose to defend the nation's executive house instead of the legislature . . ."

The captain's own shoulders twitched.

"He'd curse me for a Federalist, see if he wouldn't."

CHAPTER 21

Sam had acted impetuously, because his military apprenticeship under Andrew Jackson had made some of the General's attitudes rub off. Right at the top of the list was Old Hickory's intransigence in the face of an enemy. Now, though, Sam had to make good on his boasts. He was all of twenty-one years old, and the captain's epaulet on his right shoulder wasn't even official yet.

His first step was clear enough. In point of fact, the carriages of the two twelve-pounders *were* in splendid condition, and the guns could quite easily be hauled the one mile distance to the Capitol simply by having militiamen and Barney's sailors haul them by hand.

But then what?

To make things worse, now that the impulse of the moment had passed, Sam was beginning to fret over the situation with the children. Major Ridge and John Jolly had *not* sent their children to Washington in order for Sam to lead them into the middle of a pitched battle.

But what was he to do with them? There was no chance of finding a proper family in Washington who would take in the children. Certainly not at the moment. Half of the city's proper families had already fled, and the rest were huddling fearfully in their homes. That would have been true even if the children in question had been white, much less Cherokee.

And even if he *could* find someone, the chances were slim to none that he could get the children themselves to agree.

Nancy Ridge . . . maybe. But her brother John and her cousin Buck were at a fever pitch of excitement, the way only twelve-year-old boys can be. Whatever Sam's qualms, *they* were looking forward eagerly to the prospect of a battle. The tales they'd be able to tell when they got back! The status they'd achieve!

The Cherokee weren't a "warrior tribe" in the same sense that some of the tribes on the plains were, or the fierce Chickasaws. But they bore precious little resemblance to Quakers either.

And Tiana!

Sam glanced at her, riding her horse not far away. The sixteen-year-old girl might be wearing modest American lady's attire, but the easy and athletic way she sat the horse would have made her Indian origins clear to anyone, even without the coppery skin tone. Not to mention the way she'd hoisted the dress above her knees, to leave her legs clear!

Her eyes were literally gleaming. If Sam tried to place her out of harm's way she'd be likely to stab him. Nor did Sam doubt that she had a knife hidden somewhere in her pack. Possibly even a pistol.

Fortunately, Sam's newfound adviser stepped into the breach.

"I don't see much chance of getting your wards anywhere to safety at the moment, sir," Driscol said quietly. "But the Capitol's quite the huge place, you know, and very solidly constructed. I'm sure we can find somewhere sheltered enough for them. They should be safe, unless the enemy breaches the walls."

Uncertainly, Sam eyed the great buildings they were marching toward. It was late in the afternoon by now, and the sun was beginning to dip toward the west. The golden rays reflecting off the Capitol made the twin edifices seem even more imposing than usual.

"What if the British *do* breach the walls?"

Driscol shrugged. "That's as may be, sir. But I don't think you've much choice. And—ah . . ." He cleared his throat.

Sam smiled. "Yes, Lieutenant Driscol, I know. I should be focusing my attention on planning the defense, not worrying about what might happen should my plans fail. Still, I do have a personal responsibility here."

He came to a decision. After all these weeks of travel, he'd come to know Sequoyah pretty well. The lamed Cherokee might be prickly about his condition, but underneath he was quite a levelheaded fellow. So long as his honor was respected, he was willing enough to be practical.

"A moment, please, Lieutenant." Sam turned his horse and trotted over to the Cherokee.

He returned with a sense of relief. "He's agreed to take charge of them once we get there," he told Driscol. "We'll need people to reload anyway, he reminded me, and take care of the wounded."

Driscol studied the children dubiously, for a moment. "But will *they* agree?"

Sam smiled ruefully. "Tiana, who knows? Especially once the battle starts. But the others will. Have you much experience with Cherokees, Lieutenant?"

"None at all, sir. Precious little with any of the tribes, even the Iroquois."

Sam nodded. "Well, don't believe most of what you hear. The children will be rambunctious, but they'll listen to Sequoyah. And now, Lieutenant, what's next?"

"We should place the cannons between the buildings, sir. That'll give them a clear line of fire at the approaching enemy, with excellent protection on their flanks. With this many men at our disposal we'll be able to erect solid breastworks for the guns, too."

Sam looked around at the little army that they'd assembled.

Not so little, actually, not any longer. Most of the militiamen who'd been gathered at the president's house had chosen to join them. Not more than a couple of dozen had followed the accountant Simmons toward Georgetown. Between those who had stayed and the volunteer Baltimore dragoons Driscol had brought, and the dozens of sailors from Barney's regular naval unit, they'd started down Pennsylvania avenue with a force of some three or four hundred men.

To be sure, calling that mob a "force" was a little ridiculous. There wasn't a semblance of order among them, leaving aside Barney's sailors and, to a degree, Driscol's young Baltimore dragoons. Still, the men seemed determined enough—even eager.

The ones who'd chosen to accompany Sam were those who hadn't been completely demoralized by the rout at Bladensburg. Clearly enough, they intended to redeem themselves, now that someone had taken charge and proposed to lead them into battle instead of further retreat.

The farther down Pennsylvania Avenue they went, the more men they picked up, too. The broad boulevard that formed the spine of the capital city was full of troops slogging disconsolately toward Georgetown. From what Sam could determine, American casualties at Bladensburg had been light. There were enough men here, if Sam could rally them, to create something for which the name "army" wouldn't be a joke.

He gave it his best, speechifying to the retreating troops from the saddle all the way down the avenue. By the time they drew up before the Capitol, his voice was hoarse.

"Well, that's that," he said to Driscol glumly. Sam was learning for himself what experienced commanders had known for millennia—routed soldiers, even if not badly mauled, were usually too demoralized to be of any use for a while. Most of them had had enough of fighting for one day.

Sam looked over the milling mob—there was even less in the way of order now than ever—and estimated he had not more than a thousand men. "It's not much," he said. "But it was the best I could do."

Driscol was half astonished and half amused at the gloominess in the young officer's voice.

Not much!

The lieutenant had known marshals in Napoleon's army who'd have done well to rally a portion of the men that Houston had, under the circumstances. The big captain was a wizard at the work. He'd been able to project just the right combination of breezy self-confidence and good cheer to turn the trick.

Even wit, for a wonder.

To be sure, the captain's frequent citations from the *Iliad* probably seemed odd to most of the soldiery. They would have understood the references well enough. The Greek classics, along with the history of the Roman republic, were the staples of education at the time. But precious few of *them* would have taken the time and effort to memorize most of Homer's epic poem.

Still, if the citations made the captain seem a bit eccentric, they also made clear that he was an educated man—always something that Americans respected. Better still, it had shamed those among the crowd who were likewise educated, reminding them of their duty.

There were quite a few of those, too. Many of the volunteer units who had assembled in Washington to participate in the battle of Bladensburg were militias drawn from the city itself or nearby Baltimore. They included in their number many young men from the educated classes.

Best of all, though, had been the jokes accompanying the citations. By itself—

> Let fierce Achilles, dreadful in his rage,
> The god propitiate, and the pest assuage

—might have rung hollow. But coupled with "So, I am told, cried General Winder as he galloped westward! Who can refuse such a call?"

It drew quite a laugh, even from men such as these. And another fifty or so turned aside and joined Houston's forces marching toward the Capitol.

A thousand men, where Driscol had thought five hundred the best they could hope for. With a thousand men, and a commander to inspire them—and a fortress to defend, always far easier for untrained troops to manage than an open battlefield . . .

"Never you mind, sir," he rasped. "We can *win* this thing."

Houston's eyes widened. "D'you think so? Really?"

"Oh, aye, sir. I've no doubt of it at all."

Within an hour after they arrived at the Capitol, Sam was thanking—silently but no less fervently for all that—the great good luck that had brought Driscol to him. On his own, there wasn't a chance in the world that Sam could have brought order and discipline to the mob of soldiers who poured into the twin buildings.

Driscol managed it easily. There was just something about the squat Scots-Irish soldier that settled everyone down.

Steady. The word hardly scratched the surface of the matter. You might as well describe a mountain as "weighty." Driscol's blocky forehead and jaws exuded the sureness of theologians; his cold, pale eyes, the certainty of damnation if his dictums were not followed. Even the missing arm added to the effect.

Had anyone had any doubts, Driscol settled them within five minutes of their arrival at the Capitol.

"I must insist that my detachment be assigned to defend the Senate, sir!" blustered a florid-faced young militia lieutenant. He swept off his hat and waved it dramatically. "Ours is the senior unit of the brigade, and we should be assigned to defend the senior house!"

For a moment, Sam was too astonished by the absurdity of the demand to know what to do. But then Driscol was there, and it all became a moot point.

"McParland!"

Driscol's bellow was an odd sort of thing. Loud and penetrating, not so much because of its volume but its sheer menace. As if a file peeling away metal had taken on a human voice.

The young private who seemed to be Driscol's inseparable companion was at his side in an instant. "Yes, Serg—uh, sir."

Driscol jabbed a finger at the militia lieutenant. "Aim your musket at this insubordinate."

The musket came up. Firmly couched against the private's shoulder, it was pointed squarely at the lieutenant's chest. The muzzle of the gun seemed almost as wide as the militia officer's eyes, though it was not as wide—not nearly—as his gaping mouth.

"Arm your musket."

Click.

Driscol's icy gaze had never left the lieutenant's face. "You have five seconds," he rasped, "to obey orders."

He added no threat, made no reference to the alternative if the lieutenant disobeyed. To do so would have been . . .

So, so unnecessary. No one present at the scene doubted that

Private McParland would pull the trigger on Driscol's command. Instantly and unquestionably.

The lieutenant himself might have been too shocked to manage Driscol's five-second time limit. Fortunately, another member of his unit grabbed him by the arm and jerked him away. Then hastily led the lieutenant and the rest of the unit toward the House of Representatives.

Driscol moved off, seemingly as unconcerned as a housewife who had just finished sweeping the floor.

"Steady," Sam murmured to himself, some time later, as he stood between the two buildings and surveyed the ground that sloped down to the east of the Capitol. Even to his inexperienced eye, it was obvious that his jury-rigged military force had the advantage of position. Not only did the two buildings of the Capitol provide a ready-made and solid fortress, but the terrain over which the British would have to launch an assault against it was superb.

Superb, at least, from the American point of view. Sam didn't doubt that the British soldiers who'd have to come across in the face of heavy fire would hate it. Washington, D.C., had been created out of what amounted to something of a swamp. Much of the city's ground still wasn't far removed from that condition. After a rainfall, Sam had been told, even Pennsylvania Avenue was likely to turn into a sea of mud. The ground east of the Capitol hadn't been worked on much, and it was wet and soggy almost all of the time.

Close to marshland, in short. That also meant there wasn't much in the way of trees or even tall brush to obscure the field of vision, as Sam's men aimed their cannons and muskets at the advancing enemy. The British would have to cross hundreds of yards in the open, on treacherous footing, before they reached the Capitol—and then, they would have to make the final charge uphill.

"A perfect killing field." So Driscol had named it, with a cold satisfaction in his voice that almost made Sam shiver.

There was something primevally savage about the lieutenant, beneath the tightly disciplined exterior. Sam had no trouble at all imagining Driscol as an ancient Scot or Irish warrior, charging his enemy stark naked to display his sneering courage, armed only with blue paint covering his body, and a great claymore.

Certainly his Cherokee companions hadn't missed that lurking essence of the man. "One of the old true-bloods," he'd heard James Rogers murmur to his brother John, not long after they'd met Driscol.

John had nodded—and Tiana, also hearing the exchange, had given Driscol a long and considering look. So long and so considering, in fact, that Sam had felt a little surge of jealousy.

He shook off the thoughts, and went back to watching the lieutenant at work. Driscol had the two twelve-pounders already in position, and Barney's sailors were directing a veritable horde of soldiers in creating proper breastworks to shelter the guns. The interaction between the lieutenant and his men had become easy and relaxed.

There'd been no repetition of the incident with the militia officer. Once Driscol's authority had been firmly established, the troops at the Capitol had discovered other qualities to the lieutenant who served as Sam's second in command. Driscol was usually gruff and sometimes sarcastic, but he also had a sense of humor. A sarcastic remark, following some soldierly foolishness, would invariably be followed by a relaxed and matter-of-fact solution to the problem. If Driscol would brook no insubordination, he also held no grudges.

Most of all, he exuded confidence. He didn't exactly inspire men, the way Sam himself could. Driscol simply wasn't the man to give speeches and appeal to lofty sentiments. But he provided them with the surety they needed, after the momentary elation produced by speeches began to fade. Like a solid boulder, exposed by a receding tide, to which men could anchor themselves.

They needed that boulder, because even those mostly inexperienced soldiers knew full well that war was ultimately a deadly and practical business. The finest exhortations in the world couldn't conceal that reality for very long. Soon enough, the men had to face the real problems—a fortress that wasn't *really* a fortress; units that weren't yet *really* an army; guns that were short of ammunition; an oncoming enemy that was not a bard's insubstantial spirit.

But, always, Driscol was there to lead them to a solution of those practical problems.

He did so again, in the next five minutes.

* * *

When they'd arrived at the Capitol they'd found two eighteen-pounders already positioned there. But jubilation soon gave way to frustration. They discovered that Commodore Barney's sailing master John Webster had hauled off two of the four cannons that had originally been there, after Winder ordered him to bring the cannons to Georgetown. Unable to round up enough wagons to draw more than two of the guns, Webster had spiked the other two in order to prevent them being used by the enemy.

"Any chance of getting them back in service?" Sam asked the sailor who'd more or less placed himself in charge of Barney's gunners.

To Sam's surprise, that had been one of the black sailors among them, Charles Ball. Ball's fellow white gunners made no objection, either.

Sam had heard that the U.S. Navy, unlike the army, did not restrict Negroes from joining the service. But he hadn't realized the full extent of it. For naval artillerymen, it seemed, competence was more important than skin color.

Ball shook his head gloomily. "Webster knows what he's about, Captain. He spiked the guns with rattail files. Hardened metal like that . . ." The sailor shrugged. "We could drill them out, eventually. But it'd take forever, and we'd need a big supply of drill bits to begin with. Which we don't have a one."

Someone tugged at Sam's sleeve. Turning his head, he saw it was the black teamster who'd handled the wagon that had brought Driscol to the president's mansion. He didn't know the man's name. Had completely forgotten about him, in fact.

"I used to work at Foxall's Foundry, Captain. There's drill bits there, and it's not too far away."

Ball shook his head.

"Still wouldn't do no good, sir. It'd take *hours* to get the spikes out of those guns. Prob'ly couldn't do it at all until sometime tomorrow." He swiveled his head to the east, the direction from which the British would be arriving. "We won't have enough time before they get here."

Ball brought his gaze back to the teamster. "There's guns there, too, though, idn't there? We could use those. And we could sure as creation use more ammunition and shot."

The teamster looked dubious. "Well . . . my wagon's big enough to haul powder and some shot. *Some* shot. And I guess we could hook up a gun or two to the back of the wagon. But . . ."

The expression on his face was very dubious now. So, for that matter, was the expression on the face of the black gunner's mate.

Suddenly, Sam understood the problem. A white man entering Foxall's Foundry and hauling away materials would be presumed to be going about official and legitimate business. That would be true even if he wasn't wearing a uniform, since many civilians had been providing assistance to the army.

A black man would be presumed a thief—or, worse yet, a runaway slave providing supplies to the enemy. He'd likely be shot, or hanged on the spot.

"What's your name?" he asked the teamster.

"Henry Crowell, Captain."

Sam nodded. "Here's how it'll be, Henry." He glanced around and spotted Driscol's young companion, standing not far from the lieutenant.

"Private McParland!"

McParland trotted over.

"You already know Henry, I believe."

"Yes, sir." McParland gave the black teamster a cordial smile.

"I want you to provide him with an escort. He'll be going to Foxall's Foundry to bring us some supplies. I'll need you to verify his credentials, in the event someone might question his purpose. I'll write you out some official orders, which you can show anyone who asks. If they won't accept that—"

"I'll shoot 'em, sir. Not a problem." The private's bland assurance gave way to uncertainty. He glanced toward Driscol. "But—"

"I'll inform the lieutenant," Sam said firmly. He started to add something else, but saw that Driscol already was coming over.

Once Driscol was apprised of the situation, he immediately agreed with Sam. "But we can do better than that. We can round up some more wagons along the way, with enough men. Most of them are just standing around doing nothing now, anyway."

He turned to McParland. "Find Corporal Pendleton. Tell him and his unit of Baltimore dragoons to go with you. That'll give you enough men—in fancy uniforms, to make things perfect— that you'll be able to sequester some more wagons. Bring back as much as you can." He nodded toward Crowell. "For the rest, just do whatever Henry tells you to do."

McParland left, with Henry Crowell in tow. The teamster was

still looking a bit dubious, but Sam spotted a little gleam in his eyes, as well. It wasn't often that a black man had a unit of white soldiers not only providing him with an escort but, effectively, under his command.

Chuckling, he turned back to Charles Ball. The gunner's mate also seemed amused. Or, perhaps, simply gratified.

"That'll do us good, sir," he said eagerly. "Real good. Foxall's is the biggest gunmaker in the country."

Sam nodded. Then, examining the useless eighteen-pounders, he sighed heavily. "May as well add these to the breastworks, I guess."

"Might as well," agreed Driscol. "If the heavy bastards can't shoot, they can still stop enemy shot."

Driscol left, then, to oversee the men who were bringing some smaller guns into position alongside the twelve-pounders.

There were six guns, all told. On either side of the twelve-pounders, Barney's sailors were wrestling into position four other cannons that Sam had been able to round up from retreating troops who had chosen to join him. None of them were bigger than six-pounders, true, and there were but two of those. But what was probably more important was that the pair of six-pounders had been in the possession of some more stray sailors from Commodore Barney's unit. Stubborn—and still furious over the debacle at Bladensburg—the sailors had insisted on saving their guns and hauling them all the way back to Washington.

They'd be put to good use now, and there were finally enough of Barney's sailors in Sam's impromptu army that he could be confident his artillery would be handled with professional skill. With a battery of six guns, protected by the hastily erected but solid fortifications, the American force holding the Capitol could inflict some real damage on the enemy.

Sam would catch hell for those fortifications, in a day or two. Breastworks required wood, brick, or shaped stone to form suitable berms for the artillery, even if most of the material was dirt.

The only such substances ready-made in the area were the fittings of the Capitol itself.

For the most part, the men had been able to use wood planks taken from the covered walkway that ran between the buildings, once they tore it down, or the timber used for the flooring of the public galleries. It was amazing, really, how quickly that many men could tear something down, when they put their minds to it.

Still, for much of the underlying frame of the breastwork that would be shielding the twelve-pounder on the north, near the Senate building, they'd had to use the broken-up mahogany desks and chairs of the senators themselves.

But that was just furniture, when all was said and done. The real trouble would come from the House of Representatives. Sam was as sure of it as he was of the sunrise.

Alas, before Sam or Driscol noticed them doing it, some enthusiasts had taken it upon themselves to tear down the eastern entrance doors and add their heavy wooden substance to the breastworks.

"Oh, splendid!" Driscol had snarled at them, pointing an accusing finger at the now-gaping holes of the doorways. "In the olden days, enemies were required to use battering rams. Nowadays, we have cretins to do their work for them."

Abashed, the guilty soldiery avoided his glare. After a moment, Driscol snorted.

"Well, it's done. Now—"

His stubby finger was still pointed at the House, like a small cannon.

"Go in there and find something we can use to replace the doors. Something that will—ah, never mind. The Lord only knows what you'd come up with. *I'll* find it. Just follow me."

Find something, he did. And such was Driscol's grim and certain purpose that not even Sam dared to object.

One door of the House was now blocked by the great stone frieze which had once hung over the statue of *Liberty*. Only a portion of the bald eagle depicted on that frieze could be seen from the outside, since the eagle's wings spanned a good twelve feet—and it took a dozen men to shove it aside whenever someone actually needed to use the door.

The *Liberty* itself had done to block the other door. Once the mob of soldierly fortifiers had put it in place, of course, the door had become effectively impassable. The marble statue was bigger than life-size, what with *Liberty* herself seated on a pedestal, her left hand holding a cap of liberty and her right a scroll representing the Constitution.

It was a foregone conclusion that if Sam survived this battle, he'd catch merry hell.

"I heard the sculptor worked on it for years," Sam had heard one of the soldiers say to another, as they manhandled the great thing into the doorway. "They say he was coughing up blood at the end, from the consumption that killed him."

"I can believe it," grunted another. "I'm like to be coughing up blood myself, soon enough, just from moving the blasted thing."

Oh, merry hell indeed. But it still beat giving up the Capitol without a fight.

Shortly before eight o'clock of the evening, the British army arrived and took up position about half a mile to the east of the Capitol. By then, the sun was starting to set, but the enemy forces were easily visible. There were great flames rising from the nearby Navy Yard, which added their own light to the scene. The nation's premier naval arsenal and shipbuilding facilities had been set afire by its so-called defenders, long before the enemy arrived. By now, the place was a raging inferno.

That had been done by orders from above, apparently.

Houston damned General Winder yet again.

Just as the sun was going down, a British officer and two soldiers appeared on the ground east of the Capitol. The officer was waving a white flag and the soldiers were carrying a man on a stretcher. Sam sent one of Ball's gunners out to provide them with assurances of a safe conduct.

When the gunner got back, the British lagging behind due to their burden, he was practically hopping with glee.

"It's Commodore Barney!" he shouted. "It's the commodore!"

Sure enough. The two British soldiers carried him up to the breastworks and deposited the stretcher on the ground. Then made a hurried exit. The officer didn't leave, however, until he'd taken a little time to examine the newly-erected fortifications. From what Sam could tell from his expression, the officer—a captain, if Sam was interpreting the insignia properly—seemed both surprised and concerned by what he saw.

The commodore was gravely injured, from the wound in his thigh he'd received during his valiant stand at Bladensburg. But he was still conscious, and lucid.

Even cheery, once he saw the preparations that were in progress.

Several of the artillerymen picked up the stretcher and carried Commodore Barney into the central chamber of the House of Representatives. There, they lowered him gently onto one of the settees that had been brought into the chamber. Following Driscol's suggestion, Sam had designated the central chambers of both buildings to be the areas where the wounded would be taken. Fortunately, the enthusiasts hadn't initially thought to include upholstered furniture in the breastworks—and by the time they did think of it, Driscol was there to stop them.

"How did you convince them to let you go, sir?" asked Charles Ball.

Weakly, but actually smiling, Barney shook his head. "There was no need for me to convince anyone, Charles. After having one of their surgeons treat my wound, the British volunteered to let me go. General Ross and Admiral Cockburn themselves came to visit me. Very fine gentlemen, I must say! General Ross was especially effusive with his praise for our gallant stand at Bladensburg."

Ball and the small crowd of artillerymen swelled with pride. But out of the corner of his eye, Sam saw Driscol scowling. The Scots-Irish lieutenant, clearly enough, thought the phrase "very fine gentlemen" fit English generals and admirals about as well as it would the devil himself. Driscol, unlike Sam—but very much like Andrew Jackson—positively hated the English.

"Oh, yes," Barney continued. "We chatted a bit, and then General Ross told me he was giving me parole, and I was at liberty to go either to Washington or to Baltimore. I chose Washington, and Captain Wainwright—another very fine gentleman—volunteered to see to it."

The commodore looked away from the little mob of his admiring artillerymen and brought Sam under his eyes.

"But enough of that! Who are you, Captain? And am I right in assuming that you intend to defend the Capitol?"

Sam took the questions in reverse order. "Uh, yes, sir. We do, indeed, plan to defend the Capitol. I'm Captain Sam Houston, from the Thirty-ninth U.S. Infantry. I'm on detached duty here in Washington, at the orders of General Andrew Jackson. Just arrived in the city this morning, as it happens."

Sam hesitated then, but only for a second. With another man, he might have left it at that. But Joshua Barney—his reputation even more than his clear and inquisitive gaze—required a full and honest answer. As a young naval officer, the commodore had been one of the new republic's heroes during the war for independence. Now in his fifties, his conduct during the current war had shown that the decades had not taken a toll on his spirit. So Sam continued.

"My rank as captain hasn't been approved yet, though, by the War Department."

"But it was approved by General Jackson. That should be good enough, I think." The commodore's shrewd eyes moved to Driscol. "And you, sir?"

"Lieutenant Patrick Driscol. I'm from General Brown's Army of the Niagara. General Scott's First Brigade." He lifted his left stump. "Lost this at the Chippewa, and I was in Baltimore recuperating when the word came of the British landing."

"So, naturally, you hurried down to join the fight." Barney lowered his head to the cushion, closing his eyes. For all his good spirits, the commodore was obviously still very weak. "God help a nation which can produce such splendid junior officers—and such a sorry lot of generals."

Both Sam and Driscol cleared their throats simultaneously. Still without opening his eyes, Barney smiled. "Oh, please, gentlemen. You can be certain that I exempt Generals Jackson, Brown, and Scott from that blanket condemnation. But, alas, they are elsewhere. Here we are blessed with such as General William Winder—and that arrogant ass Armstrong. Perhaps the only secretary of war one can imagine who would neglect the defenses of his own capital city."

Sam wasn't sure if that was outright insubordination on the commodore's part. Normally, of course, for an officer to publicly ridicule his superior authorities would be considered so. But Barney was in the navy, and thus fell under the command of Secretary of the Navy William Jones, not Armstrong. And he hadn't said anything sarcastic about President Madison.

Not that Sam cared, anyway.

"Be that as it may, sir, we still propose to defend the Capitol, whatever it takes."

Barney's eyes opened, staring at the domed roof of the chamber far above. His gaze moved from one to another of the multitude of square plateglass sunlights.

"The roof's pinewood, but it's clad in sheet-iron. Not many

people know that." His eyes moved to the semicircular interior walls of the chamber and the fluted Corinthian columns above them. "Those are decorative, but the outer walls are worthy of the pharaohs. You may not be such a lunatic as you think, Captain Houston."

The commodore closed his eyes again. "Lunatic or not, however, you have my blessing. I'll not have the enemy come into the capital without bleeding on the way. I believe I am the senior officer present?"

"Yes, sir."

"Very well. I'm too badly injured to participate in the fight personally—nor could I do so in good conscience in any event, given the terms of my parole. But my wound gives me an honorable way to remain here, so long as I take up no arms myself. And, in the meantime"—here he spoke loudly enough to be heard by any of the several hundred soldiers and sailors who had crowded their way into the chamber—"you have my full confidence and authority, Captain Houston. Do the best you can."

CHAPTER 22

"Good God!" Rear Admiral George Cockburn exclaimed gaily, as he peered through his telescope. "Your captain was quite right. They *do* have a statue perched in one of the doorways. Great ugly thing, too." He lowered the telescope, chuckling. "One must grant this much to Cousin Jonathan—he certainly has a flair for the dramatic."

General Robert Ross wasn't going to let the matter slide so easily as all that. "And was Captain Wainwright also correct in his *other* observations?"

He already knew the answer to the question, since Ross possessed his own telescope. But the question served to remind Admiral Cockburn that the task which Cockburn had so breezily assured everyone would be as easy as a London promenade was proving more difficult by the moment—and, from Ross's viewpoint, it was bad enough already.

Since Cockburn's only response was a twist of the lips, Ross plowed on.

"It's all very well, Admiral Cockburn, to make sneering jests about Cousin Jonathan's capacity for headlong and panicky flight. But it wasn't your sailors who paid the butcher's bill at Bladensburg. It was *my* men—and the bill was disturbingly steep."

"We won handily, didn't we?"

Ross restrained his temper. "Oh, to be sure, all the historians will say so, when this is all over and done. A decisive victory, indeed. But historians don't pay butcher's bills either. Resounding victory or not, the fact remains that the American casualties at Bladensburg were light, and the casualties of my infantry brigades were anything but."

Cockburn avoided the general's hard gaze. Annoyed still more, Ross pressed home his point.

"It might be true that Cousin Jonathan is prone to panic—though there's always the hammering Riall took recently on the Niagara to prove that needn't be so. But American infantrymen are also liable to be remarkably good shots, for the few rounds they manage to fire before running away. And whatever the shortcomings of American infantry—do I need to tell an *admiral* this much?—we've been continually surprised since the war began at the professional level of American artillery. If the enemy infantry is often feckless, the artillery almost never is. Commodore Barney's men proved it once again at Bladensburg. They were as staunch as they were deadly, too. At the end, some of them had to be bayoneted with the fuses still in their hands."

What is it about sailors, Ross wondered, *that seems to make it necessary for them to keep learning the same lessons, over and over again?* Did the citrus juice in the drinking water pickle their brains?

By now, one would think, they would have learned how perilous it was to underestimate American gunnery. Mighty the British navy might be, compared to the tiny upstart rival that Cousin Jonathan had put to sea in the war. Still, in engagement after engagement, the Americans had demonstrated that their gunnery, if nothing else, was consistently superior to British.

Cockburn *still* hadn't answered the original question. Ross cleared his throat. "Did you hear me, Admiral?"

"Yes, yes," Cockburn replied, waving his hand impatiently. "Cousin Jonathan *does* have some guns up there, as well."

"Among which are two twelve-pounders. And are they as well fortified and positioned as Captain Wainwright stated?"

Cockburn simply shrugged. As always, the rear admiral wasn't a man to let minor impediments stand in the way of his enthusiasms.

"Please, General Ross! You know as well as I do that the forces holding those grotesque buildings can't be more than the shattered fragments of disparate units. They'll have neither leadership nor morale, be sure of it."

"I am sure of no such thing!" Ross snapped. Courtesy toward naval colleagues was well and good, but there were limits. Ross was a general who, for all his skill and capability, was solicitous toward his men. He was willing enough to lose soldiers for a good purpose, but he balked at doing so simply because a bloody admiral had a pet peeve and was an arrogant ass to boot.

Even the admiral's choice of terms betrayed his invariant bigotry. "Grotesque." Ross himself thought the Capitol was quite majestic in its design and appearance, even if he was rather amused by the fact. The pugnacious little American republic was every bit as prone to erect grandiose public structures as any king or emperor of Europe.

He pointed at the edifice in question. "No doubt the Capitol is now manned by men from disparate units. But where do you conclude from this that their leadership and morale are wanting? I conclude the exact opposite. *Somebody* had to have rallied those men, and the men themselves will be self-selected by the very process."

"It's *Cousin Jonathan,* for the love of God!" Cockburn snapped angrily. "A windbag gave a speech and empty heads were swayed by it. What else do you expect from a sorry lot of republicans?"

It was all Ross could do not to roll his eyes. *Sorry lot of republicans,* was it? Like the same republicans who, not so many years ago in France, had sent packing every monarchical army that attacked them? The same sorry lot of republicans who, less than three months earlier, had broken superior British forces at the Chippewa?

There were times he found Cockburn well-nigh insufferable.

Alas, while Ross had become Cockburn's superior as soon as British forces set foot on land, he was still subordinate to Admiral Cochrane. And, alas again, Cochrane had supported Cockburn every step of the way.

"The vice admiral wants those buildings taken, General Ross. Taken, then burnt to the ground."

Burnt to the ground—as if brick and stone were flammable substances! To be sure, Ross could wreck the Capitol, assuming he could take it in the first place. But without spending time and effort they couldn't afford to blow them up—not to mention a huge supply of powder, which they didn't possess either—there was no way that he could do more than have the buildings gutted by fire. If Cousin Jonathan was skilled enough to have erected that magnificent structure in the first place, he would certainly have it rebuilt soon enough after the British left.

And leave they would—and none too quickly to suit Ross. This raid concocted by admirals never would have worked at all if the American secretary of war hadn't been astonishingly slack at preparing his capital city against attack. In that regard, if nothing else, Ross would allow that the Navy's intelligence had been quite accurate.

Still, not even the admirals thought the British forces who had landed on the shores of Chesapeake Bay could possibly hold the area for any length of time. Cockburn and Ross had only a few thousand men under their command. By now, American reinforcements would be pouring toward Washington. Within a few days, if they didn't extricate themselves, the British would be swamped and forced to surrender.

Ross tightened his jaws with exasperation. The sole purpose of this flamboyant raid was to "make a demonstration." *Of what?* the general wondered. British talent for arson?

"Do you hear me, General?"

"Yes, I heard you, Admiral Cockburn."

"Look on the bright side, Robert," Cockburn said, smiling again. He pointed toward Ross's army. "We must outnumber them by at least three to one, even leaving aside the gross disparity in training and professionalism."

That . . . was true enough. Even Ross found some comfort, following the admiral's pointing finger. His soldiers were taking up their formations with experienced ease and skill. The red-coated ranks and files, with their shakos high and their bayonets higher still, seemed to ooze with confidence.

The problem was the terrain, combined with the solidity of the Capitol. For all practical purposes, the houses of the American legislature were a ready-made fortress. If Ross were meeting the enemy on an open field, he knew full well he'd brush them aside. But his own long experience in the peninsular campaign and other theaters in Europe had taught him just how difficult it could be to storm a fortress held by resolute and well-armed men. Disparity in number and skill be damned.

However, there was nothing for it. The attempt had to be made.

He took a long, deep breath. Then: "Very well. I'll order the assault."

"Are they mad?" General Winder bellowed. "I gave *explicit* orders for all units to abandon the capital and regroup here in Georgetown!"

His eyes ranged wildly about the tavern where he and several of the nation's cabinet had set up a temporary headquarters. More in the way of a momentary resting place, actually for the secretaries of war and the treasury.

President Madison and his cabinet had called a hasty emergency meeting at the president's mansion, after the disaster at Bladensburg. They had determined that the nation's executives would quickly disperse, lest the British invaders capture them all at one swoop. Madison, accompanied by Secretary of the Navy Jones and Attorney General Richard Rush, had already left Georgetown. His intended destination was Wiley's Tavern, some sixteen miles to the northwest, where the president's wife, Dolley, awaited him.

Secretary of War Armstrong and Secretary of the Treasury George Campbell had been about to leave the tavern when word arrived that forces of the United States were making a stand at the Capitol. They'd delayed their departure in order to discuss this unexpected turn of events with General Winder and Secretary of State Monroe.

"Who is in command over there?" Winder demanded. "I'll have him shot for insubordination and treason!"

Armstrong exchanged glances with James Monroe, who was sitting across the table from him. Despite the smoke and dim lighting in the tavern, Monroe's expression was clear enough. The secretary of state's tight jaws made it obvious that, had he the authority, he would be more inclined to have General Winder placed before that firing squad.

So would Armstrong himself, for that matter. He was a ruined man, and he knew it. He would accept responsibility for neglecting the capital's defenses, for which, in truth, he'd done little more than create the impressively named "Tenth Military District." But of all the poor decisions the secretary of war regretted, the one he regretted the most was having made William Winder the commanding general of the newly formed district.

It had seemed a clever enough idea, at the time. A former general himself, Armstrong hadn't really expected the British to attack the capital in the first place. So what did it matter which officer was placed in charge?

Armstrong *still* didn't understand the military logic behind their operation, in fact, since Baltimore offered a far more suitable target.

Rational or not, though, the British had chosen to attack Washington instead of Baltimore. General Winder had made a complete hash of the business, as one might expect from a man whose only previous military accomplishment had been his ignominious capture at the battle of Stoney Creek. Giving command of the Tenth Military District to Winder had seemed a sensible way at the time to enlist the political support of Maryland for strengthening the defenses of Baltimore. William Winder was a prominent attorney in Baltimore; better still, his uncle Levin Winder was the governor of Maryland. But Armstrong was deeply regretting that decision now.

All in the past.

"I *can't* undermine him now, James," Armstrong murmured softly to the secretary of state. "Bad as Winder might be, to shred the military chain of command under these circumstances would create the worst situation possible."

Monroe glared at Winder. The general took no notice, since he was far too preoccupied with roaring outrage and indignation and shouting threats of bloody punishment to be paying any attention to the cabinet members who were whispering at their table in the corner.

"You told him *yourself* the Capitol would make a splendid fortress," Monroe hissed to Armstrong. "And I agreed with you. Just a short time ago, when we all met there after that farce at Bladensburg."

Armstrong shrugged uncomfortably. True, he had. The fact had been obvious to anyone with real military experience. It had been equally obvious to Monroe, who'd fought in the Revolution. But Winder had been on the verge of hysteria, after Bladensburg, and Armstrong hadn't felt it possible to press the matter.

"What difference would it have made?" he asked Monroe softly. "Yes, the Capitol would have been a fine place to make a stand—but not under Winder. Certainly not in the condition he was in at the time. What was I to do, James? Relieve him on the spot? And who should I have replaced him with?"

Monroe sighed. "Curse the luck that Winfield Scott's wounds proved too grave for him to take the post."

Armstrong nodded. The brilliant young brigadier had been everyone's first choice for commander of the Tenth Military District. Unfortunately, the injuries Scott had received at Lundy's Lane were taking months to heal. The brigadier was still recuperating in New Jersey.

"We do what we can, James. The question that now faces us, is: What do *we* do?"

General Winder's bellows provided one answer.

"I'll have him shot! I swear I will! What is his name?"

A hesitant voice answered. It was the accountant, Simmons. "Huston, I believe. I'm not sure of his first name, General. Sam, maybe. He's got some wild injuns with him, too. Frightful-looking creatures."

"Well then, General Sam Huston will go before the wall! See if he won't!"

Armstrong frowned. He had a good memory for names, and there was no General Huston serving in the U.S. Army. Nor in any of the state militias, as far as he knew. And what would a group of Indians be doing accompanying a general, anyway?

He cocked an inquisitive eye at one of his secretaries, seated at the same table. The efficient young man was already flipping through the files he'd salvaged from the War Department.

"Huston, Huston," the clerk muttered. "There's no Huston of any rank in—oh, wait."

"Yes?"

The clerk looked up. "There *is* an officer by the name of Sam *Houston,* sir. From Tennessee. He's in the Thirty-ninth Infantry, and apparently conducted himself very well at the Horseshoe Bend. But he's certainly not a *general.*"

"What is he, then?"

The clerk looked back down at the file. "Well, there's some question about that. Technically, he's just an ensign. General Jackson gave him a field promotion to captain, but the recommendation hasn't yet been approved by the War Department."

Armstrong almost laughed at that, despite the circumstances. *One of Jackson's frontier roughnecks, and an ensign to boot!* It figured, though. Say what you would about Andrew Jackson, the man was a fighter. Had he been in command of the Tenth Military District, the British would have had to contest every inch of soil from the minute they landed.

Monroe and Armstrong looked at each other for a long moment. They weren't on good terms personally. None of the Virginians in Madison's cabinet had much of a liking for the secretary of war, who'd been a New York senator. Most of that was just typical Virginian clannishness, Armstrong supposed, though he'd allow that some of it was due to his own abrasive personality.

That, too, was all in the past. Armstrong's political career was finished. He'd be the one who'd take most of the blame for the disaster here, of that he was certain.

All that remained was to salvage what he could of his own honor.

"I can't undermine Winder, James," he repeated softly. "Until we've formally replaced him, we have to leave him in charge. At least publicly. Or we'll have pure chaos."

He gave Monroe a long look from lowered brows. It might almost be called an accusatory gaze; it was certainly a challenging one.

"That's because I'm the secretary of *war,* and therefore his direct superior. You, however, are not." With that, his voice took on a challenging note, and he peered expectantly at Monroe.

Who, in turn, stared back at Armstrong. Then, looked away for a few seconds. Then, looked back.

"Can you keep him distracted?"

Armstrong smiled thinly. "Oh, yes, James. That I can do. With Winder, it's not even difficult."

Monroe nodded. "I'll be off, then."

The secretary of state rose from the table and moved as quickly as he could toward the tavern entrance, without moving so quickly that Winder might notice his departure.

No fear of that, really. Winder was now bellowing the details of the firing squad, down to the caliber of the muskets. Armstrong watched him for a while. It seemed, under the circumstances, as good a distraction for the general as any.

Outside, in the tavern courtyard, a servant brought up Monroe's horse.

"On to Frederick now, sir?" asked the lieutenant in charge of the small force of dragoons who escorted the secretary of state.

"No. We're going back into the city. The Capitol, to be precise."

CHAPTER 23

Since John Ross had no idea what he should be doing, he simply attached himself to Sam Houston. He trotted along with him as the young maybe-captain charged back and forth from the House to the Senate to the artillery battery emplaced between the two and gave speech after speech.

Houston was a superb speechifyer, too. Even a Cherokee like Ross, accustomed to the eloquence of chiefs' councils, was impressed.

John had no idea if Houston was citing the quotations from the *Iliad* properly. He'd read the poem, once, but he certainly hadn't impressed it to memory. On the other hand, it hardly mattered. John was quite sure that none of the soldiers manning the Capitol had memorized the poem, either, so who could argue the matter?

And if Sam's rendition of the *Iliad* was his own half-remembered words instead of those of Pope, then the breezy youngster from Tennessee was something of a poet himself.

> *Shall I my prize resign*
> *With tame content, and thou possess'd of thine?*
> *Great as thou art, and like a god in fight,*
> *Think not to rob me of a soldier's right.*

It sounded splendid in the House of Representatives, regardless of whose words they actually were. And it seemed to lift the spirits of the men.

When he said as much to Houston, as they hurried across to the Senate, Sam just grinned at him.

"Not too appropriate a citation, perhaps. They were disputing over a captured woman, you know, not a nation's capital. But it seemed suitable to the occasion, so long as I kept it to a few lines."

Suddenly the grin was replaced by a frown. "Speaking of women, where *is* Tiana now?"

It was John's turn to grin. For all the martial speeches, the only actual *battle* Houston had fought so far had been his desperate struggle to keep Tiana Rogers from accompanying him everywhere he went. Partly because he was worried about her safety; partly because Tiana would inevitably distract the men; but mostly, he confided to Ross, because he was in enough trouble as it was. If Tiana remained at his side during the battle, the gossip would have it afterward that she was his concubine. So fornication would be added to the charges of treason and insubordination!

Americans were odd, John mused, when it came to sex. Cherokees were far more rational on the subject. Marriage was taken seriously among them, and adultery was frowned upon, of course. But it was also taken more or less for granted that energetic and curious youngsters would inevitably do what they would do, and where was the harm? Granted, such a relaxed attitude was easier for a matrilineal society than one that, like the American, granted ridiculous authority to fathers and husbands.

"Bastardy," an obsession for the whites, was almost a meaningless term for Cherokees. A child's place came from the mother's position, not the father's.

"She's sulking in her tent, I imagine," John replied.

Sam flashed another grin. But they were already striding into the Senate, and it was time for another speech.

"And will we be become one with the Trojans, boys?" Sam bellowed, gesturing to the soldiers.

> *"My heroes slain, my bridal bed o'erturned,*
> *My daughters ravished, and my city burn'd,*
> *My bleeding infants dash'd against the floor—"*

"No, sir! No, sir!" came the responding roar.

"Henry?"

The exclamation, coming unexpectedly out of the shadows, literally made Henry Crowell jump. Except for a few lamps here and there, there was no illumination in the cavernous foundry at night.

Not this night, anyway. On some other nights, in the past, work crews laboring on a rush order would have kept the foundry lit just by the nature of their work. In years past, Henry had put in a fair number of sixteen-hour days himself.

He peered into the darkness. That voice . . .

"Is that you, Mr. Kendall?"

A figure came from behind one of the furnaces, dressed in heavy work clothes, a musket in his hands. "Yes, it's me all right. What are *you* doing here, Henry?"

Kendall's voice wasn't *quite* suspicious, and the musket wasn't *quite* pointing directly at him. Still, Henry figured a quick explanation was in order.

"I was sent here by Captain Houston, Mr. Kendall. Me and"—he turned and gestured behind him—"these other men."

Henry had been the first one through the door, and he was relieved to see Pendleton coming forward. Even in the poor lighting, the young volunteer's uniform was flamboyantly visible.

"The captain's in charge of the Capitol's defense," Henry elaborated. "He instructed me and these Baltimore dragoons to come to the foundry and see if we could find some ammunition and shot. Maybe some ordnance, too."

He completed the introductions. "Corporal, this here is Mr. David Kendall. He used to be my foreman, when I worked at Foxall's."

By now, Kendall was relaxing. He even seemed pleased to see them. He leaned the musket against a pillar and slapped his hands together. "Defend the Capitol! Yes, you'll need some shot and powder for that. Be right down magged without it!"

He turned and headed toward the interior of the foundry, waving for Henry to follow. "I've got better, too. There's a couple of three-pounders just finished and ready. You can take them back with you."

Even with his limp, Kendall soon outdistanced the men who were following him. It had been several years since Henry had worked in Foxall's, and he'd half forgotten the complicated layout of the place. There were too many half-seen obstructions for him to want to risk getting bruised—or worse. The only soft thing in a foundry is human flesh.

"He seems to like you well enough," Pendleton commented. "Lucky thing, eh?"

Henry shook his head. "Well, I suppose he ought to. He got that limp some years ago when a blank rolled onto his leg. Liked to have crushed it completely, 'cept I picked up one end of it so's he could get out from under."

Pendleton looked puzzled. "Blank?"

"One of them." Henry pointed at a solid bar of iron they were moving past. It was over six inches in diameter and several feet long.

Pendleton ogled the thing. "That must weigh . . ."

"Don't know how much, exactly. A lot. Thought my back would break by the end."

Now Pendleton was ogling him.

"I'm powerful strong," Henry said, half apologetically.

He needed that strength, later. One of the three-pounders got stuck while the dragoons tried to haul it out through the dark foundry, after they fit it onto its carriage. Henry freed the wheel by the simple expedient of lifting it up.

"Remind me not to arm-wrestle you," Pendleton murmured.

Kendall barked a laugh. "I can't remember anybody being dumb enough to arm-wrestle him since the first week he started working here. How old was you then, Henry?"

"Sixteen, Mr. Kendall."

"Well, you haven't lost it, even living that easy new life of yours as a teamster." He patted Henry's heavy shoulder and gave the dragoons a friendly nod. "Good luck, boys, and do the best you can."

Before he'd gone more than two blocks, two well-dressed, middle-aged white civilians armed with muskets accosted Henry on the lead wagon. The only real trouble came after they left the foundry.

"What're you doing, boy?" demanded one of them.

Henry didn't need to answer. Pendleton trotted his horse forward, holding up his own musket and glowering as fiercely as a youngster can.

"You there! We're on official military business!" he snapped. "Now move out of the way!"

Seeing other dragoons coming up behind him, as well as two more wagons, the civilians backed off. One of them, however, didn't move quite fast enough to suit Pendleton.

"Keep dawdling like that," he snarled, "and we'll make you arm-wrestle Henry here."

"You'll look good," another dragoon commented, "your arm in a sling. All busted up the way it'll be."

Tiana wasn't sulking in her tent. In fact, she wasn't sulking at all.

Not any longer, anyway.

She'd given in to Sam's demands that she remain behind while he dashed to and fro rallying the soldiers. No sooner had he left, however, than her sullen resentment had turned impish.

Houston had told her and the other children—as if *she* were a "child"!—to remain in the Senate. So, naturally, as soon as he had left with John Ross in tow, she led them across to the House of Representatives. Even Sequoyah didn't argue the matter. She thought he was a bit disgruntled himself, at being left out of the battle.

It had been a fortunate move, even if driven only by rebellious impulse. In the Senate, she and the Ridge children had just been underfoot. But, once in the House, she discovered Commodore Barney, lying wounded on his settee. The small mob of admirers who had earlier surrounded the commodore was gone, and he was looking a bit forlorn. He was obviously in considerable pain, too, now that the excitement of his arrival was past.

Tiana needed something to keep her mind off the coming battle. So she decided to tend to the commodore's injuries.

The man seemed surprised—even a bit shocked—by the easy and casual manner in which she went about the business. *Why?* she wondered. Injuries, even injuries taken in battle, were messy and undignified by their very nature. The scars to come would be suitable objects for boasting, but the open wounds themselves were simply ugly.

"They did a good job," she pronounced, after lacing and buttoning the commodore back up. "I don't care for that poultice, but I suppose it'll do."

"You speak English?" he asked, still rather wide-eyed.

Tiana snorted, then muttered something in Cherokee.

"I'm sorry, lass. I didn't understand that."

Tiana decided the mutter was probably best left untranslated.

"Of course I speak English, Commodore. I can read it, too. My father's a Scotsman, and he's hardly the only one in my family tree. Many Cherokees speak English."

She pointed to the Ridge children. "They can read and speak the language, too. They've been studying with the Moravians."

Barney's eyes moved to the youngsters. Nancy Ridge smiled shyly. John Ridge and Buck Watie just looked solemn.

"Indeed." The commodore cleared his throat. "A day of many surprises for me, then—or perhaps I should say, considerable learning."

He looked back at Tiana. "What are you doing here, if I might ask, in the company of Captain Houston?"

Tiana stood up, grinning. "Major Ridge—he's one of our chiefs and the father of John and Nancy here—wanted his children to get a better American education. So he asked Sam to bring them to Washington with him and find them a proper school. I came because . . . Well, I felt like it."

Like a small whirlwind, Sam Houston and John Ross came blowing into the chamber, followed by a gaggle of soldiers who seemed to be serving them as an escort. Sam's eyebrows went up a bit, seeing Tiana and the children in the chamber, but—wisely—he just went on his way. Tiana could hear him start speechifying again as soon as he left. His booming voice penetrated back into the chamber from one of the adjoining rooms.

"To human force and human skill the field:
Dark show'rs of javelins fly from foes to foes;
Now here, now there, the tide of combat flows—"

"Does that silly chatter really do any good?" Tiana wondered.

The commodore smiled. "Oh, yes, lass. A great deal, in fact. Not so much the words—never much liked Homer myself, the truth be told—but just the fact that he's spouting them so surely. Terror is the great enemy, in a battle. The first duty of a commander is to slay the monster, which is what your fine young captain is about. And doing splendidly well at it."

Tiana shook her head dubiously. "I'd think—"

She fell silent. Another officer had come into the chamber. This one, with a pace that could be better described as that of the tides.

She met his eyes across the room. Quite pale in color, those eyes had been earlier, when she'd seen them in the sunlight. Now, lit only by the lamps in the chamber, they seemed very dark.

The darkness was the truer color. *Asgá siti,* that man was. More so than even Major Ridge, she thought.

An American girl might have been repelled by that knowledge. Tiana, Cherokee, was not. In the end, nations lived and died by such men.

So she met his gaze calmly and levelly. It was he who looked away.

Ha! He *was* attracted to her! That was . . .

Interesting.

Barney's eyes had now moved to the new arrival, as well.

"Lieutenant Driscol," he said. "What a great pleasure to see you here."

Commodore Barney knew very little about Lieutenant Patrick Driscol, beyond the man's name. But he was far too experienced a commander not to recognize what he was, just from watching the way the lieutenant had carried himself thus far.

A great pleasure, indeed. There wasn't a single naval engagement Barney had won in the war of independence—he'd fought thirty-five, in all, and been defeated only five times—that hadn't, in the end, been won because of men such as Driscol. If captains like Houston could rally a broken army, it was only because lieutenants like Driscol provided it with a spine that had remained intact. The Driscols of the world could be beaten, surely. Broken, never.

Barney gestured toward the man, inviting him to approach. It was obvious that the lieutenant had entered the chamber for that very purpose, although—

Barney glanced up at Tiana, and suppressed a smile. Now that he was here, clearly enough, the good lieutenant had found another item of interest in the place. Even if he was doing his level best not to make it evident.

Driscol came forward, to stand beside the settee.

"May I be of any assistance, Lieutenant?"

"Yes, sir. It's the rockets, Commodore. I was wondering about them."

The lieutenant looked a bit embarrassed, for an instant, the way a master craftsman might when he is forced to confess that he lacks a certain bit of knowledge concerning his own trade.

"It's simply that I've never faced them, sir. The Congreves are a newfangled device, and we never had to deal with them on the continent when I was in the French army. Nor did Riall have any at the Chippewa. But they started using them at Lundy's Lane, and I've heard that Cockburn and Ross seem to have brought shiploads of the things."

The continent. That explained a great deal.

"You were serving with the emperor, I take it?"

Driscol nodded. "Aye, sir. For a goodly number of years."

Barney nodded, then extended a hand toward Tiana. "Help me up, would you, lass?"

A moment later, he was sitting erect. Tiana's grip surprised him with its strength. He was even more surprised at the instant way she acceded to his request. A white girl would have wasted time insisting he was too weak to move.

"Don't worry yourself about the rockets, Lieutenant, at least not beyond the question of morale. The truth? Congreves are frightening, when you first encounter them, but their effect is almost entirely upon the mind. As actual weapons, they don't amount to much."

Driscol's blocky face showed no expression at all. "I'd come to suspect as much, from the accounts I'd heard. Inaccurate, I take it?"

Barney chuckled. "If I was one of the men firing them, I'd be as concerned that the blasted things might decide to land on me as on the enemy. Not to mention the fact that they're bloody dangerous to fire in the first place. From what I've seen, they're far more likely to blow up in your face than even the most poorly made cannon."

Driscol and Barney simultaneously scanned the chamber. They were both gauging the walls that lay beneath the fancy trappings.

"The rockets have no real breaching power, either," Barney stated. "To take the Capitol, firmly defended, the British would be far better off with some real siege guns. But I saw no such at Bladensburg."

The stump of Driscol's left arm twitched, as if he'd begun an old gesture that was now impossible. A moment later, with a rueful little smile on his face, the lieutenant brought up his right hand to scratch his chin.

"The big guns from a ship of the line would do the trick," he commented. "But can you imagine the difficulty of taking such out of a ship, and hauling them here all the way from the coast?"

Barney smiled. "I'm a naval officer myself, Lieutenant Driscol. That's not a chore I'd want to be assigned, for a surety." He shook his head. "No, I don't think you need worry about siege guns. As I said, I saw none at Bladensburg. In fact, I saw little proper artillery at all in the possession of the enemy. Just a barrage of Congreves. Less than a handful of field pieces—two three-pounders and one six-pounder, nothing more."

His good humor faded. "Mind you, the Congreves did quite well when it came to panicking our troops. But that was on an open field, with little enough in the way of shelter. Worst of all, of course, was that our top command was—"

He cleared his throat. "Well. Inadequate to the task, let's say."

Barney peered up at Driscol. The lieutenant was not tall, but he seemed as wide and solid as an old oak.

"I daresay that won't be a problem here."

Driscol's answering smile was a cool thing, just barely this side of cold.

"No, sir. That'll not be a problem here. Captain Houston's not got much in the way of experience, but he's stalwart—and I believe I'll be able to make good his lack when it comes to the rest."

"Yes, I imagine you will." Barney glanced around the chamber again. "It's possible that one of the rockets might by great poor chance come through one of the windows—and then, by still greater poor chance, explode at that very inopportune moment. If so, you'll suffer some bad casualties. But even then, the havoc will be confined to one room of the building."

Driscol nodded. "I've already seen to a surgery, sir. As it happens, there were several doctors among the Baltimore volunteers. Enough to staff surgeries in both wings of the Capitol."

"Proper doctors, is it?" The commodore decided to keep his true feelings to himself. "Well. That'll bolster the men's confidence."

From the momentary look that flashed across the lieutenant's face, Barney suspected that Driscol shared his own low opinion of "proper doctors." In truth, for all that the Cherokee girl's immodesty had startled Barney, he was rather inclined to think that her savage Indian methods of medicine were less likely to produce bad results than those of educated white doctors. For many years now, Barney had noted that the death rate of wounded men taken to a hospital was worse than it was when they were tended on an open field, or even left to their own self-treatment.

"Humours," the doctors claimed, were at the bottom of all illness and disease. If so, Barney was convinced, the "humours" which seemed to follow doctors around were worse than any other.

Lieutenant Ross came in, this time alone. "Captain Houston would like to see you, Lieutenant. He thinks the enemy are beginning their attack."

Driscol departed at once. Barney was pleased, but not surprised, to see the way the man moved—with a tread that covered ground swiftly, but still seemed sure, rather than hurried or nervous. The commodore knew that tread, allowing for the difference between one learned on soil and one learned on a rolling ship's deck. Just so had he himself moved, in times past, when battle loomed.

"Damned if I don't think we'll *win* this thing," he said softly to himself. "And wouldn't that be a wonder, to save a day I'd thought already lost in ignominy."

The pain and weariness threatened to overwhelm him, now. He gave Tiana a pleading look, and within seconds she had him lowered back on the settee. She was a very graceful girl, he thought, as well as a strong one.

"When this is over," he murmured, "I'll speak to some people I know. I'm quite sure a good school can be found for the children."

Tiana's expression bore a sudden undertone of anger. Barney chuckled. "Oh, please, girl. For *you,* of course, something more suitable would have to be arranged."

That seemed to mollify her.

But what? he wondered, closing his eyes. There was a notable shortage of finishing schools for Amazons. Nary a single one, as far as he knew.

He heard a familiar hissing sound, muted by the walls, but quite audible nonetheless.

"Well, it's started," he said.

"Are those the Congreve rockets you and the lieutenant were talking about?" asked one of the Cherokee boys.

"Oh, yes. Nasty-sounding things, aren't they? But don't be afraid."

"I'm not!" insisted the lad stoutly. "Just curious."

The commodore didn't believe that for an instant. He himself, for all his experience, had been a little shaken by the dragon fire when he first encountered it. But the boy seemed to believe it, which was all that really mattered.

Joshua Barney couldn't have recited a single verse of the *Iliad* to save his life or soul. Yet he had no doubt at all that, thousands of years earlier, boys in bronze armor standing atop and in front of the walls of Troy had assured themselves that they were really not afraid.

All lies, of course. But lies that they made true, because they believed them.

All traces of twilight were gone by the time Monroe and his escort reached the president's mansion. But, even in the dark of night, it was impossible to miss the Capitol. That would have been true even if the Naval Yard hadn't been burning like an inferno. A barrage of rockets was blazing down upon the seat of the nation's legislature, adding its own flaring illumination. Clearly enough, the British had decided to soften up the defenses by a bombardment, before trying to storm them.

"Are you certain about this, sir?" asked the lieutenant. The young officer nodded nervously toward the Capitol. "Be a risky business, that, trying to get in."

James Monroe hesitated, before he answered. Now that the task of smuggling his way into a fortress under siege was actually at hand, he found himself hesitating a bit. What sane man wouldn't?

On the other hand, ambition and honor impelled him powerfully forward.

Ambition, because as secretary of state he was widely considered President Madison's logical successor. Armstrong would take the blame for this disaster. If Monroe took his stand with the men defending the Capitol, he would come out of it smelling like the proverbial rose. Assuming he survived, of course. But that was always a risk for one who chose to lead a nation.

Even more, there was honor at stake, too. In the end, perhaps, the survival of the nation itself. Monarchs and their courtiers might flee their capitals easily enough, because their legitimacy was a matter of blood. But if no leading elected official of a republic placed himself beside the valiant junior officers who were resisting the enemy in that republic's very capital, when given the chance, could such a republic deserve the name at all?

"Yes, I'm quite sure. Lead the way, Lieutenant—and quickly. If we arrive before the British fully launch their assault, we should be able to make an entry through one of the western doors."

CHAPTER 24

The moment Driscol emerged onto the open area between the twin buildings of the Capitol and looked across the ground to the east, he knew that the Sassenach were, indeed, forming up for the attack.

Even in the relative darkness, they were an impressive sight. The scarlet uniforms weren't bright, of course, the way they would have been in daylight. But the martial color was clear enough, in the red glow reflected from the low clouds that now covered the sky. The huge, flickering flames from the Navy Yard reflected off the metal trimmings and the gun barrels and the brassards on the shakos, making the assembled force seem even more menacing than it would in daylight.

There was something demonic about the appearance of that half-visible army threatening the Capitol; as if those lobster uniforms were filled with great clawed monsters in fact, instead of men.

Driscol took a deep breath, as he always did before a battle in which he faced British soldiers. He needed that breath, to still an old terror. The very first time he'd seen that sight had been on the road from Randallstown, where the Sassenach had broken the men of County Antrim. Sixteen years old, he'd been that day, armed with nothing better than a pike.

He'd spent the night that followed hiding in the fields, while the British hunted down the United Irishmen and slaughtered them without mercy. Prisoners, the wounded—the Sassenach had murdered them all, and dumped the corpses in a sandpit. One of the bodies had been that of Driscol's older brother.

As always, that one deep breath was enough. His eyes ranged the artillery battery, taking satisfaction in what he saw. The guns themselves were manned by Barney's sailors, which meant he'd have no fear that they'd be handled fumblingly. Nor were these men who would be wondering how soon they should flee.

Better still, the space between the guns was occupied by naval marines. Captain Samuel Miller had led those marines at Bladensburg, and by all accounts they'd acquitted themselves as well as Barney's artillery. There were close to a hundred of them—almost the entirety of Miller's unit, in fact, except those who had been killed or wounded at the earlier encounter.

Unfortunately, Miller himself had been one of those wounded at the battle, so he was not present. But the marines had fallen immediately into practiced formations, and they were accustomed to working closely with Barney's gunners.

So Driscol left them to their own devices. He'd been far more concerned with organizing and steadying the soldiers who'd taken positions inside the two buildings. Those soldiers, sheltered by the walls of the Capitol, were in considerably less danger than the artillerymen and marines. But they had nothing like the experience of the veterans manning the big guns.

Houston came trotting over, the moment he spotted Driscol, with John Ross just a step or two behind him. He looked concerned, but no more so than any commander making his preparations on a battlefield. Driscol couldn't detect so much as a trace of fear in the captain's face.

He wasn't really surprised. He'd learned enough of Houston's actions at the Horseshoe Bend to know that, whatever weaknesses the captain might have, lack of courage was certainly not among them. Driscol had participated in enough headlong frontal assaults in his life to know what it took for a man to be the first over the wall in the face of enemy fire. In sixteen years of almost continual warfare, Driscol had managed the feat only twice. Houston had done it in his very first battle.

"What d'you think, Patrick?" Houston asked as he came up to him. "How soon should we open fire?"

Driscol glanced at Charles Ball, who was standing by the twelve-pounder on the House side of the battery emplacement. In the darkness, it was impossible to discern the black artilleryman's expression, but something about his stance practically quivered exasperation. Houston must have been pestering the poor man since he first spotted the enemy assembling for the attack.

"Might I suggest, sir, that you leave that decision to Ball and his men. They know what they're doing."

Houston looked a bit confused. "But shouldn't I be the one to give the command?"

"Oh, certainly, sir. But the way this works, you see"—*here anyway,* he told himself—"is that Mr. Ball will give you the meaningful eye, and then you solemnly instruct him to do what he plans to do anyway."

Houston peered over at Ball. "I see. Well, that makes sense."

"And, ah . . ." Driscol cleared his throat.

Houston grinned in response. "Oh, Patrick, please. I assure you I'm not really a fool, even if I've been charging all over foisting citations from the *Iliad* on people as if they were patent medicine. I won't pester Charles any longer. I promise."

"Splendid, sir."

For such relaxed good sense, a reward seemed in order. "It's perfectly acceptable, of course—when Ball lets you know the time has come—for you to bellow the order in a fine Homeric manner."

"Oh, good. I was looking forward to that. And where will you be, if I need you?"

"It's hard to say, sir. Wherever the troops seem to be the shakiest."

Houston nodded. "You'll have McParland with you, of course. If I might make a suggestion of my own, why don't you ask James and John Rogers to join you, as well?" He pointed to his left. "They're right over there, lurking in the shadows out of old habit. Just tell them I sent you."

Driscol cocked his head a bit, in a questioning gesture.

"Just trust me, Patrick. Whatever McParland can't manage in the way of intimidation, they will. And if it comes to fighting hand to hand—I'll be blunt here—you've only got one arm left. The Rogers brothers will make good the lack. Especially James."

Driscol looked down at his stump. He suddenly realized that he hadn't given that any real thought at all. To be sure, he was right-handed, and he had a pistol stuffed in his waistband. But that was good for only one shot. How was a one-armed man to reload the bloody thing in the middle of a melee?

His eyes moved to the shadows against the wall of the House. He hadn't even spotted the two Cherokees there. That wasn't because of their skin color, which wasn't really all that much darker than a white man's. Like their half sister Tiana, the Rogers brothers probably had as much Scot as Cherokee ancestry.

It was because they were completely still. Even now, when he was *trying* to spot them, he could barely do so.

For a moment, Driscol felt a little disoriented. His experience at gauging fighting men was extensive, and based on long-standing experience. But he now realized that, as with his missing arm, he'd been blind to what should have been obvious. True, those two Indians might not be of much use standing in a line, armed with muskets. But if the British breached the walls, and the affair was reduced to a desperate business in the rooms and corridors of the Capitol . . .

"I'll do so, sir. And thank you."

A sudden hissing sound burst upon them from the east, accompanied by a flare of light. Turning their heads, they saw the first volley of rockets coming toward them.

It was as good a time and place as any to find out if the commodore was right. So Driscol never moved. Never so much as twitched a finger. Beside him, Houston did the same, taking his cue from the lieutenant. So did John Ross.

They're certainly spectacular-looking things, Driscol thought, during the few seconds it took the Congreves to make the flight. The sight and sound of them was positively fearsome. But—

The rockets began landing, those of them that hadn't exploded in the air from short fuses.

—impressive *looking* and *sounding* was just about the limit of it. One of the rockets landed not far from the six-pounder, on the northern end of the battery. But as well protected as the battery now was, by the breastworks, the burst caused nothing in the way of casualties, and there was no harm to the gun.

Two others managed to impact the walls of the Senate. By sheer luck, one exploded just as it hit the wall, but it didn't do any real damage beyond shaking loose some of the sandstone cladding. The other one exploded prematurely, so that what hit the walls were simply bits of rocket debris. With walls like that, the British might as well have been throwing pebbles.

There was another rocket that hit the corner of the House, but it caromed off harmlessly into the darkness and exploded a few seconds later, after it had landed on open ground.

Most of the rockets accomplished nothing. Some of them landed far short, others veered wildly to the side, and two sailed over the Capitol entirely.

"Sound and fury, signifying nothing," Houston murmured.

"Is that from the *Iliad* as well, sir?"

"No, Lieutenant. It's from Shakespeare's *Macbeth*."

"Didn't know they had rockets in his day."

"I don't believe they did. But he was more or less meditating on the folly of excessive ambition. I only saw the play performed once, and I suspect the troupe which put it on took some liberties with the text. But I liked that line, and I looked it up later in a copy I found in the possession of a traveling salesman. *That* line is in the play. I couldn't find the horse race anywhere, though. Or the bearbaiting scene."

The British fired another volley of rockets. Driscol decided that a pleasant literary discussion, conducted in the midst of a rocket cannonade, would have a splendid effect on the troops. Several hundred of them now had their heads sticking out of the windows. And while many were ogling the oncoming rockets, most of them were anxiously watching to see how Houston and Driscol and Ross were behaving.

So he turned away from the oncoming rockets and ignored them completely.

"I've never seen a horse race—much less a bearbaiting—performed on a stage. That sounds rather hard on the flooring."

Houston laughed—and, to Driscol's complete satisfaction, he was still laughing when the second volley of rockets began to land. "Oh, it wasn't performed on a *stage.* They held it at the race grounds in Nashville. Horse racing is all the rage in Tennessee, you know."

"Cherokees are fond of the sport, too," Ross chimed in. "Not as fond as we are of our ball game, of course."

Out of the corner of his eye, Driscol saw a third volley fired.

"That's quite fascinating," he stated, as if he cared passionately about the entertainment habits of frontiersmen and Indians.

Houston turned to face Driscol squarely now, leaning over the shorter man as if they were both engrossed in conversation. As a display of what the French called *sangfroid,* it was as good as any Driscol had ever seen on the part of a commander in battle.

Twenty-one years old. Great God, what this man could accomplish with his life! And probably the same for Ross, who's not much older.

Some distance to the east, General Robert Ross lowered his telescope. Then, took a long, slow breath.

This would be no Bladensburg—and Bladensburg had been costly enough.

He hadn't been able to make out the features of the three figures in the distance who seemed to be the American commanders. Even in full daylight, he couldn't have done so. But there'd been enough illumination to make their comportment obvious.

With officers like that to lead them, Ross had no great hope that a simple headlong charge would rattle the enemy enough to send them scampering. He'd been able to do it at Bladensburg because the few stalwart units among the American forces had been left isolated on the open field, after most of their fellow soldiers were routed. Eventually, they'd had no choice but to retreat.

Here, with a fortress to shelter them . . .

Still worse, he was reasonably sure that the soldiers who'd been rallied at the Capitol *were* stalwart units, in the main. Ross had rallied troops himself, in the past, and that was almost invariably the pattern.

"Damn all admirals and their cocksure schemes," he muttered under his breath.

But there was nothing for it. Ross had proposed a flanking attack, but Cockburn had objected—and given Admiral Cochrane's support for this expedition, Ross hadn't felt it possible simply to override the objection.

"A flanking attack? That'll take half the night! No, no, Robert—just roll right over the bastards. A few volleys of the Congreves and one staunch charge, and it'll be all over. Cousin Jonathan will be scampering up Pennsylvania Avenue and we'll follow him to burn their president's mansion."

Nothing for it.

Ross took another deep breath and turned his head. "Send forward the Fourth," he commanded his aides. One of the two immediately sped off.

Ross would have preferred using Thornton's Eighty-fifth Foot Regiment. A *very* stalwart force, that. But the Eighty-fifth needed a rest. The regiment had been handled roughly at Bladensburg, storming a bridge under American artillery fire. Thornton himself had been severely wounded a bit later by grapeshot. The Fourth, on the other hand, had faced only militiamen, who'd soon enough run away.

Looking over the terrain, Ross knew it would soon be covered with carnage. If the Americans held their ground . . .

His remaining aide said it aloud. "This may prove something of a desperate business, sir."

Do tell, Ross thought sarcastically. *A direct frontal assault on a fortress, with riflemen in every port and heavy field artillery well positioned in the middle. And me with nothing but Congreves and three light field pieces.*

As if on cue, the six-pounder and the two three-pounders opened fire. That was the entirety of Ross's "battery." It was a pathetic sound, compared to the ferocity of the hissing rockets. But, glumly, Ross knew full well that what little damage the field pieces would do against the heavily built Capitol would probably exceed the effect of the Congreves.

The British general wasn't fond of the cantankerous rockets. Yes, the things were splendid for the morale of his own men—and sometimes shattered an opponent's nerve. But, as actual weapons, he thought they were more trouble than they were worth.

Wellington, he knew, had come to the same conclusion in the course of the Peninsular War. But this expedition fell ultimately under naval command, and admirals loved the blasted things. So, whether he liked it or not, Ross had been saddled with a multitude of rockets, instead of the one good battery of real guns he would have preferred.

Again, as if on cue, one of the Congreves exploded not more than a second after it was fired. Fortunately, the rocket had traveled far enough not to injure the men who had fired it. Ross could only hope that the fragments didn't land on the backs of the Fourth marching across the field.

A flash of white caught his attention, and drew his eyes back to the center. He saw Admiral Cockburn prancing his horse not far behind the men of the Fourth, exhorting them onward. The conflagration at the Navy Yard was now great enough to spill a devil's light over the entire area. The admiral's gold-laced hat and epaulettes gleamed quite brightly.

Cockburn favored a white horse, in a battle. The admiral was nothing if not a showman. For one brief, savage moment, Ross found himself fervently hoping the animal would provide the enemy with an especially clear target.

But that was an unworthy thought, and he drove it under.

Besides, unless Ross was much mistaken, he'd soon enough be joining the admiral. Surpassing him, in fact, because when the battle was most desperate Robert Ross had always been a general who'd led his men from the front, as he had at Bladensburg and many places before it.

He'd do so on a brown horse, though. Courage was essential for a commanding officer—but there was no reason to be *stupid* as well.

"Bring me my horse," he commanded. The second aide sped off.

"Damn all admirals and their cocksure schemes," Ross muttered again. Louder this time, since there was no longer anyone to hear.

CHAPTER 25

A wave of relief swept over Sam Houston when Charles Ball finally nodded to him. Even the delay at the Horseshoe hadn't seemed as long as the time that had just passed. The Thirty-ninth Infantry at the Horseshoe had waited for an hour and a half before beginning their assault, yes; and the time that had elapsed since the British began their assault on the Capitol hadn't taken but a few minutes. Still, those minutes had seemed endless.

Seeing Ball and the gunners placing their hands over their ears, Sam did the same. "*Fire!*" he bellowed, in his best imitation of an Achaean captain ordering a charge.

Sam supposed—

The roar of the battery was enough to numb his mind for an instant.

—that his anxiety was due to the intrinsic difference between being on the defense versus the offense. However long they might have waited at the Horseshoe, they hadn't been worrying that the Creeks were going to attack *them*. It was one thing to settle your nerves when danger was an abstraction. Quite another to do so when danger took the form of a red-coated machine, grinding steadily toward you in the flickering illumination of a massive bonfire.

Sam peered intently into the darkness, trying to discern what effect the salvo had had on the British. It was hard to see much of anything, since his eyes were tearing up. He'd been standing not far away from Ball's twelve-pounder when it went off, and a little gust of wind had blown the acrid and sulfurous gun smoke back into his face.

After wiping the tears away, Sam glanced at Ball and saw that his eyes looked quite normal.

Ball glanced back at him, then smiled. "Next time, sir—if you'll pardon my boldness in saying so—I suggest you close your eyes. That powder never burns completely, and it can blow anywhere."

Sam nodded. "I'll do so, be sure of it. But what effect did we have? Can you tell?"

"Oh, very good, sir. It's perfect range for grapeshot, and those poor bastards don't have any cover at all. They'll be hurting now. Not enough, of course. Not yet."

As Sam and Ball had been conferring, the gun crews had hurried through their practiced motions. Sooner than Sam would have thought, they were ready to fire again.

At least, *this* crew was. Looking up and down the line of the battery, Sam's vision was still too impaired to tell if the same was true for the other guns, as well.

He decided he'd done his Homeric duty well enough, for the moment. "Mr. Ball, why don't you take charge of the battery from here on?"

"If you say so, Captain." Ball's eyes flicked back and forth, checking the dispositions of all the crews. Then—

Sam hastily covered his ears again—and closed his eyes.

"Fire!"

Ball's voice was suitably Homeric, too, Sam observed. More so than his own, he suspected, feeling more than a bit chagrined. Embarrassed, too. Belatedly, it also occurred to him that a commander who insisted on doing his men's work for them was a blithering nuisance.

"And yet again," General Ross sighed. American artillery was going to be just as murderous on this field as it had usually proven to be, since the war began.

His horse had been brought to him, by now. He moved immediately toward it. There wasn't a chance in creation that this assault was going to succeed if he wasn't seen by his men in the lead.

Damn all cocksure admirals and their schemes.

James Monroe and his party of dragoons drew up to within a hundred yards of the western side of the Capitol. There were no enemy soldiers anywhere to be seen, although Monroe assumed the cannon roar they'd just heard emanating from the other side of the buildings indicated that the British were beginning their assault.

Now was the time to make their final dash for the Capitol, therefore. Even going up a hill, they'd be within the relative safety of the buildings in less than a minute. They'd have to leave their horses behind, of course.

Alas, one problem remained. The young dragoon lieutenant put it into words.

"How do we keep our *own* people from shooting us?"

A bit ruefully, Monroe pondered the problem. The illumination thrown over the area by the burning Navy Yard wasn't sufficient enough for the soldiers who were crouched at the windows to distinguish friend from foe, certainly not at a distance.

This would all become a humiliating farce—quite possibly a fatal one—if the secretary and his party were to be driven off by gunfire from the Capitol's *defenders*.

He decided to risk a straightforward and open approach, moving forward alone and waving a white handkerchief. One man would be less likely to be considered a threat.

Then he heard the sound of wheels coming up the street. Heavily laden wagons, from the clatter they were making.

"Into the shadows!" he hissed, guiding his horse into the darkness that lay between two nearby buildings. His dragoons quickly followed suit.

Half a minute later, they saw three wagons rumbling onto the ground just below Jenkins Hill. The wagons were, indeed, heavily laden—with ammunition, Monroe thought, and there were a couple of three-pounders being towed behind the first two wagons. The driver of the lead wagon was a Negro. The two others were driven by white men wearing some sort of uniform. There were other white men riding escort, all wearing the same uniform.

"They're ours," Monroe stated firmly. The British army had a variety of uniforms beyond the well-known red coats, but these uniforms—for such young men—were too elaborate and fancy for British dragoons. They were exactly the sort of flamboyant uniforms that well-to-do militia volunteers would design for themselves.

There came the sound of another cannonade. Monroe realized that whatever decision he was going to make, it had to be made now. Once the British assault neared the walls of the Capitol, entry would be impossible.

He set his horse trotting forward into the half-lit street.

"Hold!" he cried. "We're Americans!"

Startled, the black driver stopped the lead wagon and stared at him. A couple of the more alert soldiers raised their weapons. Monroe was both amused and relieved to see that the white dragoons, as if acting by sheer reflex, looked to the Negro for guidance.

That was a familiar reaction to a Virginia farmer and slave owner like Monroe, and one he was quite sure he'd not have seen from British soldiers. Many times in his life—he'd done it himself—he'd seen white men engaged in some enterprise about which they knew little turn to a slave to show or tell them what to do. As if, for an instant, the relationship of master and slave was reversed. He'd once commented on the matter to his good friends Thomas Jefferson and James Madison, and discovered that they had observed the same thing—and, in the case of both, found yet another subtle sign from Providence that slavery was a dubious institution. For *any* nation, much less a republic.

Monroe wasn't sure about the matter himself, although he'd learned never to underestimate the philosophical acuity of his two friends. But unlike Jefferson and Madison, Monroe was not inclined toward theoretical ruminations on political affairs. His prominence in the new nation's politics was due to hard work, practical ability, skill in the daily business of legislative committee work, a tightly-focused mind—and the fact that most everyone liked him, because he was a likable man.

All qualities that would be of good use here, as well, especially the latter. Monroe gave the wagon driver his most winning smile and trotted forward in a confident and relaxed manner, as if he had every right and reason to be there, and there was no cause for anxiety on anyone's part.

All of which happened to be true, fortunately. Monroe wasn't really a good liar, despite his years as an ambassador.

"I am James Monroe, the secretary of state," he announced loudly.

The dragoons' eyes grew wide. Those of the driver narrowed.

"By the Lord," the black man said, "so you are. I recognize you, sir!"

Monroe nodded graciously. The driver sat up a little straighter. Clearly enough, he was relieved himself to discover that Monroe and his party of soldiers were not the enemy.

"I've seen you any number of times, sir," the man continued. "My name is Henry Crowell, and I make regular deliveries to the State Department. The War Department, too."

Now that Monroe had pulled up alongside the wagon, he realized that he recognized Crowell himself, although he hadn't known the man's name. He'd seen Crowell a few times, making deliveries. That wasn't surprising, of course. For all that it was the capital city of a nation, Washington, D.C., was still more in the way of a large town than a small city.

He glanced into the wagon. Ball and powder, as he had surmised, along with some tools. He pointed toward the Capitol. "I assume you're taking these supplies in there."

"Yes, sir. I told Captain Houston I was pretty sure I could make the trip and be back before the British attacked."

Captain Houston, then, indeed. And how delightful it was for Monroe to discover that at least *one* piece of their intelligence had been accurate!

The sound of a third cannonade rolled over the buildings.

"Lead the way then, Crowell, if you would."

"You're coming, sir?"

"Oh, yes." Suddenly, Monroe heard the lighter and sharper sounds of a multitude of muskets being fired. The British must be close now.

"And best quickly, I think."

Robert Ross's horse was shot out from under him by a salvo from the American guns. A grapeshot that shattered the poor beast's skull. It was no new experience for the general, so he landed safely and was on his feet within seconds. He never even lost his grip on his sword.

He could even, for a moment, bless the soggy ground that was causing so much trouble for his advancing soldiers. The mucky soil had cushioned his impact.

His aides were at his side already. One of them started brushing the mud from the general's uniform.

"Leave that alone!" Ross snapped. "Get me another horse."

He *had* to get in front of this charge and lead it, or it would collapse. The American gunnery was proving even worse than he'd feared. He was certain now that he faced the worst eventuality he might have faced. Those were U.S. Navy sailors manning the guns.

Most British army officers derided Americans as "Cousin Jonathan." But, with a few exceptions like Cockburn, British naval officers did not, and for good reason. Not after the *Guerriere* and the *Frolic* and the *Macedonian,* and Lake Erie.

A horse was brought up. Another brown one, of course. Ross's aides knew his habits.

Once mounted, Ross waved his sword and charged forward. The front line of his army was now within seventy yards of the breastworks, and he could sense them wavering.

They'd suffered fearsome casualties already. The treacherous and slippery ground had slowed the advance, and they'd had to cross hundreds of yards in the face of enemy fire. The fact that it was a night attack hadn't helped them, either. The terrain provided no cover, and the illumination from the burning Navy Yard was enough to provide the enemy gunners with clear targets.

Very heavy fire. As they had demonstrated many times since the war started, American gunners could work their cannons faster than British ones.

Suddenly, the lighter and sharper sound of musket fire was added to the hell's brew. The Fourth had come within range of the multitude of enemy riflemen Ross could see in every window of the two Capitol buildings.

A *lot* of musket fire. British casualties would start mounting still faster.

"Follow me!" he bellowed. *"I'll dine in the Capitol tonight, or in hell!"*

Driscol had been waiting patiently, in the Senate room where he'd taken his position with a single platoon. The lieutenant had made no effort to stop the rest of the soldiers, in the other rooms, from firing their muskets whenever they chose, even though he knew most of them would start firing long before the enemy was in range. He'd have had no way of controlling them anyway, scattered as they were throughout the building. Maintaining volley fire wasn't as important in defending a fortress as it was on an open battlefield, anyway.

But he *could* control that one platoon, and he'd done so easily.

No need to bring the threat of McParland and the two savage-looking Cherokees to bear. Driscol didn't even think of them. The troll was in full presence, now, and that was more than enough.

"Easy, boys, easy." He didn't shout the words, didn't need to. Even over the thunder of guns and muskets, Driscol's voice carried easily through the chamber. "Won't be long now. Sassenach officers are vile beasts in every other respect, but they don't lack courage. He'll be coming along any moment. And we'll kill him."

Monroe's final dash to the western doors proved simple. American soldiers were stationed and ready there, of course, and they were indeed anxious. But their anxiety was directed at wondering whether or not Crowell's supply run would make it back in time.

"Let me, sir," Crowell whispered to Monroe, as they neared the Capitol. Realizing the wisdom of the words, Monroe let the driver lead him the rest of the way up the hill. A black face in the fore would mean only one thing to the sentries.

Sure enough, before Crowell had even reached the building—he'd headed for the House—soldiers were coming out to greet him. Unarmed to boot, because they were already racing toward the wagons drawn up below, to help the dragoons unload them and bring in the munitions and other supplies.

So, Monroe's entrance into the Capitol proved something of an anticlimax. None of the soldiers paid any attention to him as they poured out in a little flood. He'd been identified as one of Crowell's companions, which was good enough for his bona fides. For the rest, the soldiers cared only about the black man's precious cargo.

In fact, Monroe had to more or less force his way past them and into the building. Once there, not knowing where else to go, he headed toward the central chamber. By now, the sound of musket fire was continuous. The assault was clearly reaching a climax.

Driscol had good eyes, and particularly good night vision. He'd been hoping for the sight of a white horse, since he detested Cockburn more than he did most Sassenach. But he spotted the brown one easily enough, wasn't fooled for an instant.

"That bastard!" he called out. "The one on the brown horse,

charging forward. D'you see him, boys? Look for the sword and the gold fancywork."

Some of the men in the platoon called out their answer, but Driscol didn't need it. He watched the way most of their shoulders shifted slightly, the way those of riflemen do when they've spotted a target. Holding their muskets in a line, these men would probably prove pitiably wretched. But most of them had grown up hunting. If they didn't really know how to fight, they did know how to shoot.

"On *my* command," Driscol growled. "Any man fires before that, I'll grind his bones for my soup."

He waited, cold and merciless, hunched at one of the windows and gauging the range.

Quite a splendid officer, that was. Fearless and resolute. Probably the very commander himself, Robert Ross.

Which was even more splendid. *The best way to kill a snake is to crush the head.*

"Fire!" Driscol roared. More of a snarl, really. He controlled his voice, because the acoustics in the chamber were far better than those of a battlefield—and one of his full-throated roars would have startled such men. Might throw off their aim.

Two seconds after the volley went off, Driscol straightened up.

"I'm proud of you, boys," he pronounced.

Two chances saved the life of Robert Ross. The first was that his horse reared up just before the musket volley fired. Startled, probably, by a round from one of the twelve-pounders that flicked its ear. By now, the American gunners were firing canister.

Most of the volley hammered into the horse, killing it instantly. One round struck Ross in the shoulder. The left shoulder, so he retained his grip on the sword. Another struck him in the rib cage, breaking two ribs and channeling down them to exit from his lower back. A third struck him in the right forehead, a glancing shot, not fatal. Not even a serious wound, really, although a bloody one.

But it was quite enough to daze the general. And so it was a senseless man in the saddle as his horse collapsed, not one who could throw himself free. A horse weighing half a ton will crush a man that it falls upon.

The second chance came into play. One of the musket balls passed between Ross's leg and the horse. It did no worse than bruise the general's calf, but it cut the saddle girth as neatly as a razor. The saddle came loose and the horse's dying spasm flung Ross off to the left.

He landed on his side, his right arm crossed below him. Unfortunately, old reflexes had kept an iron grip on the sword, so his already-injured rib cage had a terrible laceration added from the impact of his body upon the sword hilt.

He lay there, limp and unconscious.

"The general's down!" cried one of the aides.

The Irish-born Ross was a popular officer. One of the most popular in the British army, in fact. In an instant, half-a-dozen men were there to bear him away from the field.

Thirty yards to the rear, and somewhat to the left of the field, Admiral Cockburn heard the cry. Cursing, he drove his horse forward to rally the men. Even to an admiral without Ross's experience in such matters, it was obvious that the assault was on the verge of breaking.

"Ah, there he comes," said Driscol with great satisfaction. He swiveled his head back and forth.

"D'you see him, boys? The fancy-looking bastard on that fancy white horse? That'll be Cockburn himself. And I want him dead."

Cockburn gave Ross's body no more than a glance as his horse drove past the group of soldiers carrying the general to the rear. Dead, apparently. Gravely wounded, at least.

At the moment, all that was irrelevant. All that mattered was taking the Capitol. Arrogant and cocksure the admiral might be, but no one had ever accused him of lacking courage or willpower. He himself never gave such matters a single thought.

"Follow me, men!"

For a moment, after the volley was fired, Driscol had his hopes. But then, seeing soldiers carrying Cockburn away, he had to restrain himself from cursing his platoon.

Cockburn wasn't being carried the way Ross had been, like a sack of meal. The admiral was still on his feet—with a man under each shoulder to steady him, true. But Cockburn was still bearing most of his own weight. The admiral had lost his fancy hat, and his steps seemed a bit uncertain. But it was quite obvious that he hadn't been badly wounded. He was probably just dazed, and winded from falling off the horse.

No time for a second volley, either. Not only was Cockburn himself being hustled away quickly, but the entire British line was falling back. It wasn't *quite* a rout. But a retreat so hasty that within a few seconds Cockburn's figure was completely lost in the fleeing mass.

Ah, well. Charles Ball and his gunners were still firing, of course. Ball was no more the man to show mercy on defeated enemies than Driscol himself. A most fine fellow. So there was always the chance that a stray round still might kill the admiral on his way.

Nervously, one of the volunteers cleared his throat. "Sorry, Lieutenant."

There was a time to browbeat men, and a time to do otherwise, and Driscol knew the difference.

"Never you mind, lad," he said, straightening up from his crouch again. "The chances of war—and we beat the bastards back. A piece of advice, though."

His head swiveled back and forth, giving his men a look that was stern, but not condemning. "*Next* time you shoot at a man on a white horse, do try to hit the man. Not the horse."

The whole platoon stared out of the windows. Even in the half darkness, the carcass of the horse was easy to spot. Although it was no longer exactly in one piece.

Driscol should have warned them, he supposed. In the darkness, that great gleaming target must have drawn their eyes like a magnet.

"Ah, well," he repeated. He knew the quirky chances of war. No man knew them better.

From their position in the back of the room, where they'd be out of the way of the militiamen, the Rogers brothers watched Patrick Driscol carefully.

Very carefully, just as they had been for hours.

Not because they were concerned about his safety, though. Their new assignment as Driscol's bodyguards had turned out to be almost meaningless. That night, at least. There was now little chance that the British would manage to break their way into the huge building, where the hand-to-hand combat skills of the two brothers would come into play.

Little chance—largely because of Driscol himself.

So, as the night wore on, James and John Rogers had been able to devote more and more of their time to considering Driscol from an entirely different viewpoint.

Within the first hour, his courage and resolution had become obvious. So had his practical intelligence. Thereafter, it was other things they looked for.

A good sense of humor, of course, was the most important thing. He'd need it.

Eventually, after observing the sure and relaxed way Driscol handled a mass of nervous and uncertain soldiers, they were satisfied. For all the lieutenant's grim demeanor, the Rogers brothers hadn't missed the fact that he was far more likely to settle down a young soldier with a jest rather than a curse. Or break up a quarrel with sarcasm, rather than threats.

"He'll do," James pronounced softly.

"Do?" his brother whispered back. "He'd be *perfect*. Except he's ugly."

Driscol came over to them a short while later.

"It seems you won't have to do much tonight, lads."

They nodded. Then John asked:

"Have you met our sister Tiana, Lieutenant?"

Driscol stared at him for a moment, before looking away. He seemed intent on examining a nearby window. Odd, really, since there was nothing to be seen through it except the night.

He cleared his throat. "Ah. Yes, I believe I have. In a manner of speaking."

James smiled pleasantly. "Oh, that won't do at all. 'A manner of speaking.' No, no. A real introduction is called for. As soon as possible, after the battle."

"We'll see to it," John added. The same serene smile had appeared on his face.

They waited. There was one last thing that needed to be known.

Finally, Driscol cleared his throat again. His eyes never left the window. "Thank you. I'd appreciate that. Very much."

"Consider it done," James said.

CHAPTER 26

Monroe entered the crimson-draped chamber of the House just as a roar of applause went up. The secretary of state had to push his way through a crowd to see what was happening. The chamber seemed to be packed full of soldiers, many of whom had obviously just arrived themselves. All of them were still carrying their muskets, and the soldiers were so full of excitement that Monroe hoped none of them would fire a shot by accident—or even, in the fervor of the moment, fire a celebratory shot into the ceiling.

The assault had been driven off, clearly enough. As soon as the roar began to subside, a penetrating voice rang out.

> *"These ills shall cease, whene'er by Jove's decree*
> *We crown the bowl to Heav'n and Liberty:*
> *While the proud foe his frustrate triumph mourns,*
> *And Greece indignant thro' her seas returns."*

Monroe thought he recognized the passage. If so, a speech given by Hector to his brother Paris predicting the victory of Troy was perhaps unfortunate. If the secretary recalled correctly, Hector himself would be slain by Achilles not long thereafter.

Still—

The soldiers seemed pleased with the sentiments, and Monroe doubted if many of them understood the irony of the citation. Besides, Monroe was six feet tall. Now that he had finally pushed his way into the chamber, he could see well enough over the heads of most of the men to examine the one who'd given that little classical peroration.

So this was the mysterious "Captain Houston." Monroe

couldn't stop himself from barking a little laugh. Great God! The man even *looked* the part!

Houston was standing before the Speaker's canopied chair, at the south end of the chamber. For a moment, Monroe thought he was standing on a stool, until he realized that the captain himself was simply very tall. Tall, broad-shouldered—and powerful, judging from the nearby soldier half reeling from Houston's friendly clap on the shoulder. Houston's blue eyes, powerful blunt nose, and wide grin radiated confidence and good spirits. The mass of rich chestnut hair the captain exhibited when he swept off his hat capped the image perfectly.

"We beat 'em back slick, boys! I'll be scorched if we didn't send the bastards east of sunrise! It won't convene for them to be marching on us again any time soon!" He gestured with the hat, waving it about flamboyantly. "Let's have three cheers for our *Liberty*!"

The cheers came—enthusiastically, not dutifully—and there were quite a few more than three. By the time the soldiers subsided, Monroe's ears were ringing.

He'd kept pushing forward, and finally made it to the front row. Thankfully, there seemed to be an open space of some sort at the center of the mob. Once the secretary pushed his way there, he saw the reason for it: Joshua Barney was lying on a settee, attended by a very large and striking Indian girl. Several other Indians were gathered around the settee as well, all but one of them children. Even the excited soldiers had been respectful enough not to crowd the commodore. It was obvious at a glance that Barney was badly injured, and feeling the pain of his wounds.

The presence of the Indians was a mystery, but the commodore himself didn't seem concerned over the matter. Badly injured or not, Barney was conscious and alert. He spotted Monroe at the same moment the secretary of state spotted him.

"Mr. Monroe!" the commodore called out. "Welcome to what is *still* the Capitol of the United States."

Captain Houston had been about to launch into another peroration, but hearing Barney's words he blinked and closed his mouth. Then he peered intently at the newly arrived figure.

The commodore levered himself up on an elbow and pointed. "It's Mr. James Monroe, Captain. The secretary of state. Mr.

Monroe"—the finger pointed the other way—"may I introduce Captain Sam Houston?"

Houston was no older than his early twenties, the secretary gauged, and—for the first time since Monroe had spotted him—he finally looked a bit unsure of himself.

This was *no* time for uncertainty. Monroe strode forward, bypassing the commodore's settee, his hand outstretched.

"A pleasure to finally meet you, Captain!" he boomed. "And let me be the first to extend to you the congratulations of your grateful nation and government." Monroe would allow himself a little fib here. "Mr. Madison asked me to convey his regards, as well. Alas, he was tied up with matters too pressing to come himself."

That last part was likely true, at least. The president was probably lost, halfway to Wiley's Tavern. The area surrounding Washington was still, in many parts, not far removed from a wilderness. Given the confusion of the moment and having to travel at night—the skies were lowering, too, with a storm in the offing—Madison and his party would have had a rough go of it.

As for the rest . . .

Well, the secretary was quite certain the president wouldn't begrudge him the little lie. James Monroe and James Madison had been friends for decades, a mutual regard that had not really faltered on those occasions when they'd found themselves on opposite sides of a political dispute or even contesting against each other for the same political position.

Besides, Monroe was quite sure that if Madison *had* been present at the tavern in Georgetown, he would have agreed to send Monroe to the besieged Capitol. He might very well have tried to come himself, and his cabinet would have had to dissuade him.

Houston's handshake was firm and confident, betraying none of the self-doubts and apprehensions the young captain might be having.

No, not *might*—was surely having, from the questioning look in his eyes.

The secretary of state was normally reserved in his demeanor, but this was a situation that called for some unbending. So, in addition to the handshake, Monroe clapped a hand on Houston's shoulder and drew him close enough to speak quietly.

"I think you may relax, young man. True enough, the last I saw of General Winder, he was bellowing words which did not bode well for your future. But I daresay the general's influence is already low, and plunging lower by the minute."

Houston's response was a slight grimace. Monroe decided he might as well test the captain's honesty, while he was at it. "You *did* know General Winder had ordered a general retreat?"

Houston blew a little hiss through his lips. "Well, sir, yes. Although I suppose in my defense I could argue that the man I heard it from—William Simmons, his name—turned out no longer to have any official connection with the government. But I didn't have much doubt—none, really—that he was telling the truth."

"William Simmons." The proverbial bad penny. Monroe's own lips pursed, as if he'd tasted a lemon. "Yes, I know the man. President Madison dismissed him for bitter hostility and rudeness to his superiors—whereupon that wretched accountant blamed Secretary Armstrong for persecuting him."

He released the captain's shoulder, smiling broadly. "It's not a bad defense, actually. I speak as a lawyer of considerable experience. In the confusion of the moment—all the military staff unfortunately gone when you arrived in the capital—when *did* you arrive, by the way, and for what purpose?—hearing of the order to retreat only from a cashiered accountant, who had no authority over you whatsoever—seeing the obvious chance to rally troops at the Capitol—yes, it's a splendid fortress. Secretary of War Armstrong himself tried to convince Winder of that just this afternoon, but Winder's a blithering fool, and you never heard me say that—you acted on the spur of the moment, according to your duty as you saw it. Yes, that'll do quite nicely, Captain. In the unlikely event of a court-martial. Which is getting more unlikely by the moment. Now that I'm here, your action essentially has the imprimatur of the government, if not its formal sanction and command."

By the time he finished, Monroe's smile was wide indeed. Houston shook his head, and managed to extract the questions out of the flurry of legal points.

"I arrived—we arrived—just this afternoon, sir. The rout from Bladensburg was already under way, with soldiers streaming down Pennsylvania Avenue." He looked uncomfortable. "I should inform you that it's possible—uh, likely, in fact—that in the course of my addresses to the troops on the avenue I may have—well, did—juxtapose General Winder's name to various heroes of the *Iliad* in a manner which might possibly be construed as derisive. That is, perhaps even insubordinate."

Monroe burst into laughter.

Houston flushed.

"As to your other question, sir, I arrived as an escort for a party of Cherokees, at General Jackson's behest. In fact—"

Houston turned aside and beckoned someone forward. "May I have the honor to present Lieutenant John Ross. The rank is that of a U.S. officer, but he's a Cherokee. Not a chief, but well regarded by his people nonetheless. Distinguished himself at the Horseshoe."

Monroe was one of the very few members of the nation's eastern seaboard elite who had spent considerable time in the western territories. So he wasn't surprised to see standing before him shortly, in the person of a Cherokee notable, a man whose red hair, blue eyes, and pale skin would have fit well upon any Scotsman.

Ah, the Scots. Monroe had always found it amazing that the dour northerly tribe had somehow managed to foist off onto more Latin folk the reputation for rampant concupiscence that was rightfully theirs. Scots went everywhere, and bred madly wherever they went. Not forgetting, of course, to spout stern Presbyterian homilies all the while.

The young lieutenant had his hand out, and Monroe clasped it with his own.

"A great pleasure to meet you, Lieutenant Ross. Welcome to Washington—though I wish your arrival hadn't been so awkwardly timed."

"The same, sir. And may I extend the best wishes of my nation."

Perfect, fluent English, too.

Monroe looked back at the commodore and his Indian companions.

"I assume these youngsters are with you also?"

"Yes, sir. Their parents have asked us to place them in suitable schools. Major Ridge, in particular. He's the father of the younger girl and one of the boys, and the uncle of the other boy. Uh, he used to be called The Ridge, but you probably never heard of him under either name."

Monroe had heard of The Ridge, actually, but he couldn't recall whatever else he'd heard about him beyond the name itself. Dealings with the Indian tribes fell under the purview of the Department of War, not the Department of State.

"Well, I'm quite sure something suitable can be found. And now, Captain, might I inquire as to your plans?" He turned back, smiling again. "Your immediate plans, I refer to. Regarding the"—he pointed a finger toward the eastern wall—"enemy."

"Oh." Finally remembering the hat he'd snatched off to lead the hurrahs, Houston placed it back on his head and gave a little tug to set it firmly.

"Well, sir. It's like this."

He seemed to be stalling, his eyes looking toward the entrance that led to the adjoining Senate building. A moment later, whatever he saw seemed to cause a trace of relief to come to his face.

Monroe turned and saw another officer coming into the chamber. Almost an apparition, really. Where the six-foot-tall and strongly built secretary of state had been forced to push his way through the mob of soldiers by main force, the middling-height and squat lieutenant seemed to pass through them like Moses parting the waters of the Red Sea. And with only one arm, to boot, where Monroe had had two.

"May I introduce Lieutenant Patrick Driscol, sir. One of Brigadier Scott's officers. *Distinguished* himself at the Chippewa."

The slight emphasis on the word made it clear that this time Houston was not using it simply as a gallant pleasantry.

Distinguished himself.

Studying the approaching lieutenant carefully, Monroe thought that Captain Houston was quite wrong. "Distinguished himself" wasn't the right phrase, and he was certain the man Driscol himself would have scoffed at it. He had all the earmarks of a soldier risen from the ranks. Monroe had known men like this, in his youth. At the battle of Trenton; again, at Monmouth; most of all, during that terrible winter at Valley Forge.

Officers and gentlemen fought battles and distinguished themselves. Men like Driscol made and broke entire armies, and did so with no more thought than a blacksmith shaping iron at an anvil.

He had his hand extended before the one-armed lieutenant had even begun to raise his. James Monroe was a gentleman born, and of the Virginia gentry at that. But he'd been taught his manners as a twenty-year-old subaltern by a general named George Washington. A ruthless and hard commander, who'd whip an insubordinate or shoot a deserter in an instant, but never once sneered at the men who made him what he was.

"A pleasure, sir," Driscol said, as he took the secretary's hand. He even seemed to mean it.

Houston cleared his throat. "Patrick, the secretary of state was just asking me what my plans were. As they relate to the current conflict."

"Well, Captain, as we were discussing just before the British began their assault"—it was all Monroe could do not to laugh—"you'd planned to give the men some supper after they'd beaten the bastards off. In rotation, of course, following the system I'll have set up, so that we keep sentries in place at all times. In the event of another attack."

"Supper, yes." The captain looked about, doing his best—rather well, in fact—not to look puzzled.

"There's not much, I'm afraid," Driscol continued, every inch the respectful lieutenant, even if Monroe thought his rasping voice could have filed away stone. "Nothing in the Capitol itself, of course, beyond an occasional bottle of spirits hidden away here and there."

Monroe chuckled. "Knowing my legislative colleagues, Lieutenant, you'd have found quite a few of those."

Driscol smiled at him thinly. "Well, yes, sir. About every other desk. I had them all sequestered and stashed away in the Library of Congress. Under a reliable armed guard."

Monroe must have looked a bit skeptical. Driscol's smile thinned still further. "Oh, you may lay your fears to rest on that account, sir. Private McParland will shoot any man who tries to force his way in. And he'll refrain from disobeying my orders himself, you may be sure of it. I executed the lad, once, and he's been the very model of discipline ever since."

Monroe raised one eyebrow. But Driscol was already turning to Houston.

"Captain, there'll be enough food in the packs of the men—some of them, not all, of course—to go around well enough for tonight. No one will eat well, but as long as it's divided evenly—I'll see to that—they'll go hungry, but not famished. And we'll pass around a tot of spirits later. Not enough to inebriate any man, just enough to cheer them up."

"Very well, Lieutenant." Houston seemed oriented again. "But how are we with regard to powder and shot?"

"Well enough for the battery. Ball and his men are experienced. Between what they brought themselves and Henry's supplies, we should have enough to last the night, even if the Sassenach are lunatic enough to try another frontal assault. I doubt that, though. They suffered a fearful slaughter. Still, I've got sentries posted. If they come again, we'll have plenty of warning."

The lieutenant sounded mildly disgruntled at the thought that the British *wouldn't* attempt another assault. Between the man's demeanor and the Ulster accent, Monroe understood. Driscol was one of those Scots-Irish immigrants whose hatred for the English was corrosive and unrelenting. Under other circumstances, that could pose a problem. Under these—

As secretary of state, it would be Monroe's task to make peace with the enemy, eventually. The more men like Driscol bled them, the easier that task would be. Problems of another day could be dealt with then.

"We're less well off with the muskets, I'm afraid," Driscol went on, now looking a bit exasperated. "There was no way to keep the silly bugg—ah, militia volunteers—from blasting wildly at anything in sight. Or *not* in sight, often enough. Some of the men are out of shot or powder entirely, and many of them are low. On the other hand, a fair number never fired their muskets at all. I'll see to a redivision of what we have left, sir. We'll have enough."

He glanced at the secretary of state. "For tonight, that is, and assuming we do nothing more than simply hold the Capitol. But I don't recommend any sallies—and I couldn't begin to predict what the morrow might bring."

Very smooth, this rough lieutenant with the voice like a file. Monroe couldn't have passed the initiative up the chain of command any more slickly himself.

Fortunately, at the age of fifty-six and with many years of experience as a senator, a state governor, an ambassador to three major nations, and a member of the executive cabinet, Monroe was no stranger to finding the initiative deposited firmly in his lap.

"If the British make another attempt on the Capitol, Captain Houston, I shall rely upon you and your men to beat them off. But that is *all*."

Driscol's mention of a "sally" had almost made Monroe shudder. The thought of Houston leading untrained and inexperienced men, collected from the pieces of dozens of shattered units, into an assault of his own upon British regulars in the open field . . . at night, even worse than in broad daylight . . .

Monroe *did* shudder, just slightly. Houston flashed him a smile.

"Please, sir. As I've once had the occasion to inform Lieutenant Driscol, I am not actually a fool. I've no more thought of leading a sally against the British tonight than I do of leading a charge against the tides."

His humor was fleeting, though. "But will simply holding the Capitol be enough? It's possible the British may leave things where they are, but I doubt it. There's really nothing stopping them from burning the rest of the city. The public buildings, at least. They may spare the private homes."

Monroe shrugged. "So be it. And so what? Captain, the sole purpose of this British raid was to manufacture a political demonstration. It was designed to humiliate us and undermine national morale, that's all. There's no conceivable *military* gain for them here. On that subject, at least, I was quite in agreement with Secretary Armstrong, even if—"

He broke off the rest. This wasn't the time nor the place to air the dirty linen of the cabinet. "The point being this: They can burn everything else in the capital, starting with the president's mansion, but this—*this alone,* never think otherwise—is the seat of the United States government. So long as the Capitol stands against them, they have accomplished nothing but to brand themselves publicly as arsonists and thieves. Petty vandals, no more!"

Deliberately, Monroe had spoken slowly and loudly enough to be heard all through the chamber. A fresh roar of applause went up from the soldiers.

"Just hold the Capitol, Captain Houston," Monroe added quietly. "Do that, and you will have done extraordinarily well. Trust my judgment here, if you would."

"Certainly, sir." Houston hesitated; then: "General Jackson speaks well of you, Mr. Monroe. I, ah, just thought I might mention that."

That was . . . interesting, although Monroe wasn't really surprised. Before the recent rise to political prominence of western figures such as Henry Clay and Andrew Jackson, Monroe had been the one major politician in America who had generally been attentive and friendly to western interests.

Interesting.

Monroe pondered the matter, as Houston and Driscol went about preparing the troops for a possible new British attack. In less than two years, Monroe would most likely be the new president of the United States. It had become something of a tradition in the new republic for the secretary of state to succeed to the presidency.

Whether the current war with Britain was won or lost, he was well-nigh certain that the western states and territories would dominate many of the concerns of his administration. If the war was lost, as rambunctious grievers and grousers; if it were won, as rambunctious triumphalists. Either way, they'd be an opportunity and a monstrous pain in the neck at one and the same time.

His friend Thomas Jefferson had once said of James Monroe, "Turn his soul wrong side outward and there is not a speck on it." Like all encomiums, especially coming from a personal friend and political ally, Monroe knew that the statement needed to be sprinkled with some salt. But he liked to think it was true enough—and he certainly strove to maintain it as a principle for his own conduct.

So he decided to postpone contemplating the fact that he'd cemented the allegiance of southern and western frontiersmen by his actions this night. For the moment, he'd be guided solely by his assessment of the needs of the nation.

There would be time afterward for a consideration of the political implications. He'd give the matter some real thought then, of course. An upright and honest politician still had to be a politician, or republics would be as fantastical as unicorns.

CHAPTER 27

"There will *not* be another frontal assault against those murderous guns," Robert Ross hissed. He was in no mood, any longer, to be polite. "I've lost enough men already, Admiral Cockburn, thanks to your headstrong ways."

He rolled his head on the cot in the surgeon's tent, bringing Colonel Arthur Brooke into his field of vision. Brooke was the senior brigade commander and would now have to lead the British army units.

"D'you hear me, Colonel Brooke?" Ross pointed a finger toward the glowering Cockburn. "I am *not* relinquishing command to him. You will have to lead the men in the field, but my orders are final."

Though enfeebled by pain, Ross matched Cockburn's glare with one of his own. "The *admiral* may advise you. That is all. You will *not* attack the Capitol again. Not frontally, at least. We shall begin siege operations."

Cockburn rolled his eyes. He knew as well as Ross did that there would be no time to carry through a successful siege of the Capitol, before the British army would be forced to retreat back to the ships on the coast. The most Brooke could do would be to harass the defenders and keep them from sallying.

Still, Ross felt it necessary to add the directive. He did so because siege preparations would tie up the bulk of his forces, which meant that Cockburn would not have them available for his own uses. Brooke was a solid enough man, but once he left Ross's immediate presence—or Ross lost consciousness again, which was quite likely—Cockburn might be able to sway him to folly. Not a direct attack on the Capitol, to be sure. Given Ross's explicit orders, Brooke would refuse to do that, no matter what Cockburn said. But who was to say what *other* folly

Cockburn might seize upon? The rear admiral's determination to punish Americans wasn't altogether rational.

Great folly, at any rate, which might produce great casualties. Ross would allow the admiral his little pleasures, so long as his men were not placed seriously at risk. If for no other reason, because Ross wanted to get Cockburn away from Brooke and unable to influence him.

"What is the time?" Ross asked.

"Just after ten o'clock of the evening, sir," Brooke replied.

Ross closed his eyes. Pain and exhaustion were threatening to take him under again.

Not yet.

"If you intend to burn the president's mansion, Admiral Cockburn, I would suggest that you get started. You may take a few hundred men with you." His eyelids lifted slightly. "Not more than three hundred, mind. We'll need the rest for the siege."

"Siege!" Cockburn barked sarcastically. But even the admiral understood that Ross would be unmovable. Angrily, Cockburn turned on his heel and stalked out of the tent.

"Follow him, Colonel," Ross ordered. "Let him have enough men for his evening's arson, but that's all. *Three hundred,* no more."

"Yes, sir." Brooke hurried out.

Once they were gone, the surgeon stepped forward.

"You *must* let me take the bullet out, General. The longer we wait, the worse the risk. As it is, gangrene . . ."

Ross shook his head. "Not till this business is over, and I'm sure my men have been removed from peril."

He didn't add—not to the surgeon—that he didn't dare allow himself to be entirely incapacitated. Not yet. If Ross were unconscious for hours, during and after surgery, and therefore unable to lead his men any longer, Cockburn might claim that command of the ground forces fell to him.

The surgeon's expression was exceedingly anxious. "General—"

"Oh, be done with it!" Ross snapped. "I understand the risk, Doctor, and the responsibility is mine. If I die, I die."

There's no reason to be rude to the man, Ross chided himself. *He's simply doing his job.*

"Consider the bright side, Doctor," he added. "At least I'll return home in good spirits, which is always something an Irish-man treasures. Well. Navy rum, at least. Admittedly, it's not my favorite potion."

The doctor smiled crookedly. It was the custom of the empire to return the corpses of top officers to the islands, rather than burying them where they fell. They kept the bodies from rotting during the long voyage by immersing them in casks of rum. It was perhaps undignified, but . . . it worked.

Colonel Brooke came back into the tent a few minutes later.

"The admiral's gone, sir. On his way to the American president's mansion."

Ross nodded. Then, finally, he relinquished his hold on consciousness. Darkness was peace, and a blessing.

"Got himself another white horse, I see," Sam Houston said wryly. He lowered the telescope through which he'd been peering from an upper window on the south side of the House. "There's a man who is set in his ways."

"It *is* the admiral, then?" asked Driscol. He'd been almost certain, even without the aid of a telescope, but not positive.

The conflagration at the Navy Yard was still growing, and had begun spreading to nearby buildings. They could hear the sound of collapsing structures, as well as periodic explosions as the roaring flames encountered munitions. As impressive as the fire was, however, the Naval Yard was too far away for those flames to pose a direct danger to the Capitol—which also meant that the illumination was still far poorer than daylight.

Sam shrugged. "I could hardly distinguish his features at this distance, even with a glass and even if I knew what he looked like. But unless there's another British naval officer with that much gold braid and a devotion to white horses, I'd say that has to be Cockburn."

Driscol leaned out of the window and looked down. Hungrily, he studied the three-pounder that Ball and his sailors had positioned to guard the southern flank of the Capitol.

"Leave it be, Patrick!" Houston said, laughing and clapping the smaller man on the back. "Clearly he's learned his lesson. He's staying well out of range. Even with a twelve-pounder, it'd be sheer luck to hit the bastard."

Driscol didn't leave off his calculations. "Now, yes. But

maybe when he returns he'll get careless." He straightened and pushed himself away from the window. "No harm in being prepared, after all. With your permission, sir, I'll see to it."

Still chuckling, Houston agreed and waved him off. Driscol headed out the door immediately, McParland and the Rogers brothers in tow.

As James passed through the door, he looked back at Sam and grinned.

"Asgá siti," James said cheerfully. "Just the way it is."

Houston brought the telescope back to his eye and returned to his study of the enemy movements. He lacked Driscol's experience, but he had no trouble understanding what the British were about. Most of their men had begun setting up their own fieldworks on the ground facing the eastern side of the Capitol. But now they were moving detachments into place, threatening—well, guarding, anyway; they weren't really much of a threat—the northern and southern flanks as well.

At least, looking out from a window on the south side of the House, Sam didn't have to listen to the sounds of injured and dying British soldiers on the grounds to the east.

That was . . . ghastly.

The heavy musket balls were bad enough. They shattered bones whenever they struck a limb squarely, mangling arms and legs so badly that amputation was almost always required if a man's life was to be saved. But most of the casualties had been inflicted by Ball's cannons, and they'd been firing grapeshot during most of the British assault.

What Ball and his men called "grapeshot," at least, even though Ball had explained to Sam at one point that it wasn't really the nine-shot cluster that the term technically signified to naval men. Apparently, such wired clusters of very large balls caused too much damage to cannons for them to be favored much in land battles. What Ball's gunners were calling "grapeshot" was really just heavy case shot: three-ounce bullets as opposed to the balls weighing half as much that were used in regular canister.

The technical details aside, the heavy balls were utterly deadly within four hundred yards. The British soldiers had been forced to advance that far with no cover whatsoever, over muddy and slippery terrain that they couldn't see well because of the darkness. By the time they'd gotten near enough for Charles and his gunners to switch to canister, they'd already suffered casualties so bad that one volley of canister had been enough to break the final charge.

There were still hundreds of them out there. Many were dead, of course, but the majority were merely injured—if the term "merely" could be applied to the most horrible wounds imaginable.

Thinking about those men, Sam came to a sudden decision. He didn't begrudge Patrick Driscol his feelings toward the English, but Sam simply didn't share them. He closed the telescope and strode from the room, his mind working on who he should send. He'd go himself, but . . .

No. If Driscol didn't strangle him, the secretary of state probably would.

When Brooke came back into the surgeon's tent, Ross had only recently returned to consciousness. Considerably to his regret, actually.

"Yes, Colonel?"

"Sorry to disturb you, sir. But the Americans have sent over an envoy under the flag of truce."

"Send him in, please."

A few moments later, a very young and nervous-looking American officer was ushered into the tent. A militia lieutenant, judging from the flamboyant uniform.

"And how may I help you, sir?" Ross asked politely.

The young American swallowed.

Then: "Captain Houston—uh, Secretary of State Monroe agreed, too—sent me to ask you if you plan another assault tonight." Apparently realizing the question was absurd, the flustered youngster hurried on. "Not exactly that. He doesn't expect you to reveal military plans, of course. But, well, he told me to tell you that if you *don't* try any—uh, I think he said something about respecting the flag of truce—then, uh—he said it looks like a storm is coming, too—uh—that'll make the misery still worse . . ."

The youngster ground to a halt, desperately trying to reassemble his thoughts, which now bore a close resemblance to a shipwreck.

Ross took pity on him. He seemed a harmless enough lad, and besides, Ross was touched by the gallantry involved. There was often much to like about Cousin Jonathan.

"Yes, I understand. Your—captain, was it?—Houston is extending an offer to cease-fire while we collect up our dead and wounded from the field."

Relieved, the young officer nodded.

"Certainly," Ross stated, as firmly as he could manage. "You may assure your commander that we will make no attempt to take advantage of his gracious offer. See to it, Colonel Brooke, if you please. And send the men out unarmed."

"Yes, sir."

As Brooke left, the American militia lieutenant made to follow. Ross called him back.

"One moment, Lieutenant. You didn't answer my question. Am I to understand that your commander over there is a *captain*?"

"Uh, yes, sir. Captain Sam Houston. From the Thirty-ninth Infantry."

Ross didn't recall any Thirty-ninth Infantry being stationed in or near Washington. Of course, military intelligence was never perfect.

Apparently sensing Ross's puzzlement, the youngster cleared up the little mystery. "He's from Tennessee, sir. The Thirty-ninth is with General Jackson down there. Captain Houston was just in Washington by happenstance."

A captain. Here by happenstance.

That would be the same Andrew Jackson whom Admiral Cochrane and Ross expected they'd be facing later in the year, when they finally made their move into the gulf after sufficient reinforcements arrived from England. It was all Ross could do not to wince.

Of course, the odds were essentially nil that Ross himself would still be in command of the ground forces by then. Even if he survived the next few days, it would take him months to recover well enough to reassume command.

Still, it was a grim prospect. Ross wondered who would be sent over as his own replacement. Pakenham, most likely. A good commander, to be sure, but with something of a headstrong reputation. If he could, Ross would do his best to instill a bit of caution in him. *Above all, stay away from frontal assaults against that horrid American artillery.*

"Thank you, Lieutenant. Please pass along my regards to Captain Houston and Mr. Monroe. I take it the secretary of state is in the Capitol also?"

"Yes, sir. Oh." The young militiaman looked chagrined. "I shouldn't have said that."

Ross would have laughed, except for the pain. "You may set your mind at ease, Lieutenant. I assure you I have no intention of launching another assault with the sole purpose of seizing Mr. Monroe, estimable gentleman though he is. But do pass along to him a request from me, as well as my compliments."

"Sir?"

"I'd appreciate it if he'd give your fine captain a promotion. He well deserves it, anyway, and it would do wonders for my self-esteem. Driven off by a *captain*. No, no, it won't do! A major, I could live with. A colonel would be better still."

"Do it," Joshua Barney growled, after the militiaman returned and conveyed Ross's words. "And make it 'colonel.' "

Monroe, sitting on a chair next to Barney's settee, shook his head. "Commodore, you know perfectly well I don't have the authority to promote army officers."

"Make it a brevet rank, then."

"I can't do that, either. Secretary of *state,* remember?"

Barney closed his eyes. "It's a pity Washington, D.C., isn't a state. We could haul the governor out of his bed and get Houston a fancy rank in the state militia."

Smiling, Monroe started to respond, but the same militia lieutenant was coming back into the chamber. Looking more worried than ever.

"You'd better come see, sir." The youngster swallowed. "They're burning the president's mansion. It's a fearful sight."

From an upper window on the western side of the House, Monroe watched the flames devouring the central buildings of the executive branch of the United States. He couldn't see any details, at the distance of a mile, but it was obvious nothing was being left untouched.

"The bastards," Captain Houston growled, lowering his telescope and offering it to the secretary. "They're burning everything over there, it looks like. Although I think they might be sparing the Patent Office."

Monroe shook his head, refusing the telescope. He had no desire to see buildings he'd worked in and come to know well over the past years go up in flames. He could imagine it all well enough in his mind, in any event.

There'd be no shortage of kindling in the president's mansion. The Madisons had inherited twenty-three rooms of furniture from Thomas Jefferson and previous inhabitants. Exquisite things, most of them: sofas, writing tables, chairs and tables of all sort, beds—many of them finely ornamented. There were three dozen gilded chairs with red velvet cushions in the oval room alone, all hand-carved in Baltimore. Not to mention that the entire mansion was festooned with fancy drapes and curtains, all of which would go up in flames.

Still, Monroe controlled his anger easily enough. He wasn't a hot-tempered man. His worst characteristic, in that regard—and one he did his best to guard against and control—was a tendency to let resentment fester silently. Especially when the slights were personal.

But this wasn't a personal issue, and, besides, he knew the British were blundering badly here. He was a little surprised, actually, since General Ross had the reputation of being a cool-headed man, as well as the sort of officer who was popular with his men.

Houston spoke again. "I'm fairly certain that Admiral Cockburn is leading the detachment that's burning the executive mansion and offices, sir."

"Well, that lends support to a theory I'd just been in the midst of constructing."

Houston cocked his head. "Sir?"

"I'd wager that Ross was somehow incapacitated in the earlier assault, and is having difficulty retaining control over his forces. Cockburn may have gone off on his own, or Ross may have sent Cockburn off just to get him out from underfoot."

"Oh. Well, as to that, sir—it is indeed true that Ross was badly hurt. May well have been killed, in fact."

"He was seen to fall?"

Houston looked a bit uncomfortable. "Lieutenant Driscol took command of a platoon and had them personally fire on the general when he reached the front ranks. So, yes, he was hit. Badly enough that they had to carry him off."

Monroe nodded. That sort of deliberate targeting of an enemy commander lay well within the rules of war, of course. True, most gentlemen would consider it ungallant. But most of America's gentlemen were still of English extraction, not Scots-Irish. That was changing, now, as men from the western states and territories—men like Andrew Jackson and Houston himself—began coming to the fore.

Monroe turned back to the window. He had mixed feelings on the subject. The growing prominence of the Scots-Irish was inevitably introducing a harsher element—not to mention a more raucous tone—into the politics of the United States. But as a committed republican, Monroe could hardly object, even though he knew full well that if he became president he would have many occasions to clash with the breed.

"Why do you think that, sir?" Houston asked. "The business about Ross wanting to get Cockburn out from underfoot, I mean."

Monroe pointed at the buildings burning in the distance. "Because that is a bad mistake, Captain, and not one I'd have expected General Ross to make."

From the captain's expression, it was clear Houston wasn't following him. Monroe elaborated. "Oh, I have no doubt that burning the president's mansion was part of their *original* plan. But the logic only holds if they'd been able to take and burn the Capitol as well. Then they'd have inflicted a most humiliating defeat upon us. It would be of no great military value, to be sure, but one which might have had quite profound political effects. Now . . ."

He shrugged. "The Capitol is the key. Your stand here will turn it around—and make this a political triumph. So that"—he pointed again to the west—"is reduced to simple arson. The populace will be furious, even in New England. And the Federalists won't be able to claim that it demonstrates the hopelessness of the war.

"They'd have done better to simply retire from the field after being repulsed from the Capitol. That would still have been a victory for us, but purely a defensive one, and not something that would have greatly aroused the public. And if Ross were still in full command, that's what I expect he'd have done. Mind

you, Captain"—Monroe gave Houston a wry little smile—
"these are all theories on my part, and unlike Misters Jefferson
and Madison, I am not renowned as a theorist. So I could be
quite wrong."

Houston returned the smile. "Let's just call it clear thinking,
then. It sounds good to me, sir." His eyes became a bit unfocused for a moment.

"I was wondering, sir," he continued, "if I might impose upon
you further in that regard. I have a slight—well, not so slight—
problem of my own to figure out."

"By all means, Captain," Monroe said graciously. He glanced
out the window. "There's not a thing we can do about that situation, certainly not until the morning comes. So why not distract
ourselves from the unpleasantness."

The discussion which followed was one of the most peculiar in
Monroe's life. Most peculiar, perhaps, because it did not seem
so then. He would ascribe that, later, to the fury of the times and
the temper of the moment.

Still!

To begin with, there was the youthful naïveté of the captain,
to whom it never seemed to occur that divulging the plans of
General Jackson might stir up a tempest. Jackson had *no* authority to strip the Creeks of half their land. True, the administration had appointed him to negotiate with the Creeks along with
the Indian commissioner Benjamin Hawkins—but he'd been instructed to follow the guidelines developed by General Pinckney. And those guidelines certainly had not contemplated any
such sweeping land transfer.

But Monroe kept silent, on that issue. Unlike most of the nation's elite, the secretary of state had traveled extensively
through the area, and understood the realities on the frontier.
The settlers pouring across the mountains would take that Indian land, come what may, by force or by fraud—or simply by
crowding the Indians aside and destroying their hunting
grounds. No government in North America, be it colonial or native, had ever been able to stop them. It was an issue that had
driven presidents half mad, just as it had done to colonial gover-
nors before them.

The problem was insoluble, and for the simplest and crudest

reasons: there were just too many settlers, and not enough
ldiers to keep them in check. Nor could the size of the sol-
ery be increased to change the equation.

Monroe wasn't surprised to learn that Houston understood
at much, given his patronage. Unlike many of the nation's po-
ical elite, Monroe was not prone to assuming that Andrew
ckson was either stupid or unsophisticated.

". . . have to build an army as big as the tsar's. That's what the
neral says, anyway."

"He's right," Monroe grunted. "The idea is grotesque. Oppo-
ion to a standing army—certainly a large one—has been one
the tenets of our Republican Party since the beginning."

"Even the Federalists wouldn't support it, the general says."

Monroe nodded. "He's right again, if for no other reason than
mply the enormous cost involved. There's nothing in the
orld so hideously expensive, even leaving aside the inevitable
aste and corruption that comes with it, as maintaining a large
my, even in peacetime."

Monroe gazed out the window, pondering the intractable
oblem yet again. Given the impossibility of creating an army
rge enough to control the settlers, that left . . .

Houston filled in the thought. "Look, Mr. Monroe, what it
eans in the real world is that it'll always be the champions of
e westerners and southerners, people like General Jackson,
ho'll ultimately win. I come from the frontier myself, and I
now."

"Yes," Monroe sighed. "The government in Washington can
oclaim what it will, disavow what it will, denounce what it
ill, disclaim what it will. Andrew Jackson and men like him
ill still wield the whip. In the end—like every continental gov-
nment in North America has done for two centuries—the na-
onal authorities will acquiesce to their wishes. Tacitly, if not
penly."

He made a face. "It's perhaps dishonorable; it's certainly un-
leasant. But it remains a fact. It will become a fact here, once
gain."

Monroe studied the captain, while the earnest young officer
ontinued expounding his problem and his first attempts, shaky
nd uncertain though they seemed, to uncover a solution. As he
id, one thing became clear to the man who was now the secre-

tary of state and would, in two years, most likely be the ne
president of the country. If there was any graceful way to sid
step the problem, it would have to come from frontiersm
themselves. Men like Houston.

There was always this, too, Monroe reminded himself. With
bit of an effort, because he was by no means completely free
the common prejudices and attitudes of the eastern gentr
From a distance, Monroe realized, the people of the weste
waters seemed nothing but crude and violent frontiersmen. Y
it was also true that, day to day and year to year, they interact
with the native population of the territories in a multitude
ways that were unknown to the East. And if many of those i
teractions were brutal, many others were not.

Houston was not the first white settler boy to have bee
adopted by Indians, after all. And Monroe had only to wa
down to the chamber of the House to see, gathered arou
Commodore Barney, still other fruits of that interaction.

That was a beginning, at least. Possibly even a foundation.

"That Lieutenant Ross of yours," Monroe interrupted. "He
a coming man among the Cherokee?"

"Yes, sir." Houston smiled crookedly. "Even though he's n
really much of a warrior. When I introduced him as having 'di
tinguished' himself at the Horseshoe, I was perhaps bending t
truth. He was there, yes, and certainly he didn't conduct himse
badly. But John would be the first one to tell you he's no gre
shakes in the soldiering business."

Monroe chuckled. "And how is that a problem? It's enoug
that he was there, to establish his bona fides. For the rest, polit
cal sagacity is what's needed here, Captain. Warriors—white
red, either way—won't come up with an acceptable solution.

"As a strictly military proposition—and you know this
well as I do—the only solution that will ever be found with r
gard to relations between whites and Indians will be the exte
mination of the Indians. If it comes to it. But everyone I kno
would very much like to avoid that extreme."

That was nothing more than the truth. Attitudes toward the i
digenes were often harsh, even among easterners. But Monro
had never known a single prominent and powerful man in th
political life of the nation—and he'd known all of them, begi
ning with George Washington—who hadn't understood that

policy of exterminating the Indians would destroy the United States as a nation. Destroy it utterly, because it would destroy its soul.

Monroe was a practicing politician, and an experienced one, so he knew full well that governance was often a callous business. But some things were simply too barbarous to consider. To be sure, barbarities aplenty had been committed upon the Indians, but they were neither systematic nor the product of national design. More often than not, they were the result of local clashes, local greed—or that greatest of all sources of social cruelty, simple negligence. It was all too easy for the nation's authorities to become preoccupied with other matters, while actual policy was determined on the spot by crooked Indian agents or hot-tempered young thugs.

"That's well said, sir," Houston stated forcefully, "and a fine sentiment. But I will tell you what else is true—and you know it as well as I do. Any *just* solution—" He waved an impatient hand. "Oh, let's not call it that, because no solution will be 'just.' Any *rational* solution, that everyone can live with—that'll cost money, sir. And plenty of it."

Monroe grimaced. Houston was speaking no more than the truth, alas. *Money* would indeed be the choking point—with a Republican administration even more than a Federalist one. Some Republicans had even protested the very favorable Louisiana Purchase, even though it had been negotiated by Republicans. Monroe himself had been one of the two envoys sent to meet with Napoleon, and the purchase had been approved by the recognized founder of American republicanism, Thomas Jefferson. They'd not simply objected to the money involved, either, but had objected on grounds of constitutional principle.

Still . . .

Monroe was startled to hear the sound of a cannon being discharged. "Are they beginning another assault?" he asked.

Houston was already at the window, leaning out and looking to the south. When he brought his head back, he was smiling crookedly again.

"No. It's just Lieutenant Driscol, taking a gamble. Admiral Cockburn must be on his way back from his evening's plunder and arson."

Monroe looked at his watch. "It's later than I thought, then. I

should be returning to the chamber, I think. In the meantime
Captain, I have no ready answers to the problems you've
raised."

"Don't really think there are any, sir."

"No, I'm afraid there aren't. But that's why men like me—
and soon, I think, you and your companion John Ross—are kep
in business. So let us begin with small steps. First, do me the fa
vor of corresponding regularly, in the future."

Houston's eyes widened a little. The captain wasn't so naïve
as all that, then, and he understood that such an invitation, com
ing from the secretary of state, was tantamount to an offer of
patronage. It carried a tremendous amount of influence, at the
very least.

Monroe could practically see the wheels turning. If Houston
had the ear of both Andrew Jackson and James Monroe . . .

There was no derision in the thought. Monroe himself, as a
young man, had sought the same sort of patronage. Sought it
and gotten it—from Washington, Jefferson, and Madison, just
to name three. He was where he was today because of it.

Patronage alone was not *enough,* of course. The corridors of
power were littered with the political corpses of once-young
men who'd made the mistake of thinking so. Monroe had never
made that mistake—and if he thought young Sam Houston
might be prone to it, he wouldn't have extended the offer in the
first place. But one of the reasons for Monroe's political success
was that he was a very good judge of men.

"And secondly, Captain . . ."

Monroe hesitated, for a moment, then shrugged. If nothing
else, it would be an interesting experience.

"Until this current affray is over, I think it would be appropri
ate to have an officer assigned to serve me as an aide. The secre
tary of war could hardly object to that, under the circumstances."

He didn't need to finish the thought. Houston smiled—not
crookedly at all, this time—and nodded. "Indeed, sir. And I
think you'll discover that Lieutenant Ross is a very capable
young man. John is perfectly fluent with written English as
well."

"Splendid. An illiterate aide would be awkward. We'll consider it done, then."

Driscol came into the room then, his expression sour. "I'm

raid we missed him, Captain. The range was just too great, en if we'd had better than a three-pounder."

That was as good a reminder as any, Monroe thought. Never a od idea to *really* infuriate the Scots-Irish. Once their bitter stility was aroused, they were a folk to make Huns look like ristians.

CHAPTER 28

Ve've found the president!" Colonel George Minor called out, soon as he entered the tavern where John Armstrong had ent some of the worst hours of his life.

Weary as he was, the secretary of war came to his feet imme- ately. "Where?"

"He was at Salona, sir." The colonel came striding over. magine! And here we've been looking for him as far afield—"

"Never mind that!" Armstrong snapped. "Is he coming here?" he estate owned by Reverend Maffitt at Salona was but a few iles away.

Colonel Minor's face grew stiff. "Yes, sir. Of course he's ming. Be here in less than an hour, I should think."

Armstrong silently cursed his own abrasive manner. Now e'd offended the commander of the Sixtieth Virginia militia giment, too.

But he couldn't bring himself to offer an apology. Minor's en hadn't made it to the battle of Bladensburg at all—because Iinor had allowed an officious junior clerk at the armory to de- y him endlessly with pettifogging accounting procedures be- re he'd release the arms and munitions the regiment needed. rmstrong's career was sinking fast, in part because of men ke this.

So the secretary swiveled his head and brought the figure of

General William Winder into his view. Much the same way a ship of the line brings its guns to bear for a broadside.

Winder had finally tired of planning Houston's execution, and he'd spent the rest of the night issuing plans and directives that contradicted themselves from one moment to the next. Just as well, though, because the confusion he'd created had kept most of the military units from leaving the area. It was utterly laughable. Armstrong thought Winder might be the first commander in the history of the world who had to keep his army from headlong rout—even though *all* of his directives had had precipitous retreat as their sole unvarying element—by confusing them into sheer paralysis.

However that might be, the forces were still at hand. And Armstrong had had enough of Winder. *Respect for protocol be damned.* Once the president arrived, Armstrong could leave all other matters in his hands and take direct and personal control of the army as the secretary of war.

It was now—Armstrong checked his watch—almost daybreak. If the Capitol was still standing . . .

No way to know that for sure. So rumor had it, but rumor was rumor. Armstrong needed direct and certain confirmation before he could finalize his plans. Unfortunately, on top of everything else, Winder had created such hurly-burly on the part of his subordinates that Armstrong had been forced to enlist a civilian to scout the matter for him.

At that, Armstrong had more confidence in the civilian he'd sent than he did in most of the officers who hovered around Winder. Francis Scott Key, a Georgetown lawyer to whom Armstrong had been introduced by Congressman John Randolph. A solid and reliable man, Key, even if he did fancy himself something of a poet. In the time since the British landing, most of Washington's population—military and civilian alike—had fluttered about in panic like leaves in the wind. Key, however, had efficiently organized the evacuation of his family and personal possessions, taking them to a place of safety, and then had come back into the city to see what use he might be to the republic. He'd wound up guiding General Smith and his First Columbian Brigade to the battle of Bladensburg, even helped him map deployments.

If the Capitol was still standing . . .

*   *   *

ncis Scott Key hadn't arrived at his post of observation in
ficient time to witness the British assault on the Capitol, nor
repulsion. But the excited inhabitants of the town house from
ose roof he'd been able to watch everything since had de-
ibed it to him well enough. They'd even possessed a tele-
pe with which he'd been able to examine details of the
matic aftermath.

o, although he hadn't been an actual eyewitness, Key was
e to write a good report. It helped, of course, that he was a
t, and thus fluent with a pen.

*. . can observe many bodies of British soldiers still strewn
bout the ground to the east of the Capitol. The attack which
ccur'd was most clearly injurious to the enemy, & they have
ow retired from the scene. The battle seems to have settled
nto an exchange of fire at a distance, which the sturdy walls
f our Capitol should withstand readily enough. I think it un-
ikely the British will renew their efforts before tomorrow at
he earliest, & they may have been repulsed entirely.*

> *I am, your obedient servant,*
> *F. Key*

The report done, Key handed it to the teenage son of the fam-
who owned the town house. The lad had already agreed to
e the message to the secretary of war, since Key didn't want
leave his post, lest something else occur.

"He should still be at the tavern in Georgetown. It's lo-
ed—"

"I know where it is!" cried the boy, and he was already racing
. Whatever reluctance he had to miss any of the action, it was
re than offset by the excitement of being directly involved in
ch momentous events.

His duty done, Key could now indulge himself in his most
artfelt wish—to craft a patriotic poem that would suitably
mmemorate the dramatic occasion.

Dramatic it was, too, all that a poet could ask for! Fortunately,
light cast by the burning Navy Yard would be enough that
'd be able to see the words he'd be scribbling in his notebook.

ratching more often than scribbling, he realized with dismay,
me time later.

Alas, "Marble *Liberty*" was a well-nigh impossible phrase fit into proper verse. For perhaps the hundredth time that ni he cursed the soldiery holding the Capitol—yes, yes, gall fellows, but he had a *poem* to write—because they had thought to raise a flag over it to replace the one which had b carried away by a Congreve rocket.

Blast it! Something as simple as *that*. Key had long ago figu out how he could have fit "star-spangled banner" into the poe

True enough, the first two lines worked splendidly:

> Oh, say can you see, by the dawn's early light,
> What so proudly we hailed at the twilight's last
>   gleaming?

Excellent meter, which fit the well-known tune of "Anacre in Heaven" to perfection.

But then what?

> Whose broad wings and fierce eyes, through the
>   perilous fight,
> In the doorways we watched, were so gallantly . . .

Gallantly *what?*

Yes, yes, "gleaming" would work—but he'd already used word in the previous sentence, and he would *not* give up "tw light's last gleaming." No poet in his right mind would.

The cretins! Were there a banner, he could have it *streami* But "streaming eyes" wouldn't do at all! And "streami wings" was simply meaningless.

An explosion from the Navy Yard distracted him for a n ment. Key glanced back over his shoulder. Another store of m nitions must have been set off, although the conflagration on river to the south was finally starting to burn itself out.

No business of a poet's, though.

He turned back to the notebook, beginning to despair. Fr the look of the skies, the first light of dawn was beginning to a pear, and a fierce storm was in the offing. Once that sto broke, poetry would have to seek prosaic shelter.

Perhaps . . .

He was gripped by sudden excitement, and began scribbli hastily again. If he went back and changed . . .

Yes! Forget the eagle entirely. The bird was mostly a scavger anyway. Concentrate on the statue.

Whose bold gaze and sure brow, through the perilous
    fight,
At the gates as we watched, were so gallantly standing?

Yes, that'd work! From there . . .

  And the rockets' red glare, the bombs bursting in air,

He hadn't seen that himself, but the inhabitants had described
Now . . . a bit of fudging . . .

  Gave proof through the night that our dame was still
                there.

He could get away with that, surely. True, the British had
opped the bombardment of the Capitol hours earlier, but
ey'd fired off an occasional rocket now and then. More for
ow than anything else, obviously, but that was a pedestrian
atter that a poet could safely ignore.
Then . . .
Oh, those mindless soldiers and their imbecile Captain Hous-
n! Key had the *perfect* closing couplet for the first stanza.

  O say, does that star-spangled banner yet wave
  O'er the land of the free and the home of the brave?

No banner, alas.
Key sighed. Nothing for it—once a poet begins with an im-
e, he has to remain true to the thing, bloody awkward though
be. So . . . a little scratching and scribbling here and there . . .

  O say, does she stand still, our belov'd Liberty,
  In the doorway of the brave and the home of the free?

Yes, that worked, although the meter was damnably awkward
the first line of the couplet. He'd have to work on that some
ore. But at least he'd kept the high Cs in the tune.

                *   *   *

A gleam of light struck his eye.

The first ray of the sun, just now peeking over the horizo With a guilty start, Key realized he'd tarried a bit. His messe ger would be back from Georgetown soon, and it was time got started on a second report.

Francis Scott Key stood up, tucking away his pen and no book for the moment while he stretched his arms and legs. gazed at the Capitol, its eastern walls now showing clearly—i cluding the scars left on it by the British bombardment. T American battery was still there; so, in the doorways of t House, were the eagle and the statue.

Key doffed his hat in salute. "You are a poet's despair, Ca tain Houston. But a patriot's delight."

"Get the men ready to move out," Ross commanded. "I want well out of the city before that storm breaks."

"But we'd planned—"

"I know what we'd *planned,* Admiral. But among those pla we did not include being bloodied and repulsed at the Capit Now did we?"

Cockburn looked mulish, but said nothing.

Ross was relentless. "Boldness is one thing, recklessness a other. As soon as the news spreads, the Americans will ra quickly enough. Be sure of it. Our plans to spend a day he wrecking every public building to demonstrate the U.S. gover ment's fecklessness are now moot, Admiral. *Moot,* d'you hea

"For that matter, so are our plans to attack Baltimore. V can't afford any more such losses, if we're to take New Orlea later in the year—and New Orleans is the key to the war. So. is now time to extricate ourselves from Washington before t Americans can bring enough might to bear to force our surre der. I have less than four thousand men left. Enough for a bo raid, if all had gone well. Not enough—not nearly enough—f anything further.

"We shall retreat, then. Immediately. We're in a trap tha about to be closed. You and Colonel Brooke will lead the r treat, Admiral. I'll stay behind until the last moment, to keep t men steady."

Headstrong as he was, Cockburn wasn't actually a fool. took a breath, held it, then sighed. He even managed somethir of a rueful smile.

"As you wish, General. I do regret not having the opportunity to wreck the *National Intelligencer*. The foul slanderers!"

Ross nodded, graciously enough. He had no desire to get into any further disputes with the admiral. They *had* to get out of Washington, and quickly enough that they'd be too far out of the city for Cockburn to commit any further mischief, once Ross gave his final order.

Thinking of that final order, he had to repress his own sigh.

The commander of an army had many responsibilities, some of which were unpleasant in the extreme. But Robert Ross had never shirked his duty, since the day he'd enlisted in the Twenty-fifth Foot right after graduating from Trinity College in Dublin. Nineteen years old, he'd been then, and a professional soldier ever since. Wounded in battle three times—make that four, now—and the veteran of campaigns in Spain, Egypt, Italy, and the Netherlands before he came to North America. One of the very few men in the British army who had worked his way up the ranks to major general by sheer professional skill, without family influence.

Ross reminded himself that honors enough had been showered upon him, in the course of it all. Three Gold Medals, the Peninsula Gold Medal, and a Sword of Honor. So he could hardly complain, now that duty was knocking on the door, bearing the bill.

Cockburn left the surgeon's tent. As soon as he was gone, Colonel Brooke turned to the general.

"Are you *certain* about this, sir?"

Ross nodded toward the surgeon. "Ask him."

The surgeon shook his head. "The only chance for the general's survival now lies with the Americans. Delaying the surgery as he did"—the surgeon still sounded aggrieved—"I can't possibly do the work well enough in the course of a retreat. I doubt the general would survive the rigors of the march, in any event."

Brooke still looked dubious.

"Just get the men out of here, Colonel," Ross said. "Once the march is well under way, you can inform the admiral—no, I'll send an aide myself, so you can pretend you didn't know—that I was forced to remain behind. By then, not even Cockburn will be rash enough to turn around.

"Damnation, Arthur, I *will* get my men out of here, whatever else."

That braced the colonel. "As you wish, sir. I'll see to it."

Then he was gone, leaving only the surgeon and young Captain Smith still with Ross in the tent.

"I'll let you choose the aide in question, Harry, if you'd do me the pleasure of remaining behind until the transfer is done."

"Of course, sir." But the captain also looked dubious. "Are you so sure the Americans will behave properly, though?"

Ross waved his hand. Very weakly, now. "They will or they won't, as it may be. I have no great fears on the matter. Cousin Jonathan's manners may be rough at times, but he's hardly a brute. Captain Houston has certainly conducted himself gallantly enough—and we'll surrender me into his hands when the time comes."

As chance would have it, President Madison entered the tavern not two minutes after Armstrong finished reading Key's report. Finally, the secretary of war had all he needed to take action.

General Winder came over to say something to Madison, but Armstrong's quick steps blocked his path.

"Mr. President, I've just gotten the word," the secretary stated. "The Capitol is still in our hands. I propose to rally the men and begin a counterattack."

Over his shoulder, Armstrong could hear Winder's gathering protest. He drove right over the first blustering sentences. "General Winder here, of course, is needed *immediately* in Baltimore. To prepare the city's defenses."

Madison stared up at him. The diminutive president—he stood not much over five feet tall, and weighed perhaps one hundred pounds—had no expression whatsoever on his face. But he knew perfectly well that the commander of the troops in Baltimore was Samuel Smith, who was both a senator and a major general—which meant he outranked Winder, as well as despising him.

"A splendid plan," the president stated. "General Winder, you must be off at once. Baltimore must be protected at all costs."

Whatever protest Winder might have made died aborning.

"At once," Madison repeated.

As soon as Winder left, the president turned to Armstrong. "And *do* you have a plan, John?"

The secretary of war shrugged. "That word would be too

grandiose, perhaps. But I don't really think any complex schemes are needed here, Mr. President. We still hold the Capitol, and have since the British arrived in the city. Mr. Monroe is there himself, in fact."

Madison's eyes widened at this unexpected news, but he simply inclined his head, inviting Armstrong to continue.

"That gives us the rock we need around which to rally our men, Mr. President. No better rock possible. There are still enough soldiers in and around Washington to turn the day. More than enough—some of them still intact units and ready to fight." His eyes flicked across the room, looking for—

There he was. Armstrong pointed to a young naval officer, seated in the corner.

"That's Captain David Porter, Mr. President. He rushed down here from New York at the secretary of the navy's behest, as soon as word came of the British landing. Brought all his surviving crew with him, too. I spoke to him earlier this evening, and he volunteered to lead a relief column to the Capitol."

Madison nodded respectfully at the captain. Porter was one of the young heroes whom the navy had produced in the war. The many heroes, where, alas, the army had produced precious few. Porter's frigate *Essex* had ravaged British shipping until the British had finally destroyed it with overwhelming force off the coast of Chile. He and the surviving crewmen had just returned in April, after a prisoner exchange.

If apologies were difficult for Armstrong, he was willing enough to make amends in other ways. "And I'm sure Colonel Minor and his Sixtieth Virginia will volunteer to join the sailors. Valiant men, those."

In another corner, the colonel in question straightened his shoulders. "Most certainly, Mr. President! I've six hundred infantry and a hundred cavalrymen under my command, all present and accounted for."

Even armed, now, Armstrong thought sarcastically. *Let's hope they don't run afoul of another officious clerk who might disarm them.*

But he didn't say it aloud, of course. Besides, even if they did run across such a fearsome foe, Armstrong could rely on Porter to deal with the matter. Porter had fought the Barbary pirates, after all, who were not much less rapacious than clerks.

Since the president still seemed a bit hesitant, Armstrong quickly ran through the roster of forces he knew to be present, willing, and able to fight. Added together, it was quite an impressive list—even if more than half of the units were still in disarray and often enough absent their commanding officers.

"One great push now, Mr. President," Armstrong concluded softly. "That'll do it—because we still hold the Capitol."

Madison nodded. "Yes, I understand. The Capitol will do, where our generals didn't. Speaking of which . . ." The president stopped himself and waved his hand. "Never mind. Now is not the time for that, I suppose. Very well, John. You have my approval. For that matter—"

"That would be most unwise, sir. There's always the possibility you might be captured. Best you remain here, I think, and use this tavern for your temporary headquarters. And . . ."

Bad news was best dealt with promptly.

"I'm afraid your own home is now destroyed, sir. The British bypassed the Capitol after their repulse, and burned the executive complex. Everything. Your mansion, the War and State Departments—according to the report, about the only thing the bastards didn't set fire to was the Patent Office."

Madison winced. "Dolley will be most upset. But at least she managed to salvage the most valuable items. I . . . think."

The president started to run fingers through his hair, but stopped the thoughtless motion halfway through. He was old-fashioned in some ways, one of them being his insistence on still powdering his hair. Whatever dignity that might have added to his appearance, it made certain ways of quelling nervousness rather difficult.

He satisfied the urge with a simple profanity. Even muttered as it was, that spoke to the president's distress.

"So be it. Very well, John. I shall remain here while you take charge of the matter. You will send word, though, as soon as the Capitol is secured?"

"Yes, Mr. President. As soon as it's safe for you to come, I'll let you know."

"They're leaving, Captain," Driscol pronounced.

Houston leaned out of the window and examined the distant British army. The enemy force was going through the compli-

cated evolutions of a well-trained professional army preparing
to leave the field. Driscol knew full well that to Sam's inexperienced eye, it would just look like . . .

Well, anything.

"You're certain of that? No chance this is a feint of some
kind?"

By now, the soldier from County Antrim had developed a profound respect and liking for the young officer from Tennessee.
Fortunately—or he'd have been tempted to reply sarcastically.

*I've fought battles and engagements across half of Europe.
D'you think I can't recognize a retreat when it's under way?
Not to mention that fancy clever stunts like the Trojan Horse
work only in fables. Try that in the real world, ha! If I'd been in
Troy—any Scots-Irishman; even a bloody Sassenach, for that
matter—the first thing I'd have done is order the thing burned
where it stood. See how clever Odysseus is when he's roasting.*

But he left it all unspoken, where it belonged. Houston had
earned the right to display a little anxiety, now that it was all
over. Earned it, and then some.

"Yes, I'm certain, Captain."

Houston would never twitch for long. "Call me 'Sam,' would
you? I'm a rude frontiersman, y'know. We're not prone to formalities."

Driscol smiled. "Not on the field, sir. Besides, if the reports I
hear are accurate, you informal westerners *are* prone to dueling
at the drop of a hat. I'd be afraid I might offend that very fine-
tuned sense of honor."

"I've never fought a duel in my life," Houston protested.

"And you are—what? Twenty-one years old?" Driscol's
smile widened. "Give it another year or two, and who knows?
They might be laying your victims—honorable foes, sorry—
down in rows. But modest and humble Patrick Driscol will not
be one of them."

Houston started to grin, but the easy expression faded. "It has
been a great pleasure and honor to make your acquaintance,
Patrick," he said softly. "Do not ever think my sentiments otherwise."

There seemed no ready answer to that, so Driscol simply nodded and remained silent. The only appropriate answer, in any
event, would have been to reciprocate the words—which

Driscol would do willingly enough, but not until the battle was over and done. The British were retreating, yes, but they were not gone. In fact, one of their tents was still on the field.

Anthony McParland, along with James and John Rogers, had been studying that field while Driscol and Houston had been talking. Now, McParland turned away from the window and spoke.

"There's someone coming out of that tent, Lieutenant. He's waving a white flag."

Driscol understood what that meant immediately.

"Damnation," he growled. "This is *exactly* why I refused a commission." Glumly, he examined his left stump. "Until I had no choice."

Houston was clearly lost. Grimacing, Driscol nodded toward the window. "It'll be General Ross in that tent, sir. He'll have been too badly wounded to join the retreat."

Houston looked at the window. "Well. In that case, we shall have to provide him with good medical care."

The rest was a foregone conclusion. "Patrick . . . I'd go out there myself, but . . ."

"Yes, I know. A commanding officer does not leave his post." Driscol sighed, accepting the inevitable. "I'll handle the matter, sir."

As he headed for the door, a cheery thought came to him. "As it happens, Captain, I know just the doctor to recommend for a Sassenach general. Very fine fellow. Studied under Benjamin Rush himself."

CHAPTER 29

It was fortunate, thought the secretary of state, that Captain Houston was a good-humored man, and in both senses of the term: generally cheerful in his disposition, as well as possessed of a ready wit. A solemn or humorless fellow might have been chagrined, even upset, to receive the thanks and congratulations of a grateful nation in a form which was so completely . . .

Sodden. Try as he might, Monroe could think of no better term.

The storm had finally broken, and had proven more ferocious than any Washington storm that anyone could recall. At the height of it, a tornado had swept through parts of the city, adding nature's havoc to the destruction wreaked by human foes.

On the positive side, the rain had squelched all the many smoldering fires left over from the British ravages, as well as the self-imposed arson of the Navy Yard. But if that added to the capital's safety, it did nothing for its appearance. There was nothing quite so miserable-looking as half-burned buildings whose embers looked more like jagged excrescences than man-made edifices.

By midafternoon, the nation's capital was drenched—as were those of its inhabitants who had chosen to brave the elements to come to the Capitol.

Half the remaining population, Monroe estimated—and a far higher percentage of its political classes. As soon as word arrived that the British had been driven off, those latter had come racing back into the city. Rain be damned. They'd kept one wary eye out for tornadoes, of course, but the other—and warier—eye had never left off scrutinizing the new political situation.

Soaked to the bone or not, looking like cats tossed into a pond or not, every holder or would-be holder of public office who was anywhere near Washington wanted to be seen that day, at some point or other, standing alongside Captain Houston and his valiant men.

Houston, for a marvel, even spotted the frequent hypocrisies, and seemed simply amused by them. Most young men of Monroe's acquaintance—he did not exempt himself, at that age—would have been too full of themselves to notice. Or, if they had, they would have reacted with youthful self-righteousness.

"I suppose there's always this to be said for despotism," the young captain murmured to Monroe at one point. "The despot himself serves to draw all courtier flattery and insincere praise, thereby sparing the innocent."

Monroe chuckled. "Surely you're not likening our glorious republican customs to flypaper, Captain?"

Another newly arrived congressman came forward to vigorously shake Houston's hand and assure him that he was the pride of the nation; a true son of the republic; etc.; etc.; etc. *Your obedient servant, sir, and should you desire anything, simply call upon me—*

And off he went, without even taking the time to dry his clothes or finish wiping the mud from his boots. No doubt he was looking for military units from his district, upon which he could shower like-minded encomiums.

Houston handled it perfectly, as he had handled all such from the moment the crowd began pouring into the Capitol. A firm handshake, a friendly smile—modest, but not *too* modest—and, most of all, a few well-chosen words that deflected the praise onto the soldiers and sailors who had stood with him.

It was well done.

Very well done. A man like this, Monroe knew—provided, of course, he had no as-yet-hidden weaknesses or vices—could go as far as he wanted in the republic, with some patience and good sense. The fact that he came from modest birth would not stand in his way, either. It might have, were he uneducated, but Houston had already disposed of *that* problem.

Indeed, he disposed of it again that very moment. The Capitol was still full of soldiers and sailors, too, and now—for the fifth time, if Monroe recalled correctly—several of them sent up the cry.

"A speech, Captain, a speech!"

Houston was never at a loss for words, either. A moment later he was back up on the desk that he'd appropriated some time earlier for his speechifying, and launched into it.

Monroe listened to the speech, as he had to all the others, the way a master craftsman gauges the work of a very promising apprentice. A sure and self-confident craftsman, to boot, who has no trouble accepting the fact that the apprentice, at least when it came to the specific skill of oration, was more naturally gifted than the master himself.

Granted, there wasn't much in the way of real substance to the speech. But substance was too much to ask from the young—indeed, would have made Monroe a bit suspicious. In the secretary of state's experience, twenty-one-year-old men who had achieved *substance* in their public pronouncements usually did so by seizing upon formulas and simplistic schemas. To be sure, that was a natural condition, the philosophical equivalent of measles or mumps. Still, there was always the risk they'd never outgrow the condition.

No danger of that here, though. Houston's speech contained enough in the way of the standard phrases to make it clear that the young captain was a staunch Republican. *Abasement of monarchy's pretensions; staunch yeomanry the base of public virtue; the common man the pedestal upon which Liberty rests,* etc.; etc.; etc. But there was no gratuitous attempt to turn the matter into a partisan one.

It was a speech to make Federalists frown, not one to make them snarl. There were enough references to states' rights to please any Republican in the crowd, certainly. But Houston didn't go out of his way to sneer at such Federalist enthusiasms as internal improvements—which tended to be popular in the West, anyway—or manufacturing tariffs.

Thankfully, he avoided the issue of a national bank altogether.

In short, it was a speech to salute a nation's victory, not one to deepen its rancorous political divisions. Under the circumstances, splendid.

President Madison had come up to stand beside the secretary

of state partway through the speech. "A good Republican, it seems."

"Oh, yes, Mr. President. I've spoken to him at some length in private, and I can assure you he's solidly with our party."

And then some, Monroe thought wryly. It was perhaps best he warn the president. "Mind you, sir, he does have some radical notions. He's much influenced by General Jackson and his people."

Madison nodded. "Well, that's to be expected. He's from Tennessee himself, after all. Still . . ."

The president looked toward the settee where, in hours past, Commodore Barney had rested. The settee was now spilling over with congressmen and senators, since Barney himself had finally been evacuated to a place where proper medical attention could be given him.

"I wouldn't have thought, from their reputation, that one of Jackson's men would have been accompanied by a party of Indians. What happened to them, by the way?"

"The children went with the commodore. He'd more or less taken them under his wing by then. The quiet one named Sequoyah went with them also. I believe the others are somewhere upstairs with Lieutenant Driscol."

The speech had come to what Monroe now recognized as the inevitable Homeric portion.

> *The weapon flew, its course unerring held;*
> *Unerring, but the heav'nly shield repell'd*
> *The mortal dart; resulting with a bound*
> *From off the ringing orb, it struck the ground.*

"And have you met this mysterious lieutenant, James?" Madison asked. "For all that Captain Houston has been effusive in his public praise for Driscol, I've not yet caught so much as a glimpse of the man."

How to answer that? As the night had passed, Monroe had come to take the measure of Patrick Driscol, as well. He couldn't claim to *know* the man, certainly. Men like Driscol were difficult to know, especially if you were a man of Monroe's own class. But he understood him, well enough.

It was all very good to give speeches about staunch yeomanry and the stalwart common man. But what got lost in the fulsome

phrases was the fact that such men often bore terrible scars, and
the fierce and unforgiving hatreds that came with them. Hatreds
which, often enough, were too deep and bitter to make fine distinctions. To a man like Driscol, a president could look much
like a king; a secretary of state, much like a royal courtier. And
gentlemen, not so very different from noblemen.

True, the lieutenant had punctiliously discharged his duty to
escort General Ross into the Capitol, where the British officer
could begin to receive the medical care he so desperately
needed. But if others—Sam Houston among them—had showered Ross with praise for his gallantry and courage, Driscol had
not. He had even refused to let himself be introduced to the
British general, simply stalking out of the chamber once his
duty was done.

Monroe sighed softly. That subtlety was enough to transmit
some of the truth to the president. James Madison and James
Monroe had been friends and close associates for a very long
time, and knew each other extremely well.

"Sulking in his tent?" Madison asked. Nodding toward Houston, who was now coming to the end of his speech: "Jealous of
the captain's acclaim?"

Monroe shook his head. "Oh, not that, surely. Envy is not the
vice of a man like Driscol. I'm quite sure he doesn't begrudge
young Houston anything. It's simply . . ."

Houston was closing his speech with another Homeric citation, which provided Monroe with the cue. "Let me put it this
way, Mr. President. Patrick Driscol is surely not sulking in his
tent over some perceived personal slight. He's no petulant child.
But I daresay he could teach Achilles the true meaning of
wrath."

"I see."

"He's from Northern Ireland, Mr. President," Monroe elaborated. "I've heard bits of the story from Houston. It seems
Driscol's father was one of the United Irishmen. A blacksmith
in a small town near Belfast. You may recall that, when the
British decided to squelch the insurrection in its early stages,
they made blacksmiths a special target. Driscol's father was one
of them."

Madison grimaced. British tactics in Ireland had been . . . severe.

"Oh, yes. Since the British knew that blacksmiths were making most of the arms for the rebels—pikes, more often than guns—they seized all blacksmiths in the towns and chained them to tripods in the town squares. Then, lashed them until they revealed where the weapons were hidden."

"As many as five hundred lashes, I heard. How does a man survive that?"

Monroe took a deep breath. "As a rule, he doesn't. Even those who speak under the torture. Which, apparently, Driscol's father never did. He died, silent."

There was a pause. Houston clambered off the desk. Sprang, rather. He was quite a graceful man, for one so large.

"Such is Patrick Driscol, sir. A lesson for the world—does it really need it?—that destroying a father may seem a sensible measure at the time, but not a generation later." Monroe nodded toward the east. "As several hundred British officers and soldiers discovered this past night. General Ross himself was felled by a volley from a platoon at Driscol's orders. He did his best to kill Admiral Cockburn, also."

The president grimaced again. Unlike Monroe, who had fought in the Revolution under Washington, through its most dire moments, Madison had little personal experience with warfare. He tended to be more delicate-minded about these matters. The man who was now a secretary of state had once been a subaltern of cavalry. Monroe had been one of the two officers who led the charge that captured the critical Hessian guns at Trenton, at the junction of King and Queen Streets. He could still remember the bloody fury of that charge—and the long months of pain that followed, as he recovered slowly from the wounds he'd received.

Gallant foe was a phrase for afterward. At the time, Monroe's sole and single purpose had been to saber Hessian artillerymen, butchering them as pitilessly as he would have butchered animals—but with a venom that he'd never have visited upon mere beasts. Ugly emotions, yes, looking back upon them—but the act of looking back was itself their fruit. The trick was in being able to set them aside, when the time came.

That was easy enough for a man of Monroe's class. Not easy, often, for a man who did not come into the world with the easy perquisites of a gentleman.

"Much like Andrew Jackson, then," Madison commented.

"Yes." Jackson's mother had died during the Revolution.

From privations she'd endured after the British drove them out of their home. Like Driscol, Jackson had been a teenager at the time. And, like Driscol, Jackson had never forgiven the British.

And never would, in all likelihood. Monroe could understand the matter, well enough. It was still a problem for the republic. Nations could no more be guided by unthinking hatreds than unthinking enthusiasms.

"Your captain was right, by the way," the president added. "I just spoke to John, and he tells me he received word two days ago from Hawkins. Jackson did, indeed, force the Creeks to sign away half their land, in a treaty early this month."

Monroe nodded. As secretary of war, in charge of relations with the Indian tribes, Armstrong would have received the news first. Naturally enough, he hadn't raised the matter at the cabinet meeting the day before, which had focused entirely on the British assault on the capital.

"And so, once again, Mr. President, we are presented with an accomplished fact," Monroe said. "Whether we like it or not. If *we* nullify the treaty, now that Jackson coerced the Creeks into signing it, we'll infuriate every settler west of the mountains, and every southerner below the Carolinas."

"And half the Carolinians," Madison muttered.

"Yes. And those are the same people—Andrew Jackson himself, first and foremost—whom we have to rely upon to repel the British. The theater of war will shift to the gulf, now."

The president sighed. "That's why we have made him a general in the regular army. It's a strange way, one would think, to punish a man for insubordination."

Monroe said nothing, for there was nothing to say. Events on the frontier were being driven by forces far too powerful for any government to control. All the more so because Andrew Jackson was not even the source of it, ultimately, simply its representative and visible face. Behind Jackson, lifting him up, driving him forward, were hundreds of thousands of nameless folk. Nameless, at least, to the eastern gentry and northern merchant class. Scots-Irish immigrants, in the main, now known as "the people of the western waters."

Relentless, implacable. Much like—

A thought came to Monroe. "Excuse me for a bit, Mr. President. I have something to attend to."

He turned around and beckoned to John Ross. The lieutenant

had been standing just a feet away; close enough to be ready for any task the secretary might require of him, but distant enough to allow Monroe privacy of conversation. In this, as in every other respect the secretary had seen thus far, the Cherokee was proving to be as adept and subtle as any white assistant he had ever had.

Houston. Ross. Driscol. Perhaps some others . . .

Always Jackson, of course, for good or ill.

James Monroe subscribed to the sweeping principles of republicanism, and had done so all of his adult life. But he also firmly believed that problems were solved by men, not abstractions. Specific men, in specific places, in specific combinations. Just so, as a young officer, had he seen George Washington forge a nation. Just so, as a man coming into his own maturity, had he seen that nation grow and swell, when other men did the same.

With Ross in tow, he intercepted Houston as another gaggle of congressmen were coming forward to extend their congratulations.

"A moment of your time, Captain, if you'd be so kind. Where is Lieutenant Driscol? I'd like to have a word with both of you." He glanced to the side. "The three of you, actually."

Staring out of an upper-floor window of the House at the rain-drenched and wind-battered city to the west, Driscol thought his mood matched the sight. Bleak and bitter, just like Washington itself, even if both he and the city were supposed to be celebrating a victory. That victory, however, was being marred not only by the weather, but by the rumors of a slave insurrection.

The rumors had grown so wild that even a freedman like Henry Crowell, who'd played an important role in defending the Capitol, had been forced into hiding. In his case, fortunately, that wasn't hard. He was sitting on a chair in a corner of the same room Driscol occupied. McParland and the two Rogers brothers were squatting in the same corner, having a quiet and friendly conversation with the wagon driver. That was probably enough to reassure Henry that he had nothing to fear, as long as he stayed with the lieutenant and his men in the Capitol.

Driscol was startled by a soft, feminine voice. "What's that expression you use? 'A penny for your thoughts,' I think."

His eyes shied away from the source of the words. Not because he didn't want to look, but because he did—and was afraid of that feeling.

When the Rogers brothers had offered to introduce him to Tiana, he'd felt his heart surge in a way he hadn't felt since he was a teenager. And the same again, when they'd made the "real introduction" less than half an hour earlier.

There'd only been one woman in his life who'd ever produced that feeling in him. A young Irish girl by the name of Maureen. He'd been sixteen at the time, and so had she. The same age Tiana was now.

He'd never seen Maureen again, after he'd been forced to flee Ireland. For all he knew, she was dead.

In the years that followed, he'd pretty well squelched that side of his soul. There just hadn't seemed to be any place for it in his new life as a soldier. Now . . .

"My thoughts would hardly be worth a cent," he said harshly, his lips half twisted. "I'd not pay a half cent for them, myself."

"Look at me, Lieutenant."

That startled him even more. Softly spoken or not, the tone had been utterly . . .

Imperious, was the only word.

He looked. Up. Standing right next to him, all of Tiana Rogers's height was evident. The girl was about six feet tall, topping him by several inches.

"What is the matter with you, Patrick Driscol?" she asked quietly. She didn't seem cross, so much as puzzled. "Do you think I'm blind? Do you really think I needed my brothers to make a formal introduction? When you think I'm not looking, I can feel your eyes on me. Yet when I look, you look away. If you keep it up, I'll start thinking you're a lecher."

Now, a smile came. "An old and decrepit lecher, at that, too worried about his capacities to do more than leer at a distance."

Driscol flushed. There was just enough truth in that statement to make him uncomfortable. He wasn't, in fact, a lecher—and he knew full well that his *capacities* were still those of a young man. Still, he couldn't deny that the Cherokee girl aroused him, in ways he found hard to understand, much less explain.

Sheer beauty was part of it, of course. The athletic grace of her body even more than the face. Perhaps it was the combination—or, rather, the contradiction. Tiana Rogers was *exotic*. Half white, half Indian, never seeming one or the other to

Driscol. The same with her bearing. At one moment she could act like a princess, the next like a hoyden, the next like a . . .

Farm girl? Squaw?

And where, precisely, did one end and the other begin? He'd heard her brother John praise her talents at gutting and dressing a deer. His mother had possessed similar, plebian skills. So had Maureen.

It was that confusion, not lust, which had kept him so constantly off balance around her. He simply didn't know what to make of her. Had he not been so attracted to the girl, of course, none of it would have mattered. Given that he was, he'd reacted the way Patrick Driscol usually reacted to being puzzled.

That thought finally allowed him to smile. Houston, he suspected, would accuse him of sulking in his tent. Not because of a conflict with a king, but because Patrick Driscol *resented* being confused. Kings he could deal with. Nothing easier, at least in theory. Just cut their throats and bleed them out.

Alas, such well-worn and simple tactics were quite unsuited to this problem.

He tried to find the words to explain, as best he could. Fortunately, a welcome interruption came. Houston strode into the room, followed by Secretary of State Monroe and John Ross.

The captain was smiling cheerfully, as he so often was. And, as it so often did, the smile warmed Driscol. His brother had smiled like that, before he died on the road from Randallstown to Antrim, and had been tossed into the sandpit by the Sassenach. Such a smile would never come to Patrick Driscol—and might not have, being honest with himself, even if his life had been different. But seeing it on Houston's face reminded him of all the many families in the world that had not been destroyed.

"Mr. Monroe's made me a proposition, Patrick—and it involves you."

After he'd heard what Houston had to say, all of Driscol's earlier bleak thoughts returned. Rude though it might be, he went back to staring out the window. For a moment, his sentiments were so hostile that he was unable to speak.

Perhaps I shouldn't speak at all, he thought. *What's the point?* He'd probably just ruin his own chances, small as they were already with an arm now missing.

But a lifetime's stubbornness wouldn't let him remain silent.

He reminded himself that a man who advocated letting the blood from monarchs should at least have the courage to speak the truth to a secretary of state. And face the prospect of being broken from the ranks with the same unyielding courage he'd faced lines of Sassenach muskets.

So he turned back and looked at Monroe. "Fine words, Mr. Secretary. I'm sure they came from you, even if young Sam here gave them a heady and enthusiastic lilt. But I'm no great believer in airy sentiments."

He pointed into a corner of the room. "I'm sure you didn't notice him when you came in. But you might ask yourself why Henry Crowell is huddling over there."

Everyone turned to look in the corner, where the black wagon driver was sitting. Just as startled as everyone else had been by Driscol's words, Crowell's eyes were wide.

"Oh, aye," Driscol said, half snarling. "It's not safe right now for a freedman in the city. Any man with a black skin. It seems there are rumors of a slave insurrection, and half the soldiery is out there charging about to put it down." The rest, he did snarl: "While the Sassenach, needless to say—the ones who *did* burn and loot and plunder—make their escape with no pursuit."

He kept the finger pointing, as steadily as a musket. "So Henry Crowell, who brought the munitions which held the enemy at bay, cowers here in a corner. Not knowing, even, what's happened to the wagon which is his sole means of earning a livelihood. And slavemasters give speeches about the glories of republicanism in the chamber below, and come up here to propose schemes for bringing just settlements to the Indians. Well, there's nothing I can do about it. But I fail to see why Patrick Driscol should lend himself to the furtherance of the lies and hypocrisies of gentlemen."

Driscol's pale eyes were cold, but all the hot, boiling anger surfaced in the words. "Oh, aye, it's always *class* that tells, isn't it? You'll ladle praise onto a stinking Sassenach general for his gallantry. But let me ask you, Mr. Secretary, when you were governor of Virginia, did you ladle the same praise onto the man named Gabriel when you hung him? And if not, why not? What crime was he guilty of, other than opposing the tyranny of his so-called betters, with arms in hand?"

The anger was all encompassing, now. The cold, pale eyes moved to John Ross.

"And *you,* Lieutenant. What is *your* complaint? That the white man won't let you remain on your plantations, lording it over your own slaves?" He jerked his head toward the Rogers brothers. "Just a few hours ago, they were telling me—boasting, to call things by the right name—that most of your chiefs have plantations as fine as any white men. Your Major Ridge, I'm told, is a great man—and nothing proves it so much as his twenty slaves. So you, too, are nothing but lordlings who, like all lordlings since the dawn of time, seized their status by theft and murder and then used the plundered goods to prove the status. And now—*now*—have the unmitigated gall to claim that you are the victims of injustice."

He turned away. "Be damned to all of you. Do what you will. But do not ask me to give it my blessing, much less my active participation."

His eyes searched the city below. Looking for a dwelling wretched enough that he might be able to afford it—on whatever income a discharged lieutenant might have.

Sergeant, he reminded himself. His promotion to lieutenant had not been approved as yet by the War Department. And now, of course, surely wouldn't be.

CHAPTER 30

Monroe glanced at Houston. For the first time since he'd met him, the young captain was obviously at a complete loss for words. In fact, he was almost gaping like a fish. Whatever else he'd expected from Driscol, clearly enough, Houston hadn't anticipated that coldly furious tirade.

No, not tirade, Monroe cautioned himself. It was the lieutenant's harsh words—the tone, even more than the words themselves—that had infuriated some part of Monroe. That part of him which was Virginia gentry by birth, and whose status had grown great with time.

Yet the fact remained that Driscol had said nothing which, in substance if not with the same pitiless condemnation, Monroe hadn't heard said time and again. He'd even said as much himself.

It was indeed true, as Driscol had charged, that as governor of Virginia, Monroe had had to sentence the leaders of a slave insurrection. Would-be insurrection, to be more accurate, since—as was usually true in such cases—informers had revealed the slaves' plans before they could set them into motion. Monroe had been astonished, at the time, at the hostility which his lenient policy had generated from most of his fellow gentlemen. He'd hung the leader Gabriel and several others, because as governor he was charged with maintaining public order and existing laws and property relations. But that had seemed enough, to him, for the purpose. To go further would have been simple cruelty—yet that had been precisely what many others wanted. Why? For no better reason than Driscol's very accusation—they'd been gentlemen, aggrieved by the impudence of slaves, demanding vengeance for their injured dignity.

Monroe took a deep breath, calming and dispelling that stupid, vicious, gentleman's anger. Driscol's charge cut to the very soul of the nation, after all—and Monroe knew it. If most men might not wrestle with the problem of slavery, the greatest of them did. George Washington had done so, in his own austere way—and, in his will, he had freed his slaves. Thomas Jefferson, in his far more voluble—some might say, histrionic—manner, had done the same. He'd once concluded a denunciation of slavery with the words, *I tremble for my country when I reflect that God is just; that his justice cannot sleep forever.*

And Madison, too, in his quiet manner. He'd already told Monroe that once he was no longer president, and could finally retire from public life, he hoped to convince Dolley to move to Ohio. So he could, at least in his own person, finally be rid of slavery.

The president hadn't had much hope of success, however. His wife Dolley was Quaker-born, not southern, and had no theoretical attachment to the peculiar institution. But she also had an improvident son, and enjoyed her wealth. And slavery *was* profitable.

Money. In the end, Monroe knew, it all came down to that. For him, as much as any man of his class. Nothing else, nothing more. Certainly nothing more exalted. Just the endless, well-nigh irresistible seduction of Mammon—who was surely a demon.

He almost laughed, then. Leave it to Lieutenant Patrick Driscol to call a gentleman a demon worshipper, and do it to his face!

That wry thought was enough finally to bring the statesman to the helm.

"Actually, Lieutenant," the secretary of state said calmly, "your objections strike me as speaking well for your qualifications in this mission. *Very* well, in fact."

Driscol's eyes narrowed, and his head turned partway from the window.

"You must be joking."

"Not at all." Monroe couldn't convince a man who wouldn't look at him. His years as an ambassador to France and England and Spain—failures and successes alike—had taught him that. "Please, Lieutenant Driscol, will you simply listen to me?"

Courtesy—especially when it came unexpectedly—did the trick. Driscol turned completely away from the window and faced him squarely. True, the man's eyes were still cold, and his slightly lowered brow could have butted a bull senseless, but . . . he was listening. And Monroe knew how to talk. Far better, if not in formal speeches, than a youngster like Houston.

"All of it is a Gordian knot, Lieutenant. All threads tangled together. A republic which rests in good part on slavery—yet it *is* a republic. Which means, among other things, that it must respect the property of its citizens until such time as those citizens decree otherwise. Or would you have me take the power, and wield it like a despot? And if so, why do you think the end result would be better? How well did Napoleon do, after he became emperor? You served under him, I believe."

Driscol's jaws tightened. "So I did. I left his service . . . after some time in Spain. Just butchery, that was."

Monroe nodded. "The contradictions continue, on and on. The United States is also a nation coming into being by robbing the lands of other nations—yet it *is* a nation, and one that you would see grow yourself. Why else did you come here from Europe? Did far more than that!" He pointed at Driscol's stump. "Gave that nation your own arm."

"It'll all unravel," Driscol growled. "See if it doesn't."

"Perhaps it might," Monroe allowed. "But in what manner? I'd gladly see it unravel myself, if I could be sure all the threads wouldn't be lost, the good along with the bad."

"You don't unravel a Gordian knot."

"Precisely." Now, finally, it was time for a smile. One of Monroe's best—and he was good at smiling, even if he did it rarely. "A Gordian knot needs to be *cut*. So who better to ask than someone like you, Patrick Driscol?"

After the secretary left, a few minutes later—dragged away by his aides once they found out where he'd gone—Driscol glared at Houston.

"How in the name of creation did he talk me into this madness?"

Houston had recovered his own equilibrium by now, along with his good cheer. "Patrick, you can't be *that* iron-headed. Do you think a man has the career he's had—with the presidency still to come, most like—if he doesn't know how to talk people into things?" He placed an arm over Driscol's shoulder and gave him a friendly, reassuring little shake. "Think of it this way. You can always console yourself with the knowledge that you were swindled by an expert."

Driscol grunted. The sound was half sour, half . . .

Not.

"It's an interesting idea, I'll give it that. The core of it's yours, I assume? Monroe's too much the proper gentleman to have come up with it, even leaving aside his English heritage. Only a daft Irishman would think this scheme could work."

The lieutenant's pale eyes moved to John Ross. Always a sergeant's, those eyes, never an officer's. "*You* won't have agreed, of course."

Hesitantly, Ross shook his head.

"No, of course not. So far I don't see where"—he shot Houston an apologetic glance—"it's fundamentally any different from what's been proposed many times before. We move across the Mississippi—and you take our land." He shook his head again, this time more firmly. "It's simply not *just*. It's our land, and you can't even claim the right of conquest. We've been your *allies,* most of the time."

Houston was a little afraid that the Cherokee's bluntly stated opposition would deter Driscol. Instead, it seemed to have just the opposite effect.

"Oh, it's justice you want from the white man, is it? Well, it's good to see the Irish have no monopoly on blithering idiocy. You might as well expect an Irishman to get justice from a Sassenach, as so many did and do. Let me explain something to you, my proud young Cherokee. Looking for justice from the mighty is the work of fools. You'd do far better to look for re-dress in the form of vengeance. Or haven't you figured out yet that's really Houston's scheme?"

Ross's eyes widened.

So did Houston's.

"I never—"

Then Sam realized what Patrick meant. At which point, his eyes widened still further.

"I know the stories," Driscol continued, "even if I can't cite the verses. So, tell him, Sam. Tell him what finally happened to the Trojans, in the end." His eyes swept the room. "Tell *all* of them. Henry, too. He's got as much right to know as any."

Everyone was staring at Houston, now. He cleared his throat. "Well, it's just a story . . ."

"They're *all* just stories," Driscol rasped. "Which means one's just as good as another—if people act by it."

"Well, ah . . . true enough. According to the poet Virgil—he was a Roman, not a Greek—some of the Trojans survived and fled to Italy. After many adventures. And . . . they founded Rome."

"The *whole* story."

Sam sighed. Driscol was glaring again. He was *so* glad he'd never been a soldier who'd had to serve with Driscol as his ser-geant. The man was a veritable troll!

"Well, yes. And in the end, of course, the Romans conquered the Greeks. So the Trojans got their vengeance. Mind you, it took about a thousand years, and there were a lot of twists and turns."

There was silence, for a moment.

Then, suddenly, James Rogers laughed. "That's ridiculous!"

He held up the war club that seemed to be inseparable from him, practically an extension of his arm. "I can fight as well as any Cherokee. But the idea that we'd ever be able to *conquer* the Americans. It's just ridiculous. There are too many of them. Kill one, and ten more step forward in their place."

But Sam could finally see what Driscol was hinting at. "A thousand years, remember. With lots of twists and turns. And then the Greeks turned the tables again, because the Romans all wound up speaking Greek and quoting Greek philosophers."

James shrugged. "So?"

"So 'conquest' is a word with many different meanings." But Ross was the key here, not the Rogers brothers, so Sam turned to him. "Here's how it is, John—and I'll do my best to talk you into it. You and all the others, in the time to come. Stay where you are, and you'll be crushed out of existence. There's no way around it. But move—move *yourselves,* like men, rather than being driven like beasts—and you stand the chance of forging something powerful out there. Something which can shape its own destiny."

"And who knows?" Patrick added. "You may end up shaping your enemy, too. Create a nation powerful enough, in a place you can do so, and over time you'll begin changing the nature of your neighbors." He looked a bit uncomfortable then. "Now that it's all over, I'll admit that Robert Ross seemed a fine enough fellow. Of course, he *was* born in Ireland."

John Ross just stared at him. Driscol shrugged. "Look, lad. I hate the Sassenach as much as any man. But the fact is, I speak their language. So do most Scots or Irishmen. The same language in which the Declaration of Independence was written—and humbled the bastards in their own tongue."

He gestured toward the door through which Monroe had departed. "It was that, in the end, which convinced me. The man's right enough about that. Let two generations pass, and the threads are all tangled up again. So now we Irishmen speak English, and the English argue with themselves about Ireland. Sometimes they even listen to Irishmen. And their cousins here in America—English, Scots, Irish, all tangled together—intrude rudely into the dispute with opinions of their own, which they mostly derived from Englishmen, but didn't hesitate to impose by force of arms when needed."

*   *   *

Patrick Driscol took a deep breath. The quite unexpected reaction of a Virginia politician had cracked, perhaps for the first time in his life, his unyielding animosity toward gentlemen.

Well, not the first time. Another Virginian named Winfield Scott had done that. But Scott had been a general, and Driscol always gave more leeway to soldiers.

"My point is this, John. After a time, it all becomes something of a family quarrel. And now, for good or ill, and whether you asked for it or not, your Cherokees have become embroiled in it." He looked Ross up and down, then glanced at Tiana Rogers and her brothers. "And not just embroiled in the quarrel, either. You're now embroiled in the family itself."

Ross cocked his head. "Granted. Sequoyah's even talking about creating our own written script. To add to all the rest—the mills, and the separate houses, and raising livestock. Yes, slaves, too. I suppose we're adopting all the white vices, as well as the virtues. But we're *still* different, and we want to stay independent." He also glanced at the Rogerses; then, smiling a bit, down at his own hand. "Even if we're none too fussy about who we mate with."

Driscol snorted. "I'd say so, given the way you mate with the Scots-Irish. Pack of ruffians—and I know whereof I speak."

Driscol flushed a bit, then. He carefully avoided looking at Tiana. All the more so, because he suspected she was grinning at him.

"Those fancy stories of the ancients, Greek and Roman both. What I think? If you could trace it all back, you'd find some sordid family dispute at the heart of them. Properly dressed up, of course, as the centuries passed. Gods and heroes, the lot. Somebody cuckolded somebody else—probably a cousin—and they got their revenge, and then their children struck back, and they're still arguing about it to this day even if nobody can remember what it was all about in the first place. Because it just doesn't matter, any longer."

He took another deep breath. "I am not a fool. I know perfectly well that my blessed Scot and Irish ancestors were a pack of brawling clansmen, mostly illiterate and always pigheaded. More than willing to kill each other and steal each other's sheep at the bidding of some mangy clan chief whose 'palace' wasn't much more than the biggest hut in the village. The English played us all for fools. Played this one against the other—most any clan chief was always willing to be bribed—"

Seeing Ross wince, Driscol snorted. "Yours, too, eh? I'm hardly surprised. And so what?—if, in the end, our demands for justice are couched in the Englishman's tongue. More than that—are couched in English ways of thought. But not entirely, because we shape them for our own purposes. And then—"

Grudgingly: "They pay some attention. Some. Even start to think a bit differently themselves. Not because they want to, but because they're forced to. That's always the problem with a family quarrel. You can't ignore the bastards, because they're yours. Especially if they're mean, tough bastards with a house of their own. And that's the heart of Houston's plan, when you get down to it. Move *now,* while you can still do it as a solid and intact nation, not a band of refugees. Build a house of your own *now,* in a place where you'll have enough time to build it strong and big."

Ross was following him intently, but obviously still not convinced. He stared out the window, for a moment. Then, looked back at Houston.

"It will never happen without a break, at some point. Some place, some time, where a line is finally drawn. 'This far and no farther.' "

Houston nodded. "Sure. Let people push you and they'll push you forever. But the other mistake is to push back when you're standing on thin air. Which is where you are today, John—and, if you're honest, you know it yourself. General Jackson will strip you of your land, sooner or later, don't think he won't. And how will you stop him? On *that* land?"

"And you'll support him," came the accusation.

Houston didn't flinch. "If it comes to it, yes. I'll fight for a worthy cause, John, but this one is already lost. And in the meantime, my own nation—the only republic on the face of the earth—needs that land to grow. Which is *also* a worthy cause, and one which is *not* lost." He shrugged. "I don't claim that it's 'just,' because I couldn't begin to figure that out. 'Justice' mostly depends which side you're on—and I'm an American, when all is said and done.

"Give yourself another cause, though, John, and you can count on me. My word on it."

Ross's gaze came back to Driscol. "And your word?"

Driscol snorted. "Do I look like a bloody gentleman? My word! That wouldn't buy you a pint of whiskey. But I will give you my advice, as a soldier. Any commander who insists on standing his ground when the battle is lost is a fool and a blunderer. Worse than that, he's a killer of his own men. Retreat's never pleasant, but there are times when it's necessary. Retreat, regroup, and fight again on ground that favors you."

He looked at Tiana. She and her brothers. If she'd been grinning earlier, she wasn't now. Neither she nor her kinsmen. Driscol continued. "I don't know much about your nation, but this much is obvious—you're in no condition to even fight this battle, much less win it. So do what's necessary. Retreat in order to buy yourselves the time you need. Whether you use that time wisely or not, of course, will be up to you. But that's no business of mine."

"What *is* your business, then?" Tiana interjected, before Ross could say anything.

Driscol shrugged, uncomfortably. "What I agreed to." He jerked a thumb at Houston. "Help this young idiot buy you the time."

"That's not what I meant. What is your *business?*"

He stared at her blankly. "I'm a soldier, girl."

She shook her head. "That's a trade, not a business. You could have chosen to take the English king's colors. Plenty of Scotsmen and Irishmen do. And don't tell me otherwise! My father was a Tory soldier in the Revolution, after he came here from Scotland." Impishly: "Although he'll never admit it today."

Driscol's mind was a blank. "I still don't understand the question, girl."

"I'm sixteen years old. And Cherokee. So I'm *not* a girl."

She gave her brothers a quick, fierce, warning glance. Wisely, they kept their peace.

Then, with that impish smile that Driscol could feel pulling him like the tides: "What I think, Patrick Driscol, is that your business is lost causes." She gave Houston a cool, dismissing sniff. "Whatever *he* thinks about it."

Private McParland burst into the room.

"Dolley Madison's back! And she says there's going to be a *victory ball.*"

* * *

"And how did I get talked into *this,* too?" Driscol grumbled.

Houston had no sympathy at all, as could be expected from a man who was not only the favored dancing partner of the evening but who could also—was there *anything* the blasted youngster wasn't good at?—dance superbly well. He was only at Driscol's side to hear the grumble, in fact, because he was taking a moment's break.

"Stop grousing, Patrick. You could learn to dance, if you wanted to. All that stands in your way is that surly peasant attitude." He mimicked Driscol's rasping voice: " 'Dancin's for stinkin' decadent gentlemen. Damme if I will.' "

He gave Driscol a grin, and then was swirled away by yet another Washington belle. Her matronly dame, rather, who plucked Houston off with expert skill in order to introduce her daughter.

Or daughters.

Or nieces.

Or several of each, all at once.

It was almost laughable. Not only was Houston the young and glamorous hero of the hour. Sooner than Driscol could have imagined possible, the word had spread through the city's distaff elite—most of Baltimore's, too, it seemed, British threat be damned—that he was a *bachelor* to boot. Dolley Madison's sponsorship of the evening's affair would have guaranteed a large crowd, anyway. With the added attraction of Houston . . .

—he's got Monroe's favor, they say—

—Jackson's too, I hear. Of course, he's a roughneck—Jackson, I mean; they say Houston's quite the gentleman—but still—

Driscol did chuckle, then. Why not? Like his brother had been, Houston was a man who found women just as charming as they found him. Driscol might feel completely out of place here, but Houston was in his element. And if there wasn't much chance that he'd be successfully wooed tonight, or even in the few weeks before they'd have to leave for New Orleans, there was always the possibility that the basis might be laid for later success. Marriages in America's high society rarely proceeded with any great speed anyway. Calculating matrons always knew they had time on their side, after all.

Whatever else he might be, Houston was obviously ambitious. That was considered a virtue in the new republic, not a vice—but it still had to be done virtuously. That meant marriage, among other things, and at a reasonably early age. The commonly held attitude, among men and women alike, was that if a man was still unmarried in his thirties, he was suspect for some reason. Whether because he was riddled with vice, or simply unwilling to assume the responsibility of an adult, who could say?

But any hope of a political career would start plummeting thereafter—and in the United States in the year 1814, there was no real distinction between a political career and most others suited to a gentleman. Officer, lawyer, planter, merchant—they all wove in and out of the political corridors.

So, Houston would have to make a suitable marriage, sooner or later. That was a given, and matrons could calculate accordingly. If he dillydallied for a few years—which he very well might; he was only twenty-one, still young to be a husband—there were always younger daughters or nieces coming down the line.

Driscol's wry observations were interrupted by a hand on his shoulder. The left shoulder, which surprised him. Most people were gingerly about—

Most people. He knew who owned the hand before he even looked. *She'd* not care, he realized. Neither about the missing arm, nor about whatever sensitivities he might have regarding the loss.

Well enough. It struck him as a reasonable bargain. If she'd accept the missing limb, he'd accept the fact that she didn't care about it.

"And what may I do for you, Miss Rogers?"

"You still haven't answered my question, Lieutenant. Neither one, in fact."

Driscol tried to remember the first question. He couldn't. Couldn't remember the more recent one, for that matter. It was a bit frightening, the way the woman could muddle his mind.

She wasn't smiling impishly, though. Smiling, yes, but the undertones seemed a bit melancholy. Without warning, she changed the subject.

"Can you teach me to dance? Like this, I mean. I don't dare go out there and start dancing the way we do at the Green Corn ceremony."

Driscol stared at the city's upper crust, busy with their elaborate . . . whatever it was. *A quadrille,* he thought. He wasn't sure.

"No, I suppose not. They'd be scandalized."

He was having a hard time—a *very* hard time—keeping his eyes on the dance instead of Tiana. Somewhere, somehow— Driscol suspected the subtle hand of the secretary of state at work—Tiana had managed to get herself outfitted in a real gown. It was the first time he'd ever seen her in clothing designed to be decorative, rather than utilitarian, and he'd been struck by her beauty even in such.

Dolley Madison had transformed fashion in Washington, ever since her husband had become president. She favored French fashions, in particular what the French called the "Empire" style. That was their own, somewhat more flamboyant version of the Greek Revival fashions that had swept Britain for the past few years.

Tiana's gown was a fairly typical example. White in color, very simple in design, it was patterned after the flowing lines of ancient Greek robes. The soft muslin fabric clung to her body and was so thin it was almost sheer. For all the fancy lacework and geometric designs that decorated the hems—also patterned on ancient Greek models—the gown was basically a very expensive nightgown.

Anywhere except at a formal ball, Tiana would have been wearing a chemisette underneath for modesty. But here, she wasn't, and the low-cut square décolletage and the high waist of the gown emphasized her very feminine figure. She wasn't an especially bosomy woman, but with her size and firm musculature, it hardly mattered. The bare flesh of her shoulders and upper chest was . . .

Dazzling. All the more so because the long and slender lines of the gown as a whole made her stand out even more than she would have anyway. Tiana was the tallest woman there—and made no attempt to hide the fact.

Dolley Madison was perhaps thirty feet away and having a conversation with several other women. Tiana glanced at them and smiled wryly. Then, stroked fingers through her long black hair.

"At least I'm not wearing a turban, like they are. As if they were Cherokees! I think I scandalize these people enough as it is."

Driscol felt a moment's anger, as he always did when confronted by hypocrisy. The scandal wouldn't be caused by Tiana's *Indian* heritage. Full-blooded Indians had been appearing at fancy affairs in European dress for two centuries now, in Europe as well as America, and no one thought anything of it.

But Tiana was obviously a half-breed. Her hair, her skin color, her features—the blue eyes that were so startling against those prominent cheekbones and dark complexion—all these were signs, to a gentry that preferred to think otherwise, that the lines they drew around themselves blurred at the edges.

It was mostly a southern gentry, too, which made it all the worse. None of those proper Virginia and Maryland matrons wanted to be reminded that, often enough, some of the children of their slaves had a readily recognizable father.

He could feel himself starting to slip into an old, familiar bleakness. Vileness, everywhere he looked. But Tiana's little laugh pulled him out.

"But that's not what I'm worried about!" Again, she sniffed. It was quite an impressive sniff, too; no proper matron could have done better. "I don't care what *those* people think. It's when I got back! The Green Corn Festival is a religious affair, you know. Well, no, you probably didn't. But it is. If my people found out—" She shivered slightly. "I'd never hear the end of it."

Driscol realized again how little he knew about the Cherokees, or any other Indian tribe. "Well, look on the bright side. They wouldn't be able to say much of anything to you, for a few years. You'll be in school up here. By the time you get back, they might have forgotten."

She shook her head. "I'm not going to school. I'm going back with you and Captain Houston next month."

Driscol's startlement must have been obvious. "Ah."

"Didn't Sam tell you?"

He tried to control the sudden excitement that filled him. Confusion also. He'd been assuming that in a few weeks, after he left for New Orleans, he wouldn't see Tiana again for . . .

Who was to say? Months, at the very least. Quite possibly forever.

He'd become reconciled to the fact. Even relieved, in some ways. Now, realizing that he'd be in the woman's company, indefinitely, he didn't know what to think.

Or do.

Or feel.

Well, that last was a lie. He knew exactly how he *felt*. He'd never been so thrilled in his life.

"No," he said, almost choking out the word. "He didn't."

"I'm not surprised." Her eyes moved across the crowd. Not for long, since Houston was easy to spot.

Driscol couldn't determine what was in those eyes. Sadness? Anger?

Perhaps neither. The fact that Driscol thought all people were essentially the same beneath the skin didn't mean they all thought alike. Otherwise, why would he have spent half his lifetime in the single-minded pursuit of slaying his English "brethren"?

"I only came here on a whim, really," she said softly. "Call it a childhood's fancy."

Driscol knew about the girl's oft-proclaimed intentions with regard to Houston. James and John Rogers had been with him through most of the battle, and they were fond of joking. Indeed, they joked about most everything.

Tiana studied Houston for a bit. He was swirling everywhere, passing from one dancing partner to another, and obviously enjoying himself immensely.

"There's no place for me here," she said, even more softly. "I want to go home."

Driscol's mind went back. "Then why did you ask me if I could teach you to dance?"

Her eyes came to him. Still with that same look in them he couldn't quite fathom. "I'm not a white girl, Patrick Driscol. What you call 'romance' is a silly business to me. I fancied Sam Houston for a time, because he's a man to fancy. But if you think for one moment I'm going to pine away"—again, that majestic sniff—"I'd as soon waste my time pining over the moon, when there's a harvest to gather or a deer to be dressed. Not likely, ha!"

Finally, he understood. They were simply calm eyes, accepting. Not liking what they saw, perhaps, but accepting it nonetheless.

"Can you read?" he asked. Not thinking, until he blurted the words, that she might be offended by them.

Fortunately, she wasn't. "Oh, yes. Quite well, the Moravians tell me."

"Ah. But I imagine you prefer prose to poetry?"

The little smile widened. "For a man who insists he's no gentleman, Patrick Driscol, you dance more than any gentleman I can imagine."

Much more Tiana-like, the smile was now. "Why did I ask you if you could teach me to dance? The simplest reason of all. I wanted to hear what your answer would be. Not because I cared, one way or the other, about the dancing."

"Ah." It occurred to Driscol that if he said "ah" one more time, he'd never hear the end of it. Or, still worse, *might*—because he'd never hear that voice again at all.

Either prospect was suddenly unbearable. His mind cast wildly about, for an instant, until it found a safe and secure refuge in . . .

Patrick Driscol. Where it damn well properly belonged.

"No," he said gruffly, "I can't teach you to dance. But I do have a social obligation I've been remiss in carrying out. I was wondering, Miss Rogers, if you'd do me the pleasure of accompanying me?"

"I'd be delighted."

He extended his arm. Alas, the wrong one. He still hadn't quite adjusted. Probably because the bloody blasted thing still felt like it was there. It hurt enough, anyway.

She grinned at him. "I'd look like a proper fool, being led around by a stump."

"Sorry." He swiveled, bringing his right arm into position. A moment later, her hand tucked into his elbow, he led her toward the door.

No one noticed them leaving. All eyes were on Sam Houston.

General Ross was out of surgery, and awake.

"And your own defense was most gallant as well, Lieutenant," he said pleasantly. Ross cocked his head on the pillow, studying Driscol. "I suspect we've met before. Have we?"

Driscol cleared his throat. "In a manner of speaking, sir. I was across the field at Corunna. And, ah . . ."

Ross chuckled drily. "Took part in the very vigorous pursuit afterward. You have the look of a relentless man."

Driscol must have looked uncomfortable. Ross chuckled again, very drily, glancing at his heavily bandaged shoulder. "I had a feeling that volley was targeted. You, I presume."

"Ah. Yes, sir." Before he'd ushered them in, the doctor had

told Driscol that Ross would most likely survive. But he'd need to spend months recovering, and would never really be able to use that arm very well again.

And . . .

Patrick Driscol would do it again. In an instant.

Looking into Ross's eyes, he knew the man understood. So, a crack that one gentleman officer had started, and a gentleman politician widened, was widened still farther by a third. And this one a Sassenach general, to boot.

Driscol began to fear for his soul.

"I was surprised at the time by the professional quality of the Capitol's defense," Ross went on. "Not to detract anything from Captain Houston—a very estimable young man—but that wasn't his doing."

"Ah. No, sir."

Ross nodded. "Good. I feel much better. It's embarrassing to be repulsed so decisively by an inexperienced militia officer. Now, at least, I'll be able to say I was defeated by one of Napoleon's veterans. Even if he was a lieutenant."

"Ah. I'm not exactly a lieutenant, sir. That's a field rank, which still hasn't been confirmed by the War Department. Properly speaking, I'm still a sergeant."

"Better still!" Ross actually grinned. "One of the emperor's *sergeants*. A lot of trolls, everyone knows it. Fearsome brutes."

They both chuckled, then.

"Belfast, from the accent?"

"Not the town, sir. But, yes, County Antrim."

"I see." Ross was back to studying him. "I'm from County Down," he said abruptly. "Not far south of there."

Driscol didn't know what to say, so he said nothing.

Again, Ross seemed to understand. "But I went to Trinity College, and you did not."

"No, sir. My family was not Church of England."

"Yes. Mine was. And so I became an officer of the British army, and you became my foe. Such is the working of Providence."

They were very keen eyes, even in a man who must be throbbing with pain. Driscol had no difficulty, any longer, understanding Ross's reputation as a soldier's general. Had . . . Providence not ruled otherwise, he'd not have minded serving under him.

"I'm afraid I'm a bit tired, Lieutenant Driscol, Miss Rogers, so I'll have to ask you to excuse me." He smiled thinly. "Or I shall have that miser—ah, fine doctor—nattering at me again."

"Of course, sir." Driscol started to turn away, extending his arm to Tiana.

"One thing, though, Lieutenant. It seems important to tell you. We've met twice now, and—who knows?—may meet again. But we never met before Corunna."

Driscol cocked his head. "Sir?"

"What I mean, Lieutenant—Sergeant, rather, for this purpose—is that I was in Holland in 1798."

"Ah."

"You understand, *had* I been in Ireland, I would have obeyed orders. Whether I approved of them or not. But, as it happens, I was not there."

Driscol thought about it. And decided that was good enough.

"A pleasure to make your acquaintance, General Ross. Our best wishes for your recovery."

He probably said it too stiffly. But Tiana's smile made up the difference.

Tiana was silent, most of the way back to the Capitol. That was unusual, for she was not a quiet young woman by temperament. Driscol suspected she understood that he was lost in his own thoughts, and was accepting of the fact.

When she did finally speak, of course, she made up for it.

"I warn you, Patrick. If you keep saying 'ah' all the time, I'll start making fun of you."

CHAPTER 31

SEPTEMBER 18, 1814
*Mobile, Florida, territory disputed
between the United States and Spain*

"It's definite, General," John Coffee stated as soon as he entered the room where Jackson had set up his headquarters. "We just finally got word from Major Lawrence. Fort Bowyer is still in our hands, and the enemy force was driven off."

Jackson looked up from the papers he was reading. "That explosion we heard?"

There'd been a ferocious blast of some sort coming from Mobile Bay, three days earlier when the battle was fought. They'd heard it all the way in Mobile, thirty miles off. Jackson had worried that it meant the British had seized the fort, and had blown it up—although there was no logical reason for them to have done so. Fort Bowyer was located on a sandpit commanding the entrance to the bay. If the British had seized the fort, they'd surely have manned it themselves rather than destroying it.

"It turns out that was a British vessel blowing up," Coffee replied. "The *Hermes*. Lawrence says a lucky shot cut its anchor cable and the ship was swept by the current right under the guns of Fort Bowyer. The enemy finally set it afire themselves, after our guns hammered it into shreds. The flames ignited the magazine."

Jackson grunted, and looked out the window across the town of Mobile. The view faced south. Jackson had picked that house for his headquarters, despite the fact that it was more modest than many in the Spanish Florida town. It gave him a good view of the direction from which the enemy would come.

The Spanish inhabitants took that as a sign that Jackson was being moderate, Coffee knew, although it was nothing of the sort. Had the finest mansion in Mobile given him a better perspective, Jackson would have sequestered it and driven out the owners with no thought at all.

But the Spanish were rather inclined to be favorable toward Jackson anyway. Not because they liked the American general who'd seized their town, which they certainly didn't. But, by now, word had spread throughout the Floridas of the conduct of British soldiers who had seized Pensacola. The British had been invited to land at Pensacola by the Spanish governor of Florida, González Manrique, to protect the town against attack after the Americans had seized Mobile.

He'd had no choice, really. Spanish claims to the Floridas were a mere legality now, and every power in the world knew it. The United States had already stripped Spain of west Florida, on the grounds that the territory was included in the Louisiana Purchase. Those were shaky grounds, legally speaking. Under the terms of Napoleon's treaty with Spain, the French emperor had had no right to sell any Spanish territory in the New World in the first place.

But that didn't matter. The Americans chose to interpret the thing as they did, and the Spanish had no real military power to oppose them. Everyone knew it was only a matter of time before the United States would move on to seize east Florida, which had definitely *not* been included in the purchase. The only way the Spanish could resist was to become—whether they liked it or not—the legal proxies for the British Empire. Britain *did* have the power to fight the Americans along the gulf, and was quite willing to do so.

Though they were in Pensacola as guests of the Spanish, however, the British commander Major Nicholls and his marines had behaved as if they were conquerors. They'd treated the Spanish populace far more roughly than Jackson had treated them in Mobile.

The thing about Jackson that so many people failed to understand, Coffee reflected, was that his flamboyant reputation for violence had both a limit and—because of that limit—often redounded unexpectedly to his credit.

The limit was simple: Jackson could be every bit as rough on his own as on anyone else. If he told his men they would refrain from any atrocities—even rudeness—then they would damn well obey him, or he'd have them shot. So, when people discovered that the *terrible Jackson* . . . wasn't actually so bad once he finally got there—could even be downright gracious and charming, if he chose—they had a tendency to flip-flop and declare him a fine fellow after all.

The world was often an odd place. Oddest of all, perhaps, was the man sitting at the desk.

By temperament, Andrew Jackson would have made a legendary tyrant. Not one like Nero or Caligula, to be sure, because there was nothing decadent about him. But he could certainly have matched Diocletian or Constantine. Or possibly even Genghis Khan, come down to it.

Yet, for whatever quirk of fate—perhaps Providence, who knew?—the same man was imbued with deeply republican principles, and held to them just as rigidly as he did anything else.

Jackson's head turned away from the window. Then, suddenly, he grinned and slammed his hand down on the table.

"It's going well, finally. Have you read these yet?" The hand that had just slammed the table scooped up a batch of newspapers and dispatches.

Coffee shook his head. "I haven't had the chance, General. Although I've heard the gist of them, of course." He grinned himself. "Who hasn't?"

"Who hasn't indeed? *Ha!* One of our boys, the hero of the hour." Jackson began reading one of the newspapers. From the quick and easy way his eyes scanned the print, it was obvious he'd read it several times before. Savored it, more precisely.

"He chose to defend the Capitol, you know," Jackson gloated. "A Republican, that boy, through and through."

"Yes, sir, I heard."

"They made him a colonel, too. That must have been Monroe's doing. Madison would have waffled, as always, and Armstrong's useless." Jackson cleared his throat. The sound had a certain gloating quality to it also. "*Was* useless, I should say."

Coffee raised an eyebrow. Jackson smiled at him. "Yes, of course. If you haven't read the dispatches—the newspaper accounts rather—you wouldn't know. It seems the good John Armstrong is resigning as secretary of war. Monroe's to replace him."

Coffee looked out the window. That was certainly good news. "Then who's to be the secretary of state?"

Jackson shrugged. "Nothing's definite. If the newspapers are to be believed, Monroe will remain on for a time as the acting secretary. But he'll be devoting himself primarily to the War Department."

Better and better.

It was a sunny day outside, which matched the mood in the room. Both Coffee and Jackson thought rather highly of James Monroe. They didn't know him that well, true, but Monroe had always been the main voice in the Madison administration calling for strengthening America's military forces. And, for an easterner, he was unusually sensitive to the situation of the settlers in the West.

Jackson cleared his throat again. The sound, this time, lacked the earlier gloating quality. Again, he held up a newspaper. "You should know also that Houston's Cherokees apparently participated in the fight with him. That Lieutenant John Ross is named specifically in several of these accounts. It seems he's even become one of Monroe's aides. He got a promotion, also, to captain—as did one other officer. Fellow by the name of Driscol."

"Don't know him," Coffee grunted.

"Neither do I. They even jumped him to major, from first lieutenant." Sourly, now: "And it's no brevet rank, either."

Coffee thought it was best to move past that issue. Jackson was disgruntled that his recent promotion to major general had been a brevet rank only. His permanent rank in the regular U.S. Army was to be that of brigadier. There was a good chance that Jackson's major generalship would become permanent, since rumors continued to swirl that Harrison would resign. That would free up one of the major generalships authorized by Congress—and Jackson would be the one to get it.

But, for the moment, he was still prickly on the subject.

"This Driscol must have done superbly well for himself in the battle," Coffee commented hurriedly.

"I suppose." Then, shaking his head as if to clear it of unworthy thoughts, Jackson went on: "Must have, yes. Not surprising, though. It seems Driscol was one of Scott's men at the Chippewa. Lost an arm there. That certainly speaks well of him. *Very* well."

Coffee's eyes widened. Jackson's approbation, he knew, didn't come from the missing arm itself. Limbs were lost in battle, it was a given. An honorable matter, certainly, but no more than that. But the Chippewa had occurred early in July and the battle at the Capitol late in August . . .

Coffee did the calculations almost instantly. "Good heavens. Seven weeks after losing an arm, he helps lead a successful battle against British regulars? The man must be tough as iron."

"So it would seem," Jackson said. Whatever resentments he might have felt earlier were gone now.

"Pity we don't have him down here," Coffee said. "We could use him."

"Oh, but we will!" Jackson was back to grinning, and, once again, slammed the table with his hand. "Well, if the newspaper accounts are accurate—which is always a dubious proposition. But, if they are, Houston—*Colonel* Houston now, remember— is to lead a force down here to join us. Most of them volunteers, of course, but it'll include a unit of artillery—*regulars,* John, mind you. The Lord knows we could use them! And apparently this Major Driscol will be serving as his executive officer."

That was *very* good news. If the intelligence they had was accurate, Admiral Cochrane would be bringing somewhere close to ten thousand British regulars to invade and conquer New Orleans and the outlet of the Mississippi. To oppose them, Jackson would have a force no larger, most of which was made up of militia units. One of the most ragtag assemblages of odd bits and pieces in the history of military affairs would have to fend off an equal or superior number of Wellington's veterans, possibly the best soldiers in the world.

"What about the Cherokees, General?"

Jackson shrugged. "Ross will be coming with them. But whether Houston can convince Major Ridge or any of the other chiefs, who knows?" He tapped the papers on his desk. "They'll be passing through Cherokee Territory, apparently. I assume Houston planned it that way to give him a last chance to persuade them to renew the alliance."

Jackson rose from the desk and went to stand before the window, his bony hands clasped behind his back. "He'll be a problem for me, you know. Houston, I mean."

Coffee was one of Jackson's closest intimates, so he understood the meaning of that cryptic remark. He glanced at the pile of papers on the desk. Buried somewhere in that mass would be stiff notes from the War Department, scolding Jackson for hav-

ing assumed far too much authority in his sweeping land grab
from the Creeks.

Buried at the very bottom, no doubt. The general had simply
ignored the letters. The Treaty of Fort Jackson was now an accomplished fact. Whether the jittery authorities in Washington
liked it or not, Jackson had persuaded the Creek chiefs—coerced them, to speak honestly; they'd been voluble in their
protests at the time—to cede twenty-three million acres to the
United States. That was enough to enlarge the state of Georgia
by a fifth, and enough to create most of the proposed new state
of Alabama. Already, settlers would be moving onto the land—
and once they did, no power on earth could dislodge them. Coffee doubted if even the tsar of All the Russias had an army big
enough to do so. The United States certainly didn't.

It was an unfortunate turn of affairs for the Creeks, of course.
Coffee, by nature a more genial person than Jackson, felt a moment's sympathy for the tribe. But only a moment's. At bottom,
he viewed the matter the same way Jackson did. The growth of
the United States was the world's best hope for republicanism—now more than ever, with Napoleon broken and the
British installing monarchical regimes all across Europe. If that
required dislodging a few barbarian tribes from their land, then
so be it.

There was other land for them to the west, across the Mississippi, to take from *other* barbarian tribes. And why not? They'd
been doing it for centuries. The Creeks, like the Cherokees,
were a tribe that had migrated into the area from the North,
breaking and swallowing other tribes that had stood in their
way. They could do it again, if they chose.

They'd have no choice, anyway, because Jackson would drive
them out. All of them, allies as well as enemies. He'd bide his
time, where he had to, to deal with political opposition. But he'd
discussed his long-term plans with Coffee, and Coffee knew
Jackson would never swerve from them. Sooner or later, he'd
drive all the southern tribes across the Mississippi—the Cherokees and Choctaws and Chickasaws who'd fought alongside
him just as surely as the Creeks and Seminoles who'd fought
against him.

Indians who chose to remain as individuals could do so, but
there'd no longer be any independent Indian statelets east of the
Mississippi, to challenge the authority of the new state govern-

ments that would emerge as the United States expanded its territory.

It was a cold-blooded plan. Even a treacherous one, looked at from one angle. But Jackson was willing to be cold-blooded, and his loyalties were to his own nation. Because, in the process, the United States would become a power encompassing a third of a continent. If they could defeat Britain in the current war, then drive the Spanish out of the Floridas altogether—that was Jackson's plan, whether the government in Washington fiddle-faddled or not—the security of the nation would be assured. Canada could be ignored, thereafter. Give the thing another two or three generations, and the American republic would be so powerful it could thumb its nose at all the kings and noblemen of Europe.

That said . . .

"You can't be sure what he'll do, General."

Jackson chuckled. "Yes, I can. You watch, John. The only thing that will stop Sam Houston from becoming a monstrous headache for me will be his own ambition. I'll wave the rose of fortune under his nose, of course, when the time comes. But . . . I don't think he'll take it. The boy who stormed the barricade at the Horseshoe Bend would have. But the young man who defended the Capitol? No. I don't think so."

His tone was one of complete satisfaction. Jackson turned back from the window, hands still clasped, and peered at Coffee past slightly lowered brows.

"You watch," he repeated. Gloating over the words. "He'll refuse the rose."

CHAPTER 32

"You'd best come get him, Lieutenant," said Henry Crowell, his tone full of concern. "Or he'll land in some trouble. Again."

The teamster glanced at the new insignia on Driscol's uniform. "Sorry. Major, I should have said."

Driscol smiled thinly. "Don't apologize. I forget the new rank myself. And it's all ridiculous. I'm a *sergeant,* blast it. Never intended to be anything else."

He levered himself up from the padded chair, and placed the book he'd been reading onto the small table that stood next to it. Thomas Paine's *Common Sense,* that was. Driscol wasn't quite sure why he was reading it again, since by now he practically had the book memorized. Probably just to fortify his soul, given the situation he'd be finding himself in, once he got to New Orleans.

He paused, and studied Henry for a moment. The big teamster was carrying himself differently these days. He seemed taller, and broader, as if he was finally coming to accept his own size. He still retained much of the self-effacing diffidence of a freedman, of course. It would be dangerous to do otherwise. Even in New York or Boston.

Still, his bearing was subtly different. More self-confident. Even, at times, almost swaggering.

And well it should be, Driscol thought. Leaving aside the public acclaim Henry had received due to his role in the defense of the Capitol—the *National Intelligencer* had even devoted two paragraphs of an article to his deeds—what was more important was that Henry was on the verge of becoming one of the very few prosperous black men in America.

"So how drunk is he?"

"Falling-down drunk, Major. Me and Charles would have just carried him out of the saloon, but . . ."

Driscol nodded. "Yes, I understand. He would have raised a ruckus."

"Oh, he's not a *mean* drunk, sir. Not at all. It's just . . . well . . ."

Again, his voice trailed off; and, again, Driscol nodded. He didn't think there was a mean bone anywhere in Sam Houston's body. The problem was that, in drunken bonhomie, Sam would have simply insisted that Crowell and Ball join him for a friendly drink. Or ten.

In a saloon, where the only other black people were servants; where all the customers were prosperous white men, half of them politicians; and in a capital city that was every bit as southern in its attitudes as Richmond or Charleston.

Driscol couldn't help but grin a little. "Would've been a fight."

"Yup." Henry's grin was a more rueful thing. "Sam Houston challenging some rich congressman to a duel. 'Cept it wouldn't have been no formal duel. He'd a just started swinging."

"True."

If Sam didn't have any mean bones in his body, he didn't have any bashful ones either. The only reason Houston might be able to avoid fighting a duel sometime in his life—leaving aside his habits with a bottle—would be his sense of humor and his lack of touchiness about matters of "honor." It certainly wouldn't be because he was *afraid* to fight. On two recent occasions now, that Driscol knew about, Sam had cheerfully joined into a tavern brawl.

Fortunately, those had been brawls in lower-class saloons. The sort of places where getting a bloody nose with a drink was more or less taken for granted, and nobody would even think of meeting at dawn with pistols. Following one of those brawls, the man Houston had flattened had bought him a drink afterward, and bragged for days that he was a drinking companion of the Hero of the Capitol. Of course, the fact that Sam had bought the next three drinks hadn't hurt any.

The saloon he was getting drunk in today was different. It was one of the taverns that catered to Washington's elite, and its clientele was predominantly southern politicians and their hangers-on. Plantation owners, almost to a man.

Now that Driscol had gained some experience with the breed, during the few weeks he'd been in Washington, he had developed a mental list—a very, very long list—of reasons he detested wealthy southern slave owners. A concrete and specific list, not the general condemnation he had leveled onto the breed in times past from abstract considerations.

Somewhere near the top of the list—probably third, he thought, after their brutality toward their male slaves and their lies and hypocrisy on the subject of how they dealt with female slaves—was their endless posturing and braggadocio concerning their "honor." As if the term could be applied to armed robbers and rapists in the first place.

He ascribed it to idleness. They did not toil. Their Negroes toiled for them. In their fields, by day; in their beds, by night. So they were able to spend their time giving longwinded speeches on the glories of republicanism and issuing challenges to each other over the pettiest slights imaginable.

They were, he had concluded, a breed of men so foul that they *had* to elevate "honor" to absurdly mystical proportions. Or they couldn't have looked at themselves in a mirror at all.

Houston possessed none of their faults. Unfortunately, he thought they were very good fellows, and liked to drink and carouse with them.

And he could not handle his liquor.

"Bah," Driscol snarled. "Animals, the lot of them."

He was looking forward to leaving Washington. Sam would sober up—hopefully—and Driscol would no longer have to rub shoulders with men he despised. Frontiersmen had their faults, true enough. They were frequently illiterate, had many crude habits, and they owned slaves themselves, many of them. But Driscol had come to realize from talking with Houston and Tiana and her brothers that slavery on the frontier tended to have a different flavor than it did in the settled society of the eastern seaboard.

He was still utterly opposed to the institution, under any circumstances. But he had begun to understand that in the West it was more akin to the sort of traditional thralldom that his own Celtic and Norse ancestors had practiced than it was to the cold-blooded profiteering of large plantation owners. Especially among the Indian tribes, who generally didn't share the white man's obsession with race.

"They're not all so bad as that, sir," Henry said quietly. "I think well of Mr. Monroe. Don't know a single black man who doesn't. And I never heard of any black woman raising one of his bastards."

It was all Driscol could do not to glare at him. The man from County Antrim liked things *simple*. The fact that there were men like Monroe, who were exceptions to the rule—nor was he the only one, not by any means—didn't sway him at all.

Damn all exceptions to the rule. Ought to hang them first, because they provide the others with a mask.

Then he took a deep breath of air, and his mood lightened. It had been doing that more often, lately, much to his surprise. Tiana ascribed that to her good influence on him.

So did Driscol.

"Let's go get him," he said, a hint of amusement creeping into his voice. "Lead the way, Henry."

He took the time, before leaving the hotel room that served him as official living quarters, to plant his new major's hat on his head and buckle on his sword. It wouldn't do to march into that fancy saloon without all the paraphernalia of his rank.

"Not that it'll do much good," he grumbled on the way out. "Never met a rich slave owner yet who wasn't a colonel of some sort."

They'd reached the street, where Charles Ball was waiting for them. The gunner heard his last remark and grinned.

"'Tain't true, sir. There's supposed to be a big plantation owner somewhere down in the Carolinas who's only a captain. Course, it's just a wild rumor."

More seriously, he added: "Those are militia ranks, Major. They hand them out like candy to kids. In the North just as much as the South. Your rank is a real one—and *they* wasn't at the Chippewa and the Capitol."

That was true enough. As he walked up the street toward Pennsylvania Avenue, Driscol noticed more than one person stopping briefly to stare at him.

He was becoming used to it, more or less. His own role in the Capitol's defense was well-known, by now, even if he'd never attained the sheer celebrity of the glamorous Houston.

That had become especially true after the *Intelligencer* had published a long article that amounted to an interview with Robert Ross. Without taking anything away from Houston's role, the British general had made it quite clear that he thought the assault itself had been turned back because of Driscol's professional skill and leadership.

Sensing that some sort of rancorous personal dispute might be in the offing, the *Intelligencer* had immediately raced to Houston to see what *he* thought about the matter.

At that point, whatever hopes Driscol might have entertained for remaining reasonably anonymous had gone sailing out the window. Houston had not only expressed his full agreement with General Ross's assessment, but had added to it in his own inimitable style.

Sam Houston had a way with words. So now, whether he liked it or not, Patrick Driscol was labeled with the public cognomen of *America's one-armed Odysseus.*

"Bah," he snarled again, speaking to no one in particular. "I'm a *sergeant.*"

From the window of her own hotel room, Tiana Rogers stared down over the city below. Like almost all of the U.S. capital beyond the stretch of Pennsylvania Avenue between the Capitol and the president's mansion, the city looked like a small boy wearing adult clothing. A "capital city" whose grandiose plans laid down by a French architect were still mostly a fantasy. The city's population still wasn't more than ten thousand, of whom a fourth were black slaves or freedmen. Just beyond the outskirts of the city, in most directions, lay what amounted to wilderness.

Still, it was the biggest town Tiana herself had ever seen. Much bigger than Knoxville, which was the only other major American town she'd visited. That had impressed her, at first. But now, after weeks in Washington, she'd come to the conclusion that the main difference between a city and a village was simply that dirt accumulated in a city three times as fast as it did anywhere else. Now that she'd experienced the joys of city living, the "rough frontier" seemed as clean as fresh creek water from melting snows.

Washington was always dirty. No, *filthy*. Muddy after a rain, dusty after two days of sunshine. And, in these summer and early autumn months, sweltering and fetid whether it rained or shined.

She'd be glad to leave. Would have left long ago, in fact—

forcing her brothers to take her away, if she had to—except for Driscol.

"Well?" James asked, from behind her.

"Don't hurry me. I'm still thinking about it."

That was a lie, actually, at least insofar as her own sentiments were concerned. What was really happening was that Patrick was still mulling over the matter, and Tiana was willing to wait for him to finish doing so.

James saw through it at once. "That's silly. You're even claiming he's not ugly these days."

"He's *not* ugly."

"Giddy as an American girl!" her other brother laughed.

"I'm not *giddy*."

She turned and glared at them. James and John were both sitting cross-legged on the floor, disdaining the plush armchairs in the fancy hotel room. They claimed the floor was more comfortable, except the carpet was too soft.

And that was a lie, too. At home, on John Jolly's island, they were just as prone to luxuriate in whatever American furniture could be obtained as any sensible Cherokee would. Her brothers' ridiculously exaggerated attachment to "traditional customs" since they'd arrived in Washington was just James and John's way of shielding themselves against the same uncertainties that plagued Tiana herself.

Mixed blood, mixed ways, mixed customs—everything *mixed*. It was hard to know what to do.

"I never thought he was ugly," she said softly, almost sadly. "I really didn't. Not once."

That much was true. Her brothers wouldn't understand, because they were men. A man's definition of "handsome" just wasn't the same as a woman's.

Not that even Tiana had ever thought Patrick Driscol was *handsome*. But the blocky, craggy features that men described, as if he were some sort of monster, just seemed very masculine to Tiana. They had, even from the beginning.

They did so all the more now, as she'd spent more and more time in his company. She'd come to understand that the grim bleakness of that face was more a thing of his soul than of his flesh. As if all the scar tissue in his heart had been transplanted onto his features. Patrick Driscol's way of shielding himself. No different, really, than James and John's insistence on squatting on a floor, and walking about the streets of Washington in full and traditional Cherokee regalia.

"It's not that," she said, still speaking softly. "It's that he's not Cherokee. And never will be."

John cocked his head. "Do you care? I know you don't want to spend any more time in American schools. But do you really care if you wind up living in an American town, instead of one of our villages?"

"I wouldn't like it much."

"Who would?" chuckled James. "From what I can see, they measure 'civilization' by how much tobacco they spit. Still and all, do you really care?"

She shook her head. "It's not whether I'd care. It's whether he wouldn't."

They didn't understand. She couldn't blame them, really, since she was only groping at it herself.

She'd try it a different way.

"How long do we stay married?"

James and John looked at each other.

"Until the women throw us out," said James.

"Unreasonable creatures," John added.

Tiana smiled. Very sweetly. "And how long do *they* stay married?"

James winced. John shuddered a bit.

"*That's* the point, brothers of mine. And don't think that Patrick Driscol isn't a white man, just because he hates a lot of what white people do."

She turned back to the window. "I wouldn't mind, I don't think. But I don't know if he'd feel safe enough. Happy enough. I don't think he knows, either."

There was silence, for a moment. Then James asked: "And do you *care*?"

"Yes. I do."

She felt, again, the shivery sensation that started somewhere in her feet and ended up in her loins. That was a new thing, too. One of the other ways, she now realized, that there was a big difference between being thirteen and being sixteen years old.

She'd been insisting for a year now that she was no longer a girl. Well. *That,* at least, wasn't a lie.

She looked down at the street. It hadn't gotten any cleaner, or less ugly, in the minutes that had gone by.

So be it.

She'd wait. She *wanted* Patrick Driscol.

Henry and Charles waited in the street while Driscol marched into the saloon.

Three minutes later, he came back out, with Houston draped over his shoulder. He was staggering a little.

"I'll carry him," said Henry.

"Damn right you will," Driscol muttered. "You're the only one big enough and strong enough."

He passed Houston over. "Lord, he's heavy. If he starts getting fat, he'll be as great as an ox."

Henry handled it easily, though. Now that Driscol had been around the teamster long enough to see past the somewhat shy exterior, he'd come to realize that Henry might well be the strongest man he'd ever met.

Few other men of Driscol's acquaintance, certainly, could have carried on a conversation while toting such a great burden on his shoulder.

"Got two other boys signed up, Major," Henry said cheerfully. "That'll do it."

"Good ones?"

"Oh, sure. Isaac and Rufus Young. They're first cousins, not brothers. I've known 'em for years. Both good drivers, and both of them steady men."

Driscol glanced at Houston. His head was hanging down near Henry's hip, and he was drooling a little.

Better to ignore that. Driscol had known plenty of drunks in his life. Precious few of them had had any of Houston's other qualities.

If Driscol hadn't already respected the young colonel, he would have done so after watching the battle he put up for the logistics of the new unit he'd be leading to New Orleans.

Henry Crowell was there when nobody else was—so he gets the contract.

And I'll raise Jesse in the press—no, in Congress!—if anybody foists some chiseling nephew on me!

An empty threat, in some ways. Driscol had no doubt at all that the capital's newspaper editors—not to mention most of its senators and congressmen—were no more taken by the idea than the horde of angry businessmen who'd been bypassed for the plum contract. All the more so, because most of those were, indeed, some editor or politician's nephew.

Or cousin, or brother, or uncle—the nepotism of Washington was notorious.

But Houston was still the Hero of the Day, after all. And, in what had probably been an even more decisive development, James Monroe was now the secretary of war, and he'd given Houston his quiet but firm support behind the scenes.

In the end, Driscol was fairly certain, the decisive argument in the private conversations of the city's elite had been that anything that lessened Washington's large population of freedmen was a blessing. So let that too-big-for-his-britches Henry Crowell and his gang of black teamsters take the contract. It'd get them out of the city, if nothing else.

Freedmen were always a thorn in the side of slave society. Neither fish nor fowl. On the one hand, always a quiet reminder to gentility that its vaunted republic rested on a dark and shaky foundation; on the other—worse still—always a temptation to the slave. More often than not, the first step of a runaway slave was to vanish into the anonymity of the little-known freedmen societies of the nation's larger towns and cities.

Let them go to New Orleans. That depraved city had the largest freedmen community in North America, given the slackness of its French and Spanish inhabitants. Hopefully, they'd all choose to stay there, after the war was over.

They probably would, too. Driscol knew that was Henry Crowell's plan. Still shy of thirty he might be, built like Hercules to boot, and half literate at best. But Crowell was proving to be quite the shrewd businessman. He and the freedmen partners he'd organized to handle this very lucrative government contract stood to come out at the end with a very solid stake. And New Orleans was the one city in the United States where a free black man could set himself up in business with relatively little in the way of obstruction.

Some, of course. Even New Orleans expected a white man to be the visible face of the business. But for decades the city had institutionalized ways to deal with that, Henry had learned. There were supposed to be any number of white lawyers in New Orleans willing to place their name on a partnership—some without even charging exorbitant fees—so the black men who really ran the business could do so unmolested.

Driscol's eyes turned to Charles Ball, who was striding along-side and looking very cheerful. All of the black sailors in Barney's unit had volunteered for Houston's expedition. They were all veterans, so Driscol doubted very much if that was because they were eager to join another battle. They, too, probably planned to stay in New Orleans after the war was over. Why not? They'd most likely be demobilized anyway, and in New Orleans they wouldn't face the same difficulties they would elsewhere. Fewer difficulties, at least.

"Looking forward to New Orleans?" he asked.

Charles grinned, as he so easily and often did. "Yes, I am, Major. Best city in the world, people say. Sure as creation for a Negro. Think I'll stay there, after the war, like Henry's planning to."

Houston came back to consciousness after Henry lowered him onto the bed in his room. He was staying in the same hotel Driscol was quartered in.

He peered blearily up at Crowell and said, "Thanks, Henry."

Then, more blearily still—almost teary-eyed, in fact—he gazed accusingly at Driscol.

"You stole my girl."

"You didn't want her," Driscol rasped. "I asked."

"Wasn't fair. I didn't have any choice."

"Yes, you did. And you made it. So don't whine."

Houston started crying. There wasn't any real emotion to it, though, just the easy tears of a man in a drunken stupor. Driscol knew that Sam was a bit jealous concerning the situation between himself and Tiana. He also knew that the jealousy didn't run very deep, and that Houston would get over it, easily enough.

Within a minute, in fact, Houston was unconscious again.

Driscol sighed. "Whom the gods would destroy . . ." he murmured.

He'd wondered, in times past—a bit jealous himself—if there was *anything* about Sam Houston that was flawed. In so many ways, the youngster seemed like someone out of Greek legend.

Well, now he knew. And wished he didn't.

"You've got the Irish curse, lad," he said sadly.

Henry, always quick to be charitable, shook his head. "Lots of people drink too much, Major."

That was true enough, of course. Foreign travelers to America were always a bit stunned at the level of alcohol consumption throughout the new republic. People—men, especially, but a fair number of women, too—drank whiskey as if it were water.

But Driscol knew drunkenness backward and forward, and he knew he was looking at the curse.

So did Charles Ball. His personality was a lot more acerbic than Henry's. "Don't fool yourself, Henry. By the time he's forty, Sam Houston will either have quit drinking, or he'll be lying in the gutter. Or just be dead. The major's got it right. It's the Irish curse."

Henry was stubborn, though, in his quiet way. "Lots of black folks drink too much, too, Charles."

The gunner snorted. "Sure. That's 'cause most of us are part Irish. My grandfather was a white plantation owner, name of O'Connell. Course, he never fessed up to it. But he freed my grandmother, in his will, which is how I got to be born free."

"How good of him," Driscol growled. "I notice he didn't free her until after he died."

"Course not. If he a freed her sooner, his bed woulda been cold at night. His wife had died years earlier." Charles shook his head admiringly. "She was a powerful good-lookin' woman. Chirk and lively, too. Still was, even when I knew her."

"I can't *wait* to get out of this stinking city." Driscol was now almost literally growling. "A nest of snakes, it is."

Despite his color, Ball didn't share much of Driscol's animosity toward the world's injustices. He was frighteningly good-humored about it, in fact.

"We better get out fast, too," the gunner said, grinning. He pointed down at Houston. "Before our handsome and dashing young colonel figures out that if he stops crawling into the taverns with the boys, he can be crawling into the beds of half the girls in town."

Driscol rolled his eyes to the ceiling. "I did *not* need to hear that, Charles."

"Hey, Major, you know it's true. They falling all over him, every chance they get. Sam Houston's the prize bachelor, right now. You think those prim and proper matrons ain't figured out the oldest way known to man to get a fella to the altar? You think their prim and proper daughters won't be willing? Enough of 'em, anyway."

Driscol was still staring at the ceiling. The paint was peeling in one of the corners. In case he needed a reminder that appearances are usually a veneer. Especially in Washington, D.C.

"I did *not* need to hear that."

"Look on the bright side. Couple of months, we'll be in New Orleans. Most sinful city in the New World. They'll *love* Sam Houston."

"I did *not* need to hear that."

CHAPTER 33

OCTOBER 9, 1814
Washington, D.C.

Winfield Scott arrived in Washington to assume command of the Tenth Military District just in time to see the newly promoted Colonel Houston and his party off on their expedition to New Orleans.

"I see you've made quite the name for yourself, Patrick," he said to Driscol, shaking his hand vigorously. "My deepest congratulations. Nothing more than you deserve, of course." He didn't even seem to notice Houston, who was standing not three feet away.

Driscol returned the handshake with a smile, letting no sign of his irritation show. As much as he admired and respected Scott, there were times he found the man's thin-skinned vanity downright aggravating. Especially because it was so childishly transparent.

Driscol was no threat to Scott's status, of course. For all the private and public praise that had been heaped upon the man from County Antrim over the past few weeks—not to mention a double promotion that had well-nigh astonished him—no one thought of Patrick Driscol as a dashing hero the way they did

Sam Houston. Now people were speculating that Houston might soon become the youngest brigadier general in the U.S. Army—a status heretofore enjoyed by Winfield Scott.

Irritating, truly irritating.

Worse than that, it had far-ranging implications, under the current circumstances. Monroe had seriously considered sending Scott to reinforce Jackson in New Orleans, now that the brigadier had recovered well enough from his wounds to resume active duty, rather than keeping him in Washington for what would be a purely administrative post. The secretary of war had even, privately, asked Driscol for his opinion on the matter.

Soon enough, he'd pierced through Driscol's circumlocutions.

"So you think he and Jackson would clash constantly?"

"Well, sir. Yes." Driscol had no doubt that he had looked uncomfortable. "I can't be sure, of course, since I don't yet know General Jackson. General Brown managed to get along with the brigadier quite well, mind you. But, ah, Brown is . . ."

Monroe nodded. "A politician, and a very good one. And not a man to begrudge his subordinate getting the lion's share of the praise. Which"—here a grin—"ha! Is *certainly* not true of Andy Jackson. He's even pricklier about his public image than Winfield."

"Yes, sir. Such is my impression."

Monroe had studied the papers on his desk, for a moment. Not looking at the print, simply using the familiar sight to concentrate his thoughts. Then, sighing, he continued. "Scott's already beginning to clash with Brown, actually, and over the pettiest issues imaginable."

"Yes, sir. So I had heard. Since you asked for my opinion, Mr. Secretary, here it is. Said bluntly, if you'll pardon my presumption. Put Winfield Scott on a battlefield, and he's superb. He's also possibly the best trainer of troops I've ever encountered. For that matter, give him a straightforward administrative task and let him have his head, and he'll give you all you could ask for. But assign him to play the loyal subordinate to another commanding officer as vain and headstrong as he is, and you're asking for trouble. They'll likely spend as much time and energy quarreling with each other as they will fighting the enemy."

"Yes, you're probably right. Very well, then. We'll keep Scott here. It's not as if he won't be of real use, after all. I don't expect the British to attack the area again, but who knows? And, in any event, since we've now got this Tenth Military District, we ought to have it organized properly."

Eventually, of course, Scott acknowledged Houston's presence. Even then, with words of praise that were abbreviated and a handshake that was barely this side of cursory.

Fortunately, Sam Houston had a different temperament. He'd kept his expression bland throughout, but by now Driscol knew the young colonel well enough to know that he was probably amused by Scott's behavior. Houston was one of those people blessed with a self-esteem so thoroughly grounded that he had no need for the reassurances of others. A liking for it, certainly—what man didn't? But its absence spilled off him like water off a duck.

"And when will I see you again, Patrick?" Scott asked, turning away from Houston once again. "You know there'll always be a place for you on my staff. And I'll see to it, rest assured, even in the teeth of the demobilizations which are bound to come once the war is over."

"Thank you, sir." Driscol didn't doubt that Scott would live up to his promise, too. He was also certain that without Scott's patronage, he'd likely be finding himself eking out a meager existence on the income of a retired officer. Nonetheless, the offer held no attractions whatsoever.

How to say it, though?

He cleared his throat. "As it happens, sir, I've been giving some serious thought to entering civilian life. After the war is over."

Scott cocked his head, in a gesture which was half quizzical and half skeptical.

As well he might, Driscol thought ruefully. Until a very short time ago, the idea of *Patrick Driscol, civilian* would have been as laughable to Driscol as to anyone. But . . . a very short time could sometimes bring some very real changes. And the fact was that, for the first time since he'd been sixteen years old, Driscol had started thinking seriously about what a life might look like without killing Sassenach at the center of it.

Best to sidestep the matter, however. "Well, sir, it's like this. Once the war is over and we win it, how will I find any Sassenach to fight?"

Houston was giving him that same cocked-head look, now. In Houston's case, though, it was all inquisitiveness. Alas, it'd be difficult to sidestep the issue with *him*.

For the past week, Houston had stayed out of the taverns and bustled about, getting his column ready for departure. Driscol was thankful for the sobriety, but the cost of it was that Sam was back to his normal, keen-eyed way of observing things. His brains were awfully good, when they weren't pickled in whiskey.

Sure enough. No sooner had Scott bade his farewells and left, than Houston turned on Driscol.

"Out with it, Patrick!"

Seeing Driscol's mulish look, Houston laughed. "Oh, for the sake of all that's holy! D'you really think no one beside me has noticed the daily promenades you've been taking with Tiana the past few weeks? The last time I saw General Ross, even *he* made a little jest about it. A very friendly one, mind."

Driscol was flushing now. He'd wound up, to his surprise, visiting Ross several times. Always with Tiana at his side. How are mighty trolls fallen . . .

Houston's expression suddenly became serious. "Patrick, one thing you should understand. She won't leave her people. Don't ever think she will."

Driscol happened to know that Tiana's sentiments were by no means as clear-cut as Houston made them seem. By now, in many ways, Driscol knew Tiana far better than Houston ever had, or would. The basic reason was that Sam still thought of her as a girl, and Driscol had never once thought of her as anything other than a woman.

He knew her attitude on this specific issue because . . .

Well, because she'd told him. Tiana was to "subtlety" what the Mongol hordes were to decorum.

And he was getting peeved, now. "If you're speaking of Miss Rogers, sir, what does that have to do with anything we're about?"

Houston went back to that aggravating head-cocking business. "You? Living among the Cherokee?" Suddenly, the head came back up. "Well, why not? Plenty of other white men have never given a damn about the opinion of refined society. So why should you?" Grinning: "*Especially* you—whose secret wish is to fire grapeshot at refined society, anyway."

Driscol returned the grin with a cold smile of his own. "Canister, sir. For really up-close, bloody, personal work, you always want canister."

Houston laughed at that. He started to say something, but paused to let his eyes roam over the column that was forming up on Pennsylvania Avenue. "Caravan of gypsies," might be a more appropriate term. The military force that Houston was about to lead out of Washington was as polyglot an affair as Driscol could have asked for.

At the head of the column—they'd insisted—rode the volunteer dragoons from Baltimore who had once been officially part of Stansbury's regiment. They numbered some two hundred now, having had their ranks fleshed out fivefold by new volunteers eager to share in the fame and glory, instead of the few dozen woebegone lads whom Driscol had rescued from ignominy a few weeks earlier. But they still had their flamboyant uniforms—and didn't look much more soldierly than they had before.

Ah, well, Driscol mused inwardly.

"They'll do, well enough, when the time comes," he said aloud. "We'll have weeks of the march to shape them up."

"Well, I imagine that'll be true of the Baltimore lads. Our newly commissioned *Lieutenant* Pendleton has the makings of a fine officer, it seems to me."

"With a bit more blooding," Driscol gruffed.

Houston got a sly look on his face. "I'm not so sure about some of our other promotions, though. I still think seventeen years old is a bit young to be a sergeant."

Driscol sniffed. "You let me worry about McParland, sir. Seventeen years old means he hasn't picked up any habits, either—except the ones I give him. He'll do just fine."

The heart of the column was marching past now, and its true fist—one hundred and twenty artillerymen and almost as many marines. About half the artillerymen were taken from Commodore Barney's unit, after having been formally transferred from the navy to the army. The other half consisted of Captain Burch's Washington artillery unit, which had also acquitted itself very well at Bladensburg.

Burch himself, now promoted to major, was in command of the entire unit. Better still, from Driscol's point of view, was that Charles Ball had been formally promoted to sergeant and was recognized—informally, if not formally, since the United States had only one rank of sergeant—as the unit's master non-commissioned officer. As far as anyone knew, Ball was the only black man with that rank anywhere in the U.S. Army, even if the equivalent wasn't unheard of in the navy. There'd been more than a few opposing voices raised, when Houston first proposed it. But again Monroe had given it his quiet support, once he was assured that Burch had no objection.

Following the artillery came another unit of volunteers, this one formed from scratch out of veterans of the fight at the Capitol. There were almost three hundred of them. Driscol had rather high hopes for that lot. If they lacked the fine apparel of the well-to-do dragoons, and displayed even less in the way of military order, they had the virtue of being self-chosen by men who had displayed real fighting spirit when the time came.

The name of the unit itself reflected that: the *Liberty* Regiment. Technically, it was the First Capitol Volunteers—the unit being a regiment in no real sense of the term—but the men had made stick the requirement that only those who had fought in the Capitol on that now-hallowed night were eligible for membership.

Next came the little group composed of Tiana Rogers and her Cherokee companions. There were only four of them present at the moment, since the Ridge children were staying behind at a school found for them by Commodore Barney, and Lieutenant Ross was still serving his last moments as Secretary Monroe's aide.

Finally, and making up the most singular sight, came the logistics tail of the column: some sixteen wagons, all of them driven by black freedmen, with Henry Crowell's in the lead. Twenty-six wagons, if you included the much scruffier ones that served to haul the families and personal belongings that most of the teamsters were taking with them.

Houston finished with his examination. It hadn't really been an "examination" in the first place, Driscol knew, just a way for Houston to collect his thoughts.

"Do you know how a Cherokee proposes to a girl?" he asked abruptly.

Driscol set his jaw. "I do not recall asking, sir," he rasped. "Nor do I see—"

"Stop it, Patrick!" Houston said, his voice unexpectedly stern.

"Whether you're ready to admit it to yourself or not, I don't think I've ever seen a man so smitten by a woman. It's the main reason I stopped being jealous. I know you're not playing with her, and . . . well. I wish her the best, which . . . well. Wouldn't be me."

Driscol started to snarl an angry response, but . . .

Ah.

Couldn't.

"Thought so," Houston chuckled. "Well, it's like this. The most important thing is whether or not the girl is interested. She'll ask for advice, of course. She'll listen to the women's council more carefully than anyone else, probably, but she'll listen to her family, too. Uncles and brothers more than fathers, insofar as she listens to men at all. Be prepared to wait a bit. Maybe quite a bit, depending on this and that. Cherokees usually don't do anything without discussing and wrangling first, and they like to talk and wrangling's the best kind of talk. Do you follow me so far?"

"Aye," Driscol said grudgingly. "Sir."

Houston's teeth flashed. " 'Sam,' Patrick, 'Sam.' The march hasn't started yet, and this surely qualifies as a personal discussion."

"Fine. Sam."

"Good. But despite all that, there *are* some formalities. The most important is that the young fellow involved—using the term 'young' loosely, and keeping in mind that it's not that uncommon for a Cherokee girl to marry a man twice her age—first announces his intentions by placing the carcass of a slain deer in front of the girl's home."

Driscol's mind went blank.

Houston's grin widened.

"Oh, yes. It's tradition, Patrick. Demonstrates that the fellow is a good provider."

Blank as a field of snow.

"Patrick . . . have you had much experience as a hunter?"

Driscol cleared his throat. "Oh, aye. Not since I was a youngster back in Ireland, of course. I've been too busy since at the soldiering trade."

Houston cocked an eyebrow that could be called *quizzical,* only in the sense that open derision could be called *skeptical.*

"It's true!" Driscol insisted stoutly. "The potatoes in my family's patch quaked at my coming. I can still hear their shrieks of fear. Course, I slaughtered them without pity, nonetheless. Skinned 'em myself, too."

Houston chuckled. "Well. You'll think of something."

He went off, then, to see to the final preparations. Driscol remained behind, his mind still blank as a field of snow.

Well, not quite. He knew what a deer looked like. A very small, skinny cow. With absurdly complicated horns.

"Well, that's it, then." Monroe extended his hand. "You've done exceedingly well as an aide, Captain Ross, and I shall miss you."

John returned the handshake. "It's been a pleasure serving you, Mr. Secretary."

That was no more than the truth. Monroe was one of those men who carried authority with such ease and grace that they never felt it necessary to run roughshod over their subordinates. Whatever might come in the future, whatever clashes John Ross and his people would have with James Monroe—and there'd be many, certainly, if Monroe came to the presidency—John would always respect him as a person. *Like* him, for that matter.

"You understand," Monroe continued, "that my offer for correspondence was more than a polite formality."

"Yes, sir, I do—and I shall. Be assured of it."

Monroe smiled. "I suspect I may come to regret that offer, from time to time. But it stands nonetheless. I want to establish my own conduit to your people."

"You understand on your part, Mr. Secretary, that I can speak only on my own behalf. I hold no formal position among the Cherokees."

"No *formal* position." Monroe shrugged. "I don't claim to know your nation, Lieutenant—but I'd be very surprised if it's all that different from my own in many regards. One of which is that formal position and real influence are not the same thing." His hand waved toward the window of the temporary office he'd set up close to the Capitol, while work began on rebuilding the president's mansion and its adjoining executive offices. "I can name a dozen men out there, not one of them holding an official title of any kind, whose opinion carries more weight than all but a handful of senators or congressmen."

John nodded again.

"Furthermore," Monroe went on, "you're still very young. Give it a few years, and I'll be surprised if your status doesn't become formalized."

"And do we *have* a few years, Mr. Secretary? Or, should I say, Mr. Soon-to-be-President."

Monroe didn't blink at that, although he himself had never mentioned his own prospects.

"Yes, Lieutenant, you will have a few years. That much, I can promise you. If nothing else—" He cleared his throat. "Well. Let's just say that Andrew Jackson will be preoccupied else-where, for a few years."

John knew what that meant. Jackson would go after the Span-. ish next. Drive the Dons off the continent entirely. That would keep him in the Floridas, for a time, hundreds of miles from the Cherokees and farther still from the Choctaws and Chickasaws.

"But eventually," Monroe went on, his tone harshening a lit-tle, "that'll be over. So, yes. You have a few years. But no more than a few. After that, the vise will be tightening again."

For a moment, his eyes softened, and Monroe slid into rare informality. "Understand something, John. There are many things I can regret, as a private person, that I cannot oppose as an official of the republic. That's a cold business, in the end, whether a man likes it or not."

It was a threat, however politely veiled. But John could appre-ciate the courtesy with which it was extended. The same cour-tesy—no, respect—that Monroe had extended by not trying to bribe him, as so many clan chiefs had been bribed in the past.

So. He would be able to tell Major Ridge that, if nothing else, James Monroe was a man they could talk with. And bargain with.

Not trust, really. As Monroe himself had just made clear, as president he could only be trusted by his own people. Which, looked at one way, was no different from Andrew Jackson. Sharp Knife or not, Monroe would still cut when he saw no al-ternative. Or hold the victim, while another wielded the blade.

Still, he hadn't tried to bribe him. That meant if a bargain could be made, he'd most likely not try to cheat afterward.

A bugle sounded from outside. Off-key.

Monroe smiled ruefully. "The perils of a republic, Lieu-tenant. Always especially shaky in the beginning."

Then, much more seriously: "Remember this one thing I will

say to you, John Ross, if nothing else. It's a lesson I learned when I was even younger than you are today. I was with George Washington when he crossed the Delaware, and later at Valley Forge. This republic of mine—this *nation*—was not born out of glorious victories and triumphal marches in the bright summer sun. I was there, and I know. It was born out of retreats, in the bitterness of winter."

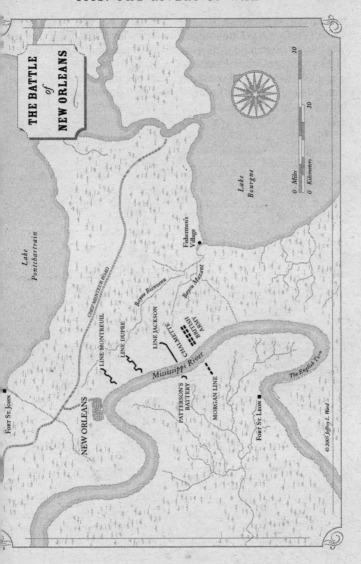

THE BATTLE
of
NEW ORLEANS

Lake
Pontchartrain

Lake
Bourgne

0 Miles 10

0 Kilometers 10

FORT ST. JOHN

NEW ORLEANS

CHEF-MENTEUR ROAD

LINE MONTREUIL

LINE DUPRE

LINE JACKSON

Mississippi River

PATTERSON'S
BATTERY

MORGAN LINE

FORT ST. LEON

Bayou Bienvenu

Bayou Mazant

CHALMETTE

BRITISH
ARMY

Fishermen's
Village

The English Turn

© 2005 Jeffrey L. Ward

Part V

~

THE MISSISSIPPI

CHAPTER 34

As he was led toward General Jackson's headquarters in New Orleans, Sam Houston found himself fighting the urge to laugh. Jackson had set himself up in the Cabildo, the former Spanish colonial administration center that fronted on the city's main square. The Cabildo was a huge building, and they were still, he guessed, a corridor or two away from Jackson's office. And . . .

He could already hear the general hollering.

"Be damned to your poltroon concerns, sir! Those men have volunteered to fight the enemy, and so they shall! D'you think I care about your tender sensibilities?"

Mumble, mumble. That would be the voice—voices it sounded like—of whoever was coming under the lash of Jackson's fury.

Sam could practically see the sneer on the general's face that so obviously came with the next holler.

"And where are your volunteers, sir? You—damn all rich men!—who tell me you cannot serve in your country's colors because you have to remain on your plantations to keep your slaves in order. But—but!—insist that I cannot put arms into the hands of freemen of color who are willing to step forward bravely and serve their country. And why? Because they might inspire insurrectionary thoughts in the same slaves who keep you paralyzed! Was ever such a monstrous logic advanced in the supposed service of a republic?"

Mumble, mumble—cut very short, this time.

"Get out! GET . . . OUT. Now, sir. And take the rest of these wretched traitors with you! GET OUT!"

Sam took the arm of the nervous officer who was leading him and Driscol, and drew the man to the side of the corridor. Major Driscol quickly followed suit. A moment later, a dozen men came pouring past. They weren't *quite* stampeding.

"He's a brute!" Sam heard one of them hiss to another. "Just as we were warned!"

After they were past, the young lieutenant shot Sam an apologetic look. "The general's been in a picklish mood these past few days. Ever since the ruckus started after he accepted Governor Claiborne's proposal to allow the free men of color—that's what they call some of the niggers down here, sir—to go ahead and form the two battalions they offered to set up."

Dubiously, he added: "Can't say I think much of the idea myself. The plantation owners are up in arms about it all over Louisiana."

"Why?" Sam asked. "If I've got this right, no one's proposing to arm any slaves."

The lieutenant shook his head. "Still. The niggers will get ideas."

Sam marveled at the stupidity of the lieutenant's statement. As if slaves needed to "get ideas." Hadn't the young idiot ever heard of the great rebellion in Santo Domingo? Or the dozens of much smaller slave insurrections that had taken place across North America, over the past century or so?

"Has it ever occurred to you, Lieutenant, that the 'idea' of rebellion is instilled in a man the moment you put him in chains? It doesn't really take anything more than that, you know—although, to be sure, whipping him on a regular basis will speed the process marvelously."

The youngster gaped up at him.

Doesn't understand a word.

Oh, well. Perhaps the practical aspect of it . . .

"Leaving that aside, if I understand you correctly, you feel we should allow the British to defeat us today—they *will* take the slaves themselves, you know—lest victory take them from us on the morrow. That is the logic of the plantation owners, yes?"

The youngster was still gaping.

Not a word. I might as well be citing the Iliad *to him, in the original Greek.*

Oh, well.

Best to remind him of the most practical side of all.

"As it happens, General Andrew Jackson is in command here. Not you, and certainly not a passel of plantation owners who refuse to fight. And as I recall, he instructed you to bring me to him. Yes?"

Sam gave him a friendly smile and made a shooing motion with his hands. "Best we be about it then, eh? The general tends to get riled when his orders aren't followed. If you hadn't noticed."

The lieutenant literally jumped. Two inches off the floor, by Sam's estimate. "This way, sir!"

Whatever residual fury Jackson might have been harboring vanished the instant he saw Houston and Driscol.

"Sam!" he exclaimed, rising from his desk and coming around to greet him, hand outstretched. "I was beginning to worry that you might not get here before the fighting started. You blasted dawdler!"

But the words were said with a grin, and the vigor of Jackson's handshake matched the expression on his face.

"We had a long ways to come, General," Sam pointed out mildly.

"So you did. And how many did you bring with you?"

Sam ran through a quick sketch of the forces that had marched into New Orleans with him that morning.

"No Cherokees?" Jackson asked, frowning.

"They'll be coming along presently, sir. Captain Ross and Major Ridge, at least—but John told me he thought Major Ridge would be able to convince some two hundred of his tribesmen to volunteer. I expect them within a day or two."

"Two hundred . . ." Jackson mused, his eyes a little unfocused as his head turned toward the nearest window. "Well, I can use them. I've got some Choctaws, but not many. And— well, come here, Sam, I'll show you."

Houston followed the general, with Driscol in tow. Once they got to the window, Jackson leaned over the sill and pointed to the southwest. The line of his finger passed over the Spanish-style buildings that fronted the main square, aimed at the countryside beyond. Sam could see a stretch of the Mississippi to his right, but most of what Jackson was pointing to just looked like a mass of luxuriant vegetation. Cypress swamps, mainly, with the more regular patterns of sugar or indigo plantations close to the river.

"Ever seen this country?"

"No, sir."

"Well, except for a narrow stretch of plantations along the bank, it's almost all swamps and marshes. Bayous, and the like. How familiar are your Cherokees with that sort of terrain? Fighting in the wretched stuff, I mean."

Sam shrugged. "Not as familiar as Choctaws, of course. But they'll do well enough. Woods are woods and water's water, however you mix them up. There's plenty of both where they come from. And they're used to fighting as irregulars."

Jackson smiled coldly. "Which the British are not. So let's see how well the bastards handle wild savages on their own ground." The smile widened, slightly. "Begging your pardon, Colonel. Congratulations on the promotion, by the way. And my compliments for your gallant stand at the Capitol."

Jackson thrust himself away from the window and turned to face Driscol. His eyes flicked to the stump. "And you'll be Major Driscol, I assume. My compliments to you as well, sir."

Driscol nodded. "Pleasure to make your acquaintance, General."

Jackson studied him for a moment. Then, abruptly: "I've been told—in the form of a letter from General Scott forwarded to me by Mr. Monroe—that you're possibly the best trainer of troops in the United States Army. How well do you get along with darkies, Major?"

If the sudden shift of topic confused Driscol, there was no sign of it. "Well enough, sir."

Sam's smile must have been more apparent than he thought—or he'd simply forgotten how perceptive Jackson was, under that bellicose exterior. The general's eyes moved to him instantly.

"You seem amused by the major's response, Colonel. Why?"

Sam hesitated a moment. Most white men would be offended at the notion that they had any special affinity with Negroes. Driscol . . .

Wouldn't.

"Patr—uh, Major Driscol gets along famously with the fellows, sir. A considerable number of the artillerymen we brought are black sailors, as well as the entire logistics train."

"So I'd heard." Jackson frowned. "You took a hellish risk there, Sam. I'm surprised half of those darkie teamsters didn't run off with the goods. They may be a servile race by nature, but they're always quick enough to steal."

Sam started to reply, then decided there was no point getting into an argument with Jackson on the subject. If the general was often prepared to countenance measures that other white men would shy away from, he didn't really differ that much from accepted opinion on the various races which inhabited America. Black people were servile; shiftless; stupid; lazy; and generally unreliable. Indians were certainly not servile, but they were just as shiftless; in most regards, just as stupid; and even lazier and less reliable.

Sam shared none of Jackson's opinions with regard to Indians, and as time went on he was becoming increasingly skeptical of the standard view of Negroes. Whether or not the race was servile by nature, it was simply impossible to determine. Most of them were born into slavery, after all, and even the freedmen were usually given little chance to demonstrate their abilities. So who could really know?

As for the rest, the main conclusion he'd come to was that broad racial categories were too often swamped by the wide variations between individuals to mean very much.

That was a safe enough place to differ with the general, he decided.

"That's as may be, sir. But I have confidence in Henry Crowell—he's in the way of being my quartermaster—and I let him pick the rest."

Jackson grunted. "Well, true enough. I've got several hands on my plantation I never worry about. And when it comes to it, one of the darkie blacksmiths in Nashville is more reliable than most of the white ones. Does better work, too. Don't even think he has any white blood, either."

His thin smile returned, as he looked back at Driscol and jerked his head toward Houston.

"May I assume, Major, that you share the heretical notions of young Sam here?"

Driscol restricted himself to a curt nod. Houston chuckled. "I think you'll find, sir—assuming you can get Patrick to open his mouth—that Major Driscol's notions are generally a lot more heretical than mine."

Jackson grunted again. "Well enough. The reason I ask, Major, is because I believe we have something of an opportunity here—if I can find the right man to shape it up. Have you gotten word of my little dispute with some of the local notables—as they see themselves—over the issue of the free men of color?"

Sam cleared his throat. "It was difficult not to overhear, sir. Though we don't know any of the details."

"Ha! Heard me, did you? Good. I hope I was hollering loud enough for them to hear me all the way across Lake Pontchartrain." He strode over and resumed his seat, clasping his hands on the desk.

"Here's how it stands. New Orleans has a large number of free Negroes. I'm not talking about the usual run of freedmen, either, but people who've been free for generations. The Spanish and French are lax about such things, you know. For all practical purposes, many of the freedmen here are black Creoles to match the white ones. Some of them are wealthy—some are even slave owners themselves."

Sam had never been to New Orleans before, but he already knew that much. The black Creole population of the city was rather notorious among southerners in the United States.

Jackson's eyes were now on Driscol. "The point's this, Major. The two battalions I've got are made up of such soldiers. One of them is a battalion of native-born men—that's under Major Pierre Lacoste—and the other is made up of black Creoles who fled here recently from Hispaniola. Major Louis Daquin's in charge of that group. But that still leaves a large population of free Negroes in the city who are not enrolled at all. Some are Creoles, some came here from elsewhere in America—and most of them aren't more than a generation removed from slavery."

Jackson's lips twisted. It was half a sneer, half a grimace at the folly of men. "The free men of color are quite full of themselves, you see. Those black Creoles, from what I can tell, will parse the various shades of color more tightly than a white man. They'd not be partial to allowing common darkies to join their battalions. D'you follow me?"

Driscol nodded. "What sort of men are these others, sir? Field hands? Laborers?"

Jackson shrugged. "A fair number. But a lot of them have a trade. Ironworking, usually, since New Orleans has a lot of that work."

"And how much time would I have to train them?"

Jackson took off his hat, laid it on the desk, and ran fingers through his stiff, sandy-gray hair. "Not long, I'm afraid. Just a few days ago, Admiral Cochrane crushed the little fleet of gunboats I had on Lake Bourgne. Luckily, from reports I've gotten, it seems the British don't have enough flat-bottom boats to move on New Orleans through Lake Pontchartrain. I've lost track of their movements since then, but they'll have to land somewhere in the bayous and march on New Orleans from Lake Bourgne. I expect we'll begin engaging the enemy within a week or two."

Apologetically, insofar as Jackson could manage such a thing: "I realize it's not much time, Major. I don't expect miracles. Still, I can use anything I can get. Once General Coffee and General Carroll get here, I'll have several thousand good troops. Militiamen, but they're mostly veterans from Tennessee. Other than that, my forces are the most gol-derned collection of odds and ends you can imagine. Some navy regulars, Creole battalions—white as well as black—other volunteers. Ha! I've even accepted the offer of the Lafitte brothers and their Lake Baratarian Algerines to fight with us."

He peered at Driscol intently. "So. Can you do it, Major?"

"That largely depends on you, sir. I'll need a core to build on. Without that, it'll be hopeless in the time available. But with the right core—and we brought them with us—then . . . yes, I can do it. Mind you, it's not a force I'd want to rely upon on an open battlefield. No chance at all I could train good line troops in so short a period of time."

"Core?" Jackson was puzzled for a moment. Then, as he understood, he started to frown. "You're speaking of the artillerymen you brought with you. Tarnation, Major, I was counting on those as an addition to the main force."

"I don't need most of them, sir. Just Charles Ball and the other black sailors. And one of the twelve-pounders, and two six-pounders."

Houston cleared his throat. "That'd still leave you most of the naval artillery unit, General. And the marines."

Jackson nodded, but he was still frowning. "I can spare the men, but . . . the cannons? I hate giving up any guns for a long shot."

"I have *got* to have them, sir." Driscol's face seemed blockier than ever. "Give raw recruits a core of veterans—*and* some impressive ordnance that the veterans can use—and I can form a unit around them that won't collapse at the first contact with the enemy. Without them, I can't. Not in two weeks, General."

Jackson sighed. "Fair enough. All right, you can have them. What else do you need?"

"I've been told—we've heard rumors, I should say—that you offered the free men of color a bonus in addition to their regular pay."

"Yes, I did. One hundred twenty-four dollars and one hundred sixty acres of land." Jackson winced a little. "I'll manage the money. Whether I'll be able to come up with the land after the war . . . who knows? The local notables will object, of course."

"Land won't be much of an incentive anyway, for the men I'll be looking to recruit," Driscol said. "Can you increase the dollar bonus? I'll be wanting tradesmen, mostly, and a big enough bonus to allow them to set themselves up in business will be a major incentive."

Jackson winced again. "How many men do you expect to get?"

"I can't be sure, until I get to know the city better. But I'd be aiming for three hundred. Maybe four. I think that's possible."

Jackson's eyes widened. "*That* many? Major . . ."

Something in the set of Driscol's features caused Jackson to trail off. "You actually have a plan, don't you?"

Driscol shrugged. "Not as such, sir, no. But I've a lot of experience at this sort of thing—and I know Ball and his artillerymen very well, by now. I also know Henry Crowell and his teamsters. I expect most of them will sign up, also—if there's a big enough bonus. That gives me upward of two dozen men to serve as recruiters, and they can start immediately."

"They're new in the city."

"True. On the other hand—I've learned this much from the past months in their company—freedmen have their own societies, in every place they live. New to the city or not, they'll manage in hours what it would take me weeks to accomplish—if I could do it at all. But I need the core, and I need the money."

Jackson ran fingers through his hair again, disheveling it still further. "Two hundred dollars? I can go that high, I think—but there will be no land grants to go with it."

"That ought to be enough, Patrick," Sam said. "Most of them will be forming partnerships anyway, pooling their money. Just the way Henry put together the logistics train."

Jackson looked back and forth between the two men, then he chuckled. "You've become quite the experts, haven't you?"

Sam had to fight down a moment's irritation.

"There's not really much expertise required, sir. Just common sense and eyes to see. A freedman doesn't have much to hope for in the United States, when you get right down to it. His best chance is to learn a trade—and then set himself up in his own business, which precious few of them can manage. Poor as they are, they almost always have to do it with partners."

At least one of whom better be a white man, he almost added. But he didn't say it aloud. With his unthinking prejudices, Jackson would simply assume that it was because black men couldn't run their own business.

The real reason was to avoid the grief that was usually visited on black businessmen by white society. Shakedowns from the authorities, threats from white competitors—often enough, just the surliness of a mob disgruntled at uppity Negroes who didn't know their place. A prominent white partner usually diverted all that.

"All right, then," Jackson said, "see what you can manage, Major.

"And now, I'm afraid I'll have to break this off." He jabbed an accusing finger at the papers stacked up on his desk. "I've got a pile of complaints and wheedles I've got to say no to. In writing, unfortunately. Most of them haven't got the nerve to brace me in person."

The young officer who'd guided them to Jackson's office was waiting for them in the corridor. As soon as Sam and Driscol emerged, he started showing them the way out, moving much more quickly than a "guide" really should. The lad seemed eager to get out of Jackson range.

Sam let him trot ahead. He knew the way out anyway.

"Don't lie to *me,* Patrick. You do have a plan, don't you?"

"I don't know as I'd call it that," Driscol rasped. "A 'plan' suggests logic and order—both of which are in short supply here. Let's just say that it occurs to me that if I wind up a civilian, I'd do well to have a ready-made business to walk into." He glanced down at his stump. "I can't do the work myself anymore, of course. But I do know how a blacksmithing business operates—and Henry, you'll remember, worked in the nation's largest foundry."

The young officer, having noticed that his charges were falling behind, came trotting back anxiously. Sam and Driscol just moved right past, ignoring him completely. By the time the jittery youngster managed to match his pace to theirs, they were out of the Cabildo and stepping out into the sunshine that was spilling across the main square. Depending on whether the speaker was French or Spanish, the square was called the Place d'Armes or the Plaza de Armas.

Sam took a moment to admire the St. Louis Cathedral. "I think we'll manage well enough from here, Lieutenant."

"Uh, yes, sir." The lieutenant pointed to the west. "Being white men—real white men, I mean, not Creoles or Dagoes—you'll want to seek lodgings—"

"*Dismissed,* Lieutenant." Houston had had enough of this dolt.

After the youngster jittered off, Sam gave Driscol a long, considering look. "How did you ever become so cold-blooded? The ambition, I can understand. Isn't a Scots-Irishman born doesn't fancy himself emperor of the moon."

Driscol chuckled. "How is it that I'm cold-blooded? First, I prey upon the fears of black folk, in order to parlay myself into what will soon enough be the largest foundry and armory this side of Cincinnati. Between me and Henry and Charles, we can manage it, you watch."

"You've got *Charles* roped into this, too?"

"Charles and every one of his black gunner mates. And why not? What great prospect do *they* have after the war is over? Most sailors get tired of life at sea after a few years, but what else is there for them? Doormen at hotels? Laborers? Stevedores?"

"True enough," Sam grunted.

"Then," Driscol continued, "if need be—the notables of New Orleans will probably object to our presence, after a time—I plan to prey upon the fears of the wild savages to get them to let

me move the entire operation somewhere across the Mississippi. When the time is right, you understand, which will be a
ways off. Probably in Arkansas, I'd think. But I don't know the
land myself yet, so I'll worry about that later."

He stopped and gave Sam a level stare. "Oh, aye, it's a plot a
Sassenach would admire. In my defense, I *will* point out that it
provides me with a livelihood, and it gives Henry and Charles
and their folk a better prospect than anything else they're looking at."

Driscol's eyes were paler than ever. It was an unseasonally
sunny day. Perhaps that accounted for it.

Then again, perhaps not. Sam Houston had long since come
to the conclusion that Anthony McParland was right. Patrick
Driscol *was* a troll.

Fortunately, a troll on Sam's side. "All right," he said. "And
what about Tiana?"

"What about her?"

Sam sighed, exasperated. "Stop being obtuse. Does *she* know
about your plans?"

For one of the few times since Sam had met the man from
County Antrim, Driscol grinned. A genuine, good-humored
grin.

"Well, I'd think so. Given that she was sitting right there
when her father and I came up with it. Did I mention that Captain John Rogers will be one of the partners, too?"

Sam rolled his eyes at that. They'd stopped off for three days
at John Jolly's island on the way to New Orleans. He'd noticed
that Driscol had spent most of his time with Tiana's immediate
relatives. Naïve romanticist that he was, Sam had assumed the
Scots-Irishman had been pressing his suit.

He said as much. Driscol laughed, but sidestepped the issue.
"Don't forget the lady's heritage, Sam. She's as much Scots-
Irish as she is Cherokee—and they're both, in their different
ways, a practical folk."

That was true enough, actually, even with regard to the
Cherokee. Because he'd spent his teenage years living with
them, Sam still tended to think of the Cherokees in a teenager's
terms. It had been their free and easy life that he'd enjoyed and
admired so much. But, in the end, they were the largest and
most powerful Indian nation in the South because they were
also hardheaded.

He pondered, for a moment, what that nation might look like in the future, if it became something of a hybrid with Scots-Irishmen like Patrick Driscol and Captain John Rogers—whose nickname was Hell-Fire Jack. Then toss in for good measure a hefty leaven of freedmen like Henry Crowell—and Charles Ball, who commanded twelve-pounders with the same ease a Cherokee commanded a canoe.

An *asgá siti* nation, whatever else.

"Good Lord," he muttered.

"That remains to be seen," Driscol rasped. "That's why I'm a deist, and make no bones about it. Judging from all available evidence, I think the Lord needs a bit of nudging, here and there."

CHAPTER 35

DECEMBER 18, 1814
New Orleans

The next day, Jackson ordered a review of the troops in the Place d'Armes. It was more in the way of a public spectacle, really, held as it was in the city's central square, rather than on a training field. The purpose of the event was to bolster the morale of the citizens of New Orleans and the surrounding area. Which . . .

Needed it badly.

Sam had concluded as much on his own, just in the short time since he'd arrived. New Orleans was a city with shaky loyalties and a multitude of social divisions. The white population was still primarily Creole, of French and Spanish extraction, many of whom spoke no English at all—and few of those who could did so by choice. They'd been U.S. citizens for only a few years, following the Louisiana Purchase, and no one was yet sure whether their new national identity would withstand the pressure of a British onslaught. Not even, Sam suspected, the Anglo American officials and new settlers who had recently come into the area.

But Jackson had driven over that problem the same way he drove over most problems. He'd simply ignored it, officially, while conducting himself with such energy and confidence that he boosted the spirits of everyone around him.

"Of *course* they'll fight the British," he said to Sam, as they prepared for the review. "Why shouldn't they? They're French, mostly—no love there for England—and the ones who are Spanish won't feel much different. Especially because they'll remember Badajoz."

The siege of Badajoz, during Wellington's campaign against the French in Spain, had happened less than three years earlier. After breaching the walls, the British troops had run amok and sacked the city, despite the fact that the population was mainly Spanish, and they were supposedly liberating the city from French occupation. Murder, rape, looting—the incident had become notorious, and had added to the reputation of British troops, which had been none too savory to begin with.

As much as anything, it was fear of a similar incident that inclined the citizenry of New Orleans to support Jackson, whatever they might think privately of being part of the United States. At least Jackson kept his troops under control. But continued support would depend entirely on the citizens' assessment of Jackson's ability to fight off the oncoming enemy.

Hence the review, which was somewhat silly, from a purely military standpoint.

At least, Sam thought it was silly. The big square looked more like the site of a festival—New Orleans had been celebrating Mardi Gras for over a century—than a stern military affair.

For Sam, the highlight of the march came when Major Ridge, John Ross, and about two hundred Cherokee warriors arrived that morning, just in time to join the festivities. And join them they did, with typical flair and panache.

Because of their late arrival, the Cherokees formed the tail end of the parade that passed before General Jackson's reviewing stand. And if their ranks had none of the precision of the Creole battalions, or even Jackson's own Tennessee militia, they made up for it with their warlike appearance. Except for Ross and Ridge, who wore U.S. Army uniforms and took their place with Jackson on the stand, the two hundred Cherokees who passed below were dressed and painted for battle.

Sam was particularly amused by the fearsome manner in which they brandished their spears and war clubs. He knew full well that the first thing Major Ridge was going to do was start negotiating for muskets and ammunition. Cherokee warriors might still use traditional weapons, but they were quick to adapt to new military methods.

Sam also was amused to observe that Major Ridge did not think the affair was silly. He didn't seem to think it was quite sane, but not silly. He was no stranger himself to the sometimes preposterous displays a chief staged in order to bolster the morale of his warriors.

So for the first hour, as the march proceeded past the reviewing stand, the Cherokee chief just stood there looking very solemn and dignified. But once that was done and Jackson had started his speech, he tilted his head over toward Sam, who was standing right next to him.

"How many muskets can we get?" he asked. To anyone but Sam, Ridge's half whisper was covered by the shrill sound of Jackson's voice, as he continued his peroration.

"—fellow citizens of every description—"

Sam restrained the urge to scratch. It was an unseasonably bright and sunny day in New Orleans, and the heat was making him sweat under the heavy dress uniform. But colonels, he suspected, weren't supposed to scratch in public.

"—country blessed with every gift of nature—for property, for life—"

"Don't know," he murmured in return. "There's a shortage of good firearms. Jackson's been screeching at just about everybody over the problem for weeks now, from what I heard. Promises come in from everywhere—but still precious few guns make it into town."

There might have been a trace of a smile on Ridge's lips. "You mean we're not the only ones who find that the white man's promises are usually empty?"

Sam made no attempt to suppress his own smile.

"Oh, not hardly. You know how it is—and don't try to tell *me* the same thing doesn't happen among your folk. Every chief makes his brag in the council—and then goes home and starts thinking about how he really needs to keep this and that for himself, instead of throwing it to the winds."

"—opulent and commercial town—"

Major Ridge grunted. "True. But I need at least fifty guns to start with. We can get the rest from the enemy, I think, now that I've seen the land we'll be fighting on."

"You didn't bring *any* guns?" Sam asked, already pretty sure he knew the answer.

There was no question that Major Ridge was smiling now, even if it was a thin sort of business. "Of course not. Needed to keep them for ourselves, back home. In case the Georgians showed up again."

Sam chuckled. "Has there ever been such a ragtag army in the history of the world?"

But Jackson didn't seem to share his doubts—not publicly, at least, on that square on that day. The general's shrill penetrating voice kept spouting sure and confident proclamations throughout Sam's little exchange with Ridge.

"—and for liberty, dearer than all!"

A goodly part of Jackson's speech, needless to say, dwelt on the despicable nature of the foe.

"—who vows a war of vengeance and desolation—"

Actually, the British had done no such thing. Indeed, they'd assured the citizens of their safety, and claimed simply to be defending international law from American thievery. They had a point, too, since Napoleon had promised the Spanish he wouldn't sell any of their land in the New World.

"—marked by cruelty, lust, and horrors unknown to civilized nations—"

Sam thought that was a nice touch. Absurd, true. Not even Driscol would claim that the Sassenach were worse than the ancient Greeks and Romans, who had thought nothing of sacking a city by way of a summer's pastime. But, Sam wasn't inclined to argue the matter. Demon-spawned or not, there was no doubt that if the British succeeded in taking New Orleans, they'd refuse to give it up again, regardless of the terms outlined in any subsequent peace treaty.

And with the outlet of the Mississippi under British control— formally Spanish, of course, but that meant nothing—they'd have their hands on the throat of all commerce to the western states of America.

The Federalists could prattle all they wanted about the glories of state-built roads and canals, but every settler and merchant west of the Appalachians knew that there was no genuine substitute for the Mississippi River.

Jackson was winding down his speech, showering the thousands of citizens who were assembled in the square with praise for their courage and strength. *Another nice touch,* Sam mused, given that the population of New Orleans was famous across the Western Hemisphere for many things. Decadence, lewdness, moral laxity—the list went on and on. "Courage and strength" were conspicuously absent from most accounts.

But skeptical men never led armies to victory, and Jackson could and would.

"—the prize of valor and the rewards of fame!"

Major Ridge grunted approvingly, after Sam had translated that final Jacksonian promise. "He'll forget it all by next year," the Cherokee chief murmured. "But most won't remember any of the promises, other than victory."

No skeptic there, either. But Major Ridge had also led men to victory, and would again.

Sam looked toward John Ross, who was standing not far away. "Have you come to any decision?" he asked Ridge.

The Cherokee chief shook his head. Anyone who didn't know him would have missed the gesture entirely. "No." He glanced at Ross himself. "Neither has he, really, although you've got him talking persuasively."

Sam was neither surprised nor discouraged. He hadn't expected Major Ridge—much less most of the Cherokee chiefs— to make their decision quickly. And he knew full well that Ross was still riddled with doubts concerning the proposal that had been sketched out in Washington between Sam, Driscol, Ross, and Monroe.

Nor could he blame Ridge, really. Easy enough for someone like the secretary of state to issue philosophical pronouncements regarding the course of a nation's destiny. Especially when it was someone else's nation. It was something else again for that nation to agree to give up its material land in the here-and-now, all for the sake of an abstract future.

True, the offer was more sweeping than any the United States had made before, to any Indian tribe. The Cherokees would be given somewhere over one hundred thousand square miles, an area larger than the territory they currently occupied. The exact boundaries would be determined in later negotiations. Furthermore, the United States would provide the Cherokees with the weapons and tools they needed to secure and develop that land, along with other material assistance to the amount of several million dollars. And Monroe had promised that the government would bear the financial burden of the relocation itself.

Promises, promises. Coming from a United States which had—being honest—a wretched track record for keeping its promises. And which, as this looming battle illustrated once again, had just as wretched a reputation for interpreting promises without much regard for the facts. After all—being honest—Napoleon *hadn't* had the right to sell Spain's Louisiana territory.

"We'll *still* keep it," Sam growled to himself. Because, right or wrong, millions of people whom Europe had despised would create a life for themselves on that land. And what was so great about Europe, anyway, riddled as it was with kings and noblemen? If the world's only republic swelled into power as much by swindling and theft as by glorious feats of arms, so be it. The same could be said for every dynasty of Europe, down to the tiniest German robber baron who'd been put back in power by the Congress of Versailles, after Napoleon's defeat.

Driscol didn't participate in the gala affair at the Place d'Armes that Sunday, because he was still recovering from a different sort of gala affair that had taken place the previous night.

More precisely, because his newly forming unit was still recovering. Driscol had the sort of iron constitution that would have allowed him to march even after a full night's carousing, but Charles Ball and his artillerymen didn't.

So they claimed, anyway. Driscol wasn't inclined to argue the point. First, because he'd already warned the general not to expect the new "Freedmen Iron Battalion" to be parading past the reviewing stand, not that Jackson had really cared.

"Just as well," the general had grunted. "I'd have to listen to more squawking from the plantation owners—and the free men of color would probably whine at me, too."

Secondly, because while Driscol *could* have marched that morning, he certainly didn't want to.

Patrick Driscol rarely drank liquor. But when he did, he tended to drink a lot.

"My head hurts," he complained to Ball after he woke the gunner up. That feat had been relatively simple. It had required no more than stumbling to his feet, taking three steps, and giving the artillery sergeant's shoulder a vigorous shake.

Driscol, with a lack of sensibility that would have shocked any proper citizen of the United States, had fallen asleep—become comatose, rather—on the floor of the same dilapidated house in the freedmen's quarter of the city as the chief noncommissioned officer of his unit. And done so, moreover, with no regard for other delicate aspects of the business.

True, the floor was covered with a carpet of sorts. But those same respectable citizens would have been aghast to note that it was Sergeant Ball, not Major Driscol, who occupied the only bed in the house. They would have been scandalized further by the fact that the sergeant's head was well cushioned on the bosom of a lady who, in addition to suffering from the shame of Ham's lineage, did not seem any too virtuous. Judging, at least, from her clothing, which was both flamboyant and—for the most part—flamboyantly absent.

Bad enough that Driscol would get drunk with darkies; worse yet, that in his drunkenness, he would fall asleep on a darkie's floor. *Positively insane* that he wasn't the one sleeping in the bed with the voluptuous darkie who owned the house.

Driscol essayed an erect posture. Giving that up as hopeless, he resumed his crouch and gave Ball's shoulder another shake.

Ball uttered some sort of incoherent protest.

"It's for your own good, Sergeant," Driscol insisted. "If you don't pry yourself loose from Marie, your leprosy will get worse."

Ball chuckled, but his eyes remained closed. The eyes of the lady in question, however, popped wide open.

"Who you calling a leper, Patrick Driscol?" she demanded. "You watch yourself, or I'll curse you. See if I don't!"

That was no idle threat, either. Though only in her twenties, Marie Laveau was already a well-known voudou queen in New Orleans's colored quarters. Everywhere in the city, in fact, because quite a few white people followed at least some of the voudou rituals. That was especially true of the women who employed Marie as their hairdresser.

Driscol probably didn't believe in voudou. On the other hand, it was a faith he knew little about, and he saw no reason to take unnecessary chances. Besides, whether she could hex him or not, he'd seen enough of Mademoiselle Laveau to realize that smiting a man with a blunt instrument was well within her capabilities. His lily-white skin be damned. This was the black side of Ramparts Street, not a plantation in Georgia.

"It's not *my* opinion," Driscol added hastily. "I'm just passing on the advice of a famous doctor."

"Doctors!" Marie pried Ball loose and sat up in the bed, seemingly oblivious to her half-bare chest—quite an impressive chest, too—and Driscol's presence.

"Doctors!" she repeated. "The priests ought to ban the lot of them, seein' as how suicide is a sin."

Driscol smiled at her. "You'll get no argument from me."

After a moment, Laveau returned the smile. Then she gave Ball's shoulder a shake that was a lot more vigorous than either of Driscol's. "Get up, Charles! Before the major has you shot for insubordination."

" 'E wouldn't do that," mumbled Ball, struggling to rise. "Not a fellow sergeant! 'Sides, I'm a friend of his."

Which . . .

Was true enough. Driscol didn't make friends easily. But when he did, it was usually with another sergeant—and, in the months since the battle at the Capitol, he and Charles Ball had become quite close, as these things went.

So much for established wisdom. That commodity, never valued too highly by Driscol, had suffered still a further decline over the past period. Weeks—no, months now—in close proximity with Indians and Negroes had demonstrated to Driscol that the official certitudes of white American society were as shaky as a badly made roof.

As was always the case, those certitudes and their results were written down by literate men of the upper classes. Granted, taken as a whole, the certitudes described social affairs well enough. But social affairs are never taken as a whole. The very notion was an abstraction. In the real world, in the literary shadows where people of the lower classes met and mingled, the truth could be quite different.

* * *

Not everyone saw it the way he did, of course. Often enough, not even members of the lower classes were involved. That had been made pretty clear the previous evening.

"Oh, that's just silly!" Marie Laveau had snorted at one point in the drunken conversation that had taken place around her kitchen table. "Patrick Driscol, every lynch mob I ever seen or heard about was mostly made up of the poorest white trash around. You won't see hardly any rich men around."

"Sure," Driscol replied. "So what?"

He took the time, politely, to pour Charles Ball another drink. That took quite a bit of time, because by now his hand was very far from steady.

"Same was true in Ireland. The Sassenach could always get plenty of dirt-poor Irishmen to do their dirty work for them. But they were the ones who called the tune, not the slobs—and they could have stopped it in a minute if they'd wanted to."

" 'E's right," Charles burped. "You know it well's I do, Marie. Mos' o' the time, anyhow. There's a lynching, there's rich men gave the signal for it. And they sure always the ones see to it nobody gets punished afterward."

Marie glared at him. "Since when do you start spoutin' this crazy Scots-Irishman's radical notions?"

"You only known me a short while, girl," Charles protested.

Marie's glare never wavered. After a bit, Charles grinned and shrugged. "Didn' say I did. But 'e's right about that. And I'll tell you what else."

Ball clapped a friendly hand on Driscol's shoulder, spilling some of the liquor from Driscol's glass onto his lap. But nobody noticed. It wasn't as if those were the first liquor stains on the now-bedraggled uniform.

"This here fine Irishman ain't the first white friend I've ever had. Been several of them, before, in the navy. Still got some, in fact—three o' our new unit is white, just 'cause they more comfortable with us than they was with the others. And you know what, girl? Not a one of those white-boy friends of mine had any bigger pot to piss in than I did."

"Aye!" Driscol exclaimed, gesturing dramatically with his glass. The liquor stains on his trousers expanded. "*That's* the point, Marie. I didn't say poor people were virtuous. I've known far too many of them to think any such foolishness. All I'm saying is that they *can* be—because the money isn't standing in the way."

He pointed to her hand. "Look there, woman. If that skin is 'black,' I'll eat this fancy officer's hat."

"High yeller, we call it," Ball said. He did his best to keep a smug tone out of his voice. His best was . . . not very good.

Marie's lips twisted. "There's a lot more white in me than black, is the truth of it. Not that it matters any."

"Aye, and *that's* the point, also. It didn't matter to somebody else, either, or you wouldn' be here at all."

"You livin' in the clouds! Maybe it didn't matter when the blood was running hot, but it sure mattered afterward. Not a one of those white forefathers of mine ever married one of those black foremothers." She hesitated a moment, taking a drink from her own glass. "Well. All right. I know that one of them wanted to, and lived as if he did. But the law didn't allow for it."

"Aye. And who *passed* the law? Poor men, or rich men?"

Driscol rose from the chair. He needed to use his remaining arm to brace himself, and still had trouble. He was very, very drunk, he realized. Drunker than he'd been in years.

"Feels good," he muttered, thinking not of the drunkenness but the reason for it. It was nice to have lots of friends again. That had been missing, since Ireland, except for a few stretches in the emperor's army.

"I'll be to bed now, so's to leave the two of you to yourselves. You don't mind, I'll just use a part of your floor."

Marie nodded. There was a certain air of satisfaction about the gesture, as if she'd just scored a point in the debate.

"You best do so! You try makin' it back to your officer's quarters, in your condition and this late at night, you won't get there. Not in this part of New Orleans. Not without being robbed, for sure, and maybe havin' your throat cut. And it won't be no evil rich white man do it, neither. Be one of those virtuous poor niggers you blathering about."

Driscol grinned at her. "Did I ever say I thought being stepped on made a man a saint? Not hardly!"

He drained his glass and set it down carefully on the table. "Leave it at this, Marie. I just feel more comfortable—always did—in the midst of outcasts. Lot more than I ever do with the so-called proper classes, that's for sure. Maybe that's my ideals at work. Maybe it's just my contrary nature. Whichever, it's the way it is."

She looked up at him, coolly and consideringly. Marie had drunk a lot less than he or Ball.

"Good enough for me. Help yourself to the floor, Patrick Driscol. I recommend somewhere there's a carpet. Thin as it'll be, it'll be better than nothing. And there'll be some breakfast for you in the morning."

Ball managed to sit fully erect. "Lordie," he muttered. "Marie, what poison you give us last night?"

Marie was on her feet now, wrapping herself in a robe and heading for the kitchen area of the apartment. "Poison! I told you Criollo Jim's so-called whiskey was rotgut. Maroons make it, out in the bayous. What you expect?"

Maroons were runaway slaves who lived in the semi-impenetrable waterways and cypress swamps west of the city. There were entire little towns of them out there, according to the stories Driscol had heard.

He was inclined to believe the tales, being a veteran of Napoleon's Spanish campaign. Periodically, the authorities made sweeps through the bayous, but it was always hard to catch the maroons. If they were pressured too much, they'd simply drift further west, finding shelter among the scattered fragments of Indian tribes. In the meantime, they maintained a lively traffic with the large slave and freedmen population of the city.

The black city-dwellers provided the maroons with needed tools and other manufactured goods; in exchange, they got the products of the swamp—moonshine always being a popular item—as well as, for the slaves, a potential escape route, should they ever need it. Most slaves were inclined to remain in bondage, though, since—in practice—most New Orleans masters were smart enough not to make that bondage too oppressive. But there were always some stupid or vicious masters whose slaves would eventually decide that the bayous were preferable.

There were some white people out there, too, or their mixed-blood descendants. Like any great seaport, New Orleans had a constant trickle of crewmen who jumped ship, as well as indentured servants brought over from Europe. For such white men and women, the cypress swamps were often their best refuge, as well. One of the stories Driscol had heard the night before had amused him simply because of its rampant race-mixing—what proper American citizens called "amalgamation." It seemed that, in the previous century, fifteen people had been accused of plotting to run away together to the Choctaw lands. Among the accused had been a teenage Indian slave, a teenage African slave, a French sergeant, a Swiss soldier, and a twenty-seven-year old French woman sent to Louisiana against her will in a forced marriage.

Amalgamation, indeed—and a lot more of it happened than polite society recognized and its antiquarians recorded. The history of families, formal and informal, whose members were semiliterate at best and thus beyond the pale of Official History as practiced by the world's respectable scholars.

Marie started cooking up . . . something. Driscol wasn't inclined to inquire as to the details. Food was food, and he needed it.

"So when you goin' to propose to that Indian girl of yours, Patrick?" her voice carried clearly from the kitchen. "I'm warning you, she must be crazy. First, to come all the way here. Second—really crazy—looking for the likes of you."

"Does *everybody* in the world know about my private affairs?" Driscol grumbled. He shot Charles Ball a very unfriendly look.

The gunnery sergeant raised protesting hands. "I didn' say nothing last night! 'Sides, you were there. In all that commotion in the Place des Nègres, who could have heard me anyway?"

There was just enough truth to that claim for Ball's protest to fall into the range of the Scottish jury verdict. *Not proven.* The Place des Nègres, on New Orleans's northern outskirts, had been established for a century as the locale where the city's black population—free or slave, either way or both—could create its own market. At night, the place also served as an informal outdoor ballroom. The beat of the *bamboulas* and the wail of the *banzas* were enough to drown out most anything, even leaving aside the congeries of dancers.

"You talked well enough in that same ruckus to wheedle your way into Mademoiselle Laveau's good graces," Driscol pointed out darkly.

Hungover or not, Ball shifted his defense with all the grace of a mountain goat leaping the rocks on a hillside. " 'Xactly so! How could I have been preaching on your private business when I was sweet-talking a voudou queen?"

The look he gave Driscol combined reproach and the injured innocence of a cherub. How Ball managed that, with his rugged sailor's face, was a mystery to Driscol. "You think that's so easy, Major Patrick, *you* try it sometime."

He spoke loudly enough for Marie to hear him in the kitchen. "Sweet-talking is right!" her voice rang out. The tone was half angry, half amused. "I can't believe I let a black curree like you sample my golden charms."

"Did more'n sample 'em," Charles said smugly—but, this time, too softly to be overheard by her. The quadroon in the kitchen was a fearsome woman in her own right, and now she was armed with kitchen implements, to boot.

Before he could continue, there was a knocking at the door.

"Answer that!" Marie hollered. "Tell whoever it is I don't have enough for his breakfast, too." Something in a skillet made a sizzling sound that was way too loud for any respectable food-stuff Driscol was familiar with. But, again, he didn't inquire, simply went to the door and opened it.

Outside, standing on the open-air stairs that led up to Marie's second-floor apartment, was Henry Crowell.

Grinning. Below him, the street seemed to be jampacked with young black men. Most of them dark-skinned, but with a sprinkling of that "high-yeller" color that usually denoted a black Creole in New Orleans.

"Oh, no," Driscol croaked.

"Good morning to you, master and commander!" Crowell boomed. "The Freedmen Iron Battalion is present and accounted for, *sir!*"

"We are *not* marching in any parade today," Driscol croaked.

"Course not, sir! These are *fighting men.* They're here today to begin their training."

Crowell's grin was wide enough to scare a shark.

Charles Ball staggered over to stand next to Driscol, and gaze dumbfounded at the mob below.

"Where they come from?" he groaned.

"You recruited them last night, Sergeant! You and the major!" Driscol had a vague memory of some speech making at the

Place des Nègres. The memory was so vague he'd passed it off as drunken fantasy.

"I did *what*?" protested Ball. He waved a feeble hand toward the kitchen. "Couldna. I was busy sweet-talking a voudou queen."

"Yes, sir! Your valor impressed the men deeply, sir!"

"*Will* you stop shouting, Henry?" Driscol's croak was beginning to resemble a respectable growl. "Listen, just keep them there. We'll be down in a minute. Or ten."

"Sir!" Crowell ripped off a salute that came from no army known to Driscol. Perhaps the teamster had learned it in another life, if the Hindoos had it right. The Fantastical Moola Scimitars of the High Panjandrum of Somewherestan. Who could say?

Driscol closed the door and gave Ball another glare.

"So. Speech making, when you were supposed to be sweet-talking a voudou queen. Who knows what *else* you were babbling about last night?"

Marie came out of the kitchen bearing plates full of . . . something. Driscol decided he could eat without looking, even with only one hand.

"You didn't answer my question, Patrick," she scolded. "When you goin' propose to that Indian girl of yours? She's waiting for you at the Trémoulet House. Her daddy must be rich, putting up there. Most expensive hotel in New Orleans. Didn't know any Indians were rich."

"Her father's not an Indian," Driscol grumbled. "Captain John Rogers is a thieving, swindling, conniving Scotsman—and a blackguard to boot. He got the rank of captain fighting for the Tories in the Revolution."

"Oh." She set the plates down on the table. Now that he had a better view of the contents, Driscol *really* didn't want to look. If that was meat, it had way too many legs for a proper Scots-Irishman.

"She's got one of you Scots-Irish for a daddy and wants to marry another? Somebody put a grigri on that poor girl. You send her to me and I'll lift the curse."

CHAPTER 36

DECEMBER 21, 1814
Lake Bourgne, Louisiana

"Are you sure this Duclos fellow is telling the truth?" Admiral Cochrane's tone was skeptical.

The young British army officer who'd brought the report started to shrug. Then, remembering the august company he was facing, Lieutenant Peddie caught himself and turned the gesture into a straightening of the shoulders. "The interrogation was most rigorous, sir. Unless the Frenchman's a lot better liar than I think he is—"

General Ross interrupted him. "He's not lying. But he's not telling the truth, either."

Cochrane swiveled his head to peer at Ross. The movement was done carefully. Cochrane was normally a vigorous man, and had he been in his own expansive quarters on his flagship, the admiral would have swung about dramatically. But in the very cramped quarters aboard the schooner he was using to supervise the landing of his troops at Bayou Bienvenu, his movements had become downright cautious. He still had a bruise on his forehead from the time he'd banged his head, having forgotten that a schooner's dimensions were not those of a ship of the line. The first of three occasions.

"Explain, Robert, if you would."

Ross had no need to watch his own movements. The general was still so weak that even sitting up in a chair was difficult.

"What I mean is that the man undoubtedly *thinks* he's telling the truth. But he's wrong." Ross looked at the lieutenant, swiveling his eyes only. "Duclos is a civilian, you said?"

Peddie nodded. "Yes, sir, for all practical purposes. All the men we captured were part of the Louisiana militia, under the command of a certain Major Villeré—who is also a civilian in all but name. The son of a wealthy local planter, from what we could determine. Apparently, Jackson ordered Villeré to send a detachment to guard the outlet of the bayou, and—"

Ross interrupted him again. "I'd think Jackson would have ordered the bayou obstructed, as well."

"Well, sir, he may well have done so. Duclos was vague on the matter. I suspect his commander Villeré made it clear he was not too happy at the notion of interfering with the waterways." Lieutenant Peddie smiled thinly. "The Villeré plantation is located along the bayou, and he may have been concerned that damage would result to his own property."

Admiral Cochrane chuckled. "I almost feel sorry for Jackson. Imagine having to command such a pack of vagabonds calling themselves an 'army.' "

For perhaps the hundredth time since he'd returned from his captivity, Ross had to suppress a remark. *Like the pack of vagabonds who broke our charge at the Capitol?* No matter how hard he tried, Ross had simply found it impossible to get Cochrane to take the enemy seriously.

Seriously enough, at least. Of course, Cochrane didn't have a crippled shoulder to remind him constantly of the folly of doing otherwise.

But this wasn't a good time for another argument with the admiral. Ross was still in no condition to resume active command of the army. He was accompanying the New Orleans expedition solely as an adviser to Cochrane and General John Keane, who'd replaced Ross until Major General Pakenham could arrive from England. At that, Ross had had to use all his powers of persuasion to get Cochrane to agree to let him come along, instead of returning him to Britain for a long convalescence.

Ross didn't really know himself why he'd insisted so vigorously. Partly out of concern for his soldiers, of course. Partly, because he was a stubborn man by nature, and hated to leave any business unfinished. But some of it, he suspected, was simply curiosity. He just wanted to see how it would end, this war with a peculiar—and peculiarly resilient—young republic.

"I've never known a civilian who could estimate the true size of an army," Ross continued. "It's in the nature of things. How many civilians ever see thousands of men, assembled in one place? Precious few, whereas soldiers witness the phenomenon regularly. Put five hundred men in a town square and they look like the hosts of Egypt to an inexperienced civilian eye."

"True enough," Cochrane allowed. "So what's your estimate, Robert? I take it you think Duclos's numbers are off a bit."

"More than a bit. He claims there are fifteen thousand men in New Orleans under Jackson's direct command—and another three thousand at the English Turn. Is that correct?"

"Yes, sir," Peddie said. The lieutenant cleared his throat. "That *does* match some of the other accounts Captain Spencer and I heard when we scouted the area."

Ross was tempted to make a sarcastic remark, but restrained himself again. With greater ease, this time. First, because he was never as impatient with junior officers as he could be with senior ones. But also, because he admired young Peddie's boldness, if nothing else.

Several days earlier, Peddie—normally a quartermaster officer—had accompanied the naval captain Spencer on a reconnaissance up Bayou Bienvenu. The two British officers had disguised themselves as civilians and questioned some of the Portuguese and Spanish fishermen who lived on a tongue of land just a short distance inland from the bayou's mouth. "Fishermen's Village," they called it—insofar as a dozen rude cabins could be called a village at all.

Spencer and Peddie had even managed to hire a pirogue in the village, along with two fishermen who'd rowed them up the Bienvenu to the branch called Bayou Mazant. They'd made it all the way to the Mississippi and walked along the east bank of the great river.

"The accounts of fishermen," Ross specified, "who are even less experienced at gauging the size of armies than most civilians."

"True enough, sir. And it's also true that the estimates of the fishermen themselves varied wildly. Some claimed Jackson had no more than a few thousand men under his command."

"That'll be off, as well," Ross said, "but closer to the truth." He looked back at Cochrane. "Consider the matter, Admiral. The Americans probably never managed to amass fifteen thousand troops, even at their own capital. How would they have done it here? Especially when Jackson expected us to attack through Mobile or Pensacola, and march overland to New Orleans, rather than go at the city directly."

Cochrane scowled. "We *were* planning to attack via that route."

Ross suspected the admiral's scowl was directed more at him than at the distant figure of an enemy general. Indeed, Ross was gently reminding him not to underestimate Jackson, and Cochrane knew it. The British had been forced to relinquish their plan to invade the gulf through Mobile because Jackson had moved quickly and forcefully to block them—and hadn't cared at all that he was violating Spanish territory in the process.

So here they were. Forced to find a route into New Orleans through cypress swamps and truly horrible weather. The gulf in late December was nothing like the balmy Caribbean paradise so many of the troops had expected. When the British army had landed on Pea Island in Lake Bourgne, they'd been greeted not only by a torrential rainfall but with temperatures much lower than anyone had imagined. There'd even been frost the next morning.

The terrain was bad enough. What worried Ross still more was that the conditions for disease were worse than any he'd ever encountered in Europe. By now, just from the rigors of ferrying from the fleet's anchorage at Cat Island, a large number of the soldiers were coming down with a variety of illnesses.

"How many does he have then, Robert?" asked the admiral.

Ross's shrug was a weak thing. He was sick himself, and had been for days. "At a guess ... Jackson won't have more than seven thousand men, in all. Not all of whom will be with him at New Orleans, either. He'll need, at the very least, to keep detachments at Fort St. Leon to guard the English Turn, at Fort St. Philip to guard the river farther south, and at Fort St. John in case we manage to get into Lake Pontchartrain."

"Seven thousand," Cochrane murmured.

"Probably closer to five, actually. And most of them will be militia units."

Cochrane sat up straight, after a quick glance to assure himself there was nothing to crack his head against. "We can manage that. Easily, I should think."

Manage it, yes.

Easily, no.

Something of Ross's skepticism must have shown. The admiral eyed him for a moment, his face expressionless, and then said abruptly: "That'll be all, Lieutenant Peddie."

As soon as the lieutenant was gone, the admiral's earlier scowl returned. "Do we need to argue this again, Robert? I have no choice, and you know it. We can't attack from the north because we're lacking shallow-draft boats, and we can't come up the river because of the forts. That leaves no alternative but Bayou Bienvenu or its equivalent—and Spencer and Peddie report that the equivalents are all worse."

Ross's headshake was as weak as his shrug. "That's not the point, sir. The route, we can manage—*if* the thing is led properly."

"You can't *possibly*—"

Ross shook his head again. "I realize full well I'm in no condition to lead it myself." With a wry smile: "I'm struggling as it is just to keep from sliding off this chair. What bothers me is that . . ."

He'd come to the edge of the issue that he'd thus far skirted, out of politeness for fellow officers.

Cochrane grunted. "You've no confidence in Keane."

"That's putting it much too strongly, Admiral. John Keane is a fine officer. But as a commanding general, which he is now for the first time, I fear he'd be too cautious."

"Too *cautious*?" Cochrane threw up his hands with exasperation—banging the knuckles of the left on a bulkhead. Muttering under his breath, he pulled out a kerchief and dabbed the blood. "Robert," he growled, "as I recall you have been the one all along urging caution on this expedition. Now you choose to complain of its *excess*?"

"My cautions, sir—and I believe I made this clear—all had to do with the *strategic* aspects of the problem. What I am now referring to is the likelihood that General Keane will be excessively cautious when presented with a tactical situation."

"Surely you're not suggesting that Keane is a *coward*?"

"Oh, for the sake of God!" The moment he blurted it out, Ross cursed himself. Whatever chance he'd had to persuade Cochrane had just been diminished again by that angry outburst.

No help for it but to plow on, however.

"My point was certainly not to question Keane's courage, Admiral. But a man can be personally brave and still not have the wherewithal to push forward a charge at the right moment. Were that not true, any good corporal would make another Alexander the Great."

"Damn you, Robert! On the one hand, you tell me Keane will be too cautious. On the other, you think Pakenham will be prone to recklessness. Yes, I know you've been veiled about it, but I am not stupid. What do you want? For me to wait until I have the perfect army assembled?"

Cochrane was glaring, and it was all Ross could do not to scowl just as ferociously in response. The admiral certainly wasn't stupid, but he had a habit of playing the innocent, which Ross sometimes found immensely aggravating.

"I have told you already—several times, Admiral—that I simply think we'd be wise to postpone the assault. For a few weeks, at least, although I'd prefer two or three months."

He fought off the weakness and sat straighter, leaning forward. "I never said I thought Pakenham was reckless. But you know as well as I do that he has the reputation for being . . . ah . . ."

Cochrane's scowl faded. He even chuckled, albeit drily.

"Yes, I know. '*Bold,*' I believe, is the term most commonly used." More seriously: "On the other hand, he *is* considered a superb general by most of the officer staff, Robert. He didn't become a major general in his mid-thirties simply because he's Wellington's brother-in-law, you know."

How to explain? Ross did not, in fact, doubt that Pakenham was a very talented general. But he was also young, and talent wasn't the same thing as experience. Add to that a certain reputation for rashness, and . . .

"Admiral, Pakenham won't arrive to take command until the very last moment. What I fear is this: Keane is an excellent subordinate officer, but he's never been in command before. His initial approach will therefore almost certainly be too cautious, too tentative. No fault of his own, really; simply lack of experience. But that will give Jackson enough time to prepare himself—and that's what Pakenham will face when he arrives. If you then push Pakenham to move immediately, he'll almost certainly err on the side of being too aggressive."

"Robert, I hardly think it's necessary for our generals to maneuver perfectly in order to defeat an amateur like Jackson."

Fiercely, Ross controlled his temper. It would do no good at all to start shouting.

"Admiral Cochrane, you *must* stop underestimating Andrew Jackson. He is a genuinely dangerous opponent, not simply a jumped-up militia general. An amateur he might be, by the professional standards of a British or continental army. But history is full of battles won by gifted amateurs against professionals.

"Amateur or not," he continued harshly, "Jackson has consistently outmaneuvered us in the months leading up to this attack on New Orleans."

Ross paused, giving Cochrane a level gaze. Cochrane was obviously angry at those last words. But, just as obviously, he wasn't prepared to dispute them.

He couldn't. Robert Ross had been privy to all the plans, and he *knew*.

Just to drive home the point, Ross decided to make it specific.

"Admiral Warren's initial plan relied upon a powerful force of Creeks to be allied with us. But Jackson broke the Creek Nation at the Horseshoe Bend, before the alliance could be carried out."

Sourly, Cochrane nodded.

"And what happened then, Admiral? After you replaced Warren in command in the gulf, you decided on an initial landing in Mobile. Which I fully agree was the right thing to do. That would have circumvented all the horrid terrain south and east of New Orleans. Again, however, Jackson reacted quickly. He ignored Spanish sovereignty and moved into Mobile in force— and so our initial thrust was broken at Fort Bowyer."

Cochrane sighed. And nodded again.

Ross shrugged. "For a short while, there, I hoped that Jackson had outsmarted himself. The American general seemed so certain that we'd attack Mobile that he remained there, even while our expedition moved on to Lake Bourgne. But . . ."

He left the rest unspoken, since it was obvious. *But Jackson corrected the error in time. And he's in New Orleans now.*

He could tell that Cochrane was still unconvinced, unfortunately. Or, at least, not convinced enough.

Again, how to explain, Ross asked himself desperately, in words that would be calm and coherent? The long and painful months recovering from his terrible wounds at the Capitol, now added to by this new illness, had left Ross too muddleheaded to say anything clearly. In truth, he felt—had he the strength—like grabbing Cochrane by the shoulders, shaking him, and screaming: *Take your enemy seriously, you fool! What sort of arrogant ass thinks you can put a man in command, a week before a battle—Pakenham or Caesar, it matters not—and expect him to defeat the likes of Jackson?*

Ross could see it all unfolding. Pakenham would arrive just in time to inherit the poor tactical position left him by Keane—and, from frustration and inexperience, he'd try to overcome it with a direct assault. Assuming, unthinkingly, that the British veterans who'd broken Napoleon on the open field of battle would easily sweep aside these American militiamen.

And so, indeed, they might, if it weren't for that terrifying American artillery. The same artillery that Ross had seen batter his forces at Bladensburg, and shred them in front of the Capitol. Cannons fired more quickly and accurately than any British battery had ever managed, in Ross's decades of experience.

He sighed. "I simply wish you'd postpone the thing until Pakenham's been here for a bit, Admiral. At least give him the chance to learn the terrain and size up his enemy properly."

Cochrane wasn't an ill-tempered man, by nature, so his earlier anger had faded away. "I *can't,* Robert. I'd like to myself, as it happens, but I simply can't."

He hesitated a moment; then: "I'll ask you to keep this in confidence. I've just received word concerning the latest developments in the peace negotiations at Ghent. Underneath the formal language, the gist of it is that our envoys are stalling, to give us a chance to seize New Orleans before any treaty is signed."

"I see." Ross grimaced.

The peace negotiations, which had been taking place between Britain and the United States in the Belgian city of Ghent, had been going on for many months now. If they were finally close to a settlement . . .

The war with the United States wasn't popular in England—all the more so now that twenty years of war with France had ended. That did, indeed, place Cochrane on the horns of a dilemma. Since Britain had never recognized the legitimacy of the Louisiana Purchase, the treaty would not settle that question. If Britain *already* held New Orleans when word of a peace treaty arrived in the gulf, they'd keep it. Under the legal fiction of returning it to its proper Spanish owners, of course.

But given the war weariness in Britain, there was no chance of starting a new war with the United States, even under the pretense of rectifying an injustice done to Spain. So if Cochrane was going to take New Orleans, he had to do it quickly.

"They can't stall for very long, I take it."

"No, Robert, they can't. It's not just that our populace is growing restive. The situation on the continent is none too well settled, either. There is still a great deal of Napoleonic sentiment in France, you know. The government isn't as confident as everyone else that we've seen the end of that conflict, and if that's the case, no one wants to have a large body of British troops on this side of the Atlantic."

"Yes, I can see the logic behind that. So, in essence, they'll stall at Ghent just long enough to give us one chance at a quick victory."

Cochrane nodded. "I wouldn't be surprised at all to discover that the ink is drying right now on the treaty. We've only got a few weeks, Robert. If we're to do it at all, it has to be done now. And that's all there is to it."

Cochrane rose from his chair, moving carefully. "Enough, Robert. You need to get some rest. You're looking—well, terrible, to be honest. If you contract yellow fever in your condition . . ."

Ross struggled to his feet. "Yes, I know. I'll die."

"Look on the bright side," the admiral said. "Pakenham can probably manage. But whether he can or can't, I'm ordering the men into the landing boats tomorrow morning."

"Three days before Christmas," Ross mused. "Well, let's hope for the best."

DECEMBER 21, 1814
Ghent, the Low Countries

Glumly, sitting at his writing table in the lodgings he occupied in Ghent, John Quincy Adams studied a copy of the treaty which had finally been arrived at. Only the long and stern habit of a man raised in the puritanical environment of one of New England's premier families kept him from cursing aloud.

Months, he'd spent, slowly persuading the other members of the American delegation that this treaty he had before him was the best the United States could hope for. *Months,* while the other members of the delegation—Albert Gallatin, Henry Clay, James Bayard, and Jonathan Russell—kept stalling, hoping for some sort of miracle.

What miracle? Adams wondered. The only bright moment had been when news arrived that the British assault on Washington had been driven off, and the Capitol had been spared. Savagely, Adams almost found himself wishing the assault had succeeded—since, from his perspective, it had simply kept Gallatin and Clay and Bayard and Russell suspended in midair for perhaps a month, empty-headed with braggadocio.

Almost . . . but not quite. Adams was a patriot, and he couldn't deny the deep satisfaction he'd felt when the news had arrived. The same sort of satisfaction he'd felt at the news of the *Guerriere*'s capitulation, or the news of the battle at the Chippewa.

The problem had been that his fellow envoys simply couldn't understand that such satisfaction was *all* that the United States could realistically hope to achieve in this war. The conflict with Britain had always been a preposterous exercise, in purely military terms.

It was no doubt a very fine thing for the morale of a young republic to see a handful of plucky American frigates defeating a handful of British frigates. But the cold, hard, cruel strategic fact remained that the tiny U.S. Navy boasted no ships larger than a few 44-gun frigates—and the British Navy had over a hundred two-decker 74-gun ships of the line.

It was no doubt excellent from the standpoint of that same young republic to see—finally!—one of its armies defeat an equal force of British regulars on the open field of battle, as Brown and Scott had done at the Chippewa. But the moral splendor of the feat could not, to a sane man, disguise its triviality in cold military terms. The total forces engaged at the Chippewa had been less than five thousand—a clash which, for the past twenty years on the continent, would have been considered a skirmish rather than a battle.

In the campaign that had finally defeated Napoleon, culminating in the Battle of the Nations near Leipzig, more than half a million men had met on the field.

Splendid, yes—certainly!—the pluck of Captain Houston

and Lieutenant Driscol and their men at the Capitol. But what did it really come down to, in the harsh, brutal, realistic terms of political geography? One thousand men armed with a few cannons kept a small invading force with no artillery to speak of from taking Washington, D.C.

Splendid, splendid. No doubt many fine poems and songs would be written to commemorate the event. The fact remained that Napoleon had brought seven hundred field guns to Leipzig—but the Allies had fielded twice that number. Just as the fact remained that no sane man gave even a moment's thought to the possibility that the United States might land an army on British soil to threaten *London*.

Adams sighed, left off his pointless study of the treaty—he had every clause in it memorized by now—and rose from his desk. Then he moved to a window that faced to the west, toward the Atlantic and his nation beyond.

He was forty-five years old, and had spent many of those years living in Europe. As a student, an assistant to American diplomats—his father among them, before John Adams became the second president of the United States—and then later as a diplomat himself. The son of the second American president had often, as a young man, sat at the dining table with its first, listening carefully to George Washington's shrewd assessments of foreign affairs.

Since then, John Quincy Adams had sat at many other tables with the world's most powerful men, in most of the major capitals of Europe. He'd been, at one time or another, America's ambassador to Britain, France, Holland, Portugal, Prussia, and Russia. He spoke and read French easily and fluently, and had once translated Wieland's *Oberon* from German into English. He was one of the most well-educated and well-read men in the United States—the world, in fact—and had the personal library to prove it.

All for nothing, quite possibly. Partly, because Gallatin and Clay and Bayard and Russell were fools. Partly—Adams was usually as harsh in his self-criticism as his criticism of others—because John Quincy Adams had never been good at suffering fools gladly. So, over the months, he'd increasingly alienated his fellow envoys, while their light-minded frivolity led their nation into a very possible trap.

Again, he restrained himself from cursing. They could have signed that same treaty months ago. *And why not?* To this day, the British still refused to concede anything concrete, when it came to the official casus belli the United States had proclaimed as the causes of the war. The issues of impressment, boundaries, fisheries, neutral rights—all ignored or swept under the table. For all practical purposes, the United States was agreeing in that treaty to the same conditions that had existed prior to the war.

And so what? The only possible victory America could have obtained in this conflict was simply the moral victory of going to war in the first place. And that had already been won, long since. The cold equations of national power hadn't been changed an iota, except in the one—often critical—variable of national respect. Whatever else, none of the great European powers would any longer regard the transatlantic republic as something of a bad joke.

Months, it had taken him to convince his fellow envoys. Precious, precious months—while Adams watched anxiously as Britain finally defeated the great French power which had kept it preoccupied for decades and could now send part of its true might across the Atlantic. *Months,* during which the territorial integrity of the U.S. could have been protected simply by signing the same blasted treaty they were going to sign now anyway.

Months . . . while the British were able to assemble the powerful task force which now lay somewhere near New Orleans and the critical outlet of the Mississippi. Might even, for all John Quincy Adams knew, already be enjoying a conqueror's feast in the Cabildo. It took weeks for news to cross the Atlantic, even from his native New England, much less the distant Gulf of Mexico.

It was all up to Andrew Jackson, now. Jackson and the same sort of rude, crude, uncouth southern frontiersmen who composed his army.

Sternly, John Quincy Adams reminded himself that he had chosen long ago, exercising his God-given free will, to devote his life to the service of his nation. Knowing from the very beginning—he'd hear no excuses, from himself least of all—that his nation was a republic. It wasn't as if dozens of monarchists hadn't told him for years he was a fool. Some of them had even read as many books as he had.

Not many, of course.

CHAPTER 37

DECEMBER 23, 1814
*A mile upriver of the Villeré plantation,
near New Orleans*

Colonel William Thornton decided to try one last time.

"I beg you, sir," he said forcefully, "consider that every single piece of evidence leads us to believe that we've caught Jackson completely by surprise." Dramatically, he pointed a finger ahead of them, to the northwest. "The prize is but a few miles away, sir! One vigorous push now, and we can be into the city before Jackson can organize its defense."

General Keane replied with an equally dramatic finger pointed to the rear. Specifically, to the Villeré plantation house that was still visible to the southeast.

"Every piece of evidence?" the general demanded. "Hardly that, Colonel! Villeré himself escaped from captivity this morning, did he not? By now, he'll surely have brought warning to the enemy."

Thornton silently cursed the fluke of chance that had allowed that to happen. As time went on, Thornton was learning how astute General Ross's assessment of the Americans was—even if that assessment often ran counter to the established wisdom of British officers.

"Don't fool yourselves, gentlemen," Ross had said. "They *are* our cousins, and lack neither courage nor intelligence. Sluggish one moment, they can be decisive—even daring—the very next. So you will do me the favor of not matching Cousin Jonathan's carelessness with carelessness of your own."

Those words, said in a tone that was unusually harsh for the normally mild-mannered Ross, had sobered his officers. Ross had gone on, in a more congenial manner, to elaborate.

"The key thing is that the Americans are *brittle* in war. But brittle is not the same thing as soft. Indeed, some of the finest alloys can be quite brittle. The trick is to catch them by surprise— to strike at the haft of the American blade, as it were, and be sure to miss entirely the edge. Because that edge can be very, very sharp, gentlemen. Don't ever forget that."

Very sharp, indeed, as they'd discovered in the failed assault on the Capitol. In truth, Thornton had already discovered that earlier at Bladensburg. "A rout," Bladensburg would be called in the historical records. But the Eighty-fifth had been the unit which encountered the edge in that battle, when Thornton had led his men across the key bridge near Lowndes Hill.

The bridge had still been standing in the first place because of American incompetence. Any professional army would have destroyed it. But, just as Ross had said, having blundered one moment, the Americans had rallied the next. The defense their artillerymen and riflemen had put up for that bridge had been ferocious. Thornton could not remember ever coming under such heavy fire from an enemy, even if it hadn't lasted that long before the Americans broke.

Sharp edge, indeed—but the haft was brittle.

And today, only two days before Christmas, Thornton knew that the British expedition, if it moved quickly and decisively, could strike Jackson's sword before the American general could bring the edge into position. They could snap that brittle blade at the haft.

Wait a day, and the opportunity might be lost.

"No, Colonel," General Keane said, shaking his head. "We'll halt the advance here and bivouac while we wait for the rest of our forces to arrive. By now, Villeré will have carried the warning to New Orleans. I am *not* so reckless as to attempt the city with only a portion of my army, and with my lines of supply stretched as badly as they are."

Nothing for it.

Thornton walked away obediently, almost grinding his teeth.

The small mistake of allowing Villeré to escape was about to be compounded, he thought, by the huge mistake of allowing Jackson to escape.

Such an odd fellow, Cousin Jonathan, as if two completely different men inhabited the same skin. Up till the moment of his escape, Major Gabriel Villeré had been a laughingstock to his British captors. A commanding officer caught on his own porch, smoking a cigar!

Yes, a farce, all very comical—and all very typically American. Amateur soldiers who'd disobey orders in order to safeguard their own property, and lounge about whenever they felt like it.

Even Villeré's sudden bolt for freedom when his British guards grew slack had been amusing enough. Especially comical had been the sight of Villeré's faithful dog, racing across the yard after its master, barking excitedly.

But Thornton and his men had not laughed some minutes later, when they'd found the dog's body in the swamps. The poor beast's throat had been cut. By Villeré himself, obviously. Feckless Cousin Jonathan had been cold-blooded and ruthless enough to kill his own loyal dog, rather than run the risk of having the excited beast give away his location to his pursuers.

Damnation! Colonel Thornton desperately wished that Robert Ross was still leading this army, instead of lying close to death on a ship in Lake Bourgne. Ross would have understood immediately that they had the chance—*now, this moment,* if they *moved*—to capture Andrew Jackson on his own figurative porch, smoking a cigar.

But Ross was not in command, alas, Keane was. And while Keane was certainly a courageous enough commander, he was neither an imaginative nor a particularly intelligent one.

If Keane let the American general escape, allowed him that one carelessly unguarded moment . . .

Villeré had cut the throat of a dog. Jackson would cut the throat of an army, if they gave him the time to bring that brittle but very sharp blade into position.

Hiding nearby in a cypress swamp, Major Arsène Latour studied the British positions as Keane's army began its bivouac. Latour and another military engineer, Major Howell Tatum, had left New Orleans that morning. General Jackson had commanded them to scout the terrain in the vicinity of the Villeré plantation. Partly, to determine the current position of the British; partly, to assess the possibility of erecting good field-works in the area.

Well, they'd done both.

The Mississippi River coursed east by southeast from New Orleans for some fifteen miles before it began the bend that cul-minated in the English Turn. The English Turn was blocked by Fort St. Leon on the opposite bank—and the fort itself was pro-tected by the cypress swamps that surrounded it. Coming up by the bayous from Lake Bourgne, therefore, the British would have no choice but to follow the east bank of the river, in order to reach the city.

It was a truly terrible route for an invading army. Any part of the area between the Chalmette and Villeré plantations would make superb terrain for the Americans, allowing them to erect fortifications to defend the city. There was less than a mile of open ground at any given point, with no easy possibility for the flanking maneuvers a British professional army could manage so much better than Jackson's largely volunteer force.

To the southwest lay the Mississippi, impossible to cross without boats—and Jackson had a small flotilla under Com-modore Daniel Patterson to prevent that from happening. To the north and east, at distances varying from half a mile to a mile from the Mississippi, the thick cypress swamps filled most of the land between the river and the lakes. Those swamps weren't exactly impenetrable—Latour knew that Jackson's Indian allies and many of his frontiersmen would manage in them quite handily. But they might as well be, for an army organized and trained to fight great formal pitched battles on the continent of Europe.

Earlier in the day, Latour and Tatum had decided to recom-mend to Jackson that he make his stand at the Rodriguez Canal, just west of the Chalmette plantation. The terrain there was ideal for a defending force. The cypress swamps encroached more closely upon the river there than elsewhere, choking the passable open ground to a stretch perhaps half a mile wide. Bet-ter still, the canal itself could easily and quickly be turned into a moat, with solid fieldworks behind it. The British would need scaling ladders and fascines to surmount such a fortified line— which they'd have to bring with them across a narrow open field after enduring heavy American fire as soon as they came into range.

Almost perfect. On the chance they might find something still better, however, Latour and Tatum had continued on. No sooner had they gotten to the next plantation, De la Ronde's, when they met several people racing westward who told them that the British had already reached the Villeré plantation. Had apparently captured Gabriel Villeré himself, in fact.

Tatum rushed back to New Orleans to inform the general that the British were much closer than anyone had suspected. Latour, meanwhile, forged on ahead to do a reconnaissance of the enemy forces.

To his surprise—and immense relief—he discovered that the British were preparing to bivouac, despite the fact that it was still early in the afternoon, and they could easily have managed to march the remaining ten miles to New Orleans.

That was a bad mistake on their part, he thought. Neither Jackson nor his troops at New Orleans were at all prepared to fight a battle that day. If the British had pressed on, Wellington's veterans would have had the upper hand, storming into an open city where the largely amateur defenders would have difficulty organizing themselves in the chaos of city streets overrun by panicked civilians.

But . . . apparently they were going to give Jackson a day to prepare.

The idiots.

A man might as well give a tiger advance notice that he's about to be bagged the next morning.

So be it. Latour would exploit the opportunity to study the British field positions. Unless he was very badly mistaken, Andrew Jackson wasn't going to wait until the morning. This was his jungle, and tigers can prowl at night.

Latour chuckled, as he carefully began jotting down the locations on his notepad. Especially when some of those tigers were Cherokees and Choctaws, who were already beginning their rituals for battle. The two engineers had taken the time that morning before they left the city to watch, fascinated, as the wild savages painted themselves openly on the streets of New Orleans.

Tatum had been goggle-eyed where Latour had not, of course. Latour was a French Creole and, thus, vastly more sophisticated than his companion. The Anglo-Saxon Tatum wasn't much more than a wild savage himself. Latour had learned his engineer and architect's trade at the Paris Academy of Fine Arts. Where had Tatum learned? Who could say. Probably in a rude schoolhouse in some wretched frontier village, made entirely of logs.

Latour shrugged the matter off. The Americans who were now the masters of New Orleans were barbarians, true enough. But at least they weren't *Englishmen.* Latour continued jotting down his notes. In French, which he'd have to translate for the barbarians later.

By the time Latour got back to New Orleans, it was late in the afternoon. As he'd expected, he found the city in an uproar— but it was the sort of uproar that showed a resolute and energetic commander in charge, not the panic of leaderless soldiers and civilians.

Jackson had made a bad mistake, of course, underestimating the ability of British regulars. But if the tiger had been sleeping carelessly, the beast was wide awake now. Awake—and roaring.

Latour came into Jackson's headquarters, pushing his way past officers rushing in the other direction. No easy task that, the way those officers were moving. Fortunately, Latour was a very big man. Even so, his progress was slow, and he could hear Jackson shrieking long before he caught sight of him.

"I will *smash* them, so help me God! By the Eternal, they shall not sleep on our soil!"

The general was even blaspheming, something he normally seemed to avoid. The Americans were odd, that way, as one could expect from superstitious primitives. They'd use profanity in a coarse manner no Creole would stoop to—the Anglo-Saxon terms "fuck" and "shit" and "piss" and all the rest rolled off their tongues casually, often enough even in the presence of women. But they used the silliest circumlocutions to refer to God and His works.

Latour could still remember his puzzlement the first time he heard Americans talking about someone named Jesse, and another fellow named Sam Hill. Especially when they often seemed to use the names to refer to locations instead of people. When he'd eventually realized the truth, he'd been astonished.

Did the barbarians really think that naming Satan and his domain openly would bring a devil's curse down upon them? That damnation would be avoided by calling it "tarnation"? That the omniscient deity who had created the universe would be fooled if they asked someone named "Gol" to "dern" their enemy—instead of, honestly and forthrightly, asking God to damn them?

Perhaps so. They were Protestants, after all—of one or another of the multitude of creeds that promiscuous heresy generated—and thus lacked the benefit of Latour's sane and rational Catholicism.

Still. At least they weren't *Englishmen.*

Latour finally pushed his way into the room, bearing his precious notes.

Driscol spotted the Creole engineer the moment he came into Jackson's headquarters. Latour was an impossible man not to notice, between his great size and skin, eyes and hair which were darker than many Indians.

He spotted the notepad clutched in the big engineer's hand an instant later, and smiled thinly. Latour was an obnoxious Creole snob, but he was also very competent at his trade—not that Driscol would use the lowly term "trade" in front of Latour himself. The Creole engineer would immediately shower him with voluble protests, and remind them that he was a graduate of some fancy academy in Paris. As if Driscol cared where a man learned to do anything, so long as he did it well.

That notepad would be full of jottings placing the British positions, unless Driscol was badly mistaken. Written down in Latour's flowery French and fussy handwriting—but dead accurate, nonetheless.

"Well, that's a relief," he commented quietly to Houston, who was standing next to him.

The young colonel spared him a quick glance. He and Driscol were standing in a corner of the room, waiting for their turn for Jackson's instructions. "It's always hard to tell, with that stone face of yours, but I had a feeling you weren't very happy with the situation."

"That's putting it mildly. Two hours ago, I thought we were probably on the verge of disaster."

He didn't add *because Jackson blundered badly, out of overconfidence. Something the general has a tendency to do, from what I've seen thus far.* Long habit would have kept Driscol from openly criticizing his commanding officer, even to Houston. He certainly wasn't inclined to do so with a commander like Jackson, for whom he had developed an immense respect.

"Disaster?" Houston frowned. "Do you really think it was that close a thing?"

"Oh, aye. If the Sassenach had been smart enough to keep coming. Not even Jackson, for all his ferocity, could have rallied these mostly inexperienced soldiers in a handful of hours. Not well enough to withstand a British assault with no prepared defenses."

He shook his head firmly. "Not a chance. Not when those troops are Wellington's veterans, with decades of war under their belts. I've seen British regulars smashing their way into a city, once the defenses were breeched. The most frightening thing about it was that they maintained their order and discipline even under the conditions of street fighting."

Houston was still frowning. "Really? But what about—"

"Forget Badajoz. That was the exception, not the rule. The reputation they've gotten due to the sack of Badajoz and a few other incidents is misleading. As a rule, even in a sack, British regulars remain professional—and their officers are quick to execute any man who misbehaves."

"Well . . . That was true in Washington, I agree. After the British left, we found the body of a British soldier. Executed at Cockburn's own order, apparently, from the accounts of an eyewitness. The man had been caught robbing American civilians at gunpoint, while Cockburn had been burning the president's mansion. The admiral had him shot immediately."

"I heard about it. The reason I hate the Sassenach isn't because they're a pack of howling savages. Oh, no. It's because they're such cold-blooded and calculating savages. They'll commit atrocities as bad as any Hun—but they'll do it under orders, given by the haughtiest noblemen in the world."

He had to restrain himself from spitting on the floor. "An army like that will tear apart the amateur defenders of a city, once that city's defenses are breeched. Rip them to shreds. If the British had gotten into New Orleans, Jackson would have been in the position of trying to lead panicked chickens against a pack of very professional weasels."

"Why didn't they, do you think? March into the city, I mean."

Driscol shrugged. "Excessive caution on the part of the commander, I suppose. That'll be Keane, until Pakenham gets here, and he's new to top command."

Jackson's waving hand summoned Houston, at that point. While the colonel hurried over, and before Driscol got his own summons, he had the time to ponder that last statement.

He'd come to regret the thing personally, but . . .

I'm glad I had Robert Ross ambushed at the Capitol.

The thought of Robert Ross being still in charge was too grim to contemplate, so Driscol left it aside. What mattered was that Ross was *not* commanding the army that was advancing upon New Orleans. He was probably on a ship crossing the Atlantic back to Britain, by now.

Driscol had gotten a letter from the general, telling him that he'd been exchanged and would be released soon, and that he thought his shoulder had mended well enough to allow him to travel. The letter hadn't finally caught up with Driscol until he'd reached New Orleans, so the information was weeks out of date. The workings of the American postal service could be peculiar, but it was usually persistent.

More peculiar, however, had been the fact that it wasn't until the day after he'd read the letter that it had occured to Driscol that his reaction itself was the most disconcerting thing of all. Patrick Driscol, from County Antrim, had smiled with pleasure as he learned of a British general's continuing recovery, from a terrible wound Driscol had inflicted upon him with murderous intent.

Ah, well. Driscol's found himself not worrying about it, because his soul seemed to have grown considerably lighter these past months. He could still summon the troll, whenever he needed it, but he found himself nowadays spending less and less of his time in that dark monster's lair.

That was Tiana's doing, mostly. The girl respected the troll, but had no liking for the creature. Still, Driscol would admit—even to himself—that the British general had something to do with it, too.

A man could surely spend half a lifetime slaying Sassenach, and spend it well. But when that lifetime, he finally realizes, constitutes but thirty-two years, he has to ask himself whether the same righteous work can fill three-fourths of a lifetime. Possibly even four-fifths, given Driscol's iron constitution.

For Patrick Driscol, at least, the answer was coming to be no. Amazingly enough, the soldier from County Antrim was growing weary of the killing trade.

Of course, there'd still be some fine moments, before he retired, with a commander like Andrew Jackson.

The same impatiently waving hand summoned Driscol. In less than a minute, Jackson gave him his orders, tersely and concisely. Then, sent him on his way.

As he headed out the door, Driscol heard Jackson erupting again.

"I will smash them, so help me God! By the Eternal, they shall not sleep on our soil!"

By Driscol's reckoning, that was the eleventh time Jackson had shrieked those same two sentences that afternoon. It would have all been quite comical, except that the time between the histrionic shrieks Jackson had spent issuing a blizzard of orders to his subordinates. Every single one of which had been coherent, logical, intelligent—and had, as their sole invariant purpose, smashing the enemy and driving him from American soil.

CHAPTER 38

"And what's this?" demanded Tiana's father, the moment Driscol entered the salon of the suite where he and his family had set up residence in the Trémoulet House. Captain John Rogers waved a vigorous hand at the window. His left hand, not his right—which held a glass of whiskey rock-steady all the while. "I'd have thought you'd be out there with the rest of them, playing your part in that desperate business tonight."

Driscol glanced at the window. There wasn't much to be seen, since night fell early this time of year. Still, even with the window closed to fend off the winter chill, the cannonades to the south were quite audible. Naval guns, from the sound of it. Jackson had ordered Commodore Daniel Patterson to bring the schooner *Carolina* down the river after nightfall, to begin bombarding the British camp on the Villeré plantation, while Jackson launched his night attack.

"None of my business, that," Driscol grunted. "When the general asked, I told him my men would be well-nigh useless in that sort of fighting."

"The darkies not up to it, eh?" Rogers jeered. As was so often the case, the captain's tone was half ridicule and half . . . something else. Hell-Fire Jack was a rogue, sure enough. But he was also, Driscol had come to conclude, a very intelligent and cold-blooded sort of man. The constant jests and jibes were his way of probing friends and enemies alike.

So, as he invariably did when dealing with Captain John Rogers, Driscol refused to take the bait.

"Of course not," he responded mildly, without even a hint of irritation. "They've had less than a week's training, and there's nothing more difficult to carry off than a complicated three-pronged night attack like the one Jackson is attempting. I'll be doing well if I can get my artillery unit ready to stand firm in broad daylight."

"So Sharp Knife is a madman, is that what you're saying?"

"No, actually, he's not. His plans *will* all fall apart, of course. I doubt if even the emperor's Imperial Guard could manage what Jackson is asking his army to do. He'll have to call off the assault eventually, when it starts coming to pieces.

"But that doesn't matter. All that matters tonight is that Jackson is responding immediately to the British landing. Whether he wins or loses this battle, his assault will stop the British from driving forward. That will buy him time to get our forces ready and our defensive positions erected."

Without waiting for an invitation, Driscol took a seat across from the divan where Tiana was resting. She smiled at him but said nothing.

It was a very serene smile; almost astonishingly so, on such a young face. If nothing else, Tiana had inherited her self-confidence from her father. Even at the age of sixteen, she was quite capable of watching a test of wills such as the one that was taking place between her sire and her intended husband, without worrying herself over the outcome.

Intended husband. She'd made that clear, too, without saying it in so many words. Driscol still had no idea at all why she'd made the decision, but he didn't doubt the decision itself. He certainly didn't doubt his own reaction, once it had finally seeped into his bones. It was the most profound desire he'd ever felt for anything. As if a man drowning in darkness had suddenly found a lifeline.

Of course, when the drowning man's name was Patrick Liam Driscol, he'd seize the lifeline in his own unique manner. A sergeant with sixteen years experience in war is not a man to do anything without considering all the angles first. Any intelligent sergeant would see it that way and, being honest, Driscol was the most intelligent sergeant he'd ever met. He was even smart enough to have gotten himself promoted to major without starting to think like an officer.

Captain John's eyes—the same bright blue as his daughter's—flicked back and forth from Tiana to Driscol. The half-grin never left his face; somehow, he even managed to keep it in place while downing a sip of the whiskey.

"So when's the wedding, then?" he demanded. He waved the same vigorous hand at his two sons, who lounged only a few feet away. James was leaning against the salon's dining table, while John was sitting on one of its chairs. "I realize these two heathens won't have pressed you on the matter, even though such is their brotherly duty. Cherokees and their stupid customs. But—!"

Rogers issued a majestic *harrumph.* "You and I are civilized Scotsmen, Major Driscol—well, allowing for your bastard Irish brand—and we should conduct ourselves accordingly."

Driscol glanced at the two brothers. James and John wore that same serene Rogers smile on their faces.

There was a battle won. A campaign, rather, since there'd never been any actual conflict. Somewhere, sometime, somehow, in the months since Sam Houston had assigned James and John Rogers to serve as Driscol's bodyguards in a battle, these two Cherokee warriors had shifted their clan allegiance to the figure of their new chief.

They were even smart enough to realize that Driscol intended to forge an entirely new kind of clan.

"You rotten bastard!" Captain John exclaimed, still with that same half-grin. "Bad enough that you intend to strip me of my

beloved daughter. I can at least console myself with the thought
that, sooner or later, somebody would have done so."

He paused for a moment, and the half grin faded to a quarter
grin. "But you! You intend to strip me of my slaves, too, don't
you?"

Driscol just smiled. "How could I hope to do that?" He made
a dismissive gesture at the officer's insignia he wore on his uniform. "I'm really just a sergeant, you know."

That was nothing but the truth. A very experienced and savvy
sergeant, who had no intention of letting a potential opponent
know what he was planning.

Another cannonade from the naval guns actually rattled the
window. Tiana's head turned toward it. "Well, *I'm* glad you're
not out there tonight."

When her head turned back, the serenity in her smile was in-
fused with a great deal of warmth. "And I'll be glad when this
war is over."

There was just the slightest emphasis on the word *this*. That,
even more than the warmth in her smile, filled Driscol with love
for the girl. The woman, rather. This one would make a *wife*.

"So will I," he said quietly.

"What a fucking mess!" exclaimed the Tennessee militiaman
angrily. The man was floundering in the cypress swamp not far
from where John Ross was doing his best not to fall off the log
he was trying to sidle along. That would have been hard under
any circumstances, much less in the dark with guns firing everywhere.

John silently agreed with the man's sentiment. Granted, the
British soldiers they were fighting in this chaotic melee were
floundering more badly still. American frontiersmen and
Cherokees were somewhat accustomed to this sort of terrain,
but it was completely foreign to Wellington's veterans.

Still, the only people who seemed to be enjoying themselves
were the twenty or so Choctaws who'd been brought to the fight
by Captain Pierre Jugeant. For the Choctaws, this was familiar
ground, and a setting in which they were as deadly as alligators.
John was glad to have them here, even if relations between
Cherokees and Choctaws were usually none too friendly.

A gun flash not far off drew his eyes. Was that friend or foe?
It was almost impossible to tell. A large number of the casual-

ties they were incurring were being inflicted upon men by their own side. In the dark, the uniforms worn by some of the British highlanders were hard to distinguish from the hunting shirts worn by most of Coffee's Tennessee militiamen.

So John froze, trying, as best he could, to balance himself motionlessly on the slippery and unstable log. He could sense the same militiaman who'd issued the curse a moment before doing the same. Only, in this case, the man had both the advantage and disadvantage of standing in pure muck.

A figure moved forward in the darkness. Slowly, stealthily, John raised his pistol.

Suddenly, plaintively, the figure called out: "Are you the Ninety-third?"

Immediately, the Tennessee militiaman replied: "Of course!" Stinking wet or not, angry or not, the man was quick-witted. He even had a passable Scot accent. That wasn't surprising since, like most American frontiersmen, he was probably only a generation—if that—removed from Scotland or the Scot settlements in Ireland.

Sighing audibly, the figure moved forward.

Within seconds, John could tell that he was one of the enemy highlanders. He was about to fire his pistol when the militiaman surged out of the water like an alligator and pressed his musket against the British soldier's chest.

"You are my prisoner!" he cried.

John was not surprised at all by the highlander's response. An even deeper sigh of relief.

"Well enough," the British soldier muttered, extending his own musket butt first. "Anything to get out of this fucking mess."

"Damn those guns!" Colonel Thornton snarled.

Another broadside from the *Carolina* swept a shower of grapeshot across the soldiers of the Eighty-fifth Regiment who were trying to find cover at the levee. Even in the dark, the American gunners were deadly. Thornton couldn't see it, of course, but he was quite sure that the huge and muddy Mississippi was stained by the blood of his men. The Americans had the only gunship on the river, and the cursed thing had turned the area by the banks into a field of carnage.

He turned to one of his aides. "Find General Keane and tell

him I can hold the riverbank from assault, assuming the Americans are stupid enough to launch one. But I can't do anything to drive off that schooner. They've got six-pounders on that ship—two twelves, as well, I think—and all I've got are these useless three-pounders. I might as well be throwing rocks against that hull."

He didn't bother to add that he no longer dared to fire the three-pounders at all, since the American gunners would instantly target them. Nor did he bother to add that the rockets he *did* dare to fire at the ship—he'd fired plenty of those—were as useless as the cannons.

"Might as well be throwing rocks," he growled again, "except the rocks might actually *hit* the bloody thing." Gloomily, he watched another Congreve skitter somewhere across the Mississippi. It made a fine hissing sound when it splashed into the water. Many, many, many yards away from the *Carolina*. Perhaps an American fish had been slain.

The aide scrambled off, keeping as low as he could.

"What a bloody mess," Thornton snarled.

The marines and artillerymen who'd been moving forward, down the high road alongside the river, recoiled from heavy fire coming from the British lines. Several of them were hit, so the marines began falling back quickly. The artillerymen, encumbered by the awkward weight of their guns, were slower in doing so.

Too slow. A British contingent charged out of the darkness, rushing to capture the guns.

General Jackson and his staff rode forward, through a hail of bullets. "Save the guns, boys!" Jackson shrilled at the marines. "Save the guns!"

The general made for the imperiled guns himself, even dismounting to help haul them away. Rallied by the sight, the marines followed. So did a company of the Seventh Infantry. Between them, they were able to level enough fire to hold off the British long enough for the guns to be extracted.

"What a frightful mess," Major Reid hissed. Inadvertently, he spoke loudly enough for the general to hear him.

But Jackson took no offense. The general just gave him a savage grin, before ducking to evade another volley of British fire.

"To the contrary, Major!" Jackson cried out when he straightened. "We're learning to bow properly in high society."

* * *

But once the guns were safe, even Jackson shook his head. "I should probably call it off, I think." His tone made it clear, however, what he thought of the idea.

Reid agreed wholeheartedly. Jackson's energy and combativeness were an enormous asset to the United States, but they always carried the risk of overreaching. The major had entertained his doubts from the beginning that Jackson's complicated battle plan would work—and, sure enough, it had frayed badly and quickly. Still, they'd bloodied the British this night, and Reid suspected that would be enough to cause the enemy to postpone any further advance. At least for the moment.

In the end, that was really all that mattered. Not even Jackson thought that his pieced-together army was capable of defeating British regulars on an open field of battle. He'd been willing to gamble on this attack because he was fighting at night, and still facing only a portion of the enemy's forces. But the fundamental goal remained what it had always been: create a strong defensive position and force the British to attack the Americans in a frontal assault, where they couldn't maneuver on the flanks. It was the British who were on the offensive, after all. Jackson had only to hold New Orleans, and he'd win.

"Yes, sir. I'm thinking we've gained enough time tonight to turn the Rodriguez Canal into something of a fortress."

Jackson nodded. "I do believe you're right. Send word to the men to start withdrawing from the field."

John Ross had always thought bayonets were a flashy but fundamentally silly weapon. Sticking a skinny foot-and-a-half-long knife on the end of a heavy and clumsy musket seemed a preposterous way to design a spear. Nothing at all like the graceful weapons favored by the Indian tribes.

That night, groping his way through the dark woods of the cypress swamp, he stumbled into another highlander from the Ninety-third Regiment, and the man quickly showed the Cherokee captain the error of his thinking.

John simply hadn't taken into account the fact that such men would be *trained* to use a bayonet properly. The musket might be clumsy and heavy, but the butt stroke the highlander delivered to start the fray was all the more powerful because of it. John was sent sprawling in the muck, his left arm badly bruised and paralyzed. A moment later, his right arm just beneath the shoulder was ripped open by the bayonet.

He would have died then, except the swampy muck and the darkness made the highlander miss his next thrust. He speared a half-rotted log instead of John, and then made the mistake of trying to pry the bayonet loose. That gave John the time to scramble back to his feet and fire a shot from his pistol at point-blank range.

The pistol misfired.

John's dowsing in the swamp had soaked the powder in the flashpan. But at close range a pistol made a decent enough club, especially when wielded by a man who was half terrified and half enraged. Wounded arm or not, he kept clubbing the high-lander until the man collapsed—whether dead or simply uncon-scious, John had no way of knowing.

Under the circumstances, the difference was probably moot. The man's head slid beneath the water, and by the time John could catch his breath and haul the highlander onto what passed for dry ground in the cypress, the man had probably drowned, even if his skull hadn't been shattered. There was no way to tell.

Between John's exhaustion, confusion, and the urgent need to bind up the flesh wound before he lost too much blood, he gave no thought at all to examining his enemy. By the time he fin-ished dressing the wound, his only purpose was to get back to his own lines.

Wherever they were. In the course of the fighting, John had gotten completely lost and separated from the Cherokees and Tennesseans he'd been fighting alongside. So, he just made his best guess and started slogging through the swamp. He was worried that he might accidentally be shot by one of his own, but he was a lot more concerned about the effect of the blood loss. Or perhaps it was simply the cumulative effect of the most terrifying night in John's life. Either way, he felt as if he might lapse unconscious any moment.

And if he did, in that muck, he would likely drown.

Eventually he heard some noises up ahead. He paused, trying to gauge the sound. Voices, he thought, and moved forward as silently as he could.

After a few yards, he recognized the voices. The words, if not the speakers.

Cherokees. He felt more relieved that he ever had in his life, and managed to croak out a few words in Cherokee himself.

He finally collapsed, then. When he came back to full consciousness, he found himself being levered powerfully forward by a man who had John's left arm over a thick shoulder, and was carrying at least half of Ross's weight.

Major Ridge, he realized. He was even stronger than John had imagined.

"Thank you," he murmured. His badly bruised left arm was hurting a great deal now, from the awkward position more than anything else. But John issued no complaint. Ridge was propelling him out of that wretched cypress swamp as surely and certainly as a buffalo. An aching arm was a small price to pay for that blessing.

John heard Ridge chuckle. "Next time you fight an alligator," he said, "try to keep your arm out of its maw. We don't have that many promising young diplomats that we can afford to have them eaten."

"Was a highlander," John croaked.

"Scotsman, alligator—what's the difference?"

"That's it, then," Driscol said. The sound of the cannonades had faded away and finally ceased.

"Did we win or lose?" Tiana asked.

"We won. Or it was a draw, more likely, which amounts to the same thing under the circumstances. If we'd lost, you'd still be hearing the sound of fighting. Jackson would muster a delaying action for every mile the British had to cross to get to New Orleans."

Captain John grunted. "To allow the citizens time to evacuate."

Driscol shook his head. "No, to allow the men he left behind time to set fires, and burn the whole city. Whatever else, Jackson will not allow the British to take New Orleans. A pile of smoldering ruins, perhaps, but not the city."

For once, the jeering grin vanished from the face of Tiana's father. "Good God. Do you really think he's that cold-blooded?"

Driscol smiled thinly. "Oh, I'm positive. The instructions he gave me were quite precise."

CHAPTER 39

DECEMBER 27, 1814
Lake Bourgne

Major General Sir Edward Pakenham, Knight of the Bath, arrived from England on Christmas Day with three thousand fresh troops. He spent that day and the next familiarizing himself with the situation on the battle line at the Mississippi, before scheduling a conference of the top commanders of the British forces in the gulf. The conference was held in one of the rooms of the Villeré plantation house, and included his second in command, Major General Samuel Gibbs.

Pakenham and Gibbs had worked together in the Peninsular War. In fact, many people considered the two generals to have been Wellington's most capable lieutenants during that long and bitter struggle in Spain against Napoleon and his marshals.

Admiral Cochrane came from Lake Bourgne. So, ignoring his illness and continuing weakness, did Robert Ross. He had insisted, and despite the fact that he no longer had a formal place in the chain of command, no one was prepared to tell him otherwise.

Pakenham's assessment was blunt, forceful, and to the point.

"We're in a bloody bottleneck," he growled. "I can't imagine worse ground to launch an assault." Since General Keane was not present at the conference, Pakenham saw no need to spare his feelings. "Keane blundered badly, on the twenty-third. He should have kept driving forward while the Americans were still confused and disorganized."

He shook his head irritably. "Yes, yes. I understand his reasoning. I'm not accusing the man of anything improper, mind you. Looked at from one side, his caution was commendable.

He only had a portion of the army available, and some of the intelligence he'd received led him to believe the American forces in New Orleans numbered as many as fifteen thousand troops."

Robert Ross couldn't quite stymie a choking sound. Pakenham cast him a shrewd look. "I take it you didn't give any more credence to that figure than I do, Robert?"

Ross shook his head. "We heard the number from several sources, but the sources were all suspect. What's more important, how could the United States possibly have assembled such a force in so short a time? It's a republic, you know."

Ross didn't share the sharp hostility toward republicanism that was common among Britain's officer corps, but he was still no great admirer of the beast. A republic was a clumsy form of government in time of war, especially when that republic was further burdened by the creaking joints of America's intricate federal structure.

The same General Winfield Scott who had acquitted himself so well at the Chippewa had been ignominiously captured in an earlier campaign in the war because the boats that were supposed to ferry his army back across to American soil had been lodged on the opposite bank of the Niagara. The boats were under the control of the New York militia, and the militiamen had stoutly insisted that their sole responsibility was to defend the soil of *New York*—and Scott and his men were in Canada. So, placidly, the soldiers of one state in the union had watched federal regulars captured on the opposite bank because they refused to row across a river.

It took a peculiar sort of genius to make the armed forces of such a ramshackle nation fight effectively. Unfortunately, Andrew Jackson was just that sort of genius. There'd be no obstreperous militiamen to grease the skids for the British army here. If speeches and harangues didn't work, Jackson would simply have them shot.

There was a reason, after all, that the word "tyrant" originated from the ancient Greek republics. Who else but a tyrant could make such a risible form of government work at all, in times of crisis?

Pakenham sighed, and ran fingers through his hair. It was an easy, natural gesture. Somewhat to Ross's surprise, Wellington's brother-in-law had proven to be remarkably free—so far, at least—of any trace of the haughty stiffness he had expected.

Albeit tentatively, Ross decided he rather liked the man, for all of Pakenham's handsome looks and flashy reputation.

Like Ross himself, Pakenham came from Ireland—although, in Pakenham's case, from the upper crust of the Anglo-Irish aristocracy. He was only thirty-seven years old, but, again like Ross himself, he had been fighting for many years. With his family connections, he'd become a major in the Ulster Light Dragoons before his seventeenth birthday.

Thereafter, Pakenham's rise through the ranks had been based upon his own ability. His reputation had been made solid by his impetuous headlong assault against the leading French column at the battle of Salamanca. Wellington's great victory there had opened the road into Spain during the Peninsular War.

But it was becoming obvious to Ross that beneath that reputation lay a very fine and capable military brain. And one whose experience was almost as extensive as his own.

Pakenham was still looking at Ross, the man he was replacing. The relationship between the two men was potentially fraught with difficulty. They both knew it, even though not a word had been said by either on the subject.

So, making his movements appear more weak than they needed to be, Ross levered himself upright in his chair and shook his head. "I wouldn't presume to advance any tactical opinions, Edward. You've seen the lay of the ground, and I haven't. But from what I can tell, I'd think we'd be wise to extract ourselves and try another line of attack entirely."

Pakenham took a slow, deep breath. The young general was doing his best to maintain his even expression, but Ross could tell that his words had come as a considerable relief.

"Exactly what I was thinking!" Pakenham stated forcefully, almost barking the words. He nodded toward Gibbs. "And he as well. That ground alongside the Mississippi is a slaughterhouse waiting to happen. We should pull our men out and come at New Orleans through Lake Pontchartrain, where we'd have more in the way of dry ground and room to maneuver. Instead of—blast Keane's caution on the twenty-third!—being bottled up between one of the world's biggest rivers and a cypress swamp, with less than a mile of front. With Jackson and his men busier than bees—oh, yes, I saw them myself—erecting solid fieldworks to block the way at the Rodriguez Canal."

Admiral Cochrane was now looking distinctly unhappy.

"General Pakenham, we don't have the requisite number of flat-bottom boats to go into Pontchartrain. We all agree that would be the ideal invasion route, but . . ." The admiral spread his hands. "It's simply not possible."

Pakenham and Ross exchanged a meaningful glance. Providing the proper water transport for this campaign had been the Royal *Navy's* job.

It dawned on Ross that the awkwardness of his relationship with Pakenham could just as easily become an asset. If the two of them worked together . . . Ross advancing the objections in a sharp manner, since he had no need to directly coordinate his work with the admiral, thereby giving Pakenham the leeway to compromise as need be.

"You're asking General Pakenham to lead his men into a charnel house, Admiral," Ross snapped. "And most likely a pointless one, to boot. There simply is no way any army the size of ours is going to storm fortifications like the ones Jackson is erecting at the Rodriguez Canal. Not with Jackson in command, and guns manned by professional American artillerymen and sailors. Pakenham will lose hundreds—no, thousands—of officers and men, for no purpose whatever.

"Just as," he growled, "I lost hundreds of men in front of the Capitol—which, I will point out, was a far weaker fortress than the one General Pakenham now confronts."

Admiral Cochrane was becoming angry, but Ross decided to rub salt in the wounds. He was still quietly furious at the arrogance of the naval officers.

"I'm told, by the way, that the same Captain Houston who led the American stand at the Capitol is now on the scene in New Orleans, as well, along with many of the veterans of that affair. They've promoted the young man to colonel, in fact. And among those veterans is the same Lieutenant Driscol—now promoted to major—who provided Houston with the professional expertise needed to organize the gunners."

Blithely ignoring Cochrane's glare, Ross slumped back in the chair. Again, making the movement seem feebler than it needed to be.

"I met Major Driscol, by the way, while I was in American hands. Quite an impressive fellow. One of Napoleon's veterans. I can assure you, Admiral, that you'll not be breaking the likes of Driscol with a mindless frontal assault."

There. That should do it.

Pakenham cleared his throat, causing all eyes to turn in his direction.

"I'm afraid I have to agree with General Ross, Admiral." Pakenham gave Ross what was, to outward appearance, a reproachful glance. "Perhaps he's putting the thing too crudely, but his basic point is inarguable. We are, indeed, in what amounts to a trap. The conditions are horrible for the men. They've eaten up what food they could forage from the nearby plantations, and are now reduced to their rations. The weather is much colder and wetter than we'd been led to expect, and illness is making steady inroads into our ranks.

"If there's an outbreak of yellow fever—which is all too likely, under the circumstances—the army will be effectively destroyed. And the only way out of the trap—on *that* miserable terrain—is a frontal assault against an army which, whatever its other weaknesses, has demonstrated well enough that it can handle such tactics."

Again, he cleared his throat. "We need to face reality, Admiral. This is now a siege, not a battle, and we're in the wrong place to wage a siege. For all practical purposes, the Americans have *us* under siege."

Cochrane slapped his hands on the arms of his chair with exasperation. "But what else *can* we do, General Pakenham?" He shot a stern look of reproach. "Or does General Ross propose that we simply abandon the campaign entirely?"

In point of fact, Ross had come to the conclusion that abandoning the campaign wasn't such a bad idea at all. The more he considered it, the more it seemed to him that this entire gulf campaign was a disaster in the making. They were no longer fighting a war, really. The British forces in the gulf—especially the army—had been given the thankless task of being cutpurses rather than soldiers. They were supposed to quickly grab the outlet of the Mississippi before the advent of peace made that impossible. As if the tactics of armies on campaign could be reduced to the simple tactics of armed robbers!

Bah. Neither the terrain nor the nature of the enemy made such a quick grab of terrain possible—or, if it *was* possible, at all, only by suffering horrendous casualties. What looked plausible to statesmen in London looked very different to a general on the ground half the world away.

Since he couldn't say all that outright, Ross went about it indirectly. "I've said no such thing, Admiral. Allow General Pakenham to plan a *campaign,* and I have little doubt that he will hand you New Orleans, along with control of the Mississippi."

He didn't add the deadly words: *sooner or later.* All that Ross had said was true enough. If Britain was prepared to fight a *war* for the Mississippi, Pakenham—or Ross himself, if his health returned—could win the thing. But that would require a patient and carefully planned campaign, not this hasty and ill-planned attempt at a quick victory. And the fact was that Britain *wasn't* prepared to wage the war much longer. For all Ross knew, a peace treaty had already been signed and was on its way across the Atlantic.

So, he'd concluded, under the circumstances his chief loyalty was to his own men. Robert Ross would not see his soldiers sacrificed, simply because of the carelessness and stupidity of politicians, or the thoughtless arrogance of admirals.

Pakenham wouldn't see things the same way, of course. For Pakenham, this assignment was a chance to cap his career with a final moment of triumph. Still, it was already obvious to Ross that Pakenham was no more willing than he was to throw away the lives of good soldiers.

Cochrane shook his head. "Robert, I have already explained to you that we don't have the time to consider a completely different campaign. We either do this thing now, or we might as well abandon the enterprise entirely."

"Let me propose a compromise," said Pakenham. "The one weakness in the American position is that they are lightly guarding the opposite bank of the river. Plenty of artillery, but little in the way of infantry to support them." He chuckled harshly. "Of course, they don't *need* to, since as long as they've got the only warships on the river we can't cross it anyway. But I believe that situation can be remedied."

Cochrane winced, and Ross actually felt a moment's sympathy for him. He knew the admiral wasn't at all happy at the showing the navy had made in the campaign thus far. True, they'd defeated Jackson's flotilla on Lake Bourgne, but given the absence of flat-bottomed boats, the victory had been meaningless. So, once again, what should have been a naval matter was being handed over to the army to solve.

"How do you propose to do that, Edward?" Cochrane asked.

Pakenham looked to Gibbs.

"By the simplest of all methods, Admiral," said Gibbs. "We propose to haul the big guns out of our naval vessels and transport them to the Mississippi. The eighteen-pounders, at least. Our artillery officer, Colonel Alexander Dickson, tells us that he thinks he can destroy at least one of the American ships tonight just with hot shot from the twelve-pounders we already have in place. Give Dickson a battery of eighteen-pounders, and we believe he can clear a way across the river for us."

Cochrane was starting to look intrigued. "You do realize you're proposing to haul enormous cannons across tens of miles of bayous and swamps. Your men won't thank you for it."

"I imagine they'll curse me for days." Pakenham shrugged. "And so what? Cursing officers is a soldier's favorite pastime anyway. They'll still do it."

Where the admiral had raised a military objection, Ross raised a naval one. "And how do you propose to cross the river itself, assuming we can clear away the ships and the defending battery? There's no point sending a few men across. I'd estimate we'd need at least a regiment to do the job properly. Do we have boats to transport that many men?"

"In fact, I propose to send over a thousand men. Between now and then, Jackson may well send some reinforcements across. The Eighty-fifth—Thornton's our best regimental commander, I believe—with the Fifth West India in support. Plus a party of marines and sailors to handle the guns once they're captured. And to answer your question, I think we can round up enough boats to ferry the men across. Mind you, they'll be a lot of little boats, not the few big ones I'd prefer. That'll introduce an element of disorganization, obviously, but I don't believe the problem will prove to be critical."

Ross was becoming intrigued himself. A thousand men— and, yes, Thornton and the Eighty-fifth would be the best. With the gunners to properly use the captured American cannon . . .

"I see," he mused. "Then you'd have Jackson's right flank under enfilade fire across the river, instead of him having our left." He sat up straight, completely forgetting to exaggerate his condition. "Yes, it just might work. If Jackson has an outstanding weakness, it's the other side of his strength. He tends to focus on a problem too narrowly, for all the energy he brings to solving the problem itself. Consider how he delayed so long at Mobile. He must have been convinced that we intended that as our invasion route. Right now he seems focused entirely on his front, along with keeping enough forces in the north to guard against a thrust we might make up the Chef Menteur Road. He may well be oblivious to the danger from across the river."

Pakenham nodded. "I think he is, in fact. The battery over there is solid, yes. But without good infantry to protect it, even the best battery can be overrun."

Admiral Cochrane, sensing the growing eagerness of the three army generals, looked back and forth from one to the other. "I'm still a bit puzzled. The fact is that a force on the west bank of the Mississippi *can't* take the city. So what good does it really do us, even if we capture that side? We still have to break through Jackson on the east bank."

Pakenham and Ross stared at him, then glanced at each other. Gibbs, more diplomatic, simply gazed off into space. Admiral Cochrane would have understood instantly the significance of a warship crossing the T on another. But it didn't seem to occur to him that the same principle applied to land warfare.

Ross cleared his throat. "Admiral, if Thornton can seize the American battery across the river, they've got eighteen-pounders and at least one twenty-four pounder over there. With enough men to shift them upstream, he can bring Jackson's entire line on the Rodriguez Canal under enfilade fire. The American right wing at least. It's one thing to defend breastworks against fire from the front. It's another thing entirely to do so when round shot is ripping your lines from an unprotected flank."

He moved his gaze to Pakenham and Gibbs. "If it can be done—*if*, I say—then a well-planned and determined frontal assault on Jackson's lines could indeed carry the day. But it would all depend on our success across the river."

Ross was tacitly offering Pakenham and Gibbs a bargain. If Pakenham agreed not to launch a frontal assault without a prior success on the west bank, Ross would support him fully—not only here in the gulf but back at home if need be, once they returned to England—in the event the campaign failed. Understandably enough, Pakenham and Gibbs were concerned for their reputations. But if Ross, whose injuries and illness made him no longer liable for whatever failure might occur, gave them his full public support, then the two generals had much less to worry about. Ross and their patron Wellington could shield them from any public criticism or censure.

Pakenham understood the nature of the bargain, clearly enough. He nodded, a bit stiffly, and said: "You may rest assured that I will not subject your men to needless casualties, Robert. If the assault on the west bank fails, I won't send the rest of the army forward."

He gave the admiral a look that wasn't quite steely, but bordered on it. "In that event—damn the treaty and its awkward timing—we'll have no choice but to withdraw, and begin preparing an approach from Lake Pontchartrain. Flat-bottom boats *can* be built, after all."

He didn't bother to add the corollary: that doing so would require weeks, quite possibly months. Which, of course, would in all likelihood make the whole thing a moot point. By then, presumably, the war would be over.

Cochrane wasn't a stupid man. He studied Pakenham for a moment, then Gibbs, then Ross, and clearly realized that he'd pushed them as far as they could be pushed.

Again, he slapped hands on the arms of his chair. "There it is, then! We're all agreed."

Pakenham launched the first stage of the new plan at two o'clock on the morning of the twenty-seventh. Having moved their guns into position under cover of darkness, Dickson's artillerymen began heating their shot in hidden fires. Shortly after daybreak, they opened fire on the *Carolina*.

Incautiously, because they assumed the British still had no heavy artillery, the Americans had kept the 230-ton schooner moored well within range of the guns.

"They were safe against the three-pounders we had before," Dickson said to his commanding officer. He was practically chortling. "They aren't safe from *this* battery."

Pakenham followed his artillery officer's admiring gaze. The British forces on the river now had a battery consisting of two nine-pounders, four six-pounders, two 5.5-inch howitzers, and a 5.5-inch mortar. They'd be using heated shot, to boot.

Dickson's veteran gunners found the range quickly. The nine-pounders fired the heated shot while the six-pounders raked the schooner with antipersonnel munitions. The howitzers and mortar added solid shot and shell. Long before the startled Ameri-

cans could get the ship under way, the British gunners brought
down the *Carolina*'s rigging.

The schooner was helpless, trapped with no means of escape.
Then a round of heated shot fired in the second volley from the
nine-pounders struck squarely.

Soon enough, the *Carolina* began to burn.

Cochrane was watching the action with them. "I think the
round lodged in the hold under her cables, where it couldn't be
quickly removed," he guessed. "If so, they'll have to abandon
the ship—and they'd best do it quickly."

He proved to be right. Not more than half an hour after the
bombardment began, they saw the Americans start leaving the
ship. Their captain, obviously enough, had no choice. He and
his sailors clambered into boats and made their escape to the
western bank of the river, shielded from British fire by the bulk
of the burning schooner.

At nine thirty in the morning, the *Carolina* blew up. Andrew
Jackson had only one ship left to defend the waterway—and
Dickson's gunners turned their attention to it. The sixteen-gun
sloop of war *Louisiana* was moored more than a mile farther up
the river. Still within range of the British guns, but far enough
away that the quick destruction they'd made of the *Carolina*
would be unlikely.

Still, the wind and the current both kept the *Louisiana* from
moving upstream. With persistence . . .

But if Jackson had been caught napping, he must have awak-
ened quickly. From his headquarters on the Macarty plantation
house, he must have sent orders immediately to get the ship out
of danger, whatever it took.

Soon enough, Pakenham could see a small fleet of boats setting out from the shore and attaching cables to the sloop. Within
a few minutes, rowing like mad, the Americans had the
Louisiana well out of range. From what Pakenham had been
able to discern at the distance, Dickson's battery had struck the
sloop with only a single shot, which hadn't done much damage.

"Well, that's it for the moment," Pakenham announced to
Cochrane, lowering his eyeglass. "We'll have to wait until you
can get the eighteen-pounders to us."

"That'll take a week, I estimate," the admiral said confidently.
"Not more than ten days."

Pakenham brought the glass back up and began studying the American battery across the great river. "Good. Then we'll take those guns, and New Orleans with them."

That same morning, in Ghent, John Quincy Adams stood on the docks staring out over an expanse of water that dwarfed even the mighty Mississippi. The North Sea, which was but an extension of the great Atlantic.

The ship carrying the peace treaty had left those docks two days earlier. Two days—and it would require weeks for it to cross the ocean, even if the ship encountered decent weather. Fortunately, it wasn't hurricane season. But the Atlantic in winter was still no sailor's paradise.

The American ambassador had come down to those docks the morning it sailed, and both mornings since, moved by an impulse that he fully recognized was pure superstition but could not resist. A ship was driven by winds and currents created by the will of God, not the heartfelt desires and wishes of a mortal human diplomat.

"Weeks," he sighed. "Six weeks at best, before the news can reach the Gulf of Mexico. If Jackson can hold New Orleans and the Mississippi until then . . ."

Pure superstition. So, as he had for three mornings, Adams scolded himself for his lapse into savagery, turned away from the ocean, and began walking toward his lodgings. He decided he'd spend the rest of the day—as he had the three previous ones—reading the Bible.

CHAPTER 40

JANUARY 1, 1815
*The banks of the Mississippi
near New Orleans*

Robert Ross listened to men discussing his fate.

"Is it yellow fever?" asked one. *Pakenham,* he thought.

A voice he recognized as the doctor assigned to handle his illness replied: "I don't believe . . . no jaundice evident . . ."

Ross could sense the doctor shrugging, if not see it. His eyes were closed, and the effort of opening them seemed too much at the moment. The fever made it hard to think, especially with the sound of cannon and musket fire drowning half the sentences.

"Who knows . . . is, General?" continued the doctor, his tone one of helpless exasperation. "This whole land . . . festering ground . . . diseases of all sorts."

A cannon salvo obliterated the next sentence or two. Then: ". . . never have remained here . . . should have . . . back to the ships."

Ross heard a chuckle. That came from yet another man. *Gibbs,* he thought.

"Fine for you to say so, Doctor." Yes, that was Gibbs. His voice penetrated clearly. "Have you ever tried to get Robert Ross to do anything against his will?"

Pakenham spoke again. His voice carried well also, much better than the doctor's.

That was the habit of officers who needed to call commands across the cacophony of a battlefield—of which it sounded like a small one was raging. Mostly a cannon duel, Ross judged, from the sound.

"Robert's a general who cares about his men," Pakenham

said. "He refused to leave until this business was over, and I wasn't about to deny him the privilege. He knew the risk."

Ross felt a powerful hand close on his shoulder, and give it a gentle squeeze. "Besides," Pakenham's voice continued softly, "I found his presence a comfort. And his advice, invariably helpful. He's a soldier, and a splendid one."

The hand withdrew. "What are his chances, Doctor?"

". . . here?" There came a snort of disgust, which seemed to blend with the distant musket fire. ". . . may as well haul out . . . rum. You'll be shipping him home in a cask . . . two days. At most. He should . . . to the ships."

That was madness. The advice of an overworked doctor just trying to remove a hopeless case from his docket. The festering conditions aboard the ships anchored in Lake Bourgne would be even more deadly for Ross than the conditions in the army camp.

It was time to open his eyes, difficult as the task was.

"No," he croaked. "I can't do anything further here, anyway. Send me across to the Americans."

He could see Pakenham now. The young general was staring down at him.

"The Americans?"

Ross tried to nod, but found the gesture impossible. It was all he could do to keep his eyes open and speak.

"They'll give me better care in New Orleans than you can possibly do here—or Cochrane on his ships."

"Perhaps—"

For some reason, shaking his head was within Ross's capacity, where nodding had not been.

"No, Edward. Admiral Cochrane is in no position to detach one of his vessels simply to carry a stubborn general back to England. I would refuse the offer anyway, even if he made it. You need every ship you have."

Pakenham looked away, his attention momentarily distracted by a particularly loud salvo. The artillery exchange that had gone on alongside the Mississippi for days had settled into the routine of siegework, but it still had its occasional peaks.

"You're certain of this, Robert?"

"Oh, yes. It's not as if I haven't been in American captivity before, you know. I can assure you that it is not a fate worse than death." He managed a half smile. "I rather like Cousin

Jonathan, as a matter of fact. Quite a bit, in the case of some of those obstreperous fellows."

Five minutes after Driscol arrived at the fieldworks on the Rodriguez Canal, he was shaking his head. Not so much in disbelief as in pure wonder. Whatever God there was, He was clearly a whimsical one.

"Ross? *Here?*" Driscol raised his head and peered over the fortifications at the British lines hundreds of yards away. He did so cautiously, with the habit of a veteran, even though a ceasefire was in place.

There was nothing to see, really. The ground between the American and British positions had once been the fields of a plantation. But the first thing Jackson had done was cut down all the crops, to remove any cover for the oncoming enemy. All that was left between the cypress swamps and the river was barren soil and stubble.

The only reason Driscol had looked at all was simply because he'd been so surprised by the news.

He crouched back down. "What in the world is Ross doing here? I thought he'd be back in England by now."

General Jackson shook his head. "I've got no idea, Major. But I sent Colonel Houston across in response to their request for a parlay, and he assured me that it is, indeed, General Ross."

Driscol glanced around.

"Houston's not here now, Major," said Jackson. "I sent him back across to arrange the transfer."

"You're agreeing to the British request, sir?"

"Of course I am!" Jackson scowled. "I despise the bastards. But for that very reason, I'll not have them claiming after their defeat that I was ungallant."

Driscol kept a straight face, although he felt like grinning. That was . . . a very Jacksonian response. Odd, how a man who could be so practical and ruthless one moment could be moved to quixotic acts the next, if he thought the matter touched on his personal honor or his sense of chivalry.

"Yes, sir. And what do you want *me* to do? Forgive my presumption, but I assume that you summoned me for some purpose."

Now, Jackson grinned.

"Ha! You're to be the good British general's nursemaid, it

seems. Ross put in a specific request to be handed over into your custody—assuming that wouldn't interfere with your military duties."

Driscol stared at him.

The general's grin widened.

"It would, of course. But Houston tells me that Ross added the qualification that if your—I believe he used the word 'intended'—was present on the scene, that she would do even better."

Driscol transferred the stare back to the distant British lines. "That stinking rotten bastard."

"Oh, I shouldn't worry about it, Major. From Houston's description of his condition, I doubt very much if General Ross is in any shape to be competing with you for the lady's affections. By the way, when will I be introduced to this mysterious fiancée of yours?"

Realizing his mouth was open, Driscol snapped it shut.

"She's not my 'fiancée,'" he growled. "It doesn't work like that, with Cherokees. And that's not what I meant."

Belatedly, he added, "Sir."

"A Cherokee lass, is it? You and that blasted Injun-lover Houston!" Jackson cocked his head. "In that case, I shall have to *insist* on an introduction. I won't have one of my officers consorting with common squaws."

But he was still grinning when he said it.

Driscol had come to know Jackson well enough by now to realize that he was a much more complicated man than most people assumed. In this, as in all things, Andrew Jackson was a living contradiction. At one moment, he could speak of Indians and black people as if they were beasts—and, often enough, treat them the same way. The next moment, speak of them— and treat them—far better than most white men would.

The same Jackson who thought nothing of referring to black freedmen as "niggers" had also championed their right to bear arms, overriding the vehement protests of slave owners. He'd furthermore insisted that the men of the black battalions would receive the same pay as white soldiers.

A bully, a bigot—sometimes a brute—but still one who could suspend all that at times because he could see the men beneath their skins. In short, Driscol had concluded, exactly the sort of man the very contradictory American republic would hoist up as a leader. Sooner or later, the United States would have to resolve its own contradictions. But, for the moment, Andrew Jackson was the best they had.

"I should be honored to introduce you, General. Her name is Tiana Rogers, by the way. She's the daughter of Captain John Rogers."

"Hell-Fire Jack's girl? You're a bold man, Major!" The grin faded a bit. "Sometimes I don't think I approve of half-breeds. Then again, other times . . ." He shook his head, an unusually pensive expression coming to his harsh, gaunt face. "Ah, who's to say? Maybe, in the end, that's what God has in mind for this great republican experiment of ours. I'm told that's what Colonel Richard Johnson thinks, anyway."

Pensiveness wasn't a mood Andrew Jackson would remain in for more than a moment. Now, he was scowling. "Of course, Johnson's a race-mixing, amalgamating rascal. Hero of the battle of the Thames or not."

Driscol's nod was a noncommittal thing. He'd never met the famous—and notorious—Colonel Johnson, so he reserved his own judgment. One moment the colonel was hailed as the killer of Tecumseh, a hero for all frontiersmen—then denounced in the next for his openly conducted affair with a black woman named Julia Chinn. No acceptably discreet master-slave affair, either. Johnson considered the relationship a marriage, even though such a marriage was prohibited under Kentucky law.

If rumors were true, people who visited Johnson on his Kentucky plantation either had to accept the presence of a black woman sitting at the dining table as the mistress of the house— or Johnson would make clear to them that they were not invited at all. He'd even been reported to have said that he was only doing openly and honestly what Thomas Jefferson hadn't had the courage to do.

Yet . . . that same Johnson was a plantation owner. If a black woman sat at his dinner table in the place reserved for a wife, other black people labored as slaves in his fields.

"Yes, sir," however, was all he said. "I'll send one of my men back to the city, and inform Tiana and her people that they'll be entertaining a new lodger."

"Do they have the room?"

"They'll manage. Cherokees are very good at that, I've learned."

*   *   *

Sam Houston had taken advantage of the time he spent in the British camp to discover what he could about the enemy's dispositions. He was somewhat disturbed by what he saw.

"They're up to something, General," he reported to Jackson, after he returned.

Jackson shot him a sharp look. "What, do you think? An advance up the Chef Menteur Road?"

Privately, Sam thought Jackson had become somewhat obsessed with his fears regarding the Chef Menteur Road—an obsession that prevented him from considering other possible dangers. To be sure, a British advance up that road would—in theory, at least—provide them with a way to outflank the Jackson Line, and reach the much drier ground north of the city. But in practice, it would be a roundabout slog through cypress swamps, with Governor Claiborne's troops in position to slow the British down long enough for Jackson to shift the American defenses. That done, it would be just as easy to turn Marigny's Canal into the same sort of fieldworks that he'd contructed on the Rodriguez Canal, with the added advantage of having Fort St. John directly threatening the British flank.

But Sam was careful to keep his skepticism from showing on his face. Jackson would listen to arguments, but he was thin-skinned. He'd simply get stubborn if he thought someone was being derisive.

"That's possible, sir, but I don't think so. They kept me as far north as they could, so I couldn't see very much. But I saw enough to get the feeling they're working their men like dogs to widen the canals south of their lines. Why would they do that, if their intentions were to advance up the Chef Menteur?"

Jackson gazed toward the British lines, frowning. "Why would they do it at all? They can't possibly widen those canals enough to bring warships through from the lake. Small gunboats, maybe, but those would be no match for the *Louisiana*."

The general swiveled his head, gazing across the river.

"Are you sure about what you saw, Colonel? The only purpose I can see would be to bring through enough small boats to land an offensive force across the river. But what's the point of that? They can only attack the city from *this* side of the Mississippi."

"No, sir, I'm not *sure* about it. But if we were gambling, I'd give it five-to-one odds."

A bit exasperated, Jackson took off his fancy hat and ran fingers through his hair. "But *why*? Even if they did land soldiers on the other side, General Morgan . . ."

Jackson's words trailed off into silence, a sour look coming to his face. The American commander wouldn't criticize another general in front of junior officers. Not openly, at least. But Sam was quite certain that Jackson's opinion of General Daniel Morgan wasn't too different from his own.

When the British made their landing from Lake Bourgne, and Jackson launched his counterattack on the night of the twenty-third, Morgan and his three hundred and fifty Louisiana militiamen had been stationed downriver of the British position, guarding the English Turn. When the battle began, Morgan refused to march north on the grounds that he hadn't received any explicit instructions from Jackson. He'd finally moved, long after the fighting started, because his men threatened to go without him.

Even then, he'd led his men only as far as the Jumonville plantation. As soon as he came under fire from British skirmishers, he'd halted, kept his men idle in a muddy field until three o'clock in the morning, and then retreated to his initial position at the English Turn.

Morgan's wretched leadership on the night of the twenty-third, in fact, was probably why Jackson had decided to move him across the Mississippi. Jackson didn't expect any British threat to that side of the river, so it was a convenient place to dump a useless officer who was too well connected politically just to dismiss outright.

"Morgan . . ." Jackson muttered. He clamped the hat back on his head. "Morgan."

"Yes, sir. That's really all we've got over there, other than the artillery. General Morgan and his Louisiana and Kentucky militiamen."

Jackson clasped bony hands behind his back and rocked forward a little on his toes. There he stood, for perhaps a minute, silent. Then he turned to Houston and said quietly:

"I'm not very confident in Morgan, Sam, to be honest—although I'll ask you to keep that in confidence. I still don't think there'll be a problem, but it can't hurt to be ready. Make quiet preparations that would enable you to ferry your forces across the river in a hurry, if need be."

Sam nodded. "Does that include Major Driscol's new unit, sir?"

Jackson thought about it for a moment. "Yes—but let's move them over right away. With their inexperience and with guns to haul, they'd probably get underfoot if we had to move them quickly. Whereas if we add them now to the battery over there, they'll have the advantage of getting some live training."

"Yes, sir. I'll let him know."

"Well, it's about time," Driscol grumbled.

"You're always such a ray of sunshine, Patrick. Have I ever told you that?" Sam smiled as brightly as he could—which was very brightly indeed. "I knew you'd be happy to be able to give your recruits some live training."

"It's not that. I meant it's about time the general realized that he's got a potential disaster waiting for him across the river."

Sam frowned. "That seems a little excessive. I admit the British could make a foray in force over there, but so what? They can't reach the city from that side."

Driscol shook his head. "Why does it take a low-minded sergeant to see the obvious? Colonel Houston, if the British brush Morgan aside—which is about as hard to do as brushing aside cobwebs, if you ask me—then they could quite possibly seize the *battery*. And if they do that, what's to stop them from shifting the guns upriver and bringing them to bear on *our* lines? Twenty-four pounders firing enfilade down the whole length of the Jackson Line could very possibly weaken our defenses enough to make an otherwise suicidal frontal assault from their main forces over there carry the day."

Houston's eyes widened. "But surely Morgan—"

"Surely Morgan *what*?" demanded Driscol. In a low, rasping voice: "Hold off a British assault long enough to allow the battery to extract the guns from danger? Sam, the man is a *coward*. He's craven, not just incompetent. He'll break the instant the British come at him. And while I don't question the courage of his men, they're just a poorly trained militia. I've never seen a militia yet that would stand its ground against disciplined regulars, unless it had officers like Jackson or Coffee in command. Neither have you."

They were standing in the corridor of the Trémoulet House just outside the door that led to the suite of rooms occupied by the Rogers family—and, now, General Ross. Sam's eyes ranged down the corridor, noting but not really paying any attention to the richness of the trappings.

He was seeing something else in his mind. The vivid image of the carnage twenty-four pounders could wreak on the American soldiers behind the Jackson Line—all of whose fieldworks were designed and built to protect the men from fire coming from the *front*. Not from across the river.

To be sure, the river was so wide that it would take the British artillerymen a bit of time to find the range. But those were the same veteran gunners who'd found the range to the *Carolina* in less than a minute.

"We could fall back to the Line Dupre," he protested. "Or the Line Montreuil."

Jackson—very wisely, in Driscol's opinion—had prepared two lines of fallback defense in the event the Jackson Line was overrun. But the major wasn't assuaged.

"So? The British—if they command the opposite bank—could shift the battery more quickly than we could shift an entire army. They'd just do the same to the Lines Dupre and Montreuil that they did to the Jackson."

He gave Houston a little shove. "Best you get about the general's orders then, eh? I have a feeling the day will come—and soon—when my life and those of my men will depend on how quickly you can get across the river."

Houston stared at him. "You won't break, I know. But will your men?"

"They'll stand until you arrive," Driscol rasped. "They won't dare do otherwise."

Even in daylight, the plush corridor was a rather gloomy place, despite all the fancy decorations. With such lighting and with *that* expression on his face, Driscol looked more like a troll than ever.

"A ray of sunshine," Sam muttered.

"The world has enough sunshine. I provide it with the needed thunderclouds.

"Go, lad." Again, Driscol gave Sam a shove, not so little this time. "I'll stand. You get there in a hurry. 'Tis really no more complicated than that."

CHAPTER 41

JANUARY 4, 1815

Robert Ross's fever broke two days after he was moved into the Trémoulet House. By the next day, although he was still somewhat feeble, he felt better than he had in many weeks.

Disease was a peculiar thing. He'd thought he was far more likely to be dead by now. In truth, the main reason Ross had insisted on being handed over to the Americans was because he knew he'd simply have been a burden to the British forces if he'd remained behind, either in the camp or on the ships.

Ross had always been blessed with a rugged constitution. But—perhaps it was mere fancy—he preferred to ascribe his astonishing recovery to the salutary effects upon a man of having such a beautiful young woman attending to him.

Very stately young woman, too, for all that her apparel was often a bit bizarre. It wasn't that Cherokee costume was significantly less modest than that worn by white women. Indeed, it was considerably less risqué than the clothing he'd seen on some Creole women in the street below, on the two occasions Tiana had allowed him to walk about the room a bit.

But if she generally wore Cherokee costume, it was never a complete ensemble. This or that would clearly be of American design and make. Just the day before, for whatever reason, Tiana had chosen to wear an entirely American costume. No simple settler woman's garment, either, but a rather fancy dress he was certain she'd purchased very recently, right here in New Orleans.

She wore it easily and splendidly, to boot.

Then there was her father. The sire was like a mirror image of the daughter, with the proportions reversed. Captain John Rogers normally wore American clothing, but never without Cherokee accoutrements here and there. He was just as likely to wear a turban as a hat, for instance, and Ross was almost certain that the man wound it about his head himself, requiring no one's assistance.

Ross hadn't seen enough of the two sons to get more than a vague sense of their preferences in costuming and dress. James and John Rogers seemed to be largely inseparable from Major Driscol, and Driscol was almost never around. Ross had seen him only twice since he'd been brought into New Orleans, and on only one of those occasions had Driscol taken the time to speak to him, albeit briefly.

That wasn't rudeness, of course. Patrick Driscol was an officer in an army fighting off a siege, and had plenty to keep him busy.

Hybrids, then. Ross wondered what would come of it all, in the end.

Though not a gardener himself, he'd grown up in gardening country. Hybrids were unpredictable. On the one hand, always dangerous. A hybrid could ruin a line, or an entire garden, or simply prove too feeble to survive. On the other hand, always an opportunity. More than one hybrid had grown into a flourishing new line, which brought strengths to the world hitherto unknown.

Everywhere he looked, Ross could see those hybrid shoots growing in the United States. Here in its southern regions more than in the northern ones, he thought. That was because of slavery, banned in the North but flourishing in the South. There was a grotesque irony there. To a considerable degree, it was their common trafficking in black people that gave white and Indian people a ground on which to intermingle. Tiana and her brothers had been sent by their family—which was itself half white and half Cherokee—to study in American schools. But they'd been able to pay for it, in large part, only because of the money generated by their slaves.

Patrick Driscol entered the room.

"Good afternoon, General. Miss Rogers tells me you're doing much better. I'm very glad to hear it."

Ross rolled his head on the pillow to examine the American major. Out of Ulster, by way of France and the emperor's armies. Another hybrid, this one made by grafting old stock onto new.

"I never thought about it much until I came here," Ross said abruptly, "but I've had plenty of time since, recuperating from my wounds. I've come to the conclusion that I disapprove of the institution of slavery. Wilberforce and his people are right. I'm not sure about Buxton and his outright abolitionists."

Driscol's blocky face was creased, for a moment, by a smile. That was always a bit peculiar to see, on that visage, as if a stone head suddenly moved.

"I detest slavery. Wilberforce and his followers are craven weaklings. Buxton . . . A good enough fellow, I think. Better than the rest of that puling lot in the Anti-Slavery League, certainly."

Ross rolled his head back, staring at the ceiling. "The day after the night battle—I was told about this, I didn't see it myself—a black slave came into our lines. He'd run away from his master and was seeking refuge among us. He had a sort of horrid torture device clamped about his neck. We removed it, of course. Ghastly thing. It was shown to me afterward."

Driscol nodded, and moved to the window. There, with a finger, he shifted the curtains aside and gazed down at the city. "Yes, I know. I've seen them myself. The plantation owners around here are partial to the things. A collar lined with spikes, facing inward, which barely prick the skin. So long as the man stands and works, the pain is minimal. But if he lays down his head, it becomes agonizing—it could even kill him. They'll leave it on the slave for days, until by sheer exhaustion he no longer cares if he lives or dies."

Ross studied the back of the major's head. "And yet you—a United Irishmen, no less—choose to serve such people."

Driscol shrugged. "And who else would I serve? The British?" He swiveled his head, giving Ross a view of his profile. From the side, Driscol's face looked even more like a stone crag than ever.

"Don't play the innocent, General Ross. Your British army has been distributing handbills all over this area since you arrived. Assuring the slave masters that their property will be respected by England, in the event of victory. Good of you, of course, to remove that collar from the man. But I wonder how much he'll thank you when you hand him back to his master and he gets another—along with a savage whipping for running away. It would hardly be the first time Britain has betrayed the Negroes, when you found it convenient."

Ross couldn't help but wince. He'd seen the handbills himself, and . . .

Being honest, had approved of them. Undermining political support for Jackson was simply a logical move in a war.

Driscol turned away from the window.

"There are precious few innocents here, General, just as there are precious few anywhere in the world. But the one thing that *is* different here—to a degree, at least—is that this nation is undermining the distinctions of class. Often, without even realizing it. And that's the key."

In a now-familiar gesture, Driscol lowered his head a bit. The way a bull will, considering a charge. "*Class,* General Ross. That's always the key ingredient when it comes to injustice. Two breeds of men may dislike each other as much as they wish. They may well spill blood and commit outrages because of it. But it's only when one of those breeds become a *class,* elevated over the other, that injustice and brutality become locked into place. As they have been in Ireland for centuries now. Even though, you know as well as I do, the real differences between breeds of Irishmen—or Irishmen and Englishmen, for that matter—are tiny compared to the differences among breeds of men here in America."

Ross thought about it. Driscol's words were certainly true, insofar as they bore on Ireland. What differences really existed, between the boy Robert Ross had been and many of his playmates? Nothing, in terms of blood—or precious little. Centuries after the English conquest of Ireland, any man who claimed he knew how much Anglo-Saxon blood ran in his veins, instead of Celtic, was either a fool or a posturing ass. Usually both.

Ross chuckled. "You've such a cold way of looking at the world, Patrick. But I'll grant you there's a great deal of truth in it. Put a Calvinist and Catholic and a proper Church of England man in the same pasture and they'll quarrel, right enough. But it's only when the Anglican becomes the owner of the land that the Calvinist and the Catholic will make regular visits to the gaol or the whipping post. Mind you, the same would happen if you made the Calvinist—or the Catholic—the landlord and master."

"Oh, aye." Driscol shrugged. "A man doesn't become a superior being simply because he's exploited or oppressed. Often enough, if he reverses the situation, he'll do the same himself. Or worse. It'll only end when a nation arises that can finally abandon the barbaric business of class rule altogether. Not by becoming angels—no chance of that, in this world—but simply because they agree to change the rules."

Ross looked out the window. It was a gray and cloudy day, as was common for this time of year in New Orleans. "Do you really think your Americans can manage that?"

"Not easily, no. Certainly not quickly—and there's no chance at all it'll happen without bloody conflict. There will be at least one civil war waged on this continent before it's done. Of that much I'm certain. And I suppose, in a way, it'll never be entirely done. I suspect class arises naturally, like weeds in a field. The key is to develop a society that knows how to pull up weeds before they take over the garden. That's what Thomas Jefferson meant, I think, when he once said that the price of freedom is eternal vigilance."

Ross chuckled again. "So you see yourself here as a knight leveling his lance against the inequities of class, do you? Forgive me, Patrick, but I'm afraid that reminds me more than anything else of Cervantes's man from La Mancha. He was the Spanish knight who tilted at windmills, if you've never read *Don Quixote*."

"Please!" Driscol snorted. "I'm no knight of any sort. Certainly not a snooty Spaniard one. I'm a *sergeant,* General. So I'll go about it the way a proper sergeant would."

Ross examined him for a moment. "You've come up with a campaign plan, then?"

"I wouldn't dignify it with the name of 'campaign plan.' Generals design those fancy things, and—I told you—I'm a sergeant."

Driscol was still standing next to the window. He turned and gazed through it, out over the city.

"I'll build a redoubt, here in New Orleans. A fortress of sorts, you might call it, although it won't exactly be a military one. I don't have the wherewithal to plan and lead a campaign. Someone else will have to do that. Maybe Sam Houston, as he ages nd matures. He's got the mind and the will and the heart for it, f he chooses to. Or someone else. But whoever it is, Patrick Driscol will see to it that his general has a bastion upon which ne can anchor his forces. If I can manage that, before I die, I reckon I'll have lived a good enough life to be allowed into whatever paradise God has set aside for sergeants."

Ross laughed. "Lord in heaven, Patrick! What I'd have given o have had you as *my* master sergeant, in any force I've ever ed!"

Still looking out the window, Driscol smiled. It was an unusually gentle smile, on such a face.

"Well, I'm afraid that's not likely to happen. But when the war is over, in the years ahead . . . If you've the time and the inclination, Robert, do come visit me, would you?"

It was the first time Driscol had ever addressed the British general by his given name. Perhaps the oddest thing of all that had happened to Robert Ross since he came to the New World was the sudden, deep warmth that gave him.

"You tried to kill me!" he protested.

"Oh, aye. Did my level best. And I'd do it again, in an instant, if I saw you coming at me with a sword in your hand, leading men in redcoat uniforms. Don't take it personally, Robert. I'd do the same for any bloody officer coming at me and mine with class in his heart, and damn the color of the uniforms."

Tiana came into the room, then. "Sergeant Ball is here, Patrick. He says the battalion is ready to—"

She broke off, flashing Ross an apologetic smile. "Go where you're supposed to go," she finished.

"Good lass," Driscol murmured. He lowered his head again, giving Ross a very stern look. "Never impart information in front of a Sassenach officer. Injuries, illness, death's door—all that be damned. The treacherous fellow is likely to be feigning it. Ready in an instant to leap from his bed, cut whatever throats he must, and race back to his own lines with the news."

Ross grinned. "Pay no attention to him, Tiana. Just another sullen Irishman. I'm too weak to cut the throat of a mouse, and if I tried to leap out of this bed I'd be lucky to roll off on the floor. Still, I'll not pry. Not even after the brute is gone."

Tiana grinned herself.

Driscol didn't, but he gave Ross a friendly nod before he and Tiana left the room.

*   *   *

After they were gone, Ross went back to staring at the ceiling. All traces of good humor faded away quickly, as he pondered the matter.

The battalion is ready to go where it's supposed to go.

Driscol's battalion.

And where would that be, I wonder?

Ross had never met any of the men in Driscol's new battalion, but he'd seen a few of them when they'd accompanied the major on his visits to Tiana. One of them, in particular, had caught the general's eye. He was a black man, like all the rest except one young white soldier, but seemed to carry himself with an unusual degree of poise.

When he'd inquired, Driscol had told him that was Charles Ball, a veteran from the U.S. Navy. The man who'd been in charge of the American artillery at the Capitol.

A freedmen's battalion, it was, made up almost entirely of former slaves who were now mostly ironworkers. The lowest stock of all, other than outright slaves, who'd need time and experience to develop the self-confidence that such men would naturally lack from their life's experience.

Normally, Ross would have dismissed such a formation without a thought. A unit made up of men like that would usually break in an instant, without lengthy training, once the crush of battle fell upon them. But with men like Charles Ball to serve as a crystallizing core for the force . . .

And Patrick Driscol to lead them! Ross had seen him do it, from the receiving end. Driscol could impart *confidence* to common and uncertain men like no other sergeant in his experience.

Oh, that was another matter altogether. If they fought behind defensive lines, at least, where they wouldn't need the months of training in the intricate steps and practices needed to maneuver and fight on the open field of battle in a hail of destruction.

Ross closed his eyes.

Where are they going? Where is Jackson placing them?

It was possible, of course, that Jackson simply intended to fit them somewhere into the forces already in position at the Rodriguez Canal.

But Ross didn't think so. The fieldworks at the canal covered little more than half a mile of front, and by now Jackson had thousands of soldiers available. Not the fifteen thousand Keane

had feared, no, but both Ross and Pakenham were sure that
Jackson had amassed at least five thousand men on that line—
and plenty of artillery with them.

Driscol's unit would just be an encumbrance there. His men,
still poorly trained, were more likely to get in the way of other
units than do much good.

So where else?

Fort St. John was a possibility. Quite a good one, actually. If
Jackson had the usual American distrust of the capabilities of
black men as combatants—unlike the British, who had many
black units in uniform—he might very well decide the fort on
Lake Pontchartrain was the best place to put them.

Except . . .

With anyone other than Driscol in command, Fort St. John
probably was where Jackson would put them. But Driscol *was*
in command. Jackson wouldn't have had the success he'd had as
a general—not leading mostly militia forces, certainly—if he
wasn't a good judge of an officer's caliber as a combat leader.
By now, Ross would give very long odds that Jackson had sized
up Driscol and come to the same conclusion that Ross had.

*And I'd have put that man in charge of whatever unit might
come under the fiercest blows, on any battlefield in my life.*

He opened his eyes. The ceiling was a blank, cold, empty bitterness.

Jackson was moving Driscol and his freedmen battalion
across the river. With their ordnance. Ross was well-nigh certain of it. Just as he was almost certain that Jackson would have
made plans to reinforce them, if necessary. As had happened so
many times before, the British had *almost* caught Jackson napping.

But not quite in time.

Robert Ross sighed. On a battlefield, "almost" was more
deadly than grapeshot. Nine battles out of ten were won or lost
because something *almost* happened—but didn't.

Ross rolled his head slightly so that he could peer out of the
window. It faced toward the British army, where Pakenham
would even now be crouching like a tiger, ready to pounce.
He'd be launching the assault very soon, within a few days.

"Please, Edward," he whispered. "Oh, dear God. *Please.*"

He knew exactly what thoughts—emotions, rather—would
be filling Pakenham's breast. The same that would have been

filling his own, had Ross still been in command. Doubts, hesitations, fears, second thoughts, quibbles, uncertainties—all those, Pakenham would be burning on the altar this very moment. Purging them from every corner of his soul, steeling himself for what was coming.

There was nothing harder for such a general to do, once he reached that needed state, than to call it all off and just walk away. He had once overheard an officer remark that Robert Ross on the edge of a battle was like a satyr on the edge of a seduction. Consequences be damned.

He'd chuckled, at the time, and taken no offense. He still didn't, because it was largely true.

"Please, Edward." Pakenham would most likely die himself, of course. So would Gibbs. Probably Keane. Not the least of the reasons that the British army was the most feared in the world was that the casualties of its top officers in a battle—won or lost, it mattered not—were usually worse than among the soldiery.

But it was Ross's soldiers that he cared about. If officers died in a battle, they did so with all the perquisites and honors of their class. Statues would be erected, here and there, honoring their memory. A moment of silence would be held in churches across the land, perhaps even in Parliament. Their names would be remembered for generations, sometimes centuries.

Soldiers simply died. Within a few years, no one remembered their names except perhaps a widow, or orphans, or parents grieving an old age without a child. Often enough, no one remembered at all. Their regiments would celebrate their example, true; but the name that went with the example would be forgotten, even in the regiments.

The hardest thing, for a leader of men, was to understand when a battle was lost, sometimes even before it began. That the only thing he could do that made any sense, as inglorious as it might be, was simply to retreat. Find another place, another ground, another time, where another battle might be won. Not to confuse a battle with a campaign, a campaign with a war, or to forget that even a war has an ending—and that the wars to come would begin with *that* ending as their opening ground.

Ross could only hope, now, that Pakenham would be able to find that rare, precious wisdom.

*   *   *

Several miles to the southeast, another man had come to the same conclusion. John Ross had hesitated for months, torn between two impulses. In many ways, every instinct he had was repelled by Houston's scheme. It was inglorious, unjust—and it amounted to giving up the battle before it was even fought. Before, really, more than a few minor skirmishes had taken place.

But . . . Reality was a stubborn thing. John could also see no point in starting a war that couldn't be won.

Having made his decision, he'd come to stand beside Major Ridge. Ridge was studying the British forces across the field from the vantage point of the fieldworks. Chalmette, that expanse was called, named after the plantation.

The place where the American fieldworks were located had once been called the Rodriguez Canal. But it was called the Jackson Line now, and for good reason. A modest and sleepy little waterway had been turned into a moat, with solid fortifications behind. To break that line and defeat the American soldiers who held it, the British would have to cross a ten-foot-wide waterway and clamber up the fieldworks it fronted.

They'd have to climb at least fourteen feet, twice the height of a man, from the bottom of the moat to the crest of the fortifications, with thousands of American soldiers pouring fire on them. They could do it only by hauling ladders and fascines across more than four hundred yards of open field, with eight American batteries manned by the best gunners in the world raking them with round shot and grape all the way. Canister, at the end—to match the musket fire of thousands of riflemen, which would pour out in a flood once the British got close enough.

Most of those riflemen were Tennesseans, too. Militiamen, technically, but they were the veterans of Old Hickory's campaign against the Creeks. They might not be quite as good as regulars—wouldn't be, certainly, on an open field—but good enough for the purposes of this battleground. More than good enough.

If the British came across that field in a frontal assault, they would be slaughtered. John was as sure of it as every American on that line, and the knowledge gave them the confidence that would make them even more deadly when the fight came.

"We can't win," he said quietly to Major Ridge, "any more

than the British can. Where we are now, the Cherokees are facing a Jackson Line just as hopeless as this one."

Ridge swiveled his head, to give John a calm gaze. Ross was relieved to see that there was no anger in those dark eyes.

He hadn't thought there would be. A very subtle but unmistakable change had come in the way Major Ridge looked at John Ross, after that night battle on the twenty-third. Prior to that time, Ridge had been friendly to John. Even praised him, now and then, for his shrewdness and acumen, while he dismissed with amusement the fact that Ross was obviously much better suited to be a diplomat than a warrior.

But not after that night. That night, John had finally entered the full darkness of the pit that warriors spoke of publicly as the glory of battle. And had come out of it, in the morning, with the knowledge that he now understood had been possessed by such men as Ridge for many years.

Battle was not glorious in the least. It was dark, bloody, terrifying, confusing, painful, and exhausting—to the soul even more than the body. The real glory—the only glory, to a man worthy of the name—was simply that he had survived it without disgracing himself.

The only moment in that night that John remembered with any real pride was the moment he'd hauled a highlander out of the water. He'd done his level best to kill the man first, and the man had probably died afterward, in any event. But in the darkest moment of his life, John Ross had not forgotten that he was a man and not a beast.

That was truly glorious, in its own way, he thought. A very quiet sort of glory, to be sure. But John was now certain that the only glory worthy of the name was the sort that took place silently, in the dark places of the soul, where there was no one to see the deed but the man who did it himself.

John hadn't mentioned the incident to anyone, except Major Ridge. And then, only to wonder if the highlander had died. But Ridge had seemed to understand; and, since then, he had made no jokes about diplomats and warriors. Not because he thought John was his equal as a warrior—very few Cherokees were— but simply because John was now a part of that brotherhood.

"You want my support," Ridge stated.

"Yes. It won't work without it. If I tried—which I would, whether you agreed or not, because I've made up my mind—I might succeed. But not without, most likely, tearing our nation in half."

Ridge nodded. "Probably. Give it a few years, with your talents, and I think you'll have more influence over our people than anyone. But I already have a lot, and I won't lose it."

The words were said with a stolid surety that matched Ridge's powerful frame. His gaze ranged up and down the Jackson Line. "I'm glad I agreed to come here," Ridge murmured. "If I hadn't . . ."

He snorted, softly. "Who knows what foolishness might have come into my head? A Jackson Line doesn't look like so much when you're facing it. See it from its own side, though, and you see the real thing."

When he turned back at John, he had a rare smile on his face. "Agreed, young John. You sweet-talk the stubborn folk, and I'll growl at them. Between us, we ought to get it done well enough. It'll take a few years, of course. By then, my son and nephew ought to be old enough to help, too."

That was true—and it would be a blessing. Ross had seen more than enough of John Ridge and Buck Watie in the course of their journey to Washington to know that they were as bright and capable as any youngsters the Cherokees had produced. Given their own abilities, and being the son and nephew of Major Ridge, they'd form the core of a generation that would have to carry on what was started here.

The clouds opened enough to let through a ray of sunlight. For a moment—not a long one—the dismal field at Chalmette shined brightly. The symbolism of the moment, coming when it did, finally broke the quiet melancholy that had engulfed John Ross for months. It allowed him, for the first time, to see the future as a prospect, instead of a bleak necessity.

Just like the Jackson Line, the future looked very different from that vantage point. The Cherokees would give up their beloved land, true. But they'd move to a new land as a nation, not the broken pieces of one. They'd move with a leadership that was united, not tearing at itself savagely and bitterly. They'd move with the resources and the material goods they needed—John Ross would squeeze the Americans for years before they left; every drop of blood he could get, out of that damn stone—to forge a new place for themselves quickly, not bleeding and battered and stripped to the skin. Give them a few decades to build from *that* start—John was sure they'd have that much time, even with American land hunger—and who was to say what they might not accomplish? And what pressures of the future they could then withstand? Or, at least, compromise with well enough to make "survival" more than a word applied to hungry refugees huddled in shacks and tents.

A Trojan retreat, indeed. He understood now what the cheerful youngster Sam Houston had been groping at—and the grim older troll Patrick Driscol had seen so clearly.

That was another thing. They'd have Houston as an ally, and Driscol, too. Each in his different way.

"We can *win* this," he said, surprised.

"Yes, we can," growled The Ridge, his expression fierce for an instant. "It'll take quite a few years, of course." His smile came back. "But years are our greatest resource, when you think about it. The Americans are too impatient to use them properly. Wars are fought with maneuvers over time, even more than territory. We can outmaneuver them. Watch and see if I'm not right. The Americans are *too* powerful. It makes them stupid."

Jackson appeared, on his horse, trotting down the line and shrilling orders. His whipcord body seemed to thrum like a sword.

"Of course, they *are* powerful," Ridge allowed. "So we'll just have to be a *lot* smarter."

CHAPTER 42

Charles Ball was waiting for Driscol in the salon, along with Tiana's brothers. All three of them were standing by the door that led into the corridor beyond.

Driscol nodded at them as he entered. Then, after hesitating a moment, he cleared his throat.

"I'd appreciate it if you'd wait outside for me. I'd like to speak to Miss Rogers alone."

John Rogers, his face expressionless, immediately opened the door and stepped through. His brother followed at once. There might have been a slight smile on James's face.

Ball's face seemed to undergo a brief spasm. Driscol realized the gunner was struggling mightily to keep from grinning.

"Not a problem, sir," Ball said, half gargling the words. "The battalion's still getting into formation. Won't actually be ready to move for maybe half an hour."

That said, he hurried after the brothers. The door closed behind him with a firm click.

Driscol stared at the door. Now that he had the moment he'd wanted, he wasn't quite sure . . .

Tiana moved past him. Her graceful, long-legged stride struck Driscol even more powerfully than usual. She opened the door and stuck her head out.

Ball and her brothers were standing a few feet away, in the corridor.

"Wait *outside,* please."

She closed the door and turned back to Driscol. The smile on her face was so wide it was almost a grin.

"I was hoping," she said. "But with you, I always wonder a little. And I'm tired of wondering, even a little. By now, it's just silly."

In the corridor, the Rogers brothers glanced at each other. Then, simultaneously, they looked at Ball.

"You'd best do as she says, Charles," said John.

He gazed back at them, frowning. "And what about you?"

James smiled. "Oh, we'll be along, soon enough."

"We just want to make sure everything's all right." John was also smiling. "We might not be able to hear anything, outside."

"Of course, we might not be able to hear much here, either," James added. "That door's pretty thick."

His suspicions now fully aroused, Ball looked back and forth from one brother to the other. His gaze did not fail to take in the war clubs belted to their waists.

"I think maybe I should stay—"

"Why?" James snorted. "You think John and I are going to

smash down the door to defend our sister's virtue?" He gave his brother a shake of the head. "Poor fellow's been spending far too much time with white people, you ask me. It's starting to muddle his mind."

John was always less sarcastic than his brother. "We just want to make sure, Charles, that's all. Tiana told us months ago to find her a suitable husband. We think we did. But the next few minutes ought to prove it, one way or the other."

Ball was still suspicious. "What's going to be proven? In half an hour, Patrick Driscol—with *his* stiff-necked ways—won't manage more than—"

James started to chuckle. Then, as if worried his sister might hear the sound, choked it down. "And you think Tiana will *let* him?"

By then, Tiana had Driscol pinned against the table in the center of the salon. She managed that feat without laying a finger on him, simply using the ancient tactic of the hoplites.

Inexorable advance. As if one sixteen-year-old girl was an entire Spartan phalanx.

She was now standing less than a foot away from him, looking down. The four inches she topped him in height seemed more like four feet.

Driscol cleared his throat.

"You might be dead in a day or two," Tiana said, softly but firmly. "We may never see each other again."

"Well . . ."

"It's time, Patrick. Do you *want* me?"

He looked up into her solemn eyes. Their bright blue color, as always, stood out sharply against her coppery skin. Set in those striking cheekbones, they seemed like two sapphires.

"Answer me."

With a vast sense of relief, Driscol realized it was time to surrender.

"Yes. Oh, dear God, yes."

An instant later, she had him in an embrace, her lips open and already on his mouth. It seemed as if he could feel her whole body pressing against him, from the ankles up.

He returned the kiss just as eagerly. He gripped her slender waist with his arm, wishing he still had the other to stroke her hair.

By then, his erection had come. More fiercely than any he could ever remember.

Even with the heavy woolen trousers, as tightly enfolded as they were, the fact was obvious.

Tiana gasped a little laugh, her mouth still on his. "Oh, good!"

For all that she was on the slender side, Tiana was incredibly strong. Driscol wasn't tall, and he wasn't fat. But as stocky and muscular as he was, he still weighed close to two hundred pounds.

It didn't matter. She lifted him two inches off the floor and carried him several feet. Before Driscol understood what was happening, Tiana had both of them sprawled across the big settee.

Her mouth never left his the whole way. It was the most passionate kiss Driscol had ever experienced in his life.

Once they were on the settee, Tiana's fingers started working at the buttons of his trousers. She was having a hard time of it. Partly, fumbling from passion. Mostly—so much was obvious—fumbling from inexperience.

Some last, Driscolish part of his mind tried to put a stop to it all. "We can't, lass. You might—"

She finally broke the kiss. "Shut up," she growled. "Make these stupid things work."

Driscol gave Driscol a firm boot to send him flying. He didn't care any longer. He *wanted* the woman.

His own fingers made short work of the buttons and getting his trousers down.

Tiana made even shorter work of getting her dress up.

The mating that followed was more like a pure rut than lovemaking. It had been long months in the making.

Tiana didn't really seem to know what she was doing, at least not in precise detail. But as eager as she was, she managed well enough. Again, the simple tactics of the ancient phalanx. Inexorable copulation.

He slid into her easily, almost instantly. Driscol thought she was probably still a virgin. But as active a life as Tiana had led, her hymen had long since become a thing of the past.

Not that he cared in the least. He'd come from a world where women were either maidens or whores. But that had been many years ago. Many lands ago. Tiana was what she was, and always would be, not what someone else would make of her.

Very soon, he could feel her shuddering with an orgasm. He'd been disciplined enough—just barely—to wait for it.

"Dear God, I love you!" he half cried out, as he ejaculated. Tiana's response was a hiss so loud it might have come from a steam engine.

Outside, in the corridor, Ball's eyes still were fixed on the war clubs belted to the waists of the brothers. The gunner was cursing himself for not having brought a pistol, though there'd seemed no reason to do so.

That door wasn't close to being thick enough. The sounds coming through it couldn't have been mistaken by an idiot.

He was pretty sure all hell was about to break loose. Even with a pistol, dealing with James and John Rogers would have been a chancy business. Especially James.

He heard John clear his throat. Startled, Ball looked up.

The two brothers were exchanging a look of some sort. James had his arms crossed over his chest. John had his planted on his hips.

"I think we should go," John said.

James nodded solemnly, and uncrossed his arms. "Yes. We should respect our sister's privacy."

With no further ado, he started walking down the corridor toward the stairs leading to the lobby. John followed, shaking his head.

"Who cares about *that*? If she finds out, we're dead men."

Ball brought up the rear, also shaking his head.

If Tiana's father had been there, the situation might have turned explosive. Although it was hard to tell. Captain John had adopted many of the Cherokees' attitudes, for all that he jibed at them for their heathen ways.

But he wasn't there. He'd left the city again, on one of his never-specified "expeditions."

Ball was pretty sure that Cherokees were all crazy. On the other hand, they were crazy on *his* side, so he wasn't going to worry about it. Even if the craziness did seem surprisingly infectious.

In the middle of his dark musings, in his own room, Robert Ross heard Driscol's half cry, if not the words themselves. Tiana's response came through the door even more clearly.

The meaning of the sounds was . . .

Well. Obvious.

He smiled at the ceiling, feeling his gloomy mood lighten. The Church of England wouldn't have approved of the doings in that other room, of course. Indeed, no church that he knew of would. But, for Robert Ross also, his childhood upbringing had been many years ago. Many worlds ago.

Ross *approved* of that couple. So let the preachers and parsons be damned.

There was silence in the salon, for perhaps two minutes. Driscol and Tiana just nuzzled each other, too exhausted to do anything more.

As the seconds passed, Driscol found himself—for the first time in months, really—deeply missing his absent left arm. His right arm was pinned under Tiana, and as tightly as they were embraced, there was no way he could pry it loose.

Nor did he want to, for that matter. But he *did* wish he still had another hand, to caress that beautiful and precious face.

"I love you," he murmured, looking into her eyes. Her face lay not more than two inches away.

"Good." Her eyes crinkled from a smile. "I'd hate to think you were just taking advantage of my girlish enthusiasm. Not that I didn't enjoy that more than anything I've ever done before in my life."

The smile remained, but her gaze became solemn again. "Come back to me, Patrick. *Please.*"

There was no sensible answer to that. Driscol would survive the coming battle, or he wouldn't—and very little that he did would have much effect on the matter. Battles were chaos incarnate, ruled by whimsical gods who struck down whomever they wished.

But he was pretty sure Tiana understood that. The plea was just her way of expressing her own love.

He slid out of her, finally. Half regretting the softness, and half cherishing the prosaic intimacy of the moment. If he survived the next few days, there'd be many such moments in the future.

Tiana, obviously, shared his sentiments. "Next time—and all the times after that—let's get *all* our clothes off first." A long, bare leg stroked down his own, twitching a bit once it got past the knee. "Wool's *itchy.* And I'm not too fond of all those buttons and hooks on your tunic, either."

He hadn't had time to remove the coat, beyond pushing it up and out of the way. It did, indeed, have a multitude of buttons—purely decorative, those—along with the eyelets and hooks to keep it closed. Far more than it needed, really, for practical purposes. The military just naturally seemed to dote on the things. That was true of every army Driscol had ever seen.

Of course, if he'd taken the time to remove the coat, the vest underneath it was woolen also.

"All our clothes," he echoed. He was able to lift himself up enough to stop the things from pressing any longer into Tiana's chest. She started to hold him back, by reflex, but not for very long.

Passion spent, the rest of the world was coming back, with its insistent demands. Driscol could hear, again, the sounds of the battalion in the street below getting ready for the march.

He could hear them, he belatedly realized, because the window was open.

Seeing his startled gaze, Tiana's eyes followed. "Oh, who cares?" she said. "It's not as if everyone doesn't know where babies come from."

The mention of babies caused Driscol to wince. Then, wince again, when he felt the wetness of their still-intimate contact.

Which was *very* wet. In every sense of the term, that had been the most explosive coupling of his life.

"Ah . . ."

"You and your stupid 'ahs'!" she laughed. "Stop worrying, Patrick. Or if you must, worry about staying alive in the battle."

But Driscol had adhered sternly to duty his entire life. "What if you get pregnant?"

Stern duty would not allow any fiddling with tenses, either. "*Are* pregnant."

Even lying on her back, Tiana's shrug was graceful. "I might be. It's close to the right time of month. And so what if I am?"

She stroked his cheek. "Patrick, I'm a Cherokee. There's no such thing as a bastard among us. The baby would be brought up like anyone else in the clan. And would give me something to remember you by. The best memory I could ask for."

It wasn't the first time Tiana had made Driscol feel as if she were twice his age, instead of the reverse. Fervently, silently, he pleaded with whatever God might be to allow him a full lifetime to spend with the woman.

The prayer came with some apologies, too. Not apologies for what they'd done, but for some of his past thoughts.

Not about Tiana, but her people. Other than his personal attachment to Tiana and her brothers, Driscol had shared none of Houston's fondness for the Cherokee. Just another tribe of barbarians, to Driscol's way of thinking, who'd added the civilized vice of slaveholding to their native ones.

Now, belatedly, it was occurring to him that the girl he so deeply loved had not appeared out of nowhere. Athena might have sprung full-blown from the brow of Zeus, but Driscol didn't live in the world of Greek myths. However many of Tiana's qualities were her own, something—*somebody*—had to have cast the mold in which they'd been able to form.

So, too—and not for the first time—Sam Houston seemed much older and smarter than he, at times. There could be a great stupidity brought on by too much scar tissue on the soul. Driscol had seen it in other people, and could now see it in himself. Sam's cheerful and friendly attitude toward the human race, as foolish as it might sometimes seem, was ultimately a much wiser way of passing through a life and its work.

So Driscol suspected, at least. What he *knew,* for a certainty, was that testing that hypothesis was a far more attractive prospect than continuing to amass evidence for its opposite.

Driscol wasn't just tired of the killing trade. He was increasingly getting tired of the whole business of hating altogether.

It seemed . . . empty, in the end. Where the young blue eyes gazing up at him were like pools of clear water with no bottom at all. He could swim in them for a lifetime, and be refreshed every day. Cleansed every day.

"I love you," he repeated. "But I must be going now."

"Yes," was all she said.

Once outside the hotel, Driscol tried to project the troll's fearsome countenance.

It was . . . difficult.

The assembled ranks of the soldiers on the street by the Trémoulet House were too precise, the shoulders of the men too square, their eyes too much to the front, their gear and weapons held too properly and too well.

Driscol glanced up at the window of Tiana's suite.

Wide open.

An entire battalion was doing its level best not to grin from ear to ear. Or even burst into outright laughter.

"Damn the bastards," he growled, trying desperately to catch the troll before he fled the scene altogether.

He glared at Charles Ball. The sergeant avoided his eyes, but there was a trace of a smile on his face.

"What are *you* grinning at, you black ape?"

"Nothing, sir. Just, ah, pleased to note that your sweetheart took your departure so well. She's a plucky lass."

In the end, Driscol couldn't think of anything to do other than smile himself. Under the circumstances, the troll seemed as ridiculous and out of place as a warthog at a wedding. Or a christening.

"Yes. Indeed, she is. A very spirited woman."

He even looked back—twice—as the battalion marched off. And made no attempt to hide the fact from his troops.

They were very long looks, too, since Tiana was now standing in the window. It might be the last time he would ever see her.

After the battalion had marched out of sight, Tiana went to Robert Ross's room and knocked on the door.

"Come in," he said.

Once she entered, she looked around, almost hopping from one foot to the other. Then, not seeing anything better to do, she sat down on a chair next to the general's bed and clasped her hands in her lap.

"I was wondering if I could stay here, for a bit. Might be quite a bit."

Ross looked up at her. "Of course, my dear. Stay as long as you'd like."

Her fingers started twisting. She managed to stop them after a few seconds.

"Tell me about your life, Robert," she said abruptly. "Not your military career. Your *life*. Your boyhood. Your wife. Your children. Living things."

After a moment, she added: "Please."

CHAPTER 43

"Bunch of niggers. They'll be useless, you watch and see."

Commodore Daniel Patterson swiveled his head to stare at the marine who had made that remark to a man standing next to him. Both men were part of the battery Patterson had placed ashore on the west bank of the Mississippi. They were watching Major Driscol and his "Freedmen Iron Battalion" as they disembarked from the ferries that had carried them across the river.

Patterson was about to issue a reprimand when the marine's companion made it unnecessary.

"Maybe not, too," the man said sharply. "And what do *you* know about it, anyway?"

He was a sailor, not a marine. The U.S. Marine Corps didn't allow black freedmen to join its ranks, but they were common in the navy. No one knew for sure, because no records were kept detailing the navy's racial composition, but somewhere between fifteen and twenty percent of the naval ranks were composed of freedmen—and the percentage was often much higher in the combat units.

Watching Driscol and his men as they energetically dug themselves in and prepared their positions, Patterson felt whatever doubts he'd had himself vanishing. Driscol's implacable determination was obvious, as was the fact that he'd successfully transmitted it to the men who followed him. Patterson was a bit astonished at the discipline of the unit, in fact, since he knew that they'd only had the benefit of less than a month's training.

Being a white man, it was hard for him to know exactly what went on in the minds of black men. But Patterson knew from a friend that Captain Isaac Hull, in his report on the *Constitution*'s victory over the *Guerriere,* had remarked that the black gunners who'd made up a sizable part of the *Constitution*'s crew had fought even harder and better than the white ones. Determined, it seemed, to prove themselves.

Patterson suspected he was seeing the same thing here. The more so since Driscol obviously had established a rapport with his men, despite the major's grim demeanor. He was the sort of white officer who could lead black soldiers well, because he was able to maintain the needed discipline without making his men feel that he was distrustful of them. Indeed, he seemed able to instill confidence in them and the conviction that they could succeed.

So by late afternoon, Patterson was in a far better mood than he'd been just a few days earlier. A good part of that was because, in a rare moment of military good sense, General Morgan had ordered Driscol and his battalion to take position on the right flank of Morgan's line.

Praise the Lord.

"General Morgan likes to call it the 'Morgan Line,'" Patterson told Driscol, when they had their first private conversation that evening. He and the major were standing on the open ground next to the riverbank, which gave them the best possible view of the terrain.

He kept his voice and facial expression impassive.

So did Driscol.

"Does he now?" mused the newly arrived major. His pale eyes moved up and down the trench in question. "I'd think the 'Morgan Scratch' might be a more suitable term."

Patterson had to choke down a laugh. Where Jackson, on the east bank, had turned the Rodriguez Canal into a formidable line of fieldworks, Morgan on the west bank had been satisfied to dig a shallow ditch and call the piled-up dirt behind it a "breastwork." The fieldworks were so shallow that men had to crouch or even lie down in order to be protected by it. And that "moat" could be leaped by a ten-year-old girl.

Driscol's gaze came to rest on the left wing of the "Morgan Line," next to the river itself.

"That seems solid enough, though," he commented.

Relieved both by the major's competence and his ability to

keep a straight face, Patterson decided he could speak more openly.

"Yes, I agree. It's the only bright spot in the picture. Morgan's got two six-pounders positioned there, along with a twelve-pounder. The gunners are a mix of Louisiana militiamen and navy regulars, with other Louisiana militiamen on hand to provide infantry protection. Best of all, they're under the command of Lieutenant Philibert of the navy. They'll do well enough, I'm sure, when the fray starts."

Driscol nodded. "The real problem is on the right, where the line ends at the woods."

Patterson teetered forward a bit, his hands clasped behind his back, and examined the woods in question.

The *jungle,* it might be better to say. The west bank of the Mississippi, like the east bank, was flanked by huge cypress swamps.

"General Morgan believes the swamps will be an impassable barrier to British soldiers."

"Ah," said Driscol. "I take it General Morgan has never actually *fought* any British soldiers."

Patterson smiled. Very thinly.

"On the other hand," the major continued, "I *have* fought British regulars. They won't handle that terrain well. But I doubt very much if the veterans who managed to fight their way across the rugged country of Spain in the teeth of Napoleon's armies will be stopped by it."

Driscol's cold eyes came to rest on the troops who were lazing about their campfires at that end of the line, next to Driscol's own unit. They consisted of a few hundred poorly armed Kentucky militiamen who had arrived on the scene only two days earlier. They were part of the contingent of two thousand Kentucky volunteers who'd staggered into New Orleans on January 4, under the command of Major General John Thomas.

The Kentuckians had little of the experience of Jackson's Tennessee veterans. Most of them had come without weapons, in fact, because the captain of the ship carrying their supplies had refused to bring his vessel any closer than Natchez. Jackson, in a fury, had sent a detachment upriver to arrest the captain and bring him back in irons.

"They're a sorry-looking lot," he commented.

"Afraid so," Patterson agreed. "The Kentuckians got here in

such a ragged state and so bare of provisions that the Louisiana legislature had to enact emergency relief just to provide the men with blankets and clothing to ward off the winter cold. Jackson immediately put the five hundred of them who *had* brought guns on the Jackson Line. The rest, as they scrounge up weapons in the city, he's been adding in dribs and drabs. Most of them on our side of the river."

He didn't add the word "unfortunately" to the end of the last sentence. With Driscol, there was no need to underline the obvious.

Patterson would no more have relied on such men to fend off an assault by British regulars than he'd have relied on a pack of half-starved and shivering mutts to fend off tigers. The cypress swamps that Morgan thought would serve them as a shield from the British would simply provide the Kentuckians with an attractive escape route when the fight began. Fortunately, they now had Driscol and his battalion as an anchor—not, of course, that the Kentuckians viewed those black soldiers with any more enthusiasm than the marine gunner had.

Niggers. They'll be useless.

But it didn't really matter what they thought. What mattered was how much shot those black gunners would level on the oncoming British, once the assault began. And from what he'd seen, Patterson had high hopes.

Sometime later, after parting from Driscol on a very cordial note, Patterson left. He needed to rejoin his own battery, which was located a considerable distance to the rear of the "Morgan Line," its guns facing across the river.

Like most of Morgan's dispositions, this one made no sense. Where Jackson, on the opposite bank, had a genius for concentrating his forces, Morgan had an equal genius for dispersing them—even though he had far smaller forces to begin with.

He had Patterson's battery, the best and strongest unit under his command, positioned so as to provide covering fire for Jackson across the river. So far, so good. But for reasons incomprehensible to anyone with any military sense, Morgan had placed most of his forces so far forward of the battery that it couldn't provide his *own* defensive line with any protection.

Then, apparently not satisfied that he'd inflicted enough damage upon himself, he'd dispersed his forces even further by sending some of the Kentuckians downriver to "defend" the bank of the Mississippi at the Jourdan plantation. As if 120 militiamen, armed with fowling pieces, would be able to do anything in the face of a British landing.

Madness, all of it. It wasn't in Patterson's nature to think ill of another man without solid evidence. But, by now, he was almost sure that the problem with Morgan went beyond simple military inexperience. There was something frenzied about Morgan's incompetence. He reminded Patterson of the way a man who is fundamentally scared to fight will sometimes, facing a set-to, start waving his arms about and shout wildly in the attempt to assure himself that he is really a very bold fellow after all.

Hopefully, Driscol and his men would make the difference. At least now the far right of the Morgan Line would be anchored by solid troops, with real artillery, to match Lieutenant Philibert's unit on the far left by the river.

Once he reached his own battery's position, Patterson nodded to his men but kept walking farther upriver. Just fifty yards or so, to the spot where Driscol had left the one white sergeant in his battalion. Anthony McParland, that was, whom Driscol had given a special assignment.

Patterson had wondered about that. Perhaps Driscol had left McParland behind because he was so young and Driscol didn't quite trust him in a battle. But McParland had been at the Chippewa, and apparently done well enough that Driscol—a hard man, that, too—had seen fit to promote him. So that didn't make sense.

Perhaps it was because, being white, Driscol trusted McParland to handle a task that he feared one of his Negro soldiers would fumble. But that didn't make much sense, either, because the task itself was as simple as any task gets: when the time came, light a flare. Any plantation owner routinely assigned far more complex chores to his slaves.

Patterson came upon McParland unawares. The teenage sergeant, fuse in hand and ready to be lit in a nearby campfire, was chatting away pleasantly with some of Patterson's sailors.

"—so then I told the general, straight to his face, that my da didn't raise me to shine another man's boots, and he could damn well shine them himself or have a lackey do it." Forcefully, McParland spat in the fire. "I was a soldier, tarnation, not a blasted servant."

A grin creased the youngster's face.

"A word to the wise, boys. Old Winfield's a wizard on the battlefield, but he's a nasty old woman any other ways. Well, he like to have a fit. The next thing I knew he had me in front of a firing squad with none other than my own Sergeant Driscol—yeah, he was just a sergeant back then—in charge of the business. And I *knew* the sergeant would do it, without blinking an eye."

Another gob of spit unerringly struck the flames.

"Driscol's not exactly human, you know. Mostly human, sure, but there's some troll blood in him. There's trolls in Scotland, and that's where his family comes from originally."

One of the sailors was bold enough to argue the point. "Ah, I don't think so. My family's from Scotland, too, back when, and they never talk about no trolls." Hastily, seeing McParland's gathering frown, he added: "I don't doubt you, mind. Not about Driscol! I've *seen* him. But don't forget that Scots got a lot of old Viking blood in us, too—and, sure as shooting, there's trolls in Norway and places like that."

Two or three of the sailors nodded sagely.

Mollified, McParland continued. "Well, yeah, you might be right at that. Anyway, there I was, standing in front of a firing squad. General Scott himself was watching, sitting on his horse. I looked him square in the eye and said, '*Fire away and be damned!*'"

McParland paused, chuckling.

"What happened then?" asked one of the sailors eagerly. He looked to be no older than McParland.

"Well—heh—I was young and stupid, in those days. I didn't think they'd actually do it. But Driscol—he's a troll, didn't I tell you?" McParland looked momentarily aggrieved. "Why, the bastard took *my own words* as the signal and ordered them to fire. Next thing I knew I was knocked off my feet by the blast. 'Sa good thing—I found out later—Driscol had told all the men to aim no higher than my chest, or the powder burns would have scarred me for life, point-blank range like it was. But the guns were loaded with blanks, it turned out. General Scott's mean as a snake about some things, but he's still a general as good as they come. He just wanted to establish what was what. As it was . . ."

He shook his head. "Well, let's put it this way, boys. General Scott never told me again to shine his boots, but if he had, I'da done it and not given him no back talk. Don't think I wouldn't. And I never again doubted that Patrick Driscol would do exactly what he said he'd do. You might as well argue with a rock as argue with *him*."

Silence fell on the little group squatting about the campfire. Then, as one man, they all looked at the squat flare positioned not twenty feet away.

"So, you gonna do it?" asked one of the sailors. "We all heard General Morgan, when he come by earlier, telling you not to fire it unless he gives you the order."

McParland hawked, spat. Another gobbet caused a small hiss in the fire. "Don't matter what Morgan says. The sergeant—ah, Major Driscol—told me to fire that flare the moment I think the British are coming for sure. And start waving that big flag over there."

There was a furled banner resting against a nearby tree. Patterson hadn't noticed it earlier.

Hawk. Spit. Hiss.

"So General Morgan can go fuck himself, for all I care. If he hollers about it afterward, the troll will eat him."

Smiling, Commodore Patterson walked quietly away. He didn't believe most of that story. Someday, if he had the chance, he'd ask Driscol what really happened. But he didn't wonder any longer why Driscol had left McParland in charge of the flare.

The sun was setting now.

It would happen tomorrow. The commodore had spent most of the day downriver, watching the enemy with an eyeglass, making their preparations. Patterson knew that Jackson still thought they'd do no more than send a token force across the Mississippi; a feint, essentially, to distract him while they launched a massive frontal assault on his own lines. But Patterson had seen the effort the British had put into widening the canal over the previous week. That was no feint.

The enemy would strike here first, and they'd strike hard and fast, with their best units. He was sure he understood their battle plan: overwhelm the Americans on the right bank, seize Patterson's big guns and turn them to fire enfilade on the Jackson Line. And only *then* start their assault on the east bank.

They might well succeed, too, given the weakness of the American forces on the west bank and the incapacity of its commanding general. But, if nothing else, Patterson was now confident that Driscol would hold them off long enough to allow Patterson to destroy his own cannons. Whatever else, the British would *not* use those splendid American guns against American soldiers. And without those guns, any victory on the west bank would be ultimately meaningless. They couldn't reach New Orleans from this side of the river. Not when Patterson still had the *Louisiana* anchored there to destroy any attempt to cross over.

"Are the spikes ready?" he asked his chief gunnery mate.

"Yes, sir." The sailor nodded toward freshly dug pathways leading to the riverbank. "And I've got everything ready, like you said, so we can pitch the guns into the Mississippi after we've spiked them."

Patterson nodded. He hoped he wouldn't have to, of course. But . . .

Just like McParland, and Driscol, he'd do whatever needed to be done.

Across the river, Colonel Thornton lowered his eyeglass slowly. He hadn't been able to get a good view at any time over the past two days, as the new American unit had arrived to reinforce Morgan's forces. Just enough to know that they were an artillery unit, which seemed mostly composed of black soldiers.

That probably meant U.S. Navy regulars, which was the *last* thing Thornton wanted to encounter after he crossed the river. At least, he knew of no other American forces that had large numbers of black soldiers who handled cannons with such apparent familiarity.

Damnation.

The key to the whole assault was *speed.* It wasn't enough to just defeat the Americans over there. They had to be *routed.* Sent scampering in such haste and confusion that they wouldn't have time to spike the big guns or pitch them into the river. Or haul them out of danger altogether.

Until that new unit had arrived, Thornton had thought he had an excellent chance of doing so. British intelligence was quite good now, with a number of American deserters coming across the line, in addition to the runaway slaves, and Thornton had known that most of the forces over there were militia units. Some of them newly arrived from Kentucky, ill trained, inexperienced, and apparently almost completely unsupplied.

Now . . .

Thornton did his best to look on the bright side. Even if he failed to capture the guns, he was still confident that he could seize the west bank. In that event, the siege would simply settle in. Over time—not without great difficulty, but it could be done—the British could transport the big guns from the naval vessels on Lake Bourgne, down the canals and across the river. Step by step, day by day, if they controlled the west bank they could keep shifting those guns closer and closer to New Orleans, forcing Jackson to retreat to the city. Wellington's veterans had plenty of experience with sieges—far more, after all the years in the Peninsular War, than the Americans did.

Thornton shook his head. He wasn't privy to the inner councils of the British high command, but he knew that Cochrane and the top generals thought a peace treaty was in the making. However good the British army was at fighting sieges, it was still a fact that sieges took time. And time was probably the one essential item of which they were in the shortest supply.

"Well, Colonel?"

Thornton almost jumped, he was so startled. He turned to find General Pakenham standing behind him.

"Sir. Sorry, I didn't hear you coming."

"Yes, I know. You seemed quite lost in your thoughts. I'd appreciate knowing what they are."

Thornton hesitated. He wasn't familiar enough yet with Pakenham to know how much his new commander would welcome in the way of frankness. Robert Ross had always encouraged his subordinates to speak their mind, although he'd never shuffled the responsibility for making a decision onto them. But many British generals regarded a contrarian view from subordinate officers as just a hair short of treason—or cowardice in the face of the enemy—both of which were capital crimes.

Pakenham was personally intimidating, too, in a way that the relatively lowborn, plain-faced and easygoing Ross had not been. He was tall, handsome, vigorous, poised—the spitting image of an Anglo-Irish aristocrat. Add to that his own reputation, and the fact that his sister had married Wellington . . .

Pakenham smiled, slightly. "I am quite aware of your splendid reputation as a commander in battle, Colonel Thornton. I really would appreciate hearing what you think."

"Yes, sir." Thornton nodded across the river. "They've added a new artillery unit over there, sir. They've got a twelve-pounder and at least one six-pounder. Somewhere around three hundred men, as near as I can determine. Most of them seem to be black soldiers. That probably means U.S. Navy regulars."

Pakenham gazed across the Mississippi. There was nothing to be seen over there now but darkness, with only the last moments of sunset to illuminate the area.

"Possibly. But I think not. Just this morning, two more runaway slaves arrived in our lines. From the city itself, these, not one of the nearby plantations. They tell us that Jackson had a new battalion of freedmen formed up, less than three weeks ago. That's probably them, in which case they'll be even more inexperienced than the usual militia force."

Thornton started to speak; then, still hesitant despite Pakenham's tacit reassurance, closed his mouth.

"Yes, Colonel?"

"Something still doesn't make sense here, sir. A new black battalion wouldn't be given *guns*. Muskets, at the most, and probably the poorest ones available. But twelve-pounders? There has to be more involved."

Pakenham nodded. "Oh, surely. From what we can glean from the runaways, the unit indeed has a core of U.S. Navy sailors. But nine-tenths of them are completely new. Former slaves, mostly, who were employed in various crafts throughout the city."

"I see. Do we know the name of the commanding officer?"

Pakenham shook his head. "The slaves—as usual—knew precious little in the way of details."

The tall British commander paused. He was looking down at Thornton in a peculiarly stiff-necked way that made the colonel uneasy, until he remembered that Pakenham had suffered two neck wounds in his career. The first, according to rumor, had given his head a peculiar cock to the side. The second, fortunately, had done the same on the *other* side. So now Pakenham's head sat unerringly straight, but to the natural stiffness of an Anglo-Irish aristocrat was added the immobility of matching wounds. Under other circumstances, it might all have been quite amusing.

U.S. Navy regulars . . . black sailors . . . an unknown commander. Thornton had an uneasy feeling he knew who they were. Might be, at least.

His own Eighty-fifth, blessedly, had not suffered badly at the Capitol because Ross had chosen to give them a rest after Bladensburg. So he'd used the Fourth as the lead regiment in the assault there.

Used them up, it might be better to say. The Fourth had suffered terrible casualties in that assault, even during the brief time it had lasted. The American battery positioned between the two wings of the American legislative house had been murderous.

"Sir, have you considered the possibility—"

"Yes, Colonel, I know. It *might* be the same men who were at the Capitol. And with the same commander. Driscol, if I recall the name properly. Ross told me about him. Still . . ."

Pakenham studied the darkness across the river. "War is always a murky business. It might not be them, too. And even if it is, there aren't more than a dozen or so veterans in the lot. Most of that unit will be greener than an Irish spring. We have no choice other than to press forward as we planned, and I'm confident we can handle the worst."

He paused, for a moment. "Still, let's not be foolhardy. I was trying to decide anyway, and now I have. I'll add one of the two new regiments to your assaulting force, Colonel, along with some of the West Indian troops. That'll give you about two thousand men. Even if that new unit is in fact Driscol's, you'll outnumber them heavily."

That would be a help. A *tremendous* help.

All the more so, because of the quality of the reinforcements. Major General John Lambert had just arrived with the Seventh Fusiliers and the Forty-third Light Infantry: seventeen hundred men, in all. Both were veteran units, fresh from the campaigns in Spain and southern France and covered with laurels from them. Like Pakenham himself, Lambert had served under Wellington and was one of his young protégés.

The colonel's spirits were rising quickly. Thornton was a very experienced combat commander, and he knew full well that the single most important factor when it came to winning battles was usually the crudest and simplest. *Numbers*. With two thousand men instead of a thousand, he'd have an overwhelming force, once he got across the river.

That assumed, of course, that he'd be able to send the militia forces scampering. But Thornton was quite confident on that matter. It was the American artillery units over there that worried him. With two thousand men, though, he should be able to simply overrun them. And he'd have enough men to be able to afford heavy casualties, if that was what it took to do the job.

"The Forty-third, I think," Pakenham mused. "They're light infantry and will move faster. I'd planned to keep them in reserve, but if your assault fails, they'd probably prove useless to me anyway."

"Yes, sir. I'd much appreciate that, sir. And . . ."

Pakenham's smile, this time, was not thin at all. "Oh, you needn't be concerned about that, Colonel. I shall make it clear to the Forty-third's commander—that's Colonel Rennie, by the way—that you are in command."

Thornton nodded. The one problem with adding a new unit on the eve of an operation was that quarrels might arise between the commanders. All the worse when, as in this instance, Thornton hadn't even known the name of the Forty-third's commander, so recently had the regiment come into camp. But Rennie would be familiar with Pakenham—and Thornton, to his considerable relief, was discovering that Pakenham had the same sureness as a commander that Robert Ross had possessed. He'd make clear enough to the fellow that Thornton was his superior officer in the coming assault.

"You'd best get ready now, Colonel Thornton," Pakenham stated. "I want your men starting into the barges as soon as the sunrise fades."

CHAPTER 44

The British assault started falling behind schedule almost immediately. Admiral Cochrane had insisted from the beginning on having his sailors widen the canals, where the British soldiers would have preferred simply to haul the barges across land using rollers and brute force. Unfortunately, Pakenham had chosen not to dispute the issue with the admiral—and now Colonel Thornton was paying the price.

The British engineers and sailors had labored round the clock. They'd erected a dam across the canal a short distance from the river, and left a levee standing between the end of the canal and the Mississippi. The plan was to load all the soldiers in the barges, and cut the levee. The canal was lower than the Mississippi, so the water rushing in would reach the dam, be blocked, and quickly fill the lower portion of the waterway, enough to enable all the barges to sortie as one.

After his men had clambered into the barges, the levee was cut and the waters rushed in. To his horror, Thornton watched the dam collapse. In their hurry to make the deadline, the engineers had been sloppy in their work. The thing was just too flimsily made to withstand the sudden pressure.

To make things worse, the banks of the canal also caved in at several points. Looking up and down the line of the canal, Thornton saw that most of the barges were hopelessly stuck in the mud.

"God damn all admirals and their schemes," he hissed.

"What was that, sir?" asked one of his aides.

Thornton shook his head. "Never mind. Nothing for it, now. We've got no choice but to offload the barges and haul them down to the river by brute force."

He didn't add what he could have, which was that the army could have done that from the very beginning. In fact, that *had* been the army's proposal, but Cochrane had overruled them.

So the soldiers would wind up doing it their way anyhow—except now they had to do it waist-deep in mud. Cocksure naval officers had cost Thornton hours of precious time. And by the time he got his men onto the river, they'd be exhausted from the labor.

It was as bad a way to start a battle as he could think of.

"We've only got thirty barges ready so far, sir," protested the same aide, several hours later.

"I know," Thornton growled. "That'll just have to do. It's already three o'clock of the morning. We can't afford to wait any longer. We'll start the attack with the men we can fit into those thirty barges. My own Eighty-fifth, of course. The Royal Marines, also."

He turned to Colonel Rennie. "You'll have to follow us with your Forty-third Light Infantry and the West Indian troops, when you can. As soon as I reach the opposite shore, I'll start my march to the north."

"You'll have less than a thousand men, sir."

It was all Thornton could do not to snarl: *I know that, you idiot! D'you think I can't do simple arithmetic?*

But he restrained himself to a simple nod. In truth, Rennie had proven to be a most competent and helpful subordinate, showing none of the resentment that Thornton had feared he might. The man was just doing his job, pointing out problems to his superior.

"Just join me as soon as you can, once you get across the river."

Once you get across the river.

Such a simple and innocuous phrase. But no sooner had Thornton gotten his force fifty yards into the river than he encountered yet another unexpected problem. The British navy had never been able—never really tried, actually—to force its way up the Mississippi past Fort St. Philip. So the British had little experience with it. So Thornton and his men were discovering what he suspected any competent American riverboat captain could have told them: that the slow-moving, muddy Mississippi had currents far more powerful than it seemed.

Thornton watched helplessly as his flotilla of barges was swept downstream. They'd cross the river, sure enough—but they'd finally make landing almost a mile farther south than they'd intended.

The British had planned to land their force about three miles from Morgan's main line of defense. Just far enough away that Morgan couldn't get a solid force to the bank soon enough to drive off the barges, but close enough that the British could undertake a forced march on his position as soon as they arrived. Instead, they'd land so far away that if Thornton tried a forced march in full gear, his men would be too tired to fight once they reached the American lines. Especially since they'd be starting off already tired from the labor of getting the barges to the river.

In that respect, at least, this new unexpected delay yielded an advantage. Whether Thornton wanted it that way or not, the current was giving his soldiers a longer period of rest than they would have had if things had gone as scheduled.

Trying to eke what little solace he could from that thought, the colonel adjusted his plans. He had no choice now but to give the Americans more time to prepare their defenses. He wouldn't be able to get his men in place until well after daybreak.

No choice, no choice. If the assault on the west bank was delayed *too* long, the Americans would have the time to extract the precious guns, or destroy them. Moreover, Pakenham would have to delay his own assault on the east bank. No commanding general wanted to start a major attack with that much of the day already gone, if it could be avoided. Certainly not Pakenham on January the 8th of the year 1815, on the field of Chalmette. Even if Pakenham broke the enemy line, Jackson had created two fallback lines of defense. If Pakenham was forced to halt the advance because of nightfall, the enemy would have the time to regroup—if not at the Line Dupre, then at the Line Montreuil. Thornton knew that Pakenham wanted to break the Americans where they were, and then pursue them relentlessly all the way to New Orleans. But to do that would require a full day, not half of one.

So be it. Thornton was still leading some of the best soldiers in the world, against some of the worst.

Some of the worst. Thornton wished he knew for sure how true that would prove to be. The black water of the Mississippi at night reminded him that he still didn't know the nature of that new artillery unit.

*   *   *

Charles Ball trotted up to Driscol. "Just got the word from
Henry, down at the river. He says the racket they're making—
they been hollering all night, he says, every time they got another barge into the water—this has got to be it."

Driscol nodded. He'd sent Henry Crowell and three other soldiers to scout for him, although he hadn't done so until after
nightfall. That wasn't because he cared if the British spotted
them, but because he saw no reason to get into another argument
with the idiot Morgan. The general had explained to Driscol—
clearly, explicitly, and at amazing length—that Driscol's unit
was raw, untrained, unfit even if they had been trained since
they were darkies, and under no circumstances were they to act
as skirmishers or leave their position.

Driscol had nodded sagely, keeping silent and not arguing the
point with the good general. Why bother? Driscol had realized
long since that one of the advantages to having black troops was
that they were hard to spot at night. Provided, of course, that
their uniforms were dark also. Since official uniforms were
scarce these days in New Orleans, Driscol had had his unit design their own and have them made by seamstresses in the city's
Negro quarters. Who were, often enough, their wives or mothers or sisters.

I don't care what they look like, he'd told them, *except they'll
have no shiny buttons—nothing shiny—and they'll be blue.
Dark blue.*

"Morgan didn't spot them, I assume?"

Charles grinned. Despite his part-Irish ancestry, the gunnery
sergeant was very dark-skinned, even for a black man. At four
o'clock in the morning, in that uniform, his teeth shone like bea-
cons. "Major, *I* can't spot 'em thirty feet off."

He glanced at James and John Rogers, who were standing
nearby. "Maybe Cherokees or Choctaws could. But Morgan
don't have any."

Driscol scratched his chin. By now, that gesture was smooth
and certain. He'd gotten so used to the missing arm that he
didn't think about it much anymore. Much sooner, in fact, than
he would have thought possible. He was pretty sure that was because Tiana never seemed to notice its absence at all.

For the first time in his life, on the eve of a battle—except that first battle outside Antrim where his brother had died—Driscol found himself fervently hoping he'd survive.

Tiana . . .

But that was a treacherous thought. So, ruthlessly, he ground it under.

"All right, then," he stated firmly. "I don't want to wait any longer than I have to. If McParland fires that flare after sunrise, Houston might not spot it. Right now, though—any time within the next hour—there's no way he couldn't. So get up there as fast as you can, making sure that jackass Morgan doesn't—"

A bright yellow plume flared into the sky, in the distance to the northwest.

"Never mind," said Driscol. "Nice to see young McParland's alert."

'You won't do it," stated one of the sailors. Like the others, he was half hidden behind a nearby tree. But he said it very uncertainly.

McParland sneered, advancing toward the flare. The fuse was now burning. The teenage sergeant had lit it in the campfire, after giving the fire the benefit of another gob of phlegm.

"Think I care about Morgan? The sergeant—ah, major—given me my orders. Nobody but a fool would think all that noise down there"—McParland jerked his head toward the south—"is anything but what it has to be. And my mama didn't raise no fools."

For all his braggadocio, when McParland tossed the fuse into the gaping maw of the barrel-shaped flare, he did so gingerly and from a distance—and then scampered away.

Fortunately, the thing did what it was supposed to do, instead of just blowing up. McParland hadn't been at all sure it would work, even with Driscol's assurances. Still, better to get blown up than cross the troll.

"Wow!" hissed one of the sailors. Like all the rest, only his head peeked from around the trees. "That's some Roman candle!"

Now that he was sure that the flare would burn out without any harm to him, McParland was back to braggadocio. He stepped out into the open—no trees for him—and stood there, hands planted firmly on his hips.

"Yup. It's the salt, you know." His tone was that of an expert sure of his trade, even though he was no such thing. "Driscol said that just adding salt to the gunpowder would give it tha' color."

Bright yellow, flaring briefly into the night.

"You gonna wave the flag, too? Can't nobody see it across the river yet."

But McParland was already moving toward the furled banner. "Course I am! Like I said, my mama didn't raise no fools. A troll tells you to do something, you do it. Unless you wanta be soup."

Thornton also spotted the flare. *"Damnation!"* he shouted. And why not? He'd been completely unable to keep his frustrated men from maintaining silence since midnight. Now, quite clearly, silence was pointless. He might as well give vent to his own exasperation.

Sam Houston was dozing in his tent, so he didn't spot the flare. He'd finally had to force himself to try to get some sleep, so he wouldn't go into the battle having gotten no rest at all. He was normally a heavy sleeper, but tonight he was so keyed up with excitement that he woke up instantly when John Ross came into his tent.

"Driscol's sent the signal," Ross said.

Houston sprang to his feet. "Did you tell the general?"

John shook his head. "I came to you first. But I sent a courier to give him the word."

Houston wondered if he should wait to hear from Jackson before starting across the river. But his hesitation was brief. Jackson had agreed to the plan already, and Houston was no General Morgan to dither and dally using the excuse that he hadn't been given explicit orders at the moment.

Besides, there was no time to waste. Because of the danger of hot shot fired from the British artillery, the ferries that would carry Houston and his men across the river were waiting several miles upstream. They'd have to march for an hour upriver, then cross, then march the same distance back down before they could reinforce the American troops on the other side of the Mississippi.

He clamped on his colonel's hat. He'd slept without taking off anything else, even his boots.

"Let's go, then," he said, stooping and passing through the tent flap.

Jackson hadn't seen the flare himself. The general, sure that the British would launch their final assault on the morning of the 8th, had not slept much that night either. But he had finally managed to nap for a short time on the couch of the Macarty plantation house where he'd set up his headquarters.

Major Reid shook him awake. "Sir, the flare went off across the river a short while ago. Colonel Houston's already pulled out of the lines, to reinforce Morgan."

Jackson sat up, shaking his head to clear it.

He wasn't surprised that Houston hadn't waited to receive permission to cross the river. Would have been surprised if he had, in fact. Still, though he wasn't irritated by the youngster's initiative, he was a bit disgruntled by the situation.

Jackson didn't think the British intended any serious assault over there. He wasn't sure, of course, which was the reason he'd agreed to Houston's proposal. But Jackson thought the young colonel and his men would be spending most of the day doing nothing more valuable than crisscrossing the river. Soon enough, once it became clear that the British thrust across the Mississippi was just a feint, Houston would be marching his men back.

By the time they returned to the Jackson Line, however, the battle would probably be over—and they'd most likely be too tired to fight anyway, even if it weren't.

"Oh, well," he murmured. He was philosophical enough about the matter not to dwell on it. Houston had left his artillerymen behind with Jackson, since they'd move too slowly with their guns to be of any use to him. In truth, by now Jackson had so many men on the line that he'd been keeping the rest of Houston's regiment in reserve anyway. A reserve that he really didn't expect he'd need.

Pakenham would need a miracle to get his men across the killing field at Chalmette—and God, Jackson was sure, was on the side of America.

Besides, even if the British attack on the west bank was a di-

version, Jackson didn't want to see his forces defeated across
the river. Which they were almost bound to be, if the British
landed in any numbers. Even leaving aside his doubts concerning Morgan, Jackson knew full well that most of the Kentuckians over there were in no shape to fight.

He muttered under his breath.

"What was that, sir?"

Jackson rose from the couch, shaking his head more vigorously still. Not to shake off weariness, but in sheer disbelief. "I
still can't believe those Kentuckians arrived without guns, the
most of them. Talk about miracles! I never in my life seen a
Kentuckian without a gun, a pack of cards, and a jug of
whiskey."

Once they finally reached the shore, Thornton got his men into
marching order very quickly. The Eighty-fifth was a superb regiment. The veterans knew what to do, even without the officers'
orders.

Captain Money and his Royal Marines, he was pleased to see,
got into formation just as swiftly and surely. Now that the fight
was finally at hand, Thornton could feel all the frustration of the
past hours vanishing. Late or not, behind schedule or not, he
was leading one of the finest fighting forces anywhere in the
world.

"We'll win, by God!" he almost shouted.

He spoke loudly enough for Money to hear him, as the marine
officer trotted up to get his final marching orders.

"So we will, sir," he said, smiling. "I assume you'll want us to
leave most of our gear behind?"

"Yes. The men will have gotten some rest from that overlong
voyage on the river. But if they have to undertake a forced
march for miles, with all their equipment, they'll be too exhausted at the end to fight well."

Money nodded calmly, even though he knew that meant
they'd be fighting with just a few rounds of ammunition for
each man.

"Be a lot of bayonet work," he predicted.

"Yes, it will." Thornton's grin was savage now. "Cousin
Jonathan is about to discover that the facts of life are made of
cold steel."

* * *

Miles upstream, Sam Houston was cursing the weather. As was not unusual in New Orleans for that time of year, the river was half obscured by fog that the rising sun had not yet burned away. It was a good thing Driscol had set off the flare before daybreak. Had he set it off now, it might well never have been seen on the east bank.

"Don't dare risk it, sir," said the captain, for the tenth time since the ferry left the shore. "Got to move slowly and carefully, under these conditions."

For the tenth time, Houston was tempted to curse the man along with the weather—or just toss him overboard and pilot the boat himself. But . . .

Piloting a ferry on the Mississippi was a real skill, and not one that Houston possessed himself. Nor, as far as he knew, did any of the men who were following him. Certainly the Cherokees didn't. Whether he liked it or not, he had no practical way of overriding the captain's caution.

So he distracted himself by pestering his men, making sure they were all prepared for the coming fray. The young Baltimore dragoons and First Capitol Volunteers took his fretting fairly seriously; Major Ridge and his Cherokees paid him no attention at all.

Finally, the ferries started coming ashore. Houston was the first off the boats, charging onto the pier on the west bank like Achilles storming off the waters of the Aegean at Troy.

After striding three steps later, his boot caught on a loose plank and he was sent sprawling. Flat on his belly, Sam glared at the wooden flooring. He was feeling quite indignant.

Achilles hadn't tripped within ten feet after landfall.

Of course, Achilles hadn't had to deal with the hazards of a hastily constructed pier. On the other hand, Achilles had certainly stormed ashore waving his sword, and Sam was mightily glad he hadn't.

An ignominious end, that would have been, to a glorious life just barely under way. *Alas, in his enthusiasm, the Young Hero of the Capitol skewered himself dreadfully at the beginning of the battle. His remains were interred—*

It didn't bear thinking about. Just didn't.

* * *

Hours, they'd lost! Precious *hours.*

It was past nine o'clock in the morning and Major General Edward Pakenham, Knight of the Bath, was practically exploding with frustration.

Pakenham knew, from somewhat-veiled comments offered by Admiral Cochrane, that Robert Ross had expressed strong reservations concerning the wisdom of launching directly into battle with a new commander in charge of the army. Even though Pakenham understood that the reservations didn't actually involve his own abilities, he'd still resented them a bit.

Now, he was coming to realize just how wise Ross had been, with his greater experience. The army under Pakenham was a very good one, and he knew that he was a very good general. But the fact remained that war was a messy business, always full of unexpected difficulties—and there did not yet exist the smooth interaction between himself and his subordinates that would have come from weeks or months of working together on a longer and better-planned campaign.

The result had been a series of setbacks and mishaps. Most of them fairly minor, in themselves. But, added together, they were beginning to undermine the entire plan of the battle.

He was doing his very best not to take out his frustration and anger on his subordinates.

And succeeding, for the most part. The only officer who'd received the full brunt of Pakenham's wrath had been Lieutenant Colonel Thomas Mullins, the commander of the Forty-fourth Foot. The Forty-fourth had been charged with the task of carrying the fascines and ladders that the rest of the army would need to storm the Jackson Line, and by eight o'clock it had become obvious to Pakenham that the man was hopelessly incompetent. The fool hadn't even bothered to check if the fascines and ladders were actually in place where they were supposed to be, even though he'd been explicitly instructed to do so the night before.

But, General Pakenham. I made inquiries and was told—

Told by whom? *And why didn't you look for yourself? The entire attack plan* depends *on those ladders and fascines, you— you—*

Pakenham had experienced a nightmarish vision of his soldiers piling up at the Jackson Line, and being ripped to pieces by American fire, with the means of storming the fieldworks somewhere lost in the rear because a blithering idiot who only held his command due to the fact that he was the son of Lord Ventry had not taken so simple and obvious a measure with regard to so critical a matter as to look for himself.

You are dismissed, Colonel Mullins. Inform your subordinate that he is now in command of the Forty-fourth.

Dismissed, *I said!*

For the tenth time that morning, Pakenham resisted the urge simply to launch the assault across the field of Chalmette, regardless of where things stood on the opposite bank. It was a difficult urge to resist.

Very difficult. Pakenham, like the hapless Mullins, certainly owed the start of his career to family connections. But his rise thereafter had been due to his own ability and temperament. Even by the standards of Wellington's army, Pakenham was an aggressive general. Every instinct he had was shrieking at him to begin the attack.

He probably would have done so, in truth, had it not been for Robert Ross. Partly due to Ross's words of caution based on his own experience at the Capitol; partly based on the deep respect Pakenham, like all officers in the British army, had for Ross as a general. And partly, in the end, simply because he had made a personal promise to the man.

So he took a long, slow, deep breath, controlling his urges.

"Perhaps I was a bit hard on Mullins," he said to Gibbs.

His second in command's jaws were tight. "You saved him from a court-martial, sir. I just got word from Lambert. The ladders and fascines *weren't* in place."

Pakenham's face turned pale. "Good God."

"Yes. Can you imagine what would have happened?"

Pakenham could, all too well. A pure massacre.

"Good God," he repeated.

Tiana Rogers had been watching Robert Ross for almost an hour, sitting silently in the chair in the corner of his room where she often spent time while tending to him. The British general was normally courteous—even mildly flirtatious, at times, in the harmless way that a middle-aged man will sometimes be with a young woman. But today he had been completely oblivious of her. Other than a glance he'd spared when she'd come into the room that morning, all his attention had been directed at the open window.

He must have opened it himself, before daybreak, since she'd left it closed the night before to ward off the winter cold. Ross had been lying in his bed staring at the window ever since.

His eyes were open, but they weren't really seeing anything. He was listening. Trying, with his very experienced ear, to gauge the progress of the conflict now starting to unfold miles down the Mississippi.

"Would it make you feel any better if we waited down by the river?" she asked. "Mind you, it'll probably rain—drizzle, for sure—and it's already cold and damp. So if you take ill again, it's your own fault."

Startled, he looked at her. Then smiled.

"Sorry. I've been very rude, I'm afraid. Yes, dear girl, it would make me feel immensely better."

He looked back at the window, cocking his head a bit. "From the sounds of the street, though, I'd say I'll be in greater danger of being slaughtered by frenzied females, than dying of a chill."

Tiana barked a laugh. "Those hens! They're all rushing about in a tizzy because they're sure they're about to be raped by on-coming hordes of Englishmen. Slaughter's the last thing on their minds, or they'd be doing something useful like sharpening their knives." She rose from her chair, smiling in a rather predatory manner. "I sharpened mine days ago."

Ross flushed. "I realize the reputation of the British army suffered badly after Badajoz. But I can assure you, young lady—"

"Spare me, Robert. British soldiers are no more saints than any other. What will happen, will happen. The one thing I can assure you is that if any gang of soldiers tries to rape *me,* the second or third man in the party might succeed. The first one will either be dead or singing falsetto. Probably the second, too."

Ross chuckled. "You are a formidable creature, have I ever told you that?"

"Yesterday. Again. After I told you—again—that you were welcome to empty your own chamber pot any time you were stupid enough to decide you're fit and hearty. Which you aren't."

She shrugged on her shawl, which was a very attractive Creole one. Before they got outside, Ross knew, she'd supplement it with a Cherokee blanket. Tiana Rogers simply didn't care what other people thought of the way she dressed or carried herself. To be sure, as young and beautiful as she was, she didn't really need to. But Ross was quite certain that she'd be the same way as an old woman.

"Formidable," he repeated, as Tiana helped him out of the bed.

She did not, thankfully, offer to help him change from his bedclothes into his uniform. She was formidable enough to do it, if he'd needed the help. But he'd manage well enough, and it would have embarrassed him. It was bad enough that she did the sort of unpleasant chores for him that a servant should properly do. Cherokees were odd, that way. They'd employ slaves for productive labor as readily as white Americans, from what Ross could tell, but didn't seem to feel that personal servants were appropriate.

One woman on the street did shriek, seeing Robert's uniform. Then, scampered away in panic, insofar as an overweight matron in her fifties could be said to "scamper" at all. Several others gaped at him.

None, however, advanced upon him with mayhem in their hearts. Ross decided he would survive.

Down by the riverbank, he couldn't really hear what was happening all that much better than he could have staying in his hotel room. Still, he felt relieved being there, out in the open of the Plaza de Armas. They were fairly comfortable, too, soon enough. Tiana bullied a Creole baker whose shop fronted the city's main square into providing them with a small table, two chairs, pastries, and a pot of tea. The tea in New Orleans was even good, unlike the normal American travesty.

"There fails only a parasol to ward off the drizzle," Robert chided.

"Suffer," she replied.

CHAPTER 45

When the first line of Americans began firing on the Eighty-fifth Foot, Colonel Thornton ordered the regiment to launch an immediate bayonet charge while still in column formation. There would be no forming into a line and firing volleys. Just cold steel, in a headlong assault. Thornton was sure he could sweep aside this first screen of skirmishers, and he didn't want to lose the time or the ammunition that volley fire would require. Until the Forty-third Light Infantry and the West Indian troops could rejoin his regiment with the supplies he'd left behind at the debarkation point, he needed to conserve his ammunition.

His assessment proved correct. Almost absurdly so, in fact. The skirmishers fired not more than a round each—many of them, not even that—before racing off into the swamps. A fair number of the Americans dropped their weapons before they ran, and not a single one died at the point of a bayonet—or any other mishap caused directly by British action. One man did break his neck when he tripped over a root and slammed head-first into a tree.

"And will you look at this, sir?" crowed one of Thornton's sergeants gleefully, holding up a gun left behind by an American. "It's a bloody fowling piece!"

So it was. If that was typical of the weaponry Jackson had given his forces on this side of the river, Thornton could hardly blame them for running away.

He shook his head, and reminded himself that they'd encounter deadlier arms up ahead. There was ordnance there, for a certainty. Still, this easy victory had done wonders for the morale of his regiment. The men had been, as always, obedient and disciplined. But the cold and the drizzle and the hours of muddy labor during the night had left them tired and disgruntled. Now, with the sun finally burning away the mist, their spirits were improving rapidly.

"Forward, lads!" he cried, waving his sword. "We'll chase the cowards all the way into New Orleans!"

As the distant sound of skirmishing fire faded away—very quickly—Robert Ross lowered his cup of tea onto the table.

"That'll have been the Eighty-fifth brushing aside a line of skirmishers, I think. These pastries are quite good, by the way."

"Would you like some more?"

"Yes, please."

Tiana rose and walked toward the bakery. Her long-legged stride made the colorful heavy skirt she was wearing flash like a banner in the breeze.

But Ross didn't watch her for more than a second or two. His head turned toward the south, cocked slightly to the side to bring an ear to bear.

As soon as the first Kentuckians came into sight, racing like mad toward the "Morgan Line," General Morgan clambered upon his horse and rode out to meet them. He was waving his sword so vigorously that Driscol thought he might injure himself. Perhaps even badly enough to require evacuation for medical care.

Alas, no such luck.

"Stand your ground, you cowards! Stand your ground, I say!"

The Kentuckians dodged around him without missing a stride. The first ones reached the "Morgan Line," bounded over it like deer leaping logs in the forest, and continued racing toward the north.

The ones who followed continued to pour around Morgan, ignoring him like the others. The general had his horse pivoting in circles while he continued waving his sword and screeching commands that weren't so much "commands" as simple curses. At one point, he took a swipe with the sword at a fleeing militiaman who was perhaps twenty feet away.

"Think he'll fall off?" Ball wondered.

"Doubt it," Driscol grunted.

"He's a fair horseman," James Rogers pointed out charitably. "I'm still hoping for a good gash in the thigh, though."

Again, no such luck. After the last of the Kentucky skirmishers had leaped over the ditch, Morgan sent his horse racing after them. The horse, by now becoming exceedingly exasperated, did its level best to throw its rider as it vaulted the ditch.

But Morgan stayed in the saddle. Within seconds, he was out of sight, pounding off in pursuit of his fleeing men. Still screeching incoherent commands and still waving the sword.

"Ah, well," Driscol said. He just shook his head. Charles Ball did the same, and the Rogers brothers were actually grinning.

The men of the Iron Battalion would be watching the four of them closely, at this moment, especially Driscol and Ball. The sight of the Kentucky militiamen racing to the rear would have unsettled even veteran troops. Most of the men in the battalion were completely inexperienced in combat, and their nerves would be *very* jittery. If either Driscol or Ball showed any concern at all, they might start to break.

The quite evident good cheer of the two Cherokees helped also. Indians were rather exotic to most of the men in Driscol's unit. Indian warriors, at least. Much like easterners did, the black soldiers ascribed to the Rogers brothers a great deal more experience in warfare than they actually had. If the "wild Injuns" didn't seem worried, why should they be?

After a few seconds, Driscol could see that the troops were settling down nicely. He and Ball exchanged a glance. What a pleasure it was, to have such a fine subordinate under his command! As good a top sergeant as any Driscol had ever known.

He gave his head one last humorous shake, just for good measure. "At least he's out of our hair for a while."

Sure now that his men had been steadied, Driscol turned back to face the oncoming enemy. He couldn't see the British, but he could hear them. The still-invisible soldiers were moving fast enough to make their gear clatter. From the sound of it, though, he thought they'd stripped away everything but the essentials.

"Grapeshot, I assume?"

"Yes, sir." Like any good sergeant, Ball knew when to shift to military formalities. "All the guns are loaded with grapeshot. I told the men not to use canister until I gave the order."

Driscol eyed the distance. The British would be in a direct line of sight for more than two hundred yards before they could reach his fieldworks—and Driscol had taken advantage of the past two days to turn his section of the "Morgan Line" into something deadly serious.

"They'll probably launch a bayonet assault immediately, Sergeant. So they'll get here more quickly than they normally would. We'll shift to canister after the first round."

"Yes, sir." Quickly, Ball left to pass along the order.

He was back within half a minute or so. Driscol's section of the "Morgan Line" was more in the way of a bastion than anything else. In fact, his men had started calling it *Fort Driscol*. Deliberately, almost sure that the Kentuckians would break, Driscol had designed the bastion so that it could protect his men from three sides. Only the rear was left open.

Of course, the fieldworks had been hastily erected, using nothing more elaborate than dirt and logs. But his freedmen had set to the work with a will, and had managed to create something quite substantial in a very short time. Best of all, before they'd left the city they'd somehow scrounged up—stolen, most likely—a fair amount of wrought-iron fencework. The fancy fake spearpoints that tipped those fences had been designed for decoration. But, embedded into the walls of the bastion and slanted outward, they made an effective barrier. Decorative iron was still iron.

The three hundred men of the Iron Battalion were anchored on the twelve-pounder, with the six-pounders positioned on the flanks. Driscol had placed the remaining ordnance—three four-pounders and two three-pounders—in the spaces between. About half his men would work the cannons, under the direction of Ball and his naval veterans. The other half were armed with muskets, pikes, and swords.

The pikes had been made up in the iron shops. The "swords" were rarely that. Most of them were just the biggest knives the men could find, although some of them were armed with cutlasses that Houston had sweet-talked from Lafitte's Baratarian pirates. The Baratarians had been willing enough, since Jackson was using them as artillerymen on the Jackson Line.

Driscol thought the pikes and blades would be more useful than the muskets. He'd concentrated his training on the cannons, of course. There really hadn't been time to train men properly in the use of muskets, as well. And freedmen, unlike white frontiersmen, didn't grow up with muskets in their hands.

So Driscol had simply taught them how to load and fire a single round. Some of them, either from a bit of experience or simply because they had the knack for it, would probably manage to reload and get off another shot. Most of them, after firing the first round, would drop the muskets and take up simpler weapons.

On an open field, Driscol's battalion would have been mincemeat. But here, especially facing the headlong bayonet charge that Driscol expected, he thought they'd do quite well. They were nervous, of course, but they were also burning with a determination to prove themselves—a sentiment Driscol had spent the past weeks nurturing as assiduously as he could.

Which . . . was assiduous indeed. If soldiers had been flowers in a garden, Patrick Driscol would have been reckoned one of the world's finest gardeners.

The British were almost here, he thought. He had just time enough left for a little speech.

"All right, lads." His rasping voice, half-shouting, carried superbly well. "There is nothing complicated about this. There are no maneuvers required of you. All you have to do is stand your ground and fight."

His pale eyes ranged across the faces of his watching soldiers. Their attention was riveted on him.

"The enemy will attack and try to kill us, or drive us off. The first might happen. *The other will not.* We will win on this ground, or we will die on this ground. But whichever it is, we will not retreat. It's nothing but stand and die, or stand and win. Do you all understand?"

A wave of nodding heads came in response. There was no hesitation.

He smiled then. That thin, cold smile of his, but a smile nonetheless.

" 'Tis normally at this point in my little speech that I threaten my men with the consequences, should they fail me. Grinding bones for my soup, and such." A tittering little laugh swept the soldiery. "But I'll not do that here. Not today. Not with the men of the Iron Battalion. There's no need. You will do what your mates and your nation require of you, I am certain of it."

He paused, wondering what he might add.

Nothing, it seemed. Henry Crowell, standing with a ramrod by the twelve-pounder, swept off his cap and waved it in the air.

"I saw the major break the bastards at the Capitol, and he'll do it again today! A cheer for the major, boys!"

Driscol was genuinely astonished at the cheer that went up. Loud, vigorous, full of confidence and enthusiasm. More than he'd ever hoped for, in truth.

To be sure, he thought the cheer itself was ridiculous. As if the simple name *Driscol* chanted over and over again was some sort of magical talisman.

But he made no protest. Perhaps it was, to such men.

As soon as he caught sight of the American line—much more substantial, this one, ranging across hundreds of yards of front—Thornton paused just long enough to assess the thing. The American left, anchored on the river, would naturally be the strong point. There'd be some regulars there, manning the battery. Musketeers and a handful of light ordnance were spread across the middle. There would be the weakest point, but he didn't want to charge with batteries firing on him from the two flanks. Even if he broke through, his casualties would be severe.

He studied the solid-looking fieldworks to the left of the field. That was where the new freedmen battalion was positioned. For a moment, he was tempted to turn the charge to head directly for them. As a rule, a unit like that would break easily. But . . .

He was mindful of the possibility that the Capitol veterans might be there. Probably were, in fact, now that he finally got a good look at their fieldworks. Someone with determination and authority was in charge there. Remembering the carnage in Washington, he decided that a direct assault would be too risky.

"Right," he said to his aides. They clustered about him while the men took a moment to rest. "We'll avoid the American right, and make our drive along the river. That new unit looks to be solid—but with as little training as they've received, they'll be like lost lambs once the line gives way. If we can break the American line at the river, the entire line will come apart. The freedmen and militia won't retreat for the good and simple reason that they don't know how. They'll run like rabbits, and we'll hunt them like hounds."

He waited just long enough to see if any of his lieutenants had any doubts they wanted to express. As he expected, none did.

"Right, then. Nothing fancy." He raised his voice so it could be heard by the men at the head of the column. "It'll be a column charge with bayonets, lads! We'll do or die!"

A cheer went up. *A very good one,* Thornton thought.

He drew his sword, held it high, and took his place near the head of the column.

"To victory!"

"Damnation," Driscol growled, seeing the British angling toward the other end of the line. He'd been expecting them to attack him at once, and had prepared accordingly.

But Ball was already giving the order to replace the grape with round shot. At the range the British column was keeping, all the way across the field, grapeshot would be a hit-or-miss affair.

Ball's method for switching rounds was simple and sanguine. The entire battery fired the grapeshot that was already loaded, and then started reloading with round shot. "Hit-or-miss," after all, isn't the same as "miss."

If the freedmen battalion was poorly trained with muskets, they knew how to deal with heavy ordnance. Very soon, they were ready to fire again.

"Rake 'em, boys!" Charles Ball yelled. "Rake the bastards!"

Again, the battery erupted, all but the one six-pounder that was too far out of position on the right. It was as neat and sweet a volley as any Driscol had ever seen.

Grazing shots, too, the most of them. Ball had veterans aiming the guns. The cannonballs hit the ground in front of the column, and skipped into the mass of men at waist level. The effect wasn't as devastating as it would have been if the cannonballs had struck stony ground, scattering splinters of rock to accompany the balls themselves. But not even the soggy ground along the banks of the Mississippi could keep those balls from caroming into the British column with deadly force.

One ball missed entirely, from what Driscol could tell through the cloud of gunsmoke. But the rest hit the enemy column like mauls wielded by a giant.

The only thing that kept the casualties from being worse was that Driscol had only a few guns and was firing on the British column from an angle across the field. "Enfilade fire," as it was called, was usually devastating against a line, because the shot could strike so many men. But it was much less effective against a column that was no more than a few men wide. If Driscol's guns had been firing head on, a single ball might have slain and maimed a dozen British soldiers. As it was, Driscol saw one of the balls—must have been from the twelve-pounder—pick up four men and hurl their broken and shredded bodies into the river.

Ross could feel his face tighten. Two volleys, fired like thunderclaps. Even from the distance, there was no mistaking the thing.

That'll be Driscol, he thought. The man like a stone.

Near its head, Thornton ignored the havoc being wreaked on the center of the column. He'd known his men would take casualties from the other American battery while they charged the one by the river. At the moment, he was far more concerned about the damage he was taking from straight ahead. The battery they were charging was doing quite well itself.

Grapeshot killed two men in what was now the front rank. Thornton simply leaped over their bodies. The battery on the American left was within fifty yards. Thornton knew how terrifying a mass of bayonets would be, coming at the run. That battery would *break,* so help him God.

"Forward!" he cried. He was no longer waving the sword. Now, he had it gripped for the killing stroke.

"Rake 'em, boys, rake 'em!"

Ball was doing a splendid troll imitation himself, so Driscol let him be. The one time he started to move forward to assist, John Rogers held him back with a hand on the shoulder.

"Just stay here, Patrick." The Rogers brothers had no use at all for military protocol. "He's doing fine, and if you get crushed by a cannon recoil scurrying around like a fussy hen, me and James will never hear the end of it from Tiana."

Driscol didn't try to fight off the restraining hand. John's words were true enough. The first bit, at least. The idea that Patrick Driscol would let himself get carelessly behind a cannon being fired was just ridiculous.

"Rake the bastards, you blasted currees! You got no excuse to miss since they ain't firing back! Any crew misses its shot I'll cut your ears off and fry 'em up! My voudou queen got one hell of recipe for it, too!"

Granted, Ball's version involved a lot of unseemly leaping about, but Driscol made allowances. You couldn't reasonably expect African trolls to have the same customs as northerly ones.

And he was getting the result they needed. Between Ball's energetic leadership, and the sure confidence of the core of veterans from Barney's unit, the men of the Iron Battalion were going about their work swiftly and effectively. Even, to all appearances, calmly. The sweat now coating their dark faces and bodies was simply that caused by the heat of the rising sun and the work of firing cannons.

It was everything Driscol could have hoped for. He might lose this day—die this day—but not before gutting the Sassenach.

Stoically, Robert Ross sipped his tea. The sound of the batteries was almost continuous now. But, always, with that regular punctuation. One battery maintaining volley fire while the other simply blazed away as best it could.

Miles away, out of sight, Ross could see it as if he were there. Thornton had done exactly what he would have done—avoid Driscol's unit and attack the American line across the field. By the river, probably. He'd suffer bad casualties in the doing, of course. But once the hinge was shattered . . .

Yes, it might work.

Undoubtedly *would* work, if Thornton had enough men. Once the flank gave way, men as inexperienced as the Kentucky militia and the hastily trained freedmen would be lost. Orderly retreat, disciplined regroupment—all that would be completely beyond their grasp. They'd simply break and run, peeled away like rind from a fruit.

"Unless," he muttered.

Tiana gave him a blank-faced look. In fact, there'd been no expression on her face at all, since the battle began. "Unless what, Robert?"

Ross took a deep breath. "Unless Driscol does what I damn well think he's going to do, the stubborn Scots-Irish bastard. Simply stand, like a stone. He'll *force* Thornton to come at him."

There was still no expression on her face. "Stand and die, you mean."

The British general reminded himself sharply that the man he was speaking of was loved by the girl across the table. Deeply loved, in fact. Of that, he was by now quite certain, even if he often found her Cherokee way of expressing it puzzling.

"Perhaps. You never know, in a battle. Believe it true, Tiana. You simply never know until it's over."

When Sam Houston encountered his first Kentuckian, fleeing from the battle he could hear in the distance, he neither shouted nor waved his sword. He wasn't holding his sword in the first place, having recognized what a dangerous practice that was in a long march so forced it was almost a run. He simply grabbed the man by the scruff of the neck as he raced past, spun him around, and sent him sailing back toward the front lines.

"You so much as look back at me once, and I'll break your neck! You *will* fight, so help me!"

The militiaman didn't look back.

Encouraged by Houston's example, other men in his regiment used similar methods of persuasion as they encountered more fleeing militiamen. By the time Houston and his men reached Patterson's battery, they'd rallied perhaps a hundred of the Kentuckians.

"Thank God you've arrived!" Patterson cried. "They're fighting hot and heavy down there! Don't know how much longer they can hold!"

"Then why are you still here?" Sam snarled.

Patterson gave him an odd look. Confusion, mainly, not anger. Sam stopped, planted his hands on his knees, and took some deep breaths. He needed a rest. And if he did, so did his men.

"My apologies, Commodore." Sam had spoken unfairly, and he knew it. Sam didn't doubt Patterson's courage any more than anyone else did, and he knew Patterson's chief responsibility was making sure that whatever else happened, the big guns didn't fall into enemy hands. His battery was positioned directly across the river from the field of Chalmette. If the guns of the battery were seized by the British before Patterson had a chance to spike them, it would take only minutes to shift them upstream far enough to start ravaging the Jackson Line.

His wind back, Sam straightened and peered across the river. The British forces over there were in position to launch an assault, but hadn't so far made a move to do so. They were waiting, he guessed, to see what happened on the west bank.

Then he looked at Patterson's battery. "Give me the two three-pounders and enough men to haul and fire them. Even if the enemy seizes them, they won't do much damage firing across the river. But I can use them downstream."

Patterson didn't hesitate. "Yes, certainly."

Five minutes later, rested, Houston and his regiment were off again. Almost running now, with two three-pounders bouncing along behind.

From the second-floor window of the Macarty house, watching through an eyeglass, Jackson saw the British break the hinge of Morgan's line of defense by the river. The battery put up a stout fight, but before long it was overwhelmed.

The rest of the line started peeling away, Kentucky militiamen scattering like chaff in the wind.

He swiveled the eyeglass far around, looking north. Yes, there was Houston, coming fast. *Thank God.*

Swiveled it back. It was hard to tell much, more than a hundred yards past the riverbank. But he could see clouds of gunsmoke, billowing like clockwork.

That'd be Driscol and his freedmen, solid as a rock.

The general lowered the glass and hollered something. None of his lieutenants in the room understood a word. They couldn't have, anyway, since there really weren't any words. That had been just a shriek, half glee and half fury.

Still clenching the eyeglass, Jackson turned from the window and stalked from the room. Down the stairs, and out of the house.

He shook the eyeglass toward the southeast. "Come at me, Pakenham! Tarnation, *come at me!*"

Pakenham was standing next to a tree, near the riverbank. Watching. Softly, steadily, like a metronome, he kept pounding the trunk with the bottom of his fist.

He'd wait before ordering the assault here at Chalmette. He wouldn't act until he knew what was happening across the river.

He'd wait.

So help him God. The God who ruled battles, and all else. He . . . would . . . wait.

CHAPTER 46

The American lieutenant died at his post, after firing a last round of canister from his twelve-pounder that killed three British soldiers and wounded several more. In their fury, no fewer than four of Thornton's soldiers bayoneted the man repeatedly after they reached him, practically ripping his body into shreds.

Gasping for breath, Thornton looked down at the corpse. The lieutenant still gripped the smoldering fuse in his hand.

Sometime later, Thornton knew, he'd feel admiration for the man. The unknown lieutenant had just added to the splendid reputation which the little U.S. Navy had gotten in the course of the war. But at the moment, he felt more like stabbing the corpse himself, with his saber. That battery had hammered the Eighty-fifth worse than Thornton had expected.

After a few more breaths, Thornton regained his wind. Amazingly enough, in that last charge, he hadn't himself suffered as much as a scratch, even though he'd been in the lead much of the way.

But what next?

A round from the battery still firing on the American right killed another British soldier and scattered his squad, right in front of Thornton's eyes. *Damnation!* Against all logic and reason, that bloody unit was still in place and still firing its cannons with the same rate and accuracy that had ripped the Eighty-fifth throughout the charge. The rest of the American line had peeled away and raced to the rear, even before the assault overwhelmed the artillerymen on the riverbank. But the other battery hadn't so much as flinched.

So much for logic and reason. As often, applied to military affairs, they'd proved to be treacherous beasts.

Quickly, Thornton considered his options. None of them were good.

"Shall we charge them, sir?" asked Lieutenant Colonel Gubbins, Thornton's immediate subordinate, nodding toward the American battery a few hundred yards away.

Thornton thought about it—quickly, because the battery was continuing to fire on them. Now that the Eighty-fifth had reached the redoubt on the riverbank, the men were somewhat sheltered. But not enough, and certainly not against fire that accurate.

Standard procedure would have been to silence the battery before pressing onward. No commander wanted to leave an enemy bastion threatening his rear. But Thornton decided to risk it. He *had* to take the main American battery, farther to the north, with its big cannons. And he had to do it quickly.

"No, we'll keep pressing on. However good that new American unit has proven to be, I don't think its commander will risk a sortie against our troops on the open field. And if he does, we'll turn and crush him."

Gubbins scanned the area, then nodded. "Soon enough, too, we'll be out of their range. Out of sight, for that matter, once the column moves a few hundred yards off."

Thornton saw that Gubbins was right, and his grim expression lightened considerably.

The American commander had established his line at a place where the cypress swamps were fairly distant—exactly the opposite of what Jackson had done across the river. Just a few hundred yards north, the swamps closed in again, leaving an open area not more than two or three hundred yards wide between the cypress and the waterway. Once the British column reached that narrow neck, they'd be out of sight of the American battery altogether.

"Do you want to leave a detachment behind, sir?" Gubbins asked.

"Yes. They'll serve to guide the Forty-third and the West Indians, once they arrive." Thornton looked over the guns they'd seized from the naval detachment. One twelve-pounder and two six-pounders, neither of which the Americans had found time to spike. For a moment, he was sorely tempted to take the cannons with him. But they wouldn't be enough to affect whatever battle started across the river on Chalmette field; and, in the meantime, the detachment he left behind would need those guns to defend themselves against the American battery that was still in place.

"Leave as small a detachment as we can manage, but not so small that they might be overrun by those bloody bastards over there. Make sure they've enough experienced men to handle the guns we leave behind, as well."

Gubbins moved off. Thornton began organizing his regiment to make a rapid movement out of the shelter of the redoubt. Such as it was.

"Give it to 'em, boys!" hollered Ball. "Any crew slacks off I'll have their legs in with the rest of the shrimp in Marie's pot!" Brandishing a cutlass, he glared at the crew of the twelve-pounder. "Don't you be grinning at me, Corporal Jones! Those long legs of yours'll fit, too! That voudou queen got the biggest cook pot in New Orleans!"

Ball was demonstrating that his superb performance at the Capitol had been no fluke. He had as much of a knack for handling novice recruits as he did the veterans he'd had with him in Washington.

Better still, Driscol knew, the men themselves were blooded now—and in the best possible manner. Bloodlessly, for them. They'd been able to prove to themselves that they could inflict damage on an enemy before that enemy could attack them directly. When and if the British came at them, they'd have confidence that fighting back would make a difference, even in the face of a terrifying bayonet charge.

When, he thought, correcting himself. There'd be no "if" involved.

True enough, from what he could tell the British commander was getting ready to push onward, leaving Driscol and his battalion behind. But it was obvious that they'd faced only a portion of the British forces, thus far, not more than a regiment. There had to be more coming.

The British were pushing this assault far more vigorously—almost recklessly—than they ever would have for a simple diversionary movement. Driscol thought there would be at least another thousand soldiers arriving now on this side of the river. They'd be here soon enough.

In the meantime—

"Look, Sergeant! The bastards are leaving!" Excitedly, one of the gunners pointed toward the river, where the head of the British column could be seen moving to the northwest. "They're running away!"

Ball was there in an instant, swatting the man. Fortunately, he did it with his bare left hand, not the cutlass. "And what do I care, you stupid curree? Get back to your post! Fire on 'em, boys! *Keeping firing, the Lord damn you!* I want those bastards bled and gutted every step of the way!"

Splendid, splendid. Driscol wondered if Jackson's quirkiness would extend as far as to allow Driscol to promote Ball to a commissioned rank.

Maybe. You never knew, with Jackson.

After the sound of the guns faded, Robert Ross looked at Tiana, sitting across from him at the table on the square. Her face had remained expressionless, but seemed tighter than before.

He started to open his mouth, prepared to reassure her, but stopped almost at once. He brought the cup of his tea to his lips, to disguise the moment's lapse.

How *could* he reassure her? Driscol might well be dead by now.

Or not. Battles were unpredictable things. There had been many times in his life when Robert Ross had thought the peculiarly abstract nature of military terminology—those fussy and precise terms like *enfilade* and all the rest, often enough drawn from a foreign tongue—served the main purpose of shielding soldiers from the raw certainty that battles were nothing but chaos, carnage, ruin, and agony. Battles would be unbearable, faced without that prism to shield the human heart and mind.

"He's dead now, isn't he?" There was no tone at all in Tiana's voice, though the voice itself seemed brittle.

Robert shook his head firmly. "There's no way to know, girl. Trust me about this. There is simply no way to know."

Steadily, like a metronome, Pakenham's fist kept pounding the tree trunk. Very gently, now.

"I wonder if he's being wise, sir," commented Gibbs, watching the British column that was continuing north along the riverbank.

Pakenham shook his head firmly. "We shall not be second-guessing Colonel Thornton, General. He knows he's far behind schedule. No fault of his own, of course. So he's leaving that bastion behind, and going for the critical guns. What other course can he follow?"

Pakenham wondered what he might have chosen to do, in Thornton's place. He didn't wonder more than a moment, though. The very same thing. Err on the side of aggressiveness, if err you must.

"A splendid regimental commander," he pronounced. "I'll see him knighted, so help me God."

Jackson was back at his window, studying the battle through his glass. Once the British column moved past the naval battery they'd overrun, he lowered the glass and shook his head.

"I will be good goddamned," he stated, lapsing into blasphemy. "The niggers *held*. The only ones that did except the regulars, goddamn all Kentuckians."

He swiveled his head and glared at his aides. "What's the name of Driscol's chief sergeant over there? The black one, I'm talking about—black as the ace of spades. The fellow he brought with him from Washington."

The aides glanced at each other. Reid cleared his throat. "Not sure, sir. 'Ball,' I think."

The glare was joined by a grin that was, if anything, more ferocious still. "Well, he's *Lieutenant* Ball now. Army regulations be damned, along with the whole state of Kentucky."

Jackson turned back to the open window, leaned out of it, and shook the eyeglass in the direction of New Orleans. "Take *that*, you trembling bastards! Take *that*, you craven curs! Rot on your stinking plantations, you treacherous cowards!"

He continued in that enthusiastic vein for a time, becoming more vulgar and profane as he went. Andrew Jackson, in a mood for cursing, was extraordinarily good at it.

When Houston saw the oncoming British column, he skidded to a halt. "Hold up!" he shouted. "Form a line!"

Fortunately, the sailors from Patterson's unit were veterans, so they had the three-pounders in line quickly enough to give the rest of Houston's regiment an anchor point. The three-pounders were positioned directly across the narrow dirt road that led up the riverbank. Houston placed his Baltimore dragoons on either side, and extended the Capitol volunteers in a line stretching toward the nearby swamp.

There was no time to make breastworks, of course. The British weren't more than three hundred yards away by now. But Sam was sure that, firing in a line against a narrow column, his men would at least be able to hold the British for a few minutes.

That left Major Ridge and his two hundred Cherokees.

"Can you get through that cypress?" Sam asked.

Ridge glanced at the swamp. "It'll take a bit of time."

"Sure. I'll give you the time. You get in there and hit them on the flank." He peered into the distance. "There's not more than two hundred yards between the river and the swamp, where I'll stop them."

Ridge left immediately, fading swiftly into the underbrush with his Cherokees in tow. John Ross went with them, without waiting to hear what Sam wanted him to do.

Sam was a little surprised by that. John was normally punctilious about military protocol, even if his own status in the U.S. Army was somewhat anomalous. But, clearly, the young Cherokee captain had decided his identity here was with his own nation.

So be it. Houston wouldn't really have known what to do with him anyway. The situation was about as clear and simple as it could get: the American regiment would start firing on the British once they got within a hundred yards, and keep shooting until it was all over.

"We'll stand here, boys!" he shouted. Belatedly, he remembered his sword. A moment later, he had it waving about. "We'll win here or we'll die here, but whatever else, *we shall not retreat!*"

The regiment sent up a cheer. A bit too wavering a cheer, to Sam's mind.

"D'you hear me, blast it! We'll stand and win, or stand and die!"

His mind raced through the *Iliad,* then raced back again to the beginning. Yes, that verse would do nicely.

> *"Since great Achilles and Atrides strove,*
> *Such was the sov'reign doom, and such the will of*
> *Jove!"*

Most of the veterans from the Capitol burst into laughter.

"I'm getting a little predictable," Sam muttered.

But . . .

Being predictable, he decided, was probably a good quality for a military commander. To his men, at least, if not the enemy. And besides, that laughter from the veterans seemed to have braced the morale of the rest even more than the preceding cheer.

He wondered why that should be so, other than the general quirkiness of the human soul. But he didn't wonder for long. The British were coming fast, now. They'd be breaking into a full run any moment. The oncoming rows of bayonets made them seem not so much like an army, but a single beast. A great huge snake, making its strike.

"All right, boys, let's kill that snake!" They were in range now, Sam decided. Certainly for the three-pounders. "Let 'em have it!"

The cannons went off before he finished the sentence. Grapeshot shattered the front lines of the column.

"Let 'em have it, I say!"

The first musket volley was fairly done, if somewhat ragged. But the men shot straight enough, the most of them. And if their ensuing fire was ragged, it didn't slack off. They had the inevitable advantage that a line always has, firing on a column. There wasn't much coming in the way of return fire, to rattle his inexperienced troops.

And—though Sam didn't know it—those first volleys decapitated the snake.

Colonel Thornton's shoulder was shattered by a grapeshot. The blow spun him around. Reeling but still on his feet, his face pale with shock, he stared at Gubbins.

"Keep the men—"

Whatever Thornton's last command might have been went unspoken. A musket ball penetrated the back of his head and blew out his left eye.

Gubbins wiped the gore off his face. "Forward, damn you! Forward, I—"

He choked, clutching his throat, torn by a musket ball. Blood spewed out instead of words. Another musket ball struck him in the ribs, spinning him sidewise; then another passed through his jaw, smashing out most of his teeth along the way.

Gubbins collapsed. On a dirt road by the Mississippi River, he bled to death.

"You're in command, sir!" cried the pale-faced young lieutenant of the Eighty-fifth. "Colonel Thornton and Colonel Gubbins have both fallen."

Captain James Money of the Royal Navy stared at the head of the column, some fifty yards or so in front of his own marines. The column was bunched up, now. No longer a column as much as a ragged lot of men trying to form an impromptu line, with no officers and a narrow front to boot. The charge had stumbled to a halt. Bayonets wouldn't do it here, clearly enough.

Money looked back at the rest of the column.

"Right. No help for it, then. We've got to form a line and fight it out. Lieutenant, I want—"

A musket ball struck his left shoulder and drove him to his knees. Turning his head, his mouth open, Money saw a wave of wild savages pouring out of the cypress swamp. The Indians had begun their charge with a volley, apparently, as soon as they emerged from the trees.

A volley of sorts, at least. Money's mind was too dazed to remember exactly what he'd heard. All he could do was watch as the savages slammed into his unprepared men. They fired again, once—no volley there; just each savage as he would, those who had muskets—and then began killing with war clubs and spears.

Captain Money *detested* this idiot war in the gulf. The terrain and climate were the worst he'd ever encountered. Nothing that happened in the next half a minute caused him to reconsider his opinion. Certainly not the war club that shattered his skull.

"Back! Back to the woods!" Major Ridge's voice, like Driscol's, was eminently capable of carrying across a raging battlefield. *"Get back now!"*

For a wonder, the warriors obeyed him. That alone, John Ross knew, as he plunged back into the cypress along with the others, was enough to make clear Ridge's status. Cherokee warriors weren't terribly prone to discipline. Ferocity, yes. Obedience in the face of commands—

He actually chuckled, once he reached the dark safety of the trees.

Not hardly.

Apparently Ridge heard the chuckle. John had stayed close to him throughout the charge out of the swamp, and the quick retreat back into it.

He gave the younger man a crease of a smile. "Amazing, isn't it? But it only worked because they aren't stupid."

John nodded. The attack had caught the British completely by surprise, and had inflicted a lot of casualties on them. But John's own experience in the swamps on the night of the twenty-third had taught him how dangerous British soldiers could be, once they were planted and ready to fight. There were still at least twice as many enemy soldiers on that road as there were Cherokees. If Ridge had tried to stand and slug it out, they'd have started getting butchered.

"What now?" he asked.

Ridge was peering through the trees at the British column on the road. John, doing the same, could see British officers racing up and down, bringing order to their troops. Faster than he would have imagined possible, the enemy was forming a line to defend their flank.

"We'll just wait a bit," Ridge answered. "Let Houston do whatever he's going to do first, and then we'll see what things look like. If they come at us, here in the swamp, we'll rip them. The same would happen to us, if we were stupid enough to charge back out there against that line."

It made sense to Ross. So, he took the time to reload his pistol. He'd even hit an enemy soldier with the round he'd fired during the charge, he thought.

That wasn't much of an accomplishment, of course. Not at point-blank range, against a mass of men caught with their backs to the river. John added the experience to the long list he was compiling, which was proving to him that there was something ultimately absurd about war.

Or, at least, the way men talked about it.

Why did men boast so, about a field of endeavor whose greatest achievement was to do the crudest thing imaginable, in as simple a way as possible? No Cherokee woman, after all, would have bragged that she'd made the ugliest garment in the world, using the fewest possible stitches.

"Shall we charge them, Colonel Houston?" Lieutenant Pendleton asked eagerly. "We bloodied 'em good!"

Sam took a moment from his study of the enemy to glance at the young dragoon officer who was standing next to him.

He was tempted to say, *Do I look like an idiot?* The British, their charge having been broken, were forming a line about one hundred and fifty yards away. He was amazed at the speed and precision with which they'd done so. Sam knew perfectly well his own regiment would have made a dragged-out mess of the business, if they could have even managed it at all after suffering such casualties.

And he could practically *feel* the savage eagerness of the British soldiers to see him marching toward them. Oh, they'd get some of their own back, then! Surely they would.

"No, Lieutenant. Face facts—that's the first thing an officer has to learn. Those are regulars over there, and we aren't. So we'll not be so foolish as to try matching them line against line. Tell the men to start digging in and form a breastworks, and tell the three-pounders to hold their fire unless the enemy advances. They'll be getting low of ammunition, anyhow. We'll just stand here. That's really all we need to do. If we keep the enemy away from the commodore's guns, we've done our job."

It was almost comical, the way Pendleton's face fell.

"*Now,* Lieutenant."

"Yes, sir." Pendleton raced off.

Well. Slouched off hurriedly. But Sam wasn't inclined to chide him over his posture. Now that the immediate danger was past, he was worrying about Driscol and his men.

Were they still alive? If so, they were trapped back there—and Sam didn't dare charge to their rescue as long as the British had that line across the road. If the enemy broke his charge, which they most likely would, there'd be nothing between them and Patterson's guns.

"Why is everything so quiet now, Robert?"

Somehow, she'd still managed to keep her face expressionless. But Ross thought the lines of the face itself were tighter than any drum he'd ever seen.

"The assault's been beaten off," he said, trying not to sigh. "For the moment, at least."

He suspected that his own face was as tightly drawn as Tiana's. Under the circumstances, *for the moment* was a meaningless phrase. Ross knew the battle plan Thornton had been following. The thing either had to be done quickly, or there was no point in doing it at all.

The tree was starting to shed bark, under that softly but steadily pounding fist. Gibbs was genuinely amazed. He'd never seen Pakenham able to restrain himself to such a degree in a battle.

Wellington, he knew, would have been pleased to witness Pakenham's unwonted control. The duke had won the Peninsular War because he'd always been able to contain himself, when the need be. Something few of his immediate subordinates could have managed.

Including Gibbs. If he'd been in command here, despite his own great doubts about the prospects, the men would have started across Chalmette field at least an hour earlier.

They might have even carried the day. Who was to know? Leading a charge was so much easier than being the commander who had to order it—or refrain from doing so.

Another piece of bark fluttered to the ground.

"Come at me, blast you," Jackson hissed. He was back on the line now. He didn't need a glass to see the British formations, hundreds of yards away. Not when all he had to do was look across the bareness of Chalmette field.

He'd cover that beautiful empty field with red-coated corpses, if they came across. He knew it as surely as he knew the sun would rise on the morrow.

CHAPTER 47

By the time Colonel Rennie and his Forty-third Light Infantry came ashore, Rennie already knew the expedition on the west bank was in danger of disintegrating. He'd seen enough from the barges while crossing the river to know that much. The continuing sound of gunfire from the north told him that Thornton was stalled somewhere upriver.

The delay in ferrying all the troops across had badly scrambled the original plan of action. Instead of hitting the enemy with a solid mass of two thousand men, they'd been forced to feed their troops into the action piecemeal. Thornton and his Eighty-fifth were already engaged before Rennie's men had even finished climbing into the boats.

As soon as all the men were ashore, Rennie started the march. He was so preoccupied with the situation to the north that he completely failed to realize there was still an active American battery on the scene. The first thing he saw as his column entered the wide area in the swamps where Morgan had constructed his feeble breastworks were the British soldiers manning the overrun American battery by the riverbank.

The men were waving a banner. A bit frantically, it seemed. Perhaps they were coming under attack.

Rennie started to order the column to step up the pace when the bastion he'd overlooked on the far left of the field erupted with cannon fire. An instant later, round shot was ripping into the head of his column.

Perfect grazing shots, too.

"What a bloody fucking mess," he snarled.

"Give it to 'em again, boys! Give it to 'em again!" Charles Ball was bouncing about as if he were a ball in truth. "Forget those bastards over there!" He waved his cutlass at the British battery across the field, somehow managing to make it a derisive gesture. "We've already pounded them silly. Keep your feeble minds on these new bastards!"

Ball's derision notwithstanding, Driscol kept his eye on the enemy battery. True enough, in the time that had elapsed since the main force of the Eighty-fifth marched off to the north, Driscol's men had won the artillery duel that had followed. They'd dismounted one of the enemy's six-pounders from its carriage and battered the crew of the twelve-pounder so badly that it had been out of action after the first few minutes. But the last six-pounder was still intact, as far as he knew.

He paid little attention to the newly arrived British column, other than to note that they were shifting from column to line formation. Soon enough, they'd be charging across the field. But Ball could handle the business until then, well enough.

Driscol was getting worried, although he did not think any of that showed in his expression. Very little ever did, after all.

He was wrong, though. The Rogers brothers had become quite familiar with him over the past months. John Rogers put his worries into words.

"Do you think Sam should have been here by now?"

Perhaps oddly, hearing his fears expressed aloud calmed Driscol. "No, not quite that. It's true that we're coming into the time range during which I expect him to show up. But that range is one of at least two hours, and we're just coming into it. Besides, battles are always unpredictable. I've never seen a precise time schedule yet that didn't get shredded once the fighting started."

How are mighty trolls fallen. Driscol hadn't fretted during a battle for years. Like his unwonted desire to survive, that was Tiana's doing.

Seeing the crooked smile that appeared on Driscol's face, James Rogers cocked his head inquisitively. As he had since the engagement began—his brother John also—James had never been more than ten feet from Driscol's side. The reputation Indians had among white men for being unreliable certainly couldn't be proven here. As bodyguards, the Rogers brothers were like barnacles.

"I was just worrying about the fact that I was worrying," Driscol explained. "It's your sister's fault."

James nodded. "She's always been a nuisance, that way."

Ball sprang from the six-pounder to the twelve-pounder and back again. "Round shot! One more time! Goddamn you bastards, you've got plenty of time for another round before we change to grape! Don't tell me you don't. *What was that, Jones?* Say that joke one more time and you're in the cook pot! Marie will salt and pepper you good, she will!"

"At a guess, I'd say your man is still alive," Robert Ross murmured. "Would you care for some more tea?"

Tiana shook her head. "Why do you say that?"

"That sudden eruption of artillery. Can you hear the solidity of those volleys? That's an American battery—has to be; my people couldn't have ferried across much in the way of guns—with a hard commander in charge. Who else would it be but Driscol?"

Tiana swallowed, and swiveled her head to the south. "It could be someone else. Charles Ball, maybe. Patrick thinks the world of him, even if he won't say it out loud."

Ross tried to place Ball in his mind. "Ah, yes. The very dark sergeant he often has with him. Seems a solid man, true enough. But he's still a sergeant, not a commander. Trust me, Tiana. If Patrick had fallen, his battalion would be too unsteady to maintain such a fire."

"You can't be sure."

"No, of course not. It's simply my educated guess. But on this subject, my guess is extremely well educated. I've been at war for almost thirty years."

She looked back at him. "Why? It seems a stupid thing for a man to do."

"Family tradition got me started. Thereafter . . ." He shrugged. "It's a career, and I'm quite good at it."

"You should learn to do something else."

"And what would that be, young lady?"

"Something that wouldn't get you killed. I'd miss you, Robert. I really would. Patrick would, too, even if he'd never admit it. So would your wife and children. So would probably lots of other people, I'm sure of it. You should learn to do something else. You're almost fifty. Too old for this, but not too old to change your life."

It was his turn to swallow. Ross hadn't seen his family for almost a year now. There'd been many times since he'd arrived in the New World when he'd been sure he never again would.

"Well." He cleared his throat. "We shall see. Between my injuries"—he shifted his half-crippled arm a bit—"and the threat of peace breaking out before I can return to service . . ." He raised his cup and took a sip. The tea was really quite good. "Perhaps. I may have no choice anyway."

There came a distant hissing sound, as if a giant snake lurked somewhere in the swamps to the south.

"That'll be the Congreves. Yes, I'd say Patrick Driscol is still alive. See how angry they sound? Only that stubborn Ulsterman could enrage British rockets so."

* * *

"Forget those silly fucking rockets!" Ball hollered. "Just forget 'em, God damn your souls! We sneered at 'em at the Capitol, and you'll damn well sneer at 'em here!"

Finally, as Driscol had been expecting, the six-pounder in the British battery fired.

"Take that gun out for me, if you would," he said quietly to the crew of their own six-pounder, which was facing toward the river. "You can do it, lads. I know you can. Quickly, mind you. The British will start their charge soon."

As the crew of the six-pounder went about their newly assigned work, Driscol gazed back across the field. Three minutes, he estimated. Then the enemy would be ready to start the charge. Given the confidence with which his gun crew was operating, he thought the enemy's six-pounder would be silent by then.

"Iron Battalion indeed!" he said, loudly enough to be heard all over the bastion. The pace of his gunners seemed to pick up a bit.

"I have no *choice,*" Rennie said to the commander of the West Indian troops. He was almost growling with frustration. "That battery is far too effective to leave in place. We've got to cross that field in the face of their fire anyway, if we're to reinforce Thornton and the Eighty-fifth. So we may as well do something besides die while we're at it, eh?"

The men of the Forty-third were poised in line formation, by then. "It'll be bayonets, lads! We'll not waste time matching muskets against six-pounders! Just a taste of cold steel and Cousin Jonathan will be off and running!"

He would have shouted anyway, simply for the effect it would have on his men's confidence. But the hiss of the Congreves as they darted off, and the roar they made as they landed, gave him no choice, if his words were to be heard at all.

"I wish we had real artillery," growled the West Indian commander. Another Congreve exploded somewhere in the swamps, slaughtering the American cypress.

So did Rennie. But such was fortune.

"Charge!"

"They're pulling back, Colonel Houston!" said Lieutenant Pendleton. "Look at 'em run!"

In point of fact, the British were doing no such thing. Pulling out, yes. But the smooth precision and discipline with which the enemy began marching to the rear was as far from "running" as Sam could imagine. Especially after having watched hundreds of Kentucky militiamen give such a splendid demonstration of the term "rout" a short time earlier.

"Should we charge after 'em, sir?"

Sam glanced at the sailors who were standing by the nearest three-pounder. The chief gunner was almost glaring at him. Sam could easily read his mind.

The gunner, a veteran, knew perfectly well what would happen if Colonel Houston was foolish enough to order his half-trained regiment to "charge after" a regiment of British regulars undertaking a well-ordered retreat. The same thing that would happen to a hound dog who went into the brush "charging after" a wounded bear.

The bear would turn and—*chomp*—the dog would learn the difference between a mutt and a monster.

"No," he said. "We will pursue them, but at a steady march, and maintaining line formation. The gun crews will set the pace."

The chief gunner made no attempt to disguise the relief that swept across his face. "You heard the colonel, boys! Let's get this gun moving forward."

Thereafter, the biggest problem was restraining the enthusiasm of the Baltimore dragoons, who insisted on helping the artillerymen move their guns. They had no draft animals, so it had to be done by hand—with, now, a hundred pair of them getting in the way.

But they managed, well enough. The British regiment was retreating rapidly, as Sam had thought they would. From the sound of gunshots, war whoops, and occasional screams, they were being harassed along the way by Major Ridge and his Cherokees, darting in and out of the cypress on their right flank.

Driscol would just have to hold. Sam would get there as soon as he could, without risking the loss of his regiment. As long as Houston's regiment kept the British away from Patterson's guns, the battle was won. And if Driscol's battalion got shredded in the process, well, Sam was quite sure that Driscol would make the British pay for it dearly. They might overrun him, but if they did, they wouldn't be in any shape to fight further that day.

* * *

"Give 'em the grape, boys, give 'em the grape!" Ball wasn't bouncing around any longer. He was just standing behind the twelve-pounder—far enough to the side not to be struck by the recoil, of course—and quivering like a bowstring. "Give it to 'em good!"

That first round of grapeshot struck the British line hard. Driscol didn't think a single gun crew had missed its mark.

"Reload! Reload! Goddam you, Jones, you can move faster than that!"

In point of fact, Corporal Jones was doing a quick and splendid job, as were all the men at the twelve-pounder. Driscol knew it was the grin on his face that kept riling Ball. Quiet and solemn Henry Crowell was on the same gun crew, and Ball hadn't yelled at him once.

The crews had their guns reloaded as fast as any gun crews in Driscol's experience. "Iron Battalion indeed!" he shouted.

"Fire!"

The Forty-third staggered under the blows, but kept pressing the charge. Rennie was appalled at the casualties they were taking, but also as proud of his men as he'd ever been. The line of bayonets was leveled and gleaming in the sun, as unwavering as any commander could have asked for.

"At them, men! We'll have them at cold steel before you know it! And we'll butcher the bastards!"

They even gave out a cheer. *God, what a splendid regiment!*

"Oh, yes, Driscol's alive, I'd say." Robert Ross looked at the teapot and decided he'd had enough for the moment. He'd learned to ignore the demands of his bladder, up to a point, over the years of campaigning. But once he reached that point he'd have no choice but to leave the square for a time. Something he couldn't imagine doing while those raging sounds kept coming from the south.

The battle down there was reaching a climax.

Finally, to Sam's relief, the retreating Eighty-fifth broke into a trot. That was partly the cumulative effect of the Cherokees tearing at their flank. Mostly, though, it was the sound of the battle ahead of them. They were almost back to the original

American line, and the British soldiers knew as well as Houston did that their reinforcements had been stymied by Driscol's battery. They intended to join the fray, to see if they could turn the tide.

So would Sam.

"Pick up the pace!" he shouted.

The Whale loomed up in the dimness of the cypress trees.

"I've been down there," he said to Major Ridge and John Ross. "Driscol and his men are going to be hit hard before too long. Real hard."

Ridge nodded, and glanced through the trees at the retreating British column.

"We'll let this group be, then. Let's go see how well the British down there can fight."

Quickly, in their undisciplined but vigorous manner, two hundred Cherokees slid through the swamp toward the beleaguered American battery.

"Canister! I want canister, boys!" Ball held his cutlass below waist level now, lashing it back and forth like the tail of an angry leopard. "You know what canister looks like, don't you? Black ugly little beads—just like your balls will look in my voudou queen's soup, if you fuck up and piss me off!"

Driscol found it necessary to add an element of dignity to the affair. For the first time in his life, ha!

"The Iron Battalion will stand! As surely as its name!"

This officer business is treacherous, he thought. If a man wasn't careful, it'd rot his brain. He'd die, in the end, from terminal pomposity.

Close enough. *"Now, lads, now! At the charge!"*

The Forty-third raced toward the bastion, which stood less than fifty yards ahead. A great broom of lead swept two dozen of the men aside, but the rest never flinched.

"We'll have our blades in the bastards!"

Sam thought it was time to throw caution to the winds. The Eighty-fifth was spilling into the open area beyond "Morgan's Line," their ranks starting to fray a bit. If his men charged now . . .

He glanced at the gunner chief standing a few feet away, alongside one of the three-pounders. The man, who'd been watching him, nodded.

"Yes, sir. I think we can push our way into that battery redoubt. That'll give the men an anchor point."

Houston had been thinking the same thing.

If 'twas to be done, best to do it quickly.

"All right, boys! *Now* we'll charge them."

He set off at a trot. Eagerly, their confidence filled like a great sail, the Baltimore and Capitol dragoons thundered after him.

Thundered past him.

Hollering and whooping and running *way* too fast.

"Slow down, you idiots! Or you'll be gasping for breath when a British bayonet empties your lungs. You cretins! *Obey me, blast you, or I'll—*"

He charged after them. *"You stupid fucking bastards! I'll skin you alive!"*

The three-pounder crews brought up the rear, laughing all the way.

"One more round! You got time, you lazy currees! You got time! See if you don't! Wipe that grin off your face, Jones!"

Driscol wasn't sure the gunners *would* have the time for another round. Maybe. The iron grillwork might stall the British who came clambering up the breastworks, just that little bit needed.

After that—

He swiveled his head, bringing his pale-eyed glower to bear on that half of his battalion that had been standing by, while the gunners did their butcher work.

"One round from the muskets, that's all. Then it'll be the pikes and blades. D'you understand me, lads?"

"AYE, SIR!"

It was quite a splendid roar. "Gallant," Driscol would have called it, if he'd been a bloody fool of an officer.

The reckless charge of the Baltimore and Capitol volunteers didn't break the retreating Eighty-fifth, much less rout them. But the sheer enthusiasm of the thing did make the British regiment recoil—and far enough to expose the battery by the riverbank.

Seeing his chance, Houston and those men he still had paying any attention to him overran the battered British artillery unit within seconds. There was no quarter asked, nor mercy given. Those gunners who didn't flee just died next to their guns, by gunshot and bayonet and saber.

What was left of the guns, anyway. After a quick inspection, Sam realized that only one of the six-pounders could be put into action.

Patterson's gunners saw to that, while they brought the two three-pounders to bear. Sam left the bastion and did what he could to impose order on the milling mob of volunteers who were now on the open field, blazing away at the British.

He needed to do it quickly, too.

Ten feet to his left, a Capitol volunteer dropped to his knee and shot a redcoat some thirty yards away. It was a fine shot, in and of itself. The British soldier collapsed to the ground, hit in the chest. But it was obvious that the volunteer wasn't even thinking about working with his mates, trying to put a volley together.

Worse yet—much worse—was that some of Sam's soldiers were starting to grapple with the enemy in hand-to-hand combat. The results of that were a foregone conclusion. Even as Sam took a deep breath to bellow out an order, he saw a British veteran expertly butt aside a Baltimore dragoon's awkward lunge, and rip the man's throat open with his own bayonet.

"Form a line, damn you! Form a line!"

Most of Sam's men began to do so. But, with a sick feeling in his stomach, he could see they wouldn't manage it in time. The British had already formed their own line facing him, and their muskets were coming up for a volley.

There was a crash like thunder, and the sight of the enemy was obscured by a huge cloud of gunsmoke. At least a dozen of the American soldiers were struck, many of them knocked flat to the ground.

It was a real, hammering, professional soldiers' volley. For a moment, Sam was sure he'd see his volunteers crumple under the blow.

Yet, they didn't. Their responding volley, fired at Sam's command, was a ragged thing. But it was fired nonetheless—and even the men who hadn't joined the volley were still blazing away on their own. Not one soldier, as far as Sam could see, was even thinking about running away.

Glory be.

Under most circumstances, they would have. But their fighting spirits were high, and they could sense a victory in the offing. Houston's men had driven off the Eighty-fifth, and hounded them down the road—and now, by God, they wanted some real blood.

So, for the next three minutes, a half mob of American soldiers exchanged ragged half volleys and individual fire for the professional volleys that were coming from the enemy. It should have been no contest at all, but it was turned into one by the sheer determination of the amateurs.

Sam never did bring any real order to his ranks during that stretch. He didn't even try, after the first half a minute, realizing that he had no time, and he'd most likely just confuse his men. He simply stood his ground and kept bellowing the order to fire.

A meaningless order, in itself, since his men had every intention of firing anyway. But he'd been told that if a commander was seen to be resolute by his men—sounded resolute, anyway; the gunsmoke covering the field made "seeing" almost meaningless—that their spirits would be bolstered.

It seemed to work, too.

Then the six-pounder and the three-pounders opened up, and grapeshot started tearing at the Eighty-fifth's flank. Finally, finally—Sam thought almost all of their officers were dead or injured by now, except low-ranked ones—the regiment gave way.

Even then, they weren't routed. But the Eighty-fifth had had *enough.* Their retreat off the field and back to the barges waiting downriver was as precipitous as you could ask for.

Pakenham finally stopped pounding the tree trunk.

"The Eighty-fifth is in full retreat, sir."

"Yes, I can see that." The view across the river was quite good, even without a glass, now that the mist had burned away.

The battle was lost. Today's battle, at least. There was no chance—certainly not at this late hour—that a charge across Chalmette field could carry the day.

Perhaps tomorrow. The Forty-third and the West Indians were still in the fray. Perhaps if they seized that battery—*finally!*—something might be possible on the morrow.

"Tell the men to stand down. There will be no assault today."

*   *   *

Jackson just stared, from the window of the Macarty house. He'd finally come to realize that the British attack across the river had been no feint at all. No diversion. Houston had driven back one of their regiments, but at least two others were still in action. The only thing standing in their way, beyond Houston's few hundred men, were Driscol and his battalion.

Why hadn't he recognized the danger that the British might go for Patterson's guns? He cursed himself for an idiot.

The curses were silent, of course. Andrew Jackson was as good at cursing himself as he was at cursing anyone else. But he didn't do it out loud. He might be an idiot, from time to time, but he wasn't a blasted *fool*.

Tiana rose from her chair and went to stand by the riverbank. Ross remained seated, staring at an empty teacup. The noise from the south was like a constant roll of thunder.

CHAPTER 48

The ironwork Driscol's men had embedded in their breastworks did stall the British charge just that extra bit. The last round of canister, fired from Ball's guns at point-blank range, wreaked havoc on the regiment again.

By now, it was a badly battered regiment. But the enemy had arrived and were finally at the throats of their tormentors, and they'd have blood, by God.

Colonel Rennie started up the last little slope, just behind the front rank of his soldiers. Two canister balls ripped open his left thigh, severing the femoral artery. He stumbled and fell, blood gushing like a fountain.

A young officer stooped over him, his face pale and tight.

"Help me up!" Rennie shouted.

"Sir—your leg. We must—"

"Get me up, damn you, or I'll see you hang! *Get me up!*"

The officer did as he was commanded. The colonel took two steps and was knocked down by a soldier who was falling back. The man's chest had been torn open by a pike blade. It was a hideous wound.

"Get me up!" Rennie shouted again.

The officer did as he was told. Rennie stood, and started to raise his sword. But the blood loss from a severed femoral is enormous, in a very short time. His face suddenly turned white, his eyes rolled up, and he collapsed in a heap.

The young officer's desperate attempt to staunch the mortal wound would have been hopeless, even if the body of another soldier falling back from the rampart hadn't knocked him aside and left him pinned for half a minute before he could get back to his stricken commander.

The fight at the line of the guns was as ferocious a hand-to-hand melee as any Driscol had ever known. Hundreds of men, stabbing and hacking each other with bayonets, pikes, and the motley assortment of blades the Iron Battalion had managed to acquire.

Charles Ball proved as adept with his cutlass as with his tongue. Not that he ever stopped using the first.

"Give it to 'em, boys, give it to 'em good!"

Henry Crowell was astonished to see a British soldier clamber over the writhing body of another soldier who'd gotten impaled on the ironwork. So astonished that he didn't even feel any fear when he saw the man was preparing to leap at him with his bayonet extended.

The big teamster's position as spongeman for his gun crew was just in front and to the right of the twelve-pounder. Henry stepped back a pace and shifted his grip on the sponge staff he'd been using to swab out the cannon and ram in another ball. When the redcoat came flying at him, he just swatted him aside. He had the reach on the man and, as strong as he was, the fact that the ramrod's tip was covered with tightly wound fabric simply didn't matter. The British soldier, stunned by the impact, slammed into two other redcoats who were struggling over the ironwork. The invader's musket sailed out of his hands, and the only damage the bayonet did was spearing yet another British soldier in the calf as *he* tried to get over the barricade.

There was something insane about it all. Despite his immense strength, the teamster was fundamentally a gentle man. He'd hardly been in any fights in his life, and those only when he was a boy.

But this wasn't really a "fight," in any sense of the term that Henry understood. It was just a huge, crazed melee where hundreds of men who didn't even know one another were doing their level best to commit murder and mayhem.

Even a racial element was absent, to give it any logic. A lot of the men coming at him in red uniforms were West Indians, as black as he was.

Yet *another* British soldier clambered over the same poor fellow stuck on the ironwork. If this kept up, the man would be killed by his own mates, driving his chest further and further onto the dull ornamental spearpoints.

Some part of Henry's mind felt sorry for him. Most of it, though, was concentrated on the task at hand. By now, so many men of the Iron Battalion were pressing forward to help repel the enemy that he realized he couldn't keep using the sponge staff as a club.

Well enough. Blunt and relatively soft though the end was, it would make a usable spear. In Henry's big hands, anyway.

So he didn't let this new soldier finish his preparations. While he was still in a crouch atop his mate's back, readying his bayonet, Henry thrust forward and smashed his face.

All the men of the battalion were fighting ferociously, but Driscol could already tell that it wouldn't be long before they were overwhelmed. They were outnumbered, first of all, by something like three to one. Then, except for Charles and his veterans, almost all of Driscol's men were still amateurs at this business, and the British soldiers who were attacking them were professionals.

Henry Crowell was handling it well, but few of Driscol's men had either Henry's strength or his quick wits. They were valiant enough, in their awkward way. But valor goes only so far in a battle. If it weren't for the breastworks, they'd have been driven under already—and those breastworks, though very well made, were still nothing more than hastily erected field fortifications.

So be it. He'd still gut them before he went down. Driscol drew the pistol from his waistband.

Slightly behind him and to either side, James and John Rogers looked at the pistol in Driscol's hand, and then looked at each other.

With three quick little jerks of his head, James silently laid out the plan.

I'll fend them off. You keep the crazy one-armed Irishman from getting killed.

John nodded. He shifted the grip on his war club.

The Cherokees had finally reached the edge of the woods. Major Ridge stopped to examine the scene, and John Ross came up next to him. Peering through the last line of trees, he could see the battle at the Iron Battalion's bastion. It looked more like a man-to-man free-for-all than what John normally thought of as a "battle."

Ridge had a thin, grim smile on his face.

"Our country, this is. I was worried a little."

It took John a couple of seconds to realize what Ridge meant. Against regular soldiers, in formation on an open field, there would have been little point in having the Cherokees launch a charge. Even with over half of them armed with guns, they'd have had no chance at all.

Here, though . . .

Yes. *Cherokee country,* when it came to war.

"How soon?" John whispered.

Ridge glanced to both sides. As dense as the cypress was, of course, he couldn't see very far.

"Two minutes, maybe. Long enough for everyone to get into position."

John nodded toward the melee, a little over a hundred yards off. "They may not last two minutes."

"Then they'll die. We're not charging out there one at a time."

There seemed no answer to that. So, John took the time to check his pistol and make sure his sword was loose in the scabbard. He considered drawing the sword before he charged, but dismissed the idea. Charging into battle with a weapon in each hand might look good on a painting. In real life, it'd be far too dangerous. He decided he'd fire the pistol, then throw it like a club, then draw and use his sword.

Hopefully, he'd get the expensive pistol back after the battle. Not that it really seemed to matter much. He might very well be dead within the next few minutes, anyway.

Sam was rather proud of the way he brought order to his victorious regiment, formed them into something you could call a "line" if you squinted real hard, and were prepared to be generous, then started them marching across the field toward Driscol's embattled battalion.

It was neatly done. At the moment, though, he was trying to figure out exactly how he'd have his men fire a volley that wouldn't kill as many Americans as British. Driscol's men and the enemy were now completely tangled up, fighting hand to hand.

He'd figure that out when they got there. From what he could tell at the distance, Driscol's men were on the verge of collapse. They'd all die, anyway, if he didn't arrive in time.

The line at the breastworks started to crumble. Not because any man of the battalion ran, but simply because the British finally started breaking through.

A British officer sabered down a gunner and sprang into the bastion. Driscol stepped forward, leveled his pistol, and shot the man through the heart. Then he stooped and picked up the saber to meet a British soldier who'd butted aside another gunner and was coming at him with the bayonet.

That was as far as either Driscol or the soldier got. John Rogers wrestled Driscol off and James Rogers, as neatly as you could ask for, deflected the bayonet thrust and clubbed the soldier down.

"Just stay out of it," John hissed into Driscol's ear after he pinned him to the ground. "You *don't* want to get my sister mad if you get killed."

Rogers was a phenomenally good wrestler. Driscol gave up after five seconds, realizing he was hopelessly outclassed.

He stared up at the Cherokee. "What difference would it make? I'd be dead."

John scowled. "Who cares? If I *wasn't*."

* * *

"Now!" shouted Ridge.

He leaped out of the line of trees and began racing toward the bastion. He wasn't bothering with a pistol at all. General Jackson had given him a new sword when he arrived at New Orleans, and the Cherokee chief was mightily partial toward it.

John Ross did his best to keep up with him. It was a little amazing how fast the stocky and powerfully built Ridge could run.

But it was only a hundred yards. Even as relatively sedentary a Cherokee as John Ross was in good enough condition to make that distance without becoming winded. Major Ridge and most of his warriors wouldn't even be fazed.

"Quick march!" Sam bellowed.

He was tempted to call a charge. Driscol and his men were going under, now.

But Sam simply didn't dare. Over the course of the march from Washington to New Orleans, Driscol had been able to give Houston's regiment some basic training. But they weren't trained well enough—especially as excited as they were now— to be able to shift easily from a charge to a volley formation. Once he started them charging, they'd keep going until they piled into the British.

Then he saw dozens of Cherokee warriors swarming out of the woods from the other side of the Iron Battalion's position, and realized it was all a moot point. By the time Sam got his men into volley range, the battle at the bastion would have become a three-sided melee. Any volley he fired would do as much harm as good.

He felt an immense sense of relief. Whatever happened, at least his friend Patrick Driscol wouldn't die because Sam didn't get there in time.

They were a hundred yards off. Close enough, for men who'd spent the last three months marching and training.

"Charge!"

Sam sped in front of his troops, leading the way with his sword. He wasn't even thinking about the *Iliad*. He just wanted to get there and hammer the bastards bloody.

Henry Crowell fell back, the last man of his crew to do so. He covered the retreat for the rest of them now, holding the sponge staff in the middle and using both ends to bat away British soldiers.

"The major's down!" somebody shouted. It was almost a scream.

Henry looked over his shoulder and saw that it was true. One of the two Rogers brothers was on top of him, apparently trying to shield him from receiving another wound. The other brother had clubbed down a redcoat and was facing three more. James, he thought. The two looked so much alike it was hard to tell them apart.

Henry was stunned at the ease with which James destroyed the three soldiers. His war club, lighter than a sword, flicked back and forth. Batting aside a bayonet; bloodying a face with a shift of the same stroke; deflecting another thrust—*crushing* that man's skull with a full, powerful backhand blow; leaping aside; striking again—a broken arm, there—then leaping back to finish the man who was wiping blood from his eyes.

He didn't think it had all taken more than a few seconds.

But he could see that it wouldn't matter. The British weren't exactly pouring through the line yet. It was more like they were seeping through, one or two or three at a time. But the seepage was happening in more than a dozen places, and more were coming into the bastion every second.

Half of them, it seemed like, were heading toward Driscol. Those veterans knew how to kill a snake. Cut off the head.

He glanced around quickly. His mates could handle themselves now, he thought.

They'd have to.

Shouting something himself—he never knew what—Henry started running toward Driscol.

"John!"

Rogers's head twisted away from the major, whom he still had pinned to the ground. James had a grin fixed on his face, like he always did in a fight. But the expression had no humor in it at all.

Looking past him, John could see a small wave of redcoats coming.

"Just *stay* here," he hissed. Then he relinquished his hold on Driscol, and jumped up to join his brother.

*　　*　　*

Major Ridge cut down a redcoat with his sword. The man never saw it coming, he was so intent on getting into the bastion. The powerful blow struck just below the neck and the blade went inches into his chest.

With a jerk every bit as powerful as the cut, Ridge extracted the blade. Took two steps, and cut off a British soldier's arm.

John Ross stopped, took one quick breath, and leveled his pistol.

He wasn't worried about missing. He was firing into a mass of redcoats, so tightly packed it would take a miracle not to hit one of them.

As soon as the shot was fired, he flung the pistol at the same mass. Couldn't miss, again.

Then he drew his sword and made to follow Ridge. The chief had already sabered another enemy soldier.

On the other side of the bastion, Sam faced a soldier who'd seen him coming. By the time he got to him, the man was in position and had his bayonet ready.

Sam's training with a bayonet had been rudimentary, at best, and he'd never been trained on how to fight a bayonet with a sword. So be it. He'd just—

A musket went off. The British soldier dropped his own weapon, clutching his leg and stumbling to the ground.

Turning, Sam saw Lieutenant Pendleton. The youngster had already lowered his gun and was charging forward with the bayonet.

"The blazes you will!" Sam shouted. He raced to get in front of Pendleton.

James killed two more British soldiers before John could get there. A third redcoat's bayonet sliced open his rib cage. He twisted aside just enough at the last moment to keep the blade from penetrating the chest wall. So the injury wouldn't be fatal. And while it was bleeding badly, no arteries had been severed.

Still, it was a spectacular-looking wound—and James gave out a shriek to match it. Half a scream of pain; half a war cry.

His face distorted with fury, he started to strike down the enemy soldier, now off balance from the bayonet thrust.

He didn't need to. His brother did it for him.

Five more redcoats were coming, their bayonets leveled.

*   *   *

Frantically, Driscol scrambled across the ground toward the saber he'd dropped when John tackled him. He was half crawling on his knees, half slithering like a snake, moving as fast as he could with only one arm.

With a shout of triumph, he made the final distance with a lunge and clasped the hilt of the sword.

Neither James nor John noticed him. Facing odds of five to two, they were paying attention to nothing except their immediate enemies. The bayonets were almost there, coming like the talons of a dragon.

Ridge clambered over the body of a British soldier who'd been impaled on the iron fencing that the Iron Battalion had incorporated into their fieldworks. Then, he sprang into the bastion beyond. He could see a knot of British soldiers to his right, charging with their bayonets, with half-a-dozen more coming to join them.

Since that seemed to be the center of the fight, he headed that way, after taking just a moment to wipe his hand on his uniform to dry his grip on the sword hilt.

That moment was enough to allow John Ross to get into the rampart behind him. It wasn't hard, really. The impact of the Cherokees had sent most of the British on that side of the bastion reeling aside.

Ross followed Ridge into the howling chaos.

Sam and his men slammed into the milling British soldiers almost directly opposite to the side of the bastion the Cherokees had already reached.

And with the same result. By now, any semblence of order in the enemy regiments had collapsed. The redcoats had been reduced to a milling mob. Ready and willing to fight—even clambering over the breastworks eagerly—but with even less in the way of formation and discipline than Sam's own men.

Under those circumstances, most of the advantages professional soldiers enjoyed against amateurs had vanished. True, as a rule, each British soldier was more adept with a bayonet than each American soldier. But that didn't matter. There wasn't enough room in that press of men to use any weapon properly. In truth, a knife was probably more useful than anything else, and Sam saw that a lot of his men had dropped their guns and were using their dirks.

He made no attempt to bring order to the melee. It would have been a hopeless endeavor—and he was far too concerned with getting into the bastion himself.

As big as he was, Sam made it up the slope by the simple expedient of leaping from one enemy body to another. Some of them were dead. Some weren't. He didn't care, either way. They were just stepping-stones. He *had* to get in there.

Henry arrived just as another three British soldiers joined the five who were now fighting the Rogers brothers. Because of the angle from which he came, they never saw him until it was too late.

There was room, here. He gripped the sponge staff like a huge club and swung it mightily. The redcoat he struck went sailing into the others, stabbing one of them in the back of the thigh with his bayonet.

The man screeched and, in sheer reflex, drove back the butt of his musket. Henry had broken an arm; that butt stroke broke the man's jaw.

Two of the other redcoats were knocked reeling. James Rogers took advantage of the opening to kill one of them with a savage blow to the skull. The soldier's shako was sent flying straight up, as if propelled by a rocket, while the head beneath turned into a mass of blood.

John Rogers slew the other. A quick belly strike followed by a short, sharp head blow that caved in the soldier's temple.

Two more were coming. Henry swung the sponge staff again, in a sweeping backstroke. He knocked the first into the second, and that man went flying to land—

On Driscol.

Just as he started rising to his feet, the saber in his hand, Driscol was knocked back down again.

Thinking he was being attacked, seeing nothing but the red of the uniform, he twisted frantically on the ground so he could bring the saber into position. Cursing, again, the fact that his left arm was missing. He couldn't thrust himself erect without letting go of the sword.

Not a chance that he'd do that. He got just far enough away

from the enemy who was lying next to him to place the tip of the sword against his chest. Then, with a powerful thrust, he sent it right into his heart.

The British soldier's eyes opened, his mouth opened—and a gush of blood like a small fountain came spewing out into Driscol's face.

He was blind, now. Had no choice. He dropped the sword to wipe off his face.

James killed another. Then staggered. He'd lost enough blood from his wound to make him a little light-headed.

The concerned glance his brother gave him lasted just long enough for a British soldier to take advantage. Finally, there was a gap in the armor of that terrifying, two-headed Cherokee killing machine.

Driscol cleared his eyes just in time to see a bayonet slide into John Rogers's belly. Moving as if time were slowed, the blade slid all the way through and emerged from his back, just above the waist.

Staring at the blood spilling off the tip of the bayonet, Driscol knew that John Rogers was a dead man. Even if no vital organs had been pierced—which was almost impossible, given the location—he'd die of infection from that sort of abdominal wound.

John knew it himself. The redcoat started to pull the blade out, but John grabbed the barrel of the musket with his left hand and held the bayonet where it was, with an iron grip.

Then, screamed. Not words. Just an incoherent cry of pain and rage that was enough to galvanize his body and spirit for one last strike.

The enemy soldier was too stunned by the sight to think of dropping his weapon. So his head was still within range, when John's war club came around like the scythe of doom.

The soldier died twice, since James crushed the other side of his skull as he fell to the ground. Then, looking at his brother, collapsed on the ground with the bayonet still held in his body by that final grip, he issued a scream of his own. The sound was so loud and so piercing that it froze, momentarily, the four British soldiers who were still coming toward him.

*   *   *

Driscol drove to his feet, the saber back in his hand, and went at one of them. Before he could get there, Henry Crowell had swatted the redcoat away.

He went for a second. But some Indian—Major Ridge, he thought—was there to cut him down.

The third, then. But that redcoat was already turning to face a new threat. Before he could get his bayonet into position, Sam Houston's sword went into his throat.

There was still a last. But he was surrendering, now, dropping his musket and raising his hands.

James Rogers was standing not more than six feet in front of him. He screamed again, leaping forward—a panther would have envied that scream—and shattered the man's skull.

There was nothing to cover the grief. No last deathblow that might remove the pain.

Staggering a little, more from sorrow than weariness, Driscol came over to John and dropped beside him on one knee.

Rogers was still alive, although Driscol could tell that he was going fast.

Still, he had enough life left to give Driscol a sly little smile.

"Know anything about Cherokee ghosts?" John asked, half whispering and half choking out the words. Blood was oozing from his mouth.

Numbly, Driscol shook his head.

"You don't want to, either. So you be good to my sister, or I'll haunt you."

His brother was kneeling next to him now, on the other side.

"You heard?" John whispered.

James nodded. Patrick thought that, from the dull expression on his face, James felt as numb as he did.

John smiled, then, and closed his eyes. He started to say something else, but died halfway through the second word.

Driscol thought the word was "forget," although he wasn't sure. The first had been "don't."

Sam swallowed, and looked away. He remembered the first time he'd ever seen John Rogers, on John Jolly's island. John and his brother had been swimming in the river. They'd both looked like seals, so swift they were.

Remembering, suddenly, that he was the commanding officer, Sam gave the area a quick and nervous inspection, his eyes ranging everywhere.

But there was no danger, not any longer. That group of British soldiers who went after Driscol and the Rogers brothers had been the last gasp of the assault. Their mates had already been falling back while it happened.

There were no British soldiers left in the bastion. None who were alive and uninjured, at least. There were quite a few corpses and wounded men.

Henry Crowell came up to him, still holding the sponge staff he'd used as a maul. "Sorry about your friend, Colonel."

"Yes. Thank you, Henry."

Sighing, Sam started to sheath the sword. Then, realized it was covered with blood. For a moment, he looked down at the corpse of the man whose blood it was, wondering if he could wipe it clean on his uniform.

But that would be just . . . horrid.

"Here, sir," Henry said softly. Looking, Sam saw that Crowell was extending the end of his sponge staff. "This'll do, well enough."

So it did.

With the sword finally sheathed, Sam went over to the breastworks. Henry came with him. They had to move three corpses aside to clear a good view. Two enemy, one of their own.

They did the work rather gently. Sam could have clambered onto the bodies, the same way he had when he came into the bastion. But now that the battle was over, that seemed unbearably wicked.

The enemy was leaving the field, moving back toward the barges that had ferried them across the river.

All of them. Gauging the numbers as best he could, Sam estimated that at least two-thirds of the British soldiers would make their escape. But those were the broken pieces of regiments, now, no longer fighting units. They weren't racing away in a rout, the way the Kentucky militiamen had done at the start of the battle. But they weren't maintaining much in the way of formation, either. Those were soldiers who'd been beaten, and beaten badly enough that they wouldn't be fighting any more this day.

"Do you think it's over, sir?" asked Henry. "I mean the whole thing."

Sam shrugged. "Your guess is as good as mine. But since we're guessing . . . Yes. I think it's over. If we could beat them back here, why would they ever think they could get across the field at Chalmette?"

The only man who really mattered, at the moment, was the one man who didn't have to guess.

Pakenham sighed, when he saw the Forty-third and the West Indians join the Eighty-fifth in its retreat. "Robert was right," he said, speaking very softly. He was really just talking to himself.

Ignoring his cluster of aides, Pakenham left the riverside and strode to a place where he could look out over Chalmette field.

He'd always known the danger of that clear, open field. But now, having witnessed that horrible American artillery in full action, and the determination of the soldiers behind the guns, he could see it as it would be. Covered with the corpses of his soldiers. A carpet of redcoats from one end to the other.

We'd have lost two thousand men, I think, before we were driven back. And I doubt we'd have inflicted more than a hundred casualties on the enemy.

No reputation is worth such a cost.

He even managed a wry little smile. In all likelihood, it'd have been a posthumous reputation anyway. *Here lies the gallant fool, Major General Edward Pakenham, Knight of the Bath.*

Admiral Cochrane came up. Pakenham gave him a cold, hard glance.

"There will be no battle on Chalmette field, Admiral. I'll start pulling out the men tomorrow morning."

Cochrane nodded. The admiral was too smart a man not to realize that he'd pushed the army as far as it would go.

"Yes, I understand. I was thinking . . . We might finally catch Jackson napping, you know. If we move fast."

Pakenham chuckled. "You're quite a good strategist, Admiral. So long as you'll agree to leave the tactics to me. Yes, I was thinking the same thing myself all morning, as I punished an innocent tree. By all means. Let us give Mobile another try."

*   *   *

After the silence had lasted long enough, Robert Ross left the square to deal with his bladder. When he came back, hearing the silence still, he ordered another pot of tea. Tiana was back at the table.

"Would you care for some, my dear?"

"No." She was finally starting to cry. "I think he's dead."

"I think he's very much alive. That's what that silence means."

It meant something else, too; little to Tiana but a very great deal to Robert Ross. That silence—continuing, and continuing—meant that thousands of his men would live to see another day, with all their limbs and organs intact.

Perhaps he *should* take up another line of work. He was beginning to think like a bloody parson.

Tiana didn't shed many tears, for it wasn't her way. And by late afternoon she was smiling half the time, in any event.

Word had come back. A runner sent by Houston to Tiana herself. Ross was surprised that such a young man enjoying such a splendid victory should have been so thoughtful.

Patrick was still alive. He hadn't even lost any more limbs, amazingly enough.

She ordered pastries, too, for anyone who wanted to sit at the table and chat.

Chat with Ross, not her. The other half of the time, her eyes blue and empty, she was staring at the river. Houston's runner had also told her about the death of her brother.

Although Tiana herself did not participate in the conversation, a number of New Orleans matrons took her up on the offer of pastries. Most of them, speculatively eyeing the perhaps-eligible British officer whose uniform had sent them screaming away in the morning.

CHAPTER 49

FEBRUARY 12, 1815
Mobile Bay

"So we finally caught Jackson napping," Admiral Cochrane said with satisfaction. From his position on the walls of Fort Bowyer, he was looking north across Mobile Bay.

"Indeed so," said Pakenham. "Almost all of his troops remain in New Orleans. Still entrenched at the Jackson Line and in Fort St. John, according to the reports I've received. Apparently, he's convinced we intend to assemble a fleet of flat-bottom boats and attack him through Lake Pontchartrain."

The admiral was literally rubbing his hands with glee. "By the time he gets here—if he even tries at all—Mobile will be ours. And with it," Cochrane gloated, "the open road to New Orleans."

Pakenham smiled. "Well, it's hardly an 'open road,' sir. And the distance is probably close to two hundred miles, the way the army will have to march."

But his own expression was sanguine, as he gazed over the bay. "Still, it's vastly superior terrain to what we faced along the Mississippi. No swamps and—best of all—plenty of room to maneuver. Let Jackson try to match us on open ground, for a change."

Two days later, before the assault on Mobile could be launched, the HMS *Brazen* arrived with the news.

A peace treaty had been signed at Ghent. The war with the United States was over.

"So it is," Pakenham remarked stoically. He watched as his men rolled two casks of rum up to the gangplank, where the sailors would take charge of them.

"I'll ask you to handle these with dignity, sir," Pakenham said to the frigate's captain. "Contained within are the mortal remains of two of the finest regimental commanders Britain has ever had serve her colors. Colonels Thornton and Rennie."

"Aye, General. I'll see to it."

As the casks were hoisted into the ship, Pakenham felt a deep sadness. Thornton and Rennie, both gone. Not to mention hundreds of other brave men—more than a thousand, counting the earlier casualties at Bladensburg and the Capitol.

And for what?

There were times he found being a professional soldier rather trying.

Cochrane, standing next to him, seemed to understand his sentiments.

"Look at it this way, General. It's just part of the cost of building and maintaining the reputation and morale of a great army. Navy, too. There'll be other wars to come, when we'll need that."

Pakenham sighed. "Yes, Admiral. Exactly what I was telling myself."

A month later, Pakenham was feeling much better. Admiral Cochrane's stoic analysis had been proven right—and far sooner than Pakenham would have thought possible.

The major general got the news while he and his men were still aboard ship sailing back to England. Napoleon had escaped from his exile on the island of Elba and landed back in France just two weeks earlier. From there, it seemed, he was making his way to Paris, rallying his forces.

The war was on again. The dispatch ordered Pakenham to report to Wellington as soon as he arrived in England.

He had to restrain himself from crushing the dispatch in his fist, out of sheer exultation.

"A *real* war, by God!" he exclaimed to Gibbs. "No more of that miserable business with Cousin Jonathan."

CHAPTER 50

MARCH 10, 1815
New Orleans

"Well, your whole country's erupting with joy, it seems like," Robert Ross remarked. "Not only is the war over, but it ended with a victory for you here in New Orleans. My congratulations, Colonel Houston."

The British general plopped the newspaper he'd been reading onto the wrought-iron table. "That calls for a drink, I'd say. My own people in England will be happy enough, too, even if it didn't end the way we'd have preferred. Still, it was never a popular war, back home, and now it's over."

Ross swiveled in his chair—also wrought iron—and caught the attention of one of the waiters who were moving among the tables on the Plaza de Armas. It was a sunny day, and the city's central square was packed with people. Fortunately, the cafés lining the square had showed the forethought to employ extra servants this day.

Houston grinned wryly. "The whole country except here." His chin swept around in a little quarter circle, indicating the crowd in the plaza. "These folks're here because it's a sunny day, is all. No end to the war in New Orleans."

Ross smiled. The rest of the United States might be celebrating the end of the war, and—a rare occasion, this!—hailing the heroic city of New Orleans for its valiant stand against the invader. But the acclaimed city itself was groaning under the lash of tyranny.

"How long do you suppose the general will maintain martial law?" he asked Houston. His casual tone made the question out to be an idle one. It wasn't a British officer's business, after all, to pry into the affairs of a republic with which his country was now at peace. Especially when that republic—one of its cities, at least—was chafing under the rule of a tyrant. New Orleans took to "martial law" about as well as a drunk takes to a temperance speech.

Sam shrugged, still grinning. "With Andy Jackson, who knows? His position is that until *official* word of the treaty arrives, he has no way of knowing whether the war is really over or not."

Houston pointed a big, accusing forefinger at the newspaper that was lying on the table. "Those are full of lies, you know. At least three-quarters full, these days, to hear the general. Who's to say that this isn't all part of a dastardly British scheme to get him to lower his defenses, while you prepare to strike a new and treacherous blow?"

His grin had steadily widened throughout. By the end, Ross was almost grinning himself.

"Indeed. I will say that I'm dazzled to discover—for the first time in my life—that we British have the wherewithal to plot and carry through such an all-encompassing scheme. Not only can we suborn newspapers—a scurvy lot of knaves, newspapermen, it's true enough—but even your own judges and magistrates, as well."

At that, Houston laughed aloud. Jackson had ordered one of the city's news reporters thrown in jail for writing an article that referred to him as a "despot." The newspaper had taken the issue to court, whereupon Judge Dominick Hall had promptly ruled in favor of the reporter and ordered Jackson to release him from custody.

Whereupon—just as promptly—Jackson had thrown Judge Hall into jail.

Houston started to speak again, but broke off when his eye spotted something.

Hastily, the young colonel rose to his feet. Rose, at least, in a manner of speaking. His stance, once he was out of the chair, was more in the way of a crouch than Houston's normally erect posture.

"Just realized that I've got a pressing errand to run. Must be off. General, my regards." A quick nod to the other occupants of the table. "Tiana. James."

And off he went. Scurrying, insofar as Houston could manage such an unnatural pace.

Puzzled, Ross peered in the direction that Houston had been looking just a moment earlier. He couldn't see anything especially noteworthy.

Well.

Except, perhaps, for a very attractive young Creole lady, moving slowly through the square. She was peering intently from table to table, examining their occupants. Her expression seemed to combine worry, eagerness, and suppressed anger, in about equal proportions.

She was trailed by an older woman. Her mother, perhaps, from the resemblance. The expression on her face was a bit similar, except that eagerness was entirely absent, and worry was overshadowed by anger. None too well suppressed, either, judging from the scowl.

"Ah," said Ross.

"You and Patrick both!" sniffed Tiana. She glanced at the two women as they slowly approached the table. "Which one's that, James?"

Her brother smiled. There was still a trace of sadness in the smile, but not much. A month after John's death, James's naturally insouciant nature had pretty well returned.

"That one's Dominique. I've forgotten her last name. Fortunately for Sam, she's nearsighted, and so is her mother. Or he'd never have made his escape."

Tiana sniffed again. "I *told* Patrick he shouldn't press the drinking issue. Sam Houston, dead drunk—in this city, anyway—doesn't get into half the trouble he can get into sober. Well, half drunk. I don't think he's had a purely sober day in weeks."

"Not one," James stated. "Not since it became obvious to everyone but Jackson that the war was over. Sam can stay away from whiskey when he needs to."

For now, Ross said to himself silently. *While he's still very young. That'll change as time passes, unless he stops drinking altogether.*

Like Driscol, he knew the Irish curse better than he wished. And, like Driscol, knew that Sam Houston's drinking habits went beyond the normal heavy consumption of alcohol, even for Americans.

But it was none of his business, after all. Just as it was none of his business if the most famous and dashing young officer in the United States—quite handsome, too, to make things worse—had as much of an eye for beautiful women as so many of them did for him.

Not the most beautiful woman in the square, though. Ross turned his head and looked at Tiana. Insofar as Ross had any personal business in America, it was the young couple he had adopted, in a manner of speaking. Not as a father, of course. More in the way of an uncle.

Tiana didn't notice Ross looking at her. As was so often the case these days, she was gazing off to the north.

In the black quarters of northern New Orleans, the lash of tyranny was the lightest. Andrew Jackson didn't care much what Negroes did, as long as they did it in their own parts of the city. So, to the nightly reveries in the Place des Nègres, the area north of Ramparts Street had added feverish daily schemes and plans since the British had been driven off.

"You get *two* shares in the business, Jones, not three," Charles Ball insisted. "You just a corporal, and wasn't no chief gunner."

"Let's see what the major says," Jones replied stoutly. "Marie, you got any more soup?"

"Not for you, I don't. That other curree you arguing with already eaten me out of house and home. I goin' turn him into a spider, I think. I can afford to keep a spider around."

The next day, still farther to the north at Fort St. John, Driscol ruled in favor of Jones.

"Why not? He kept up our spirits, didn't he?"

Ball didn't argue the point. There was no point in arguing, when the troll made a ruling.

The troll had been back, these past weeks, and in a particularly foul mood.

Jackson insisted on keeping Driscol at Fort St. John. There was no telling, after all. The British might have faked the news of the peace treaty, and be planning a surprise landing on the shores of Lake Pontchartrain. After the battle on the west bank, Jackson was as sure as the sunrise that Major Patrick Driscol could hold off the hordes of Satan long enough for Jackson to get there.

No valiant deed shall go unpunished.

So, Driscol remained at Fort St. John—and Jackson forbade Tiana Rogers or Robert Ross to visit him. The British general might be a spy, using his injuries and illness to disguise malevolent intent, and Tiana was sure to distract Driscol from his patriotic duties.

The day the news arrived, that an official copy of the peace treaty had landed in New Orleans and Jackson was lifting martial law, the wildlife of the area was finally moving about again. Spring was coming, and the human critters seemed to have stopped doing their loud and frightening rituals.

Driscol eyed one such specimen of wildlife, which had just emerged onto the open ground below the fort.

"That *is* a deer, isn't it?"

The gunners at the six-pounder he was standing beside gave him an odd look. "Uh. Yes, sir," said one. "That is indeed an official American deer."

"Oh, splendid."

The manager of the Trémoulet House was livid.

"The carpet is *ruined.* You'll pay for it or I'll have you before the judge!"

Tiana kept laughing. Captain John, back from his mysterious absence—gunrunning, whiskey smuggling, who was to know?—just reached for his purse.

It was flush, fortunately. The carpet *was* ruined; for quite a stretch, despite the canvas.

"What in God's name did he use?" he asked his son, after the manager stalked off.

James grinned. "Grapeshot. What else?"

Captain John looked at his daughter. "You're probably crazy to accept."

She shook her head, still laughing.

Captain John looked back down at the deer. "Well, then again, maybe not. Interesting times ahead of us, I'm thinking. He might turn out to be a handy son-in-law."

It was a deer, all right, as custom required. Captain John was sure of it. He recognized the antlers.

As he could, Jackson switched from devil to devil-may-care in an instant. The day he lifted martial law, he declared a festivity in honor of the upcoming marriage of one of his officers and a Cherokee princess.

Yes, he used the term "princess." In fact, if anyone else used any other term, Jackson would start hollering.

It was a real wedding, too, by white men's standards. Jackson wasn't about to settle for one of his officers just getting married according to Cherokee custom.

"Do whatever else you want to keep the savages happy," he growled to Driscol, "but you *will* get married in a blasted church. Any church, I don't care so long as it's a church. I'll not have it said that one of my officers is a squaw man."

Driscol didn't argue the point. He didn't care, neither did Tiana—and Captain John was quick to point out that being legally married according to U.S. law would provide Driscol—not to mention his new in-laws—with a wide variety of legal opportunities—close enough, anyway—which he proceeded to enumerate in detail and with enthusiasm until Driscol finally told him to shut up.

The ceremony was blessedly brief.

When they emerged from the church, however, they discovered that the "festivities" scheduled to follow would be anything but. Jackson had the whole army turned out for the occasion, along with what seemed to be half the city.

The Plaza de Armas wound up serving as an outdoor dance hall, even more crowded if not quite as loud as the Place des Nègres.

General Ross watched the festivities from a table on the side of the square. He'd had a relapse that had prevented him from being evacuated to the British ships when they left the gulf. So, as time and his condition allowed, he'd return to England—Ireland, rather, to see his family—on a commercial vessel. In the meantime, he was rather enjoying his protracted stay with Cousin Jonathan.

And with others, for that matter. His companions at the table this evening were the two young Cherokees, John Ross and Tiana's brother James. Robert had gotten to know both of them rather well, by now. He enjoyed John Ross's quiet and thoughtful assessment of things, perhaps even more than he enjoyed James's invariant wit.

The sun had set, but the many lamps that had been placed

about the area illuminated the square quite well. Smiling, John Ross nodded toward the center of the plaza, where an excellent dancer was the pivot of the crowd.

"You'd think it was *his* wedding, wouldn't you?"

James chuckled. "Sam Houston. Always the life of the party."

Houston had never been without a dancing partner, since the festivities began. The Creole matrons of New Orleans were every bit as calculating as the matrons of Washington and Baltimore, and Houston's eligible status was plated in gold.

Even if, judging from several sour faces Ross had noticed, some of them were coming to discover that hooking Sam Houston was a lot easier than landing him.

Fairly early in the evening, Tiana and Patrick came up to the British general's table.

"We'll be leaving now, Robert," Tiana said. She had Driscol's hand tightly held in her own. "It's time we, ah—"

"Got some sleep," Driscol finished.

James burst into laughter. For which Robert was thankful, since it meant Tiana's brother was the sole recipient of her glare while Robert struggled to keep from laughing himself.

Driscol spotted his doing so, but that hardly mattered. The Scots-Irishman was quite obviously the smuggest man in the world, at the moment. As well he might be.

By the time Tiana looked back at Robert, he had his expression composed.

"Of course, my dear. You must be quite tired." He rose from the table and extended his hand to Driscol. "My deepest and most sincere congratulations, Major. You are a very fortunate man."

That, at least, he had no trouble saying with a straight face. Driscol almost had to pry his hand loose from Tiana's in order to return the handshake.

"Thank you, General. For once, it seems, I was blessed with the luck of Ireland."

By the time Driscol finished that sentence, Tiana had his hand firmly gripped again. Clearly enough, she intended to maintain that clasp until they reached their quarters.

Those weren't far away, fortunately, or Driscol's fingers might have become completely numb by the time they arrived.

Whatever Captain John had been up to during his absence, it had been quite remunerative. With all the flamboyant generosity of a Scottish laird—or a Cherokee chief—Tiana's father had rented a separate suite at the Trémoulet House for the newly-weds.

Ross sat back down. "Lunch tomorrow, here as usual?"

Tiana and Driscol looked at each other.

Driscol cleared his throat. "Ah. Maybe that's not . . . Well. General Jackson was good enough to give me leave for the next week. Tomorrow . . . Ah."

"Yes, of course," Robert said smoothly.

"The day after tomorrow," Tiana said brightly. "How's that?"

"Splendid."

They were off then. But they hadn't taken three steps before James called out.

"Oh—Tiana!" He had a very wide smile, now.

She glanced over her shoulder at her brother. "Yes?" she asked suspiciously.

"Make sure you close the windows."

Tiana glared again. Driscol kept looking straight ahead. It was hard to tell, in the semidarkness of the lamp-lit square, but Robert thought his neck was bright red. An odd combination, that complexion, with the very square shoulders that looked to be leaning forward. Embarrassment, smugness, and anticipation, all combined.

Not in equal proportions, of course. That was still the smuggest man in the world. And embarrassment was being routed by anticipation.

"I'm serious!" James insisted. "It's still only the middle of March. It might get chilly tonight."

"You like to lead a dangerous life," John Ross commented, after the couple had left the square. "I don't know what that was about, but I'd say the wings of destruction brushed you closely."

James snorted. "I can still outwrestle my little sister. And she wasn't armed."

"Not tonight," Robert mused, sipping at his glass of whiskey. "Tomorrow . . ."

"I think I'll go hunting tomorrow."

"Perhaps a wise idea."

Robert set down the glass. Although he'd grown fond of the tea in New Orleans, even the best American whiskey didn't lend itself to more than an occasional sip.

The dancing and festivities in the square were still going on as vigorously as ever. Except for the people at his table, Robert realized, no one had even noticed the wedding couple's departure.

Not in the least. All eyes were on Sam Houston.

EPILOGUE

"You sent for me, sir?"

Jackson looked up from his desk in the Cabildo. "Sam! I wasn't expecting you so quickly." The general rose from his desk and, with a wave of his arm, invited Houston to take a seat in a nearby chair.

Once they were both seated, Jackson clasped his hands in front of him on the desk. The bony double fist rested atop a small pile of papers.

"I'm leaving the day after tomorrow, you may have heard. Now that Rachel's here, I see no reason to stay. Especially since, ah . . ."

"Yes, sir. I know that Mrs. Jackson hasn't found the city to her liking."

Jackson himself might be something of a freethinker, like Sam—though not as much as Driscol, of course; almost no one was—but his wife Rachel was pious to the point of religious fanaticism. She'd taken to New Orleans about as well as she would have taken to Sodom or Gomorrah.

"No, she hasn't. And I've been relieved of my duties here by the War Department anyway, so . . ."

He opened his clasped hands and gazed down at the papers. "I'm going back to Tennessee, at least for the time being," he said abruptly. "My plantation needs looking after, and, well—"

He held up one of the papers. "I received a letter from one of my close friends in Nashville just yesterday. He's urging me to run for governor or senator of the state."

"You'd win either post handily, sir." That was the simple truth, not a polite fabrication. For all that Jackson had bullied and abused his Tennessee militiamen, they were intensely loyal to him. The militia formed a tremendous political power in any state, and a frontier state more than most. Those plebeian nobodies and roughnecks had confidence in Jackson. He was their champion, and they'd sweep him into office.

Might even, someday, sweep him into the presidency.

Somewhat regretfully, Jackson shook his head. "Duty calls, Sam. Always duty. I'll see the Dons driven from our soil before I turn my ambition to anything else. If I took state office, I'd have to resign from the army. Active duty, at least. And it'll be the army—you watch and see—that deals the Dons as they deserve. No blasted politicians in Washington, much less Nashville."

"I understand, sir."

Jackson eyed him from beneath lowered brows. "Come on, Sam, you're not *that* innocent. If I can't run for office in Tennessee, there's no reason you can't. Young as you are, after the Capitol and New Orleans, you'd win in a landslide. The militia would support you just as readily as they would me."

Jackson laid down the letter and picked up another. "This is from—well, never mind. Just take it from me that I can get you an appointment as a brigadier general in the Tennessee militia."

He held up yet another. "And this letter's from another old friend, in response to a query I sent up there some weeks back. One of our state's finest judges. He tells me he can see to the completion of your education and making you an attorney-at-law. It'll take a few years, but you're still too young to run for a lot of offices, anyway. Thereafter, between that and the brigadier generalship—"

He flashed Houston a grin. "I won't even talk about your own natural gifts for orating and such. Sam, you are pretty much guaranteed a splendid public career. I'll back you every step of the way, too. We frontiersmen need people of our own in Washington."

Jackson could grin very well, when he was of a mind to do so. "You'll need to get married fairly soon, of course. But a man should get married anyway, and—ha!—you'll certainly have no lack of choices. I'd recommend a Tennessee belle, myself, but who's to say? One of those girls from the East Coast would do as well. For that matter, as good as your reputation is, you could probably get away with marrying one of these New Orleans Creole beauties, if you found one that caught your fancy."

Sam stiffened a little, at the mention of "Creole beauties." He'd gotten himself into something of a jam, on that subject. Especially with—well, and also—

His *intentions* were good, damnation! Still, it was very difficult when—especially after drinking too much—perhaps he should start listening to Patrick's nattering on the subject of whiskey and rum—

But his scattered and nervous thoughts were dispelled, the moment he spotted the thick, official-looking envelope that was also there on Jackson's desk. He hadn't noticed it earlier, because it was lying at the bottom of the pile.

"Yes, sir. I'll give it some thought, sir. But . . ."

Jackson spared him the awkwardness of asking. As if surprised, he looked down and spotted the envelope himself.

"Oh. This?" His fingers rummaged through the stack, for a moment. "Yes, I suppose I should raise it with you, also, even though I'm sure you'll decline."

He held up the envelope with two fingers, as if afraid it might be unclean. "This is a letter from Secretary of War Monroe. He's apparently decided to create a new post for handling Indian affairs—special commissioner to the secretary, or some such silliness—and wants to know if you'd be willing to accept the position. Your duties would start immediately. The salary's pretty wretched, I can tell you."

Jackson let the envelope fall to the desk. "You'll decline, of course."

Houston stared at the letter.

Jackson's eyes widened, as if in disbelief. "Sam, be serious. You *know* what a miserable job it is, being an Indian agent. Unless you're a crook, which you aren't. You'll always be caught betwixt and between. Satisfying nobody and making nothing but enemies on all sides. I can't think of a surer way for a young man to wreck a promising career before it's even gotten started."

That was all true enough. It was also—

Probably beside the point.

Not thinking of the discourtesy that might be involved, Sam rose abruptly from his chair and went over to the window. From that vantage point, he could look down onto the city's main square.

Patrick Driscol was down there in the Plaza de Armas, sitting at a table with Tiana and General Ross. That had become something of a midday ritual, so Sam wasn't surprised to see them.

James Rogers was there, too. That was a sad sight, because his brother John was absent. The two of them had been well-nigh inseparable since they were little boys.

Sam felt a little guilty about that. He and the Rogers brothers had spent a lot of time together, in the years he'd lived on John Jolly's island. If Sam had never showed up there, John Rogers might still be alive today.

John Ross also was sitting at the table, however, which *wasn't* usual. Still, Sam wasn't surprised to see him either.

Why should he be? He'd told John that Jackson had summoned him. Ross had probably made the same guess Sam had made—that, whatever it was about, it would likely have some bearing on their mutual fate.

The young Cherokee glanced up, spotted him in the window, and nodded.

Sam would never know why that simple nod triggered it off. But, suddenly, standing at a window in the Cabildo, he finally understood why he so loved the *Iliad*. It had always puzzled him, a bit. The hero, Achilles, was a repellent fellow in so many ways.

But that didn't matter, he now realized. Homer had used such a hero to make a point. A short glorious life is preferable to a long and meaningless one, certainly. But how do you measure glory in the first place?

"It occurs to me, General," he said to Jackson, turning his head to face him squarely, "that glory is a thing properly measured by duty. Not the acclaim of others."

Jackson's face went blank. "Yes," he replied.

Sam nodded. "That's what I just figured out. So I'll be accepting the secretary's offer, I think."

"Well, it's your decision." Jackson twisted his head, in a little gesture Sam couldn't interpret. Then he held up the letter. "You'll want to read it, and make your own reply. But I'll inform the secretary of your decision."

"Thank you, sir."

Jackson escorted him personally out of the office, gracious all the way. The general did that extremely well, too, when he was of a mind.

"Please give my regards to Mrs. Jackson."

"Oh, certainly. And come visit us at the Hermitage, Sam, whenever you can manage it. Rachel was quite taken by you."

In the corridor, after the door was closed, Sam paused for a moment. Jackson's last words, he realized, were the general's way of making clear that no bridges had been burned.

Good. Sam had a feeling he'd need to cross that bridge—many times—over the next few years.

Outside, he took a seat at the table.

"Well?" John Ross asked.

Sam held up the envelope. "It's done. Step one, at any rate."

Driscol said nothing. Tiana smiled. General Ross shook his head.

"Cousins," he murmured, blowing on his cup of tea. "Why is it that all families have mad cousins?"

"The English," Driscol stated. "Trace it all back, and you'll find a Sassenach to blame."

"Probably," Ross allowed. "Though I do think the Scots have some sins of their own to answer for."

"Oh, aye, to be sure. But we learned all the great crazed ones from the English. Our own native sins were too humble to scatter mad cousins across half the world, like so much gunpowder."

When Coffee came into the general's office, he found Jackson at the window, gazing down into the square below. The general had an odd, crooked little smile on his face.

Coffee came to join him. "Huh! Don't they look like a cozy lot of plotters."

"Don't they just? I *told* you he'd refuse the rose."

Coffee shook his head. "Andy, there are times I think you'd rather lose a fight—rather *die,* come down to it—than admit you were wrong to start it in the first place."

Jackson's face went blank. "Of course."

AFTERWORD

When it came time to design the jacket of this book, my editor
Steve Saffel asked me how I would describe *The Rivers of War*
and the story which it launches. It's an alternate history, obviously. But of *what?*

Well . . .

That's a harder question to answer than it seems.

On the simplest level, it's an alternate history of the Cherokees. In fact, the story originated when Steve asked me some
time ago if I could write an alternate history wherein the Trail
of Tears could be prevented.

I told him I could do it, but not precisely. "Prevented" was
simply impossible. Given the political, social, demographic,
and economic forces at work in North America by the early
nineteenth century, I couldn't think of any plausible mechanism
by which the southern tribes could avoid being driven off their
land by the expanding United States. Not, at least, without
positing some sort of time travel or science-fiction element—
and that's not what we were looking for.

Nor was that a story I would have wanted to write. Even if I
could have figured out a way for the Cherokees to make a
valiant and successful stand, retaining possession of their traditional lands, where would that lead? None of the answers to that
question genuinely interested me as a writer.

That sort of valiant effort by an embattled minority has its
precedent in world history, of course. For one example, many
of the shattered Bantu tribes of southern Africa were rallied by
Moshoeshoe in the early nineteenth century. The result was the
country known today as Lesotho, which is completely surrounded by South Africa.

But I wasn't attracted by the idea of writing a North American equivalent of the Lesotho story. I don't mean to take anything away from the accomplishments of the founders of that nation. However, the fact remains that for the two centuries since, Lesotho has been entirely overshadowed by the much more compelling story of South Africa as a whole.

The more I thought about it, though, the more intrigued I became at the idea of an alternate history in which the relocation of the southern tribes happened, but did so in a very different way. A way which, over time, would have a tremendous impact on the unfolding developments in North America as a whole.

What if, in short, an "Indian nation" emerged in the heartland of America—something more than a place where the broken pieces of the tribes were herded like cattle into a pen? This "Indian nation" would of necessity wind up becoming something of a hybrid, and would be powerful enough to withstand the blasts of later historical developments.

That was . . . plausible.

Not likely, perhaps. But "likely" isn't the business of alternate history. What matters is that the story be reasonably *possible*, and that it results in a story which will be entertaining in its own right.

In the end, Steve proposed that we call it an alternate history of the American frontier. I agreed, since that seemed as good a description as any. True, it would probably be most accurate to call it an alternate history of the United States and the surrounding territories during the Jacksonian Era and the period leading up to the Civil War. But that's an impossibly long description to fit onto a book cover.

So, *The Rivers of War* is an alternate history of the American frontier. That said, you can expect this story as it unfolds to spend plenty of time with many very unfrontierly characters, such as James Monroe, John Quincy Adams, Winfield Scott—and, for that matter, a retired British major general named Robert Ross.

The Cherokees, on the other hand, are *very* frontierly, and they are the prism through which this story will project an alternate history of North America. That's because—as the character of Patrick Driscol says at one point in the novel—this is a family saga. A tale, if you will, of the new clan emerging on the continent, with its many disputatious nations, races, factions, and creeds.

* * *

Now for the details that will be of interest to many of my readers.

First, I should explain what the break point is in this story. For those of you not familiar with the conventions of alternate history, a "pure" alternate history like this one—one without a science-fictional element that causes the change in history—is based on the notion that a single altered event is what causes the deviation from history as it actually occurred.

There are informal rules governing this, and the most important is that the author is only allowed *one* such "break point." Everything that follows has to be logically connected to that one change.

In the case of this story, the break point is simple and surprisingly modest. In the fifth chapter, as Sam Houston scales the Creek barricade at the battle of the Horseshoe Bend, his foot slips. As a result, the arrow which in real history caused a terrible wound to his groin simply produces a minor flesh wound.

And . . . that's it.

In real history, although Houston finished the battle—even led another charge which resulted in two more wounds—he was so badly injured that he was actually given up for dead. And, although he survived, he needed to spend a year recuperating from his wounds. So he missed the rest of the War of 1812.

In this alternate history, his continued activity after the battle means that he can serve as a catalyst, connecting people who would become critically involved in the basic issues dealt with in the story. And that's important, because they were *all* at the Horseshoe: Andrew Jackson, John Ross, Major Ridge, and Sequoyah—the men who would wind up being the central figures in the dispute between the Americans and Cherokees in the years to come.

Moreover, Houston's own life changes drastically. In real history, he became one of Andrew Jackson's closest associates. In fact, until his alcoholism and a terrible first marriage wrecked his initial political career, he was widely considered to be Jackson's most likely successor. And after he regained his stature as a result of the Texas Revolution, he again became one of Jackson's closest allies.

Here, however, the connection with Jackson happens much sooner, and with many unforeseen consequences. So, in one sense, this story can be viewed as an alternate biography of Sam Houston.

Beyond that, all of the major characters in the story are, with one exception, real historical figures. That one exception is the freedman teamster, Henry Crowell, whom I invented out of whole cloth. Still, even in Crowell's case, his character is based on real people of the time.

The extent to which the personalities of the novel's other characters match their personalities in real history varies a great deal from one character to the next. In the case of such characters as Sam Houston, Andrew Jackson, Winfield Scott, James Monroe, and—albeit to a lesser extent—John Ross and Major Ridge, there's an extensive historical record which enabled me to base their personalities as closely as possible on the real people. Thus, while some modern readers might be skeptical that Sam Houston's attitudes on race were as depicted in the novel, those were in fact his attitudes, and they're amply recorded in existing documents.

With other characters, much less is known. The basic facts of the military career of Robert Ross, for instance, are well established. But his personality seems to have largely vanished from the historical record. So I felt at liberty to develop his personality as it best fit the story. First, because nothing I posit stands in contradiction to what is recorded. Ross was, for instance, known for being a "soldier's general." And, secondly, because since I saved his life—in a manner of speaking—I figured I was entitled to some dramatic leeway. (In real history, after the successful British attack on Washington, D.C., Ross was killed a few weeks later leading the attack on Baltimore.)

At the far extreme, the characters of Patrick Driscol and Anthony McParland are based on real historical figures. The execution of the deserters depicted in the beginning of Part II of the novel did, in fact, happen as I portrayed it. But so far as I was able to determine, even the names—as well as the personalities—of both the sergeant and the young private involved have disappeared. So, I developed them as I needed for the purposes of the story.

Tiana Rogers occupies a category of her own. She did exist, and became Sam Houston's second wife from 1828 to 1833, when he went back to live with the Cherokee after the wreck of his political career in Tennessee. They divorced after he moved to Texas, and Tiana eventually died of pneumonia in 1838.

To the greatest degree possible, the depiction of her in the novel is true to life. Indeed, she was by all accounts very tall and, though slender, very strong. There are stories of her marching into trading posts where her husband Sam had gotten stinking drunk and hauling him out over her shoulder—and Houston was a *big* man, standing at least 6 feet 2 inches tall and powerfully built.

But there are so many legends surrounding Tiana that separating fact from fiction is simply impossible. Even her name is a matter of dispute. I chose to use the variant of Tiana, although it was probably spelled Diana or Dianna in writing, because the name would most likely have been pronounced that way by Cherokees.

However, the name on her tombstone in the officers' circle of the cemetery at Fort Gibson, Oklahoma, is spelled "Talihina." That name was bestowed on her by a journalist in the 1890s, half a century after her death—and is almost certainly wrong, because it is probably Choctaw rather than Cherokee in its origins.

But that's to be expected, since it is also a matter of dispute whether the body buried in that grave is hers in the first place. Most scholars think that it probably is, but there are a number who dispute the claim.

I made my own decision as to how I would portray Tiana during the hour or so I spent at the cemetery in Fort Gibson, contemplating her tombstone. (Which it is, after all, whether or not the body that's buried there is really hers.)

In the end, I'm a storyteller. And this is the Tiana whose tale I chose to tell.

Finally, a word on dialogue and Cherokee orthography. An author of historical fiction set in a period when people spoke an older form of English faces a peculiar problem. Readers think nothing of reading a story set in ancient Egypt or Rome, where the dialogue is all in modern English. But, perhaps oddly, if the setting is English-language, many people expect an archaic form of dialogue to be used.

I sprinkled a bit of the dialect of the time into the dialogue of my characters in this novel. But, for the most part, I simply used modern contemporary idiom, except that I avoided terms which would be obviously anachronistic.

The reason is simple. Period dialect inevitably sounds stilted to a modern reader. But those same words and phrases and sentences would *not* have sounded stilted to the people at the time. They would have sounded like modern contemporary idiom.

So, given a choice between violating the letter and the spirit of the law, I chose to violate the letter.

The same principle applies to my use of Cherokee orthography. It is the standard practice among scholars to separate all syllables in Cherokee with hyphens. Thus, properly and technically, a name I use such as Tahlonteskee should be spelled Tah-lon-tes-kee.

But I'm writing novels, not monographs. That means I deal, ultimately, more with emotions than intellect. And it's simply an emotional fact that to people raised in modern Western culture—that is to say, at least 99 percent of my audience—that words divided by hyphens look stilted, at best. Often, they seem downright comical or derisive. As if the peo-ple of the time we-ren't ve-ry bright, so they spoke ve-ry slow-ly.

Well, they didn't. Early nineteenth-century Cherokees spoke to each other in modern contemporary idiom, as well. All people do, in all places, and in all times. So, again, I chose to stick with the spirit of the law rather than its letter.

I admit, it's a low trick. But as I told you, I'm a storyteller. Ours is the oldest profession, and it's probably even less reputable than the second oldest. So what did you expect?

Eric Flint
December 2004

Read on for a sneak peek at
Eric Flint's next thrilling alternate history

1824: THE ARKANSAS WAR

available from Del Rey

The north bank of the Ohio river,
near Cincinnati
April 22, 1824

By the time they finished making camp for the night, Sheffield
Parker was exhausted. They'd been pushing hard for over a
week, ever since they'd reached the boat landing at Brownsville
in Cabell County and started traveling across country instead of
continuing down the Ohio River on a flatboat. A friendly white
riverboat man had cautioned them about it. He said they'd been
safe enough, passing down Virginia's western counties, since
there were hardly any slaves in the area. But from there on
downriver they'd have Kentucky on the south bank of the Ohio,
and several slave catching parties were active on or near the
river.

"We freedmen," Sheff's uncle Jem had protested.

The boatman glanced at their party, which consisted of Sheff
and his mother, his sister Dinah and his uncle Jem, and twelve
other people from three different families. Several of them were
children of one age or another.

"Well, that's pretty obvious. You don't never see runaway
slaves in parties this big. But look, folks, it just don't matter—
and you got to know that much yourselves. Those slave-catchers
are rounding up any black people they can lay their hands on,
these days. It's been a field day for the bastards ever since the
exclusion laws started getting enforced. They'll even roam into
Ohio to do it. They'll grab you and haul you before a tame judge
in Kentucky, and he'll bang his gavel and declare you obvious
runaways, and you'll be up on the selling block before the day's
over."

"We got papers—" Sheff's mother started digging in the sack where she kept their few valuable belongings.

"Ma'am, it don't *matter*." He flipped his hand, dismissing the idea. "Forget about anything you can call 'law' down there. If you got papers, the slave-catchers will just burn them. Then it's your word against theirs—and any judge they'll be hauling you up before would rule against Jesus Christ in a heartbeat, if he was your color."

He shrugged. "It's a shame and a disgrace, but there it is. Was I you, I'd sell the flatboat and start moving overland. Stay away from the river, as much as you can. Course, that ain't so easy, lots of places. Just be careful, is all."

They'd taken his advice, eventually, after finding someone who was willing to pay them a reasonable price for the flatboat. But it had been hard going, thereafter. The road along the north bank of the Ohio was a primitive thing compared to the National Road they'd been able to take as far as Wheeling after they'd fled Baltimore. Sheff had had to carry his little sister for the past two days, she'd been so worn out.

And then it all seemed to come to nothing. Less than an hour after they made camp, just at sundown, Sheff heard a noise in the woods that circled the clearing on every side except the river. A moment later, two white men emerged, with five more coming right after them. All of them had guns, to make it still worse. Two of them held muskets, and all the others had pistols. Nobody in Sheff's party had any weapons at all, except the big knives that Jem and two of the other men carried.

"Well, lookee here, boys. Ain't this a haul?"

Sheff stared at them, petrified, from where he was squatting by the fire. He was sixteen years old. The first eleven years of his life had been the cramped years of a poor freedman's son in Baltimore, but not really so bad as all that. Then the white people started getting crazy after some sort of battle near New Orleans that Sheff didn't understand much about, except it seemed some black men had beaten the state militia over there and moved to the new Confederacy of the Arkansas. Which was way out west; Sheff wasn't really sure exactly where.

White people had gotten mean, thereafter, a lot meaner than usual. New laws had been passed in Maryland, ordering all freedmen to leave the state within a year. Like most freedmen, they'd just ignored the law, seeing as how they were poor and didn't know where to go anyway. Most states were passing the same laws. Freedman Exclusion laws, they were called. Then the rioting had started, and they hadn't had any choice but to try to make it to the Confederacy.

And now, even that was going to be denied them.

One of the white men with a musket hefted it up a few inches. Not cocking it, just making the threat obvious. "Don't be giving us no trouble, now. I don't want to kill no nigger, on account of it's a waste of money. But I will. Don't think I won't."

One of the other men chuckled and started to say something. But he broke off after the first couple of words, startled by movement to his left.

Sheff was startled, too. He looked over to the far side of the clearing and saw that another white man had come out of the woods.

He hissed in a breath. That was the scariest-looking white man Sheffield Parker had ever seen. And, even at the age of sixteen, he'd seen a lot of scary white men. Especially over the past few months, since the killing had started.

"And who're you?" one of the white men demanded of the new arrival.

The man who'd come out of the woods ignored the question. His eyes simply moved slowly across the clearing, taking in everything. He was holding a musket in his right hand, almost casually.

The sun had set by now, and in the flickering light of the campfire, those eyes looked very dark. But Sheff was pretty sure they were actually light-colored. That scary bluish-gray that he'd come to fear and hate more than any color in the world. The color of the eyes of most of the men who had beaten his father to death just a few weeks earlier. Sheff hadn't had any trouble, then, determining the color. The men had done the deed in broad daylight, on a street in Baltimore.

He'd thought they were going to kill him, too, but they satisfied themselves with just beating him and his mother. Following which, they'd given them two days to get out of Baltimore, or suffer his father's fate.

They'd left that very night, instead, along with a dozen other survivors from the race riot the white men had launched.

"Who're you?" the white man demanded again. He began to raise his musket.

"Bring that gun an inch higher and you're a dead man," the newcomer said. Turning his head, slightly: "See to it, Salmon. Levi, if any of the others makes a threatening move, kill him."

The seven original white men froze. Partly, Sheff thought, that was because of the sight of two musket barrels emerging from the woods, gleaming in the campfire light. But mostly it was just the way the man had said the words.

Scary, that had been, like everything about him. The words had issued from those gaunt jaws like decrees from a judge—or maybe one of those Old Testament prophets that Sheff's uncle Jem was so partial to. For all the threat in the words, they'd been spoken neither casually nor in heat. Simply . . .

Stated. The way a man might state that the sky was blue, or that the moon rose. A certainty, a given, decreed and ordained by nature.

One of the other seven white men finally broke the paralysis. He hunched his shoulders and spit. "Well, tarnation, sir, who *are* you?"

In a more aggrieved tone, one of the others added, "It ain't fair! We spotted and tracked 'em first. Rightfully, the reward should be ours."

The gaunt-jawed man brought his gaze to bear on that one. "What 'reward'?"

"Well . . ." The other seem a bit abashed, for a moment. "The reward for capturing runaway slaves, of course."

That finally brought Sheff's mother out of the paralysis that she'd fallen into the moment the first seven white men had come into their camp. "Tha'ss not true! We freedmen! We was driven out of Baltimore, and we on our way to the Confederates in Arkansas."

One of the white men glared at her and started to snarl something, but the gaunt-jawed man cut him off.

"It matters not, anyway. This is Ohio. We do not tolerate the heathen institution of slavery here." He nodded toward the negroes squatting by the fire. "They are men, and thus they are by nature free. So God decrees. I care not in the least what some sinner claims in Virginia or the Carolinas. Soon enough, his flesh will roast in eternal hellfire."

He took a step forward, his musket held higher. "Begone, all of you."

The seven original white men just stared at him.

"Begone," he repeated.

One of them had had enough. He snatched his hat from his head and slammed it to the ground, then planted his hand on the pistol at his belt.

"The hell we will! I don't know what crazy notions you've got in your head, but we—"

The gaunt-jawed man took another step forward. He was now standing not fifteen feet away from the man with the pistol.

"I believe in the Golden Rule, sir, and the Declaration of Independence. I think that both mean the same thing. And, that being so, it is better that a whole generation should pass off the face of the earth—men, women, and children—by a violent death than that one jot of either should fail in this country. I mean exactly so, sir."

The man with the pistol hesitated. Then sneered. "You won't shoot."

The musket came up like dawn rising. Not quickly, no. Sheff wasn't sure, but he didn't think the gaunt-jawed man was really what people meant by a "gun man." He wasn't handling the musket awkwardly, but he didn't seem especially favored with it, either.

It mattered not at all. The dawn rises. It just does, whether any man wills it or not.

At the end, the pistol-man seemed to realize it also. "Hey!" he started to shout, before the bullet took him in the chest and hammered him to the ground.

"Hey!" two of the others echoed in protest.

The gaunt-jawed man ignored them as he began reloading his musket. "If any of them move, Salmon and Levi, slay them."

They didn't move. Even though they all had guns, too, and had the gaunt-jawed man and his fellows outnumbered.

Well . . . maybe. From the corner of his eye, Sheff could see his uncle Jem and two of the other men in their party reaching for their knives. His mother was doing the same.

Sheff wished he had a knife himself.

Halfway through reloading his musket, the gaunt-jawed man looked up. He was close enough now that Sheff could finally see the true color of his eyes.

Grayish blue, sure enough. That same frightening, cold color. But since it wasn't aimed at him, for once, Sheff wasn't so scared.

"All of you," the man said quietly to the six white men still alive and facing him, "were condemned before you were born. God is Almighty and so He decreed, for purposes of His own. I will shoot each and every one you—shoot you as dead as that one, sirs—and I will simply be the instrument of God's will. So do not think—ever—to say to me 'thou wilt not do it.' Oh, no, sirs. I assure you. I most certainly will."

They were strange words, in a way, coming from a man whom Sheff suddenly realized was quite young. Somewhere in his early twenties, at a guess, although the harsh features of his face made him seem older. Yet he'd spoken the words like one of the ancient prophets, and Sheff knew that some of them had lived to be hundreds of years old.

"I most certainly will," the man repeated. He was close to being done, now, with the reloading. "Indeed, I shall, the moment this musket is ready to fire again."

He broke off the work for an instant to point with the ramrod at one of the six white men.

"I will kill you first. After that, the others. Those whom my brothers—black as well as white—have left alive. If there are any."

Sheff's uncle rose to his feet. So did the other two black men. Their knives were all visible, out in the open and with campfire light on them.

"Won't be a one, sir," Uncle Jem predicted. "Not if your brothers shoot as straight as you do."

The eyes of the six original white men were very wide, by now.

"Hey!" one of them cried.

"Begone, I said." The gaunt-jawed man didn't look up from the reloading. "And do not—ever—come near me again."

Sheff almost laughed, watching how they ran away. His mother did, after one of them tripped over a root.

Before they slept for the night, the gaunt-jawed man insisted on leading them in prayer. Then he read from his Bible for a few minutes, until he passed it over to Jem.

Sheff didn't mind. His uncle Jem's heavy voice was a reassuring counter-tone to the white man's. And it wasn't as if they were quarreling over the Biblical text, after all.

* * *

The next morning, when he awoke, Sheff saw that the white man and his two brothers were already awake. Awake, clothed—and armed.

For the first time in his sixteen years of life, the sight of an armed white man didn't scare Sheff. Even if the man in question was still the scariest-looking white man he'd ever seen.

Once the party was all awake and ready to resume their travel, the man spoke.

"My brothers and I will go with you as far as the Confederacy. To make sure nothing happens like last night."

"It's a far stretch, sir," pointed out Jem.

The man shrugged. "We've been thinking of settling in the Confederacy, anyway. I would much like to make the acquaintance of Patrick Driscol. In a world full of sinners, his like is not often encountered."

Uncle Jem nodded. "We'd much appreciate it, sir. Ever since Calhoun and his bunch got those freedmen exclusion laws passed, it's been nigh horrible for black folks."

"Yes, I know. Calhoun will burn. Not for us to know why God chose to inflict him upon us. No doubt He had His reasons."

By the time they reached the Mississippi, almost two weeks later, Sheff had worked up the courage to ask the man's name. He was the first one to do so.

It helped that a party of Cherokees was there, ready to escort them the rest of the way to the Arkansas Confederacy. Cherokees were frightening, to be sure, but they weren't as frightening as white men.

Not even all white men were frightening to Sheff any longer. Not even *him*. He was learning to make distinctions that hadn't seemed very clear, back in the freedmens' quarters of Baltimore.

"Please, sir," he said. "I'd really appreciate to know your name."

The man nodded, gravely. Then he smiled. He had quite a nice smile, even if it wasn't often evident.

"I wondered when one of you might ask." He pointed to his two brothers. "That's Salmon. The other is my adopted brother, Levi Blakeslee. My name is Brown. John Brown."